THE CHAPEL

A NOVEL BY

S T BOSTON

For Finley and Archie

May the only monsters you encounter be the ones of fiction.

PART 1
THEN

PART 1
THEN

BEFORE THE DAY SHE WAS TAKEN, LINDIE PARKER HAD known true fear just twice in her young life. The first time had been around ten years ago, at the age of six. Lindie's mother had taken her to Plymouth shopping as a pre-Christmas treat, but it'd been busy, and Lindie, being a '*foolish child*,' as her mother had called her when she'd finally been reunited with her distraught daughter, stopped to admire a pretty pink dolly in Woolworths' Christmas display window. By the time she'd moved away from the momentary dream of unwrapping the cherubic-looking doll, with its pink dress and patent shoes on Christmas morning, she'd lost her mother in the crowd. Until her taking, Lindie had never felt so alone, with a true fear that she'd never see her parents again.

After what seemed like an age of frantically looking up at strangers' faces with tears streaking her reddened cheeks, a kind looking policeman with a slightly bulbous and pockmarked nose had finally found her. Clutching his hand, the two of them covered the high street, soon finding Lindie's mother shouting her lost daughter's name in a panic outside of Boots the Chemist. In all, and on that occasion, Lindie had been separated from her mother for just fifteen minutes, but at age six, fifteen minutes of anguish can feel as long as the longest of days. Little did she know then that her brief fifteen-minute separation was not even a dress rehearsal for the hell she'd have to endure a decade later.

The second time Lindie Parker had known genuine fear was six years ago, at the age of ten. Helen Bower, her best friend in school, but the kind of girl her mother had said, '*You really shouldn't hang around with,*' bet her a Curly Wurly chocolate bar that she couldn't ride her smart pink and white Schwinn Spitfire down a ridiculously steep slope at the Carvear Clay Quarry. It was a risky move on a few counts, for one if she did fall off and get injured, she knew there was a whole mighty heap of trouble waiting for her as the quarry was further away from home than she was allowed to wander. Not to mention the fact that they were not allowed to be in there in the first place. Trespassing was not befitting of a well-behaved young lady. However, as it'd been a Sunday the chance of getting caught was low, the temptation of the thrill, high. The quarry was a regular hangout on such days for risk-loving local kids, but on that sunny afternoon the two girls had been its only visitors, the other local youths who hung out there, mainly boys, were likely in the woods engaged in a full out game of war, using fallen ash and oak branches as imaginary guns. Miraculously no one had ever been seriously injured during those foolhardy stunts at the quarry, or worse, killed, which was surprising as Lindie had seen some mind-blowingly stupid stunts pulled by more than a few of the local kids.

Secondly, her bike might get wrecked. The Schwinn had been a present for her tenth birthday. Lindie's father, who worked as a merchant seaman, had brought it back all the way from America, and it was by far the smartest bike any girl owned at Lindie's school. It was her pride and joy. She couldn't help but grin like a maniac at the feeling as she sped through the village, the streamers on the end of each handlebar strung out behind her in the breeze. If you'd asked Lindie what that specific feeling was, she'd have told you, *freedom!*

Lindie did not want to wreck her bike, but she liked Curly Wurlys and more importantly, she didn't want Helen Bower to tell the other girls at school on Monday that she'd been a scaredy-cat, or worse a chicken-shit. So, with her heart in her mouth, Lindie struggled her beloved Spitfire to the top of the slope and made the run. Almost at the bottom and starting to think she'd bagged that Curly Wurly from Helen, her front wheel found a deep rut in the slope and the trusty Schwinn Spitfire had launched her over the chromed handlebars. Apart from a shredded tyre, and a slightly buckled wheel that Mr. Johnson at the local bike shop had fixed by adjusting her spokes, the bike survived unscathed. Lindie, on the other hand, was not quite so fortunate, and as it turned out was not quite as crash-proof as her Spitfire.

After a few blank moments of unconsciousness, she'd awoke to the tear-filled face of Helen Bower who'd proclaimed in relief, *'Fucksticks, Lind - I thought you were dead.'* Bar once overhearing her father curse when he'd hit his hand with a hammer fixing the old wooden bench in the back garden it was the first time Lindie had directly heard anyone use the F-word. She had no idea what fucksticks meant, but she was pretty sure that it was not the kind of word her mother would approve of, and likely one of the reasons why Helen Bower was not the kind of girl she should be hanging around with.

The little stunt in the quarry had earned her an overnight stay in Plymouth's Greenbank Hospital, being observed for a potential head injury, then on release a further three weeks of home detention. To add insult to injury, Lindie's eye had also been stitched up, leaving a thin scar, that even to this day resembled a half-cocked smile just above her right eye, just below the brow line.

However, those two instances had been dwarfed by the fear she'd felt on the day of her taking, and the fear that had lived with her every hour of every day since. That fear was different, it was pure, total and absolute.

The day they'd taken her, Lindie's father had been home on shore leave, and her mother, keen for them to have some quality family time together, suggested they take an afternoon trip to Charlestown. Lindie liked Charlestown, it featured a small harbour that as a young child her grandfather had taken her and her older sister fishing in. Often not catching much they'd await the ramshackle fishing boats on the quayside all scoffing toffees from the local sweet shop held in a crumpled brown paper bag. Once the tatty looking boats were docked, they'd purchase some mackerel off the sun-drenched fisherman, taking them home for her gran to gut and behead. Her grandfather never let on where the fish had come from, always letting one of the girls claim the glory of the catch. In all likelihood her gran had known, it was just one of those little things you let kids believe, like Santa Claus and the Tooth Fairy.

After a delicious fresh fish supper, her gran had always served up lashings of her self-proclaimed famous apple and cinnamon pie for dessert. The pie was always doused in a plentiful heap of clotted cream, acquired from Mrs. Hitchen, whose family ran the local farm and creamery in the next village.

Adjoining the small harbour, which held the fond childhood memories, was a beach that in the summer months saw many of the local children running and screaming in delight, kicking up water and drenching each other.

That day, not long after arriving in Charlestown, and having wandered the cobbled streets, Lindie's parents stopped into one of the pubs for a drink. Not quite yet being old enough to enjoy the benefits of the bar, or the array of delicious local ales and ciders that her father was a big fan of, Lindie had chosen to take a walk to the harbour and beach. It was early September and the weather had still been on the right side of warm. So, with the promise that she'd only be ten minutes, and that she'd be back for a lemonade, Lindie set off on her own. Reaching the shore Lindie had kicked her black Slingbacks off, collected them up in her hand and walked the length of the beach, enjoying the feel of the cool stones on her feet, and the summer-long warmed water as it swelled around her ankles. She had been wearing her favourite yellow and black striped dress that day. Her mother, far from being an authority on the fashion of teen girls, had told her she looked like a bumblebee in it, and that girls blessed with bright red hair should not be seen in such colours. Being fifteen and stubborn, naturally, Lindie took no notice of this opinion and wore it every chance she got. Her once favourite dress was now lost forever, back at the Bad Place, on the floor of the room that had been her hell since the day of her taking, and she had no intention of going back there just to get it. Besides the dress was pretty much ruined, she couldn't remember how long she'd worn it before they'd given her fresh clothes. In fact, it was fair to say that she hated the bumblebee dress now, it served as a constant reminder of that day. Lindie decided that if she never saw the dress again, she'd be the happiest girl alive. She did wish she had a pair of shoes, though. For some reason, and one Lindie never figured out, her Slingbacks had been missing when she'd awoken in her cell-like room, face down on the lumpy, dirt-stained mattress that served as the cell's only furnishing from the day she arrived until this day, the day of her escape. Since then she'd been barefooted almost all of the time, save for during the coldest months when they'd given her a pair of white ankle socks that were a little on the small side and sported some old, dry splatters of blood. Lindie didn't like to think of where the blood or the socks had come from, some things were better left unimagined.

That fateful sunny September afternoon in Charlestown the shoreline and harbour area had been quieter than normal. Walking back along the beach, her feet jostling the countless small stones and lost in a brief thought of Nigel Banks, the boy at Lindie's school who she, (and a good portion of the other girls), held a big crush on. Lindie hadn't noticed the two people making their way toward her, they'd just registered in her peripheral vision as they'd passed her by. Just two regular people enjoying the last of the summer sun before the colder months crept in. Thanks to the sound of her own feet on the shingle, and the occasional breaker that broiled its way onto the stones with a relaxing *shh-woosshhh* sound, coupled with the fact she was preoccupied with her own thoughts, Lindie had not been aware that having passed her they'd stopped, turned and began to follow her, gaining ground with every step. She didn't feel them grab her, she was simply on the beach one minute, and the next she was in the Bad Place, laid in the foetal position on that horrible mattress in the room that was to be her cell, no - her hell for many months to come. Her favourite dress had been splattered with blood on the right shoulder, more blood matted her red hair to the side of her head, just above the ear, which explained why she'd had the fiercest headache she'd ever experienced.

Lindie's memory of that day was still clear in her mind, although she had no real idea of exactly how long ago it had been since that sunny September day, the last time she'd seen her parents. Hunkering her small body down against the trunk of a fallen tree, adrenaline trying it's hardest to mask the stabbing pain that throbbed at the soles of her bare feet, she cradled her baby into her chest, the infant girl nuzzled into its mother, grizzling slightly.

"Shhhhh, baby," Lindie said softly, trying to hide the sobbing sound in her own voice, whilst doing her best to get her breath back. She'd heard the bad people pursuing her, their feet snapping twigs and crunching on fallen leaves as they came for her, but for the last few minutes the sounds of them had faded and she wondered if they'd given up the chase.

Cowering by the log Lindie looked up at the dark, ominous and towering trees. Above the looming canopy, she could see the first tendrils of dawn threading their orange light through the night sky. Lindie knew she would have to move soon, but if she hadn't stopped, she feared she would have passed out. Months of being locked in a room had not left her in the best physical shape. Her lungs were burning with every breath, and her little-used legs felt like jelly. Gently she pulled aside the grubby swaddling blanket and kissed the top of her baby's head, enjoying the comforting warmth of her body heat and the wispy feeling of the child's light strawberry blonde hair on her lips.

Lindie had only been a mummy for just over a week, and her insides and private areas, as her mother called them, still hurt fiercely from the birth, another thing that was hampering her bid for freedom. However, she felt a natural and overwhelming maternal instinct to protect her daughter from the Bad Place. Despite being a bit naive at times, Lindie Parker was not a stupid girl, she knew that her baby daughter had been put in her belly by the bad men during their strange and torturous ceremonies. Her mother, whom she missed dearly, despite her slightly out of date view on the world, had been quite conservative and had not yet broached the sensitive subject of the birds and the bees with her daughter, but Helen Bower had. Helen had told her all about how babies got into a girl's belly when they'd been twelve and sat chatting one lunchtime at the back of the school field.

Helen had delighted in telling her how her older sister, Sharon, just eighteen at the time, had once had a baby put in her belly by a local boy named Paul Fletcher, and that their father had taken a fist to her sister's belly and gotten rid of the child before it had time to become a proper person. He'd then hunted Paul down and beaten him too, and that's why her dad was spending some time at what their mother called her majesty's pleasure in Dartmoor prison. Likely another reason why Helen was not the kind of girl she should be hanging around with.

Lindie had found the very notion of child conception disgusting and made herself a promise that she would never let any boy do *that* to her. A promise that just under three years later she'd had no chance of keeping when they'd taken her innocence during the hellish ceremony. Her promise aside, as soon as she'd seen her daughter, she'd loved her unconditionally, despite the evil seed that she'd spawned from, and had no intention of letting those monsters get their hands on her.

Not long after that day, the day when they'd planted their seed into her, she'd been made to watch a ceremony. Lindie soon learned that it was no easier being a spectator, in fact watching the torturous acts of those monsters was just as harrowing as being the subject. In the early days, not long after her taking from the beach in Charlestown, Lindie would fight when they came to take her, but gradually and bit by bit they had broken her spirit. Eventually, she learned that fighting just delayed the inevitable and often landed her with a blackened eye, or a bloodied nose. At first, when Lindie could still keep track of the time she'd been away it would be a blow to the tummy, hard and harsh enough to leave her doubled over, eyes streaming with tears and her lungs on fire, fighting for every breath. But around the time every day seemed to merge into one, and time seemed to dissolve into one long living nightmare, they left her belly alone. They still hurt her, both physically and mentally, and done things to her that a girl of her age had no business being involved in, but at least the blows to the belly had stopped.

The day she'd played witness to the horrors the Minister came to her room, and as always, he'd knocked three times. Lindie never invited him in, but he always entered, nonetheless. Fearing she was going to be the subject of another hellish night at the hands of the bad men she drew her legs up to her chest, tight against her swelling tummy and hugged herself, wishing she could shrink into the walls themselves to escape the horror.

'Come, child,' the Minister had said, in his soft, almost gentle patter as he entered the room. He always spoke that way, softly and with the tone of a kind man. However, he was anything but kind, he was evil, and that night in the epileptic flickering lights of the Ceremony Room's many oil lamps she'd caught her first real glimpse of the monster he really was. *'You have nothing to fear, for today you will learn of your purpose here at The Chapel. You are truly blessed, child!'* he'd encouraged, smiling as he stalked slowly through her cell, his long dark velvet robe flowing behind him like that of a monk. His silver, grey hair was slicked neatly back on his head and his fierce blue eyes seemed to burn into her soul.

The false smile still dressing his smooth lips the Minister had taken Lindie by the hand and lead her to the Ceremony Room. She didn't fight it, like the coming of the night, it was inevitable, and besides she didn't want another bloodied nose.

There she had been handed over to the eager congregation, all of them wore faceless masks of porcelain. The participants then bound her to a high-backed chair, using a rope that felt soft against her skin, yet hurt from how securely it held her. Next, a woman, only recognisable as such as the female robes differed slightly to that of the male version by how they dropped lower at the bust, grabbed her head and held it firmly in place, while another strapped it to the back of the chair with a leather strap, fixing her gaze at the twin altars at the centre of the room, one of which had played host to her many a time.

Transfixed she watched in horror as within this pit of serpents the last of her innocents and spirit ebbed away, for here, in the Bad Place, there was no hope, this was where evil and darkness dwelt.

Behind the Minister, who clutched a bundle of something in his hands as he approached the altar, and the one they called the High Priestess who chanted spells of both Latin and English in a flat monotone voice, walked a girl with the most strikingly beautiful long blonde hair that's she'd ever seen. She was around Lindie's age, eighteen at most. It was hard to tell, her face was streaked with tears, her hauntingly beautiful grey eyes were red and puffy. She wore what looked like a white nightie, it appeared to be made of silk and dropped to her ankles where the intricate lace of the hemline was dirtied and torn as if she'd been outside.

As they led her toward the altar, she'd watched mesmerised as the girl's gown flowed and shimmered in the dancing light of the lamps. It was the first time that Lindie grasped the terrible knowledge that she was not the only prisoner at the Bad Place. When she thought about it, there had been nights, many cold and lonely nights in her hell-cell when she'd thought she'd heard distant sobbing, but she'd discounted it as if the sound were that of her own desperation reverberating through her mind. Now she knew she'd been wrong.

Transfixed by how the girl's pretty hair glistened in the light, Lindie had taken a few seconds to register exactly what it was that the Minister held in his hands. With abhorrence, she'd eventually caught the sight of the baby's angelic looking face as it wriggled and writhed in its robes, and then through the High Priestess' chanting, she'd heard it grizzle. Not wanting to watch, but at the same time for some morbid reason not being able to close her eyes, Lindie looked on as mother and child were laid down next to each other, the mother on one altar and the child on the other.

Distraught, the blonde girl had reached fruitlessly for her infant, only to have the Minister grab her wrists and bind them to the iron manacles set deeply into the altar's stone. The child, who Lindie had now seen to be a baby boy, was laid on a velvety looking black sheet, naked and squirming around, his chubby little legs bicycling the air above his tiny body.

The congregation, who had been silent, but held a palpable feeling of excitement now joined in with the chanting of the High Priestess, as if the particular spell of horror she was on was a party favourite that needed singing along to. Eyes wide, Lindie watched the Minister raise a jewel-encrusted golden dagger high above the squirming child, that now as if it could sense the imminent danger began to squawk uncontrollably. The girl, thankfully unable to see the horrific events unfolding next to her, due to her head being held in place much like Lindie's, just in a horizontal position, begged for them to stop. As the dagger reached the highest point in its arc, and the chanting reached fever pitch, Lindie saw something that at first, she thought had to be a trick of the flickering candlelight. The Minister's face seemed to change, his features moulded into one flesh coloured mound that flickered between obscurity and human, like the way the picture would sometimes roll on the old TV set in Lindie's lounge when the signal was bad. Before she could get a clear look at the illusion through her tear-filled eyes his face was normal again, and it left her wondering if her tortured mind had imagined the horrific image.

As the Minister swung the dagger down Lindie closed her eyes, but her ears served her unfaithfully, allowing her to hear the shrill pain-filled cry of the infant as the golden blade tore into its flesh. As the child's cries were mercifully and finally silenced by the dagger's blade, Lindie's head was filled with the cries of the girl, who although unable to watch was only too aware that her baby son had been slain next to her, and now lay as lifeless as the cold stone upon which his tiny body rested.

During the times Lindie had been on that altar, with the bad men doing things to her that a girl of her age and upbringing had no business being a part of, Lindie's mind had learned to shut itself down. At the times when the pain was at its worst, and the men were at their most frantic, using her body until the pain and violation were too much, her mind would allow her the comfort of unconsciousness. It was as if it had developed its own safe mode. There, in the congregation, and being made to watch the evil show her brain decided she'd seen enough and turned the horror off.

Later, day or night Lindie did not know, such things as day and night held no meaning when your world consisted of a windowless room, she awoke on the grubby mattress in her cell, as she had done when she'd first been taken. For hours Lindie had lain there sobbing, her mind filled with the terrible sound of the baby's anguished cries as it had met the eager, glinting golden blade, and the uncontrollable sorrow filled wails of the pretty blonde girl with the haunting grey eyes. From that day Lindie's fear reached a whole new level, for she now knew of her purpose, and the purpose the unborn child inside her was destined to serve. She never learned what had become of that girl and her hypnotic grey eyes. She hoped, in a kind way, that she'd died, too. A blissful release from this world of pain and nightmare. In a way, by wishing the girl dead, Lindie knew she wished the same fate upon herself. Death was not something a teenage girl often contemplated, well not those of sound mind and happy home, but things had changed, and – yes, if it meant an end to the horror, if it meant sweet and eternal peace then she wished herself there, she didn't even fear it, she only feared the pain that would precede the oblivion.

Gradually, week by week and month by month, Lindie's tummy had grown ever more outwards. From her small, bleak prison she shut herself away in her own mind, thinking of her mother and father and of her sister, of sitting on the harbour at Charlestown with her grandfather, scoffing his toffies and waiting for the fishing boats, and of her grandmother's apple and cinnamon pie. Sometimes she went so deep into her mind that she thought she could actually taste it. At times she felt guilt, guilt for the torture that her parents must be feeling. Sometimes that guilt would build to panic, panic so strong that Lindie felt as if she could almost claw her way through the walls of her room and escape. It consumed her, swelled and filled her up entirely until it felt as if there were a rabid animal gnawing at her insides. At times like that, she wanted to scream, but the sound of her own screams in that silent, lonely room just terrified her even more, so, for the most part, she kept them in her head.

Sat on the forest floor, her child cradled in her arms, that same gnawing feeling of panic began to build in the pit of her tummy again, she had the overwhelming feeling that she needed to move, even though her jelly-like legs thought otherwise. Securing the swaddling blanket around her infant daughter, whom Lindie had decided would be named Hope if they both lived through the night, she steadied herself to her feet using the fallen log for support and continued her plight for freedom.

Lindie wasn't sure how long it had been since she'd last heard their pursuing feet giving chase, and she had no idea why they'd seemingly stopped following her. Wincing as her own foot found a fallen piece of thistle, Lindie picked up the pace, the pain quelled by her longing for freedom. Hope began to grizzle louder as if she were working against her mother's attempts to be as quiet as possible.

Shushing her baby, and praying the crying would

stop, Lindie tried to navigate through the forest using what little dawn light there was. Surely soon the forest would end, and she'd break out of the woods and see a farm, a cottage, or anywhere that she could find refuge. Spurred on by the thought, and with more hope for survival and escape than she'd known since her taking, Lindie willed her fatigued legs to carry her a little further. She felt increasingly sure that now she would see her mother and her father again, she would get to taste that amazing apple and cinnamon pie cooked by her gran, and that baby Hope would get to grow knowing the warm love of her family.

Momentarily Lindie halted again and listened, there was an impossible sound that carried itself on the light breeze as it trickled its way through the trees and jostled her freshly washed red hair. Hair, that like the blonde girl's had been prepared for the main event. The sound wasn't feet or the vocal cacophony of the pursuing mob, but a single voice. His voice. Not sure if her ears had fooled her, Lindie cocked her head to one side and held her breath. The breeze chased its way through the forest once again and played with the laced hemline of her white, silk gown, and with the breeze came the voice.

"Lindieeeeeeeee," it coaxed. It was the Minister, his voice soft and unmistakable, yet at the same time mocking. *"Where are you Lindieee-Lou?"* He'd often called her Lindie-Lou when trying to coax her from her cell, she hated it. Spinning on the spot Lindie looked around frantically, expecting to see him appear from behind one of the large oak trees in his ceremony robes, his face festooned with the dark velvet of his tunic hood. But he didn't. The breeze, that was now more of a light wind, disturbed the treetops, igniting the leaves with the sound of a thousand whispers that seemed to call her name, *"Lindieeeeeee."*

Sobbing, Lindie willed her fear frozen body to move, faster now, more urgently. She felt as if every tree were watching her, working as an ally to the Minister. She felt toyed with, the way a cat might allow a mouse to think it had escaped before its paw cruelly pulled it back by the tail for more evil games.

"Lindieeeee," the Minister's voice mocked again, the leaves a conduit for his words. As if sensing her mother's terror, Hope began to grizzle louder, building into a full-on crying fit. Lindie could no longer feel the pain in her legs and in her feet, fresh fear-fuelled adrenaline had taken those minor distractions away from her. Then, in this emotional game of terror and hope, Lindie saw lights, lights from whatever building lay ahead in the clearing. Encouraged on that this nightmare was over and the voices had been nothing but a product of the terror that saturated her brain, and that she'd finally escaped the Bad Place, she broke into a run. Baby Hope squawked loudly in protest as she cradled her tightly into her chest. The thick woods began to ebb away. As she neared the building, tears of joy now streaming down her face, Lindie broke clear of the forest and dropped to her knees on the neatly trimmed grass.

"No, no, nooooo," she wailed as her infant daughter picked up her own frantic cries to a new octave. Through her tear-filled eyes, Lindie saw them all stood there. The Minister, the High Priestess, and all the others, their faces hidden behind those blank, expressionless masks of porcelain. Behind them, lights burning through its windows, the same lights that had been Lindie's false beacon of hope, was the Bad Place.

"You came back to us Lindie Lou," the Minister smiled, stepping forward. As he spoke the dawn light seemed to vanish from the sky, it grew darker, as if the encroaching sun had itself decided that light had no business here and that the night could have it back. "It's a sign, Lindie," he continued. She turned her face toward that darkened sky, a sky that held no stars, no moon, and no hope, just the abyssal blackness of infinity. "If he didn't want you, he'd let you go. Don't you see that, child?" Lindie felt his hands lifting her, she didn't resist, she was spent. "It's time to fulfil your destiny, Lindie, and become."

"Become," the faceless crowd chanted behind.

Lindie felt Hope being taken from her arms, the child screamed louder as the physical bond with its mother was broken. Her head swam in confusion, she'd ran in a straight line, never turning more than a little here and there to navigate the trees. It had been a fairly clear night, and through the trees, Lindie had made sure the bright, full moon had stayed behind her the whole time. There was no possible way she could have gone full circle.

"You didn't actually think we let you go?" the Minister said as if sensing the burning question in her mind. He walked alongside her now, cradling Hope in his arms as the High Priestess escorted her by the arm. Lindie could no longer feel her legs, like her feet they just felt dead, dead flesh that now carried her toward new horrors. "It's the ultimate test, Lindie," he continued, not waiting for her answer. "We let you escape, you see, if he didn't want you to become, he would have let you go. But he didn't!" Lindie looked up at his smooth face, his icy blue eyes danced with excitement. "He brought you back to us, Lindie Lou, he brought you back so you could *become*." And with that, they took her to the ceremony room. The room lit by the light of many oil lamps, which hung between gigantic tapestries adorned with symbols that meant nothing to her. "Tonight, child, you will be blessed." He raised his hand and wiped the tears from her cheeks. Lindie felt his cold touch on her hot skin and she wanted to retch.

"Please, d-don't, k-kill h-her," Lindie sobbed as she felt her spent body being lifted onto the altar. She had no fight left in her, the weeks and months of mental and physical abuse had taken their toll, and with tonight's cruel and false hope of freedom she could endure no more, she just wanted it to end.

"Soon you will see," the Minister said, smiling down at her as eager hands fixed her arms and legs into the manacles that had played host to her many times. "Through your child, through your offering, you will become."

Somewhere in the room, Lindie could hear the High Priestess chanting one of her spells, the Latin lost on her as it always was.

Hope cried, her squawks and wails more torturous to her than any pain they could bestow upon her.

Once again Lindie thought of the blonde girl and prayed that her suffering had ended, that she was now at peace, a peace she knew she would soon see if only she could get through the pain first, and oh how she feared the pain. But it was a necessary road, one that must be travelled for this to all end.

Suddenly the chanting stopped, and the Minister took over.

"The mother offers you this child so that she might become" he proclaimed.

"Esset facti," the others chanted.

"I don't o-offer y-you anything, please j-just l-l-let us g-go" Lindie sobbed, her voice weak, her head strapped to the altar, and her wide eyes fixed intently on the high arcing roof of the Bad Place.

"We offer you this child so that you may feast on its pure soul, and so that the mother might become," he continued, ignoring Lindie's plea.

"Esset facti," the congregation chanted in agreement.

"We offer you her body, so that you might live through her, and that she might become," he cried, his voice feverish with excitement.

"Esset facti," came the voice of the congregation, just as those at a Christian ceremony might say Amen.

Lindie could hear her baby screaming next to her.

From the ceremony she'd been forced to watch she knew Hope was naked, laid on a thick, dark velvet sheet placed on the cold stone, and that soon her daughter would meet the jewel-encrusted dagger. She tried to turn her head, tried to get one last look at her baby before the monsters took her away, but she could do nothing but stare through sore eyes at that high arcing beams that held the roof. Above her, among those old wooden beams, where the candlelight gave birth to dark shadows, she felt sure she saw them move, stir, as if alive. The shadows were excited.

The sound of the High Priestess' voice filled the room again. Lindie wondered if another innocent, as she had been, was in the congregation, being made to watch. The next victim. As the voices of the faceless ones reached new heights, she knew it was time. Lindie closed her eyes and felt the fresh tears as they rushed down her hot cheeks, tracing cooling lines on her flesh. In her head, she tried to shut herself away, mentally listening to her favourite Beatles song, Love Me Do, but through the lyrics that played in her head, she heard the pain-filled cry of her daughter as she met the dagger. Lindie prayed for unconsciousness, for her safety mechanism but it never came. Hope was quiet. Hope was gone.

"We thank you Lord of Chaos for the child, the child that we have given to you, the child that we have cast into the Abyss," came the voice of the Minister. "Now the mother will drink of its blood so that *she* might become, and so that the darkness of the Abyss might dwell inside her."

"Habitant in medio," came the chant.

Lindie felt her mouth being forced open, she tried to fight it, but forceful fingers pinched her nose. In the end, her lungs burned for air and she gasped. As she did, as the much-needed oxygen flooded her chest, she felt warm metallic liquid fill her mouth almost choking her, as she tried not to retch the room erupted in a frenzied cry of jubilation. Opening her eyes Lindie saw the Minister stood over her, his face fixed in a satisfied smile. Gagging on the taste of the warm viscous liquid she watched as he lifted a golden chalice and drank deeply from it himself. As the vessel left his lips, she saw they were painted deep crimson. Not wiping his mouth, the Minister placed it down and collected something from the altar that was out of Lindie's field of view. She soon saw what it was, the golden dagger. The glinting blade still dripping with Hope's blood was lifted high above her head. Watching through wide, frightened eyes Lindie saw his face change, as it had the day she'd played witness to the ceremony of the blonde girl with the pretty grey eyes. It softened and moulded, rolled between monstrous to blank and anonymous like the masks they wore, then back as if it didn't know which form to take.

"The blood of life from those which have died has been consumed, and now she must become," he almost sang, the words coming from his maw of a mouth as the skin morphed and quivered.

"Oportet facti sunt," came the faithful reply.

Lindie felt her head spin, the way it used to when she was a child and her father pushed her too fast on the merry-go-round at the local park. She felt almost weightless. As the life-taking dagger glinted above her, her inbuilt safety mechanism finally kicked in and she felt unconsciousness envelop her like a snug blanket, and she welcomed it.

THE DAY WAS COLD, ABOUT AS COLD AS IT HAD BEEN in November for as long as Tom Reed could remember. Iron grey clouds capped the sky for as far as the eye could see, they darkled in places portending snow and the likelihood of a harsh winter ahead.

"You're sure you can turn this place around?" he questioned, his voice coming out in clouds of water vapour as he surveyed the boarded-up, old stone building, his deep-set brow wrinkled with obvious concern.

"No," laughed his wife, Sue excitedly as she put her arm encouragingly around him and pulled him in close. "But I'm sure you can. You're the builder." She bobbed up onto her tiptoes and gave her husband a peck on the cheek, her thrill at finally seeing the place was obvious, however, it was a passion that he didn't totally share.

"Retired," he reminded her, the frown not leaving his face. Tom's well-trained brain was already working out what a mammoth, not to mention expensive task it was going to be turning this burnt out old wreck into something not only habitable but good enough for people to actually rent out and holiday in. Any renovation would have to be good, with sites such as Trip Advisor, a few scathing snippets of customer feedback could cost you, and cost you dearly. It seemed in a day and age full of keyboard warrior internet critics even something as menial as a loose seat on the crapper could earn a place a one-star rating.

Under the oxidised metal sheeting, which secured the glass-vacant windows, he could see the tell-tale signs of the fire that had gutted the property eight years before. Black tendril-like fingers of soot staining reached above the boarded off windows, marking the outer walls. A long-standing testimony to the intensity of the inferno. One of the steel shutters had worked loose, giving him a glimpse into the dark, cavernous void within. The condition of this old chapel suited the tatty grounds in which it sat. They were neglected and in need of some major work. Nature had well and truly taken over, reclaiming what once might well have been well cared for gardens. The grass, which had long since lost any signs of its last cut, was now long enough to sway in the cold November breeze. Here and there thorny bushes strangled the ground with their deep roots, whilst their sharp and oppressive branches reached toward the cold greying sky as if making their own bid for freedom from the very roots that fed them. Threaded through one of the bramble thickets was a long wooden bench. The generic long timber structure was typical of the kind found in churches and chapels across the world. This bench, however, after years of being attacked by the relentless brambles was shedding its varnish, like a snake peels its skin. One end, just visible through the thorns was scorched black, like a half-burnt stick poking out of a spent camping fire. At the far end of the building, where the overgrown grounds disappeared from view, a bell tower stood proud, looming over the apex of the roof by a good ten feet. It wasn't a tower the likes of which housed a spiral staircase that ascended its dizzying heights and could house a troop of bell ringers, it was smaller and more like the kind sometimes found on Mediterranean places of worship. No more than an extension of the building with a small bell housed in an aperture under its own small apex roof. The old bell contained within the stone had obviously seen many a year since it had last rung out across the village, and whilst Tom was far from being an expert on matters of campanology, he knew the brass would be easily restored to its former lustre and once restored it would make a nice feature point. At the moment it was the only positive he could see, and that wasn't for lack of trying. He wanted to love the place because Sue obviously did.

"Think of this as your last job, and an investment into our pension fund," Sue said, smiling at him again, it was her warming smile and sparkling green eyes that had caught his attention all those years ago.

Tom first met the woman who would turn out to be the love of his life in 1968, forty-eight years ago now, at a dance held in Salisbury City Hall. Sue was just a few days shy of twenty-two, and a legal secretary new to the area with few friends. He'd been a slightly spotty and mildly shy twenty-five-year-old, in the middle of his carpentry apprenticeship. They'd exchanged glances whilst local bands played covers of well-known rock and roll hits. The kind that neither of their parents would have approved of and put down to no more than noise.

She'd changed over the years, a little more outwards in places and her hair, which was now tied back in a neat bun, had turned from the raven black, (that had first caught his attention), to peppered grey, and small crow's feet now marked the corners of her eyes. Those light green eyes, however, still sparkled as they'd done on their first date, her warm smile had also remained the same throughout the years. Tom had known and loved her long enough to see that sparkle of excitement in those eyes and knew without a single shred of doubt that she was enthused by this run-down, burnt out old building. He just wished he felt the same optimism for the potential project.

"As you can see, and as it covers in your information pack," interjected the slightly pushy estate agent as he joined them by the makeshift double front doors, "following the fire in late 2008 the roof was replaced by the last owner as part of his planned renovations." The estate agent dove his hand into the deep pocket of his thick, grey formal coat, fished around for a few seconds before producing a set of brass keys. He thumbed through them, finally finding the one he wanted he unclipped the padlock that held the temporary metal doors closed. "After you," he encouraged, beckoning them forward.

Tom took his arm from around his wife, unhooked the heavy padlock from the hasp and dropped it to the floor. Grasping the cold metal, he pulled hard, forcing open the tatty looking steel door. It creaked painfully on rusty, little-used hinges, the strained sound of fatigued metal on metal echoing into the building and bouncing around the walls in a tortured shriek. Turning to the estate agent, who to Tom didn't look old enough to be out of school, let alone holding down a full-time job, he said, "So how many years didn't it have a roof?" Tom thought he saw a glint of frustration run through the young man's dark brown eyes as he pawed through the sales pack.

"The fire was in 08," he summarised as he scanned the notes. Tom held the same set of documents in his hand, but the property didn't exactly sell itself, so he felt like making the estate agent, who'd introduced himself on the phone last week as Karl, and now wore a white name badge confirming this, work for the sale. Karl had obviously affixed the generic white badge in a bit of a rush, it sat just above the breast pocket of his jacket but drooped to the left slightly. Tom, being more than a bit of a perfectionist, and bordering on OCD had noticed it immediately and it bugged him. He felt as if he needed to unpin it and place it back straight, the way a fussy parent might give their child a licky-licky-wet-wipe to get rid of some food left on the face after dinner. Karl fell silent for a few drawn-out seconds as he read. Finally, he looked up and said, "The roof was put on during the summer of 2011."

"That's still three years of weather and water damage," Tom replied, peering through the door and not seeing very much. The low winter sun had just about managed to struggle through one of the grey clouds, it cast a weak shaft of light into a darkness that seemed to consume it with ravenous hunger. The sudden light caught a bevy of dust motes kicked up by the fresh air now flowing in through the door and they swarmed in the winter sunlight like an excited cloud of tiny bees.

"It's old Cornish stone, Tom," Sue said as if she were on Karl's side and in for a slice of his commission on the sale. "This place will still be standing when we are both long gone, it just needs a little TLC." She rested a hand on the stone of the entrance and then patted it affectionately. Tom looked at Karl, who stayed silent. He obviously knew his trade well despite his schoolboy appearance and it was more than obvious that Sue had a real hankering to take on the place so little work on his part was needed; he was just sitting back and letting her run. "Plus," she continued enthusiastically, "that's five years it has had a roof, so much of the damp will have dried out over the summers."

"Doubtful," Tom replied sceptically, as he mentally ran through how many industrial heaters he'd need to hire just to get the damp under control. "Why did the previous owner abandon the project?" His question was directed at Karl, who shifted uncomfortably on the soles of his now slightly mud-stained black shoes. He kept glancing down at his soiled footwear as if the clinging mud was becoming a major annoyance for him.

"The previous owner, Henry Bough, acquired the site in 2010," Karl answered, moving his eyes back to Tom. "He purchased it at auction, the original owner Johnathan Deviss, who owned the site had no living relatives to pass the building on to, nor did he have a will, so the state took legal ownership. The building, from what little I know of its history, had been in the Deviss family for years. Mr. Bough did little with the building save for the roof. Despite its dilapidated appearance, the property secured a high price at the original auction. I understand there was interest in the property from the local community, but his pockets obviously ran deeper. According to his daughter, Mr. Bough's plan was to build a family home and move them all down from the city, ya know, get away from the rat-race, escape to the country, that kind of thing, but he died before the project was completed. The family held on to the place in its current state until they finally put it up for sale."

"They probably realised what a gawdawful job it would be to turn this place into something habitable," Tom laughed, noting the definite smell of damp and stagnation emanating from the darkness.

"It's a little more delicate than that," Karl replied, his eyes darting from Tom to Sue, then awkwardly down at his notes. From his paperwork his gaze fell to the mud caking the sides of his shoes again, he scraped it fruitlessly on the ground before he continued, "Mr. Bough fell to his death in the building the day he completed the works on the roof."

"Oh my God!" Sue gasped, putting her hand over her mouth. "Poor man."

Karl nodded, "I'm told by his daughter, Trudie, that he was found on the floor over there," he pointed into the darkness, giving no true indication of where the accident happened. "It appeared that his ladder toppled over whilst he carried out a few finishing touches to the beam work. The roof arcs up high as you can see from the outside, it was quite a fall." Karl now almost sounded like a tour guide, relishing in the gruesome tale of some murder mystery during a guided walk.

"And his ghost still haunts the place to this day," Tom laughed as he turned the collar of his thick, green fleece up against the cold. The sun had lost its brief fight against those dark winter clouds and had now vanished from the sky, further darkening the already sullen day. Fishing in his pocket he produced a small, but powerful LED Lenser torch, clicked it on and walked inside. The floor, the part of it that Tom could see, was tiled, whatever pattern they'd held was long gone. Even the better condition tiles had lost their glazing, many were cracked and uneven, giving the floor the appearance of a higgledy-piggledy cobbled forecourt. The whole thing would need to be re-laid. Stretching the beam toward the very back of the building the thin shaft of light caught an area where the broken tiles gave way to concrete, it looked newer than the tiles and had likely been added by Mr. Bough before his demise. That at least wouldn't need any work, but it was such a small portion of the floor it hardly made a difference. It wasn't uncommon for people with little experience of developing to attack a project in what Tom called an arse about face way, fixing something here and replacing something there. A project this big needed a plan and a structure, and someone with enough experience to complete the work. He hated to admit it, but he was the man for such a job, even if he didn't want it.

"Tom," Sue chided, giving him a nudge.

"Well a good ghost story might appeal to some," he mused, sweeping the lance of light around the cavernous and empty interior. Aiming the bright white beam upward he checked the roof. The work was good, solid oak beams held up the slate roof, the very fact the roof was on, fairly new, and in good shape would save a great deal of time and a shit load of money. He'd been in the trade long enough to know this was, without doubt, a listed building, meaning any work carried out would be governed by strict rules, and the roof was likely as close to the original as you could get. The stone of the interior walls was scorched black in many places, but the smell of the long-spent fire no longer laced the air. The visual remnants, however, were everywhere. Chasing the beam of light through the dark he did a rough count of the windows, no doubt the majority of which would need to be replaced with stained glass, in keeping with the building's original appearance. That in itself would be a costly exercise.

"It doesn't seem to say what caused the fire?" Sue questioned. Tom could see her looking around, her eyes straining through the murky half-light. Part of him wanted the challenge of bringing this mid-seventeenth century building back to life, but the other part wanted to keep the money in the bank. By the time they'd purchased the shit-tip and sank God knows how much into the renovations, there'd be a sizeable hole in their savings. It was a gamble but one that could pay off and secure them financially for life. It would also leave a nice little nest egg for their children, Ben and Lisa. Now both in their thirties they'd long since started their own adult lives and made them grandparents three times over but leaving them a good legacy for after he and Sue had gone was one of his goals, and this place done right could be just that.

Tom had celebrated his seventy-third birthday earlier in the year, whilst he still felt much younger, he'd done his time on the tools and wasn't convinced a project of this size was a thing he wanted to tackle. Retirement should be about playing golf a few times a week and taking the occasional cruise or trip to Spain, not busting his arse on a building site. That was a job for a young man.

Karl heaved open the second metal door, putting his body weight against it to get the seven-foot partly seized panel to move. The sound echoed through the empty interior; somewhere inside Tom heard disturbed wings flapping frantically. The place obviously had its own residents, no doubt using the window with its busted boarding up panel. He made a mental note to secure it at the first opportunity, the place was bad enough without having to contend with a pile of bird shit.

With the second door open the interior was much more visible. Karl joined them, although he seemed to hang back a bit, as if reluctant to venture too far in. He glanced at his notes and said, "Eventually it was ruled accidental. I think they believed it to be arson, but there was no hard evidence for it, and who the hell would be sick enough to burn down a church? This is a pretty remote village and the nearest neighbour is a good half a mile away, so sadly no one even saw the fire. By morning all that was left was the solid stone walls and a collapsed roof, nothing really for the investigators to go on."

"But the church never got it repaired?" Tom asked, puzzled.

"As you will no doubt see from your pack, this was a privately-owned building and not under the control of the church. As I said previously the building had been in the Deviss family for years; since it was built in fact. No one survived Mr. Deviss, hence why the state auctioned it."

"So," Tom said, smiling to himself, "not only is this place a gawdawful wreck, but it's killed its last two owners." In the dim light, he could see the look on Karl's face. Karl didn't know whether to take the comment seriously or not. Tom let him stew for a few brief seconds before treating him to a wide smile. "Relax, kid," he joked. "Luckily neither the wife nor I are superstitious like that - unless it gets us a few grand off the price, that is. Heck, it's an old chapel, it's probably seen plenty of bodies over the last few hundred years."

"I won't lie," Karl said, sounding relieved, "the last two clients who learned that never even put in an offer. The other prospective client was not happy that this place was never officially registered as a chapel with the church and that we were unable to prove provenance. I have conducted as much research as I can using various sites like parish register but from what I can tell this was a rare, privately owned community church. I'm no legal eagle, but its existence may have breached the Places of Worship Act, but that is reflected in the asking price – the lack of provenance. If I could find it, you'd be looking at another ten or fifteen grand." Karl was good at his job; he'd managed to spin the negative to a positive with the mention of the saving and Tom inwardly smiled at the young man's skill.

"Old buildings have history," Sue cut in, sounding as enthusiastic as ever. In the gloom, she reached for the stone wall again and ran her hand along its blackened surface. "If we didn't want history, we'd buy a new build. The lack of registration is not a worry, if the contracts and sale are legal it will suit our needs just fine. It's more the look of the building I'm after anyway over religious provenance. I'm thinking modern gothic."

Tom admired his wife's passion, but the truth of the matter was it would likely be cheaper if he looked at knocking it down, if that were an option, and starting from scratch. He didn't voice it though, because at the end of the day, despite how much of a shit-tip it looked, those old stone walls had history, and they could be restored, and life could be breathed back into the place.

"The Bough family," Karl began, cutting back into sales mode and obviously sensing a deal was close, "saw to it that planning permission for a six-bedroom property had been granted before putting it up for sale, hence why the price is a little higher than you'd expect for a building in this condition. Whilst still being below that of a registered church," he added hastily. Leaning into the thick shaft of light afforded by the double doors, Karl flashed a scaled-down version of the architect's plans in front of Tom. "Mezzanine level conversion giving you two floors, space for a games room on the lower level if you opt for a slightly smaller kitchen."

Tom couldn't deny the plans looked good. He'd only received the full sales pack through the day before they'd made the drive down from Wiltshire, but from the brief once-over he'd given the detailed plans, he'd not found much they'd need to change. The second floor was a must, the roof was high and not to put one in would be a terrible waste of liveable space. Not to mention that without the benefit of an upper floor, it would lose heat like a bitch. It was a hell of a job, but one worth doing if done properly; a phrase he lived and died by when it came to building work. Rubbing a hand over the day-old greying stubble on his face he turned his attention to his wife, who'd ventured a little deeper into the building.

"So?" she asked, raising her eyebrows in hope and turning to her husband. "It looks good doesn't it, Tom?" She paused before walking back to him, the loose tiles jostled under her feet and echoed in the emptiness.

"This has been your dream for the last ten years, if you want to take this on, I'm with you," Tom said, realising that trying to put her off was about as futile as old King Canute's efforts to halt the rising tide.

"Your husband," Karl cut in, "said you wanted to turn this into a holiday home."

"Yes," Sue said, nodding her head. "That's the plan. I grew up in Cornwall but moved east in my early twenties. It's a bit like coming home, there's always been a part of me that wanted to have a place down here."

"Well as you know it's in a fantastic location, the village is quiet although quite remote. Crime is virtually non-existent. In fact, when I searched crime figures for this postal code, I could not find a single reported crime in the village of Trellen for the last eight years, which is as far as the publicly available records go back. This is also the first property I could find in the entire village that has come up for sale in recent times, well, as far back as I could research on the internet, so this is a rare buy." Karl cast his eyes around the empty expanse as if he were viewing and selling the finished article and not a wreck. "As far as tourist attractions go, the Eden

Project is just a short drive away, and the picturesque village of Charlestown is ten miles down the road. That's your nearest decent sized town, well that and Lostwithiel."

"I think you can cut the sales patter," Tom smiled, fully aware that in the next few months, and likely when winter was at its coldest, he, and a trusted team of guys who would work for him at the drop of a hat, would be here bringing the old stone chapel back to life. "I think my wife, who obviously has watched one too many episodes of Grand Designs has made up her mind, and if it's good for her, it's good for me." Tom rubbed his hands together, trying to get some warmth into them and sooth the arthritic ache that'd slowly set into his bones during the last few years. "It's bloody freezing out here, so why don't we head back to your office, run some figures and have us a nice hot brew."

Sue, who was now clutching her husband's hand gave a small squeal of glee and kissed his stubbly cheek.

"Pleasure doing business," said Karl, his face wearing a very broad, cat-that-got-the-cream smile. He extended his hand and grasped Tom's. He pumped it up and down enthusiastically before turning and walking briskly out of the building and into the overgrown grounds.

Tom followed his wife and Karl out, stopping at the open doors he began to swing them shut whilst making another mental note to bring a can of GT85 or WD40 with him on the inevitable next trip. As the last of the winter light turned from a wide beam to a lance, and the tired hinges gave their last scream of protest, he thought he saw something stirring in the shadows at the back of the building. Something silent. Something dark and about the size of a man. Intrigued, and slightly spooked he swung the door open. The creaking hinges made him jump and he inwardly cursed himself for being childish. Straining his eyes toward the back of the cave-like interior a growing sense of unease built in

Tom's gut, as if something or someone was watching him; he felt observed. Cursing himself a second time he clicked his torch on and lit the back wall with a bright shaft of white light. The cavernous interior was empty. Still feeling uneasy Tom swung the door closed, collected the padlock up off the cold floor and snapped it shut, securing the old building in darkness once again.

CHAPTER 3

THE OLD CHAPEL HAD BEEN ON THE 'FOR-SALE Portfolio' at Winns Estate Agency for just over a year, a few months longer than Karl Banks had actually worked for the firm. At the office there was a sweepstake style prize running, thankfully which Karl was a part of, that went to the employee who managed to sell the creepy wreck of a building. The prize fund was paid into by the participants monthly, a mere five pounds each held in a big glass-style sweet jar and secured in the office safe. With his, and the other four more experienced agents paying into it every month for the last ten months the bounty heading Karl's way was two hundred and fifty pounds, a sizeable amount on his rookie wage. Added to the commission the sale had netted him, all in all, it had been a very profitable day.

Following a spell in the office with Tom and Sue Reed, who he'd taken a genuine liking to, Karl now found himself heading back out to the ramshackle old building to stick a triumphant 'SOLD' sign over the 'FOR SALE' one that had been replaced more than once during the time the building had been on their books. A property didn't look good to passing trade if the 'FOR SALE' sign outside looked like shit, even when the building it advertised was fit for demolition. Not that much passing trade went that way, and it was for all intents and purposes, the arse end of nowheresville.

Changing the sign to 'SOLD' wasn't a necessity that very day and the remote village of Trellen was a good forty-minute drive from the office in Liskeard at rush hour, but Karl didn't mind, it was his way of capping off the perfect day. Besides, it meant he got to take the new company 3 Series for another spin and really test the handling on some of the winding back roads.

The Reeds had screwed him down on the price a little; as it turned out they were only too aware of how long the place had been for sale. With them sat expectantly on the other side of his small desk, (it seemed the desks got bigger the longer you worked at Winns), sipping hot, sweet tea, he'd called the offer through to the Bough family personally. Half an hour, and a few calls later the offer had been accepted, and with the Reeds being cash buyers there was not a great deal to go wrong from here on in. Tom Reed was a builder and experienced property developer, he knew only too well what he was buying into, unlike Tom Hanks' character in that classic mid-eighties film The Money Pit, there had been no con. Yet Karl felt as if he should have been wearing a mask doing the deal.

The Old Chapel marked up Karl's most successful sale to date - not his most valuable, not by a long-shot, but the place had been on the books long enough and was proving to be a real Jonah. Karl was under no illusions that the woman, Sue, had all but hoodwinked her husband into buying the property. It was still his sale nonetheless, even if he didn't have to turn on the hard sell, something that he was getting good at.

Following the local signs toward Charlestown, and trying not to use the satnav, Karl gunned the company 3 Series down another generic, but fun, country lane. High thorny hedges lined the sides, reaching the car roof. Occasionally he would hug the BMW too far to the left, causing the nearside wing mirror to catch on the few overhanging privets. A few times, when the corner proved very tight, he had to jam the brakes on, just in case he met another mad-brained driver coming the other way. Thankfully, even at rush hour, once he'd cleared the main town, traffic was minimal. The houses and villages out here were sparsely scattered about, meaning there wasn't a glut of commuters using the old roads.

Much to his annoyance, and after close to forty minutes of driving, Karl lost his battle to not use the navigation system, and after a few too many stubborn miles he found himself pulling into the main tourist carpark at Charlestown Harbour.

Great, he thought to himself, *I'm a good ten miles out of my way now.* Inwardly cursing the local council for the lack of signs to the village he leaned forward and found Trellen on his previous routes. The helpful device informed him he was just under ten miles from his destination. He was officially off the clock in thirty minutes but on days like this, he didn't mind. Spinning the back wheels, Karl gunned the engine and left Charlestown Harbour, where forty-seven years ago a fifteen-year-old girl by the name of Lindie Parker had gone missing, in his rear-view mirror.

Navigation had always been one of his strong points, and usually, after one trip he could find his way back to almost anywhere. Karl had been out to The Old Chapel, so named by the Bough family, twice now and for some reason, he'd failed to find his way back to the strange little village on both occasions.

With the aid of the BMW's navigation system, Karl pulled the car to a stop outside of the ruined building just under fifteen minutes later, it was almost four fifteen and the light was already falling fast. Opening the boot Karl fished the 'SOLD' signs out, and feeling triumphant, fixed one to each side of the 'FOR SALE' board that was staked into the overgrown grass verge at the property's entrance. Satisfied, he stood back admiring his handiwork and wondered what he'd buy with his sweepstake win.

Behind the sign, and the very overgrown hedge that had now all but engulfed sections of the ancient drystone wall, which marked the front boundary of the place, he caught sight of the building, its dark grey stone almost silhouetted against the cold and dusky sky. A shiver chased its way down his spine, and he felt his hackles rise a little, a feeling that his old nan would say was like having someone walk over your grave. Something about the building spooked him, he was far from a believer in the paranormal and all that rubbish, but a real feeling of dread filled his gut, nonetheless. He gave the sign one more approving look and was just about to jump back in the car and leave the place behind, for what he hoped would be the last time, when he noticed the cumbersome steel double doors. They were only just visible at the end of the long drive, but with disbelief he could see that one was open. *Shit,* he thought, *I knew I should have checked that Tom guy had locked up properly.*

Karl had no intention of losing this sale, and whilst the place was in the middle of nowhere if someone got in and burnt the place out again, or somehow damaged it more than the shit-stain of a state it was already in, he'd not only be for the high jump, it could also cost him financially. He wanted the commission and he wanted his sweepstake money, and on a wider scale, he needed this job. Although in the last few months of his probationary and training period one monumental fuck up could still earn him the sack. No written or final warning, just a *see ya later kiddo* and a P45 in the post.

Trudging reluctantly down the muddy drive and soiling his shoes for the second time that day, Karl reached the door. He glanced longingly back at the BMW and wished he'd brought it down the drive. He turned his attention back to the task in hand, securing the place. The padlock was on the floor, the hasp open and the door ajar a good two feet. Karl was almost certain that he'd seen Tom Reed lock the bloody thing, he'd almost have bet his sweepstake money on it, yet here the lock was on the deck, almost in the same spot that Tom had dropped it when he'd viewed the building some five hours earlier. Fearing someone had broken in, Karl fished his phone from the pocket of his heavy grey winter jacket. Bringing the phone to life he cursed the NO SIGNAL message. If indeed there had been a break in there was zero chance of calling the police. Putting it back in his pocket he froze, someone was inside, in the darkness. He'd heard them. His heart hammering in his chest like a drum he cocked his head to the gap and strained his ears against the silence, whilst holding his breath to still the air that passed in and out of his lungs. The sound came again, a cry, no, a wail. Karl shook his head in disbelief as if the movement would remove the sound from his ears. Running a shaky hand through his thick blonde hair he breathed in slowly, holding the air in his chest once more. The sound came again. Louder this time, a definite cry, a baby's cry. The way he remembered that his little brother Josh would wail when he'd soiled his nappy or wanted attention.

"Hello, is anyone in there?" Karl called, his voice sounding anything but confident. In fact, every word sounded a little shaky as it left his lips and he inwardly cursed himself for sounding so foolish. Whoever was in there wouldn't exactly be fearing retribution with him sounding like a pussy, would they? He waited for a few seconds that ticked by like minutes. There was no reply. Just a perpetual silence that seemed to go hand-in-hand with the darkness that dwelt inside.

Just as he thought his racing mind had imagined the whole thing the crying came again, louder and more anguished. It echoed through the empty space, bouncing off the cold, stone walls. Karl felt his feet involuntarily stumble back a bit, his ankle turned on some loose stone and he almost fell. Gaining his composure, he edged back toward the door. *What the fuck is a baby doing in there?* Karl thought to himself. He scanned the darkening grounds as if expecting to see someone who could offer some help, instead only the gnarled-up mess of the thorn bushes stared back at him, dotted about the overgrown lawn before disappearing into the forest that surrounded the building on three sides. The screaming of the child came again, ending in a painful sounding gurgle. The sound hit him like a punch to the face.

Now, as if sensing something nefarious was afoot the encroaching night seemed eager to claim its hold on the land. The failing light of the day was fading by the minute and soon the whole place would be shrouded in darkness. Cursing his own stupidity, yet at the same time believing that some sicko had broken in and abandoned a child in the building, Karl found his iPhone and searched the multitude of various Apps before locating the one he was after, the one that turned his phone into a torch. Moving in reluctant shuffles toward the door, he turned it on and aimed the small but bright beam of light into the darkness.

"H-hello is a-a-any o-ne there," he stammered, his voice still not finding the courage he would have liked. With wide eyes, he followed the beam as it forced the darkness to retreat into shadow. On the second sweep, the light caught something, a white bundle of ragged swaddle cloth. Karl estimated it to be halfway into the building, and just about at the furthest point that his phone light could reach. The baby's cry came again. The bundle of cloth moved. He wanted to run. He wanted to get into the BMW and pin the accelerator to the floor and never see the damn place again, but he held firm. The child needed his help.

When Karl had been ten, Tommy Johnson, a kid in his class, had fallen through the ice down at the local boating lake in Coronation Park. All the other kids had stood by the side of the frozen water, shouting his name frantically as if just the power of their sheer will, and panic would pull him from the frozen water. Karl, however, had seen an ice rescue on the Discovery Channel the week before and knew what to do. Despite being terrified he'd spread his body weight out on the precariously thin sheet of ice, that Tommy Johnson had foolishly weighed up as worth walking over to get his ball back, and inched his way toward the stricken boy, who was trying frantically to scrabble himself free of the deadly water, hands clawing fruitlessly at the slippery frozen surface. The ice had creaked and cracked with every movement, but he'd reached Tommy, then laid out with his belly on the ice and with his weight distributed as evenly as he could manage, Karl had clasped the boy's icy hands and pulled him from the wintery lake and saved his life. Tommy's grip had been so tight, so desperate, the grip of someone holding on to the last hope of life, and on reflection that's just what he had been doing. Much longer in the freezing waters and the energy would have ebbed completely out of his small body, until it slid under the ice, where his frozen, dead eyes would have no doubt gazed up at the world from beneath the frozen tundra, as if looking through a mirror and into another reality.

Karl, now a Bonafede saver of life had become somewhat of a local child hero and celebrity in his hometown of Helston, for a short spell anyway. The episode had taught him one thing; you could be brave through fear and if someone needed his help he'd do his best to give it.

Reluctantly, and for some reason feeling far more fear than he had that day on the lake, he pulled the heavy door open further, widening the escape route if he needed it. With his insides knotting and turning in anxiety, he crept into the building.

"H-hello," he called again, but all that answered was the sound of his own uncertain voice as it echoed in the darkness. A few silent seconds slipped by then another urgent cry made him freeze. He swept the beam of his phone-torch around The Old Chapel. The place was empty, save for the small pile of squirming white rags. Inch by inch he crept closer, every time the infant cried, he stopped, his heart picking up its rhythm until he was sure it would explode out of his chest and land in a bloody puddle on the broken tiled floor.

The terrifying walk to the child was no more than fifteen yards, but it felt like a mile. Finally, stood over the bundle of rags he paused and took a deep breath that almost made him retch. The smell of decay gagged the air around the infant and the dishevelled cloth that swaddled it was stained in mottled patches that looked like blood or shit, possibly both, it was hard to tell in the light. Gingerly Karl reached down and pulled back the cloth. Lit by the bright concentrated beam of light he caught sight of the child, the source of those tortured sounding cries. As he did the cold air filled with a fresh scream, his scream. The baby had no face. Where its features should have been, was just a mould of skin that almost seemed to try and form an anguished expression as somehow it managed to wail and cry, despite having no mouth. The sound of that cry cast back the silence and filled Karl's head with a pressure that made his brain feel as if it could explode.

It's got no face, Karl thought to himself, momentarily frozen to the spot. *Where the fuck is its face. Oh Jesus, God – noooo!*

Karl reeled back and turned to run, but as he did his foot found a section of loose tile and he went spilling painfully to the floor. Hitting the tiles hard he felt his phone fly from his hand. It clattered along the ground for a few feet, the beam of light flashing erratically in angles as it went. Finally, the phone came to a stop somewhere out of his reach, but as it did the light went out.

Karl scooted back in the darkness, using his hands to move across the cold and broken tiles, the shattered masonry cutting and stabbing at his palms as he went. The sound of the disturbed tiles chinked in the darkness, but the sound of his plight to escape was not the only thing he could hear. The faceless infant was moving, he could hear it scrabbling over the broken floor after him, working its way relentlessly in chase. Feeling blindly behind him Karl's hand found the edge of his iPhone. Grabbing the handset his thumb turned on the torch App, but instead of selecting the constant beam he turned on the strobe, igniting the darkness in a rapid series of bright flashes.

Eyes searching frantically for the nightmarish image he saw it. The staccato flashes gave its movements an epileptic effect. The faceless child was clear of its blood and shit-bound swaddle, clawing its way toward him, naked and on tiny malformed and atrophying limbs. Karl tried to scream, but his voice caught in his throat. Frozen in terror and totally unable to move he watched as the tiny, twisted infant reached his right foot, then he caught a brief glimpse of its gnarled hand on his shoe. He felt its icy touch on his skin, through the thin fabric of his suit trousers. Trying helplessly to will his frozen body into action he heard it let out a triumphant sounding cry from its invisible mouth. Flash by flash he watched as it clawed its way along his leg, each time the light came it had progressed a little further. During the next series of flashes, Karl could do nothing but watch in consternation as it raised its head, presenting its featureless face. Sensing it had its quarry the thing let out another cry, the horrifyingly blank face twisted and distorted, and as it screamed the skin of its mouth tore apart, revealing a gouged maw that held no teeth, just a blackness. Karl felt, no - knew, that if this child reached his head it would suck him down into that blackness, the way a python might ingest a whole goat and he would be gone from this world to the place of nightmares, the place that had birthed this abomination.

As the infant-thing reached his knee the terror suddenly released him and the will to escape won. He kicked his leg out and watched as in a series of rapid flashes the malevolent child tumbled off and fell to the floor, emitting a cry of pain and frustration as it went. Now able to move and free from the paralysis of terror, Karl ran for the door, the screams of the demon infant echoing in the darkness behind him. Reaching the door, he kept moving, any care for securing the building now gone. The encroaching winter's night had further set in; cloaking the chapel's grounds in an ever-deepening darkness as night fully fell upon the land. Against that growing blackness the clean white paint of the BMW at the end of the long drive stood out like a beacon of hope.

Not looking back Karl ran; he'd been somewhat of a sprinter during his school days and muscle memory kicked in as he pounded his way to the car. Reaching the driver's door he wrenched it open, thankfully he'd not locked it, and with the added bonus of the intelligent ignition system the BMW knew the key was with him in the car; there was no need to fumble around for it with shaking hands. Not bothering to secure his seat-belt Karl hit the start button that was glowing helpfully, his lungs gasping for air as the engine roared to life. Not even daring a look down the muddied drive, for if he did, he knew he'd see the nightmare infant on all fours and running the distance down like a predator, he mashed the accelerator pedal into the floor and wheel span away from the horror. Working the engine hard he caused the rear end of the car to snake dangerously down the road, leaving behind two ribbons of black on the faded tarmac.

Trying to get his breathing under control Karl worked the responsive 3 Series through the gears, going far too fast to keep proper control on the narrow road. A few minutes clear of The Old Chapel he dared a look in the rear-view mirror, as if expecting to see the twisted infant now crawling its way at impossible speed down the road, it's blank face somehow rancorous and full of hate, but the view behind him was obscured by a face that grinned back at him with smooth lips and ice blue eyes. The grin on the face widened, showing a line of decaying teeth that stood out like crooked and broken gravestones from dark, blackened gums. In the false safety of the car Karl screamed!

———

"TEN THOUSAND POUNDS!" the voice of the enthusiastic local radio DJ exclaimed. "Ten thousand pounds, Cheryl – if you can tell me who owns the mystery voice, on the station that brings you all the hits; Heart Cornwall."

The lucky listener, who'd actually managed to get through, paused. In the cab of his DAF CF 220 tipper, Jim Sheers, or JIMBO as the sign in the front of his windscreen, printed on an orange number plate announced, shook his head, tutted and shouted at the radio, "It's James fucking Corden you dumb bitch!"

The mystery voice had to be identified from just one word taken from an interview, an interview Jimbo had actually heard live, during a trip from one of the area's many quarries. Which quarry precisely he could not recall, he visited most of them over the course of a working week.

The woman's trepidation to answer narked him, he also felt narked that he knew the answer, narked that he had tried to get through to the radio station practically every day for the last three weeks, and tonight had been no exception, either. Every one of his calls had been met with the enraging sound of an engaged tone.

Most of all, and above all else he was narked that his piece of shit TomTom had diverted him down some of the worst roads in the area, all because an accident had blocked one of the main arterial routes. The irony of that fact would not be lost on him in the days after his impending accident, the accident, that as he leaned forward and cranked the volume up on his stereo a notch, he didn't know was about to happen.

"Piers Morgan," Cheryl finally said.

"So, for *ten thousand pounds*," the DJ highlighted the amount, fake excitement in his voice. "You're saying it's This Morning and Britain's Got Talent host – Piers Morgan?"

"Yes, Dan."

"It's James fucking Cordon you daft twat," Jimbo shouted, the word *twat* highlighting his Welsh accent. Although frustrated at the caller's stupidity he was also glad. The woman was wrong, as wrong as putting ketchup on a roast dinner, and that meant there was still a chance he could net the ten grand when the *CALL NOW* alarm sounded, as it did three times a day. When? Well, that was anybody's guess. You had to *LISTEN TO WIN*! That particular reminder followed every song, well likely not every song, but it sure as shit felt that way.

At the same time, Karl took his eyes off the road, his attention drawn to the insidious face with its crooked teeth and black gums, Jimbo's focus on the road also lapsed. Only it was the competition that got him, and not some nightmarish image of death glaring from the back seat. It was a twist of fate, a terrible and horrific matter of bad timing, and one that would cost one life and change the other forever.

Looking down at the stereo, as if he could see DJ Dan tell the woman she wrong, the BMW heading in the other direction went wide on a slight curve and into the path of the DAF tipper, that not an hour before had been loaded with twenty tonnes of aggregate, just six shy of its maximum load weight. Jimbo faintly became aware of the headlights as he looked up, but before he could even think why some daft prick, a term he often used to describe idiot car drivers, was on his side of the road, the BMW hit him in a full head on, metal tearing, life-ending collision.

The 3 Series, that was travelling the wrong side of sixty at the time of the impact, stopped in a nano-second, the sheer mass of the DAF deciding that the car was going its way or the highway. The front of the car crumpled in the blink of an eye, forcing the engine through and into the cab, where it severed Karl's body in two. As the small BMW was forced back along the road, sparks hailing from its underbelly, the engine lost the momentum of the sharp impact and began to cook his legs. It didn't matter, Karl felt nothing. His body was now torn, twisted and crumpled in the back of the car, his neck broken, leaving his head at an angle similar to that of a person considering a difficult task, only much more pronounced, and with the added gore of his spine, that now breached the skin and stuck out in a bloodied compound fracture. His left eye had been forced from its socket by the force of the impact and now dangled down on his cheek as if puzzled at where his legs had gone.

As the BMW, now half of its original size, squealed in protest at being firmly attached to the front of Jimbo's DAF, Jimbo managed to jam on the brakes, ignoring the searing pain in his collarbone, that had no doubt been broken by the force of the impact as he'd been caught by the seatbelt's friction lock. Sparks flew from the wrecked car and ignited the ruptured fuel tank; the car began to burn fiercely before it had even come to a stop. Only the sheer weight of his tipper, aided by the size of the impacting car had saved him, that and the seatbelt, of course.

Jimbo felt as if his left arm was also broken and judging from the angle that it now sat limply at, he guessed it probably was. Using his good arm, he reached over and unclipped his belt. Wincing in pain, he'd cracked a few ribs too by the feel of it, he leant his weight against the driver's door, now buckled from the impact. The bent metal groaned in protest and he had to use all sixteen stone of his weight to push it painfully open, before he half fell to the tarmac, fresh pain igniting in his broken arm and collarbone.

Jimbo managed to stand, he wasn't sure how, all that mattered was that he was on his feet. Miraculously his legs hadn't been broken, there was pain, maybe that of a sprain or torn muscle but it paled in comparison to the other, more serious injuries.

He staggered across the narrow road, nursing his askew arm and feeling the searing heat of the fire that had now started to lick his cab with a multitude of eager, orange tongues. Finally reaching what he hoped was a safe distance he allowed his body to slump into a shallow culvert where he could do nothing but watch as the two vehicles burned brightly against the cold November sky.

PART 2
JULY 2018

THE TRAFFIC CHOKED ITS WAY SLOWLY ACROSS THE New Forest. The heat-softened tarmac of the two west-bound lanes hidden under countless cars and trucks that stretched back for miles, and from the air resembled a massive metallic slow-moving snake, glistening motionlessly in the relentless July sun, basking in the heat.

Ellie Harrison gazed nonchalantly out the rear passenger side window of her father's Peugeot Estate. Pressing her forehead against the warm glass she watched absently as they crawled past a grubby old white Ford Focus. The heat and lack of movement had proven too much for the tatty old car and it now sat slightly askew, part on the road and part on the grass verge. Its bonnet was up and a gradually increasing puddle of water leaked from the engine bay as if the car had needed to stop to take a piss. The coolant hit the hot tarmac and chased out toward the queuing traffic in tiny abstract streams. This was the third such break-down they'd crept past since hitting the jam around an hour ago; the halted traffic and sweltering heat were claiming their mechanical victims one at a time.

The occupants of the cooked Focus, a young couple who Ellie guessed were a few years older than her, were stood by the bonnet staring blankly into the steaming engine bay as if the sheer power of hope would resolve the issue and fix the radiator.

"I still don't see why I had to come," Ellie protested, looking away from the stricken car and hoping to catch the attention of either of her parents in the rear-view mirror. "I mean I am eighteen now, I'm not a kid!"

"We've been over this too many times, Ellie!" her mother, Carol, sighed from the front seat. She twisted her slender frame around to face her daughter and lifted the oversize dark lenses of her sunglasses as if to highlight the disappointment in her eyes. "This is the first and probably last chance we will get to have a proper family holiday together -"

"A family holiday," Ellie cut in, causing her mother's scowl to deepen, she hated being spoken over and Ellie knew it, "is going somewhere cool, like Florida, or at the very least Greece or Spain, not some ass-hat of a village in the middle of nowheresville!"

"What's an ass-hat?" chimed in her five-year-old brother, Henry, or Hand-Me-Down-Henry as she often called him, due to the never-ending supply of clothing that came from his cousin, Leon, who was a year older. He hated the pet name and would put on his best whining voice when Ellie teased him by saying it to his face.

Whilst Ellie's mum had been pregnant with Henry, and before they knew the sex of the baby, the bump had been nicknamed Whoops. Even then, and thanks to certain lessons in school about such things, Ellie knew enough to understand the meaning behind the name, and that Henry hadn't exactly been planned. Planned or not, just a few weeks after turning thirteen, and having spent those fun-filled childhood years comfortable with being an only child, Ellie had found herself as an older sister, and her parents, just the wrong side of forty, had found themselves once again buried in soiled nappies and suffering a seemingly never-ending stream of sleepless nights at the hands of a hedonistic and demanding infant. Unfortunately for them, Hand-Me-Down-Henry came along right around the time they also had a hormonal teenage daughter to deal with. Although Hand-Me-Down-Henry could be plenty annoying Ellie adored him, plus he was at an age where he was fun to tease. On Tuesdays and Thursdays, when Ellie had no college lessons to attend, she would walk up to collect him from his infant's school where he was in his first reception year, then on the way home take him to the local park for an hour where he could expel a little of the never-ending energy he seemed blessed with. However, her twice-weekly trips to the local park, when the weather permitted, were now sadly at an end.

The summer had arrived, and the coming of this summer had brought with it the end of her college studies, and when the summer turned to September, Ellie would find herself moving away from home for the first time as she began the next chapter of her life at Warwick University.

On more than one occasion whilst at the park she'd caught some of the mums, who seemed to move in cattle-like herds, all sporting various designer pushchairs and changing bags, flashing her disapproving looks. Obviously, they had her pegged as a young, teen mother with a child already of school age, a notion she found hilarious. Not that some girls didn't get themselves knocked-up at that age. One girl in her school named Tina Barnes, or Ten-P Tina as the boys affectionately called her, had left to be home-schooled after landing the prize of twin girls at just fourteen. On more than one occasion Ellie had been tempted to call Henry, Son, just to fully satisfy their disapproval. Ellie had no desires on parenthood for a long time and had no wanting to have the best of her years snatched away by an ankle biter. She'd seen and helped her mother with Henry from day one and knew what hard work it was, there was too much of the world to experience before she got tied down with a child of her own. If anything, being a teenage girl with a baby – turned toddler – in the house was the best sex-ed you could get and one of the main reasons she'd abstained from such carnal acts. Not that she'd not been tempted a few times, it's just the time had never been right.

Ellie watched her younger brother, who was now beaming with curiosity over the phrase, to the point where he'd even taken his attention away from the current episode of Peppa Pig that graced his tablet screen. He looked from Ellie to his mother, expectantly and awaited an explanation. "Mummy," he half winged, "what's an ass-hat?"

"Henry!" Carol scolded. "And you should know better than to use that kind of language in front of your brother!" She treated Ellie to one of her best disapproving looks, a thing she was well practised at. Carol slid a purple hairband off her wrist where she'd been wearing it like a bracelet, collected up her shoulder length dark brown hair and put it in a quick ponytail. Ellie noticed a few more streaks of grey had chased their way into her hair, and she expected the dye would come out soon and she'd have the pleasure of *doing her roots*, as her mother put it. The truth was the grey had gone beyond the roots now and had begun a full-on, you're getting old, assault on her head.

Her mother's quick and erratic movements told Ellie she was far from pleased. "Back me up a little here, Rob," she added looking at their father.

"I knew we should have taken the three-o-three and not pushed further south to the thirty-one," he muttered absently, as if unaware of the family conflict developing in the car. He expelled a long weary breath of air through clenched teeth before adjusting his weight on the car seat, arching his back as if to rid it of a niggling pain.

"Ass-hat is not exactly a swear word," Ellie protested.

"Ass-hat," Hand-Me-Down-Henry giggled his face

beaming with a wide smile at having used the word three times with virtually no reprimanding. Still chuckling to himself he went back to the screen of his tablet and started the current episode of Peppa Pig all over again. She was certain that if she had to listen to the theme tune once more, she'd be about ready to maim someone.

The last two years of Ellie's life, since leaving school, had been spent studying psychology in college, graduating with a good enough pass mark at A Level standard to carry on her passion at university. She often thought that she could easily write a paper on underlying messages in children's television shows, and if the chance came up during her fast encroaching time at Warwick, she fully planned on doing it.

"You know only too well, Hun, why we can't go somewhere *cool* as you put it," Carol said, her eyes still fixed on her daughter. "Your grandfather is not in the best of health and if the home calls we - well I, need to be able to get back. As it is five days away are the most I feel happy about leaving him for."

Ellie's grandfather, or gramps as she'd called him since being Henry's age, a name that had stuck and she still used to this day, had been in Whispering Pines Retirement & Assisted Living Home for the past three years. He'd suffered a stroke six months after Ellie's grandmother had died after a brief and futile battle with the Big C. After the stroke and being discharged from hospital it was soon clear that he could no longer care for himself. As a result of two falls and plenty of soiled trousers poor old gramps had been lodged in what Ellie thought of as God's Waiting Room ever since. Ellie hated the place, the air seemed to be laced with the constant stench of incontinence, often mixed with whatever culinary delight the kitchen staff were working on. Usually something that had the unappealing smell of overly boiled cabbage. Almost every time she visited, one of the rooms had been taken on by the next guest, its previous owner's number with the Grim Reaper having come up. In a nutshell, the place was depressing and just being there for a few hours made Ellie feel as if the life were being sucked out of her, and it depressed her that the only way to buy a ticket out of the place came with a casket.

Ellie had been very close to her gramps growing up, unlike her grandparents on her father's side who lived in New Zealand and she'd only seen twice in her life. Sure, she got the obligatory birthday and Christmas card, but she didn't feel any real connection with them. Sadly, and now at the age of eighty-five, it was looking increasingly like this year was going to be gramps' last. Deep down Ellie knew why they weren't heading further afield, and she felt momentarily bad for sounding selfish.

"And besides, Ells," her father cut in, deciding to join the conversation, "I don't really fancy coming home to find that you've wrecked the place after a big party." He winked at her in the rear-view and fired her a small but encouraging smile.

"Really, Dad?" she said, sounding a little exasperated. "I had a party to go to, tomorrow night, it's like the biggest event of the year. You do realise that just by missing it I'm practically going to be a social pariah when I get back next week."

The party was one, and largely the main reason why Ellie was so reluctant to come on this merry little family holiday to Cornwall. That, and at eighteen, holidays with your parents were not the matter of excitement they'd been when she'd been a child, and not exactly a cool reason to give your best friend as to why you couldn't attend her party. It was also the start of the summer break and even if one of her best friends, Suzie, wasn't holding a massive party that Saturday to celebrate her nineteenth, there were still plenty of places she'd rather be than here, stuck in a car in a seemingly never-ending line of traffic on her way to a place she doubted had even heard of the internet. Henry, on the other hand, had practically been bouncing off the walls of the house for the last few weeks asking every day, some days more than once, how much longer it was until they were leaving. Now they were on their way the question had switched to the obligatory, *are we there yet?* that seemed to come pre-programmed into every child under the age of ten when on a car journey that stretched out longer than a trip to the local shops, school or soft play area.

Ellie broke her father's gaze and peered around the front seat taking in the perpetual line of cars that stretched out for as far as she could see, which looked like a good mile or more. The line of halted traffic ran down the long gradual slope of the rise they were on and all the way to the top of the next. To either side the slightly brownish sun-scorched, heather-clad flats of the New Forest stretched out as far as she could see, meeting tree-lined woods on each horizon.

Occasionally a horn sounded from some impatient motorist nearby and she could see a few cars further up switching lanes as if they held some secret knowledge that the one they were jostling for was about to flow freely. Whilst undoubtedly frustrating, Ellie enjoyed people watching and was fascinated by the futile lane switching and horn beeping. Human behaviour in certain situations intrigued her; it always had and was one of the main reasons she'd chosen an educational route in psychology, something she hoped to extend to employment when she was older and eventually had to leave the snug, comfortable blanket of education.

"Just try to enjoy yourself," her mother encouraged. "If we ever manage to get there that is."

"How much further is it?" Henry asked, "I need wee-wee!"

"We're not even close," Ellie answered, discouragingly. "Lucky for you, you can go by the side of the car, I've got to hold it in until the next service station." She grinned at him, enjoying his cheeky, angelic smile.

"If I remember correctly," her father said trying to sound upbeat. "There's a Golden Arches in a couple of miles, just before Ringwood. I think we could all use a break from the car, and a burger."

"And milkshake," chimed in Henry.

"Sounds like a good deal," Ellie agreed managing a forced smile. Like it or not she was stuck with the situation for the next five days and no amount of complaining was going to change it. Grinning at Henry she held her hand up and just as she'd taught him, he smacked his tiny palm against hers in a high-five. "Good one," she chuckled, shaking her hand as if he'd hurt it.

It took them another forty minutes to cover the two miles to the next service station, and they had indeed needed to pull to the side of the road to let Henry relieve himself. Much to Ellie's amusement, he always insisted on going on one of the wheels when caught short.

Finally pulled over at the small service station, they found McDonald's carpark was rammed with likeminded travellers, taking the first opportunity since Southampton to escape the queuing traffic, pull over and hope whatever was causing the jam remedied itself whilst they were stopped.

The dry July air hit Ellie like the opening of an oven door as she left the car and she felt instantly thankful that they had a fairly modern Peugeot with good airconditioning. Even dressed in her skirt and strap top the outside air felt too hot, the smell of fumes from the gridlocked traffic hung chokingly in the air and she felt a thin sheen of sweat on her brow by the time she reached the main doors.

From what basic geographic knowledge, she had on the area she knew they were not a million miles from Bournemouth. The vibrant seaside town appealed to her much more than the converted old chapel they were heading to. She made her mind up that when she'd passed her driving test in August, she'd bring Suzie down to Bournemouth and they could have a proper weekend away. A last girls' break before they said their goodbyes and went off to find new lives at university. The fact she might fail her test didn't even feature on Ellie's scope; failing was not an option. Ellie had already purchased a car, a slightly tatty red Mini One. One of the first of the new shape to be made by BMW. She'd worked tirelessly for the past eighteen months at one of the local hair salons sweeping hair and making tea. Once she'd shown her father she could save and had half the money she'd need to buy and insure the small car, he'd put in the other half to the pot. Ellie had taken a few lessons with her dad in the family Peugeot, but he was far too stressy for her liking, yelling at her to watch out for this and look out for that. Her driving instructor was much more relaxed, and in the end, she decided paying for lessons was more favourable than learning with your father, even if it was for free.

Leaving Hand-Me-Down-Henry and her mum on the small landscaped area of greenery, where Henry was already giggling and shrieking with delight as he chased a small Minion-decorated yellow ball around, his slightly too long floppy blonde hair catching the light breeze, she headed inside with her father. Ellie left her dad at the counter, which was five deep with customers eager to eat their fill of junk-food, and headed to the toilet. The small lavatory, whilst refreshingly air-conditioned, held a smell almost akin to that at Whispering Pines Care Home. Holding her breath for as long as she could to cut out the stench of one too many toilet desperate travellers, mixed with the pungent, artificial floral scent of industrial detergent, Ellie splashed some cool water over her face. Looking at her reflection, she fixed a few wayward strands of auburn hair that had worked free of her latest hairstyle, a retro, yet modern looking bob that came just past her jawline. The sound of the next eager toilet goer rattling the door stole her from a temporary daydream, and after blasting her wet face with the dryer, she joined her father who was now at the front of the queue almost shouting his order over the cacophony of background noise.

Half an hour later and all full of stomach bloating junk food, (that although plenty tasty at the time had a habit of making you feel like shit after), they were back on the road. Traffic had eased a little and a few miles on they found the cause of the delay. A lorry had shed its load, blocking the road and causing all the traffic to use a slip lane to get around it. Police and recovery had the stricken vehicle upright and hooked to a monstrous looking recovery truck, its orange hazard lights flashing brightly despite the sunlight. Just as they'd reached the small diversion a police officer had re-opened the road fully and waved them past.

Ellie spent the next two hours of the tedious journey trying to ignore the Peppa Pig theme tune, which was proving to be a real earworm. Even whilst trying to concentrate on the level of Candy Crush that had been proving all but impossible to defeat for the best part of a week, she could still hear it in her head playing over and over.

Well behind on the time they'd planned to arrive in Trellen, thanks to the traffic mayhem in the New Forest, their father pulled them into the large tourist carpark of The Jamaica Inn. According to the map they were only around twenty miles from The Old Chapel, but with it being almost five PM and dinner time, and with neither of Ellie's parents wanting to cook with the meagre supplies they'd packed at the family home back in Reading, a stop for a pub meal was unanimously decided upon.

Henry, brimming with unspent energy, made a clumsy beeline for the wooden play area the moment he'd been released from his booster, almost tripping over his eager feet as he ran pell-mell across the gravel car park, followed at a distance by their mother who kept screaming at him to be careful. The evening sun was still strong and looking down toward the main A30 Ellie could see a heat mirage shimmering in the air, just above the sun-scorched tarmac.

The well-built timber play area was full of other children, some on swings, some queuing for the slide whilst other less patient and slightly older kids pushed in front of them. A large coach was hauled up in the corner of the car park and it looked as if the pub's museum was enjoying a few last-minute visitors.

Despite the sunny evening, Ellie was keen to head inside and check the place out. She'd seen the notorious pub on two paranormal shows over the last couple of years and it supposedly held the title of one of the most haunted Inns in the country. One of the shows, filmed a good few years ago by the Haunted Happenings team, the UK's most renown paranormal show, (yet at the same time the least creditworthy), allegedly turned up a whole host of unexplained phenomenon. From items being thrown at the crew, (conveniently always off camera), to doors shutting on their own. Ellie had half watched the investigation whilst trying to concentrate on some college work and found it almost farcical and far beyond believable. The presenter, a well-known TV celebrity named Chrissy Meadows, seemed to have the ability to lose her shit at the slightest noise. Acted or not Ellie found her borderline annoying at times. The second televised investigation she'd seen had been more recent, filmed earlier that year. The lead investigator was a guy named Mike Cross, in a show called Unexplained UK. Mike Cross wasn't a TV celebrity, according to the show his back-story was police and private investigation. Ellie wasn't sure how much truth there was in that but his small team found no paranormal activity at all, concluding that whilst the ancient Inn was a fascinating building, partly from the fame it drew by being the title of a Daphne du Maurier novel, and partly from the history of smuggling in the area, he could find no evidence of a haunting. Ellie preferred the no-nonsense style of Unexplained UK but if you were after scares against cold hard facts you were better off with the borderline comical antics of Haunted Happenings. One of the Unexplained UK team, an attractive woman called Tara Gibb, or Tig as she was usually called on camera, had supposedly heard a growl in room four. According to local legend it was the most haunted part of the building, but as they'd not managed to record it the event had been discounted.

The various paranormal investigation shows, all of differing quality and credibility, were one of Ellie's guilty pleasures and a little personal thing she indulged in a few times a week whilst squirreled away in her room. Her passion for the paranormal stemmed from when she'd been fifteen. The night that her grandmother had passed away in her sleep having finally lost her battel with cancer, Ellie had awoken suddenly in her room, or she thought she had. Truth be told she wasn't totally sure now if it had been a dream, but it had felt real, very real. Unaware at the time of her death, Ellie had seen her gran at the end of her bed. She'd looked different than normal, as if she was half there. It seemed almost clichéd, but her appearance was what Ellie considered to be holographic, there and yet not there all at the same time. Puzzled, more than afraid, Ellie watched as her gran smiled at her warmly. She'd then felt a sudden chill on her cheek followed by the overwhelming smell of her sweet lavender perfume. It hung in the air for a few brief moments like an invisible mist before the vision and the smell vanished. The next morning before breakfast, Ellie learned of her passing. To be fair she had no idea if she'd been asleep or awake when she'd seen the vision, and she was sure Mike Cross and the Unexplained UK team would debunk it as no more than a dream and a fanciful coincidence, but it had felt real to her, so very real, and Ellie was sure that her gran had stopped in on her to say goodbye.

In the days and weeks following her passing Ellie had taken a lot of solace from what she'd seen, or thought she'd seen, that night in her room. As if her gran had known she'd needed a little confirmation that she'd passed on to a better place after those months of pain. Maybe her spirit had visited in order to help her cope with what had been the first big family loss in her young life, she didn't know, but it had sparked her interest in the afterlife.

Enjoying the day for the first time since leaving home, Ellie followed her father around the side of the building and out onto the front cobbled courtyard. This had been the opening shot for both Haunted Happenings and Unexplained UK, the team leaders filming the opening link at night with the pub lit ominously behind and tendrils of mist from the moors wrapping themselves like long fingers around the building. Reaching the main door, she went inside, smiling at the idea of being stood in the exact bar she'd watched on TV not so long ago. Then and there she decided that this was bound to be the coolest part of the entire trip. From watching the shows, Ellie knew the rooms on the first floor were accessed by a small half-glazed door to the side of the bar. Whilst her father ran an eye over the menu she ventured through and took in the narrow and off-kilter looking stairs, which one of the Haunted Happenings team had allegedly been pushed down, again conveniently off camera. Not wanting to push her luck, as the door had a sign on saying, STRICTLY RESIDENTIAL GUESTS ONLY, Ellie joined her father back at the bar. Much to her annoyance, he took the drinks and menus outside and she was forced to spend most of her time at the Inn perched on a rickety picnic bench in front of the play area, where Hand-Me-Down-Henry had two little girls chasing him relentlessly around the wooden climbing frame. She wasn't sure just how many times they pursued him around that timber structure but watching the running and shrieking almost made her feel dizzy.

Following a gut-busting meal of locally made pies with mash, and just about the finest beef gravy Ellie had ever tasted, she stole herself away to the gift shop and purchased a one size too big red hoody. The front was decorated with a skull and crossbones logo, as well as the pub's name. It wasn't the kind of attire she'd wear out, but Ellie knew university life could be hard and there was no way her dorm room was going to be as lusciously heated as the family home was in the depths of winter. The hoody would be perfect for keeping warm on those cold nights. She was hoping to find a onesie, but it appeared that particular fashion faux pas had been missed by the gift shop's head purchaser.

All too soon Ellie found herself back at the car. Opening the back door, she felt a wall of superheated air hit her, with it was unpleasant smell of uneaten fast food. Stooping down she found half of Henry's Happy Meal burger in the footwell, she tossed it into the car park and helped him into his booster. Like most kids his age he'd not managed to eat the Happy Meal in the time they'd stopped for, choosing instead to run-amok in the small park area, stopping every few minutes for a chip or bite of sorry looking burger that in no way resembled the plump looking fat drenched delicacy portrayed on the menu board.

Twenty minutes later, as they reached the small Cornish town of Lostwithiel, Ellie watched her mother fish the booking sheets from her bag. "I'd better call the lady who has the key," she said scanning the papers. "I'm sure Mrs. Reed said to call when we got to Lostwithiel."

"Sounds about right," her father agreed, looking down at the forms in her mother's lap as they waited at a red traffic light. She found the part of the booking sheet she wanted and punched a number into her aging LG phone. Ellie listened to the one-sided conversation with a lady called Lucinda who apparently had the key and would let them in. After a number of apologies for how late they were, with a brief story of the accident in the New Forest threaded through for good measure the, call ended.

"She said we should be arriving in around ten minutes from here and that she'll be there waiting for us." Her mother turned around in the front seat. "Try to enjoy it, Ells," she encouraged. "It has a hot tub in one of the bathrooms, we can have a girlie pampering session."

"Sounds good," Ellie smiled, resigned to the fact that fighting it would just make the time until she could get home and start enjoying her last summer before university go all the slower.

As Lucinda had promised, ten minutes later her father swung the Peugeot into the pea-shingled driveway of The Old Chapel. At the end of the long drive she could see an Essex white, new looking Range Rover parked up. The driver, who she assumed was Lucinda with the key, was stood leaned back against the side of the car, sunning her face in the last of the day's rays. As they crept up the drive Ellie was surprised to see that Lucinda was a well turned out lady who looked to be in her early forties. She had deep red hair a shade redder than her own, that flowed to her shoulders and a waist and jawline that most women would pay top dollar to a surgeon for. Her clothes looked expensive. She donned smart fitted black trousers with a gold chain belt that looked too formal and hot for the heat of the day, finished with a lace lined white top that plunged at the front to the point of riskiness, the lace theme ran down the front and over the shoulder straps. For some reason, Ellie had assumed that anyone living this far out in the countryside would be driving a beat-up old Defender and looking like they'd just rolled in from milking the cows.

The moment the car stopped, Hand-Me-Down-

Henry was struggling the belt clip of his booster off, eager to get out and explore. Ellie helped him, leaning over to open the door. As soon as it swung open, he was off. Climbing out herself she felt surprisingly impressed by the building. It was big, easily big enough for two or three families to share. Ellie didn't know how much it had cost to rent but the idea of coming back with a good few friends and having one hell of a party did cross her mind. With the right people and enough booze, it wouldn't matter a jot that they were miles from anywhere, it might even prove to be a bonus.

Ellie wasn't good on periodical architecture, but she knew from what her mother had said that the building was seventeenth century. The old Cornish stone looked clean and bright, juxtaposed against a few newer wooden double-glazed windows, and a couple of more authentic looking stained-glass ones. The roof pitched quite steeply and at the far end an old bell tower stood century over the building. Within the tower a bell was held in place on a long steel pole. The brass of the bell gleamed warmly in the lowering sun. Ellie wondered if it actually worked or if it was just for show, she suspected it was the latter.

"Harrison family," smiled Lucinda as she stepped forward and shook Ellie's dad's hand softly.

"That's us," he replied, sounding a little flustered, obviously her striking beauty hadn't been lost on him. Ellie allowed herself a little inward smile and wondered if her mum would give him some shit later for it. She thought she probably would.

"Here is the key," Lucinda continued formally, holding out a single silver key on a large plastic fob. "When you guys leave just pop it under the mat," Lucinda pointed a well-manicured finger at the generic doormat just inside the entrance arch, just in case there was any confusion. "You have my number, there is a landline phone inside, you won't get a mobile signal out here."

Ellie took a cursory look at the S8 which she had clutched in her hand only to be met with the NO SER-VICE message.

"None of the networks have coverage here," Lucinda confirmed. "They've tried to put masts up, sure they have, but this is a close-knit community and so far we have vetoed every effort." She turned her attention to Henry who was now clinging to his mother's leg, peeking around it then ducking back when he saw Lucinda had noticed him. "Well aren't you just a cutie-pie!" She exclaimed, firing him a wink. Henry flushed the crimson red of Lucinda's hair and ducked behind his mother's leg again, pulling at her faded denim jeans. "So, you guys have any questions?" she concluded, turning her attention back to her mother.

"I think it's all in the pack," Carol said as she wrestled Henry off her leg. Ellie watched her force a smile and she knew instantly that her father's moment of fluster had been duly noted. Ellie was pretty good at reading body language and there was a definite defensive stance on her mother's part.

"There aren't any pubs here in Trellen, the nearest decent sized village is Charlestown," Lucinda continued as if she'd actually been asked. Ellie guessed she was used to the tourist guide patter. "In all, there are twelve original homes that make up the village, the recently converted chapel is number thirteen. There are no shops, no post office, just us yokels."

"Have you lived in the village long?" Ellie's father asked.

"All my life, all the families here have a long lineage to Trellen. Since Sue and Tom opened The Old Chapel up for business, we have seen the first new faces to stay here for a long time."

"Well I hope us holidaymakers don't impose too much," her mother said, still sounding a little frosty.

"Not at all," Lucinda answered obliviously. "Sure, at first we weren't too keen, but sometimes change is good. And besides it's nice to have some fresh blood around, it's breathed a little life back into the place." Lucinda paused, taking each of them in, in turn. "I'm holding a little get-together tomorrow, nothing big, just the yokels, a barbeque. Feel free to drop by if the mood takes you."

"We'd love to," Ellie's father answered before her mother had a chance to interject with an excuse that given a few more seconds she would have no doubt cooked up. "Of course, we can't stay too late, but we will come for the start, say 'til eight-ish."

"Fantastic," Lucinda beamed. "My house is next one down, you can't miss it." She pointed left. "About a quarter to a half mile that-a way, look for the stone gate posts."

"Will there be any other children there?" asked Henry, finding his voice for the first time.

"Oh, I'm afraid not, sweetie," Lucinda replied, crouching down to his level. "But that doesn't mean you can't have fun." She gave his messy blonde hair a rub and stood back up, straightening out the fabric of her well fitted black trousers. "I don't think there is much else you need to know. If you're after an internet connection, then the router and code are in the hall. We are remote but we have been dragged kicking and screaming into the modern world." Ellie watched as Lucinda turned her hauntingly green eyes to her and smiled. "Don't expect fast speeds, though. It's kinda the end of the line down her, ya know."

"You're telling me," replied Ellie. She wasn't sure why but she instantly liked Lucinda, there was something magnetic about her personality. Ellie wasn't so sure her mother felt the same way, but she knew women had tendencies to be a bit catty, especially when a better-looking model was around. Ellie loved her mum but even she could see that Lucinda, although a similar age, had it knocked out the park in the looks department, whilst her dear old mum was still on the bench, or as her American friend, Zack called them, the bleachers.

"Well," Lucinda said, rubbing her hands on her thighs. Ellie caught her father's eyes wandering momentarily to the risky plunging neckline of Lucinda's white top where his gaze hung for a split second before looking away. "I best make a move, plans to plan and bits to sort. I look forward to meeting you all again tomorrow, we can have a proper chat then."

"Shall we bring anything?" Ellie's father asked as Lucinda climbed into her Range Rover.

"Just yourselves," she beamed. The door closed and Ellie watched as she carried out a tight three-point turn, before spinning her wheels on the shingle drive and disappearing.

"Why the hell did you agree to that?" Ellie's mother asked, frowning at her husband. "We don't know anyone, it'll be – awkward."

"I just thought it was rude to say no," his face flushed a little and Ellie knew for sure her poor old dad was in for much more shit later when Henry had gone to bed and she'd retired to her room. "Anyway, let's get in and unpacked, it feels like that car is a part of me," he added, taking her away from the subject as swiftly as he could."

Ellie walked to the back of the Peugeot, lifted her pack out the boot and took a moment to survey her surroundings. The grounds were impeccably finished with small privet hedges and well-tended flower beds. Here and there narrow paths of shingle cut through the lawn. At the edges of the garden the neatly cut grass gave way to dense forest, it bordered The Old Chapel on all sides apart from the front. The building itself actually looked kind of cool, almost gothic. *Maybe it won't be so bad,* she thought to herself, now fully accepting that like it or not she was here to stay.

Ellie hauled the pack onto her shoulder and dragged her cabin-style bag behind her, the wheels jamming in protest at being used on the small stones. Reaching the heavy looking oak doors her father unlocked the left side and pulled it open. Cool air rushed out from inside, carrying with it a cocktail of smells, the old stone mixed with that of fresh paint and recent renovations.

Ellie followed her dad into the large entrance lobby. Looking up she saw the impressive beamed roof looming over her, some thirty feet above. To her front was an internal balcony, the start of the mezzanine level, and she could make out the backs of grey velour sofas and the top of a large wall mounted TV. That part of the second floor was open plan and could be accessed by stairs on either side of the entrance hall. Shaking a few stones from her wheels Ellie pulled her case further inside. Her feet were soon met by plush deep grey carpet, spanning the hall and running up both stairs. The stone walls were bare, but here and there they were decorated with large paintings or hanging tapestry style works of art.

"Wow!" Ellie's mother exclaimed following her in. "This place looks even better in real life." She joined her husband and slipped her arm around his waist, her momentary anger for accepting Lucinda's party invite, and glancing at her rather obvious cleavage, gone.

"What's that on the floor?" Henry asked, pushing past them. Ellie followed him to the bottom of the left-hand staircase, on the thick carpet laid a large wooden crucifix. Ellie crouched down and picked it up, the thing was heavy, it had to weigh a good two kilos. On the top was a decent sized iron loop and on the wall just above where it'd been laid, was a sturdy looking hook. Ellie was in no doubt that the crucifix belonged on the hook, but she couldn't for the life of her figure out how it had ended up on the floor.

"Did it fall?" Henry asked her.

"I don't know, kiddo," she replied, trying to figure out how it had managed to move off the hook. Eventually guessing someone, likely Lucinda, or whoever cleaned the place, had taken it down to dust it then forgotten to hang it again. Ellie lifted the weighty cross into position, where it sat firmly in place with a satisfying clunk.

Looking up the stairs toward the lounge area Ellie felt a little unease grow in the pit of her stomach. She had a natural inbuilt ability to get a feel for a place or situation and often prompted her mother or father to do things like getting a certain scratch card on a whim when at the shops, and nine times out of ten she won. Not big amounts, a tenner here, twenty there but they often joked she'd hit the big score one day. She was good with lost things, too. If her father lost his keys, which he often did, just visualising them often led her to where they'd been mislaid. Now, stood in the entrance lobby she had a bad feeling, like food that hours after being eaten refused to be digested. Despite the warmth of the sun that came in through the high stained-glass windows she shuddered and wondered how this place would feel when the day was spent, and the night took over.

CHAPTER 5

"Mummmmyyyyyy......"

Ellie awoke with a start, her eyes meeting the darkened room, only partially illuminated by a meagre amount of moonlight which managed to leak in from behind the heavy drapes. She lay, listening for long seconds with just the sound of her own breathing, unsure if the cry she'd heard was a product of a dream or the real world.

"Mummmmyyyyyyyyyyyyy......"

"Henry," Ellie muttered to herself, throwing back the sheet. The bed was dressed in a luxurious heavy quilt. No doubt it would have been amazing in the winter, but the night had proven too warm to even try it out. Instead, Ellie had found a light under-sheet in the linen closet and chosen to sleep under that and on top of the heavy bedding.

"Muuuummmmyyyyyyyyyyyyyy........."

Henry's cry was more desperate this time, almost frantic with definite panic woven through it. He would wake and cry for their mother in the night on the rare occasion he had a little accident and wet his shorts, but those occasions were getting rarer by the month, and this sounded different. Ellie could tell from the tone of his voice that he was scared. Likely a bad dream, then waking up in a strange room had done it. Reaching her door, she opened it and slipped out into the hall of the first floor, her feet almost sinking into the ample pile of the cream carpet as she walked. The oak beams, which held up the roof, loomed above her, partially hidden in the soot-black shadow cast by the same moon that had teased its light into her room. Her parents had opted for the over-indulgent Altar Room on the ground floor at the back of the building, so-called as in its days as a chapel that would have been where the altar stood. The Altar Room was the most lavish in the house, although none of them were too shabby. It boasted the largest and by far most corpulent of the ensuite bathrooms with a rainfall shower, that if the user wanted also doubled as a steam room. As well as the amazing shower it had a jacuzzi bath, the thing was big and raised on its own plinth at the far end of the room. Surrounding the bath and dotted around the spacious bedroom were candlesticks as tall as Ellie. At five feet each and made of heavy black iron they fitted in well with the modern yet gothic look and feel of the building. Even the curtain poles matched the décor, they were heavy looking black iron, too. Each end looked like a spearhead and seemed to be as much an item of medieval weaponry as it did a furnishing.

Ellie's room also had an ensuite, as did every one of the six bedrooms in The Old Chapel. Hers, however, was less than half the size of the one in her parents' room. Ellie's ensuite room's unique feature was another jacuzzi-bath, not as big as the one in The Altar room, that one looked big enough to swim in, but it was a cool feature, nonetheless. Ellie had taken a good hour sampling it before heading to bed, a much-needed relaxant after spending the day shoe-horned into the back of the family car with all the bags. She'd smiled with amusement at the polite notice above the bath that read, "IF USING JACUZZI PLEASE DO NOT USE BUBBLE BATH."

Covering the short distance to Henry's room she

could hear him crying, the sound getting louder with each step. Henry had been reluctant enough to sleep alone in a strange room and they'd had to bribe him with the promise of a gift during a planned visit to The Eden Project tomorrow, if he showed what a big boy he was and slept on his own. It wasn't a total shock to her that he'd had a freak out in the middle of the night. There was no way either of their parents would hear him from the ground floor, the place was too large. Reaching his door Ellie wondered what the hell had woken him. Despite his reluctance at staying on his own in a new place, Henry was generally a good sleeper and had no issues getting in a straight ten hours without waking when at home, apart from the occasional bed wetting. Normally Henry had to be woken by their mother at half seven every morning just to get ready for school. His ability to sleep like the proverbial log was one of the reasons they'd had no reservations about him being on a different floor, that and Ellie was seen as plenty old and capable enough to care for him if there was an issue. She highly suspected that they'd been segregated to the mezzanine level for the sole purpose of allowing their parents some much needed private time. The truth behind certain situations, and what that private time would entail was not always something you wanted to think about, especially when it involved your mother and father.

"Mummmmyyyyy....pleeeease........"

Ellie grabbed the handle and threw the door open. As it swung freely on low friction hinges an icy blast of air rushed out of the room and chilled her skin to goosebumps, the cold air wrapping itself around her skin like tendrils against the warmer air of the hall. None of the rooms at The Old Chapel had air-conditioning, the natural stone kept the temperature cooler than outside during the day, and the stone then seemed to retain the heat and keep it to a pleasant temperature at night. The temperature inside Henry's room was somewhere between air-con set at its coldest and the trailer of a refrigerated truck. Instinctively, Ellie ran her hand against the wall just inside the doorframe, she located the light switch and flicked it on, chasing the darkness away in an instant. Her little brother was sat bolt upright in bed, his covers were drawn up defensively over his chest and reached just below his chin, where his tiny hands clutched the thick edge of the quilt so tightly his little fingers were white. His cheeks were flushed red and tears streaked his face, Ellie wasn't sure, but she thought for the briefest of moments his rapid, panicked breathing had produced water vapour in the air, the likes of which you only usually see when outside on a cold day.

"What's up, Hen?" Ellie asked softly in a half whisper and feeling a little spooked herself. Slowly, that rotten feeling crept back into her stomach, the one she'd felt when they'd arrived, but she'd either gotten used to it, like you sometimes did a bad smell, or managed to forget about it. Momentarily he didn't seem to register that she'd put the light on, nor did he seem to be aware of her presence in the room. It was as if his brain had been caught somewhere between the worlds of waking and sleeping, like those who experience night terrors, or as the phenomenon was called in the days before they understood what caused it on a more scientific level, Old Hag.

"Ellie," he said suddenly snapping out of it. Then, like the flicking of a switch he threw back the covers and bolted across the carpet, wrapping himself around Ellie's waist so tightly it made her wince in pain. His skin felt icy cold and through the pain of his grip, she shivered again. "D-did you s-see h-him Ells?" Henry sobbed in his small voice, looking up at her with wide frightened eyes that pooled with tears.

"See who?" Ellie ruffled his hair reassuringly, then unfolded him from her waist and dropped to his level.

"H -he was in the corner, o-over there," Henry said,

his shaky voice no more than a whisper. "He went when you t-turned on the light, but I could see him, he was darker than the dark."

Ellie felt her hackles rise, every part of the sensible side of her brain told her that her little brother had been caught in one of those night terrors, where seemingly awake the things of nightmares still stalked you, making the dream all the more terrifying. Ellie had studied night terrors as part of her psychology course, she was far from an aficionado on the matter, but she knew enough, and she also knew that they were not a condition that usually afflicted him. However, the other half of her brain recalled how real that night visit from her deceased grandmother had felt, the smell of her perfume and the chill on her cheek, a chill so similar to the cold that had choked Henry's room, a cold that had suddenly disappeared. Henry's room was now inexplicably as comfortably warm as her own and somehow the temperature had risen faster than seemed naturally possible.

"I think you had a nightmare, Hen," she reassured with a lie. It came off her lips easily, as little white lies did when they were for the benefit of a small child. Ellie kissed the top of his head to secure her point, his blonde hair felt wet with sweat as did the back of his Spiderman PJs.

"I wasn't d-dreaming," he half whispered, and half whined. "I woke up f-for a weewee and he w-was there," Henry pointed to the corner of the room where a large white built-in wardrobe spanned the width of the room. "He was watching me."

"Where did he go?" Ellie asked, then immediately regretted embracing his story.

Henry shrugged his little shoulders, they shook a little as he sobbed, "I t-think he w-went into t-the wardrobe w-when you t-turnded the l-light on."

"Turned," she corrected. "Turned the light on."

"Turned the light on," he said, keen to get it right.

"Like Mike and Sully?" One of Henry's favourite movies was Monsters Inc and she guessed that putting a light spin on whatever he'd seen or dreamt would comfort him a little.

"No, Mike and S-sully aren't s-scary."

"What's say we open that wardrobe up and you'll see nothing is there?"

"Nooo." Henry winged as Ellie stood and took his hand. He pulled back reluctantly as she walked toward the white door.

"I promise you, Little Man, that no one will be in there," Ellie reached the door. As she did, she felt a shiver run down her back, she would never have admitted or shown it to her younger brother, but she was scared, about as scared as she could ever remember being. Inwardly she cursed herself for watching one too many paranormal shows. One? No more like three or four too many horror films. *If this was a horror* she thought, as she stalled at the cupboard door, *this would be the part where the audience hides behind its hands, and teenage girls bury their faces into their date's shoulder with the guy taking full advantage to slip a reassuring arm around them, an arm that won't get moved when the scare had been spent.*

Ellie gripped the handle, the sound of her heart thundering in her ears. Just as she went to pull it open a loud thump echoed up from the ground floor. Ellie released her grip of the door handle as if it had bitten her, Henry bolted into the room he'd been so keen to escape not ten seconds before and wrapped himself around her waist again, burying his face into the hemline of her PJ shorts. *And there is the scare,* Ellie thought, trying to kid herself. For a few drawn-out seconds neither of them spoke; they just stood totally still and in silence.

"It's okay," Ellie finally reassured when nothing but deep silence had followed the loud thump. "Just pipes or the building creaking, it's an old house, Hen, they make odd noises," Ellie remembered how Mike Cross and the Unexplained UK team debunked nightly bangs, bumps and creaks in an old Victorian style council house, finding the answer in both the old plumbing and wooden roof beams.

"I-it's n-n-not," Henry whimpered. "It's h-him – The Man!"

"I've told you before, Hen, The Man is just someone that mum and dad made up to make you behave."

When Henry had been around two, and of the age where he started testing the patience of their parents, The Man had been invented. A despicable character of no particular description, apart from his penchant for taking away naughty children. Won't go to bed? The Man will come. Won't eat your dinner? The Man will come. Won't listen to mum and dad? You can bet your shit The Man would come for that little faux pas, too!

"He's not," Henry protested. "He w-was here." Henry looked at her expectantly, his wide blue eyes shimmering with tears. "I'd n-not e-even been b-bad," he stammered, beginning to sob harder again.

"Listen, no one was in your room, Henry," Ellie kept her voice low and soothing whilst trying to sound sure and assertive, hoping he would take some comfort from her reasoning. More lies, as by now Ellie was pretty certain something had happened. *One too many paranormal shows, three or four too many horror flicks,* she thought to herself again. "It's an old building, it's new surroundings and you simply woke up from a bad dream. I promise. Now let's open this door and I'll bet you an ice cream that no one is in there, what do you say?" Ellie felt like some misleading government official telling members of the public that the UFO they'd just seen was nothing more than Venus reflexing off atmospheric gases released by some local swamp.

Henry didn't speak, he just chewed his bottom lip slowly, and reluctantly nodded his head in agreement.

More freaked out and scared than she felt proud of Ellie placed her hand back on the brass handle, the metal felt ice cold beneath her skin. Drawing a slow breath, she yanked open the door, fast, a little like removing a plaster. The built-in wardrobe was empty, save for a few wire coat hangers that jingle-jangled lightly to themselves in the disturbed air.

"See, empty!" Ellie tried to hide the relief in her voice.

"Can I sleep in with you, Ells, pllleeaseeee..." her brother whined in his best, *I'll get what I want eventually* voice. If she insisted he stay in his room then no sooner had she climbed back into bed and gotten comfortable then he'd be calling for her again. On a side note Ellie was certain that there was no way she'd stay in his room herself so expecting a child of five to just wasn't on, not that she was going to admit that to him. As for the loud thump from downstairs, yes this was an old building, and old buildings make odd noises, but old buildings also had history and sometimes that history stuck around. Whatever had caused it was likely something quite natural, amplified by the sheer fact she was a little freaked out. Ellie would never openly admit to it but a big part of her was glad of the company, even if Henry was only five.

"Sure, is there anything you want to bring?" she conceded.

"Just my Muddy Puddles George," he answered, already sounding better.

Ellie led him to his bed and dug around under the disturbed covers. His sheets were damp from perspiration, another good sign that what he'd experienced was no more than a dream. Finally, she located George's hiding place and she handed the stuffed toy pig to her little brother who hugged him tightly into his little chest with his spare arm.

Back in her room Henry soon made himself comfortable snuggled into her, Muddy Puddles George was also there, although he didn't take up quite as much room.

"Hen?" Ellie whispered, not sure if he'd fallen straight to sleep or not.

"Yeah."

"Why was it so cold in your room? Did you have your window open?" Ellie knew it was a nonsense question to ask a five-year-old and the night air in late July wouldn't have been as frigid, but part of her wanted some kind of answer so she could take a portion of solace from the situation.

She felt her little brother shake his head, "No, it got all cold when I saw The Man."

It wasn't the answer she was hoping for, but before Ellie had the chance to question him any further, she heard his breathing become heavy and she knew he'd fallen asleep with the speed that only a young child or a suffering narcoleptic could muster. Ellie, however, wasn't feeling tired. Reaching under her pillow she found her S8 and checked the time. It was three AM.

Ellie lay there, with Henry curled up in a tight ball next to her, her eyes fixed on the darken oak beams above as she listened intently to the sounds of The Old Chapel. Time ticked by slowly. Ellie thought she'd not sleep again that night, that she would still be gazing at the ceiling when the first shafts of morning light found their way under the heavy drapes. But around four sleep did find her, not a deep sleep, more a semi-lucid doze, a semi-consciousness where it was hard to separate dreams from reality. Caught in that strange limbo she thought she heard Henry crying again, but it couldn't have been, he was with her, and this sounded like a much younger child far off in another part of the building. Unseen by her closed eyes, the shadows above her stirred at the sound of the cries. They parted and squirmed excitedly, like a nest of silent serpents, before coming together to form one large black mass that slid and slipped silently over the oak beams. The cries came and went, ebbing and flowing the way a distant radio is sometimes caught on the breeze at the beach on a hot day. Eventually, she felt sure the sound was no more than the wind outside, or a distant fox howling somewhere in the dense forest.

Ellie was wrong.

CHAPTER 6

"IT'S NOT THAT THEY DON'T LIKE YOU," RICK Livingstone said, his accent held a hint of Australian, a testament to his family's Antipodean heritage. It came and went, sometimes stronger and more pronounced and at other times, barely even noticeable. His fair complexion and blonde hair, that bordered on containing a hint of ginger in certain lights, meant he was far more suited to a life in the more temperate climate of northern Europe than Down-Under. Rick collected a cup of black coffee up from his highly polished black-glass desk and examined the steaming brew for a brief second as if deciding whether it was safe to drink. Eventually he took a tentative sip and smacked his lips together in satisfaction. "It's just – well, how can I put it, Mike? The show hardly produced any results. If the channel wanted a history program, we'd have hired Tony fuckin' Robinson."

Mike Cross ran both hands up over his stubbly chin, closed his eyes and worked his fingertips over his eyelids. He hadn't been offered a coffee but he sure as hell could have used one. The headache that was now starting to pulse behind his eyes was no doubt due to a lack of caffeine, his one and only vice. That, and the fact he'd been up since silly o'clock, after pulling a late-nighter the evening before trying to prepare for this very meeting. A meeting where he knew he and his team would be hung out to dry.

Being too tight to pay for a hotel Mike had left his home in Arundel, on the South-East Coast, at half five in the morning just to make the eleven o'clock appointment at the UK Today and Switchback TV studio offices in Manchester's Media City. (The very same office where a year ago he'd been sat in front of Rick, the controller of UK Today, a generic satellite channel that had sprung up just over three years ago, as so many had over the years, signing the deal that secured him his own show.) A show that now looked as if it were about to be snatched away by the very hand that had given it. Mike exhaled a long breath and said, "The work I do, or we do as a team, is not exactly a measurable quantity, and as you've seen we have experienced things, it's just we were able to offer a likely and reasonable explanation for them." Mike paused, choosing his words carefully. He had a small fiery ball of anger developing in the pit of his stomach and he was trying hard not to fan the flames. "You knew my angle on this Rick, when you offered me this chance. It came off the back of my work on the Sleaford Haunting, or do I need to remind you?"

Rick held his left hand up, palm open, the way a police officer might signal a moving car to stop, "I know, Mike," he said hastily. "I love the backstory that brought you to me, and the public love a good ghost story, but one thing they love more is to see someone be discredited and made to look an idiot. That case ticked every box! The Sleaford Haunting made national press thanks to the Youtube videos that went viral, and because of the way the Jennings family whored themselves out to any bastard who'd listen to their claims. And plenty did, at having the most haunted council house in the country. So, they'd seen too many horror movies, or they wanted to have a case as renowned as the Enfield Poltergeist or the Black Monk of East Drive, who the fuck knows? Who the fuck cares? But their gravy-train had to end, and it did with you. North Kesteven council hired you in as a private investigator to consider the claims of benefit fraud and undeclared earnings off the back of their little Youtube success, not to mention the fuck-knows how much they earned from selling the story to the press..."

"Somewhere in the region of fifteen thousand pounds," Mike cut in, recalling the case that had caught the attention of the channel. "Not to mention the cash from Youtube advert clicks, that ran into tens of thousands."

"Yeah, well it takes the piss really, all the while they were still sponging off the state, makes me fuckin' sick," Rick said, leaning back on his chair to the point where it might tip back, Mike hoped it would. "Then, off the back of the financial investigation you headed up, you brought in the team to prove the entire thing was nothing but a fraud, and WHAM! You blew the lid on the whole bastard thing. You got fired from obscurity to fame, to a certain extent anyway, and now the tide is on the turn again. It's a dog-eat-dog business, Mike. Don't make this harder than it is. You're good at what you do, too good maybe."

"You knew when you contracted the show that I wanted to be different from that Haunted Happenings shit, if you were after that kind of thing maybe you should have tried to steal Chrissy Meadows and her husband away from Channel Five."

"Look, here is the issue, Mike. Yes, we want someone credible, and you fit the bill. Ten years as a copper, a Detective Sergeant by the time you threw the towel in; five, going on six years working as a PI whilst for the last three running a small team of paranormal investigators. Mixed with the personal tragedy of the loss of your wife and kid in that accident back in twenty-eleven, the very thing that got you into paranormal research. The public love that shit, they do. Serve it up on toast and they'd eat it for breakfast. But, the public who watch these shows also want to be scared."

"I'm glad my personal trauma is entertaining," Mike growled. He could feel his temper teetering on the edge. Rick was right, though. The loss of his wife, Claire and his six-month-old daughter, Megan in a drunken hit and run seven years ago had secured his obsession with trying to answer that unanswerable question. Was there something waiting after death?

Rick shifted uneasily in his expensive, but not that comfortable looking chair, obviously taken aback by Mike's outburst. He steepled his fingers in front of his mouth and exhaled through them, then said, "Look, Mike, all I'm saying is that these fuckin' shows are like a religion to some of these people. Now I know you'd have to be halfway to the local fuckin' nut house to swallow what Meadows and her team of kooks sell over on Five, I do - I get it, but that shit-house-show still has twice the viewers of Unexplained UK." Rick rubbed his hands together and fixed Mike's eyes with his. They suddenly seemed full of enthusiasm. "Look, we can still have a credible show, we just need to use a little, shall we say - artistic licence! And if you're willing to work with me, Mike, then we might be able to save it."

Mike shook his head, he'd been reluctant in the first place to get involved with a TV company, and had felt at the time as if he were getting into bed with a nest of vipers who at some point would ask him to sell his soul like some evil, devil worshipping sect, and he'd been right, here it was. "Do you know how stupid that sounds, Rick? You want to use my credibility, credibility I've worked hard to earn I might add, just to put believability on a few faked paranormal events, just to get a scare, just satisfy ratings and keep you and the board members happy."

Rick nodded, "And is it really that bad, Mike? I mean, think about it. You've seen the show, right?"

"I've watched two episodes; the Jamaica Inn one

and the Pontefract one. I'm not really narcissistic enough to get kicks out of seeing myself on TV." Which was true, Mike had dipped in and out of two episodes, just, if anything, to critique himself. Tara, on the other hand, one of his team of three, or Tig as they called her on the show, thanks to her full name being Tara India Gibb, had watched them all, and likely more than once over. Tara claimed the India part of her name stemmed from her country of conception, or so her hippy-like parents had told her. Mike didn't blame her for enjoying her obscure spell of fame, they'd spent a good few years having to pay out of their own pocket to just get through the door of most places. Being on the TV investigating was where the majority of other teams wanted to be, and having your own show sparked a fair amount of jealousy. It was fair to say that she was enjoying her five minutes of para-normal fame as much as she could, which was fine, as it looked like the clock was about to tick to minute six. After every show, she made a point of calling him up to ask if he'd watched it and if she'd come across okay on camera. Mike had known her long enough to understand her need for approval didn't come from vanity, more insecurity. At thirty-six she'd suffered two abusive relationships and she wore the mental scars of both like some singletons wear their hearts on their sleeve.

Tara India Gibb joined Mike's team around the time she'd split with her second arsehole of a boyfriend. A split eventually aided by the fact he'd been sent to the big house for a five-year stretch having beaten the shit out of her. As it turned out she was smart, pretty and well educated with a natural talent for research and a good knowledge of history, all things that her ability to fall for the wrong kind of guy had put a strangle on.

"I also saw the premier when we had the airing party here back in January," Mike added, remembering the drunken evening where by the time the credits rolled the room was rolling with them, like a ship listing on a rough sea.

"Good," Rick nodded, "So you've seen that little line at the start of the show, before the main titles roll, the one that says, *This Show Is Purely For Entertainment Purposes Only?*" Rick didn't wait for an answer before continuing, "Well that little bastard gives us licence to do whatever the fuck we want." Rick collected his coffee up again, drained the mug and wiped the back of his hand over his mouth. "Just work with me Mike, let me go back to the board and see if I can get that second season."

"You signed us up for two series," Mike reminded him, opting to use the more British term for several episodes of a television show as opposed to the more American one that seemed to be taking over.

"I know, I know," Rick straightened the large Windsor knot on his tie. Mike wasn't sure if the tie was supposed to be smart or novelty, it looked as if it were made of silk and was no doubt expensive, but it sported a number of smiling yellow faces, the kind that had featured on those eighties T-shirts with the slogan *Shit Happens* written underneath. "But in the contract, you'll see that we can pull the plug at any point if we see fit," Rick reminded him. "And after ten episodes of nothing but debunking, with a few poor EVPs that you also discounted due to the fact there's a production team with you using radios that, as you put it, 'might have caused the phenomenon,' then they see fit to pull the plug. Of course, you'll be compensated, call it a severance package. But let's not get to that point, let's try to save it. Have a chat with the team, run it past them. I'm not asking you to be Chrissy Meadows Mike, which is a good job 'cos you'd look shit in a blouse." He grinned at his own joke. "Just let us make it a bit more entertaining."

"I don't need to talk with the team," Mike said firmly. He felt his phone vibrating in his pocket, someone was trying to call him. He fished it out and looked briefly at the number scrolling across his screen. His phone told him the caller was in Salisbury, the number wasn't in his Samsung's phonebook and as far as he could recall he didn't know anyone in Salisbury or the entire county of Wiltshire for that matter. Cancelling the intrusion with one quick swipe of his finger Mike tucked the tatty phone back into the breast pocket of his shirt. "I have sole right to call the shots and make decisions, and my decision is I'd rather have no show than one that involves trickery." Mike stood up, affording him a better view of the window behind Rick's desk. The Manchester skyline stretched out behind it. "I'll have my legal team contact your team over a severance payment." His phone began to vibrate again, he ignored it this time, allowing it to ring through to voicemail.

"Maybe you could pedal your show to the History Channel," Rick said sarcastically. "Just change the name from Unexplained UK to Explained UK!"

"Fuck you, Rick!" Mike said reaching the door. It sounded unprofessional and he knew he'd regret it later, but it felt good at the time, and to be fair Rick was lucky to be finishing the meeting still in possession of his slightly too white front teeth. Leaving the room Mike made sure he had the final word and followed the 'Fuck You' up nicely by flipping him the bird before the door swung shut behind him.

FIVE MINUTES later Mike was sat behind the wheel of his Jeep, the multi-storey car park had mercifully shielded the car from the July sun. The unusually lengthy heatwave had been baking the UK since the end of May and the weather forecasters were reporting there was still no end to it in sight. Car park shade aside the air was still oppressively warm, and his blue cotton shirt clung uncomfortably to his back, and Mike could feel sweat, partly from his anger but mostly from the heat, forming on his neck and running down below the collar.

With the engine still off Mike reached up and grabbed the steering wheel with both hands. He squeezed it tightly until his knuckles turned white and tried not to let that smouldering fire of anger, which was still brewing deliciously inside him, ignite into a full-on rage. It wanted to, it wanted to badly, but with a few long deep breaths, carried out in the manner that his councillor had taught him in the months after the accident, he managed to quell it. He couldn't believe that Rick had brought up the death of Claire and Megan as if it were a bonus to his life backstory and a matter for entertainment that could be dragged out of the closet and paraded around.

The day Claire and Megan were killed, Mike had gone to work as normal, collected one of the slightly tatty looking pool cars from the force HQ where he was based, and with one of his teams other Detective Sergeants, Mark Samuels, headed to the next county for a meeting on how police forces could better share cross-border information on child abusers. A little project he'd personally spearheaded in a bid to gain evidence for his promotion to Detective Inspector. During the meeting, and whilst Mike was giving his presentation, a senior officer had entered the room and taken him aside to break the news. A drunk driver had lost control of his Ford and planted it into a shop front, at the precise time Claire and Megan were leaving the store. Mike had spoken to Claire just two hours before, whilst on his lunch break. In the call, she'd told him that she was heading to the park with Megan, who'd been cooped up inside for the past week with her first real stinker of a cold, but was finally feeling better. Claire had asked him if he fancied anything special for dinner, and before he could answer she suggested that on the way home she stop and get a couple of nice steaks. She'd often done that, asked a question then answered it herself, just one of her little traits that Mike had come to know and love in the ten years they'd been together, six of which as a married couple.

Mike guessed that she had stopped at the shop for the steaks, and maybe some nappies for Megan, who knew? The contents of her spilled shopping bags had not been the first thing on his mind that day. Mike had run through how he could possibly be to blame more times than he cared to remember. Eventually, he'd exorcised those demons and come to the realisation that the only blame to apportion was down to the selfish drunk who'd been too lazy to walk the mile home after his lunchtime drinking session, choosing instead to take two lives and ruin another forever.

That day, now just over seven years ago, still seemed unreal to him. Mike could still remember word for word the last call he'd taken from his wife and the words of the Chief-Super who'd broken the news. He could recall every wrinkle and detail of his face, the salmon pink tie he'd worn, especially the too tight looking knot, but after that, it was a blur.

His time on compassionate leave ran through to sickness leave, being signed off with depression and pumped full of various drugs, none of which he took regularly enough to be of any benefit. Counselling sessions came and went, as did the councillors who never seemed to actually help.

After several months of being locked in the family home, staring at the walls, or occasionally poring tearfully through photographs with thoughts of what might have been, Mike had his epiphany. He knew he had to change or he'd end up worse off than Claire, alive but dead inside and a shell of the man he'd once been. Confident that even with the help of his latest councillor he'd never be mentally strong enough again to do the job he loved; he tendered his resignation from the force. At thirty-six and with no other qualifications to fall back on other than those gained through the police, Mike threw himself into gaining his Private Investigators qualification. It was his way of remaining within a trade he knew and loved, whilst having the luxury of being his own boss and with none of the bureaucratic nonsense that he knew he'd not be mentally able to cope with if he'd gone back to the force. That aside, working on the child abuse team came with its own dose of other people's suffering and misery. Mike had enough in his own life, and enough to last him the rest of it, too.

He found that throwing himself into study helped numb the grief, he knew that many would be throwing themselves off the nearest bridge in his situation, or at the very least into a bottomless bottle of Jack, but that wasn't his style. It hadn't been Claire's, either. Mike owed it to her to be strong, to live the life she'd have wanted, and there was no way she'd have wanted him consumed with grief whilst sitting in a darken room pickling his liver every hour of every day on a bottle of malt. In fact, not a drop of booze had passed his lips since their passing, grief was bad enough without the demon drink along for the ride. *Nothing like a good-ole depressant to cheer you up,* he'd thought, when reading how many in his situation did turn to alcohol.

Having gained his Private Investigators licence, and whilst gradually building up a portfolio of regular clients, many of whom only needed his services the once, to catch out a cheating spouse, or partner, his interest in the paranormal was stirred. One night, whilst doing some work on his website, Mike's attention had been drawn to an American woman on a show called Ghost Stories. He hadn't intentionally put the show on, it was just background noise. He liked background noise, without it the house felt very empty, empty and sad, as if the bricks and mortar missed Claire's laughter and Megan's occasional crying fits, or those cute little giggles she'd just started to have, her tiny yet developing brain just learning when something was funny. Maybe he should have sold the place, it was too big for one. But selling it was like closing the door, finally admitting that, that chapter of his life, the one that should have been the longest, had been cut short.

The lady on the show, who looked a little like she spent too much time in Taco Bell, or Wendy's, was claiming that her twenty-year-old son, who'd been tragically killed in a car crash the year before, was still in the house with her. Leaving the laptop on the side, Mike had watched transfixed as she played audio recordings called EVPS of her son's voice from beyond the grave, recordings she'd supposedly captured right in her own home with nothing more than a digital voice recorder. That night, with the ever-faithful help of Google, Mike learned that EVP stood for Electronic Voice Phenomenon, and all you needed to capture this paranormal wonder was a basic voice recorder, much like the one the lady had used. Other snazzier versions were available, aimed specifically at those involved with paranormal study, but most investigators just used normal audio recorders, the likes of which you could buy at Argos for no more than forty pounds. Or for a few quid on eBay if you were willing to wait for delivery from China, and you didn't care too much about the quality of your product.

Reading into it Mike learned that EVP existed somewhere around fifteen to twenty hertz, and below what adult ears could hear. However, with the aid of a voice recorder which could record sound at that low level, you could pick them up, and then on playback the sound became amplified and audible. The evidence offered by the woman in the show was compelling and made Mike, who had never really had any interest in such things, wonder if his wife and child were still with him, as the woman claimed her son had been.

Trying to replicate the results caught by the lady in

the show Mike had set up recorders in every part of the house, hoping to capture just one word from his wife, or hear just one cry from Megan, wanting just one sign that they were still with him. However, no matter how much he recorded, all he tuned up was endless hours of empty hissing static. Frustrated, confused and starting the think the woman had been nothing but an attention seeking fraud he turned his attention to other supposedly haunted places, believing that if he could just capture one piece of evidence it would put his mind at rest that his wife and daughter were in a better place. Mike found that unlike many paranormal investigators, who seemed to claim that every particle of dust caught on a digital image was a benevolent spirit, he had a flair for debunking and finding reasonable explanations. In fact, the harder he looked the more blanks he drew and the more blanks he drew the more sceptical he became, almost losing all hope that they'd moved on to another life where one day he'd be reunited with them again.

Whilst researching various paranormal forums for other locations who might let him set up his equipment, that had now grown to a bank of audio recorders, some of which by now did recorded down into the infrasound, and a basic four channel portable CCTV system, Mike had found two others fairly local to him who'd been looking to join a team. Tara aka Tig, who lived just fifty miles away in North Dorset and Scotty, real name Scott Hampton who lived on The Isle of Wight, both just a stone's throw from him geographically. Scott was a big Trekkie and had given himself the nickname of Scotty when they'd first met, no one argued with him over it, and to be fair, Scotty was not the kind of guy you argued with. At just over six feet three he made Mike's distinctly average five-eleven feel small, he was also as wide as a church door and had hair that was about as black as it could be without coming from a bottle. When not with Mike and Tara, Scotty could usually be found in the gym or on the rugby pitch, and if not on the pitch in the club bar. He wasn't what you'd expect appearance wise from your archetypal Trekkie and it amused Mike to think of him at conventions dressed in his Federation replica uniform. Scotty was the youngest of the team at twenty-five. He was Mike's tech specialist and despite his oppressive appearance Mike had learned that he was really the gentlest of giants and apt to never hurt a fly.

Before being given the show, Scotty had worked for a local security firm, fitting and supplying CCTV systems on the Island, a life which it seemed now that he would likely end up going back to. In the early days, Scotty had secured them some blinding deals on equipment and helped Mike upgrade his basic eBay purchased cameras to a more professional setup. However, the kit budget they'd been given before the show started filming had seen them being able to purchase equipment the likes of which only ever made it as far as the dream list for most teams, things like full HD recording equipment and two FLIR thermal imaging cameras.

Around the time that they'd put the lid on the paranormal side of the Sleaford case, and the adult portion of the family were facing charges of fraud, benefit fraud, and tax evasion, Mike found that his approach to paranormal research had changed. Instead of longing for that one undeniable snippet of evidence, he found satisfaction in explanation, in debunking, a trait that had followed through to his show, and a trait that had ultimately been its downfall. Sure, over the time he'd been investigating he'd captured a few EVPs, it seemed they were by far the most common form of paranormal evidence up for grabs. However, in a society packed with WiFi, mobile phones, and radio waves, the evidence was too prone to contamination for Mike to hold any faith in. He certainly had never found anything as clear as the voice on the American woman's recordings, the ones that she'd claimed had been her son, and over time Mike had come to wonder if she was nothing more than an attention seeking fraud. He'd fast learned that in paranormal research frauds were about as common as crooked car salesman in the automotive industry.

Sat in his Jeep, his hands now off the wheel Mike held them before his eyes for a brief moment, almost perplexed at the way they trembled slightly, the last aftershocks of the rage that had almost consumed him now ebbing away like a tide.

Feeling more in control, and with less of a yearning to storm back into the office and grab Rick Livingstone by his stupid smiling tie and plant his face into the desk, *'cos after all shit happened*, he slid his phone from the breast pocket of his shirt and tapped the screen to life. With a few quick swipes Mike was into the call history. The second call, the one he'd ignored, was from the same Wiltshire number. He stared at it for a while, as if just looking at the digits would cause some synapse of recognition to fire in his brain. When it didn't come, he copied the number and pasted it into Google to see what information the internet held on it, a habit he had picked up from working as a Private Investigator. Mike scrolled past the first few sponsored links, the ones that asked you to list the number if it was linked to a high-pressure seller or general nuisance caller. The third link down was for the Cottage Holidays UK website and provided a sub-link through to a property on their books called The Old Chapel in the village of Trellen, Cornwall. Intrigued, Mike opened the link and scrolled through the myriad of images taken by the owner and then went on to read the well-worded description of the place. It looked impressive and whoever had carried out the conversion work, turning it from place of worship in to a holiday home, had done a top job, but he was mystified as to why he'd been called by the number on the advert. He sure as shit hadn't booked a holiday and whilst the place looked five star there was no way he'd have paid the eight hundred pounds a week price tag the property was commanding in July. Instead of going back into his call history Mike used the link on the advert to call the number back. It rang and rang, and just as he expected it to click through to answer machine the phone was answered.

"Hello, Reed residence," came a well-spoken female voice. There was the slightest hint of country to it as well, but only just.

"Hi," Mike said, caught a little off guard, he'd really expected the answering machine and not a real human. "I'm just returning your call, I had ...."

"Mr. Cross?" the lady asked tentatively, cutting him off. Her voice had a vein of nervousness laced through it now.

"Yes – although I'm more than a little confused about where you got this number from and how you know who I am?"

"You took some finding, Mr. Cross. Eventually, I found this number on a Private Investigation forum, a customer recommended you to someone looking for a discrete service into matrimonial matters. The post was from three years ago, I really didn't know if you still had the same number. I couldn't find a contact link on any websites, not even your Unexplained UK Facebook page," the lady said hurriedly. "And I didn't really want to air my story there."

"Yeah, I've been out of the PI game for just over a year," Mike answered, wondering how long it would be before he was back to chasing debts and cheating spouses. "What kind of investigation are you after, Mrs. Reed, financial, marital?" Mike bet it would be marital, people always sounded on edge when they first spoke to him about those sorts of cases.

"Umm, no – it's a little more specialist than that," the lady paused. "I'm sorry I just realised that I never gave you my first name and a proper introduction, how very rude. My name is Sue, Sue Reed."

"Pleased to meet you, Mrs. Reed," Mike replied,

"But I've had a hell of a day if you could just let me know how I may be able to help you." He sounded a little curt, it wasn't intentional, but he was still feeling riled by Rick and his stupid tie.

"Yes, of course, please accept my apologies," Mike heard Sue clear her throat nervously." I've had your number for two weeks now, the number of times I've had it loaded onto my phone with my finger over the dial button but never made the call. Well it looks like today is the day," she laughed to herself and Mike could tell she was stalling. "I'm sorry."

"It's really no problem," Mike reassured, making sure he didn't come across quite so curtly as before. "Just take your time." Mike glanced in his rear-view mirror and watched absently as an old lady in a BMW X5, that was far too big for her level of driving confidence, struggled the vehicle into a bay, taking a good ten shunts to manoeuvre the behemoth of a vehicle in straight. Having parked satisfactorily she then discovered that she couldn't open the door wide enough to get out.

"You see, what it is – umm – It's more your other speciality I need you for," Sue laughed nervously again. "But I don't want any TV cameras!" she added hastily.

"Paranormal research," Mike added.

"Yes, God - you probably think I'm some crazy lady calling you like this. But I'm not. Three weeks ago, I had never heard of you Mr. Cross, but then I began to look online for someone who might be able to help. I found the news reports on that case you explained in Sleaford first, then I found your show."

"Well the Sleaford case wasn't really a haunting," Mike cut in, not quite able to believe this was the second time the matter had been broached that day. "It was a clever hoax being run by the father of the family and a very tech-savvy fourteen-year-old son for the sole purpose of financial gain and recognition."

"That aside Mr. Cross, I have watched all of your

shows thanks to our Sky on Demand service since, and your ability to find answers is what I need."

Despite the nervous and scatty way this Sue lady was coming across Mike began warming to her more by the second, he wondered if she would mind putting those thoughts into writing, maybe on a piece of paper that could accompany a Fuck You card for Rick. "Is this about your holiday home?" he asked, cutting to the point.

There was a long pause before Sue finally answered, "How, how - could you know that?"

"I Google searched your number Mrs. Reed,"

"Sue," she cut in, "Please call me, Sue."

"No problem, Sue. As I said I Google searched your number and it came up with the booking line for a place called The Old Chapel. So, I'm guessing it's either that place or your house, but if I were a betting man, which I'm not by the way, I'd say it's your holiday let that you're calling about."

"Very good, Mr. Cross. It's that kind of foresight that I need."

"Call me Mike," he said, returning the favour.

"Okay, Mike," she laughed nervously again.

"What seems to be the issue?"

"I'd rather, if possible that is, speak to you in person. I'm not sure what your hourly rate is but...."

"The unwritten rule is that when working in the field of paranormal investigation there is no charge. It's a free service." Mike wasn't sure who'd written that rule, it was a stupid one, in fact whoever had thought that particular gem up needed a boot planting in their arse, however, it was one rule that every team he knew of, or had spoken to stuck by. Sure, he got paid by the TV channel for the show, quite nicely, too. But private and non-filmed investigations that were for the aid of a troubled homeowner were always free of charge. "I will say though, that if a lot of time or travelling is involved then it would be appreciated if you covered expenses, assuming I take the case on that is."

"I wouldn't dream of having you out of pocket, Mr. Cr – Mike," she corrected. "How soon can you come to Wiltshire? We are between Salisbury and Marlborough, a little place called Pewsey?"

Mike knew the place and was about to give a list of excuses about how he couldn't possibly make it this week due to one lie or another, but his curiosity got the better of him and after all the only thing that awaited him at home was an empty three bed semi and a tropical fish tank in major need of a cleaning. As well as that there were two things that grabbed his attention and told him that this lady was not some attention seeking nut-job. One was her instant request for no cameras and the second was her nervousness, and it wasn't nervousness at trying to trick or fool him, it was a nervousness about sounding foolish, the kind of nervousness that told Mike she didn't quite believe whatever was happening herself. He geographically ran the trip home in his head, it wouldn't be a massive detour on the way back to Arundel to go via Wiltshire, forty or fifty miles at most he guessed.

"I'm in Manchester at the moment, Sue," Mike said, still running the trip in his head as he spoke. "I'm heading south very soon, so how does around four or five this evening sound?"

"You can really come that soon?" she sounded relieved.

"What can I say, you've piqued my curiosity. Can I ask one thing, though?"

"Of course, anything."

"Do you mind if I get my researcher, Tara, to meet me at yours? I always like to have a second set of ears when being told about a case and she's not a million miles from you."

"Is that the nice, pretty young lady on your show?" Sue asked, sounding enthused. "The one you call Tig?"

"Ha," Mike laughed. "Yeah, that's her." Off camera Tara's language could be a tad more colourful, but she could reign it in when required and be professional.

"No problem at all, if you have a pen to hand, I'll give you my address."

Mike fished around in the glovebox, found a pen and jotted down the address for the Reed residence. Leaning forward he programmed his satnav. There was no signal in the concrete-box of a multi-story but as soon as he got outside it would send him the right way. Pulling out of the bay Mike found Tara's number on the call list and wondered just how he would tell her the bad news about the show, there was no doubt that she'd be devastated, Scotty too. He hoped not devastated enough to ditch him on this new case, Sue Reed and her converted chapel of a holiday home had really caught his intrigue. Her reluctance to be filmed and her unwillingness to discuss the matter over the phone just added to it.

As the Jeep broke free of the car park's shade and out into the hot July sun the call to Tara connected and began to ring.

CHAPTER 7

"THE GUY'S A TOTAL COCK SUCKER!" TARA SAID, holding the phone to her shoulder as she poured boiling hot water over the coffee granules in her favourite mug, the one that donned the caption *Drama Queen* in bright, bold pink lettering, the **D** sporting a cartoon crown. She could hear Mike was on the road and driving. In general, his Jeep's hands-free system was good, but for some reason, it had the annoying ability to cut out occasionally, and usually at a pivotal part of the conversation, and as such she'd had to have certain details repeated a few times.

"So, you're not mad that I wouldn't give in to their ideas of spicing the show up a bit by stretching the truth?" Mike asked as a car horn sounded in the background Tara didn't know if it were intended for him or not.

"No!" She replied firmly, and it was the truth. She felt gutted, sure, mixed with a few grams of disappointment and a fair scoop of anger, but none of it was directed at Mike. Hell, without him she'd have never had a shot at being on TV and would likely have spent the rest of her days sitting on her bum scanning food at Tesco for blue-rinse toting pensioners. The kind who wanted to talk to her all day about mundane subjects like how their cat was on medication for constipation, or how we needed some rain or there'd be a hosepipe ban before long.

Still cradling the phone, she picked up the milk carton that was already out of the fridge and sat on the side, and likely a few hours the right side of going sour in this warm weather. Tara unscrewed the green plastic cap and gave it a tentative sniff, it seemed fine, so she dumped a spill of it into her steaming drink.

"I know how you feel about that kind of thing," she added as she stirred her coffee. "That's not what the show or team is, was - or ever will be about. Have you called Scotty?"

"Not yet," she heard him reply through a stress relieving breath. "He'll be gutted. I'll bring him up to speed after this call."

"Well, it's not like I'm over the moon. I mean, fuck, I'm technically unemployed now. There is no way I'm going back to Tesco working the check-out and making polite conversation with lonely old people who seem to think that I'm there for some kind of social." Tara reached out and shook a cigarette loose from the half-smoked pack of Bensons and lit it.

"I thought you'd quit," Mike said instantly.

"I have, well I did," Tara replied quickly, feeling like she'd just been busted. She crushed it out, picked up the pack and thought about tossing it in the bin, then thought better of it and put it back on the counter by the warming milk. "It's just, well – that shithead Jason called me last night."

"He's out already!!"

"Looks like it," Tara said before taking a testing sip of her drink.

"They give him five years for beating the shit out of you and practically leaving you for dead and he's out in just under three. Now I know why I quit working in law enforcement. What did he want?"

"To see me."

"You're not seriously.."

"Fuck no, no way!" Tara cut in. "I told him if he called me again, I'd be making one call, to the cops."

"Good." Mike sounded relieved.

Tara guessed that once you'd lived in the world of law enforcement you always carried it with you. Mike had been away from that life for about seven years now, but it was still deeply ingrained in him. He was the type of guy she should have gone for, but never seemed able to fall for, but now wanted.

Her first serious boyfriend, Rich, who'd she'd foolishly moved in with at twenty had a liking for being violent toward her, too. Not on the level that Jason had, or with the sadistic enjoyment he seemed to glean from it, either. But enough for her to eventually pack up and leave after three years of his jealous rages and overly controlling behaviour. Rich's violent nature stemmed more from his infatuating love for her and his inability to rein in her free spirit. It came down to the fact that he'd never been able to grasp that at as a girl in her early twenties she hadn't wanted to spend every night with him, she wanted to go out and meet friends, go to the clubs that just a few years before had been off limits, unless you had a particularly good fake ID or an older sister who happened to look a lot like you. Neither of which Tara had the benefit of. By twenty-three and having been treated to a black eye for wanting to go on a girls' holiday to Spain, she packed up and left. Little did she know that Rich had just been a practise arsehole for the main event.

Jason Paxman came along when she'd been a few months the wrong side of her thirtieth and starting to feel like life, from that point on, would be a downhill ride to old age. He seemed different, nice even. He had his own business and worked hard, unlike Rich whose whole attitude seemed to be that the world owed him something and being hell-bent on doing as little as possible for maximum reward. He also had his own place that was mortgage free, a nice car and visited the gym religiously three times a week. Mixed with his charm, dark hair and tanned skin he seemed like the perfect guy, what her mother would call a real catch, a keeper, and she'd often said to her, after they'd popped in for a brew, or the occasional Sunday roast, *"You've done okay there, honey"*. Always followed by a knowing wink or gentle nudge with her elbow.

Regretfully, hiding behind that perfect guy façade was a very different monster, it took a while to surface, in fact, the first year with him had been one of Tara's happiest, but then she'd agreed to move in, and things had changed. Once living with him twenty-four seven Tara saw a different side to Jason, a side where he would burst into uncontrollable fits of rage at the slightest thing, like if he dropped or spilled something. It was always small petty stuff that stoked his fire. At first doors, walls, or much to her dismay his Springer Spaniel, Max, would bear the brunt of his anger, an anger that he almost seemed to enjoy being consumed by and gave in to at every opportunity. Unfortunately, he soon realised he had another thing he could direct his fury at, her. The first few times Jason hit her hadn't been too bad, and Tara managed to hide the marks by wearing long sleeves or applying a little more concealer. She'd fooled herself that he was a nice guy really and that usually, his rages were all her fault. But the night that had ended it all, and seen him locked up had been bad, worse than anything Rich had done, or anything she could imagine Jason being capable of.

Jason had been at work all day, he ran his own little letting agency and done quite nicely out of it, too. Maybe it was the pressures of his job that made him the way he was, maybe he was just a sadistic shit, she never really figured it out. There was a good chance it was a bit of both.

On getting home from a day at the office things had been fine, Tara cooked him dinner, as she always did if she wasn't on the late shift at Tesco. She'd even prepared his favourite dish, Spaghetti Bolognese with three slices of warm garlic bread, he always had three slices of garlic bread with it, never more, never less. It had been one of Tara's favourites too, but now just the smell of Bolognese sauce turned her stomach. Jason had been sat in his favourite chair catching up on the BBC News at six, whilst sipping at the first of his four nightly bottles of Corona with a quarter of lime rammed into the neck, (his daily routine). Jason was always big on routine. Looking back on it now she knew that part of it had been no more than mild alcoholism, and his daily drinking, although on the face of it not overly heavy, had likely contributed to the way he was.

That fateful evening she had been in the process of carrying his food through when Max the Spaniel darted between her legs, causing her to send the dish of food crashing to the floor and spilling all over the real wool rug that covered half the white oak laminate in the lounge. Unfortunately, the rug was cream and the spaghetti bolognese really did a job on it. In fact, after the beating that followed, and whilst she'd been laid half-conscious on the hard floor, she'd spent a fair bit of time staring at the spilled dinner through her two swelling eyes as it soaked into the rug. Her battered and fuzzy brain had mused that without the meat and spaghetti the red itself didn't actually look too bad, and gave it somewhat of an abstract art look, it almost brightened up the white and sterile looking lounge.

Having beaten her to the brink of unconsciousness, Jason left to take the rest of his frustrations out at the gym. That's where the police had found and arrested him, having been notified of the assault by the ambulance that she'd managed to call having regained consciousness and found the phone he'd left by her side so she could call for medical assistance. Jason was thoughtful like that! However, in his thoughtfulness, he'd never counted on her ratting him out for it. But by then she'd had enough, and being beat half to death was apt to open previously closed eyes to the truth of the matter. Jason was bad, toxic even and she needed to be free of him.

Tara spent the next two days in hospital being treated for a concussion and having x-rays carried out on various parts of her body. Jason's handywork on this occasion had left her with bad bruising and swelling as well as a few lacerations and a hairline fracture to her right eye socket. The officer who'd run the investigation had told her that it was still one of the worst beatings he'd seen from a domestic violence case and with her statement detailing a history of abuse at his hands, and photographs of her laid in hospital with two eyes almost swollen shut they'd secured a half decent sentence.

Once out of hospital Tara found that no amount of clothing, short of dressing like a Mummy, could hide the marks this time. The bruising from her two black eyes crept past the reaches that even the biggest of sunglass lenses could hide, so she'd squirrelled herself away like a hermit for three weeks, that had felt more like three years, until the marks faded to a level that she felt comfortable with and could hide under makeup. Those bruises went far faster than what it had done to her mentally, that puppy was with her for the long haul. Some nights she'd recount the beating in her head, and the thought that had played through her steadily fogging mind as the punches had rained down, *Oh God, this time he might actually kill me!*

And that had been her life, until now, one mistake after another. Tara was sure that soon she'd settle for a dozen cats and a flat that smelt chokingly of ammonia from their piss. After all, cats didn't give a shit if you went out, or dropped dinner, or if you were a bit untidy, so long as they had food, they were happy.

"It's not done and dusted yet with the show," Mike continued, snapping her away from bad memories and bad places in her mind that she hated visiting, but still went to regularly. "They will have to pay to get out of the contract, so some of that will be coming your way. The agency should start looking for a new backer, maybe one of the documentary channels. The Yanks seem to have more teams on the TV than you can shake a stick at, I don't see why Meadows and her gang of charlatans should have the monopoly on it here."

Tara could tell he was just trying to soften the blow, make her feel better. She knew the likelihood of Unexplained UK being picked up by another channel when it had been axed by a pony outfit like SwitchBack was unlikely. No one wants to purchase a dead duck as they say and TV, in general, was a pretty ruthless industry.

"Let's hope," she replied, sounding unconvinced. "I'm thirty-six years old, I don't relish the thought of having to move back in with my parents 'cos I can't afford the rent." Whilst her momentary five minutes of fame hadn't earned her a heap of cash it had proven considerably more lucrative than scanning beans at Tesco, and she'd started to become accustomed to the extra money. Not to the extent of leading an extravagant lifestyle, far from it, but it had been nice to buy the odd pair of shoes or handbag and not have to worry too much about stretching her wages out until the end of the month. Aside from the new build rented flat and few items of clothing, that were nicer and carried designer labels, unlike her usual purchases from the likes of Primark, Tara had also bought herself a little Audi A2. Not a new car by a long shot, in fact, it was eleven years old when it came to her with eighty thousand on the clock, but it was still the newest and best car she'd ever owned, even if the alloy wheels were now a little scuffed from one too many dockings with the kerb.

"I'm sure we can get you on I'm a Celebrity, or Big Brother," Mike laughed. "You must be remarkably more well-known than most of the washed-up celebs they get trying to claw back whatever scraps of a career they have left."

"Yeah, thanks," she replied a little dejectedly. "I'm not sure you can class a few episodes as a career."

"All I'm saying is it's not the end of the road, you know – one door closes and another one opens and all that bollocks. Speaking of which, what are your plans tonight?"

"Well I have a bottle of Prosecco in the fridge and there is an Ex on The Beach marathon on Spike, so – why, you asking me out on a hot date?"

"If you call a hot date a possible case then yes," Mike laughed. Wishing it were an actual date, a date where they'd end up back at his with the side of the bed that had been cold since Claire's death warmed for the first time in years. The guilt followed the thought, it always did. "And besides I definitely need to save you from an Ex on The Beach marathon, that mindless reality TV will rot your brain. You must know it's purposely designed to keep people dumbed down."

"We were reality TV," she chuckled, starting to feel a bit better.

"That's why I never watched it myself," Mike laughed.

They often had a little harmless flirtatious banter, deep down Tara wished it would progress a little further and like Mike, she'd wished the offer of a date were real. But she knew the hell that Mike had been through in the past few years, she'd had her share of it as well. However, being beaten to shit by your sadistic dick of a boyfriend wouldn't really contend with having your wife and child killed by some drunk driver in a game of relationship Top Trumps. Maybe one-day things would go further, but for now, they both seemed to skirt around it, as if afraid to take the next step.

"So, we are doing this without a TV crew then?"

"We can still go old school," Mike said. He sounded a little excited which stirred her own interest. "Don't forget your roots."

"I'm a natural ash blonde," she said with a laugh, "I

never need to do my roots." She heard Mike chuckle at the joke but then the line crackled a bit. He was likely in a poor reception area. Nonetheless, Tara picked up her coffee and went through to the lounge in case the issue was her end.

"Besides they expressively asked for no cameras," he said, his voice coming back. "I didn't go into the fact that we'd just been sacked. Anyway, it's the straight-up explanatory style of investigation that got her to call us. Unfortunately, it's not going to pay the bills but that's not why any of us got into this game."

Tara flopped herself out onto the sofa, almost slopping hot coffee over her hand. She leaned forward and placed the mug of listing liquid onto the lounge table. Then she sat back and listened with interest as Mike ran succinctly through his call with Sue Reed. The day was a scorcher and even with the windows open the heat in her small flat felt oppressive. Every few seconds the floor fan would sweep past and jostle her just past shoulder length blonde hair. It didn't put the slightest hint of a much-needed chill in the air, moreover, it just moved the already hot air around the room, but any respite from the still and humid heat was welcome.

"Sounds interesting," Tara said when Mike finished talking. "What's the place called again?"

"The Old Chapel, in Trellen."

"Let me just Google that," Tara picked up her laptop which was sat running the screen saver on her coffee table, she brought it to life and fired the name into Google. The first listing was for Cottage Holidays UK. She clicked the link, thanking her superfast connection speed as it brought up the listing as fast as the turning of a page. "Looks nice," she said flicking through the various images provided. "Pricey, too. How long have we got the place for?"

"I don't know," Mike replied. "That's what we need to discuss. The Reeds live in Pewsey, do you have a pen handy? I'll give you the address."

"I haven't said I'll come yet," Tara joked, opening Google Maps from a toggle on her screen. She pumped the postal code and house number into the search bar as Mike passed them to her, then screenshot the page and emailed it to herself.

"Of course, you'll come, I know you live for this shit."

"But what about my Ex on The Beach marathon?"

"Disk it! Be there at half four, wait for me outside if I'm not there. Traffic is looking good so I should be there by five at the latest."

"Yes, boss," Tara said jokingly. The line cleared, and she wasn't sure if Mike had just hung up the phone or had lost signal.

She spent the next few minutes flicking through the various images whilst enjoying her coffee. It was unusual for a person to contact a team directly for help, usually, they cherry-picked the most well-known locations then had to pay to get through the door. That was the clincher for her, what could be happening there that was so bad that the owner felt the need to have someone look into it? Whilst the case wouldn't pay the bills it had her excited. She checked her watch, there were six hours before the meeting in Wiltshire. Considering the hour drive she'd have, that left her five hours to get ready and do what research she could on the place and the surrounding area. Mike would expect her to be armed with it and she didn't want to let him down.

Keeping the pictures of the place loaded on a separate page that she minimalised to the taskbar, Tara opened yet another browser window and went to work.

CHAPTER 8

ELLIE HARRISON STOOD IN THE ENTRANCE LOBBY OF The Old Chapel and stared at the large wooden crucifix. Yesterday she'd rehung it onto its large and secure hook. A hook that held it firmly in place, and yet had somehow it had managed to come off that hook and land back on the floor. She'd wager that if she'd traced a line around the large crucifix yesterday, a little like American detectives drew round bodies in those old murder mystery shows, then geometrically it would be in the same spot now, and not a fraction out of place. She stared at it for a few drawn out seconds, consumed by the morning silence that hung like an invisible blanket in the building, her mind racing at the possibilities of what it could mean. Deep down she knew what it meant, someone or something had moved it, possibly The Man, or whatever it was that had been in Henry's room last night. Possibly something else! And to believe that meant you had to believe in the boogieman and the monsters who were told of in countless books and fairy tales that lurk under your bed at night. The kind ready to bite your feet off if you were foolish enough to get up and go for a wee. But those things weren't real, were they?

Whatever the truth behind it she was now almost certain that her brother had indeed been awake and had indeed seen something. Something or someone had been watching him. Ellie shivered at the thought, it started at the top of her spine and ran the length of it.

Bright shafts of morning summer sunlight streamed in through the tall stained-glass windows that stood either side of the front doors. It made her feel as if she were stood in a spotlight on the stage, like when she'd played Eliza Doolittle in the year eleven production of My Fair Lady. The stained glass filtered light would give the entrance, if viewed in a picture, the pretence of serenity. Stood in that light experiencing it, it felt anything but. The tranquil morning light seemed to be more of a mask, a mask that hid something monstrous behind its façade. She wasn't sure how she knew, she just did, she could feel dread in the pit of her stomach, the feeling wriggled and churned there, at times stronger than others. A chill ran through her body for the second time as her mind wandered back once again to the fear-frozen state she'd found Hand-Me-Down-Henry in. The chill in his room that was so unnatural against how warm her own room had been, then that dull but definite thump from somewhere in the building. The tiny hairs on her arms stood to attention as her hackles rose. Something was off with the place. It shouldn't be, the place had been a chapel, a place of worship, yet it felt rotten, like the apple given to Snow White. It wasn't what it seemed.

Ellie knew that if she voiced this opinion to her parents, they'd see it as no more than another last-ditch ploy to be allowed to head home. Even with Henry's testimony they'd never buy it. They knew she was prone to the odd hunch, but they'd think she was using it as an excuse. Either that or they'd think she'd watched one too many paranormal investigation shows and that they'd warped her young mind and made her hyper-paranoid about old buildings. Ellie had always wondered what it would be like to stay in one of the venues featured on some of her favourite shows, The Jamaica

Inn, which she'd got to visit the day before, the Pritchard house on East Drive in Pontefract and Leap Castle in Ireland had been recurring favourites and places she'd have given good money to visit. Now, stood in the entrance hall of this strange old chapel without a TV crew or team of fellow investigators she wasn't so sure she wanted any of it.

Last night Ellie hadn't managed to guess the source of that thump, the one that had made her jump as her hand had been on the handle to Henry's built-in wardrobe. Now she knew what had caused the sound, and she was looking right at it. Gingerly she bent down and picked up the weighty cross, turning it her slightly shaky hands as she had the previous evening. The wood felt sure and heavy, tactile to the touch and inanimate. No feelings passed through her as she pawed it, no psychic shock or vision, but then she hadn't expected such a thing, had she?

Not lifting it as high on the wall as it had been, she suspended it a few feet above the carpet and dropped it, the sound was identical to the one she'd heard from Henry's room. Given her closeness to it, and the fact she'd dropped it from much less of a height the volume of the thump was even close. Sure, it was far from a belt and braces scientific re-enactment, but it was all Ellie needed to be sure. Part of her wanted to hang it back on the wall, then leave the room and ask for it to be moved, just as she'd seen hundreds of times on her favourite shows, but a larger part of her wasn't that brave and instead she chose to lean it against the wall, just below the sturdy looking hook that seemed so incapable of holding it in place.

She wondered how often Lucinda found the thing on the floor when she came in to check the place after each set of guests had left. Did it freak her out, too? Or did she just accept it? Maybe she could probe her on it later when they attended the barbeque that her father had agreed to yesterday when they'd arrived. If anyone was aware of strange goings-on it would be her, after all, she was as good as the caretaker for the building. But then maybe she'd just think she was a crazy kid. Maybe it was better not to say anything to anyone. There were far too many maybes for Ellie's liking, the constant running through of the situation in her head was making it spin.

"Coffee?" Her mother's voice caused her to jump, snapping her from her racing thoughts. "You're up early," she continued, through a half yawn as she stretched her arms in front of her, causing the sleeves of her blue towelette dressing gown to creep just past her wrists.

"I didn't get much sleep after three this morning," Ellie replied, stopping herself from yawning as well by putting the back of her hand to her mouth. "Henry had a bit of a scare in the night, he's in my bed now." Ellie followed her mother, who was busy arranging her sleep-tousled dark hair with her hands through to the kitchen; the thick natural stone tiles felt cold beneath her bare feet despite the warmth of the morning sun. "Needless to say, he managed to take up most of the bed. I gave up trying to get a lay-in when I woke up with an elbow in my ribs."

"He didn't wet the bed, did he?" she asked as she searched through several identical looking oak cupboards in the monstrously large kitchen. Eventually, her mother found one that housed a fleet of generic white mugs just above the sink. She lifted two down and put the kettle on after filling it with water from the large brass faucet that creaked as she spun the handle.

"No – he – umm, he saw someone in his room," Ellie said, thinking how crazy it sounded as the words left her lips. She had an overwhelming need to confide in someone about it, someone other than a five-year-old that was.

"Bad dream then."

"No, I think he really saw someone!" she said flatly.

"He was terrified, his room was as cold as a freezer and then there's that cross in the hall out front."

"Cross?" her mother asked absently, proving that she wasn't really paying attention, and was more focused on the task of making coffee.

"Don't worry," Ellie conceded, deciding that trying to convince her sceptical mother that the place could be haunted was about as fruitless as using a chocolate fireguard. Watching her pour boiling water into the mugs she said, "You're right, he probably had a bad dream. I expect he'll want to stay in your room tonight. Did you not hear him in the night?"

"No, sorry, Ells. We both went out like lights last night. I can hardly even remember by head hitting the pillow. Probably that long drive," she said and smiled softly, the teaspoon in her hand clinked against the china as she stirred. "I did wonder about putting Henry in his own room in a strange place on the first night. Trouble is if you don't get kids of his age into a set routine, you're making a rod for your own back. He'll be fine tonight, I'm sure of it."

And that was it, case closed. Her mother worked at one of the local primary schools, not St Mark's, where Henry had just completed his reception year, but one a few miles away. Although it would have saved on travel and made things easier on her busy schedule, she'd been hell-bent on him not going to the same school at which she worked, she didn't think it was healthy. She wasn't a teacher, she worked on the reception, and Ellie didn't know how it could be *unhealthy* as her mother had put it for them to be at the same school. Her mother had some funny ideas at times, you just had to roll with it and agree, unless you wanted a *discussion*, which really meant argument.

Ellie badly wanted to tell her mum about the cross, make her listen, and make her understand the feeling that was eating away inside of her. A feeling which told her that this place was anything but good, but she had no proof, and part of her still wasn't convinced she believed her own feelings and that it was likely nothing more than a product of her overactive imagination.

Ellie sipped gingerly at her coffee not really enjoying the cheap and bitter tasting instant they'd brought with them. She was more of Costa kind of girl or Starbucks at a push. Absently she watched her mum flit about the large kitchen in preparation for breakfast. She opened the cavernous American style fridge freezer combo that looked expensive but a tad out of place, with its brushed aluminium finish against the oak and natural stone. Removing a box of eggs and placing them on the side she then produced a fresh pack of bacon and a foil-wrapped part-used pack of sausages, all of which had just about lasted the painfully slow trip from home in the cooler packed with ice.

"What's say we have a little girly pamper session and try out the hot tub bath in my room after we eat?" her mother suggested as she searched through more cupboards looking for pots and pans.

"I think I'll give it a miss," Ellie replied, blowing onto the steaming liquid before braving another sip. The first had burned her mouth a little. "I need to get some air. I think I'll take a little walk before we eat. What time are we heading out?"

"Around ten, I think your dad wants to check out the Eden Project today, so you've got a couple of hours. Do you want me to save you some food?"

Ellie took a final drink of her coffee before tossing the rest down the deep ceramic sink, the hot liquid gargled eagerly down a plug hole that seemed to be enjoying it far more than she had. She rinsed the mug before placing it on the side to drain and said, "I'll probably eat later, I'm not really feeling it at the moment."

"I'll save you some bacon and a couple of sausages, you can eat in the car," her mother replied sounding a little dejected. As Ellie reached the kitchen door her mother said, "Is this still about you not wanting to be here?"

Ellie turned to face her, forced a convincing smile for the sake of her mother who looked a bit wounded and said, "No, I just didn't sleep well. I'm fine, honest. I just need a shower and some fresh air, then I'll be good."

"As long as you're sure, just don't wander too far, and watch out for cars on those narrow lanes, they might not see you."

"I'll be fine, see you later." She took a few steps toward her mother and gave her a quick hug, hoping it would make her feel a bit better and stick a plaster over the emotional wound that she'd opened up.

Despite the consoling hug, Ellie still felt pretty much like shit, her mum genuinely looked upset at the refusal of what she'd see as some quality time together. It wasn't that Ellie didn't want to spend time with her, even at eighteen, and now starting to come out of those teen years where being seen with parents was paramount to embarrassment, she still enjoyed a little time with her, despite her sometimes strange ways and odd ideas. Ellie just needed to get out of the chapel, breathe some fresh air into her lungs and feel the sun on her face. The place was big, but for some reason inside its old walls it felt almost claustrophobic, like a reverse of Dr. Who's TARDIS, that despite looking the size of a Police Call Box was actually larger on the inside than anyone had ever really managed to figure out.

Heading up to the first floor, she crept into her room. Hand-Me-Down-Henry was still sleeping soundly, his blonde hair had been visited by the sleep fairies and seemed to be standing at a perfect ninety degrees to the top of his head. His cherubic-like face was locked in a slight frown as if something in his slumber was troubling him. Not wanting to wake him with the sound of the shower in her ensuite, Ellie collected her clothes and wash bag and headed to his room, pausing momentarily outside the door in the same spot she'd been last night. Gingerly she crept into the room, it was warm and nowhere near the frigid temperature it had been during the night. Telling herself not to be stupid, that if this place was haunted then any room would be fair game to whatever still lurked here, not just Henry's one, she headed to the bathroom and turned on the shower.

Ellie washed quickly, not taking time to appreciate the multi-jet shower heads that hit, no – more massaged you all over, like some kind of human car wash. Instead, her mind was full of movie scenes like the one from Psycho, or the myriad of other horror films where nasty things happened in steam-filled bathrooms. In fact, she left the door wide open with the sole intention of not letting it fog up. Thankfully that ensured there was no shower steam, no misted-up mirror that when cleared with the back of the hand produced an evil face glaring at you from behind in a chilling parody of any self-respecting horror movie.

Staying in Henry's room she dressed quickly in faded denim shorts, that her mother would no doubt say were just a tad short of being decent, a lime colour strap top and a pair of grey high-top Converse. Her hair was still on the wetter side of damp and smelt strongly of Fructis. Not bothering to dry it, she threw a brush quickly through the wetted hair, deciding to let the sun do the rest. Before she'd had it cut a few weeks ago her hair had been long, to the base of her back long. Just to tame it required a good hour's work. Now a quick brush and it was ready to rock.

Ellie hung the wet towel over Henry's door, something she knew her mother would tut at and move as soon as she saw it. Passing her room, she dared one more glance at her sleeping brother. He'd turned onto his back, his mouth wide open as if in the hope of catching a passing fly. Muddy puddles George was now clamped firmly under one arm. He held the toy in such a vice-like grip that poor old George would have been strangled in mere seconds had he been real.

Satisfied, Ellie padded down the stairs, glancing uneasily at the crucifix as she passed it by. Thankfully it was still propped up in the exact spot she'd left it. She had no desire to hang it up, what was the point? She knew that by the time she got home, or at some point in the day when they were out and no eyes were around to see it, it would be displaced back to the floor.

Reaching the door, she unlatched it, swung it open and stepped out into the warm, bright morning. She stopped for a few brief seconds just to enjoy the fresh air as it hit her lungs and the feel of the sunlight on her face. Closing the heavy oak door, she headed down the shingle drive, only glancing back at The Old Chapel once before she met the main road.

At the entrance to the drive, she glanced left, then right, deciding which way to go. Both looked very similar. Left would take her toward where Lucinda said she lived. Just where right would take her was a bit of a mystery. Eventually, she took a right, hoping to find a bridleway or footpath off the road and across the fields. She was certain they'd passed one such bridleway just after coming into the village, about a mile up the road. It had stuck in her brain as there'd been a very old and tired-looking roadside shrine there, marking the spot where some poor unfortunate had met their end. Making that her goal, she tipped the Ray Bans off her head and set off.

It was the start of another perfect July day, another day that the weathermen would chalk up as forming part of the great 2018 heatwave. A heatwave that baked the UK and most of Northern Europe. A real scorcher, the kind of heat that had most weather complaining Brits begging for rain while roads got so hot they began to melt.

The sky was clear of all bar a few wisps of cloud that stretched out like gossamer threads, and a gentle breeze tickled its way through the leaves. It was idyllic, but something was off. At first, Ellie couldn't put her finger on it and the feeling gnawed at her, like when you know the answer to a question but can't quite get it out. Finally, she realised what it was that bugged her, what it was that was wrong. The silence. This was about as perfect a morning as you'd find, yet in the trees no birds sang. In the thorny, blackberry-clad hedgerows no mice scurried. There was just the rhythmic sound of her well-worn All-Stars as they beat against the faded and slightly crumbled tarmac. Ellie stopped and held her breath. The only sound now, apart from the gentle pulse of her quickening heart in her ears, was the warm morning breeze as it played its way through the long grass of the field opposite and stirred the leaves on the trees. She noticed that her feeling of claustrophobia hadn't been limited to The Old Chapel, and despite now being a good half mile away and out in the open countryside, she still felt the same. Suddenly being out here on her own didn't feel right, she didn't know why, just like she didn't know why she knew there was something off with The Old Chapel. She just knew it. The Old Chapel might be a place where the nightmares of small children really came out from under your bed at night, but at least her family was there, and after all there was safety in numbers, wasn't there?

The unease gave birth to another mentally nurtured monster, panic, and she knew that once you gave into panic it was one long downhill ride to irrational insanity and it took all the will she could muster to keep it under control. *One too many paranormal shows, Ells,* she reminded herself. *Three or four too many horror films.* She cursed herself for allowing her imagination to run wild because she'd not actually seen anything in Henry's room. Sure, it had been cold, sure that crucifix could naturally have fallen off the wall, twice, and sure as shit Henry could have been dreaming. *Just like all the birds, bees and insects were having a lay-in and couldn't be bothered to be carrying out mother nature's work on a morning so fine*, her betraying brain questioned. What was it that the Unexplained UK Team said? *Just because you can't explain something, doesn't mean it can't be explained.* The tagline ran something like that. Ellie took a steadying breath, and turned to head back, trying to kid herself that she didn't feel like a walk anymore, not that she had scared herself shitless.

No matter how hard she tried her anxiety wouldn't budge; she looked around, now with the growing sense of being watched, and froze. In the field which she'd been walking parallel to on her left-hand side was what at first appeared to be a scarecrow, only the more she stared at it the more she realised that this was not like any scarecrow she'd ever seen. The figure was halfway into the smallish field, about sixty metres or so from her, dressed in a dark tunic almost like that of a monk, but it one was not the right colour to be that of a monk. It looked to be made of rich, velvety fabric and far too indulgent for a member of any brotherhood. The fabric, however, looked dirty and rotten as if it had just been dug up from the very field in which it stood. Despite its monk-like appearance this didn't feel like anything holy, far from it. It seemed to seethe insidiousness. It was facing her, watching with invisible eyes, eyes hidden inside a hood that festooned, not a face, but just darkness; Ellie felt her insides churn, the way they had when she'd once eaten some chicken that had turned the wrong side of good, her bladder felt swollen too, and she had a sudden and overwhelming need to pee. She wanted to look away, wanted to run but fear had her frozen, and in some strange way she couldn't understand part of her almost felt drawn to it, as if it were calling her and she nearly took a step forward, but at the last minute she managed to stop herself. The thing observed her, its rotting tunic seemed to hang in the air, as if being worn by HG Wells' Invisible Man, only much more foreboding than Jack Griffin had ever been.

Ellie lifted her sunglasses, blinked and rubbed her eyes with shaky hands as if the act would wash the image from her view. It did anything but. As she looked again the figure had drawn closer and with lightning fast speed. Maybe by a good thirty metres or so. Now at this distance, she could see things falling from the robe, from the gap between the hemline and the ground where the legs should have been. Beetles. Thick, black and bulbous, countless numbers of them. They crawled out from under the robe, their bristly legs clinging to the fabric for a few seconds before dropping to the floor with a soft plop, like fat black drops of rain. As they hit the long grass, she could hear their legs scurrying busily toward her, eager and relentless, their passage unusually loud against the otherwise silent morning. Slowly the figure began to glide closer, as it closed the distance the once fragrant summer air began to take on a fetid smell, that of decay, burnt human flesh and things long since dead. The stench hit the back of her throat and coated it like foul paint. Ellie instantly felt her gag reflex kick in and she doubled over, emptying the half cup of coffee she'd drunk onto the road, as well as the remnants of last night's dinner.

Grimacing, she wiped bile from her lips and as she did the first of the large black beetles scurried out from under the hedge, having covered the distance with seemingly impossible speed, its large and dangerous-looking mandibles quivering and working feverishly. Another joined it, then another, they spilled into the culvert that ran along the side of the road and began clambering up the other side toward her, like some kind of hellish encroaching tide. Ellie hated insects. All she could picture at that point was a scene from The Mummy where the Scarab Beetles snatched the life away from anyone foolish enough to get in their way by burrowing into their flesh and entering the body through any orifice that they could.

With the air clogged thick with the stench of rot, and the vehement clicking of the excited insectile hoard, paralysis released her, and now Ellie did run. She didn't look back. She wanted to, she yearned to, but she didn't dare. For she knew that if she did the figure would surely be right behind her, its cargo of bulbous beetles dropping behind it in a trail as it pursued her relentlessly. Then, just as she'd thought she was safe an invisible cloaked hand would be reaching for her, hoping to grab her and pull her down into the darkness that dwelt inside the tunic's hood.

Ellie wasn't sure how long she'd been running for, her legs burned with lactic acid and her breath felt hot as her chest heaved. Eventually, she reached The Old Chapel's gravel drive, but she held her pace, almost sliding onto her side as her Converse skidded on the shingle. Finally, at the front door, she hit at it frantically with both hands, hammering it so hard her fists burned with pain. Ellie finally looked behind her, the drive was empty. Feeling spent she pressed her back against the door for support. The wood felt cool against her hot skin. Slowly, her jelly-like legs gave way and she slid down onto the cold stone stoop. Burying her face in her hands she began to weep.

———

AROUND THE SAME time that her daughter was running from the faceless figure in the field and its swarm of scurrying beetles, Carol was in the Altar Room's ensuite bathroom freshly out of the shower and wrapped in one of the complimentary white towelled robes. Having been turned down by her daughter for the girly pamper session, she'd wanted to try the pool-sized bath out, maybe with Rob but he was still asleep. His loss. So instead and feeling a little disappointed she'd opted for the shower. She ran her hands down the soft fabric of her dressing gown. It carried The Old Chapel's logo – an embroidered copy of the building's bell tower had been sown into the fabric in royal blue cotton. The entire place was a testament to the time the owners had put into getting it just right, it was clear that no expense had been spared and that Mr. and Mrs. Reed had an acute eye for detail.

After hearing Ellie head out the front door, and before getting her shower, she'd put a tray of bacon and sausages in the large aga style oven, on a low heat to give her time. That way by the time everyone was up, most of the breakfast would be pre-cooked. Having doused her hands with water from the sink to wash off the raw meat juices, she'd headed back to the bedroom with a quick detour via the first floor to check on Henry. He'd still been starfished out in Ellie's bed, a light snoring sound coming from his partly open lips. If he had suffered a bad dream last night, he was obviously over it now and sleeping like normal. It was almost eight-fifteen and he'd be up soon. If she was lucky, she'd have a chance to get dressed before he woke and started to demand this and that for his breakfast. Satisfied that she might just have a little *me time* before he woke, she headed down the rear stairs that led from the mezzanine level and came out by their room. She tiptoed past the bed where her husband still slept, he was half in and half out the covers, his hair looking a mess and the embroidered floral design of the pillowcase imprinted on the left-hand side of his face.

The twin head, rainfall shower had been wonderful, the hot tub bath could be used later and seemed to be wasted on just one. With the temperature turned down so the water was no more than the warm side of tepid, she allowed the slightly grubby feeling of a hot night's sleep to wash down her body and into the drain.

Now stood in front of the mirror with her hair wrapped in a matching towel and her overpriced moisturiser in her hand, Carol began to dab it on her face, frowning at how, despite the forty-pound price tag, it had done nothing to smooth over the thin crow's feet that had been creeping in over the last few years. She placed the moisturiser on the sink, removed the towel and began to rub her damp hair with it vigorously. As she did a light knock came from the door.

"Five minutes," she called, a little angry that her *me time* had been interrupted.

She turned her attention back to her hair, inwardly criticising how it seemed thinner nowadays, then feeling a pang of jealousy at how Lucinda had seemingly been able to hold on to her youthful beauty, likely blessed with good genetics that freed her from the daily toils of facial moisturising with over-priced lotions. Lucinda's flowing red hair didn't look thin, tired and mumsy, neither did her figure. Rob had certainly noticed, much to her annoyance.

Allowing her frustration to flow out through her hair towelling she was caught off guard as the knocking came again, more urgent this time and at least twice as loud.

"For Christ sake," Carol shouted, throwing the towel over the heated rail. "Just give me a few minutes!" The thought that it might be Henry outside instantly made her feel guilty. "Is that you Hen?"

Silence.

"Rob?"

Silence.

"Ellie?" Carol questioned, her voice not sounding quite so sure. She felt a shiver run through her. The bathroom suddenly felt a lot cooler than it had and her skin flushed with goosebumps. She pulled the collar of her dressing gown up and re-fixed the tie around her waist.

Almost instantly the knock came again, louder, urgent and impatient. This time she actually saw the door bulge in and strain on its latch and hinges. Carol let out an uncertain breath and pulled the edges of the gown over her breasts a little more as if the fabric would offer some protection.

"Rob, if that's you it's not funny," she called in a slightly wobbly voice. Carol decided that if she opened the door and found him in the act she was going to kick his ass, and that kind of morning play fighting could lead to other things. They were on holiday after all, Ellie was out and Henry was asleep. Now smiling at the thought and feeling her body tingle with anticipation she took hold of the handle and swung the door open. Rob was in the room, but still sleeping peacefully in the exact spot he'd been in when she'd headed to the shower, totally undisturbed by the knocking which would have easily been loud enough to wake him. Fearing Henry was now up and wandering around on his own she bounded upstairs to Ellie's room. Henry hadn't even moved position.

"Ells?" she called walking back out into the hall. "Are you back?" It seemed perpetually silent, then a few seconds later the silence was broken by a loud crash and the sound of breaking glass coming from her bathroom.

Carol flew down the stairs, holding the dressing gown together as her heart hammered in her chest. As she burst into the room she found Rob sitting up in bed rubbing his eyes.

"What the hell was that?" he said groggily. "Did you drop something?"

Carol didn't answer, she shot into the bathroom only to find her jar of moisturiser broken all over the floor. The white viscous contents had starburst over the granite tiles and splattered up the wall. A large thick glob of it was also hanging from the circular LED light. It stretched out as the bulbous end gave in to gravity, finally falling to the tiles with a soft *ssspllatttttt*.

She stared at the wrecked cream, not quite able to comprehend how it had happened. The small glass container had been well away from the side, and even if it had fallen it should never have made such a God-awful mess. It looked like someone had stuck a cherry-bomb in the jar, lit the fuse and left it to blow.

Henry saw something in his room, and what about that cross? Rattled Ellie's voice in her head.

She tried to push the idea aside as preposterous, especially when considering Ellie's love of the paranormal, but her daughter's words span round and round, nonetheless. Before she had time to make her mind up someone began hammering on the front door so hard it sounded like the devil himself was trying to get in. Carol didn't quite jump the proverbial three feet in the air as the banging began, but it was close.

CHAPTER 9

HE WAS HALF DOZING AND ALMOST MISSED IT. THE lengthy periods of hissing and static that spanned between the general chat of the group always had that effect. However, some inbuilt mechanism, or more an ear for picking up strange sounds and voices instantly snapped him awake. It was there, visible on the screen, too. A slight spike in the background noise, likely not even noticeable to anyone, unless you knew what to look for. The spike was not as prominent as their voices, but then it wouldn't be. At the time, no one had heard it. The spike on the Adobe Audition edit and review screen was a clear indication of an EVP.

Electronic Voice Phenomenon was by far the most commonly caught piece of evidence by any paranormal investigation team. Scotty wasn't personally enamoured by the term, but it was as common to paranormal research as hamburgers were to McDonald's. The voices, when caught, were not electronic as such. To say they were electronic was as close, as far as Scotty thought, to saying they'd been manipulated in some way. Or required some special piece of equipment to produce, but they did not. Anyone could pick them up with the most basic of recorders. The truth behind these ghostly voices, always unheard at the time of the investigation, but audible on playback, was weirder, and one main reason why he held a good unexplainable EVP in high regard evidentially.

The voices existed below the range of human hearing, which is generally thought to start at around fifteen to twenty kilohertz, although the older you got the more your hearing deteriorated, so those numbers were often on the optimistic side for most adults. Digital voice records, however, could capture audio at those lower levels. When the recorded material was later reviewed, thanks to the modern miracle of amplification the speech became audible. The voices were there all along, it's just you couldn't hear them. It seemed the dead were with us, and sometimes they did talk, you just needed the right equipment to catch what they had to say. Whole sentences were rare, you were more likely to get the odd word, like some distant radio station coming through the static.

Some of the more complex audio recorders specifically designed for paranormal research went below the fifteen to twenty-kilohertz range and into the infrasound. Scotty had used such devices but preferred his, straight from Argos, Sony ICD. A good solid middle of the road voice recorder that did the job; and judging by the audio he'd just heard, it did it well.

Alert and focused, Scott (Scotty) Hampton adjusted himself in his large leather office chair then ran his finger across the HP's touch screen, rewound the section by a few seconds, and began the piece of audio again. He pushed his Bose headphones tightly against his ears until the lobes felt almost painful against his head, and with his breath caught pensively in his lungs, he listened.

"I heeaaarrr yoouuu!"

He let the held breath go in a slow and steady exhale as if he were defusing a bomb and caught between the blue and the red wire and not operating a reliable piece of audio editing software. Switching dexterously between the mouse and touchscreen he cut the few seconds' worth of audio and dropped it to an editing screen and hit play.

"*I heeaarrr yoouuu!*"

He felt his hackles rise. The voice from beyond the grave came through as a loud, menacing whisper. The diction was clear, the words well-formed and not in the slightest bit ambiguous. It wasn't one of those clips that five people would listen to and give you five differing interpretations. In ten shows they'd not caught one this clear, in fact, he'd never heard one so clear, ever. It was a real peach, what in the business they called a Class A EVP, and they were about as rare as rocking horse shit, hens' teeth, or whatever adage you cared to throw at it. The only EVPs they'd turned up on the show were just the odd inaudible Class C, that they then had to de-bunk due to the production teams' radios that were always playing havoc with the more sensitive equipment. That, and no one could really hear what was being said. *It's better to present no evidence than questionable evidence,* was Mike's motto, and one he'd shared since the team had blossomed from a random post by Mike Cross on paranormaluk.com, the UK's most prestigious paranormal forum, if research into ghosts could be classed as such. Mike's first post, the one that caught Scotty's attention, was him actively seeking members for his fledgling team three years ago.

———

UNEXPLAINED UK – Seeking the answer to that unanswerable question?

My name is Mike Cross, my background is in both police and private investigation. I am looking for two people to join a brand-new team. I want to keep it small, private, and we will be totally non-profit.

Ideally, I would like at least one person with technical experience transferable to the world of paranormal research, but as I am not paying I can't be too fussy! All equipment will be provided.

Interested? Drop me a direct message via the forum. Preferably applicants will be from Hampshire, Dorset, Wiltshire or Sussex, but willing to travel nationwide for investigation work.

———

HAVING SPENT years watching the various reality TV teams, some who seemed quite genuine, and plenty who didn't, and having been interested in anything paranormal for just about as long as he could remember, Scotty sent Mike a message explaining that he was a twenty-five-year-old CCTV engineer from Cowes on the Isle Of Wight with a keen interest in getting involved directly in the world of research. Mike never really said how many people responded to his post, most likely quite a few, but he'd replied to Scotty the next day asking for a few more details about his background. Scotty elaborated on his initial message saying that he held an NVQ in Electronic Engineering and worked his day job for the Isle of Wight Council, maintaining and installing the growing network of cameras. Besides his experience with camera equipment, he was also a dabhand in sound engineering and often ran booth and played bass for a local band, The Island. They'd almost had a music career two years before he'd joined Mike's team, after a song of theirs, Summer Sun, was used on a "Visit The Isle of Wight" promotional advert. The song got some airplay on mainstream TV thanks to the advert that ran the summer through across the UK. The catchy hook used in the advert saw Summer Sun make it into the Itunes top five for the best part of five weeks. It even charted in the States, too. Their rise to the heights of rock stardom had been shown the stoppers when the record company pulled the plug on the album deal. Apparently, the album didn't have a sound that was current enough, whatever that meant. It seemed that Level 42 were going to keep the kudos of being the Island's main musical export for another good few years.

The day Scotty met Mike for the first time he'd taken the Red Funnel Fast Cat across an unusually still and glass-like Solent to Southampton, then met over a coffee next to the historic Bargate building in the city centre. A little snippet of the ancient juxtaposed proudly against the modern city.

As they'd both sat in the warmth of a pleasant South Coast summer's day sipping at strong cappuccino's, Mike explained he had the other member of the team lined up, a girl in her thirties from Dorset called Tara. Tara or Tig as some called her, also had no previous experience in the field. She was, however, keen and had a penchant for history, and Mike felt that would make her vital for location research. Apart from that, she didn't seem to hold any other specific skill, but ultimately if you had someone to set up the tech, all you needed was yourself and a flask of coffee to nurse you through the night. A slight case of insomnia helped, too. Oh, and an open yet questionable mind. Mike had explained to him at that meeting how he classed himself as a sceptical believer.

"I mean, I think there is something in it, Scott," he'd said, an excited twinkle in his eyes. *"It's just I am not prepared to take every bump, creek, and bang as a sign of the other side. Or Orbs, don't get me started on fucking Orbs! I want something definitive. I don't want to be commercial and run events. I'm not in this for the money, I'm in it for answers."*

As the table waitress delivered the second coffee, Mike divulged his backstory, how he'd grown a deep interest in the paranormal after living most of his life without really giving it a second thought. Despite his relatively recent interest, his knowledge was spot on, his theories very similar to Scotty's and they agreed on a lot. It seemed that Mike had really taken a crash-course into theories around the spirit world. Enthused, he explained that he was keen to try and answer the question that had eluded man since man could comprehend his own sentience. Scotty couldn't deny why Mike had such a drive to find that answer, the guy had been through the wringer. He doubted he'd find it, though. So far many had tried but no one had. Scotty felt pretty certain no one ever would, either. He was a firm believer that some things were not meant to be learned in this life. It didn't stop him from wanting to have a crack at finding the answer, though.

How anyone could come out the other side of losing his family and still be both sane and sober was beyond Scotty's comprehension, and the upbeat and enthused way he spoke about trying to find that answer despite what he'd been through was nothing short of miraculous. Either that or the way he spoke was a façade for much darker feelings. He respected Mike for it whatever the truth. Sure, his voice had cracked a little as he recalled the story of the day of the accident and a few times he lost that sparkle in his eyes and they drifted off to sadness. Scotty guessed there'd been days when they'd spent a lot of time there. Hell, despite his large and rather rugged appearance even he'd found himself on the verge of having to wipe an eye, as Mike ran slowly through what must have been the darkest days of any man's life.

People dealt with grief and mass loss in different ways, some just ended it all and took their own lives, some drank, some even ran, as if being on the move meant the grief wouldn't catch them. If this was Mike's way of dealing with the death of his wife and child then he deserved it, hell he'd fucking earned it, and was it that strange to want to know for certain that they'd passed on to another place? With the absence of a strong religious belief, he guessed it was a reasonable question to want an answer to.

With Mike sat opposite him, that excited, and

maybe slight eccentric look in his eye that he still got to this day when worked up about something, he explained his vision for the group, how he wanted to keep it small, no more than three or four members and some of the locations he was interested in. It sounded good, the offer to work in a small team of three with all the equipment provided. Sure, from what Mike had told him it was far from the best equipment, but it was a start. Mike had funded its purchase from some of the compensation and life insurance money he'd received after the accident.

"SOME WOULD THINK I'm foolish flitting it away on such things," Mike had said, his hands wrapped around the coffee. "But I see it as an investment, I don't care if no one believes what I find. I just need to know. For me. If I had to spend it all just to know, I would." Scotty believed him, too.

He never let on how much he'd received from that compensation and insurance pay-out, and there was no way Scotty was asking. Likely enough to buy the best kit and still have plenty left, but the sheer fact that he wouldn't have to fund his own equipment was nothing short of a bonus. Back then it was hard enough on his meagre council wage just paying the rent on his small one bed flat. As it was, he used to rely on his mother's home cooked food a few times a week, okay maybe more than a few times a week, just to keep the right side of his never diminishing overdraft. Now, as head of tech on the show his financial situation had improved, not a lot but a bit. At least now when his statements dropped through the door the final balance figure didn't have a minus figure before it. Reality TV shows, especially first season ones, did not make you rich, hell they hardly made you famous, but it paid better than servicing CCTV cameras. You had to hope you'd be in it for the long run and at a later date, once you'd established yourself, just jump ship to one of the larger channels where the money was.

Scotty put his headphones on the desk, stood up and arched an ache out of his back, smiling as it made a satisfying crack. He was still hurting from the beasting he'd given himself at Puregym last night. It wasn't only his back that ached, his legs and arms were also feeling it. It was the sign of a good workout and he knew that by the time he next rolled into the gym he'd be ready to do it all again.

The fact he'd spent the last two hours glued to his chair doing evidence review hadn't helped his aching muscles, and that was just the audio, he hadn't even made a start of the video footage yet.

Ignoring the burning in his stiff legs he walked through to the bathroom, urinated, and scolded himself that the colour of his pee indicated a slight case of de-hydration. From there he went to the kitchen where he drew a pint of water from the tap, gulping it down as if he'd just spent a week walking across the desert with only his own diminishing piss as a source of hydration. He then refilled the glass and carried it back to the lounge, where he had his workstation set up on a small desk at the back of the room, near to a window that if you looked out of just right you could see the boats on Cowes harbour. In the summer with the windows open, and if the breeze was just right, you could hear the gentle *clink, clink* of rope on mast, a sound that never failed to send him off to sleep.

Back on his laptop, he saw that the HP's screen-saver had kicked in and the Unexplained UK logo bounced around excitedly in rendered luminous green 3D, like a fly caught in a jar. Catching his reflection in the glossy backdrop he chided himself over two more things; his dark hair looked messy and was a good two weeks past when it should last have been cut, and his face looked tired. Promising himself he would try and get to bed at a reasonable time, so he'd benefit from at least seven hours' worth of sleep before tomorrow's gym visit, he kicked Adobe Audition back to life. The premium rate audio editing software was one of the nice little bonuses about TV work. Stuff like that was all paid for and no real expense spared, the fact he could also utilise its licence for his own work was just another little perk.

Scotty took another long swallow of his water, placed the glass next to his laptop and snapped his headphones back over his ears. With this little finding, he was eager to get the investigation summary complete, uploaded to his Youtube channel and the link sent to the customers who'd been with him that night. If the clip went viral, he'd also earn a good few quid off the advert clicks.

Focused on the screen, Scotty highlighted the section of speech again, almost reluctant to filter it too much, it was that perfect. He felt his heart racing with an excitement that he knew only a fellow spook hunter could understand at finding a piece of rare, top class evidence. He raised the volume, then dropped out a little of the background noise and played it again.

"I heeaarrr yoouuu!"

It was clear before but now it was almost as if someone had spoken directly into the mic of his Sony ICD voice recorder. He shook his head in disbelief and quickly saved the file, Mike was going to have a bird when he heard this. He knew Moot Hall, the fifteenth-century timber-framed building that stood poignantly on Elstow Green in Bedfordshire, was going to be a good bet for an investigation. Tara had spoken to other teams whilst researching locations for the show, the place was renowned for turning up some amazing audio results. Whatever still resided or came back to its ancient walls in visitation, was very vocal. Because of her research, they had highlighted the location for show eight, but the relatively small building hadn't been given the go-ahead by the production team who'd claimed it too small to record an hour-long show in and too much of a health and safety risk once full of wires, crew, and recording kit. Eventually, Moot Hall had been replaced by The Ancient Ram Inn, in Wooton-Under-Edge. A location that whilst no doubt famous for its reported Incubus, a male sex demon who liked to get horny with female guests, was also small and pokey and likely no bigger than Moot. The whole team felt it was more a case of the production company stamping their feet and wanting only the higher profile venues. High profile locations were all well and good, but most had seen every paranormal investigation team under the sun, and Scotty felt sure that any self-respecting spirits would by now be fed up with the circus show and buggered off. Or to put it more technically, all the energies used up and just an empty shell left. The lesser known places often proved to be the gems, but as a new show they needed to attract an audience and they were pretty much at the mercy of the channel. Mike had made comments a number of times about how he felt he'd sold his soul to the devil, and to be fair he probably wasn't too far wrong. Maybe next season they'd have more clout, after all it was about establishing your brand. So, they'd smiled, agreed, then swallowed the shit pill of lies sold to them by the production company and carried on. Scotty was learning that like it or not, that was how things often worked in TV land.

With Moot Hall out of the picture and keen to check the place out for himself, he took a small team of paying customers along. It was his side-line, his little banker for the future. His official business was called Scotty's Haunts, an organised paranormal event company that ran independently of his work on Unexplained UK. Sure, when he'd had that first meeting with Mike on that sunny Southampton summer's day, organised events were not on the agenda, but then neither was ending up as a reality TV star. Times changed, and you had to roll with the punches. Scotty's Haunts offered people, many of whom were fans of the fledgling show, the chance to spend some quality time in some of the UK's most notoriously haunted places. The fact he'd set the small event company up off the back of his TV work saw him instantly able to fill places, in fact, he always had more willing participants than he had tickets. So far, the three events he'd run had been a sell-out, with every standby place filled, too. There were a whole host of people wanting to experience a slice of what they saw on their screens, with the bonus of doing it with one of the show's stars. On one occasion Tara decided to join him, which had proved popular with the guests. One balding middle-aged guy in particular who'd spent every break flirting with her outrageously, despite the rather obvious wedding ring on his finger. Other than that, Scotty ran each event with just himself and his eighteen-year-old brother, Morgan, who was always keen to earn a few quid and escape the monotony of Island life.

Now with the small section of audio cleaned he dropped it back into the main thread of speech, so it had some context with the conversation the team was having at the time. Moot Hall was split into four main rooms over two floors; on the ground floor you had a small area that now acted as a museum, the entrance hall and a small side room called A Bunyan Room, so named after the writer Robert Bunyan, famed for penning The Pilgrim's Progress in 1678. The room paid homage to the writer who'd heralded from the town. The oddly named room was supposed to represent a section of his house as it would have looked back in the day. On the upper floor was a larger room that spanned much of the building's footprint. Again, it contained a variety of historical artefacts that the paying public could snap with their digital cameras on day visits.

The clip in question had come from the last vigil of the night held in the small and rather cramped A Bunyan Room.

Scotty pushed his headphones against his ears once again and pushed play.

"*This is vigil six of the night and vigil two in A Bunyan Room,*" he heard himself say from the depths of the audio file. "*The time is three fifteen am on July tenth, twenty-eighteen. It's funny, it's not even called The Bunyan Room, it's called A Bunyan Room.*"

"*Yeah, and did you see the local walks are sponsored by Scholl foot products? Do you think that was intentional?*" said the voice of his brother. There was the sound of light laughter from the few guests.

"*I heeaarrr yoouu!*" came the voice from beyond the grave.

"*We have an ambient temperature in here of eighteen degrees centigrade and no electromagnetic interference on either the MEL or K2 meters,*" Scotty heard himself say, totally unaware that someone from behind death's dark vale had just spoken in direct response to the joke that Morgan had made.

"Unbelievable," Scotty muttered to himself as he shook his head. He had to tell someone, he felt like a kid that had just aced a test. Mike had a meeting with the channel's head honcho, so calling him was a no go. Instead, he opted for Tara's number from his most dialled list and much to his annoyance her phone was engaged. He closed the call, but before he had a chance to properly set the iPhone down on the desk it began to ring. It was Mike.

CHAPTER 10

By the time Mike ended his call to Tara he'd cleared Media City, the home of SwitchBack TV, and was heading toward the motorway. The merciless sun that hung in the deep blue sky had raised the outside temperature to an uncomfortably sweltering thirty-one degrees centigrade, according to the digital display on his Jeep, and he wondered if it would push any higher before the day was through. Not that he could feel it inside the cab of his Jeep, the aircon was cranked high and Mike was thankful for it. He'd passed a few unfortunate motorists in older vehicles with their windows fruitlessly cranked down, managing to do no more than pipe more hot air into their cars.

The BBC Radio 2 Travel and Weather News was reporting it a good five degrees hotter on the south coast. The travel report looked favourable for a clear run on his two-hundred-mile journey. There were reports of a few heat-related issues in the capital where the temperature was tipping the mercury at close to forty, closing a few of the arterial routes due to the melting tarmac. A typical sign of a country incapable of dealing with a little adverse weather. If it was too windy and wet the trains couldn't run due to leaves on the line, a little snow and the roads ground to a halt, and a bit too much of the sun and they melted. Britain, you had to love it!

The travel news ended without any reports of issues on the route he was taking. Feeling like a little music, as opposed to the rather heavy topic of infant cot death being discussed on the upcoming Jeremy Vine Show, he flipped to the digital channel Absolute 80s. Depeche Mode were singing about being unable to get enough and Mike soon found himself tapping his hands on the wheel to the classic beat. Absolute 80's always satisfied his penchant for retro music and he decided it could keep him nicely in nostalgic company all the way to Wiltshire.

The flare of anger that he'd almost been consumed by, but just about managed to keep a lid on during the meeting with Rick, was all but gone. Now he just felt a niggling annoyance, an annoyance that they would have the gall to make him risk his reputation. Mike knew that if he'd gone with their plans to spice things up a bit by using a little fakery even his reputation as a PI would be called into question. He always knew that it was likely that at some point in the future he'd to have to go back to working private investigation cases, now sooner than he'd originally thought. If his credibility was ever called into question over his work on the show that would no doubt seep over into his other line of work. Once a fraud, always a fraud as they say.

A few minutes after he'd closed the line on his call to Tara, he was cruising down a reasonably quiet Park Way heading toward the M60 which would take him steadily south-east. The early afternoon traffic was light, and it was still a good few hours before the daily rush would begin. By then he would be well into Wiltshire, even with a stop for a mid-afternoon snack on the way, as long as his bladder didn't betray him. He'd not even been given the common courtesy of a brew by Rick, so he was pretty free of diuretic laced liquids. From there the journey involved a little motorway hopping until he could pick up the M6 South at Tadley Hill. Instead of staying on the M6, and likely opting for the toll to avoid circumnavigating Birmingham, he'd have to cut close to the city to get to the M5. It was then one long run down as far as Gloucester then A roads all the way to Pewsey, where the Reed residence was situated. It was a long route, especially considering that he'd have to tackle the Pewsey to Arundel trip after the meeting unless he felt too tired, then he could maybe look at bedding down in a Travel Lodge near Salisbury for the night, then finish the drive home in the morning. Something he'd been too tight to do prior to the meeting with Rick, but now was looking like the preferable option, it just depended on how long the meeting in Pewsey was going to take. He didn't mind being on the road, in fact, he quite liked it, especially when he was on his own. It gave him time to think, to get things straight, and right now there was a lot to think about. Where he took the team from here? And what the future held for them? Questions that he didn't think he could come up with the answers to in the time it would take to do the drive, but ones he would ponder over, nonetheless. There were certain thoughts that he didn't want, ones that came stalking through his head like some unwelcome mental trespasser, but he couldn't stop them, they would come unprovoked, always whilst he was trying to resolve another issue. When the thoughts came, he always asked himself the same *what ifs*. *What if* Claire hadn't stopped at the shop? *What if* he'd not been too tired the night before to take her food shopping? *What if* the life-wrecking, drink driving son of a bitch had just stopped for a piss in the toilet before staggering to his death machine, thus stalling him for that vital extra minute, a minute that would have seen them clear of the shop? The kind of questions that could drive a man mad if he let them. He'd not let them, but there were times when he'd felt close to madness. Those times, when he had been close, they'd spun round and round for hours, like a pair of sports shoes in a washing machine on a never-ending cycle banging and bumping him toward insanity. He knew as they tumbled in his head that trying to answer those *what-ifs* was as futile as Macbeth trying to wash the blood, both real and metaphorical, of King Duncan from his hands.

Following the intriguing call with Sue Reed, he'd resisted the temptation to stall in the car park of Media City and start doing research on the location. He knew Tara would be on the case and armed with the information by the time she met him and there was no point doubling up the work, not when he had half a country to cross. When it came to digging up the past on a location, her ability to root out the facts was second to none. She had a good mind for research and investigation. A mind that had been truly wasted scanning food at the local Tesco in Blandford, a mind that had never been free to blossom to its full potential. Mike had soon come to realise that in a different life, with a few different career choices, she'd have made an excellent detective. He cringed inwardly at the thought of her having to go back to her checkout job, just another hopeful sacrificed and thrown aside by the evil world of reality TV. But unlike many of the talentless wasters that graced many of the more cringe-worthy shows, Tara was talented, and she didn't deserve this, none of them did. If the rest of his working life was destined to be PI work then maybe it was high time he got a partner, he had no doubt that she had the nuance for the job and he could even help to put her through her PI Diploma, a necessity she'd have to endure to get a licence. As for Scotty, well he was younger and had a technician career that he could fall back on, not ideal but it was something.

As his mind switched back to Tara for a few moments and how it might be to work cases with her, he inwardly smiled. They had a certain chemistry that had sparked the day he'd met her in Bournemouth after he'd invited her for a chat following her reply to his advert, just one week before he'd met with Scotty. Tara had been picked from the many hopefuls he'd had for two reasons; she was relatively local, where most interested parties had seemed to ignore his request for people from southern counties. Secondly, she was a woman. There was no underhand reason he'd favoured having a female investigator on the team, as opposed to three males, he just felt it helped balance things out.

It had been crystal clear that she was right for the team within minutes of first meeting her and Mike had taken an instant shine to her, enamoured by both her looks and her outgoing personality. Her smile was electric and sparkled in her eyes that seemed to be both blue and green, depending on how the light caught them. Even her mannerisms and the way she carried herself endeared him. It was the first and only time since the death of Claire he'd felt a real physical wanting and attraction toward another woman, and it was strong, too. After she'd left their informal chat, he'd found his mind wandering to her regularly. When those thoughts were in his head the *what ifs* always seemed to elbow their way in, as if in punishment for his feelings. It was fair to say that Mike did, and still felt guilty for the way she made him feel, for the way some nights he would lay awake and wonder how it would be to have her beside him in the bed that seemed so cold, around the house that seemed so empty. What made it harder, was the fact the attraction blatantly ran both ways. They'd just clicked, the way two people who have never met before but get thrown together in random obscurity sometimes do. Some people call it fate, but Mike didn't believe in fate. No, to believe in such things as fate meant his wife and daughter were always destined to meet their end on the way back from the park that day, having just innocently stopped at the shop to buy a few extras for dinner. No, fate could go and fuck itself. Things just happened; life was just an out of control driverless train heading down the tracks until it was time for your stop. Nothing more.

Despite working together for the last few years they'd never acted on their chemistry. Not during her last violent relationship where she'd turn up to some investigations wearing clothing that blatantly covered bruises caused by her dick of a boyfriend. Thankfully those days were before the show, times when the darkness of the location backed up the long sleeve tops, or turtlenecks she seemed to sport on a weekly basis. With guilt, he'd wanted to comfort her and take her away from that violent life, show her that it wasn't the norm for men to raise their fists and strike out, but he hadn't. The guilt was always there, a voice inside his head that told him to act on his feelings for Tara would be paramount to cheating, and no matter how hard he tried to shut it out he couldn't. It nagged at him like some annoying back-seat driver. Tara had never admitted what Jason had done, not until the very end of the relationship. The stairs or a door always got the blame, it was a cliché, a terrible one, but Mike knew. He'd worked enough domestic violence cases in his time on the force to know the signs, and Tara knew that he knew, it was just never spoken of. The elephant in the room.

Not even after the incident where she'd been beaten to shit by the loser and left on the floor of his flat had he taken her in his arms like he'd wanted to, and like he knew she'd wanted him to. He'd done no more than comfort her as a friend. That particularly nasty assault that had seen her spill her heart out to him about the abuse, but only in the manner that one friend might confide in another. It had also seen Jason the arsehole, as Mike liked to inwardly think of him, finally jailed for his handiwork and Tara set free. Sometimes shit things had to happen for something positive to bloom, and that was one of them. He'd never have wished it upon her, ever, but the changes in her confidence since his incarceration had been miraculous.

Mike just wished he could be a bigger part of that positive change, but that guilt had stopped him acting, what other reason was there? Despite Claire's death in twenty-eleven he still wore his wedding ring, he just had an inability to let go, and wasn't it that inability that had set him on the path to the place he was now? Searching for the answer to that unanswerable question. Mike guessed it was that, and maybe too much time had passed now since that first meeting for anything to blossom. They both deserved it, sure, they'd both been through a world of shit to get to the point in life they now found themselves at, but it was a sad case of another time and another place, maybe then things would have been different. No, now all they did was skirt around the attraction, the odd smile here, the odd behind the scenes flirt there, no more. How many times had he imagined what it would be like to just take hold of her when one of those looks were exchanged, kiss her and feel the warmth of her body against his? He didn't know, there had been many, and the guilt followed every time like a faithful dog.

He felt relieved that she'd taken the news about the show's future, or lack of to be exact, surprisingly well, although he hadn't been shocked at her comment about Rick being a cocksucker. Tara had a way with words like that. For a woman as attractive as she was, there was a part of her mouth that did seem to have come from the gutter when provoked, but he even liked that about her. It was an endearing juxtaposition against her otherwise feminine appearance. A little two fingers to the otherwise PC mad world that said she didn't give a shit; she was who she was and if you didn't like it you could jolly well fuck off.

Now he had to break the news to Scotty, then see if he was up for an unpaid case. He wasn't quite sure how he was going to tackle that one. He knew Scotty had pumped a fair bit of his earnings from the show into settling a few debts and starting his own paranormal event company. Kit didn't come cheap and he'd had to start buying a second stock of his own stuff, only it wasn't a case of buying one EMF meter or one set of audio ear amplifiers, he'd needed a few. Paying guests would expect to play with the cool, spooky toys they'd seen on their screens, so just having one was a no go. Mike knew Scotty had acquired, well - more borrowed, a few bits of the team's TV funded kit for his recent Moot Hall investigation, unbeknownst to the production team of course. He just hoped Scotty still had it, as the majority of the equipment owned by the channel was in storage back at Media City. Whatever Scotty had managed to swift aside, they could go whistle for if they wanted it back.

"Scott Hampton," Mike instructed his hands-free Bluetooth system as he pulled to a stop at a red light. A fully loaded aggregate lorry was coughing black diesel fumes out directly in front of him, the smell permeated the Jeep causing him to wrinkle his nose and shut down the aircon for a second. As soon as it was turned off the heat began to rise in the cab, like a fast warming fan oven. The on-screen display thought about his request for a second before connecting the call, it only rang the once before he picked up.

"Mike!" he heard Scotty's excited voice answer from the far south of the country. It filled his Jeep with its enthusiasm as it piped from every speaker. "You're not going to believe this, the channel are going to shit pine cones for not letting us do Moot."

Scotty's excited outpouring took him off guard. He swallowed, despite his mouth feeling dry and said, "What have you got?" then mentally kicked himself for not being more assertive and getting to the real point of his call. The light turned green and the lorry spewed a cloud of black smoke as it laboured to movement. As soon as it cleared, he fired the aircon up, enjoying its coolness as it hit his fast moistening brow.

"An EVP from the organised event I ran last week, and a real fucking peach of one, too. Are you in the car on speaker?"

"Yeah, listen Scott..."

"One sec," Scotty cut in, his words spilling out fast. "I gotta play it to you. I'll hold the phone to the speaker."

In the background Mike could hear Scotty messing around with wires. He heard a click and a clonk, Scotty's iPhone was put down on the table, or that was how it sounded at least, then picked up again.

"You still there?"

"Yeah," Mike replied, hating the stall his bad news was getting, but at the same time more than a little intrigued.

"Good," Scotty said, "I thought I might have cut you off, bud. I'll play you the clip, you hear the team talking then - *No*, fuck it! I don't need to explain it, just listen. If they don't give us Moot for season two off the back of this, I'll eat my hat, Mike, do you hear me? I will eat my fucking hat!"

Mike felt a pang of sadness at the mention of season two, and the fact that after his reveal, Scotty was going to be brought back down to earth with all the grace of a crashing 747. Mike heard the click as Scotty actioned the piece of audio from two hundred odd miles and one stretch of water away.

"This is vigil six of the night and vigil two in A Bunyan Room," he heard Scotty say. Despite being transmitted via a smart phone held against the laptop, it was pretty clear. The fact it was playing through the Jeep's rather expensive audio system helped matters considerably. He wasn't sure though how he was going to check Scotty's audio this way, most EVPs needed a pair of headphones and a held breath to check, then a good few minutes of arguing over what, if anything, had been

said. *"The time is three fifteen am on July tenth, 2018. It's funny, it's not even called The Bunyan Room, it's called A Bunyan Room."*

"Yeah, and did you see the local walks are sponsored by Scholl foot products? Do you think that was intentional?" said another voice. It sounded like Morgan, Scotty's younger brother. Following this little joke a few people laughed. That laughter sounded almost canned, like you used to get on those old eighties' sitcoms like The Goodlife.

"I heeaarrr yoouuu!"

"Holy shit," Mike whispered under his breath as the menacing voice filled the cab, emanating from every speaker and deepened by the Bass tube in the boot. Just as Scotty had he felt a chill run through his body.

"We have an ambient temperature in here of eighteen degrees centigrade and no electromagnetic interference on either the MEL or K2 meters," There was another click as the audio was stopped.

"You hear that shit?" Scotty babbled.

"And you're sure that's genuine?" Mike questioned. He was trying hard to quell his initial reaction, in the world of paranormal research, you often found that if something was too good to be true it pretty much always was.

"Totally, I've amplified that a bit and cut some of the background hiss out. Mike, it came in around sixteen hertz."

"But you have the original un-edited one saved, too?"

"Of course!" Scotty chided, sounding almost offended.

"Where..?"

"In A Bunyan Room," Scotty cut in before Mike could finish asking. "It's a small exhibit room at the far end of the building, ground floor. You gotta take this to the channel, Mike they HAVE to give us Moot after this, they just gotta!"

"There isn't gonna be as season two, Scott." The line

left his lips before he'd even had the chance to think about it.

"You what?"

"I said, there is no season two, we've been shit-canned."

There was a long silence that hung over the Bluetooth, where all Mike could hear was the steady thrum of the large tyres over tarmac. Finally, Scotty said, "Those mother-fuckers, just like that?"

"Well, no. Not exactly. They were willing to film and run it, but they wanted us to," Mike paused for a brief second, "stretch the truth of our findings a little. I know the team is made up of three, but I wasn't willing to even negotiate that one. I hope you're not mad."

"Mad? I'm fucking livid," Scotty almost screamed down the phone. "Not at you, no – bugger that. They want us to be another laughingstock like Meadows and her bunch of phonies – no way. I'd have told them to ram it, too. Does Tig know?"

"She knows," Mike replied solemnly. "Thank God she feels the same way you do. Like I said the team is made up of all of us but ultimately, I have to make the odd executive decision now and again. I made the call; I'm just glad you guys are with me."

"With you, Mike, if it wasn't for you I'd still be clearing bloody cobwebs from town cameras in Cowes in the pissing rain, instead of living my dream." Scotty paused. "What's the plan now? Do you think we can jump to another channel?"

"I don't know. If we've been ditched by a channel as small as SwitchBack I can't see any others taking us. I know Really love the paranormal stuff, but they are all clogged up with the Yank teams."

"Youtube," Scotty said hastily. "We own the name of the show, we have a following, we go online. With enough views and subscribers, we can make a good amount on click advertising."

It wasn't a bad idea, and Mike felt a pang of hope

cut through the otherwise shit situation. Scotty had the editing abilities and prowess to handle such a project. Sure, they'd need to source their own locations, but that was no issue. After a few years in the game, Mike had a host of locations and contacts. They could really strip it back, cut out the micro-managing and do things how they wanted, and after all, he'd never gotten into this for the money. It was nice to get paid for such work but that hadn't been the idea when he'd put that post up a few years ago.

"It's that lucrative?" Mike asked, not wanting to sound too hopeful but at the same time thinking of how much the faked Sleaford haunting had netted in revenue thanks to the monetised videos of their supposed poltergeist.

"It can be," Scotty said enthusiastically. "I get about ten pounds per ten thousand views on my videos. Okay, so at the moment I have only had just over that many views on my few investigations, but using the Unexplained UK name - Mike, some of the shit on YouTube has ten million views, do you know how that equates?"

Mike ran the sum in his head as fast as he could, which was pretty quickly, he'd always had a flair for numbers. After just a few seconds he said, "Around ten-grand per ten million."

"Right on, now if you had that many views on a number of clips, you're talking...."

"Not a bad return, and certainly enough to keep us in a bit of pocket money."

"Exactly, it's not ideal, no. But it's better than going back to scratching in the dirt."

"I think we need to have a meeting and discuss it," Mike said as he navigated the on-slip to the motorway. He gunned the accelerator and managed to join in front of an eighteen-wheeler that had been powering down the inside lane.

"Okay, I can do the editing and handle the uploads,

you source the locations and get Tara back on research."

"Talking of locations," Mike cut in. "I took a rather interesting call just after leaving Media City."

"Go on," said Scotty sounding intrigued.

"A lady by the name of Sue Reed is asking us to investigate her holiday home."

"She rooted us out for it?"

"Yes, specifically asked we bring no TV crew. I didn't tell her there was more chance of the Titanic reaching New York, obviously. Anyway, from what I can see, and I only took a very quick look, it's a converted chapel, in a village called Trellen in Cornwall."

"Ohhh, no TV crew?" Scotty said rhetorically. "The TV crew is what most people want, I guess she must be pretty genuine, it sounds interesting." Scotty was right on the money with that little observation. Mike had been contacted via the channel a few times by private homeowners, and one of the first things they asked was always would it be filmed for TV?

"I am heading to hers now, they live in Pewsey...."

"Crop circle country," Scotty cut in. Mike wasn't surprised he'd made the connection that quickly. Ghosts weren't the only thing that got Scotty's juices flowing, so to speak. He was a sucker for anything from aliens to conspiracy theories.

Mike set the cruise control at a tad over seventy, fast enough to make a bit of progress but slow enough not to excite the plod if he happened to go by a motorway patrol. "Yeah, crop circle country," he agreed. "Anyway, I am heading there now. I'm just outside Manchester so should I be there in about four to five hours, traffic depending."

"Do you want me to join you? I'd have to book the Red Funnel but I'm sure I can get an afternoon crossing?"

"It's okay. Tara is heading up from her place. She is a lot closer than you are, she's not far from the Wiltshire border. When I know more, I will give you a shout. If I take the case then I'll need you in Cornwall at some point for a tech setup assessment. I'll firm up the dates once I know if it's within our remit. How are you fixed for work?"

"We just got axed, Mike," he laughed. "I'm about as free as a bird. I have a few events coming up but nothing for two weeks." Scotty trailed off and Mike could hear the resignation in his voice that nothing for two weeks also meant no steady income for two weeks. "I'll finish up on this EVP and work on a few channel designs for you, how's that sound?" Scotty sounded disappointed at not being invited. It wasn't that Mike didn't want him there, it was more down to the fact it would be a wasted journey and a needless expense.

"Like a plan," Mike replied positively. "I'll speak to you after the meeting, tomorrow morning at the latest."

"Sure, drive safe." The line cleared and the radio came back on to Duran Duran who were singing about The Reflex.

Cruising in the middle lane Mike let his mind wander to just what might be happening at that idyllic-looking old chapel he'd seen briefly on the screen of his smartphone, and for the first time in a long time, he felt a slight pang of excitement about a venue. This wasn't some used up, media paraded, supposedly haunted location that had seen every ghost documentary and half-baked team through its doors. This was new, unknown and a totally blank canvas. Mike usually enjoyed the solitude of long-haul driving, but he found himself wishing both the time and the miles away, so he could find out just why Sue Reed had called him? Why she'd sounded so anxious? And why she'd been so set on keeping this low-key and private?

CHAPTER 11

Tig's car was already parked on the road outside of the Reed residence as Mike drove onto Wilcot Road, the back caught in the shadow of some large and well-maintained privet hedges, the front of the car bathed in the strong afternoon sun and caught in a contiguity of light and shade.

Tara was out of the car, her bum planted on the lower part of the bonnet and her arms to her sides. Her slender fingers with their perfectly manicured nails, orange this week, tapped a rhythm on the headlight glass. Her legs were stretched out, straight and locked at the knee with her attractive, and mildly summer tanned face turned toward the sun which still sat reasonably high in the sky. It would still be a few hours before it began to slip toward the horizon offering a little respite from the heat. Large Gucci shades hid her eyes and her ash blonde hair, bleached a shade lighter than normal from the sun, flowed down her back in a silky wave. There was a time when Mike knew that removing those sunglasses would have revealed another fresh, or freshened up bruise, but those days were thankfully long gone.

The sight of Tara sunning herself, and the way her body looked in her dark shorts and well-fitted red T-shirt that displayed the Hollister logo in white across her breasts, stirred the usual lust in him that he always felt when he first saw her after they'd been apart a while. That initial lust gradually ebbed away to be replaced by a steady and consistent longing, followed by the guilt, always the guilt.

He drove past her and tooted the horn lightly, snapping her from whatever daydream she'd been caught in. Tara, seemingly not at all startled, offered him an encouraging wave, and by the time he'd pulled his Jeep to a stop under the cover of the neighbouring property's pine trees, she'd reached the passenger door and was trying the handle impatiently. The door was still auto-locked, so Mike shut the engine down and removed the key allowing her to climb up into the cab. She swept an empty pack of prawn salad sandwiches, purchased at Keele Services earlier in the trip, and a drained can of Coke into the footwell before she planted her bum on the cream leather seat.

"You look like shit," she said, sounding half serious as her eyes looked him up and down.

Mike cocked his head and looked in the rear-view, he'd not shaven the night before in preparation for an early start and dark stubble now defined his jawline. His shirt, now pulled open down as far as the third button and no longer donning his tie, (that had been cast to the depths of the Jeep's rear seats), looked as if he'd slept in it. Even his hair looked a mess, out of place and, well – stressed, was the only way he could put it. Tara was right, he did look like shit, he forced a smile and said, "Nice to see you, too."

"Guess it's been a helluva day?" she half asked, and half stated with a smile. Her Skechers stirred the rubbish of the day around the footwell, the empty can she'd just added to the various wrappers and junk made a low crinkling sound as her left foot ran over it.

"Well if you define a *helluva* day as a five thirty start, followed by a drive from Arundel to Manchester, getting the show shit canned, having to break it to you guys, then driving from Manchester to the arse end of Wiltshire for..." he paused. "For, well at the moment I don't really know, likely some rich lady who has it in her head that her old church is haunted, then yes! I have had a *helluva* day, as you put it." Mike offered up a wan smile and noticed the inside of his Jeep, that had begun to smell pretty bad, a mix of half-eaten food and man-sweat, now smelt fruity and feminine. It was Tara's shampoo; the smell was welcome compared to his fousty smell. He arched his back in the seat and stretched out a travelling pain. A bone, somewhere deep in his back cracked and he felt relief wash over his aching body. Running a hand through and tidying his dark hair, he said, "Tell me what you know then?"

"You've been intrigued since you took that call, haven't you?" Then before Mike could answer Tara added. "I know you have; I know you too well. I bet it was all you could do not to pull over and get researching the place yourself at the first service station."

Mike smiled, she had him pegged alright. When he'd picked up the bland and over-priced prawn sand-wich at Keele his phone had come out, but he'd stopped himself knowing Tara would be armed with as much in-formation as the time she'd had would allow her to glean. "Look, you're right," he conceded with a smile. But I've also been in this car for almost the whole day. The seat, as comfortable as it is, almost feels like a part of me, so I'd like to get inside as soon as possible, hope-fully get a brew in as well. Service station tea always tastes like gnat's piss." Tara nodded and a knowing smile spreading across her face, it sparkled in her eyes, the way it had the very first time they'd met.

Despite the fact he'd parked in the full shade of the pines the air temperature in the Jeep had been steadily creeping up since he'd stopped. Mike cranked the igni-tion, the engine fired eagerly to life and cool, condi-tioned air began to flow from the vent.

"I've spent the last few hours kicking the case research to life," Tara began, her voice enthusiastic. Mike had been surprised at the sanguine way both her and Scotty had taken the news that the show had been cancelled and thought she'd want to talk about that first. He'd been wrong. She was focused solely on the task in hand. "And all I'm left with are more questions, questions I hope Sue Reed can answer."

"Go on," Mike encouraged, shifting his weight in the seat a little.

"Well, the place is supposed to have been a church once,"

"A chapel, but yes – close enough."

"Well there is no record of it ever having been registered as one, I mean none. I looked on parish register, a website where most places of Christian worship are registered, those not bonafide Church of England and.."

"Not a trace of it?"

"Not a single mention. I checked the Church of England site thinking it would be on there, but it's not." Tara paused as if to let the information sink in, she then sighed and continued, "So I did a little research into what is expected of churches and chapels, I mean there *has* to be some kind of regulation, right?"

"I'd have thought so, I've never been in the God squad," Mike smiled. "But in this day and age, I'm certain there must be some form of regulation."

"Right," Tara agreed, sounding enthused. "Churches with an income of over five thousand pounds are encouraged to register as charities, tax benefits and all. No such church charity for Trellen does, nor ever has existed! I then looked into a very interesting piece of legislation," (said with heavy sarcasm), "called The Places of Worship Registration Act of 1885. It basically states that any non-Church of England establishment, even if used as a Sunday School needs to be registered. It's more in-depth than that but I won't bore you. Now the holiday home website states that it was built in the seventeenth century, so it does pre-date the act, but it was also supposedly a place of worship when the act came to pass so it *should* have been registered."

"Is there a chance you missed it?" Mike asked. He looked out of the bug-splattered windscreen as two girls, both no older than ten, went skating past on roller boots, holding onto each other for support.

Tara fired him a look that said, *really, what do you think I am, a fucking amateur?*

"Okay, sorry," he added quickly, without her needing to say anything.

"Unregistered churches are common in China as Christianity is not the main religion there," Tara continued. "But here in jolly old England, or the UK for that matter, no – they are not common."

"It must have been an unofficial chapel then?" Mike asked.

"Yeah, it has to be, but why? Why would you not register it? This is rural Cornwall, breakaway factions of religion are commonplace in deepest darkest America but not here, it just doesn't add up," Tara paused again as if wondering where to go next with her reveal. Her eyes found the two skater girls who were now at the end of the road and clumsily turning around. Finally, she said, "I Google searched Trellen Chapel, Trellen Church and looked on the images tab and all I found were the pictures taken by the Reeds that are already on that rent a holiday home site. It looks like they renovated it from a fire damaged wreck. You need to see the pictures; the place was a write-off. So, having seen the post and pre-renovation photos I searched the web for news stories, I mean a church – chapel," she corrected herself, "burns down it would make the news somewhere, local Echo that kinda thing."

"Right," Mike said.

"Wrong," Tig fired back instantly, "I could only find one reference to a fire in Trellen from two thousand and eight, and that was archive records in the Plymouth Herald. It stated that a local Trellen man by the name of John Deviss is suspected dead after a fire at his home in the small village of Trellen, Cornwall. At first, they suspected it to be arson, but as it turns out it was eventually recorded as accidental. It gutted the building and no trace of Mr. Deviss' body was found. Due to the remoteness of the village, the fire wasn't seen, and no alarm raised. It didn't go into much detail, but I guess locals found it the next day. By then it was way too late."

"So, the place was never a chapel," Mike said, thinking he knew the answer. "The family who owned it, the Deviss family, right?"

"Yep."

"Thought they'd make extra money as old chapels and churches command a premium for anyone wanting to do a renovation, and they marketed the shell as such. I know it's big business, many have been converted over the last decade."

"At least eighteen thousand," Tara added. Mike was impressed, she had done her research. "And from what I can see on the various property sites there are two recorded sales of The Old Chapel since the fire, the first was at auction from the local authority. A family named, Bough bought it but obviously never done the renovations."

"It's a con, a scam then," Mike cut in, still keen to air his view. "The Reed family just bought a wreck of a building with no or faked provenance. Maybe the first family to own it decided to market it as a chapel?" He paused, thought Tara was about to chip in but when she didn't he continued, "Or the Reeds are pulling the con and have dressed up an old burnt out wreck to look like a chapel in order to add a quirky twist on their holiday home."

"If that's the case then it's the first owners who pulled the con and not Mr. and Mrs. Reed. You see the place was already called The Old Chapel when they bought it from Winn's, a local estate agency in

Liskeard," Tara took her eyes from the road outside and looked at Mike. "It's a good angle, Mike and one I'd not thought of. I have been too busy trying to prove the place was once a religious building and never considered that someone might have just made that up to add a few extra spondoonies to the price tag. Although I'm not so sure you're right, here - let me show you what I mean."

She pulled out her phone and fired the screen to life, then quickly loaded a website, before holding it out for him to see. The image on the screen was The Old Chapel as a burnt-out shell, likely taken just after the Reeds had bought it. The grounds were overgrown, and a rusty pair of metal doors sealed the front shut. The bell tower, a part of the building that Mike had noticed when he'd briefly seen the place after he'd Googled the phone number back in Manchester, and now thought was likely added during renovations, was there, at the far end of the building. Not a big deal, if the Reeds hadn't added it the first owners might have done, he found it hard to believe they'd done nothing at all with the place.

"It looks like a chapel," Tara said. "Even as a burnt-out shell the shape, size and general style of it just fits. And look here," she spread her fingers across the screen, zooming the image in so the out of control undergrowth was more detailed. The image became a little pixelated, but it was clear enough. "See that?"

Mike looked as she swept the screen to the building. He immediately saw where she was going, there was little doubt that at some point in time the windows had held stained glass. In this picture though, they held metal shutters that had been cut to size and shape yet still looked razor sharp on the edges, as if intentionally left that way to ward off anyone wanting to take hold and pry them free of the frame to which they were affixed.

"Okay, so it was a chapel, or at least it looked like

one," he conceded, still not totally happy that the evidence Tara was presenting achieved the beyond all reasonable doubt mark that he'd been so used to working to while on the force. "I'm guessing, as I said, that the Reeds will shed a little light on things. Did you check the name of the guy that died in the fire, Deviss?

"You bet, and.."

"Nothing?"

"Nothing, save for the obituary after the fire. There was no mention that he was clergy whatsoever," she shrugged her shoulders. "But that name, Deviss, I know it. I don't know where from Mike, but I do, it's been bothering me since I read it."

"It sounds kinda familiar," he said slowly, but he wasn't sure if his memory was now being led by the fact that Tara thought she knew it. Would it look familiar if he'd read it unprompted? He wasn't so sure.

"I've looked online but no dice, all I keep drawing is blank after blank. I can do genealogy on the family but that takes time, time I didn't have today, and I'd need more information to be sure. With what I have here I'd just be pissing in the wind."

"You've done well," Mike said, offering her an encouraging smile. "And it's never advisable to piss in the wind, and kinda hard for a woman unless you've got one of those SheWees."

Tara shook her head, rolled her eyes and said in a frustrated voice, "I hate being beaten by shit like this. I did warn you that all I had were more questions."

"And finally, before we head in, what does Trip Advisor say about the place? Any mention of spooky goings on in the reviews?" the sentence made him smile but he was being serious.

"It's been open for review since April, so three months. There are three reviews on there but all they say is what a good job has been done on the renovations and how comfortable the place is."

Mike wasn't surprised, that kind of thing was not

what most would mention in a public review, but it'd been worth a shot. By now he was literally dying to get out of his Jeep and have a leg stretch. He reached for his door handle and said, "Let's see if the Reeds can shed some light on things, and I hope to God she has the kettle on."

———

THE REED PROPERTY was set in modest grounds. One of the couple, or quite possibly both, had a meticulous eye for the garden, something he'd noticed in the picture of the building they were here to discuss, too. The front lawn, perfectly levelled and cut short enough to putt on, led through to the back on both sides, leaving the house itself sat like a red brick island on a carpet of uniform green. Two willow trees sprung up either side of the wide block-paved brindle drive, their signature drooping branches, now in full summer bloom hung in a magnificent canopy, trailing down far enough to tickle the grass. As they reached the front door, that was actually on the side of the building, Mike noticed a large timber-framed playhouse raised on six-foot stilts with a slide protruding from one end. He guessed it was a bespoke design and likely built by Mr. Reed himself for when the grandkids came to stay. The sight sent a pang of pain through him as he instantly thought how his daughter would never get to enjoy such a wonderful piece of play equipment, how he'd never get to hear her shrieks of joy as she careered down a slide, or begged to be pushed higher on a swing. Her life taken, robbed, before she could even walk her first step.

"Obviously not short of a few bob," Tara said in a hushed voice as she looked at the house. "How many bedrooms do you think this place has, four, five?"

"It's gotta be five," Mike replied pushing the painful thoughts aside. He was about to add that anyone with enough money to buy and rebuild a place like The Old

Chapel had to be affluent when the front door opened to reveal a nervously smiling lady who Mike guessed to be Sue Reed.

Mike had guessed Sue's age at around seventy from her voice during the call and he'd been about right by the look of it. Her hair, mainly grey, but not yet all the way gone from what once would have been raven black, was pulled back in a neat bun. Her eyes seemed to dart back and forth, from Tara to him and back. She reminded him a bit of his gran, the one on his mother's side, long since dead but she'd been his favourite and visits to hers had always been filled with treats and more sweets than his mother would ever allow. Sue had that same homely look to her, donned in a casual yet smart lemon-yellow summer dress that had likely once graced a clothing rail in John Lewis or Marks and Sparks.

"You could have used the drive," she said as they closed the small distance, the smile not leaving her lips.

"Thanks, but we brought two cars." The drive was big enough for six and Mike realised he must have sounded a bit foolish. "Anyway, we are fine on the road," he added hastily. "Mrs. Reed, I take it?" They reached the door, where she took Mike's hand and gave it an enthusiastic shake. Despite the warmth of the day Sue Reed's hand felt cold, the cold of someone with worry and stress on their mind.

"Call me Sue, please. My husband Tom is waiting for you inside," she turned to Tara. "You must be the one they call, Tig? I've seen you on the show, you're much prettier in real life."

"Tara is actually my name," Mike noticed her blush a little at the compliment, "but either is fine." Sue took her hand and another enthusiastic shake followed before they were ushered inside.

THE INSIDE OF THE REEDS' impressive home reflected the meticulously cared for garden. Mike hadn't been given the grand tour, but the walk from the reception hall through to the spacious open-plan kitchen-diner showed spotlessly clean hardwood flooring and real wood sideboards and cabinets that offered not a trace of dust. Mike wondered if Sue handled the place on her own. She probably had a cleaner, maybe two, helping to keep the house in its spick-and-span order.

Tom Reed was likely a few years older than his wife, but he had been blessed with a youthful look that if someone were to guess his age it would no doubt see them a decade out. He sat at a large oak dining table dressed in a white and blue checked shirt with faded jeans. His dark, greying hair was as neatly trimmed as the beard it flowed into. A copy of the Times daily su-doku puzzle decorated the table in front of him and the blue and silver Parker ballpoint pen in his hand rested thoughtfully on his lower lip. To the side of the paper lay a large manila file folder, not unlike the kind Mike had used himself to hold case papers in, back when he'd carried a badge.

Tom Reed looked up from his puzzle, saw Mike and Tara with his wife, smiled broadly and stood up, pushing his chair back. The feet scraped across the tiled floor, a sound that had the same effect on Mike as that of nails down a blackboard.

"Mike Cross, I assume," he said, offering a hand for another round of handshaking. Mike accepted and was met by a very firm and rough feeling grip. There was no doubt in his mind that a man with hands as rough as this had spent a life on the tools working outside. Not that he'd have pegged Tom for a common labourer, more likely the owner of a small building or development firm, one that he'd been hands-on with himself. Also meaning he had the know-how and contacts to have done the renovations himself.

"Guilty," Mike replied. "And this is my colleague, Tara Gibb."

"Pleased to meet you both," Tom said, releasing Mike's hand and switching to Tara's, which he seemed to take a little more lightly.

Much to Mike's relief the offer of a drink followed, and Sue busied herself at the far end of the cavernous yet spotlessly clean kitchen. The sound of clinking crockery emanated back as she worked, and soon she was returning to the table with a large Denby pot filled with tea. The pot was balanced a little precariously on a tray with six matching mugs and a jug of milk. To go with the refreshments, she'd prepared a plate of biscuits that she had to rush back to the kitchen to collect.

"Not really the weather for tea," Sue said, sounding apprehensive. "But my old mum always used to claim it cooled you down."

"Your old mum, gawd rest her soul, used to make a point of going to bingo if she found a money spider on her," Tom laughed, but it was a nervous one, the kind of laugh a person does when they are trying to make light of a situation that they're not sure about.

Mike took a tentative sip of his drink and sighed inwardly with relief. There was a slightly awkward silence as he waited for one of them to speak, when no one did he finally said, "I know this might be hard for you both. Reasonable people, which the pair of you seem, naturally find it a bit awkward to talk about," he paused. "The unexplained," he finally finished a little sheepishly. "But I want to assure you that just because you can't explain it, does not mean it can't be explained."

Tom chuckled slightly, the way someone might say, *yeah, right*, to a statement they thought was total horseshit. Mike looked to Sue who had her lips pursed tightly together, they formed a thin singular line across her small mouth. Sue Reed glanced nervously at her husband who gave her a look that Mike read as, *go on, you've got this one.*

"It is hard," Sue finally said. "I had it all planned out in my head; I've been running through how to tell it since I called you this morning. By the way, thank you for coming to see us at short notice."

"It's fine, really," Mike reassured. He glanced at Tara who nodded her head in agreement.

"No one is going to think either of you are crazy," Tara added in. "We have been to some of the most notoriously haunted places in the UK, heard some stories that are pretty out there, but so far we have not found anything that we couldn't explain."

"You've not stayed at The Old Chapel yet," Tom said his voice flat and devoid of any emotion. He looked up from his cup as he spoke and raised his greying brow. The statement took Mike by surprise and further sparked the seed of intrigue that had germinated inside him. He knew a similar one was growing within Tara, too.

"Just what have you seen there?" Tara asked, leaning in. She'd taken a small A5 size leather-bound notepad from her canvass Roxy bag. It was now open, and a disposable Bic pen was poised in her hand. As well as the pad she'd set her digital voice recorder in front of her. The device was on and a little red light glowed reassuringly by the speaker to let you know the mic was live.

"We bought the property back in late twenty sixteen," Tom began, obviously deciding he was going to tell the tale after all. "I had reservations about taking on such a monumental task. I'd just passed the firm over to my partner," he looked to Mike and added, "We had a construction company, Reed and Blake Developments." Mike had already guessed as much but he did like affirmation of his deductions. "It was more than a retirement project; it was an investment for our future. I've done quite nicely out of the building industry. Sure, there were some tough years during the recession; but in all, I have been lucky. However, The Old Chapel Project was still a bit of a risk."

"From what I've seen you've done an amazing job," Mike added.

"It had to be done right," Tom replied. Mike guessed it was this attention to detail and fastidiousness that had made him a successful developer. "And it took longer than I'd have liked, but that's the joys of being old, and working around the good ole British weather." Tom Reed took a gulp of his tea, ran the back of his hand over his lips and continued, "For the most part the renovations went without a hitch. We had more accidents on site than I would class as normal, but no fatalities, thank gawd." His country accent wasn't strong, but the odd word caught it every time.

"What kind of accidents?" Tara asked.

"We had three ladder tips, at times when they were secured in line with health and safety and should never have moved. I'm a stickler for that kind of thing, you see. One of those tips happened when I was working on the new windows, got myself three cracked ribs for my trouble. I say tips, but all I can say is when mine went it felt as if someone had given a good hard shove, but none of the boys were anywhere near. Tools went missing regularly, not permanently, mind. You'd put a drill or screwdriver down, or at times a tin of paint, then when you went to use it the darn thing had gone. You'd search high and low for the blasted missing item, often to find it right where you thought you'd left it. A few items turned up in obscure places, we thought we were going mad."

Mike nodded his head, the things Tom had said were odd, but far from definitive proof of paranormal goings-on. "Are you sure it's not just a case of misplaced tools and a few unsteady ladders?" he asked.

"Back then, yes – I didn't think too much of it if truth be told, but the things that have happened since have made we wonder, made me doubt – well doubt everything I thought I knew."

"Did any of your workmen see anything they

couldn't explain?" Tara asked. Mike glanced at her notepad and saw the words, *CAN PHYSICALLY MOVE OBJECTS?* had been written in block capitals and circled two or three times.

"Not as such, no. One of the young labourers, a nice lad called Theo, didn't like the place. He said it gave him bad feelings, said that every night after working there he had this dream of being chased through the woods. By what he never knew, but he said that it felt bad. He left the site halfway through the build, it bothered him that much. Plus, the boys kept ribbin' him over it, you know how lads can be."

"So, he never came back?" Mike asked.

Tom Reed looked away briefly giving Mike the feeling he wasn't sure if he should say what he wanted to say. Finally, he looked back up and said flatly, "Theo hung himself a week after he left the build. His mum came home and found him hanging out the loft hatch by a length of electrical wire."

Tara had been taking a sip of her tea as Tom dealt that revelation and she almost choked on it. "Did he have a history of mental health issues?" she managed to ask, placing the cup down.

"No," Tom said flatly. "There have been others."

"Other what?" Mike asked.

"Deaths, and I don't mean accidents, odd deaths that don't add up."

"I think you need to expand on that?" Mike said, feeling chilled despite it being oppressively warm.

"I will, we've not reached that part of the story yet," Tom replied as if stalling for time.

"What about your guests? Have any of them reported oddities? I checked Trip Advisor and so far, your reviews are good." Tara asked, getting him off the subject.

Tom shifted uncomfortably in his seat, then swilled the last of his tea around the bottom of the mug. He looked to his wife who answered.

"We have issued a lot of refunds, Tara."

"Really?" Mike said, genuine surprise in his voice.

"Not full refunds," Sue added hastily. "Partial ones, with a little extra for the hassle. You see, the place has been open since the end of April this year and so far not a single booking has stayed their entire allotted time. Well, one has, but they only rented for a weekend. I called them after the stay to see if everything had been okay, they said it was, but I could tell from the lady's voice there was something wrong, something she was not comfortable discussing."

"Just what do they think they've seen?" Mike asked. His heart had picked up its pace, his interest was now about as gripped as it could be, but what Sue told him next pushed it even further.

"Not just seen," Sue said. "But heard and felt."

Tara leaned in and pushed the recorder a few inches closer to Sue, aware that the golden nuggets of information were about to come.

"Every guest who has talked to me mentions the crying, that's the most common thing by far."

"What kind of crying?" Mike asked, his brain already working on a reasonable answer. "The place is in the countryside, surrounded by woods from what I've seen. Could be foxes?"

Sue shook her head, "It's an infant, Mr. Cross, more than one." She fixed him with her youthful looking eyes that were only betrayed by the aging face they occupied. Mike could see genuine worry behind them, worry that had transferred to the coldness of her touch in that first handshake. "Tom and I have stayed there, to try and quantify what we'd been told."

"And you've heard these cries?"

"Yes," Tom answered for her. "Usually around three or four AM, some nights much earlier and always sounding as if it's in another part of the building, but as you move toward the sound it seems to move with you. Just as you think you're in the right part of the chapel the crying is at the other end." Tom shook his head as if he were having trouble believing what his own lips were saying. "It's the damnedest thing I've ever heard. Now I'm a country man Mike, that gawd awful sound is no animal, and certainly ain't no fox. I don't know where it's coming from, but it scared the shit out of me, and that's not something I admit to lightly. I won't stay in the place now, neither of us will. Plus, we are scared of what it might do to us, to our heads."

Mike was about to ask that he elaborate for a second time when Sue cut in.

"They sound in pain," she added, Mike could see water welling in her eyes. "Those children, they can't be more than babies, it's as if someone is hurting them!" A tear escaped her eye and ran down her right cheek, she caught it with a shaky finger. "I'm sorry," she said softly. "Whatever could have happened there for them to cry like that?"

"It's fine, really," Mike reassured, as a shiver ran through his body. Someone had just walked over his grave, or maybe he was just the tiniest bit freaked out by the Reeds' story, not that he'd ever admit it. "How long does it normally last?"

"A few minutes sometimes, and others on and off for a half hour, maybe more." Tom scooted his chair closer to his wife and put an arm around her shoulders.

"Have you ever recorded it, the crying?" asked Tara.

"Never thought to," Sue answered, leaning gratefully against her husband's arm. "People have seen things, too," she said, her voice dropping as if there were un-wanted ears close by, ears that might hear her words and think her foolish. "Doors slamming when there has been no breeze or window open. I have had two reports of objects being physically moved in the master bed-room. We named it the Altar room as it was at the front of the building and where the altar would have been.

Mike shifted on the not so comfortable oak chair and asked, "What kinda things exactly?"

"First was a towel rail," Tom answered. "The kind that fits over the top of the radiator. We put them in all the bedrooms, to stop folk leaving damp towels directly on the rads. The guest, a lady doctor and her partner said it just sprang clean in the air, like someone, or something, had hit it from its underneath."

"Could heat transference have caused the metal to react that way?" Mike questioned, thinking it was a fair push and unlikely. It was still more reasonable in his mind than a spirit being responsible, though.

"I can only take the lady doctor's word for it, but she reckoned it leapt a good four feet clear of the radiator. Now I don't think heat transference could have done that, do you, Mike?"

"Maybe not," Mike admitted. It was still an experiment that could easily be re-run and he was glad to see Tara making a note. RADIATOR HANGER – ALTAR ROOM this one read; it was ceremoniously circled to match the other bullet points.

"The week after they called me, that lady doctor's husband ran a length of hose from the exhaust of his car through the window and killed himself." Mike looked at them sullenly. "One suicide I could believe as just undiagnosed mental health issues," he said. "But two, and that's not all, but we will come to the worst of it in a minute."

"It gets worse?" Mike asked in disbelief.

"Yeah," Tom said sadly. He sighed and then continued. "Guests have had personal items moved, watches, phones, jewellery. One lady said she woke in the night to see the bedside easy chair being pulled to the side of the bed, then it just stopped there facing her, and she had the overwhelming feeling that someone was in it, sat by the bed like you might sit with someone you visit in hospital." Tom looked at him earnestly. "She checked out the next day, complimented us on the place but said she didn't feel comfortable staying another day in a place where the furniture moved of its own accord. She said furniture had no business doing that."

"And physical sightings?" Tara asked, looking up from her notes. "You said people have seen things?"

"Once," Tom replied, his voice quiet. "A couple of weeks before the school holidays, a family let it out with a young daughter and a baby. The first family to stay there since opening. Before that, it had been small groups and affluent professional couples. The Rogers family, daughter was four if I recall. They booked a week but stayed two nights. The parents heard the crying on the first night, but it was the daughter's experience that caused them to leave. Like you, Mike, they tried to rationalise the crying thinking it was foxes, I think they knew it weren't but sometimes you just convince yourself."

"Right," Mike replied, still not convinced it wasn't foxes but willing to keep an open mind.

"Well the next day the mum, Janet, I think her name was, is walking past her daughter's room and she can hear her talking to someone, you know little kids play tea parties and that, gawd knows my granddaughters love to. Well, she was about to walk on by when she heard a male voice reply to her daughter, deep low and all menacing sounding."

The shiver ran down Mike's back again and he felt his hackles rise.

"Janet - Mrs. Rodgers - said she went straight into the room to find her daughter sat on the floor holding her favourite teddy bear. When she asked who she was talking to the little girl tells her the dark man, and that he'd been in her room that night watching her. She asked her mummy to tell the dark man not to come back, 'cos she was scared of him."

"Holy shit," Tara exclaimed, then added, "Sorry."

"It's okay," Tom assured her, "Holy shit is just what I thought. They stayed that night while making hotel arrangements, Mrs. Rogers said they all slept in the same bed. Nothing happened that night or nothing they saw, then they left the next morning for a bed and breakfast in Charlestown." Tom fixed Mike with eyes that were close to tearing up, he swallowed, and Mike heard the click of his throat which he cleared and said in a choked voice, "The next week that lady drowned her baby in the bathtub back at their house in York then took an overdose."

Mike propped his elbows up onto the table, in a way his mother would have once scaled him for, he ran his left hand over the stubble on his chin and took in the information. Three suicides, and one infant murder. It could be just once horrible coincidence, but he doubted it, and if he doubted it what did that mean? Did he believe that the building was somehow responsible, that it had in some way left a rotten worm inside those people's heads? The very notion went against everything he believed, and it made his own mind spin. "Who is staying there now?" he finally asked.

"A family again, the Harrisons from Reading," Sue answered. "Husband and wife, two kids. I think, from memory, the daughter is older, late teens, maybe even early twenties, the boy is younger though, like five or six."

"Have you heard from them yet?"

"No, they arrived yesterday, this is their first full day."

"And who greets them on arrival?" Mike asked, his investigative brain already looking for any possible witnesses, people he could speak to. If the Reeds had a contact in the area, someone going into the place on a regular basis he wanted to talk to them.

"A local lady called Lucinda Horner, she lives in the village," Tom said.

"And has she reported anything?

"Never," he cut back in. "Lucinda has the only other key, she is the closest thing we have to a neighbour down there, even though her place is a quarter mile away. She goes in and cleans for us and lets new guests in. She has never reported anything untoward, and I haven't told her what people have said they've seen or experienced. Nor does she know about the deaths. It's a long way to Cornwall and neither the wife nor I want to have to make that drive after every client. I'm dreading the day she sees something and throws in the towel on us."

"Has she lived in the village for long?" Tara asked.

"All her life from the little she has told us. Said she knew the Minister who ran the local community church, he lived in it too by all accounts."

"John Deviss?" Tara cut in.

"Yes, that's right. My word you have done your research," Tom noted, raising his eyebrows.

"I also know the building was never officially a place of worship, something I was hoping you could shed some light on for me."

"We knew that when we bought it, the young estate agent who sold it to us, gawd rest his soul," Tom said looking skyward, "said that the fact they couldn't prove provenance reflected the price, and it did. Although what we saved there was lumped back on as the place had planning and a new roof, fitted by the first owner."

"The estate agent is dead?" Tara asked.

"Yes, poor lad, he was only a young'un, too," Tom said, his voice remorseful. "Got himself in a head-on collision on the road that runs through Trellen, where the place is, the same day he sold it us. From what they told us, and it ain't much, he went back out to put a sold sign on, then crashed the company Beemer driving back. Probably going too fast, young fellas in fancy cars think they're invincible. Or that's what I thought at the time, now I am not so sure."

"And the first owner, do you have his details?"

"I can find you the family details, the guy himself died working on the roof," Tom paused and looked nervously from Mike to Tara, before he finally said, "His ladder fell and he split his head open."

"Fuck!" exclaimed Tara, holding her hand to her mouth. Mike winced inwardly but her foul language had either been missed or accepted by the Reeds. To be fair *fuck* was exactly what Mike was thinking.

There was a second-long pause, one that felt much longer, before Tara finally said, "So this Lucinda, have you asked her about the building? I assume that if she has lived in the village her whole life, she must have some recollection of it being a chapel?"

"Oh, sure she does," Sue said, seemingly happy to be off the subject of death. "She said she rarely saw the late Mr. Deviss, though. Save for a few times a month when he rode his bike to the next village to get some supplies. She said she'd pass him occasionally on her way home and was always terrified that he'd get knocked off his bike on those narrow roads."

Mike nodded and continued to rub his hand over his chin, feeling the fresh stubble that had formed there during the day.

"What are you thinking, Mike?" Sue asked. She was now clutching her husband's hand, their fingers were interlocked and resting on the partially finished sudoku puzzle.

"I'm wondering when we can have the place?" he said.

"You'll take the case?" she gasped, sounding relieved.

"Yes," he nodded his head thoughtfully as he spoke. "Although – you need to know that if this is a genuine haunting, and remember I, we – are yet to find such a thing, I can't fix it for you. There are those out there who claim to have the ability to do house clearances, cleansings and such things but I can't personally recommend anyone on account that I have a strong suspicion that many, if not all, are charlatans. As for the deaths and suicides, well that's not something I've ever come across before, but it seems totally implausible to me that a building can make a person do such things. I mean you two have stayed there, have you ever felt suicidal or different after being there?"

"No," Sue said quickly. "Never."

"If I'd have heard myself say this a coupla years back I'd have thought myself mad," Tom said. "But I don't think that whatever is there gets to everyone. Maybe it's a certain kinda person. You know – a person who might seem okay but has something in their head waiting to go off, like a switch. I dunno."

They all sat in silence for a few seconds while the only thing filling that void was the rhythmic *tick-tick-tick* of a clock from the hall. Finally, Sue said, "If you find rational explanations for the things we have told you I will be the happiest woman on Earth,"

"And if you confirm a haunting?" Tom added.

"Then it will be a first," Mike told him flatly. "And if we do then I guess I might have to think outside the box and use a few contacts to see if I can find someone genuine to try and clear the place, but I am *highly* sceptical about such practices."

"I appreciate your honesty," Tom said. "The Harrison family have the place for five nights, they've stayed one, as we said. If they stay the entire booking they will be leaving on Monday night. The place is yours from Tuesday. I have left a two-week gap purposely to try and get this matter resolved."

"Two weeks?" Tara asked sounding amazed. "You're letting us have it for two weeks?"

"You can come and go as you please for that time. You'll collect the keys from Lucinda after the Harrison's leave. Please don't let on to her what you're doing in there. And now we come to the topic of price. How much will you charge for your services?"

"Not a word," Mike said earnestly. "As for the cost, I believe I explained to your wife that our services are free. No team should ever charge for their services. It's kind of an unwritten rule. I would ask that expenses are covered, though."

"You will do it for free?" Tom asked looking shocked. Sue had obviously not mentioned it to him after their call earlier that day. Mike nodded and looked to Tara who did the same. "Well, I can't even begin to say how much we appreciate it. Keep any fuel receipts you incur, food as well. I'd ask you call me when your expenditure gets near to a thousand pounds. We may look financially comfortable, but all my money is tied up in this place and The Old Chapel. I would hate for you to be out of pocket, Mike."

"If we spend a thousand pounds solving this thing, I will pay the rest myself," said Mike with confidence. "In other words, I don't think for a second I will need that much; but thank you. We will look to head down on Tuesday. The team is free at the moment, and as luck would have it," *not lucky on my part,* Mike thought, "we can spend a bit of time on this."

"And remember, no TV cameras please," Tom sounded deadly serious.

"I can guarantee you that," Mike said, not going into the matter any further. "We will record but on personal digital only. You will have release rights to whatever we find, I give you my word." Mike stood and extended his hand, Tom rose and accepted it.

"Would you like some more tea?" asked Sue. Her voice sounded lighter, hopeful and as if someone had lifted a weight off her shoulders. Mike feared that all those hopes were pinned on him and the team.

"Thank you, but no. I have had a very long day, all I want to do is find a hotel and get some rest."

"The Barge Inn, down on Honey Street has a couple of nice rooms," Tom said encouragingly. "It's a community run pub, I know most of the staff and the Landlord, Bill. I can call ahead for you if you like, get you a good rate."

"A very kind offer, but I want to get back into Salisbury. I will be sure to check it out the next time I am this way, though."

Mike and Tara said their goodbyes and Sue saw them to the door. She passed Mike a card with her mobile and landline number on it. The card was glossy royal blue and had a bell tower in gilded gold leaf in the top righthand corner. One of the numbers he already had in his phone thanks to her earlier call, he tucked it into his trouser pocket regardless and promised her he'd call as soon as they arrived on Tuesday. She thanked him again, another round of handshaking ensued before she shut the door leaving them stood in the warmth of the evening sun.

Neither of them spoke until they were halfway down the drive, the smell of a freshly lit barbeque wafted on the light, yet warm breeze and the sound of children playing water fights in neighbouring gardens carried with it.

"Do you believe that shit?" Tara finally asked, looking at him as they walked.

"I think they believe it, yes."

"Do *you* believe it, Mike?"

He paused, considered the question a little, finally, and as they left the drive and arrived back at the cars he said, "Yes, I believe something is happening there, what – I don't know. I can't get my head around how all those deaths could be linked to that place, but to call it coincidence seems unbelievable, too."

"I'm a little scared," Tara said flatly. "I mean the places we have been to are known quantities, the places every team worth their salts have investigated. This is *not* a known quantity. Tom and Sue seem about as grounded as folk can get, not the kind of people to sensationalise or make things up."

"I'm sure we can find a rational explanation for what those people experienced," Tara gave him a look that said, *really, you really believe that?*

"You still remember the way to my place?" Tara asked.

"Sure, why?"

"Because you drive slow as fuck, and I'm bound to lose you on the way to mine."

"But I'm getting a hotel."

"Like hell you are, you can crash at mine tonight, we can call Scotty and work on this together over a bottle of red. I have a few in."

"But ....."

"No buts, I'll meet you there." Before Mike had time to protest, she was in her A2 and pulling away from the kerb.

CHAPTER 12

At about the same time that Mike Cross and
Tara India Gibb, or Tig as she was commonly called on
the Unexplained UK show, were getting ready for a
night of research into the very building in which Ellie
was staying; she, her mother, father and brother pulled
onto Lucinda's drive and traversed the long, winding
lane that lead to her cottage.

The day had been spent out at The Eden Project,
that back in the sixties had once been the very china
clay quarry that a certain Lindie Parker had suffered a
concussion in on a sunny Sunday afternoon, after
pitching over the bars of her white and pink Schwinn.

Walking among the various biospheres and taking in
the host of exotic plant life, Henry had shrieked with
joy as large admiral butterflies had swooped down almost landing on his head a number of times, the previous night's episode in his room seemingly forgotten
and likely in his young mind he now thought it no more
than a dream. Ellie wasn't quite so fortunate and found
herself drifting off into her own world as they wandered
around the various attractions, reliving what had happened in Henry's room and what she'd seen in the field
that morning. The only positive thing was that the
feeling of dread had eased. The longer she spent away
from The Old Chapel, and the village of Trellen in gen-

eral, the more it lifted, like some slow-moving veil. As the day reached its end, and they'd seen all there was to see and been stung for lunch at one of the overpriced eateries, the thought of returning to that place had gripped her with fear. At around five when they'd returned to the holiday let to get ready for Lucinda's summer barbeque gathering, that veil of ill feeling had descended upon her once more.

They arrived at Lucinda's sizeable two-story cottage a little after seven in the evening. It looked to have been built from the same Cornish stone as The Old Chapel, it also looked to be of the same architectural period, although instead of a steeply pitched roof and bell tower the top was dressed in dark brown thatch, topping the old stone building like a neatly made chocolate cupcake. The Old Chapel and this picture postcard cottage looked like they belonged in some kind of model village set, and Ellie suspected the other homes that made up Trellen would complete the collection if all viewed together.

The grounds to the rear were mostly masked from view by the bulk of the building, but what she could see of them looked fastidiously maintained, there was not a hint of a fallen leaf from the myriad of trees that marked the property's border and the flower beds bloomed with an array of colour that sprouted forth from an eclectic mixture of plants, the species of which Ellie had no chance of knowing. The exception to the otherwise prized garden was the grass. It was cut short, like a closely shaven haircut, giving it a neat appearance, however, in places it had started to die off in varying shades of brown, giving it a patchwork appearance. Obviously, regular watering of the large lawn was not on Lucinda's agenda, most likely due to its size. It was the kind of lawn that when in top repair would feel wonderful to run across barefoot, soft blades of grass tickling between your toes as your feet sunk into the malleable turf.

This now mottled expanse of green and fading browns began at the fence, a small four-foot picket affair that sported white gloss three-inch slats, and wrapped its way around the old cottage, disappearing off into to the rear where the building hid the rest from view. The fence, which added to the quaintness of the cottage, spanned the front of the property, reaching from either side to the looming trees at the woodland's boundary. At each edge of the building, a small matching gate sat fixed on a latch and an old bricked path hugged the side of the building like a raggedy frame of masonry. The sun-scorched atrophying lawn met the aged path with a ninety-degree edge so precise that it appeared someone had checked it with a set-square.

As with The Old Chapel thick woodland surrounded the grounds, and the edging trees cast long sentry-like shadows across the sun-scorched lawn, they lent at acute angles which would only grow taller as the sun slid slowly and steadily toward the horizon. The thickness of the woodland behind those trees, made up of tall oaks, beech, and pine, as well as bushes and shrubs, was such that it held a sullen duskiness of an hour much later. Ellie thought it likely that in the depths of that darkled woodland there would be parts of the ground that had not been touched by the sun's light for many years, where leaves decayed, and things scurried on busy insectile legs.

Earlier in the day, as they'd headed back from the Eden project they'd come into Trellen from the opposite direction to which they'd headed out, something that had puzzled her father as he felt sure he'd retraced his original journey exactly, and after all it wasn't exactly that far, ten miles, twelve at most. In the end they'd seen signs for Charlestown and having been lost on roads that all looked the same, eventually, the satnav had been resorted to, the Peugeot's built-in navigation system guiding them reliably back.

The faded tarmac road that ran through Trellen was too narrow in places to benefit from central line markings. Traversing it they'd been taken past many similar looking gated entrances to the ones on the other side of the village. Driveways that no doubt led to some of the other homes that made up Trellen. None of the houses had been visible from the road, though. All were set back and hidden from view by forest. In fact, the whole village seemed shrouded from sight, as if hiding its secrets from an outside world that developed around it.

Thanks to their journey through the opposing side of the village, Ellie had worked out that The Old Chapel must lay at its centre. As Lucinda had said there was no shop, no public-house, and no post office to be found, the lack of post office was no surprise to her in these times of austerity, but it seemed odd that there was nothing except the five or six houses sat either side of their holiday home, large expanses of woodland separating neighbour from neighbour. Trellen appeared shy, reserved and if anything, a little mysterious. Ellie wondered what secrets were hidden in those homes that also hid. Her gramps, the one now residing in that hellish Rest Home, would have called Trellen a blink and you'll miss it kind of place, or said, *'It's not quite the end of the world but you can see it from there.'*

Lucinda's quaint stone cottage wouldn't have looked out of place on a jigsaw or donning the front of those boxes of fudge that seemed to be found in any self-respecting souvenir shop. Fudge that always proclaiming to have been made locally but managed to look the same no matter what touristy part of the country you found yourself in.

"I still think this is going to be awkward," her mother said in a terse voice, as her father pulled the Peugeot to a stop behind an electric blue Jaguar XJ6 that boasted the private number plate BIZ 1.

"We were invited, I thought it would be rude to say no," her father defended. "Besides it's only a barbeque, we don't have to stay long, just a drink or two, then we can make our excuses and leave." He paused looking admiringly at the Jag parked beside Lucinda's Essex white Range Rover. "Would you look at that," he said, shaking his head as his eyes darted between them. "I guess there must be money in the area."

"Even better," Carol grumbled. Ellie couldn't see her eyes, but she knew they'd have rolled toward her brow as she spoke. "We get to spend a few hours hob-knobbing with a load of pretentious wealthy country folk. Maybe tomorrow, if you butter the right ones up, they might take you clay pigeon shooting!" She turned her head and scowled but her father didn't seem to notice, his eyes were still looking admiringly at the Jag.

"Can we play Go Fish when we get back?" Henry asked. His tablet, that seemed to be forever glued to his hands had, for once, been left behind and Ellie mused that he almost seemed to be missing a vital appendage.

"If it's not too late, Hun," her mother replied, twisting in her seat to look at him.

Go Fish had been a family holiday favourite since before Whoops, or Henry as he'd been called having breached the womb, made his appearance. Ellie vaguely recalled enjoying the natty picture card game herself as a child, now she could take it or leave it, but she'd always play to please Henry who would only whine if she tried to sit it out.

Now, at the promise of a game, if they weren't too late, he looked expectantly at their mother, smiling. He was wearing his favourite Clarks light-up shoes and a pair of dark blue jeans, which were turned up revealing the lighter underside of the material. Finishing off his outfit was a green shirt with a cartoon, and far from scary looking T-Rex embroidered on the small breast pocket. The word **ROOARRR** ran beneath the playful looking dinosaur. Ellie thought he looked like a proper little dude in his shirt and jeans and it made her smile inside. She resisted the urge to reach over and ruffle his mop of blonde hair, he hated it when she did that, almost as much as he hated being called Hand-Me-Down-Henry.

"Ellie said you had a bit of a rough first night and I don't want you getting overtired." Her voice had switched from the curt tone she'd used on her father, to a soft reasoning one that she'd often use when trying to placate Henry or prevent a tantrum.

"Will The Man come again if I don't go to bed?" he asked, sounding deadly serious, his usually cheeky little face suddenly looked sallow.

"You just had a bad dream kiddo," Ellie lied. She didn't believe that for a second and hated herself for saying it, but what else did you tell a five-year-old? Did you tell them that he might well come, that there were unexplained things contained within the walls of the otherwise idyllic looking holiday rental? Not just inside the walls if Ellie's morning walk was anything to go by. They also stalked the fields of the remote village, too. Fields that seemed to have no farm, yet had a scarecrow, one that could transform into an insect carrying, faceless nightmare. As for the thick woodland that hid the timid homes of Trellen, she didn't want to think what might be lurking in there. No, you lied, you told them that everything was okay, even if things were pretty fucking far from okay.

Twisting in his seat their father looked at Henry and with a reasonable voice said, "The Man isn't real little dude, he was just made up to make you behave." Over the last year, the threat of The Man had diminished gradually, and Ellie guessed now this was where his reign of oppression ended, maybe. It was the first time either of her parents had openly admitted to him that he was no more than a myth.

"He *is* real," Henry whined his voice pitching high to low. He kicked his Clarks against the back of his mother's seat as he spoke making the heels flash. "I saw him!"

Carol fired him a look that said, *I'd stop kicking that seat if I were you, Henry!* and as if hearing her thoughts telepathically in his head he stopped immediately and looked down at his shoes.

Ellie had wondered earlier if Henry now thought that what had happened in his room had been no more than a dream, either that or in his half-asleep state, he'd simply forgotten all about it. She'd been wrong and her little brother had obviously done no more than push it to the back of his mind, too taken up with the day's adventures at The Eden Project.

Carol smiled reassuringly at him and said, with a notable hint of uncertainty that wasn't lost on Ellie, "Like your sister said, it was just a bad dream. First night in a strange house on your own in a strange room, nothing more." Then she did something else that Ellie didn't miss, she looked away quickly as if not wanting to be caught out in a lie.

Why is she doing that? Ellie wondered as she unclipped Henry from his booster. *Has something happened to her? Something that's made her wonder if Henry had more than a bad dream?* She wanted to ask her, probe the matter further, but here was not the time. Maybe later when they got back, she shuddered at the thought, she didn't want to go back, she didn't want to spend another night in the place. But not going back was not an option, she had to, and as much as she hated it there was no choice in the matter. Besides, they'd popped back to shower and change before heading out and nothing bad had happened then. Sure, Ellie had felt that heavy foreboding return, a feeling so strong that it had its own palpability.

Once Henry had gone down for the night and her father was lost in the latest Lee Child novel, accompanied with a cold beer no doubt, maybe then she would broach the subject again, she had a feeling that this time it might not fall on such deaf ears. She had an overwhelming need to talk about it, voice her fears that now gnawed at her insides as if there were a living creature in there trying to escape.

Pushing it to the back of her mind as best she could, she undid her own belt and stepped out of the car, closely followed by her brother who had chosen to climb over her seat to exit the vehicle, rather than wait to be let out his side. Luckily for him, his shoes hadn't left a dusty imprint on the car's upholstery, their father was a little precious about such things. Once, toward the end of last winter, Henry had climbed into the front of the car after getting home from the park, he'd had a good-sized mess of dog shit on his left trainer and proceeded to mash it into the back and front passenger seat. That little stunt had bought him a half hour stay on the naughty step with the added threat that if he did it again The Man would come to take him away.

The smell of freshly lit charcoal laced the air, the scent of a barbeque yet to see food, and from the back of the cottage, a thin plume of bluish-grey smoke traced its way into the air, where at a height of twenty or so feet it dispersed to no more than a thin veil-like haze. The warm evening air carried the sound of chatter and the occasional burst of light laughter, although quite how many people were back there enjoying Lucinda's hospitality was hard to judge.

Ellie's father crunched his way on the shingle to the back of the car and grabbed a Co-op bag from the boot. Contained within was a chilled bottle of Prosecco and two small bottles of Tropicana orange juice for Henry, the smooth variety. If you tried to give him juice with bits you needed to be prepared for a kick-off, once their mother had bought the wrong kind by mistake and she'd ended up having to sieve the bits out just to make him drink it. The wine and juice had made the trip with them from home, which was lucky as the area wasn't exactly stocked with convenience shopping outlets.

We are in the back garden, just come on round read the sign written on a sheet of A4 in thick black marker, the words were neatly formed and bordering on calligraphic. It had been attached to the dark stained wooden, stable-style front door in landscape orientation. Red electrical tape held it precariously in place and the ends had already started to work their way free of the door.

Despite the sign inviting them to *just come on round,* Ellie felt like a trespasser as they walked single file through the low-slung picket gate and into the back garden, a small expedition troop heading into unknown territory. Her father took the lead, dressed in mid blue Levis commuters and a green Jack Wills polo. Ellie followed behind, her feet feeling every imperfection in the irregular surface, the soles of her second favourite pair of All-Stars, these were red, were wearing desperately thin and in need of replacing. The earlier worn denim shorts had been swapped for a three-quarter length pair of light grey jeggings, purchased the week before the trip from Primark, or Primarni as her mother called it. At the end of the day, despite the jokes you couldn't argue with the six-pound price tag, Primark always offered the pinnacle of affordable and disposable holiday clothing. The red Ramones T-shirt that hung slightly off her left shoulder had been bought the same day, bringing the total cost of the outfit to a princely twelve pounds. It certainly wasn't the kind of outfit she'd have chosen had she been at home and off to her friend Suzie's birthday, also being held that night some two hundred miles away. But for this little gathering, where the only people she knew were dear old mum, dad and Hand-Me-Down-Henry, it would suffice. Besides, she very much doubted there would be any cute boys at this particular shindig to try and impress.

Her mother, who trudged reluctantly at the rear, one hand on Henry to make sure he didn't trip on the uneven path, had seemingly made an extra effort this evening, despite her reluctance to come. She wore a light blue summer dress that ended tastefully below the knee but showed just enough shoulder to be daring. Well daring in her mother's eyes, maybe not in many others. He dark hair sat in a high ponytail held with one of Ellie's hairbands and not a rubber one as she would normally use. Ellie wondered, no more knew, that the extra effort had been made thanks to Lucinda's striking and seemingly natural beauty. Her mother hadn't wanted to spend the evening feeling outclassed, what woman would want that? Ellie felt bad for her though, as much as she loved her, in the looks department Lucinda would have likely trumped her if she'd been wearing a bin bag.

The shoes her mother had chosen were open toed yellow gladiator sandals, Ellie wasn't quite sure they rocked the dress as she intended but they were passable. She'd even braved a little makeup, not enough to make her look over the top, just some tasteful eyeliner and blue eyeshadow that went with the dress. It was probably the freshest she'd seen her look in a long time, she looked good and it was nice to see her this way, instead of tired and worn. Regardless of the motive behind it, the little self-pampering was deserved, and the little makeup had even helped to hide those thin crow's feet at the corners of her brown eyes, the ones that over the last year, with all of its stresses and strains, had become oh so more prevalent.

Her mother secretaried at the local first school until half three Monday through Friday, then before getting home, she went to the rest home to spend an hour with gramps. The drive across town alone took half an hour and was in the opposite direction to the family home, so when she did kiss him goodbye and get to the car it was even further for her to go, and by then the rush hour traffic had set in, increasing her journey time even more. A schedule like that was bound to wear anyone thin over time and she'd been living it for shy of a year with no let-up, save for the weekend and odd school holiday. Even then she went to the home every Saturday morning anyway. Saturday's she'd spend an extra hour there, taking gramps for a leisurely stroll through the pine tree-filled grounds. Ellie often joined her and would help her mother push the wheelchair. Thankfully the paths around the grounds were blacktopped with tarmac, facilitating the easy movement of wheelchair-bound guests around the various short walks that they'd done countless times, and would continue to do until whoever decided it was your time said, *"Mr. Goth, room 33 – come on down!"* That's how Ellie thought of the room numbers, displayed in white enamelled plastic above every door. It was that resident's number and a few times a week someone's number came up, just like it did when you took a ticket at the Sainsbury's Deli counter and waited patiently to be served with your weekly choice of cut meats.

Since the weekday rest home visits started her mother was always the last one home, and Ellie and her father had taken over the meal preparing mantle and the collection of Henry. The meal preparing practice was not such a bad thing considering her imminent move to university. So far she'd learned to cook a pretty mean spaghetti bolognese, she cooked a passable cottage pie and had even managed to roast a whole chicken without giving everyone E.coli or some other bout of serious food poisoning. Whilst she was still far from being a culinary goddess, a young Nigella, she knew enough so that when September came around and she left home for the first time, she'd be able to cook real food and not live off Pot Noodles and Crunchy Nut Cornflakes like so many students were rumoured to do.

Rounding the back wall of the cottage, the sound of social chatter grew louder, and the grounds to the rear fully opened up. The path led into a large patio area that could not be seen from the shingle courtyard at the front. The brick style paving was the same as the path, old looking and just a trifle dangerous. A misplaced foot in the dark would certainly see someone turn an ankle or take a tumble.

Most of the group, a good twenty or so people at Ellie's rough guess, were gathered here. A few stood chatting on the lawn where an array of sunchairs and recliners, as well as the odd table, had been placed. Ellie guess that the distribution of the garden furniture was solely down to the fact that the close-cropped and withering grass was a whole lot more level than the patio.

The lawn continued its sun-baked mottled appearance all the way to the bottom of the garden, where a small path, just big enough to fit a ride on lawn mower through, led between two oaks that stood like natural towering gateposts. The other side of the two trees it opened out into another, smaller clearing. Through those trees, Ellie could see what looked like a goodish sized stone barn. The barn, surrounded by green oak canopies and towering pines, had a dark grey slate roof that looked to be reaching a point in its life where it needed replacing. The outbuilding, hidden away as it was, seemed cut off from the rest of the property and gave Ellie the impression that it was being devoured by the forest, as if the vegetation grew in protest of its very existence.

The spacious rear garden wasn't symmetrical in the slightest, more like a large and lopsided Trivial Pursuit wedge, cleaved out of the dense forest. The barbeque was a permanent fixture, set into an outdoor kitchen that was no doubt a later addition to the property. Obviously, there was no fridge, but it did have worktops made from thick, polished marble that looked a little too modern against this period property. Ellie saw it as an odd mixture of old and new that didn't look quite right. Thankfully, with the fire hazard of the thatched roof, this impressive, if not out of place looking outside kitchen sat at the far end of the patio where stone ended, and organic life took over.

Ellie spotted Lucinda almost right away, she was flitting from one guest to the next, a bottle of expensive looking champagne in her hand. Her reddish hair shone like silk in the late evening sunshine. *She looks like a walking talking shampoo and conditioner commercial,* Ellie thought with some amusement.

Lucinda wore a one-piece black jumpsuit, although instead of full-length trousers, this ended in shorts just above the knee. Her tanned lower legs ran into sandals similar in design to those of her mother's, only Lucinda's were dark grey, and did go with her outfit, they also looked designer and expensive. The silky material hugged her figure in a way that would make a woman half her age jealous. Ellie couldn't place how old she was, mid-forties she guessed at the most, which meant she was more than twice her age, and even she felt a pang of envy at how good she looked.

Ellie watched as she filled a guest's glass, an attractive guy who Ellie pegged as being in his thirties with thick dark hair and a film star smile. The bubbly liquid fizzed in the glass and spilt slightly down the side in a single stream of bubbles. Film star smile guy nodded his appreciation and took a sip, bringing the beverage's level down enough to keep it in the delicate looking glass. He noticed Ellie and the family and nodded in greeting, adding to it a raise of his brimmed glass. Ellie smiled back and blushed a little, thinking to herself that maybe some rich, slightly older men might not be so bad, not that her mother would approve.

Noticing film star smile guy's distraction, Lucinda herself looked up and spotted them, a broad smile of her own forming on highly clear glossed lips. She plugged a cork into the neck of the bottle, grabbed three fresh glasses from a trestle table that donned a good six different styles of salad, all still in bowls and with clingfilm over the top, and made her way over.

"Welcome," she said warmly, passing Ellie's parents a glass each before placing the third in Ellie's hand.

"Champagne?" She looked at Ellie, and Ellie knew she was trying to judge her age. "If it's okay with mum and dad that is?"

"I'm eighteen," Ellie cut in quickly, making it clear that no matter what they thought she was going to get her share of the free booze. She tipped the glass toward their host who removed the cork from the bottle, it offered a small *squeak* before it broke free of the neck with a *pop*. Lucinda filled Ellie's glass first and Ellie drained half of the best tasting bubbly that had ever passed her lips before her parents' glasses had even been filled.

"Take it slow Ells," her father said, the bottle feeding its contents into his glass with slow glugs that sounded like water going down a narrow drain. "That's a Bollinger, to be enjoyed and not necked like you're at a house party."

"It's fine, really," Lucinda said smiling, "I have plenty in." She winked at Ellie and before filling her mother's glass, she gave her a gladly received top up. "That's what holidays are for, am I right?" She leaned in toward Ellie and lowered her voice a little as she spoke, her breath smelt of strawberries and champagne.

"Totally," Ellie agreed, she took another slug from her glass and said, "Although maybe not ones with your parents."

"Well, that may be so, but I'm sure they won't mind. Just don't go being sick later, it's expensive carpet the Reeds had laid." Lucinda grinned, letting Ellie know she wasn't being all the way serious.

"We brought a prosecco," her father said meekly, pulling it out of the bag. "Kinda feel a bit cheap now." He regarded the bottle a little sheepishly before dropping it back into the bag where he no doubt considered it best hidden from the view of people with more expensive tastes.

Lucinda shook her head, once again making it appear that she was a Loreal cover girl letting everyone know she was worth it. "Nonsense," she replied. "You keep a hold of that, you didn't need to bring a single thing." She bent down to Henry's height, "And how about you handsome, what would you like?"

"I brought some orange juice," he said shyly, one hand wrapped tightly around his mother's leg, he half looked out from around her upper thigh as he spoke.

"You did! Well, I have plenty of that, and Apple and even Elderflower, so if you run out just you let me know, okay?" She winked and patted him on the head, something he hated but on this occasion, he let it pass without so much as a winge or whine.

"I'm so glad you decided to come," Lucinda said, standing up and aiming her patter at Ellie's mother, who she could no doubt sense, in a way that only another woman could, that she wasn't feeling overly comfortable at the situation. "I know it might feel a bit awkward, but we're a friendly bunch, so just," she shrugged her shoulders, "mingle!"

Ellie saw her mother relax a little, she took a sip of her bubbly and said, "You have a lovely home here. Did you say you've lived in the village your whole life?"

"Born and bred," Lucinda said with marked enthusiasm. "This home has been passed down through my family for generations. When you live somewhere as perfect at this there is just no point moving anywhere else."

"It's just idyllic, do you live alone or is there a mister Horner to help out?"

"On and off," Lucinda answered, her pretty green eyes still holding an enchanting smile. She then realised that her answer would have sounded confusing and added quickly, "My husband, Seth, works for Cern, so he's away on the continent an awful lot. Things do get on top of me at times. You've no doubt noticed the grass."

"He works at Cern?" her father asked, sounding impressed. "On that collider thing?"

"Large Hadron Collider, Dad!" Ellie said in a voice that told him in no uncertain terms he was an embarrassment. She felt like adding a roll of the eyes but it might have seemed a little overdramatic.

"Yes, that's right," Lucinda added.

"So, he's a scientist?"

"Specialises in Astroparticle research and other mind-numbingly boring stuff," she said as nonchalantly as if she'd told them he fitted tyres at the local Kwik-Fit. "Trust me, it's not as interesting as it sounds. I'm sure he'd love to tell you all about it. Honestly, when he tries to tell me about the things he is working on I just about fall to sleep." She laughed lightly at her own joke, then added, "He is home at the moment, just over there talking to the Robeys and Mr. and Mrs. Wanderson. The Robeys, they live in the house right at the other end of the village. Nice couple I will introduce you later. Then there's the Lowes, they are around somewhere, they live next door. You also have the Vaughans, the Howgates, the Whittles, the Suttons," Lucinda pointed out the other villagers, although in the mingling crowd it wasn't easy to see just who she was referring to. "Just over there are the Pearsons and talking to them is Mrs. Southerns, Judy, her husband should be along later, he's a banker and works in London. The lady over there with the black hair in a bob is Celine Rutter, her husband is around somewhere. Oh, and the Utleys haven't turned up yet, but they will. I think that just about covers everyone."

Seth Horner, who stood at side profile to them around ten or so metres away, chatted animatedly to a couple in their late forties or early fifties, it was hard to tell. The female, who Ellie figured must be Mrs. Robey, had just about the longest blonde hair she'd ever seen. Save for maybe Rapunzel. It flowed down her back and over her shoulders like a mane and must have been nothing short of an absolute bitch to get in order every day. Her face, like that of Lucinda's, was clear and youngish looking and she had a feeling it belied her true age.

Seth, husband to the somewhat hypnotic and lovely Lucinda, had salt and pepper hair that looked freshly barbered to a grade two on the sides, blended to a neat crop on top. He was tall, too. Ellie had him pegged at over six three, a good foot taller than her. She wagered that he was early fifties and in good shape. He wasn't muscular but had more of an appearance of a cardio fan, over a bench pumping gym monkey. He suddenly noticed his wife with their latest guests, made his excuses and strode over, a wide smile broadening on his lips as he drew closer. He wore wire-rimmed glasses that suited the defined angles of his face, and as he approached, Ellie could see a sharp intellect behind his bespectacled hazel eyes. He wasn't what she'd class as a handsome man, but he wasn't exactly ugly, either. Nonetheless, Ellie thought he was punching a bit above his weight with Lucinda, but what he lacked in chiselled good looks he no doubt made up for with brains.

"You must be the Harrisons," he more stated than asked, his voice both soft and intelligent. A hand was extended to her father who accepted it, he pumped it up and down enthusiastically. Ellie noticed that his nails were perfectly trimmed and looked to have been manicured.

"Lucinda said you'd be happy to fill me in on the joys of Astroparticle research," her father said, both the smile on his face and the tone of his voice a sign that he was joking. "Impressive stuff, not that I have a clue what it involves. Insurance is more my thing."

"It's not as enthralling as it sounds, trust me." Seth Horner replied with a grin. "When people find out you work at the collider they seem to think you're some kind of rock and roll scientist, the truth is somewhat more mundane." His smile was a winning one and presented a line of perfectly white teeth that had no doubt seen more than one cosmetic dentistry visit.

Ellie, not being much of a drinker and a total light-weight, was already feeling the expensive champagne. The fact that Seth Horner worked at the mystery-clad LHC enthralled her. It was the topic of one conspiracy theory that she'd been steered to in the suggested section of her Youtube account. Foolishly she'd clicked the fifteen-minute presentation by Secureteam10, one of the net's foremost channels for all things unexplained, and then ended up hooked on researching it for close to a month before she'd had to ditch it for fear it would drive her mad. Lubricated by the Bollinger, and before she thought better of it, Ellie found herself saying, "Is it true that one of your experiments created a wobble in our reality and caused the Mandela Effect?" She cringed inwardly as it left her lips and she glanced regretfully at the almost empty glass that had no doubt been partly to blame for her question.

Seth Horner laughed, not a flitting laugh, but one of genuine amusement as if she'd just cracked a killer joke. He propped his glasses back up on his nose and said, "I'm sorry, I get asked all sorts of things about what it is we do down there. The conspiracy theories run from us all being a crazy bunch of satanic worshippers to insane megalomaniacs trying to punch our way through to other realities. As I said, the actual work is sadly, not that exciting."

"But you *have* heard of it?" Ellie responded; her initial embarrassment gone at his good-natured reply.

"Of course, a term coined in regard to the mass mis-remembering of facts. Initially drawn from a whole bunch of people remembering Nelson Mandela dying whilst incarcerated, and yet he obviously didn't. That's just the tip of a very big iceberg, though. This misre-membering thing, The Mandela Effect as you call it, covers everything from movie lines, movie scenes to product names and logos, the list is endless." His eager-ness to talk had put Ellie at ease and whilst she didn't expect him to come clean if they had in fact caused it, it was her kind of conversation. Seth put a hand to his mouth and cleared his throat, "The tin-foil hatters, to coin another phrase," he continued, "think that us crazy scientists," he waved his hands by his head as he spoke as if to highlight the point, "with our mystical collider went and punched a hole right through this reality and warped it with other, very similar realities, causing some minor changes." He regarded Ellie with his hazel eyes, eyes made to look larger due to his wire-rimmed glasses. There was a sudden playfulness in them, and Ellie now wasn't sure if he was indulging or mocking her. He seemed to sense her unease and added, "It's fascinating stuff, how tens of thousands, maybe hundreds of thousands of people all unconnected can misremember the same small detail. But sadly – no, I can't lay a claim to anything quite as spectacular as that." He crouched down a little, reducing his height a little closer to that of Ellie's average five foot three and said in a lower voice, "Although the multiverse theory is a widely accepted one, one I personally subscribe to and something we *are* looking at." He gave her a wink, that left her unsure of its meaning. For a serious scientist, he seemed to have known maybe a little too much about what he claimed to be a tinfoil hatter's conspiracy theory. But then she guessed he'd been asked before and had likely read up on it.

Bored of adult conversation Henry broke free of his mother's leg and darted off across the lawn to look at a pair of butterflies engaged in a dance of copulation over a blackberry bush at the edge of the woodland. He stood, head cocked, obviously trying to figure out what they were doing. Their wings beat the air furiously then seemed to become one for the briefest of moments before parting again and taking up the resemblance of a falling yellow leaf.

"Stay in the garden," their mother called after him. "If you go wandering in the woods there will be trouble!" Henry didn't bother to acknowledge her, instead opting for that sudden deafness that seems to afflict young children when the situation suited them. Turning her attention to Seth, who now had a hand around his wife's waist, she said, "Please excuse my daughter, she has a bit of an active imagination for such things."

"Well," he replied with a smile, "if you saw it on Youtube then it must be true, right? And there is no need to apologise, an inquisitive mind is a healthy mind. If there is anything that you'd like to know about the work we do while you're here just come right on over. God knows I bore poor Lucinda with it enough; it would be nice to have a willing audience."

"I will, thanks," she replied and knocked back the last dregs of Bollinger from her glass whilst wondering if there would be another refill.

"Do all these people live in the village?" Ellie asked wanting to change the subject. "We drove through the other half of it earlier and it didn't look that big."

Lucinda nodded and said, "There are twelve families who live in the village. Six homes either side of The Old Chapel. It was thirteen families until Minister Deviss died. Well I say families, he lived alone, but you understand what I mean. I or one of the others hold these little gatherings a few times over the summer months. You know what they say, a small community is a close one."

"Died!" Ellie exclaimed, "How?"

"Ellie!" her mother snapped. "Don't be so rude." Carol placed a hand on Lucinda's forearm, the one carrying the now empty bottle of Bollinger. "I'm sorry," she added.

"It's quite alright," Lucinda said and smiled a little awkwardly. "There was a fire in two thousand and eight, sadly Johnathan, or Minister Deviss as he was known to many, died."

"At The Old Chapel?" Ellie asked. The giddy feeling brought on by the champagne was gone, replaced now with intrigue.

Seth answered as Lucinda nodded sadly, although her pretty green eyes looked expressionless and failed to convey her body language. "They recorded the cause of the fire as unknown after a brief investigation. There wasn't much of the place left, save for the walls and bell tower.

"The next morning," Lucinda took over, "I went into Charlestown to get a few groceries. I saw the smoke as I drove by on the road." Her voice cracked a little, like fragile porcelain but her eyes remained clear. "As I got to the end of the drive, I could see the still smouldering remains of the building. Johnathan, Minister Deviss, lived on site, he was old and would have had little chance of escaping a fire the likes of which had gutted the building. We are so cut off here no one knew, the place just burned to the ground. Sometimes remoteness can be a dangerous thing."

"How awful," Carol said sincerely, holding a hand to her mouth.

"The Reeds renovated the place from a shell to how it is today?" her father asked.

She nodded, "Sue and Tom have done a marvellous job with it, truly stunning. It sat as a shell for so long, somewhat of a blot on our otherwise perfect village. Seth and I helped out with the kitchen, a contact of ours. The Reeds live in Wiltshire and Tom's fitter came down sick and he couldn't find another willing to travel."

"The church let it stay that way, burned out?"

Ellie could think of a few questions of her own that she'd like to ask, but this succinct history of the building was interesting enough, for now. She cast an absent eye to her brother, hoping that he would follow the rules and not venture into the surrounding woodlands, where she felt she could get lost herself. For now, he was content skiting its peripheral. Ellie kept a half eye on him, almost expecting to see a pair of dark robed arms dart out from the undergrowth and snatch him away.

"It was an independent chapel," Lucinda said sounding a little uncomfortable. "Johnathan preferred it that way, less bureaucracy. He owned and operated the chapel for the community. After it burned down, the local authority took ownership and auctioned it. Minister Deviss had no will and no family to pass it on to. I guess in a way we were his family."

"The first family who bought it never got any further refitting the roof that's now on it," Seth continued, weighing the empty bottle in his hand. "I think the job was too big for them or they ran out of money 'cos they put it back up for sale after a year or so, eventually the Reeds bought it. Whilst the fire gutted it, structurally the place was still sound." There was something in his voice that gave Ellie the impression he wasn't telling the whole truth and Lucinda looked at him warily as if she herself was afraid of what he might say. He'd also looked away from them as he spoke, only briefly but Ellie had clocked it, a sure sign that someone is either lying or hiding something. Her gramps had always told her that the old two sides to every story thing was bullshit, most had three sides. A story was a triangle and the third side was always the actual truth.

"They don't build them like that anymore," her father commented, nodding his head, and not seeing the deception. Sometimes there was a benefit in studying psychology, it taught you to read people and Ellie had a knack for it.

"No, they sure don't. We are just grateful that someone with the money and experience to turn the place around eventually took it on. Gave it a new lease of life. It's the kind of thing I'd love to be able to do, but my talents are somewhat more academic than practical. I have trouble fixing a shelf up straight," he laughed.

Henry, who'd lost interest in the copulating butterflies and their mid-flight courtship that looked more like a perilous mid-air fight to the death, now strayed to the bottom point of the garden, where the narrow path weaved through tall oak and pine trees to the barn, just visible through the foliage. He found, what looked to be a small blackberry bush and was now busy plucking the sun-ripened fruit from its thorny appendages, before popping them into his mouth.

"I'm sorry," her mother said, looking toward Henry, "It appears my darling son has decided to raid your fruit bushes."

Lucinda smiled, "It's really no problem," she replied. "The forest is riddled with them, most just go to waste, I've never been one for jam or winemaking." She glanced a little awkwardly at the rest of the guests as if she suddenly wanted to be away from them, and said, "Look, it's been great to get the chance to meet you properly, the food will be going on soon, we have fish, steak, and burgers of course. Feel free to help yourselves. If you fancy another drink feel free to leave your car here, it's not a long walk back, just be mindful of the narrow road. We don't get a lot of traffic through here but there was a very nasty accident a few years back."

"We saw the roadside shrine on our way in, and again today as we headed out," Ellie said, pushing for more information. "What happened? Was it someone you knew?"

"No," Lucinda said flatly. "As I understand it, it was the young man from Winns, the estate agency that sold the place to the Reeds. He had a head-on with a lorry from one of the local quarries the day he closed the deal. No one is really sure what happened, but I suspect he was on his phone or something. Horrible business."

One tragic event after another, Ellie thought to herself with a shudder that prickled goosebumps onto her skin despite the warmth of the evening. She suspected, no – more knew there was more to it that was being told. For one, she didn't buy that the poor man whose death place was now marked by brittle plastic florist's wrapping and a few headless flower stalks was on his phone because out here there was no phone signal. As for the death of Minister Johnathan Deviss, could that be who still resided there? Who'd turned Henry's room to ice? Was that who had stalked her in the field that morning? It didn't make sense if he'd been a man of the cloth then why had the presence felt so malevolent? Come to think of it, if The Old Chapel had been a place of worship then why did it feel so wrong? There were too many questions and not enough answers. Something told her that Lucinda, and very likely her scientist husband Seth, knew the answers and suddenly she found her initial warming to Lucinda waning.

CHAPTER 13

THE BANGING AWOKE MIKE WITH A START AND FOR A few seconds his mind, stolen so abruptly from sleep, cast him into confusion and he didn't know where he was. He had no recollection of how he'd gotten to wherever he'd woken up or what he'd been doing before he'd fallen asleep. It was a momentary confusion that he'd only suffered a few times in the past, and those had been in his younger days and usually followed a night's heavy drinking.

BANG - BANG - BANG

He sat up, arched his neck, his heart pounding against his ribs from the shock of the sudden awakening, the sound of it rushed through his ears where it pulsed with a steady *thud-thud-thud*. Looking around the darkened room he realised where he was, Tara's – this was her lounge. Then he remembered, he'd come back here after they'd visited the Reeds. On the floor sat their laptops, screens dark having long since gone into sleep mode. Scattered in a higgledy-piggledy fashion across the top of her large pine coffee table sat the congealing remains of an Indian takeaway. Jutting above plates soiled with the remnants of a very tasty Lamb Bhuna and a lone surviving onion bhaji, that now looked rubbery enough to use as a bouncy ball, stood a half-full, or half empty, depending on your life philosophy, glass of red wine. The glass next to it was empty. Mike knew the half-full one would be his, he rarely drank, and the alcohol had likely played a big part in sending him to sleep.

BANG – BANG - BANG

Mike pulled away the light fleece throw that had slipped over his legs. He owned an identical one, his, however, had never seen the other side of his airing cupboard door. Claire had purchased it, along with some natty kids' bedroom lights in Ikea just a week before the accident. The cloud, sun and moonlights still sat, all these years later in their bags abandoned in the untouched nursery that they would never illuminate. How long had it been since he'd been in that room? A month, three months? He really couldn't remember.

It dawned on him that at some point during the evening he must have fallen asleep on the sofa, and before turning in herself, Tara had covered him. Possibly even laid him down, for his head had been resting mercifully on a soft, plump pillow. He was still in his suit trousers, and his shirt was still on, although untucked and only held together by four or five buttons.

The banging came again, a set of three hard thumps, **BANG – BANG - BANG**, followed by a fourth that had a slightly different sound, one that suggested the object had been hit with something harder. Mike knew what it was, a foot. Someone was at Tara's front door and having not been able to rouse the reaction they'd wanted with fists alone, had opted for giving it a good hard kick. Something he himself had done many times, years ago when he'd been a regular uniform patrol bod and presented with the door to a slummy house whose occupants were less than keen on speaking to the Plod.

He squinted at the green of the digital clock on Tara's Blu-ray player. His head hurt, likely a mix of the wine, which never agreed with him, and having been woken so suddenly. His mouth felt dry and he considered a sip of wine to wet his palate, then thought better of it. Slowly the numbers came into focus, it was a little after three thirty in the morning. He heard someone cough, a male cough, from whoever stood the other side of the front door.

Bang – Bang – BANG!

This time the third strike was the foot again, and then a voice, muffled by the thickness of the fire-door that separated Tara's flat from the communal area, but still loud enough to make out, "Open the door, Tara – I just want to talk, that's all."

Mike stood, and his head swam briefly. He tucked his shirt in and fixed another button then walked to-ward the hall, the moonlight bathing Tara's lounge in enough silvery light to see by. He reached the hall at the exact same time as Tara appeared from her room dressed in a loose-fitting tee and a pair of red boxer-style shorts, her blonde hair was tousled by sleep yet still somehow managing to look appealing. The skin of her legs looked pale in the moonlight despite their tan. Mike saw instantly that she was shaking, her right hand was up to her lips and she bit nervously at her fingers.

"TARA, I know you're in there!" the voice shouted. The words had a slight slur to them, Mike had dealt with enough drink-related issues in his time to know when someone was either tipsy, drunk or all the way wasted. This voice was drunk but not wasted. Drunk to the level where a person might still be mostly in control of themselves, and often if the mood suited, quite vio-lent. The slight pause was broken with another loud **BANG** as the door was kicked, this time hard enough for Mike to see the bottom move inward and away from the frame, followed by the irate voice which screamed, "If you don't open this fucking door I swear to almighty God I will kick the fucker down!"

Tara fixed him with wide eyes, frightened eyes, eyes he'd not seen before but imagined she'd worn many times before her arsehole ex, Jason, treated her to a beating. A beating that in his sick and disturbed head he no doubt justified by telling himself that she'd both earned and deserved.

"*JASON!*," she half-mouthed, her voice shaking and no more than a whisper. Mike had been conscious long enough to have already reached the same conclusion and he felt thankful that he'd ended up staying the night. "He had my number, but I don't know how he found out where I lived?"

Mike knew it probably hadn't been that hard for him to figure out. One Facebook profile with slightly lacklustre security access, and the odd photo, maybe one taken outside the house, or a friend tagging themselves into your pad was all it took. But that didn't matter right now, one way or another, he had found her.

"You've got five seconds you fucking bitch then I'm gonna start kicking this thing down! You'd better not be in there ignoring me. Three years I done thanks to your testimony and I figured it was time we made even." The door was kicked hard as if to punctuate his point.

Before becoming a detective, Mike had experienced plenty of drunks, he'd also been called to more domestic disturbances than he cared to remember. Some had been no more than crossed words overheard by a concerned neighbour, some had been worse, much worse. Victims such as Tara who'd suffered the temper of a sick and twisted mind were more common than they should have been. Now, with a drunk and angry Jason on the other side of the door he felt a familiar rush of adrenalin; something he'd not felt since his days in a patrol car, responding to a job and heading into God knows what. All you knew is you *had* to go. Only this time there was something else with that adrenaline - anger, and lots of it. He'd never met Jason, he'd pictured himself dishing out a little restorative justice on his face a few times, playing out various scenarios in his head, but had never had the chance. Now here he was, just the other side of the door, the very arsehole who'd made Tara's life a living hell, who had beaten her to unconsciousness and all because the dog had tripped her, and she'd spilled food on the rug. Now that arsehole was back trying to lay the blame for his incarceration on her. Mike felt incensed, but this was more than his inbuilt moral compass for right and wrong, his anger at Jason was so strong it was palpable. He'd never dated Tara, they'd never been more than work friends, but it felt like more. There was that mutual attraction that they never acted on, the proverbial elephant in the room whenever they were together. How he felt now was proof, proof that if he told himself he liked her as no more than a colleague he was lying, and if there was one person it was pointless lying to, it was yourself.

Stood poised between the hall and the lounge, Mike lifted a hand, one that told her in no uncertain terms to stay well back. He looked into her wide eyes and she nodded in understanding. Mike stepped decisively forward, removed the security chain, unlocked the door, and threw it open.

The Man on the other side was maybe an inch taller than Mike, his dark hair was cut close to his head. *Prison cut,* Mike thought to himself. His clothes looked dirty, his white shirt that showed prison toned muscles beneath was torn at the neckline and had spots of blood on it, a sign that maybe this wasn't the first fight he'd spoiled for that night. Jason had no visible wounds to show where the blood could have come from, so Mike guessed that whomever had faced Jason prior to this had come off worse. Mixed with the blood was a good dose of dirt and Mike mused briefly that he would be a good challenge for a laundry commercial, one where the detergent claimed to get out any stubborn stains in just one wash. His jeans, once most likely a very faded blue, wore what looked like remnants of vomit as well as a good stubborn grass stain that ran down the side of the left hip as though he'd slid down a grass embankment somewhere.

Jason was more toned than well built, as if cast from

a steel girder. Mike had met enough crazed and deranged people in his life to know when he was faced with one, and now one stood right in front of him. Mike was no slouch in the fitness department, visiting the local gym as much as he could, but not as often as he would have liked. Jason had height and muscles on him that outranked him, and it occurred to him quite quickly that if he didn't assert the upper hand fast then Jason could and likely would wipe the floor with him. Mike began to wish that he had encouraged Scotty to catch the Red Funnel during his call earlier instead of telling him to stay on the Island. There was no doubt the pair of them could have taken Jason on, hell Scotty had muscles and height on Jason and just one look at him would have probably seen the shithead heading for the door. It was fair to say people of Scotty's build often won confrontations on looks alone, without the need to ever raise a fist. Mike, on the other hand, was in the camp that did have to prove themselves, not with the stature to send would be challengers running for the hills in fear of being handed a six-pack of whoop-ass.

Jason's brow creased as he stared at Mike, his mouth opened and closed a few times as if the synapsis in his brain needed to form speech wouldn't fire. Finally, he growled, "Who the fuck are you?" as he spoke spittle flew from his lips, a large glob or it arced gracefully through the air and landed on the breast of Mike's shirt.

"A friend of Tara's," Mike replied calmly, keeping his anger at the brimming point where if it were needed, he could tap into it. "She doesn't want to see you, and from what I understand you're in breach of your licence by just being here, so if I were you, I'd just leave before you get yourself nicked."

"What are you, some kinda fucking cop?" Jason asked. His breath smelt sour, a mixture of alcohol and vomit. He swayed a little on his feet and placed a hand on the door jamb for support, something Mike noticed and felt relief at. If things ended up going south then the drunker Jason was the easier he'd be to take down.

"Used to be," Mike said earnestly, his voice calm, his insides almost willing Jason to make a move that would give him the excuse to hurt him. "So why don't you – "

"No, why don't you just get the fuck outta my way before I knock you the fuck outta my way," Jason spat, springing forward and aiming to knock Mike aside.

Jason probably thought he was faster than he was, probably thought in his mind he was some undefeatable legend that could swat Mike away with sheer will, but he was wrong. Mike saw him spring forward, his drunken movement a good bit slower than that of a sober man, and in response and far before Jason had a chance to react, he punched the hateful son of a bitch square in the gut. As Jason's body buckled forward, Mike caught him by the throat with his left hand and stepping out into the communal hall, he marched him back, pinning him against the wall opposite. Instinctively Jason began to hit at Mike's arm, the one that held his neck. One blow missed and caught him on the cheek, hot pain exploded through his already pounding head, but he ignored it, the punch had been hard, but not so hard that it would put him out of the game. With his spare hand, Mike punched Jason square in the face and felt his nose explode satisfyingly under his knuckles. Mike released Jason's neck, took a step back and followed the nose strike up with one more to the gut, a short, hard and sharp jab that forced the wind audibly from his lungs in one foul smelling huff of air. He doubled over, swayed for a second on the balls of his feet, then fell forward onto his knees, his eyes streaming with tears and his right hand clenching his winded gut.

"Make one more move," Mike said, still sounding calm yet assertive, "and I'll throw you down the fucking stairs."

"You can't d – do t -that," Jason stammered, still on

his knees, his left hand now exploring the bloodied mess of his nose. "You broke my fucking nose! I'll have you arrested."

Mike laughed, genuinely amused and Jason looked at him with confusion behind eyes that ran with those inevitable tears which followed a blow to the old hooter. "Can't take a bit of your own medicine," Mike chuckled, "Is that what it is?" Jason spat blood onto the thin carpet of the communal hall, and slowly got to his feet. "As for getting arrested, yeah – maybe, but for that to happen you'd have to tell the cops just how you got your nose broken, and then you'd be sharing the cell next to me for just being here. Only long after I get out with a slapped wrist, you'd be serving out the rest of your sentence as someone's bitch back in prison. So yeah - feel free. I'll even give you my phone to make the call."

Jason eyed him with a dawning realisation that he'd lost, and that Mike was right. There was no way he could call the police. The look on his face changed from pained anger to that of a man who knew he'd been beaten at his own game. "You fucking her? That what this is about?" He sniffed back loudly and spat again. This time a thick, dark red glob of blood and snot hit the floor near to the first one.

"Just get out," Mike said firmly trying not to show his disgust whilst using the tone of voice he used to re-serve for drunken idiots who thought they would argue the toss. He took a step forward causing Jason to step back. "Get out and we will forget all about you ever being here. Come back again and I'll call the police, tell them I broke your nose if you like I really couldn't give a shit. In fact, if you plan to do that I may as well make it worth your while, I mean why stop at a broken nose?"

Jason looked at him as if weighing up the situation, but he was already edging back. He briefly tried to look around Mike and into Tara's flat, but Mike's frame was blocking his view. Now on the edge of the stairs, he ran the back of his hand over his busted nose, sniffed again and said, "You can keep the bitch, you're welcome to her." The statement of a man who knew he'd been defeated but was still intent on rescuing some pride.

"Out!" Mike said raising his voice to a shout and stepping forward, his fists clenched. He pointed at the stairs and much to his surprise, Jason placed a bloodied hand on the banister and without looking back he clumsily made his way down. Maybe Jason thought that if he didn't go of his own accord a helping shove would follow, and Mike had been tempted, very tempted, but he'd held off. A fall down the metal lipped stairs could kill a man, and he didn't want one moment of madness to land him in that particular shower of shit.

Standing century on the landing of the third and top floor, Mike watched until he heard the communal door to the apartment block close, then looking out of one of the hall windows he watched Jason stagger across the road, his fight dirtied clothes now bathed in sickly orange street light. He reached the junction, paused for a second, swayed left and right as if stood on the deck of a listing ship and then staggered off toward Tesco and the town centre.

Gone from view, Mike took a deep breath and looked down at the fist that had broken Jason's nose. His hand hurt and as he opened and closed it trying to ease the pain he noticed how badly he was shaking, not from fear, but from a mixture of adrenaline, anger and, okay - maybe a little fear. A fear that had he not been able to better Jason, had Jason have bettered him then he would have gotten to Tara. The beating he could have taken, but not her being hurt again, and not the guilt that would have followed.

Casting one more look out into the artificially lit street he turned and walked back into the flat opening and closing his throbbing hand as he went. He found Tara half in the lounge, looking out to the hall, fright still in her eyes. Seeing Mike, she stepped out to meet him and he took her into his arms, drawing her trembling body against his. She felt fragile. Not like the Tara he knew. This was a vulnerable version of her, one that he'd never encountered before, one born from the actions of the very man he'd just sent packing. He felt her move her head from his chest and reacting to her movement he met her gaze. It happened fluidly and with no awkwardness they kissed, softly at first, then more urgently, both exploring deeper, giving in to that need they'd both felt for so long, a mutual attraction never acted on, until now.

Mike ran his hands down her back and in one movement lifted her slight body off the floor and carried her through to the lounge. Sliding her down he felt Tara's hands working his trousers, he didn't protest. The guilt was there wanting to surface, but he kept it at bay, his want for her too strong. He felt his trousers fall to the floor followed by his underwear, and then her hands were on him, feeling his need for her. She moaned longingly in his ear before he pulled her down with him and onto the sofa. Kissing more urgently now she unbuttoned his shirt, pulling it off his shoulders and casting it aside. She kissed from his mouth to his cheek, where Jason had caught him with the misaimed punch, he winced as her soft lips found the bruising skin. Her lips moved away, and she allowed him to lift her loose-fitting tee over her head, exposing her breasts to the silvery glow of a moon that would soon be replaced by the first light of a new day.

Moving his hands down he ran them up her legs, to her thighs where he pulled her panties aside before lifting her up and onto him, their need for each other being felt as one, and there in the unusually warm morning air and greying light of her front room they became one. Mike rode the razor's edge of his climax until he felt her body shiver in her own orgasm before he finally and mercifully let go. For long minutes after, she stayed atop him, he still inside her, both breathing heavily, their bodies coming down from the natural high of sexual climax.

"Thank you," Tara finally said, her words a little breathless.

"I've never been thanked before," Mike chuckled, knowing what she meant, but not being able to resist it.

She nudged him playfully and slid off to the side where she rested her head on his shoulder, "You know what I mean, for what you did back there, how you handled him."

"I shouldn't have hit him," Mike replied, moving a strand of dark blonde hair from her face.

"You definitely should have hit him!"

"Maybe."

"No maybe about it." She propped herself up and looked him in the eye, then said in a breathless Marilyn Monroe voice, "You're my hero."

"Do you always sleep with your heroes?"

"Well we ain't done much sleepin'," Tara said. "But no, you're the first hero I've, umm – well you know."

Mike did know, she didn't want to use the word fuck, 'cos it had been more than that. Somewhere between fuck and make love, he couldn't think of the right way to put it. Instead, he pulled her back down so her head rested on his shoulder. She stretched her legs out and they lay together on the sofa just enjoying the feeling of being close. He kissed the top of her head and pulled the blanket around them, within minutes he heard her breathing fall into the rhythmic pattern of sleep, and as the first orange tendrils of morning light ignited the sky with a fiery glow, Mike felt his head began to lull.

Red sky in the morning, shepherds warning, he thought as he drifted off, too.

CHAPTER 14

By NINE PM ON THAT FRIDAY EVENING, ELLIE, HER mother, father and Hand-Me-Down-Henry had said their goodbyes to Lucinda and her guests and were walking back to The Old Chapel, along the faded tarmac road that ran like an old worn ribbon through the village.

Her father had only consumed two glasses of Lucinda's Bollinger Champagne and one glass of her home-made punch, as had her mother, but her parents had unanimously decided it better to leave the car on Lucinda's forecourt and collect it in the morning.

The sun was still a half hour off setting and clung to the remains of the day as if reluctant to slide back below the westerly horizon and pass it's watch to the moon. Orange light, defused by the trees, filtered through the dusky sky, giving any driver on his way through enough visibility to see them as they walked in single file, hugging the grass verge as closely as possible.

Henry rode on their father's back for the walk, having proclaimed his legs too tired to walk any further by the time he reached the end of Lucinda's drive. As it turned out he'd been the centre of everyone's attention at the gathering, attention that he'd lapped up, and come leaving time protested that he wanted to stay just a bit longer. The array of guests, whose names Ellie had been told, yet had zero chance of remembering, had doted on him. He was a cute kid, sure, but it had struck her as a little odd how despite none of them having kids of their own, well not that they brought along anyway, they'd been so keen to entertain him. Now away from the excitement of kicking a ball and throwing a frisbee around Lucinda's ample garden with anyone who was game to play, and plenty were, he looked sleepy, his eyes drooping occasionally as did his head.

Ellie had gone a glass further than her parents on the expensive bubbly and had also partaken in the punch. She felt the warm fuzzy glow of tipsiness and hoped it would help her sleep that night and that she'd awaken on Saturday morning without any further horrors. Despite the earliness of the hour, she felt unusually tired. Had she been at home and at her bestie's nineteenth she had no doubt that she'd have partied well into the small hours of the morning with ease, likely waking the next day on the sofa or lounge floor with the hope that; one - you'd not done something with some guy who would take to bragging about his conquest on every platform of social media he could; and two - you'd not made a general fool of yourself. But now she just felt drained.

Walking in front of her mother, and behind her father, she kept a wary eye on the fields opposite. She had no idea when they'd last been farmed, they lay fallow and overgrown and in the slowly fading light, she could see bees and other flying insects busying themselves around the wildflowers, eager to gather the last pollen of the day before heading home to their hives. Small swarms of midges swam hectically in the air, attracted by the four warm bodies. Elle found herself at their mercy and swatted tirelessly at them, more than a few meeting their demise on her arms and legs. She wasn't sure if any of the little vampire-like bloodsuckers had managed to breach her skin, but she itched, nonetheless.

"It wasn't that bad, was it?" her father asked, turning his head as much as he could with Henry riding on his back. "I mean, they were okay. And Henry had a good time, he's properly tuckered out."

"Not as awkward as I thought," her mother commented as Ellie wondered who the hell still used the phrase *tuckered out*, outside the pages of a Famous Five novel. "You'll have to go and get the car first thing, we want to head into Charlestown early on, otherwise we will never get parked."

"Are we going to the beach?" Henry asked, his voice sleepy.

"We most certainly are," her father replied, sounding upbeat. "It's not a sandy beach though, so no sandcastles, kiddo."

Henry made that little whining noise that seemed to come naturally to kids his age. If they'd handed out badges for that noise, as they do for knots and photography at Scouts, Henry would have earned it and then some. Sounding instantly more chipper he then said, "But I can go in the water, right?"

"Of course, but not too far out, just paddling. Make sure you take your Crocs."

"You know what they say about Crocs?" Ellie said, smiling and slapping her hand down on another pesky gnat that decided she was dinner. She removed her open palm and felt a mixture of satisfaction and revulsion at the tiny squashed body now mashed onto her skin. She picked it off, rolled it between thumb and forefinger then flicked it, the way a nose picker might launch a good booger. "The holes are where your self-respect leaks out."

"What's self-respect?" Henry asked.

"She is teasing you, Hun," her mother cut in. "There is nothing wrong with them."

Ellie caught up with her father and reaching up she gave her brother a playful tap on the arm, "You're Crocs are cool, Hen. I just don't think they make good adult footwear. I've never seen anyone over the age of ten able to rock the Croc and look good, ya know."

"We can browse the shops," her mother began, as Henry whined once again at the mere mention of something as mundane as shopping. "You can spend some of the holiday money that gramps gave you."

"All of it?" he asked brightening a little. His moods could change faster than you could flick a switch.

"Some of it, and no useless tat."

"What's tat?" He was at that age where almost every conversation resulted in a question, it was kind of endearing and annoying at the same time.

"Pointless," Ellie was about to say shit but stopped herself, "stuff," she quickly opted for instead. She wanted to point out that the souvenir shops in a place such as Charlestown likely sold nothing but pointless tat, but she didn't. She also had no doubt that many would have colourful buckets and spades hung on dangling strings outside despite the lack of sandy beach. Those kinds of places were all a carbon copy of each other, and it was a wonder they all managed to turn enough trade to stay in business.

"We might be able to get some crab lines and go crabbing," her father said. "We went once, a long time ago and before you'd remember, on a weekend trip to Dorset. I think you were about two."

"Did the crabs bite my fingers off?"

"Yep, but lucky for you they grew right back the next day," Ellie laughed. Henry giggled and wiggled the fingers of his right hand as if to check they really were there. She could remember that weekend away because she'd been about sixteen at the time. It was the last holiday they'd taken as a family staying in a large and fairly luxurious static caravan in a little place called Mudeford, not too far from Bournemouth and right next to the New Forest where she'd gone horse riding. The beaches there had been sandy and the caravan far less spooky than The Old Chapel. Why her parents hadn't opted for something similar was beyond her, it would probably have been a damn sight cheaper, too. She'd not asked how much they were being charged for the five-day stay, but a place as large and lavish as The Old Chapel couldn't have been cheap. She was in no doubt the price had been inflated by a few hundred pounds because it was summer holiday time, a time where every purveyor of tourism hiked their prices up and rubbed their greedy hands together.

"Crab fishing and fish and chips on the harbour," her father said as if cementing the plan.

Henry yawned again and said, "But paddling first."

"You bet," her father took a hand from Henry's leg and faced the palm up, Henry slapped his small hand against it in a kind of high five. "Will you come in the water, too, Ells?"

"Try and stop me," Ellie said as they reached the drive. The Old Chapel wasn't as set back as the other homes of Trellen, partly because its drive was a straight carved line through the trees. It looked as if a giant had cleaved it out of the woodland with a massive axe. When level with the drive you could just see the large double front doors and the dormant bell tower that loomed over the slate roof. The sun, now halfway below the green canopy of oaks and falling fast, silhouetted the silenced bell that looked black against the fiery orange glow.

"Home sweet home," her mother commented. "This country air has me beat. We might have to play Go Fish tomorrow, Hen. I think we could all use an early night."

"You promised," Henry whined, but his voice said that even if they played a single game he'd be nodding off before the end of the first hand.

"I said *if* we don't get back too late, and it's late. If we were at home, you'd have been in bed over an hour ago."

"*Pleeasseee.*"

"Tomorrow," her mother said firmly and in a voice

that said the matter was closed and not open for negotiation. "You don't want to be tired at the beach tomorrow, do you?" He shook his head and rubbed his eyes. The backs of his hands came away wet and she noticed the first hint of tears wetting his dark blonde eyelashes, tears he'd no doubt tried to conceal.

"If you go straight to bed you can sleep on the pull out in my room tonight," Ellie promised as they reached the heavy oak front doors. Her mother shot her a look that said she disapproved, but Ellie didn't care, there was no way she wanted another wakeup in the middle of the night. More to the point she didn't want him alone in that room.

If ghosts did indeed exist, and the evidence that she'd been unwillingly party to over the last day was pretty damning. One who stalked children in their beds at night was likely not a good and well-meaning spirit, despite the claimed origins of the building it haunted.

"Will The Man come to your room?" Henry asked his voice unsure. Ellie's skin goose-fleshed at the mention of it.

"I won't let him," she said firmly, wishing it was that simple. "You're safe with me." She'd never admit that she wanted the company as much as her brother did, sure, he was only five, but it made her feel better knowing she wasn't alone. Henry looked down at her from the elevated height of their father's shoulders, his sleep and tear-reddened eyes wide.

"This is where you get off," her father said, lifting his small body carefully down and onto the stone stoop.

"Just one night, Hen," her mother said. "I want you back in your room tomorrow, deal?"

"Deal," he replied in a small voice, then yawned.

"But you stay on the pull-out, okay? I don't want you giving your sister another sleepless night, you're all arms and legs once asleep."

It was true, he turned into a right wiggly worm once in the land of nod, a worm with bony appendages that were apt to strike you in the ribs, or those soft fleshy places that hurt and never failed to wake you up with a start. He also seemed capable of turning a full three hundred and sixty degrees over the course of a ten-hour sleep if in his own bed and left to roam the plains of sleep alone.

Ellie followed her father over the threshold and into The Old Chapel. She shivered briefly, the air inside its old stone walls was much cooler than the mugginess of that outside. Nothing supernatural, just a normal cooling caused by the natural fabric of the building.

The lowering sun, which had seemed impossibly large in the sky, as if some astral force had pulled planet Earth closer to its giver of heat and light, ignited the reproduction stained glass windows. Reds, greens, and oranges shafted light down in beams that seemed almost tangible. They hit the floor and diffused into the corpulent carpet. The evening light was akin to that of the morning, that false serenity portrayed by the coloured glass. Now, however, it was deeper, more intense and almost oppressive, not full of the promise of the new day, but full of promise for the things of the night that were soon to follow.

"You do realise by letting him stay in your room, Ells, that you're just going to have him even more scared to go back to his tomorrow. I won't have him bunking with you all week."

Ellie wasn't sure what her mother's problem was with her brother room sharing, but she'd already made her mind up that tomorrow night, and for the rest of the week, she'd go and get Henry when she turned in for bed, carry him through to the pull-out and have him in her room. She just hoped he could keep a secret as such a thing would be met with plenty of unreasonable disapproval. Her mother could be funny like that, she had no idea why the idea put such a bug up her arse, it was just one of her ways and it angered Ellie. Feeling instantly pissed off she turned to her mother, and snapped, "He is scared, Mum. You weren't there last night when he woke up, it wasn't a bad dream."

Her mother's eyes narrowed, looking almost serpentine for a second, "Keep on like that and you'll scare him silly, then he won't sleep for a week."

Ellie's father had pretty much stayed out of conflicts between her and her mother since she was about fifteen, he seemed to believe that as his daughter began knocking on the door of adulthood she was best handled by her mother, who had a fleeting chance of understanding some of the hormonal changes afoot. She was sure he'd step in if things got too heated, but so far he hadn't because things never did get *that* heated, ever. His unwillingness to get involved had earned him more than a few comments like *You could have backed me up there, Rob.* And to be fair, looking back, there were a few times that he probably should have. He obviously sensed the building tension and using Henry as his excuse to get the hell out of dodge he ushered him up the left flanking staircase and to the lounge on the mezzanine level. There he could be out of the way, but still keep an ear on things below thanks to the internal balcony that overlooked the entrance lobby.

"See?" her mother snapped. "Do you see his face?" she pointed to Hand-Me-Down-Henry as he looked woefully back at them from the third step. "You've gone and scared him to death."

"No, Ellie protested, her voice firm. "Not me, this place! Can't you feel it? I can, I felt it as soon as we arrived yesterday, and I feel it now. I tried to talk to you about it this morning, but all you were interested in was what to cook for breakfast, you never listen!"

"Nonsense."

Ellie shook her head, anger brewing in her like fire, one stoked with the help of alcohol, alcohol which also gave her the pinch of courage needed for this confrontation. The fear and emotions of the last day and a half flushed through her like hot lava. Her earlier hope that she'd be able to have a reasonable conversation with her mother about this was now in the wind, but her need to talk about it was strong and if this was how she had to do it then so be it. She clenched her fists and felt her nails bite into the flesh of her palms, the pain was reassuring, and somehow needed. She wasn't even sure why her mother's nit-picking at Henry staying in her room had enraged her so much. *It's this place,* a small internal voice whispered in the back of her mind. *It wants you this way, it likes you this way.*

"It's not nonsense?" she spat, half questioning what her mother had said and half trying to shut the whisper in her head up. But she did want to give in to the anger, she wanted to let it out, it felt good to let it out. "Last night he," she jabbed a finger toward the upper level, her nail had left a deep reddening half crescent on her palm, "he saw something! To him it was The Man because you put that ridiculous idea in his head from the moment he was old enough to understand it. Well, guess what? Here The Man is real!" She was about to tell her mother that she'd seen him herself, but she bit it back. That would be one step too far, one step further down the road of what her mother would see as plausible. "If you'd felt the air in his room, it was so cold," she said instead, and already knowing she'd never win this particular fight.

"This is an old building," her mother retaliated, her voice a low growl. It was what Ellie called a shout-whisper, it was how adults argued when they didn't want little ears to hear, but little ears often did hear because the anger in a voice travelled. "I saw you shiver when you walked in, it's a good five degrees colder in here than outside. Why you have to go filling his head with the idea of ghosts is beyond me."

"You could see your breath in the air, it's fucking July, Mum!" The mum was said with a good hint of sarcasm. Her mother gasped at her use of bad language, but Ellie didn't give her the chance to come back at her, she marched across the entrance hall, her feet leaving the tiles by the door and finding the carpet. She reached the large cross, still thankfully propped against the wall where she'd left it. Stooping down she picked it up and carried it back to her mother, who for a moment looked wide-eyed with fright, as if her daughter would lift it high and bring it crashing down onto her skull. "Twice, twice I have hung this on that hook." Ellie took the weight of the cross in one hand and now stabbed her finger at the large hook on the wall, a hook that even from a few feet away you could see was strong enough for the job. "Both times it's fallen off. Last night after Hen saw," she was about to say The Man but stopped herself, she seemed to think referring to whatever lurked here as The Man added to her mother's inability to believe, for The Man had been a purely fictional product of her imagination. Instead she said, "whatever it was he saw, I heard it fall. This morning, guess what?" She didn't give her mother time to answer, "It was on the floor. Now you tell me how this cross," she brandished it showing the strong metal hoop on the back that married with the hook when hung, "falls off that hook without a little help?" Her mother's hardened face softened a little and she caught the look of something in her eyes that told Ellie that maybe, just maybe, she'd seen something that her rational mind couldn't explain, yet stubbornly she still discounted.

"I, I," her mother stammered, looking toward the mezzanine elevated lounge as if hoping Ellie's father would come to her aid. "I don't know what's happened to you," her mother finally said in a hurt voice, tears welling in her eyes. "Why can't you just enjoy us all being away as a family? Why do you have to fight me on it? You've fought me over coming here since we booked! And now you're here you are determined to ruin it for everyone." Tears were now running slowly down each cheek and despite the anger, it made Ellie feel shitty. "If you are really that unhappy, tomorrow I will get your father to drop you at the station and you can go home. I'd rather you not be here than you be here and be like this!"

"You've not listened to a word I've said," Ellie retaliated, calmer now and sounding more beaten than anything. "Sure, I didn't want to come, but on the way here, when we were stuck in that jam I decided that fighting it would be pointless, that this was probably the last time we'd all be away like this together and that maybe it wouldn't be so bad. It's this place, you can't feel it – fine, but I can. I can't explain how or why but I can." Her head swam, and now the room did move, bringing with it a creeping nausea. She hated to go to bed on an argument, one that would no doubt leave her mother in a brooding and foul mood for the trip to Charlestown in the morning, but she needed to lay down. "I can't do this anymore," she said unsteadily. "I'll see you in the morning." She placed the crucifix back on the floor, there was no desire in her at all to hang it.

"Ellie," her mother said, but she'd already turned and reached the foot of the left-hand staircase. Using the bannister for support she made her way to the top. Henry was sat with her father on one of the large, grey sofas. They were turning the pages of a picture book about pirates, but she could tell neither were really paying any attention to the contents. Henry looked sleepy, but his bright blue eyes were reddened at the edges and tears cut clean lines down his slightly grubby face.

"I'm sorry," Ellie said to them both.

"I don't think it's me you need to say sorry to," her father said, his voice disapproving. That was about as involved as he'd get, his pearl of wisdom.

She crouched down and took Henry's hand in hers, he didn't draw away. "Still wanna bunk with me kiddo?"

He nodded sullenly, "Have you and mummy fallen out?" he asked.

"No," she lied. It was another one of those required

lies that she knew had to be used in the not so straight-forward world of adulthood that she was now a part of. "It's all fine. I think we just need to get some sleep, that's all." She looked at her father who nodded in agreement, he knew the ruse and played along.

Ellie half expected her mother to follow her up the stairs, but she didn't. She could now hear the kettle boiling away in the kitchen below, a sign that this would definitely, and thankfully now be left until the morning and that her mother was doing the very quintessentially British thing of making a nice cup of tea. A ritual often carried out when someone was upset or had suffered a shock.

Henry kissed his father goodnight, "I'll pass one on to mummy for you," he said. "And I'll get her to look in on you before she goes to bed. Don't forget to brush those teeth!"

"I won't."

"What will happen if you don't?"

"They'll falled out and I'll have to eat my dinner with a straw," he said, almost giggling.

"You know it, little dude. And it's fall out, not falled."

Ellie took his hand and led him down the long hall, away from the lounge and toward the upper-level bed-rooms. Entering her room, she felt relieved to find his PJ's folded and on her pillow. His Spiderman tooth-brush even sat neatly in the holder next to hers on the side of the sink in her ensuite, Ellie was secretly pleased that there was no need whatsoever to venture to her brother's room.

"Don't forget my tablet," he said in a low voice. "I wanna watch it before I go to sleep. It's on my bed."

Ellie felt her stomach sink. Of course, his tablet, the electronic menace that was practically a physical exten-sion of his arm. He was always permitted five minutes in bed to watch a video or do some practice spelling or math on one of the multitude of apps aimed at early years school kids. "Are you sure you want it tonight?" she asked, hoping that he'd settle for just staying in her room. "It's late, Hen, and you look tired." She glanced at the clock by her bed, an automatic reaction.

"But I *always* have it before bed," he whined as if the *always* laid it down as law.

Ellie sighed and nodded her head in resignation to the fact that she did have to go to his room after all. In truth, she wasn't sure why that should bother her. If this place was indeed haunted, then any room would be fair game. This was not the first time she'd tried to fool herself of that fact, and the second time around worked just as poorly.

She told him to get changed into his PJ's and, leaving him to the task, she padded reluctantly down the hall. Henry's door was closed and as her hand wrapped around the smooth, cool brass of the door handle she paused. She could feel the rhythmic pounding of her heart in her chest, the sound beat its steady tempo against her eardrums, *thud – thud – thud*.

From the ground floor, she could hear her mother and father talking, words obscured by the thrumming of her heart in her ears and the fabric of the internal walls and floors. Her mother sounded upset. Her father's was tone soothing as he no doubt tried to placate her. Ellie swallowed, her throat feeling dry, her head feeling woozy. In one swift movement, she twisted the handle and opened the door. Henry's room was empty, the temperature normal and there on the bed was Henry's Lenovo tablet, just where he said it would be. She crossed the floor quickly and collected the device up. Just as she turned to leave, she heard the door *click* shut behind her.

She wasn't sure how long she stood there, the tablet clutched hard into her chest, her arms drawn in a protective cross around her body and her gaze fixed intently on that door, but she suddenly became aware of a small ache in her legs. Ellie checked her watch and lines of puzzlement creased the corners of her eyes, where in thirty or so years crow's feet may well form. She'd left Henry in her room at twenty past nine, she was certain of this as she'd looked at the clock when making the comment to him about it being late, trying to dissuade him from wanting the damn tablet. She'd then walked the few feet down the hall to his room, picked up the Lenovo and immediately turned to leave. Somehow, though, fifteen minutes had now passed. The digital display of her Fitbit read nine thirty-five PM. Had she been stood there for that long gazing at the closed door? The pain in her legs told her she had.

Now she felt an overwhelming urge to rush for the door, get out into the hall, but something held her back. *What if when you reach the handle the door won't open?* Her mind questioned betrayingly. *What if you're stuck in here? And just where has your mind been for those fifteen minutes? And just what is watching you through the slats in the cupboard door, watching and waiting.* A single thought above those other questioning ones got her moving, *Henry.* Breaking her paralysis Ellie traversed the room with a few large strides and not thinking about it, the way a first-time parachute jumper might leap from a plane without a thought, for a thought might stop you, hold you back and get you to reconsider, she grasped the handle and twisted. The door opened.

In the hall, Ellie hurried to her room, and upon entering found her brother laid on top of her bed in his PJ's. Had he been calling for her in the quarter of an hour she'd been gone? Most likely he'd changed into his night clothes, climbed into her bed to wait for her and fallen straight to sleep, unaware that his big sister had been gone so long. Ellie's mind tumbled over just where her consciousness had been for those fifteen minutes. She'd once watched a show about a man in Texas who'd killed his whole family, then claimed to have no memory of it, she'd found that pretty hard to believe until now. Hell, there were plenty of cases referring to time loss in the paranormal world, particularly those who claimed the far-out idea of alien abduction. Abductees often claimed hours of lost time, some even claimed they'd been displaced miles away from the site of the alleged abduction. But Ellie hadn't moved, she'd somehow dropped into a trance-like state where she had no concept of time. No bright lights, little grey men and anal probes for her, just that missing fifteen minutes, as if someone had flicked a switch and shut her down like a malfunctioning android.

Right then and there her mother's terse offer of being allowed to head home on the train was tempting, home to where this place would be no more than a memory. She looked at her brother, his fist was clenched in a ball, the back of his hand held against the lips of his angelic face and right then she knew she couldn't go, couldn't leave him here on his own. Not only would he be devastated but she had a feeling he wouldn't be safe. She didn't know how she knew; she just did.

The nausea she'd felt whilst arguing with her mother and before going into Henry's room had passed and been momentarily forgotten. Now it rushed back, and like a fast encroaching tide, she felt it wash over her. It went racing down to the ends of her fingers that tingled with a thousand tiny pinpricks of coldness.

With shaky hands she retrieved the pull-out bed from below her own, thankfully it was on coasters that ran surprisingly freely on the thick carpet. The bed was already made up and just needed a pillow which she took from the walk-in closet. With a steadying breath she collected Hand-Me-Down-Henry up, he moaned softly in his sleep and murmured something about the wind and the trees, then with very little finesse, she dumped him down onto the pull-out. Sweat was now dampening her forehead and she wondered if she might have had a bad drumstick at Lucinda's. On the low-slung bed by her side, Henry squirmed on the coolness of the fresh sheets, then scrunched his tiny body into a foetal position and fell back into a deep and settled sleep.

Now stood by the bed, Ellie noticed the darkness filling her window and it vexed her at just how fast night had fallen. Before time had stopped for her, the grounds outside had been washed with the steady falling light of dusk. Now, however, out there was a pitch blackness so perfect it was akin to that of a deep abyssal cavern, like the blackness she'd seen inside the tunic hood of the faceless monk-like thing. She felt inexplicably drawn to it and with a shaky hand, she placed a palm flat against the glass, the night pressed a dark hand back against the pane, cooling it to her touch. With a shudder, she drew away and closed the heavy drapes, as if the fabric would help keep that unnatural darkness out, a darkness that seemed alive with a wanting to break through and fill the room.

Ellie climbed into bed and fixed her brother's tablet to the charging lead that had been intended for her phone. His battery was flatter than a dropped pancake and she surmised that he'd left it playing a Peppa Pig marathon whilst they were out. It wouldn't be the first time he'd done such a thing and come the morning he'd be impossible if it wasn't available for him to watch. She felt chilled despite the warmth of the night, the cold sweat had now crept down her back and her Ramones shirt clung uncomfortably to her. She didn't have the energy to change, instead she climbed below the light sheets, laid her spinning head on the soft pillow, and for the first time since she'd played with dolls and set up imaginary tea parties where her soft toys would sit in attendance, she left the light on while she slept.

CHAPTER 15

IN THE DREAM, ELLIE WAS NOT HERSELF. SHE COULD sense it, feel it with every fibre of her being. She did not know who she was at that point, just that the eyes through which now she saw were not her own. Ellie, although terrified by her earlier encounter in the field realised that the fear she'd felt then was what a papercut would be to losing a vital limb when held in comparison to the fear that came through this girl, who although she now seemed to share a body with, was a total stranger to her. The girl's heart raced and thundered behind her ribs, the pounding heart felt as real as if it were her own, and as if her very soul had somehow been transplanted into a new body.

In the past when she'd dreamt, Ellie had always been herself, no matter how fanciful or nightmarish the particular dream was, it was the one thing that every dream had in common, the one constant. She never even knew it was possible to dream as someone else. Sure, in a dream you might be a big music or film star, might be able to fly like Superman, or find yourself naked ski-jumping at the Winter Olympics, but you were always you no matter what persona or situation your mind put you in. But this felt different, it didn't feel like a normal dream, it had a palpability to it, a realness and a feeling that no matter how hard she tried she'd be unable to steer it the way she wanted, as she sometimes managed to do in dreams that were her own. Feeling panicked Ellie willed herself to wake, yearning for consciousness, but consciousness evaded her. This dream or whatever it was had her prisoner and she was along for the ride.

The girl whom Ellie was now passenger to was in a dense forest, her feet bare and sore, something light and squirming burdening her arms. With eyes that were not her own, she looked down at the burden. The red face of an infant festooned with strawberry blonde hair looked back. The child was no more than a few weeks old; its face showed a distressed grizzle but there was no sound coming from its lips, the child was somehow muted to her ears. She felt the wind teasing its way through the forest, it played with hair much longer and redder than her own, and with the hem of the dirtied white garment she wore. She could not decide if it were a robe, a nightie or a dress. It began in straps at the shoulders and ran all the way to just above her ankles, where delicate lace met the material, lace now splattered with greys and muddy browns. As the wind blew again a sound – no, a voice came from all around.

"Lindeee," the wind whispered woefully. *"Come back to us Lindee-lou."*

Ellie span looking left to right, then again turning in place trying to figure out where the voice was coming from.

"Lindeeee."

The voice was nowhere and everywhere at the same time, filling her head mentally as well as aurally. She looked up to the trees, whose lipless-leaves seemed to call the name, they stirred as they spoke.

"Lindeeee."

Above, the sky was as black as sackcloth. No stars shone their ancient light from solar systems light years away, no moon looked down from its lofty orbit, yet the forest somehow held a sickening grey light. Not dusk and not the light of early dawn, it was a light like nothing she'd ever seen, and in that blackness above she had the sense of things in flight, large things with massive leathery wings that when flapped caused the very wind that carried that ethereal voice.

Without forewarning Ellie's stomach lurched as if she'd suffered a sudden fall, and she felt the change. She was still in the woods, the trees topped by that cavernous darkness, but the body felt different, she didn't know how she knew, she could just feel it was so. The way she knew the body she'd been in just now was not her own. She imagined that this was how Samuel Beckett, the fictional scientist in the retro TV show Quantum Leap must have felt when he switched bodies, leaping around fixing injustices and righting wrongs.

Her arms now held another child, the face of this one different. On its head a mop of dark hair and its eyes, although wet with tears, shone brightly with an almost haunting grey.

"*Sara,*" the voice now called, it sounding once again as if it was everywhere but nowhere, carried on the breeze that played with her hair, hair that Ellie realised was now blonde.

"*Why ruuunnn, Sara? Come back to usss and become.*"

A change again, another leap, another girl, another child swaddled in her arms, another sky of eternal darkness, a vastness so great that the human mind could not conceive it, just as it could not truly conceive the infinite nature of the universe. Ellie felt that if she jumped high enough the blackness would take her from the Earth and into it, and then once in that chasm of nothingness she'd fall and fall for all eternity and be gone from the world forever, left to the mercy of the unseen horrors that dwelt there. Things not of the world she knew.

"*Lucyyy,*" the breeze sighed.

"*Come back to usss, Lucccy, this is your destiny, the destiny of your child, come back to usss and become.*"

The changes kept happening, one after the other, each coming faster than the other until the name whispered by that hateful voice of leaves hadn't had time to utter its first syllable before she was someone else. With the changes she had another feeling - time, it was as if with each change she was going further back, reeling from the present and into the depths of the past. For in the brief moments she'd settle, before the tumbling sensation gripped her insides she saw the forest change around her, the darkened trees looking younger and smaller. She felt as if soon the entire forest would soon be no more than the saplings of a newly planted wood in a time where the village of Trellen and The Old Chapel had been as new to the world as the multitude of infants had been who'd she'd cradled in her arms. So many girls, so many babies, and with that thought came a terrible dawning realisation of what it was she was being shown.

Change.

The woods were gone, now she lay restrained on the cold stone, the sound of an infant child squawked uncontrollably next to her. Ellie felt as if she were back in the first girl now, Lindie, whoever Lindie was. She tried to turn her head to find the distressed child, but a strap held her forehead in place with such force she could feel the pressure on the back of her head, pressure on her skull so strong that at any moment it might just crack like an egg and spill her brains out. With her head fixed painfully this way, her eyes were unable to do anything but stare at the high arching roof above.

Through this new nightmare, Ellie now knew without a doubt what this was, and why The Old Chapel was not the idyllic getaway it should have been, why evil lurked there still and stalked children at night. Why that crucifix could never stay on the wall. This had been a chapel, just not the kind where God dwelt, if indeed there was such a thing as God. For surely if there were, he would never allow such an abomination of a place to exist upon an Earth that he'd created.

A heart that was not her own, yet she felt as if it were, hammered in her chest and the thoughts of the mind that was not her own, and yet somehow across the bounds of time she shared in dream begged over and over, praying to a God that Ellie knew would not answer.

God, please don't let them kill her, Hope. Please.

A figure now loomed over her, the robes of his tunic dark and lusciously thick, Ellie knew the robes at once. They belonged to whatever had come to her that morning and who had no doubt been in Henry's room the night before. The Man. Only here he was in life, face fresh, skin clear and blue eyes that should have looked angelic, yet burned with an insidiousness that seemed beyond human.

Change.

She was back in the second girl, now living the same fate as Lindie had, held on that unforgiving stone the exact same way, and that same face looking upon her, smiling its reptilian smile with abhorrence.

"Through the child, you will become," his voice boomed.

"Become," said the voices of an unseen congregation.

Above Ellie watched the shadows. They squirmed and moved, the way shadows might dance in the guttering light of a candle left by an open window. Only these shadows moved with more purpose and the longer she observed them she saw how they seemed to hold an intelligence beyond the randomness of breeze. They slid and slipped smoothly over the beams with a silky ease and danced together, and although they were many, they were also one.

Change.

The third girl now, another infant bawling in terror, the same robed man stood over her as shadows danced above.

I've seen enough now, Ellie shouted in her head, the

words unable to form as speech on the borrowed lips of her host. *I want to wake up, I've seen enough.*

Change.

Another girl, and as before the changes came faster, the towering robed man always there, although now his face seemed to morph to blankness, then come back, its skin rippling as if unsure of what form to take.

Change.

Faster now, as it had happened in the wood, how many years she tumbled through she had no idea, decades, maybe centuries. But it couldn't have been that long, the face of the robed man had been pretty much unchanged with every sacrifice she'd embodied, the blankness and morphing she'd seen likely no more than a product of the dream.

This isn't a dream, Ellie, a voice that sounded like her own, although she wasn't quite sure was her own, said in her head. *You are being shown, you are being warned.*

Warned, against what? Ellie questioned herself.

With a start and the sensation of falling, Ellie awoke. Her breath came in rapid pants, the way a dog might breathe when locked in a hot car. Her room was dark, unnaturally so, especially as she'd fallen asleep with the light on.

"Henry," she said softly. There was no reply. Breath caught in her throat as she listened for the rhythmic sound of his breathing, but all that met her ears was silence. Feeling panicked she swung her legs off the bed, only instead of the floor being a few feet away, her feet met it immediately, sending pain through her heels. Her mind spun, why was she on the floor? Had she switched to the pull-out bed in the night? That had to be it. Then with dread, she realised something else was wrong, her feet were not stood on a thick, plush woollen carpet, beneath her now was hard, packed dirt.

CHAPTER 16

CAROL AWOKE WITH A JOLTING START AND NOT THE usual rise from the depths of slumber that she was used to. Her head pounded rhythmically as if a lone monkey were pedalling a bass drum over and over behind her eyes. Blinking in the bright sunlight of a new day she realised with some confusion that she was in the lounge on the mezzanine level, half sat, and half slumped on the grey velour sofa, and not in bed in the Altar Room on the ground floor where the heavy drapes kept the morning at bay. Her neck creaked and protested with all the stiffness of an old unoiled gate hinge as she sat herself up. Rob was in the matching recliner next to her; the footrest was up, and his head tilted back to an angle that opened his jaw as if he were a carnivorous plant waiting for a juicy fly. She had no recollection of actually falling asleep, nor why they hadn't made it to the bedroom.

I must have drunk more than I thought, Carol surmised as the pounding of a hangover-like headache continued, and then the argument with Ellie came back to her and she winced. Winced the way she had done many a time as a student, waking up still half drunk and remembering something of particular embarrassment that she'd done the night before.

*But I hadn't been **that** drunk last night,* she consoled

herself. *And certainly not drunk enough to fall asleep without making it to bed, still wearing my evening clothes.* Reaching beside her, Carol fumbled for her phone, locating the handset stuffed between two apparently gadget-hungry cushions. She frowned when she saw the time was 09.45. For a few long seconds, she stared at the screen as if the display were lying to her. After a few of those lengthy seconds, when it sunk fully in that it was a quarter to ten, a feeling of wrongness germinated like a fast sprouting beanstalk in her tummy. Something felt wrong. The silence which bestowed itself upon the room was consuming, she strained her ears against it as if it were a sound itself that needed to be heard over. Nothing. No running water from a shower or a bath, no tinny but chirpy music that often played from Henry's tablet, the bloody thing always up so loud that you could hear it in another room no matter how often she told him to turn it down. The chapel just had an empty feel to it, save for her and Rob. Empty the way you could sometimes tell a house was void of its occupants even before knocking the door to get no answer.

They're probably still asleep, she tried to fool herself, fighting against a mother's intuition that had her alarm bells ringing. The headache forgotten, and the yet unfounded panic flowering inside her rapidly, Carol rushed down the hall; first, she came to Henry's room, she flung the door open. Empty.

He was in with Ellie, that's what the argument was about, stop panicking yourself. By the time the thought had run through her head she was at Ellie's door, her hand on the cool brass of the handle. In a swift movement she threw the door open. Empty. Her legs went weak and she leaned against the doorframe for support.

It's late, they've likely gone to the garden, or maybe the games room, it's not time to panic yet. Carol stepped into the room, the thoughts firing automatically through her head, one running fluidly into the other. Ellie's bed had been slept in, the covers were pulled back, the pillow was at a slight angle. The images flashed before her as if viewing them as pictures and not real life. On the floor was the pull-out that she'd been so reluctant to let Henry bunk on, his covers were disturbed, too. His pillow had slid back off the low-slung mattress and now lay on the thick grey carpet. She bent and placed a hand on the mattress where his body would have slept. Cold. As if the bed had not been slept in at all. Her eyes scanned the room and found Henry's tablet on Ellie's bedside table, still plugged into the charger and next to it lay her daughter's phone. For one, Henry was always glued to his tablet in the mornings, and two, Ellie never went anywhere without her phone, even here where the nearest signal was a few miles up the road. The Old Chapel had Wifi, it worked as far as the garden if you were near the back of the property. Booster routers had been placed throughout the building and they carried the sluggish signal to every room. Ellie had been using web-based apps to stay in touch with friends at home. Carol paused, listened again. Silence. Not a peaceful silence that might be enjoyed by a parent when the kids had been offloaded to a friend or relative. A wrong silence, one that seemed nefarious.

Back in the hall she reached the far end of the mezzanine level and descended the rear stairs, her bare feet making no sound on the thickly carpeted and well-built staircase. Reaching the bottom, she came out by the Altar Room, The Old Chapel's master bedroom, the door was ajar, and she pushed it open and rushed into the gloom, the morning sun held at bay by the drapes. Empty. Silence.

Leaving her room behind she rushed down the short service passage to the kitchen. Empty. From the kitchen to the games room, the door was closed. She grabbed the handle, the panic so strong now that she felt as if it were a real beast that would birth from her throat in a scream. She swung the door open. Empty. Silence.

On legs of jelly, she retraced her steps back through the kitchen and into the entrance lobby. The internal balcony of the lounge lay above her where Rob still slept, blissfully unaware of her growing dismay. She wanted to wake him, but not yet. If she found them enjoying the morning sun in the garden, he'd think her foolish. *But you're not going to find them*, a voice whispered with silky smoothness inside her head. Carol wasn't sure if it was her own internal monologue or something more sinister.

They had to have gone out, that's it, they woke and Ellie took Henry out for a walk. She went out yesterday, remember, went out and when she got back she banged the door so hard because a spider fell in her hair, remember, it gave you a fright because of what had happened to the moisturiser. But then that other voice, the voice that spoke a truth she couldn't be ready to face said, *Ellie would have woken you, she'd not have left you to sleep on the sofa. Or if they'd gone out, you'd have woken from the sound of the door, or from Henry, he can never be quiet, never. The least Ellie would have done is left a note.* Her head reeled, she both wanted to explore the grounds and didn't want to explore the grounds, for she knew that once she found them as empty as the many rooms of The Old Chapel, she'd have to face a terrifying possibility.

She reached the heavy front door with no recollection of the trip across the lobby. It was locked. Carol didn't have to kid herself that Ellie, being the security conscious eighteen-year-old she wasn't, must have taken the key and locked the door after they'd left. Lucinda had given them one key and it hung on a hook by the door, in a place where no one – not even Rob, who in the time she'd known him had managed to lose more sets of keys than she cared to remember, would be able to misplace it. No, the key hung on the hook where Rob had left it after locking them in for the night, before the argument, and the door was still deadbolted from the inside.

Maybe she did go home, maybe she took her brother, too, maybe she is doing this to purposefully scare you. The thought was dismissed as fast as it had formed in her mind. No matter how bad the argument - and it hadn't been that bad, Ellie would never do such a thing. Sure, there were times when her daughter, now a strong-willed young adult, would come to blows with her, but it never got to that stage, never to the point where she would do something so cruel and reckless.

She grasped at the key, her hands shaking so badly that the little leather keyring caught on the hook before finally coming free. Using her left hand to steady her right she fumbled it into the lock and turned it and in one fluid movement, unlocked the heavy oak door. She then disengaged the deadlocks and swung it wide. Stepping out onto the gravel forecourt the morning heat hit her with a fist of humidity, the likes of which would have been more akin to the tropics. From its distant perch in the heavens the sun glowered down at her, threatening a day of more unrelenting heat. Hardly noticing the small stones as they prodded and bit at her bare feet, she rounded the chapel and found the lawn. Above her the silent bell tower loomed, the brass of the de-commissioned bell shone brightly as if it too possessed heat which added to the day. The lawn, green and lush thanks to a timed sprinkler system, and not like that of Lucinda's was empty. It ran as flat as a putting green to the trees where shade and shadows lurked as if afraid to venture out into a sun that would surely melt them away to nothingness.

Clinging to a last hope that Ellie had taken Henry for a morning walk she ran the length of the drive, her feet growing unignoringly sore from the unrelenting shingle assault. By the time she reached the faded tarmac road her chest heaved, her lungs burned, and her heart raced like a jackhammer. She scanned frantically left and right. The road was empty. Carol felt a loneliness wash over her. The stillness, the unnatural quietness, and the emptiness consumed her and for a moment she felt as if the rest of the world had disappeared and that she'd somehow slipped into a realm where only she existed.

Carol got herself moving, more hobbling on the stones than running. By the time she reached the step, her bare feet left small spots of blood on the warm stone. The door was still open, and she slid into the coolness of the chapel, pushing it closed behind her.

The note, she remembered. *Maybe they went out and left a note.* Carol hobbled to the kitchen, scanned the side. Nothing. Back in the lobby, she scaled the stairs, reaching the lounge where Rob still slept in exactly the same position. For a brief second, a new fear installed itself like malware into her brain. Rob didn't look as if he was breathing. Crouching down beside him she looked in earnest at his chest, breathing her own sigh of relief when she finally picked up the shallow but regular rise and fall of his chest. She scanned the coffee table behind her, no note. Nothing.

Carol had no clue what to do next, she let her legs give out and she slumped to the floor next to the recliner where Rob slept, unaware. She envied that unawareness and hated that she had to wake him, but she needed to. Not knowing what else to do and feeling more helpless than she ever had in her life, she shook her husband awake, and into what she knew would be a nightmare.

CHAPTER 17

ROB LISTENED INTENTLY AS HIS WIFE SPOKE, HER words coming quickly, conveying the panic that was so evident in her eyes. As she spoke, and as his foggy head cleared away sleep a feeling of unease grew inside him like a brick wall, each word she spoke saw another block slapped in mortar and added to the pile.

"And you're sure they're not outside?" he asked as she finished talking. Her eyes whilst wide with fear, were also reddened with tears that were yet to fall.

"I told you," Carol said as a storm brewed on her face and her voice flushed with frustration. Rob watched as her fists clenched, ragged and bitten nails no doubt biting into her flesh; he just hoped she wouldn't clench them hard enough to draw blood. "I have been around the grounds and down to the road, nothing."

He nodded, aware that she was looking to him for guidance, looking for him to be the strong one. He could and had been her emotional rock in the past, but he felt useless now and couldn't really think what to do. "They will probably be back inside the hour. I bet that Hen woke her up early, she saw we were still sleeping and took him for a walk," he finally said, feeling sure that it would all be what his mum used to call 'a big fuss about nothing.'

"You really think she'd have left us zonked out in the lounge like a couple of old drunks, or would have taken Hen out without leaving so much as a note?"

He didn't and hadn't considered that fact. He looked around the large open-plan lounge as if it would yield an answer. "What the hell happened? I don't even remember going to sleep. I do remember us in the kitchen making tea after you argued with Ells, then we brought the tea up here." He looked at the solid oak coffee table where two mugs sat half full. The tea inside, now cold for hours, had paled on the top. He ran his hands over his face as if trying to wash away the problem. "I know we'd had a drink but-"

"We weren't drunk, Rob," she placed a cold, clammy and shaky hand on his. "We weren't neglectful if that's what you're thinking."

"It's not at all what I'm thinking, and Ellie is technically an adult," he said. "Henry is fine in her care; she is a trustworthy kid. I am just trying to figure out how the hell we managed to sleep here all night. If I fall asleep at home in the chair I wake up after an hour 'cos my neck and back are giving me jip."

"That's not important now," Carol said as frustration returned to her voice. "Ellie and Hen are not here; it's knocking on for mid-morning and there is no note. In Ellie's room, the beds are unmade, Henry's tablet is on the bedside table on charge and Ellie's phone is next to it. Her bag is even hung on the back of the chair. It just doesn't feel right."

"Like I said, they have likely gone for a walk and lost track of time, she is eighteen now and despite what you may sometimes think she is more than capable of looking after her younger brother."

"Don't you think I know that! But, going out, if she – they – did go for a walk, then I know she'd have left a note. I just have this terrible feeling." Rob watched as the lines at the sides of her eyes creased, and now the tears did fall, not a downpour but two large bulbous teardrops escaped the corners of each frightened eye and raced down her cheeks as if in a bid to see which could reach her jawline first.

"This isn't the city," he reminded her, placing a hand on her shoulder and giving it a squeeze. "Whatever it is you're thinking, stop. This is the countryside," he was about to add that the worst thing that could happen is some kind of road accident and stopped himself. *What if Ellie had taken Henry out for a walk and on those narrow lanes they'd been struck by a fast-moving car or a truck? No one would know who they were, not being local kids and if they had no ID on them, which Hen certainly wouldn't have, and Ellie had left her purse and bag behind then it could take hours to ID them. Hell, probably not until a missing person's report had been filed with the police.* He didn't voice this thought, knowing that his wife had probably already visited that possibility and a hundred others. He checked his watch, it was almost ten AM. Yesterday evening whilst walking home they'd talked about going to Charlestown and the beach, something that Henry was particularly excited about. Reading wasn't as far from the coast as some places, but they didn't go to the beach much and such a trip was a real treat. There was no way under the sun that Henry would have allowed anyone to sleep in on such a day. By eight AM at the latest, he would have been waking everyone, his voice shrill with excitement and asking every few minutes when they were leaving. The more he thought about it the less likely it seemed that he'd even have wanted to go for what he'd see as a boring walk with his sister, but what other explanation was there?

Rob closed the recliner by applying backward pressure from his legs and used his hands to help haul himself up. As he stood his knees cracked, old cartilage damage from his rugby playing days in college. Not quite bad enough to warrant an operation, but bad enough to give him shit if left in one position for too long or worked too hard in exercise. His back felt surprisingly good and none of the aches and pains from what he classed as a chair sleep hindered him. His head swam briefly, causing him to sway but as he reached out for the back of the chair with a steadying hand it passed.

"Where are you going?" Carol asked, pulling herself up off the floor where she'd been knelt since waking him.

"I'm going to walk to the Horners' place, get the car and see if I can spot them on my way." He turned to face his wife and wiped a tear away from her upper cheek with his thumb. The left eye was still brewing its next one, the growing drop not quite yet of a size where gravity would take over and cast it down her face. "You're right to worry," he reassured her, taking hold of her by the upper arms and looking into her eyes. The summer dress that had looked both pretty and stylish on her last night now looked crumpled and he noticed for the first time how she stood uncomfortably on dirty and slightly blood-stained feet. "But like I said, the most rational explanation is that they went out and are not back yet. The whole village is covered with woodland. Henry was eager to go exploring it last night at the barbeque, maybe they went in and got lost. That would explain why it's so late and they're not back. I bet you right now he is whining at Ellie to get him back, so he can get to the beach. Maybe they didn't even come through the lounge this morning and just assumed we were in bed, and if they'd not planned to be out long then Ellie wouldn't have left a note." He pulled her forward and kissed her forehead, her skin felt cool and clammy, just as the skin on her hands had.

"I've just got this terrible feeling, Rob," she replied sounding helpless. "I had it as soon as I woke up. I could feel they weren't here."

"I don't understand how could you feel that?" he asked his face creasing into a frown that drew his dark eyebrows together.

"I don't know, I just could. It was so quiet. Ellie had been trying to tell me all day that there was something odd about this place, she could feel it, but as usual, I wouldn't listen despite what happened in our bathroom yesterday."

"When you dropped your moisturiser?" he asked confused, not sure how this was at all relevant to the current situation.

"I never dropped anything, I wasn't even in the room, and then there was that banging on the bathroom door when I got out the shower."

"That I never heard and never woke me, even though I was asleep in the same room?"

"You think I imagined it?" her voice now had an edge to it that suggested if she was pushed much further, she'd erupt. Carol shook her head and her face changed taking on a doubtful and defeated look. "I don't know," she whined helplessly. "I'm just trying to make sense of it all."

"I never said that you imagined it," Rob defended

"You didn't need to!"

"I'm just trying to figure out what all this has to do with what is happening now, that's all 'cos so far I've not got a fucking clue!"

Carol shrunk away from him, he rarely swore in front of her and when he did it always shocked her. His hands that had been on her shoulders fell to his side as she backed off. She looked at him, her eyes pleading and said. "I'm just saying, Ellie tried to tell me yesterday, more than once that something felt odd to her about this place, that's all. She was adamant that Henry had seen someone in his room, too."

"Utter rubbish," Rob cut in. "No one can get in here, the door is locked from the inside, all the windows are shut, and don't even ask me to entertain that he saw a ghost. How the hell any of this has anything to do with them not being here this morning is beyond me. Like I've said I'm sure they are both fine, just a little lost."

"If you're so sure that no one got in and that they went out please explain to me how the hell they magically got out of such a secure place. I hope you can because I've been trying to work it out. The front door was still locked from the inside when I went out and the key was still on the hook. The back door in the games room as well, that key is by the front door, too. How did Ellie take Henry out and lock the door, leaving the only two keys we have on the inside? Did they teleport? Walk through the wall?" her voice brimmed with anger.

"You're more rational than this, Carol," he said trying to keep his voice calm, because as she spoke, he realised she had a point. Just how the hell had they gotten out? There was always a window, he was sure she'd not checked every single one. Any window could be pushed shut from the outside making it appear secure at a quick glance, but why would you climb out the window if all you were doing was going out for some air? You wouldn't. Whatever the explanation he felt sure that when he finally found them it would be clear and something obvious they'd both missed. "Now I am going to walk to the Horners' place, get the car and have a quick drive around. You stay here. If they're not back by the time I get the car, which once I've walked there and had a quick drive around will be about half an hour, then we will call the police."

"We should call them now, this isn't right, Rob and you know it."

"If it were just Henry missing, yes. But he is with his sister, who is an adult. I know you're stressing here, believe me, I am not feeling overly calm myself right now, but we have to keep a cool head and think logically. There is a rational explanation as to how they got out, we're just not seeing it." Rob sat on the sofa, and put his Adidas trainers on, tying the laces in quick and de-

liberate movements. "They'll be back soon, I know it."
He knew no such thing, but he could tell his wife was
riding the razor's edge of a full-on panic attack and allowing himself to show his worry would just fan the
flames, the situation needed making better, not worse.
He stood and put an arm around her shoulder and bent
down, kissing her on the cheek. "I won't be long."

"Please don't be," she pleaded. Her voice wavered as
she spoke, her anger gone and replaced by vulnerability.

"I won't be," he promised. Rob descended the stairs
two at a time with Carol on his heels. He opened the
door and she held it ajar as he walked briskly across the
forecourt. "Half an hour, maximum," he said raising his
voice enough for her to hear and looking back.

"Find them," she called after him.

In a walk that was just shy of a run, Rob traversed
the drive, the sound of his trainers crunching a quick
rhythm on the shingle. Tall oaks lined the way and cast
morning shadows that consumed his as he passed from
light to shade and back again. At the top of the drive,
where his wife had stood not five minutes ago, he hung
a left and his feet found tarmac. It was no more than a
ten-minute walk to the Horners' place – maybe just over
five if he kept the pace up, yet the distance he had to
cover felt vast. the panic in his wife had spread to him
as if it were a communicable virus that he'd contracted
just by breathing the same air as her. They were right to
worry, but the chances of something bad having happened had to be slim. Reluctantly he slowed to a stop a
listened. There were no sirens to hear, and no traffic
moved through the village. Even if Ellie had taken
Henry out and God forbid an accident had happened,
he felt sure there would be emergency services vehicles
in the area. He put the thought to bed and got moving,
his breathing labouring a little more with each passing
yard. Moving as swiftly as he could Rob kept an eye on
the fallowed fields opposite and the thick darkled
woodland to his left. Occasionally he glanced back with

a feeling that someone was following him a short way down the road, each time he did he expected to see them behind him, but the road was always empty.

In all, it took him just under eight minutes to reach the Horners', by the time he headed down their long drive his right knee throbbed and sweat dampened his brow. Ignoring the pain from the mangled cartilage he kept pace, wiping his brow with the back of his hand and transferring it to his jeans. He could feel sweat running in beads down his back, too.

The front door to their picture postcard cottage still held the sign that informed guests to come on round to the back garden. He briefly surveyed the windows, noting the curtains were still drawn; not a surprise if it had been a late night. Unfortunately, this was an emergency and if Seth and Lucinda were still asleep then he'd be their alarm call, something he'd have felt more awkward about doing if they'd not gotten to know them a little better at the barbeque. He reached the door and knocked hard twice, then twice again with more gusto when no one answered. After what felt like an age, but in reality was no more than a couple of minutes at the most, he heard the door being unlatched from the inside and the sound of a key being wrestled in a lock that seemed reluctant to yield.

"Rob," Lucinda said as she swung the door open. She was dressed in a long red silk dressing gown that looked expensive, the kind of thing he'd always want to buy Carol but could never justify the cost of. She instantly noticed his reddened face and in turn, hers creased with concern. "Is everything okay, you look – flustered?"

"I'm sure it is," he half said, and half panted whilst feeling inwardly ashamed for being so out of shape.

"Is everything alright at The Old Chapel?"

"The place is fine. Look, have you seen the kids this morning?"

Lucinda's face switched to a frown that creased her

brow, wrinkling her alabaster-like skin. "No, it was a late night, the last of our guests didn't leave until gone three. We were still in bed. What time is it?"

"Just gone ten."

"Oh wow, I really did sleep in. I hate getting up so late, almost feels like you've wasted half the day," she said looking out across her forecourt as if expecting to see them. "If they went walking in the woods, then there is a good chance they've lost their bearings. The woodland is thick and runs for a good few miles behind the village. Goodness knows when I was a girl, I used to get lost on the trail ways all the time. Used to worry my mother sick, but after enough wandering about I always came out somewhere.

"That's what I told Carol, but she is prone to panic and you know how that can be."

"Spreads like the plague," she agreed nodding. A strand of her deep, red hair freed itself from behind her left ear and fell across her face and she quickly tucked it back in place.

"I told her I would get the car and have a drive around, but if they went into the woods that won't be much help."

"When did you last see them?"

"Last night, at bedtime when we got home. Hen slept in with Ellie, you know how kids are in a strange place." She nodded. "But this morning there's no sign of them, not even a note. Carol wants to call the police."

"If they are in there and as long as they don't walk circles, they will come out at one of the cottages or at the back of Culdon, that's the next village. It's a good six-mile walk from Culdon though if you take the road. I'd imagine that they would walk along the road against heading back into the woods."

"Yeah, makes sense," Rob agreed, feeling the need to get moving. He'd not been away long yet, but it didn't feel that way. "I'll drive to Culdon and see if I can find them heading back this way."

"Probably your best bet," she agreed. "Look, I will call the other villagers and let them know to keep an eye out. I am sure they will pop up somewhere. Worst comes to it I will get a search party together and a few of us will cover the woods, we all know them pretty well."

"You'd really do that?" he asked surprised.

"Of course," Lucinda replied, a smile lighting her face. "I told you this is a close community; we all help each other if help is needed. While you and your family are here you're a part of our community. Look, it will take me an hour or so to divvy them up, but if you want to call the police in the meantime it might not be a bad idea. The nearest station is in Liskeard, I think. That's a good half an hour away. We don't get much crime out in the sticks and I think the last time we had any police here was after the fire."

"Okay, thanks. I'll take the car and have a drive to Culdon. If I don't find them, I will call you when I get back."

"I'm sure it will be fine," she consoled, reaching out and placing a hand on his shoulder in much the same way he had to his wife. "I've only met your daughter twice, but she seems like a sensible kid."

"She is, which is why this is out of character for her. Look, I need to get going, Carol is going out of her mind with worry, and I don't want her on her own any longer than necessary. I really appreciate it."

"No problem, let me know. I will go wake Seth up now and rally the troops if needed."

"Thanks again," Rob watched as she closed the door, then headed to the car.

By the time he reached the road the Peugeot's in-built navigation system had found enough satellites to pinpoint his remote spot on the planet. He could see Culdon, they'd driven through it on the way to Trellen on the day they'd arrived. The large expanse of green shown in a graphic on the basic display was obviously the woodland that engulfed Trellen. He traced the route with his finger and got moving, scanning both sides of the road as he went.

About ten minutes later, and on the outskirts of Culdon, Rob passed his first car. He followed the road as best he could through the village, which wasn't much bigger than Trellen, but did have a quaint looking pub called The Goose. Eventually, he got to the point where it looked as if he'd drawn level with the boundary of the wood. With no trace of Henry and Ellie, or thankfully the accident that he'd feared so much, he turned around in a pothole infested layby and drove the same route back, feeling sure that by the time he pulled to a stop back at The Old Chapel he'd find Carol waiting for him outside with both kids and the panic would be over.

Less than ten minutes later he found that the panic wasn't over. As he swung the Peugeot into the drive, he could see his wife sat on the stone stoop, the front door sitting open behind her. When she saw the car she stood, and he could tell she was looking to see if he carried any passengers. That sight alone made his guts drop and dread swept a very cold hand across his flesh. It was half-past ten, forty-five minutes had now passed since Carol had awoken to find them gone, and he had no clue what time they'd left. His head kept going back to just how they'd gotten out in the first place. There had to be something he'd missed, believing they'd vanished into thin air was preposterous, but it was a question to which the police would want an answer if God forbid, they'd not turned up by the time an officer arrived from Liskeard.

"Please, no," Carol said as he got out of the car. Her hands were up at her mouth and he could see her nails had been fully chewed down to the quick in the half an hour he'd been away. All the colour of the summer had also drained from her skin and her face looked pale as if it were that of a person suffering a critical illness.

Rob took her by the arms and looked into her eyes which seemed sunken and dark, "I've spoken to Lucinda, she hasn't seen them, but she said the woods are easy to get lost in. I have to call her, let her know I've not found them and she will organise a search party. She is sure that's where they must be."

"It's easy for her to say," Carol spat a little scornfully. "They're not her kids." Her darkened eyes pleaded for direction and made him feel useless. "What do we do now, Rob?"

"Now we call the police," he replied.

CHAPTER 18

THE WHITE AND BLUE SINGLE-ENGINE CESSNA bounced and bobbed its way to the end of the grass runway where it swung tightly around in an arc before coming to a stop. From the glass-fronted restaurant where diners could enjoy a home-cooked style meal whilst watching the eclectic mix of light aircraft come and go, Tara heard the pilot throttle up, the monotone drone of the engine building to a crescendo that sounded like a thousand angry hornets erupting from a disturbed nest. Transfixed as she always had been by the miracle of flight, she watched as the pilot released the brake and sent the small aircraft speeding back along the grass almost looking haphazard as it progressed to a velocity where physics would take over and lift it skyward. As it drew level with the spot where she and Mike were sat enjoying a late afternoon lunch, it almost seemed to leap into the air, it climbed a little then dipped a few feet as if it had changed its mind about leaving the safety of terra-firma before the pilot smoothed out the take-off and it climbed steadily and smoothly into the perfectly blue sky. The aircraft vanished quickly from her view but after a few seconds, it reappeared, now a fast diminishing spec as it banked around and headed toward Salisbury.

"So, is this like, our first date?" she asked, her attention now back on her lunch. She forked a mouthful of her tuna and cheese jacket potato into her mouth. The food was still the hot side of nuclear and she felt it burn the roof of her mouth. She'd worried that after their impromptu session of passion, things the next day would be weird, but thankfully they hadn't been. After they'd both fulfilled a desire that had been building since the day they'd met they had both fallen asleep cuddled-up on her large sofa, waking later that morning at around nine. Before Mike had even bid her a good morning he'd kissed her, and with that kiss went all her fears of potential awkwardness. Following the kiss, they quenched their physical needs once again. It wasn't going to be awkward and there was a good chance it could be the start of something special. "Romantic lunch for two at the local airfield?" she concluded with a coy smile.

"More of a working lunch," he replied smiling back whilst pushing chunks of chicken korma around his plate with the back of his fork. "You tend to have the first date before you sleep with someone."

"Mike Cross are you implying I'm some kind of hussy?" She kicked his shin under the table, not hard, but hard enough to make him flinch.

"If the cap fits," he winked, and she kicked him again. "And anyway, this place was your idea, I'd have been happy with a good bistro pub."

"Hey, don't you dare diss Compton Abbas," she chided, cutting at her food with the side of her fork and causing fresh steam to rise from the baking hot potato. "My dad used to bring me here for hot chocolate so I could watch the planes. I was always a bit of a tomboy like that as a kid. Back then they used to load the hot chocolate up with that nasty but oh-so-tasty canned squirty cream and then throw on a handful of those mini marshmallows. I wonder if they still do it?"

"Sounds calorific!"

Tara laughed, "Are you saying I'm fat?

"Only a woman could draw that inference from such a comment," he said with a wry smile. He took a mouthful of the curry and grinned at her as he chewed. "So, this is how it's going to be with you?"

"How do you mean?"

"Difficult!"

"You'd not have me any other way," she said with a grin. She was enjoying the flirtatious banter and despite this being a supposed working lunch the subject of their up and coming investigation for Sue and Tom Reed hadn't even featured. Last night it had, heavily, but that was before Jason's visit. She still couldn't believe that the catalyst that had finally brought her and Mike together had been her drunken arsehole ex. Life worked in mysterious ways for sure. Jason, who had made her life a living hell, Jason who had beat her so hard she'd ended up in Salisbury Hospital. Jason, who through his own fuckwhittery had made her feel more excited about her romantic future than she could ever remember. She never thought she'd have been happy to see Jason the other side of prison bars and she'd been scared shitless when he'd awoken her thumping and kicking at her door in the early hours of the morning like the maniac he was, but now she'd not have swapped his drunken visit for anything. She almost hoped that one day she'd get the chance to tell him just what had happened after he'd come to exact some revenge on her, revenge that in his fucked-up head he'd justified as deserved. That was the problem with people like Jason, and the world was full of them. Sure, they weren't all abusers of women but they all thought everyone else was the problem, that it was everyone else's fault for the situation they found themselves in when the truth was, it was nearly always theirs. People like Jason never saw that *they* were the problem.

This was early days though, and during the morning, and whilst feeling like a foolish and giddy sixteen-year-old who'd just been asked to prom by the one boy in the year that all the popular girls lusted after, she'd had to reel in and put a leash on her thoughts a few times. Telling herself not to get too hopeful and not to expect too much. She couldn't help it, though. She'd had one arsehole of a boyfriend after the other, Mike had always been the kind of guy she knew she should have gone for, but now being damaged goods, she never thought she'd get. But then he was damaged goods, too. Sure, he didn't look it on the surface, but neither did she. However, scratch just below the surface and you'd see it, see the hurt and pain that he'd been through, that they'd both been through. Hell, it could even be a positive that they were both damaged goods, fucked up by life in different ways. Maybe, just maybe that's why they fit so well. She watched as he smiled back at her, his eyes seemed to sparkle at her in the sunlight that filtered through the large observation windows and his face looked both handsomely hard and kind all at the same time, hard and kind in a way that made her feel safe.

"I spoke to Scotty earlier," he said, and she felt a tinge of disappointment that he was steering the conversation toward work.

"And?."

"He is chomping at the bit to come over, I think he feels a bit out of the loop and isolated."

"Serves him right for living on that stupid island," she said before taking a mouthful of food.

"I told him we couldn't head down until next week, but he wants to head to the village, check the place out and do some local research."

"You did tell him that the Reeds don't want us talking to the other villagers, that Lucinda woman in particular?"

Mike shifted his weight on his seat, took a sip of his beer and said, "I did. I also told him that we have plenty of time to get our teeth into the case when we get there."

"Ha, so has he been doing his own bit of research?"

"Yeah, after we spoke to him last night. I think he was up late he sounded pretty knackered this morning."

"And did he manage to find anything that I missed?" Tara raised her eyebrows expectantly.

"Let's just say he's drawn as many blanks you did, and as we both did last night."

The previous night, before Jason's drunken visit and whilst they'd worked on an Indian Takeaway that would have been more suited to a party of four, Mike had Skype called Scotty and brought him up to date with what they knew so far about The Old Chapel, which wasn't much. He'd also been abridged of the meeting with the Reeds, where they'd proclaimed that the seemingly tortured cries of infants were a nightly occurrence within the walls of their holiday home, and that little girls spoke to the boogie-man whilst having tea parties, and former guests seemed prone to suicide and infantile murder after a luxurious stay. Scotty had listened with interest, his facial expressing forming an ever-changing and fluid mixture of scepticism, intrigue, and excitement and a little horror. All expressions that would never have come across on a traditional voice call.

"You believe them?" he'd asked when Mike had been done telling all there was to tell, aided with some playback from Tara's voice recorder.

Mike had told him that he believed something was going on there, but it was just too early to say. Although, the deaths were a cause for concern and maybe a little too common to put down to nothing more than some horrific coincidence. But then what was the alternative? That the building made them do it, that something inside that place had planted a worm inside their heads, one that whispered and burrowed into their brains until they snapped.

"This could be the one!" Scotty had replied, not hiding his excitement.

"I've hoped that with every investigation," Mike had told him, leaning in toward the small camera on his

Lenovo. *"Least we forget the Sleaford case. That seemed like the real deal to start with and look how that turned out!"*

"I know, I know," Scotty had said, letting a little disappointment show. *"But these guys, the Reeds, they ain't got nothing to gain – nothing. That's what tells me this is the real deal."*

The rest of the conversation had been Scotty pushing to come over and head to Cornwall four days before they could even get into the place, then looking like a petulant child denied his own way when Mike had reigned him in.

"So," Tara said, taking her mind away from the previous evening's Skype call. "After four or five hours' of research all we know is the place was occupied by a guy named Deviss, that it was a chapel, although for some reason not registered, and that it burned down in two-thousand and eight and no one really knows how or why. She paused and took a swing from her half a pint of cider and looked at the amber liquid for a few seconds as if pondering an important question, then continued. "One of Tom's builders left the site then later hung himself. The estate agent who closed the deal died in a car crash the day he sold it to them. They completed the renovations and in the few months it's been open only one client stayed the length of time they'd booked for. One gassed himself in his car, and another drowned her baby in the tub then took her own life with sleeping tablets."

Mike chewed the last of his curry thoughtfully and washed it back with the last of his half pint. He wiped a hand over the back of his mouth and said, "That about sums it up, quite the riddle we have to solve isn't it?" He put his knife and fork together neatly on the plate. They clinked against the basic white china before he pushed it aside. "Not too bad, not too bad at all," he said referring to the food.

"I told you it was good, this ain't no airport departure lounge, this is a proper restaurant." She reached a hand over the table and he willingly took it, squeezing it lightly as he played with her fingers. As he began to run his thumb over the soft skin of the back of her hand, his phone rang.

"It's Sue," he said picking the device up from the table and looking at the caller ID. "Maybe the Harrisons have checked out and Scotty will get his wish," he chuckled and stood up. "I'll take this out the front, the reception in here is a bit shit." Tara watched him weave his way through the tables and chairs. He answered the call as he passed the bar, she just about heard him say, "Hi Sue, what can I do for you?" then his voice faded, and she was left to the last of her baked potato.

Five minutes later Mike strode back in, his face looked troubled and the sparkle in his eyes was gone. He didn't come directly to the table; he first stopped at the bar and settled the bill with a young dark-haired girl who Tara guessed was peddling a summer job before uni.

"Hey, I was about to have a nostalgic hot chocolate," she said as he reached their table. "Or do you want to get me out of here before I pile the pounds on?"

"Well we can't have you letting yourself go already can we," he said with a smile that seemed false. False because it never reached his eyes.

"Is something wrong? What did Sue say?" Tara felt a ubiquitous nervousness come over her, but she wasn't quite sure why.

"There's been a development," Mike said seriously. "I'll bring you up to date in the car." She stood and he pulled the chair back for her like a true gentleman. *I'll bring you up to date in the car,* she thought to herself. The way he spoke sometimes made her smile, regimented and, well – police like, as if she were his partner in a crime-fighting duo, both part of some gumshoe type detective series like Morse. It was one of the things that made her feel safe, though. Mike was reliable and unlike her past mistakes would never do anything to hurt her either physically or emotionally.

The Cessna that had pulled off its haphazard take off as they'd enjoyed their meal was now buzzing away on a circular decent above them. It droned around like a fly caught in a room, circling frantically looking for an escape. As she climbed into the passenger seat of Mike's Jeep it buzzed low over the trees at no more than two hundred feet, before banking left and coming in for final approach.

"Well?" Tara asked feeling anxious. She suddenly felt the need for a cigarette but there was no way she'd crumble, not in front of Mike.

"It seems there may well be another riddle to solve," he said as he pulled out from the parking space and headed for the C13, the small and often treacherous road that adjoined Blandford to its neighbouring town of Shaftsbury. As they reached the junction Mike swung left out of the partly blind junction and gunned the accelerator to build speed. To their right, the Dorset countryside peeled away from the slopes of Spread Eagle Hill. On a day as clear as this you could almost see all the way to the Jurassic Coast.

"Riddle?" Tara asked hearing the Jeep's engine roar and feeling its power push her back into the seat.

"The Harrison kids are missing," he said flatly.

"Missing?"

"When the Harrisons woke up this morning both kids were gone, that was around ten AM. They thought they'd gone for a walk and got lost, but that was four hours ago and there is still no sign of them. The local villagers are about to help search the surrounding area and apparently the police are there, too."

"My God," Tara said, holding her hand to her mouth. "Those poor people, how old are the kids?"

"The girl, Ellie, is eighteen and her brother, Henry, is five."

"What's the panic, she's an adult, probably just took her little bro out."

Mike shook his head; he was obviously privy to more information. "That's what I thought," he replied, "but there is no note and its completely out of character for her, apparently. Local police will be all over it, if they are lost in the local area it won't take long to find them. I have no doubt the chopper and drone team will be carrying out searches from the air."

"So, what's the riddle?"

"When the mother saw that they were missing this morning the place was still all locked up, doors, windows – you name it."

Tara frowned not quite getting the point, "So?" she questioned.

"The doors don't lock without a key, the family had one set of keys and both keys were inside the property. The front and back doors were also internally deadbolted. Technically they have bloody well vanished."

CHAPTER 19

BY THREE PM ON THE SATURDAY AFTERNOON OF THE day that Ellie and her brother had gone missing, The Old Chapel had two marked police units sat on the shingle drive forecourt next to the Harrisons' Peugeot. Just over five hours had passed since Carol had awoken to a deathly silent building, just over five hours since she'd rushed from room to room, her anxiety building with each step and finding nothing but more silence and emptiness. Now, as she sat in a state of semi-vacantness on the sofa upon which she'd awoken, she could see from the internal balcony of the mezzanine level, down to and out of the front door which lay open. There, glinting in the sun and catching her eye was the yellow and blue fluorescent battenburging of the Police Ford Focus estate parked closest to the door. Carol placed her head in her hands as the morning's events tumbled over and over in her head, a relentless cycle of tortuous thoughts that would not abate.

———

THE FIRST OFFICERS at the scene were an older looking male PC with greying dark brown hair and serious looking brown eyes, he'd looked in his forties and his face wore the lines of a career of shift work. Accompanying him was a younger fresh-faced female PC. To Carol, the female officer looked only a few years older than her daughter and the freshness of her appearance held testimony to the fact that she'd yet to earn the same badge of service as her elder colleague.

They'd arrived thirty minutes after Rob had placed the call and had spent the first hour going through a laborious and frustrating amount of paperwork, collating everything from Ellie's phone number to usernames for her social media accounts and even enquiring about which doctor's surgery she used. A similar bevvy of questions was asked about Henry, too. However, he was obviously too young for many of the things that they believed might help to track his sister down. Carol had noted how the male officer's eyes had narrowed in what she took as suspicion or disapproval when Rob had explained how they'd woken in the lounge with no memory of having fallen asleep. Rob had assured both officers that neither he nor his wife had been drunk, but she wasn't quite sure they believed it, the male officer in particular. To be fair she didn't blame them, she knew little of police work outside of the occasional cops on the front-line type show she sometimes watched when there was nothing else on. Despite the little she knew, she knew enough to know that the lion's share of their time was taken up dealing with alcohol and drug-related incidents as well as dysfunctional families. Despite the fact she'd done nothing wrong she couldn't help but feel that they were judging her, drawing conclusions about her own family based on all the bad ones they had to deal with.

After the seemingly never-ending stream of questions had finally ended and the building searched, two further single crewed units, staffed by two male officers in their thirties had arrived, thus allowing their colleagues to return to the station in Liskeard to process the paperwork.

"I'm sure they will both be back soon," the young female

PC had said reassuringly. She'd filled out all of the paperwork under the watchful supervision of her older colleague who jumped in once in a while with a question that she'd either forgotten or had failed to get to yet. Carol got the impression that she was still a little green around the gills and likely not long out of whatever training they gave to the boys and girls in blue nowadays.

With the laborious form complete, the officers had then searched the inside of The Old Chapel. Rob led them from room to room as Carol had followed behind, feeling as if she were in a dream and observing herself from the outside. But this was no dream and no matter how hard she wished, Carol knew there was no waking up from it, no wash of relief as you rose from sleep and realised that everything was actually alright.

"What I don't understand," Rob had said to the older cop, *"is how they got out? I mean, it's as if they just went and vanished into thin air!"*

"Kids," the officer had exclaimed, slapping his palms down onto his knees. *"They can be quite ingenious at times."* His accent unmistakably local, Cornish and quite broad. *"I'm sure when they get found or turn up they'll be able to shed some light on it. I remember we had this one gurl in Liskeard who was always goin' missing. Right little troublemaker she was and getting herself into all kinds of bother. Her mother locked her in the house after six each evening and hid the keys. Wanted to stop her keep getting out and into trouble, see. But she kept right on getting out almost every night. I think I musta run a pen dry the number of times I took missing person reports for that gurl. Turned out that she'd taken an imprint of her mother's key in her little brother's play-doh and had gone and got one of her own cut."* He'd smiled and shook his head in disbelief at his own story. *"Like I said they can be ingenious."*

"No disrespect officer," Carol had said, hearing how far away her voice sounded in her own head as she'd spoken. *"But my Ellie is not a trouble maker, she's never gone*

missing before and she'd never do anything to put her brother in danger. She's a good student, off to Warwick at the end of the summer to study phycology. Now I don't know how they got out, or if this wretched place has somehow swallowed them up whole, but I do feel that something very wrong has happened to them."

The PC had nodded his head as she spoke, encouraged her not to jump to conclusions and like his female colleague he felt sure that they'd both turn up just fine and wondering what all the fuss was about. That was at the start of the search, in the games room. Carol had to hand it to them, they were thorough, no closet was left unchecked and no bed left unlooked under. By the time they'd finished with the lower level even a roach skulking in the darkest corner of a cupboard would have been found.

On the mezzanine level, they'd worked their way from room to room. As they'd reached Ellie's room there had been a knock at the front door. Carol had excused herself and gone to answer it. Stood pensively inside the front porch, on the stone stoop were Lucinda and Seth turned out in jeans, polo shirts, and sturdy footwear. Accompanying them was a couple who she'd spoken to briefly at the barbeque, Sarah and Bob Robey. Sarah's enviable long blond hair, that had been down and about as silky as a silk bedsheet was up in a tight bun and the skin of her face, pulled a little tighter by the how tightly her hair was fixed, looked like marble.

"Lucinda told us the news," Sarah had said her eyes wide and grey as if in disbelief at the situation. Reaching out she'd taken hold of Carol's cold hands. *"If they're in the woods we will find them,"* she'd reassured. *"There are others helping, too. The Piersons are heading in from their place at the other end of the village and Greg and Lucy Wanderson are doing the same. I just wanted to come with Lucinda and see you myself. I can't even imagine how out of your minds with worry you must be right now."*

Carol had smiled, an empty smile, the kind you give

someone whose intentions are in the right place, but you know can't possibly understand what you're feeling. *"Thank you,"* her distant self had said as if she were on autopilot.

"Sarah and Bob are going to head in the direction of Culdon, but drift toward my place. Seth and I will head Culdon way as well, but we will deviate more toward the Howgates, they live next cottage down. I tried to call but I think Alf already went back to London for the weekend. He's some hot-shot banker in the investment world up there. That man's a workaholic, and Erica - his wife, must be out spending some of that money he seems so good at earning." Lucinda had smiled warmly at her, *"Don't worry, though. Between those of us that are here, we can fan out and cover most of the woods even if it takes all day. You just sit tight here and be ready with the cuddles when they get back."* And with that they'd gone, walking off in single file around the lone patrol car and to the back of The Old Chapel. Carol had walked like a zombie to the kitchen and watched as they'd reached the tree line and entered the murky woodland, it swallowed them and within seconds they'd vanished from her sight, like ghostly figures being consumed by mist.

Back in the entrance lobby, she'd left the door open so anyone turning up wouldn't feel compelled to knock. By the time she'd reached Ellie's room, the two officers were busy checking through her daughter's clothes while Rob had watched on, a look of helplessness on his face. A look that said he wanted to do something, anything that might be of use, but what else was there that he could do?

"Can either of you remember what clothes she had with her?" The female officer had asked opening drawer after drawer and finding them void of clothing. Carol had told her that Ellie had been pretty much living out of her suitcase and then having retrieved it from the walk-in wardrobe proceeded to go through it with her. She couldn't be sure, but it looked as if there were no clothes missing.

"As we told you, she was wearing her Ramones T-shirt and black leggings, with red and white rather tatty looking Converse," Rob had told them a hint of desperation in his voice.

Despite an extensive search of Ellie's stuff, they couldn't locate the clothes she'd worn to the barbeque, nor her favourite Converse trainers. Everything else her daughter would normally carry and never leave behind was there, her phone, purse and favourite Holister canvass handbag. The officers had pawed through her purse with interest and both Carol and Rob had agreed that the inventory of thirty pounds, a National Insurance card, Provisional Driver's Licence, and her newly opened NatWest student bank account card were all it should contain. The female officer had leaned on the oak chest of drawers and taken down her account number and made a note in ridiculously neat handwriting that it appeared neither Ellie nor Henry had any money on them.

In Ellie's room, they also found the clothes Henry had been wearing the night before in a pile on the floor. A pair of his PJs were missing, though. Next, in his room, they found that just like Ellie's Converse, his Clarks trainers were missing. Carol could be sure with much more conviction that no more of his clothes had gone as unlike Ellie's pull along Tripp case, she'd packed his Dino-Trunki the day before they'd left. Seeing his things laid out on the bed that way, his Ben and Holly's Little Kingdom T-shirt, (one of his favourites), his cords that were a year younger in size than his actual age due to him being a little on the short side, made her eyes well up. The image caused her to fight the tears that seemed too eager and willing to fall. She'd wanted to pick them up, hold them to her face and breathe in the soft smell of him that would no doubt be ingrained into the material, but she knew if she did then the tears would fall, and once they started, she wasn't sure they'd stop. Only hours had passed since she'd discovered them missing but it felt like days, and with each passing minute that they were gone the foreboding within her grew, one intrinsically linked to the other. In the past, she'd seen tearful mothers and fathers on TV press conferences appealing for news of a missing child. Watching them had always made her feel sick, made her feel deep pity for the distraught parents, for you could only hold true empathy for others in a situation like that if you were a parent yourself. If God forbid they didn't come back, if hours turned into days and days turned to weeks she wasn't sure she'd cope. People always said it was the not knowing that got you, that not knowing drove you mad, and they were right.

"Mrs. Harrison," the male officer had said. "Do you think your daughter would have gone out in the same clothes she wore last night, or is it possible that she left with your son whilst you and your husband were asleep?"

"Went and left where?" Rob had jumped in, saving her from trying to process the answer. "As we've told you, Ellie doesn't drive. It's heck of a walk to the next village and save for a pub there is nothing there. It's goodness knows how far to the nearest train station and as you've seen neither of them has any money or means of paying for anything. There is no way in hell that my daughter would have gone anywhere with her brother at night, she dotes on that boy. I can also vouch for the fact that there is no way in the world that she would have gone out this morning without either a shower or change of clothes, or without leaving us a note. Lest we not forget here that no one has yet figured out just how the bloody hell she, – they got out."

The officer had let the outburst wash over him, no doubt he'd heard that and much, much worse more times than he'd had hot dinners. "I'm sorry, Mr. Harrison," he'd said flatly. "These are just questions I need to ask. Thankfully there are no signs of a struggle or disturbance. Now I know it's no consolation but in a way, you need to be thankful that your daughter is missing with your son. She is an adult in the eyes of the law, and despite what her agenda is I'm sure she *is taking care of him. Still, for now, and until I have checked with supervision no one else is to go in the room she was using, or the one your son was staying in, is that clear?"*

"Agenda," Rob had blurted, his face turning red. *"Are you treating my daughter as a suspect?"*

The officer had held up his hands and bit at his lower lip, he took a deep breath and said, *"I never said that. For now, they are both being treated as missing. It's just - we need to look at the most likely possibility, that's all. Your wife said she argued with your daughter last night, then this morning you both wake up and they have gone."*

"All families argue," Rob had defended his voice almost a growl.

Carol could both see and understand the angle the officer was taking. To an outsider looking in the most obvious conclusion to reach was that Ellie *had* taken Henry, possibly out of spite for the argument. A little payback. But the argument hadn't been that bad, however, they didn't know that, they'd not been there, they had to take whatever she or Rob told them as gospel. And how many times had the officer's been lied to? A lot she bet, why should they believe them?

Rob had taken a deep breath and let it out through clenched teeth, it had produced a hissing sound like gas escaping from the cranked cap of a soda bottle. *"I know my daughter,"* he'd said in a low voice. *"And my son for that matter. She would never do a thing like that. Ever."*

The officer's face had worn a frown that Carol had taken as one of suspicion, she'd glanced to his younger colleague who'd looked a bit awkward and uncomfortable with the direct line of questioning being undertaken by her more experienced colleague. In fact, she'd looked like she wanted to be just about anywhere else other than stood next to him.

"I mean no offence by what I say. I just need to cover every eventuality, that's all."

And with that, he'd shut the door to Ellie's room, produced a small roll of stickers each bearing a sequential reference number from a pocket in his body armour, then proceeded to affix one to the door and frame so that if opened the seal would break. Having secured it he took a copy of the number in a notebook and then moved to Henry's room where he went through the same routine.

As the four off them had headed downstairs to the kitchen the first of the single crewed units who were to relieve their colleagues arrived.

———

"MR. AND MRS. HARRSION?" Carol looked up taking her head from her hands. The man had approached from the westerly staircase, she'd been lost in her own mind going over the visit of the first officers at scene and hadn't seen him approach.

Carol nodded automatically and said, "Yes."

"My name is Detective Inspector Samuels." The inspector was dressed in a sharp and relatively expensive looking grey suit, his jawline defined a face that looked handsome in a slightly rugged way and was festooned by a short and neatly trimmed beard that matched his dark hair. He wasn't an overly tall man, five ten maybe five eleven at most, much like her husband yet he seemed to exuberate physical presence. He reached where Carol sat; Rob was next to her with his hand on her back rubbing it the same way a parent might console a distressed child who'd just grazed a knee. As he stood before them Rob got up and shook his hand, his grip firm and sure.

"I wish I could say it was a pleasure to meet you," Rob said solemnly.

The inspector chuckled and said, "Well usually when people come in contact with the police it's because something bad has happened. Generally, whilst our presence might be needed it's not always welcome. May I take a seat?"

Rob gestured him to the recliner where he'd slept the night before.

"Firstly," Inspector Samuels said as he sat down. "Let me assure you that we are doing all that we can to find your son and daughter."

"We appreciate it," Rob said. His voice sounded empty and Carol felt for him. While she'd all but locked herself away in her mind her husband had remained strong, answering the questions of the first officers on scene when she'd been little more than a ghost.

The inspector lifted his arm, so the sleeve of his suit jacket slid back enough to expose his watch, it was a Casio, one of those retro looking digital types that had been popular in the eighties. He glanced at it and said, "So you noticed your daughter, Ellie, and son, Henry missing quarter to ten this morning, a little over five hours ago?"

Carol nodded but didn't speak.

"Can you just run me through things, as precisely as you can from the time you woke to the time you called the police."

"Look," began Rob sounding frustrated. "I appreciate what you're doing, I – we, really do, but I have just gone over all this with the two officers who came out first."

Inspector Samuels smiled sympathetically and nodded his head, "I understand that it might be frustrating for you, but I didn't get time to speak with PC Welling and PC Stephens fully before I came over. I know the basic facts but in order for me to assess the situation I need the unabridged version."

"I woke up here in the lounge, on this sofa," Carol began, lifting her gaze to meet the inspector's eyes and mentally preparing herself to go through it all again. If it needed telling it was best done and out the way. Inspector Samuels' eyes were a deep hazel and met her gaze right back, fully engaging her, leaving her in no doubt that he was consuming every word she spoke.

"The first thing I noticed was the quiet, it just seemed, I don't know – wrong. Have you got kids, Inspector?"

"Two," he nodded. "Seven and ten, both girls. Kids and quiet don't go in the same sentence unless you're shouting at them to be quiet," he smiled.

"Then I noticed the time, it was late. Later than I normally sleep, and the fact that I was on the sofa. I listened for a few seconds, but I couldn't hear him." Carol couldn't bring herself to say her son's name, for she feared that if she spoke it, she'd lose the partial composure she'd managed to gain.

"Henry," Inspector Samuels said for her.

"If he's awake before me I can always hear the cartoons or whatever he is watching on his tablet. I went straight to his room but then remembered that he'd bunked in with his sister. Sleeping alone in an old building gave him nightmares." *Had they been nightmares?* Carol asked herself, wishing that she'd paid more attention to Ellie. *"Something is wrong with this place, Mum. You might not be able to feel it, but I can."* Her daughter's words raced through her head and she felt emotional pain flash through her like a hot lance. "The room was empty, and I know it might sound stupid, but I just had this feeling."

"A mother's intuition," Inspector Samuels agreed.

"You could call it that, Inspector - yes. I rushed through the building and checked every room, then checked outside thinking that they might be in the garden. I then went to the road at the top of the drive."

"Can you tell me about the keys?" he asked, leaning forward.

"I think it's the stone, but it keeps the place quite cool," Carol began, her voice so low the inspector had to lean further forward in order to hear. "Cooler than the night air at the moment anyway, so there is no need to open any windows, they were all locked. Your colleagues double checked that when they searched the place. The front and back door key are on the same ring, we had it hung on the peg by the front door. There is a spare back door key hung in the kitchen too, on a hook in the frame. Both doors were locked, and the keys were still on the hooks. We'd hung the main bunch up last night when we got home just before nine. What troubles me more is that the deadbolts were still in place, too."

"I see," he said and rubbed a hand across his forehead pondering the puzzle.

"It seems so impossible that they could just vanish from the building without unlocking the door and taking the key or opening a window, but I fooled myself that I must have missed something, that they had to have gone out somehow, but the more I think about it the more it bothers me."

"I spoke very briefly to PC Welling on the radio, he said that the only clothes missing are the ones your daughter wore last night and a pair of your son's pyjamas, shoe wise we are missing her red Converse All-Stars and a pair of Clarks trainers, the kind with lights in the sole that flash when walked on?"

"That's right," Rob cut in and she felt thankful for him taking over. "PC Welling, is that the male officer?"

"Yes, Brain Welling."

"He all but accused my daughter of abducting our son and leaving with him during the night. I mean she didn't even take her bag or her phone!"

"I apologise if some of the questions or inferences he drew upset you. I have known Brian for the last two years, since transferring from Sussex. He's what we call a career PC. Front-line from the day he signed up and will be until the day he collects his pension. What our front-line officers deal with every day can breed a fair bit of cynicism, comes with the job I'm afraid. He's a good officer and I can assure you he meant no offence."

"It's okay," Rob said looking down at the floor. "It was just a bit hard to swallow on a day like this."

"I'm going to be straight with you both as if I were

sat where you are now that's how I'd want it. This is a somewhat unusual case," Inspector Samuels began, sitting back in his seat and placing his palms on his knees. "We deal with missing persons every day, but most of them have either mental health issues, financial difficulties, or trouble at home, one thing or another that leads to them going. From what I can see none of those usual factors apply here. No history of domestic abuse or drug use, no previous missing reports. For all intents and purposes a happy, stable and healthy home." He paused and smiled supportively at them both. "At this time, we are grading both your son and daughter as high risk missing. That's because of your son's age, the circumstances around their disappearance, the fact it's out of character and from what we can tell they have no known means of financially supporting themselves." Inspector Samuels paused again seemingly making sure they were on board with what he was saying. "To break it down in layman's terms that means we will throw everything we have at this until we find them. I have a drone unit on route from Plymouth and NPAS, that's the National Police Air Service, lifting from Bournemouth. We have a unit at Exeter, but the aircraft is in for service, hence the delay. The Dorset craft will refuel at Exeter then head here to back up the drone unit. On top of that, I have requested a Thames Valley unit to check your home address. I will need details of any neighbours who have a key, other relatives and friends in the area, stuff like that."

"Not a problem, the Balsdon's at number sixty have a spare," said Rob. "I can get you their number If needed. As for the other details, we don't really have any other family in the area save for Carol's father who is in care. My parents are in New Zealand."

"Good, that's just in case your daughter has headed home with her brother, or gone to a friend. I know it's unlikely, but we have to check. I have also sent details to BTP, British Transport Police, and we have notified local taxi and bus firms. I trust you have recent pictures of both your son and daughter on one of your phones?"

Rob nodded, "PC Welling already had me send them to your control room via email."

Inspector Samuels clasped his hands together, "Excellent," he said. "They will disseminate those images to the likes of BTP and ensure they are shown on briefings here and all surrounding counties. If there is still no sign of them in the next few hours I want us to start looking at press releases, with your permission of course."

Rob sighed and said, "Whatever it takes, but let's hope it doesn't come to that."

"The lady who caretakes the building, Lucinda, and a few of the villagers are in the woods now looking for them," Carol added, meeting the inspector's eyes once more. "She thought if they'd gone exploring in there this morning then they'd easily get lost."

"That's good, the more hands on deck the better, so to speak. Let's hope it proves to be that simple," he cleared his throat and then added. "I have requested a dog unit, that is also coming from Plymouth. Unfortunately, the area has seen a lot of foot traffic, so it might not help, but anything is worth a try."

"Like I said," Rob began, placing his hand once more on his wife's back. "We appreciate it."

"I have also asked for digital media trained officers to come and check your daughter's phone, her Facebook, stuff like that."

"All that is great," Carol said with a wan smile. "But it still doesn't explain how they went missing in a building that was locked and secure."

Inspector Samuels frowned casting deep furrows into the lines of his forehead, "No, it doesn't. I'm being honest when I say that at first look, I would have to agree with PC Welling's initial assumption, that your daughter left with your son. It seems the most likely explanation, and we usually find that the most plausible explanation is often the answer."

"Ockham's razor," Rob said.

"Indeed, but something about the whole situation doesn't sit right with me, the keys are causing me concern. Does anyone else have a key that you know of?"

"I'm sure the Reeds have a spare, they own The Old Chapel, but they live in Wiltshire. Lucinda, the caretaker may have a spare but there is no reason that she'd give it to my daughter or come here in the middle of the night, and it doesn't explain how they got out with the doors deadbolted from the inside."

Samuels looked at them. His face appeared momentarily troubled by the riddle, "I'm sure there must be a rational explanation for it," he said. "One we are not seeing but we will speak to the Horners regardless."

"I've been telling myself that all morning," Rob commented as a light knocking came from the front door.

"Carol," a voice called up from below. The three of them stood and Carol followed her husband and the inspector to the foyer. "There you are," said Lucinda. Her face looked damp with perspiration and Seth who stood just behind her had visible damp patches around the collar of his white polo shirt and under the arms. "Sarah and Bob have gone on home, they guessed you'd have enough distractions without them barging in as well."

"This is the lady we mentioned," Rob said turning to Inspector Samuels who joined him in the large arch of a doorway. "Lucinda Horner, she is the caretaker." And then turning to Lucinda he said, "I'm guessing there has been no sign of them?"

"We have covered the woods as best we could, must have walked miles," her face creased with concern. "Not a single sign I'm afraid."

"We really appreciate it," Rob said as Carol sobbed.

Lucinda looked at her and stepping forward she

placed a supportive hand on Carol's shoulder. "I really don't know what else we can do."

"You've done more than enough," Rob told her. "Head home and we will call you if there is any news."

Lucinda nodded as a third marked police vehicle crunched its way onto the forecourt. This one had the words **Police Dogs** across the back windows in bright fluorescent blue. "Please do, we will get out of your way," she concluded.

The arrival of the dog unit prompted the two uniformed officers to alight from the air-conditioned comfort of the patrol car they'd been sat in, the other sat empty in the shade of the trees with the windows down next to a grey Vauxhall Astra that Carol guessed was the inspector's. Carol watched as the officers shook hands and relayed very succinctly what they knew about the job and shared a quick war story of a burglary they'd all recently been to where the handler's dog, or the Mighty Thor Paw as they referred to him, had found a burglar hiding under an ice cream van and practically dragged him from cover by his leg whilst he'd been screaming about police brutality.

"Well you know Thor," the dog handler, a stocky looking guy in his fifties with greying hair and a reddening face said. "His favourite food next to kibble is burglar." From the way he spoke Carol had him pegged as being ex-military. Air Force, Army or Navy she couldn't guess but his mannerisms and speech had undeniably been ingrained by one of the three. Greetings out the way he turned to the back of his specially adapted Ford Focus and lifted the boot lid.

"Boss," the dog handler said addressing Inspector Samuels as he noticed the three of them in the door.

"Greg, good to see you, thanks for making the trip."

"You know how it is," he said jovially and in a fashion of someone who had the enviable position of being able to leave all this behind him when he'd done his job. "The radio instructs, and I respond. Is there anything I need to know?"

Inspector Samuels joined the dog handler to the rear of his car, "The area has been subject to foot traffic. Some of the locals arranged a search party and went into the woods. They're out now so it's all yours. I expect the scent will have become too contaminated, though. If that is indeed where they went."

"I figured the chance of getting a track now are pretty slim. We are spread so thin that by the time I get to where I'm needed I may as well have not bothered."

Inspector Samuels nodded in understanding, "Just do what you can do."

"That's all we can do, Boss," the dog handler said in agreement as he cranked open the inner door to his mobile kennel. Carol expected to see a fearsome German Shepherd leap from the back of the vehicle, the Mighty Thor-Paw in all his powerful K9 glory, however after a few seconds there was still no Thor to behold.

"Get your arse out here Thor," the handler said clicking his fingers and pointing at the deck. Carol heard a whimper that seemed more befitting of a frightened spaniel than that of a K9 crime fighter. Curiosity drew her from the doorframe and toward the handler's van where she joined Inspector Samuels who had a confused look on his face.

"What's up with the Mighty Thor-Paw?" one of the uniformed officers asked. "Heat got to him?"

"Thor, now!" the handler commanded in a tone that could make an SAS squadron jump to attention. Carol peered into the shaded light of the purpose-built kennel. Cool air-conditioned air seeped from the van, it's icy fingers of chilled air tickled at her skin briefly before the heat of the day consumed them.

Carol saw that Thaw was indeed a massive looking German Shepherd who on a normal day would strike fear into the heart of any burglar he chased down. Only right now Thor didn't look brave or in the slightest bit vicious, he was cowered in the back of his kennel, small whimpers coming from his clenched jaw. His legs trembled, and his tail was slung up between his legs as if he'd just been scolded for taking a shit on the best rug in the house. The dog handler looked at his animal partner in confusion, which soon turned to frustration and he reached into the kennel to pull him out. Thor was having none of it, he snapped at his human master's hand and backed himself so tightly against the wall of his kennel that it looked as if he were trying to mould into the painted grey metal it was made from.

"Well if that ain't the weirdest thing I've seen all day I don't know what is," the handler said as a trickle of yellowish urine began to flow from beneath the trembling animal. It flowed in a straight line until it reached the edge of the kennel where it ran down over the bumper and onto the shingle in a steady waterfall of acrid smelling piss.

Looking at the frightened animal Ellie's words ran through Carol's head once again, *"Something is up with this place, Mum. You may not be able to feel it, but I can."*

CHAPTER 20

SCOTTY WATCHED AS THE LIGHTS OF COWES HARBOUR slowly and gradually disintegrated into the falling dusk of Saturday evening. The warmth of the day had induced a shimmering haze that sat over the Solent, one that looked like a thin smog. The Island almost seemed to sit behind a veil, one that grew thicker the further away he drew and made the lights of the distant boats and houses appear to flicker epileptically as if at any moment they might just blink out.

Through his hands, which clutched the side rail of the top outer deck, he felt a vibration run through the car ferry as its engines laboured against the swell of a departing cruise ship. The hulk of Voyager of The Seas slid past, dwarfing the Red Funnel ferry and making Scotty feel as if the two-hundred and twenty car capacity ferry were no bigger than a rowing boat. He looked up, the way someone might look up at a person stood atop a tall building and felt some envy toward the newly embarked passengers who lined the decks waving enthusiastically, and probably a little smugly. The service was busy, packed even and a few of the folk on the outer deck with him, whose trip high seas only spanned the eleven miles between Cowes and the Red Funnel terminal at the Town Quay of Southampton all waved back, Scotty too. When on such a ferry crossing it was kind of an unwritten rule that you had to, it's just the way it was. There would be no enjoying fine dining for those on the ferry, it had one small galley-style eatery where you could buy an overpriced but not overly good tasting meal, usually fish and chips. There was a bar and a small coffee kiosk to purchase drinks at an equally inflated price to that of the food. There was no point moaning about it, though. If you'd not had the foresight to bring your own refreshments and you couldn't last the hour-long crossing without food or drink you didn't exactly have a lot of other options.

Lowering his raised hand, he realised just how close the towering hull of the liner seemed. Looking up at the passengers he could make out the colour of people's trousers, see women in expensive looking evening wear, no doubt bought just for that very occasion. Many gripped cocktails or bottles of beer, likely sold at a price even more inflated than the coffee onboard the ferry.

Scotty watched the passing ship almost transfixed by how gracefully and easily she cut through the water, which was as still as glass. Slowly she began to fade into that haze, as if the boat were no more than the idea of a boat, then it vanished altogether.

The Esso oil refinery blotted the westerly shore. The eight-mile-long oil processing behemoth looked more like a city in the failing light of this hazy evening, it's lit chimneys more like skyscrapers. Scotty had been to New York once with the band for a radio interview a few years back, that was during the time when Summer Sun had charted both here and the USA and some thought that their band, The Island, would be the next big thing to come out of the UK's music industry; that was just a few months before the whole thing got shit-canned about as fast as the Unexplained UK Show. Scotty mused, and not for the first time that day about how his life had been full of almosts. Almost made it in the music industry, almost made it as one of the co-hosts of a paranormal show. Almost! But not quite.

Consolation prize for you, son, a pat on the back and a well done for being one of life's many runners-up.

Back then, when the group had arrived into a bustling Newark airport full of building excitement at what the future might hold, the distant lights of the Big Apple twinkling in the failing evening light had not been a million miles away from how the lights of the refinery looked now. Soon, when night fell, the refiners and cooling towers would be hidden by darkness and the lights would be all that you could see. When that happened, it morphed even more and if you didn't know the area you might believe that a sprawling city lay there and not one of the country's largest oil processing plants. It seemed strange that hidden behind that vast industrial centre lay the New Forest with its miles of open tracks and free-roaming ponies. Tourists, or grockles as they were affectionately called by many Southerners, loved to stop at precarious locations on the Forest's narrow roads to try and snap a shot of some dobbin munching the hedgerows, another unwritten rule or behaviour, just like the waving. When you thought about it, as Scotty often did contemplate such things, the area was a juxtaposition of marine, city, industry and sprawling countryside all thrown into one big melting pot.

Killing time, as well as enjoying the view – he still enjoyed taking in the sights from the ferry despite having done the crossing more times than he cared to remember. He sauntered to the starboard side of the ship and looked out to his east. Royal Victoria Country Park was now level with them, it had once been the site of a large hospital, used to treat injured troops brought back from the front lines of Europe during the war. Almost all the hospital had been demolished back in sixty-six. The site was now open parkland where families could relax, bike ride or walk various woodland trails. It being the summer they often had small rides for the kiddies or a bouncy castle sat in the middle of the green, where once a hospital ward had stood. Now, all that remained of the once famous Netley Hospital was its religious heart, a chapel that had no doubt been sanctum for those in their final hours or for those who had seen loved ones return from the horrors of war, only to have the Reaper cruelly snatch them away on home soil, claimed by death in the sprawling wards of that once magnificent, but now gone forever building. Maybe the odd soldier had sat on its pews and wept, looking for God again, having experienced things in battle that a loving creator should never let happen, things born from the greatest gift that God had supposedly given to his children, free will. Scotty wasn't a believer in that particular dogma, he didn't buy any religion totally. He wasn't an atheist, more an agnostic that held the belief that there was something more to this universe than he understood, yet at the same time accepted that maybe it wasn't his place to know it all in this life.

Musing over such unanswerable questions as he often did he took in the chapel's cupola. It rose into that hazy evening sky that minute by minute birthed the coming night. Lights bathed the emerald coloured dome and their glow gave the top a beacon-like appearance. The building steered his thoughts to his destination. It would be undoubtedly smaller than the grand looking chapel that lay out there on the eastern shore, but had it been a place of salvation like this had? Scotty wasn't so sure. His mind ran over the earlier conversation with Mike before he'd learned of the missing kids. Well, one missing kid and one girl of eighteen, the pair seemingly having just upped and vanished as if into thin air.

After the Friday evening call, and then having spoken to Mike and Tara via Skype earlier that morning, Scotty had wanted to head down to Cornwall and get started. Whilst Tara was the location researcher, he'd done a little digging himself and had managed to hit nothing but stone, just as she had done. He felt sure that the mysterious Old Chapel, now a luxurious holiday home, had secrets, but the kind that couldn't be learned from the comfort of your lounge. Some places required you to be on the ground and at the location before they'd allow you to learn their arcane background.

Much to Scotty's frustration Mike had insisted that in order to keep costs down he'd not even consider heading Cornwall bound until the Harrison's either checked out before the end of their stay, like so many purportedly had done, or made it to the end of their stay and went home happy. By three PM that had all changed.

As Mike spoke and relayed the implausible fact that the Harrison kids had somehow blinked out of a locked and secure building, he'd walked from his kitchen, where he'd been preparing a carbolishious dinner of tuna and pasta, and was behind his desk and firing his laptop to life. Before the conversation had ended, he'd booked a single crossing as he didn't know when he'd be back. Earlier crossings had been full, it was the school holidays after all, but the later evening ones had slots available and he'd managed to book himself and his VW T4 in for the sailing leaving East Cowes at nine-thirty PM. Later than he would have liked but save for going via Portsmouth or Lymington there wasn't a lot he could do. He needed time anyway to get the kit in order, check it, double check it and load it into his van.

There were times that Scotty hated living on an island, times when he felt cut off and remote, even though if needed he could be on the mainland inside half an hour using the Red Jet service, a fast catamaran style boat that raced foot passengers back and forth from the Island to the mainland all day, three hundred and sixty-four days a year. There were times when he'd almost upped sticks, as his mum called it, and moved to the mainland, but he could never bring himself to do it because the truth was, he loved where he lived, and it wasn't that bad. If you had to live on one of the islands off mainland Britain there were plenty that were more that were a bitch to get to than the good old Isle of Wight, even if mainlanders did rib you about in-breeding and being married to your sister.

Being on the Island had actually worked in his favour, it was the start of the school holidays, and whilst many of its residents were keen to get off what he affectionately referred to as The Rock, more were wanting to come the other way. He had no doubt that in Southampton there would still be lines of caravan towing and roof-box toting cars queuing to get a space on the turnaround service.

Scotty lifted his phone from his pocket and checked his Youtube channel. His Moot Hall EVP clip had clocked up just over ten thousand views since the previous evening. He scanned quickly to the comments section and soon found one that read, **Fake as FCUK**, its poster opting to use the popular logo that had appeared on many French Connection UK T-shirts back in the early two-thousands. The comment had a hundred likes and its own thread of keyboard warriors bitching about how it was either real or so obviously a fake that you'd have to be retarded to believe it. Then you had the Jesus jumpers who swore it was demons and meddling with that kinda stuff was tantamount to selling your soul to the devil himself.

In all honesty, Scotty didn't overly give a shit what they wrote, he knew it was real, he knew all too well that launching it into the snake pit of a public domain such as YouTube was bound to generate opinions from all sides of the spectrum. As long as people watched it and occasionally clicked on the inlaid ads he was happy.

Smiling at some of the comments he closed application and text Mike, **Be docking at Southampton in ten**, he hit send as the ferry passed what had once been Berth 44, where, in 1912 a certain ill-fated White Star liner had taken on board just over two thousand two hundred souls, fifteen hundred and three of which had signed their own death warrants by setting foot on the doomed luxury liner.

Scotty tucked his iPhone into his pocket and headed inside and down toward the vehicle deck. In a few minutes the call would go out and the free-for-all of passengers trying to get to their cars would begin.

Five minutes later he was in his T4 waiting to disembark. Whilst working for the council it had been his work van, having left for greener pastures, pastures that now weren't looking quite so green, he'd converted the back into a camper. It was a functional conversion over a posh one. His van now boasted two single beds that became a double if the centre table was used to bridge the gap between the two seats and the backrests placed together. There was a small fridge and gas cooker. He'd even fitted a twenty-four-inch LCD TV screen into the bulkhead. The van was now designed for a life on the road. In the few months it had taken to film the one and only series of Unexplained UK he'd enjoyed many a night camped out near to the location of the investigation. The channel had booked hotels and the offer of a room was always there, but there was something about the feeling of being out there in the van, self-sufficient and on his own, a sense of freedom.

The rear sleeping area of his van was now stacked with many sturdy looking black and silver metallic flight cases purchased by Switchback TV and that now, unless they really chased them, were unlikely to go back. In one large case on wheels were two four channel DVR CCTV systems that he'd adapted to be fully portable, and their cameras. The base units could run four channels at thirty frames-per-second per channel and the footage then stored on a terabyte hard drive. The cameras operated in full HD, even producing unrivalled clarity in IR mode, as such they recorded a tremendous amount of data, hence the need for the terabyte of storage per unit. Four of those cameras had even been adapted to record in full spectrum, a pricey little adaption that had been done for the team by a specialist in the States. The eight cameras themselves were not wireless, wireless was freely available and did take a shit load less time to set up, but when using delicate equipment to measure electromagnetics the less interference you had from radio waves the better. For that reason, each camera ran off a one-hundred-meter spool of good old traditional yet top quality RG59 cable. In a matching smaller case by its side were four audio boosters with four sets of Sony over-ear headphones. If the case were opened each piece of equipment would be presented to you sat snugly and neatly in cut out foam to keep it both safe and in one place. The audio boosters resembled miniature versions of the boom mikes that TV sound men carried. When rigged to the Sony headphones they amplified the background sound and allowed the user to hear EVP real time, or that was the theory anyway. They'd yet to yield any solid results but Scotty felt confident that given time, they would. In another case of the same size were three MEL meters. MEL meters were electromagnetic field testers and temperature readers developed for the sole purpose of paranormal research. There were various models available, some with additional features. The kind that Scotty carried were one of the more original and basic models that measured temperature and EMF, electromagnetic field disturbance. He'd opted for them purposely with the belief that the fewer whistles and bells they had on them the less they were likely to go wrong. The MEL meter had been developed some years ago by a grieving father called Gary Galka, an engineer whose daughter Melissa had been killed in a car crash, hence the name MEL. Like Mike he'd been looking for the same answer, the one that no one could answer but countless tried, nonetheless. Accompanying the MEL meters were four of the more traditional K2 meters that fundamentally did the same thing but only measured electromagnetic fluctuations on a series of lights, as opposed to the more accurate digital display of the MEL. K2 meters were popular with TV investigators as the light show was more noticeable to cameras recording in low light than the digits on the MEL. Sadly, whilst more visually appealing they were more prone to interference.

The next case, a smaller one that looked more like the kind of thing a beautician would carry, housed three Sony digital voice recorders and three specially adapted full spectrum portable video cameras. Two GoPro Hero 5's were fitted snugly into the foam in the corner of the case for good measure. They were about as much use as a chocolate teapot in low light but for daytime walk arounds they were the go-to bit of kit. None of the cases carried any of the fringe science equipment seen on a few of the more well-known American shows. Scotty wasn't a believer in things such as the Frank's Box, a device that in essence was no more than a detuned radio that scanned the commercial frequencies constantly. Occasionally in the static, you'd hear the disjointed voices of far-off broadcasts. Once in a while, they seemed to articulate meaningful answers to a question, but not often enough for Scotty to believe it was anything more than coincidence. To Scotty, Mike, and Tara the device was far too dependent on the influence of things from the world of the living to ever be a meaningful and reliable way of speaking with the dead. The most valuable pieces of his kit sat by him, in the footwell of his T4, wedged where there was no chance they could move. The two FLIR thermal imaging cameras belonged, like the cases and the full spectrum cameras, to Switchback. Valued at just shy of two-thousand pounds each they were worth just about as much combined as the rest of the kit put together. Scotty was in no doubt that over the next week someone from the channel would be chasing their return and when they did he'd send them Mike's way.

Finally, the roll-on-roll-off ramp dropped and the first of the vehicles began to file slowly off the ferry. Scotty was relatively near the front and he was soon creeping forward. The ramp offered a familiar sounding **CLUNK-CLUNK** as he rolled onto solid ground.

Ten minutes later he was on the outskirts of Southampton, where the urban started to give way to the open land of the New Forest. His phone rang and cut off the radio, he'd not really been listening to it and suddenly realised that he didn't even know what had been playing. Leaning forward he pinched a button to answer the call.

"Scotty, it's Mike," came the voice through the VWs sound system. The base box he'd built in below one of the seats gave Mike's voice a deep guttural sound.

"This is the call where you tell me they've turned up and to head home, am I right?" Scotty asked hoping the kids had turned up and yet not wanting to head home.

"Wrong," Mike said gravely. "I've just taken a call from Sue Reed, she just took a call from Carol, the mother. It looks like the place has been completely shut down and cordoned off. Only plod and their CSI teams in and out. The Harrisons are being put up in a hotel in Liskeard. The Premier Inn I believe."

"Have they found something?" Scotty asked, feeling his pulse rise a few beats per minute.

"Nothing, not a damn thing. That's the problem, the local police don't know what they've got. Lost kids? Abduction by a stranger? Abduction by a family member? As in the daughter, or," he paused as if not wanting to say it.

"Something worse?" Scotty filled in.

"Right," Mike said as if glad he'd not had to go there himself. "So, they go on damage limitation, worst case scenario. For now, and the foreseeable that place will be treated as a crime scene. It means we won't get a look in for a good few days or more, but it's ours when they hand it back."

"No change to the original plan then?"

"One, I've cancelled the reservation at the Saltash Travel Lodge and booked us into the same hotel as the Harrisons."

"Can you send me the new postcode, I will be stopping for food and fuel this side of Bournemouth, I'll change the destination."

"Good, we are going to be there maybe an hour ahead of you. When you arrive if you just wanna get your head down then no problem, it'll be late. We can convene in the morning."

"And tomorrow?"

"As in am I going to talk to the Harrisons?"

"Yeah."

"I – don't – know," Mike said slowly. "I think we have to play this one by ear. I want to get a feel for the situation and the only way we can do that is by being there. I have a feeling the place is going to be a media circus if those kids aren't found overnight, this is apt to be the biggest news story of the summer. The last thing that family needs is the media getting a sniff that a team of ghost hunters is checking the place out."

"I hate that term," Scotty said as if he had a nasty taste in his mouth. They weren't Ghost Hunters, they were investigators. "But I hear you," he conceded. "It's the parents I feel sorry for," he winced having said it, remembering the hell Mike had been through and hoping that he'd not freshened up a wound. There was a pensive silence from the other end of the line.

"You and me both," Mike finally said in a low voice and Scotty knew what he was likely thinking. "At least I knew," he added and confirmed his thoughts.

The Harrison kids had been missing for just over twelve hours now, and Scotty knew that with each passing hour the likelihood of them being found safe and well diminished, slipped away like sand falling through an hourglass. Although this wasn't like any normal case, this wasn't the usual child that makes the news having failed to return home after playing in the street or at the local park. Sadly, in cases like that, it was all too common for a body to be found, or arrests made a few days after the vanishing. Usually, they'd fallen foul of some predator who'd done unspeakable things. The thought made Scotty feel sick. But Henry Harrison was with his sister who was much older, he'd not wandered off alone or been snatched off the beach. He didn't know if that made it more hopeful or worse. Had it not been for the mystery of exactly how and where they'd gone he'd have firmly believed that the girl had taken her brother, maybe suffered some sort of mental breakdown. Maybe that is what had happened and something obvious had been missed, it seemed more plausible than the other possibility. After all, he didn't know the family.

"Do you buy what Mrs. Reed is selling, the fact that she believes The Old Chapel has something to do with this?" he asked, unable to suppress the need to push for Mike's take on it and wanting to cast the thoughts of what might have happened to the back of his mind. There was another silence, one that told him that maybe Mike hadn't decided, maybe he was on the fence and considering the impossible.

"Honestly," he finally said. "I don't know. This started out as just another case but now it has a different feel to it. I always trust my gut, but even that is undecided at the moment." There was a pause and Scotty heard him talking to Tara, but he couldn't make out what was being said. "I guess we will know more tomorrow morning," Mike added. "We just need to tread carefully. If they don't show this will be a major police investigation and I don't want to tread on anyone's toes. I know that so far, we have been unable to prove anything quantifiable with our work, but I still believe there are things out there beyond our comprehension.

And if you could have seen how the Reeds were in that meeting," he paused as if remembering it. "Honest level-headed people don't call for our kind of help unless they are scared, and they were scared, Scotty, scared enough to seek us out. I know from experience the police won't even consider the fantastic, it doesn't feature on their radar. However, I don't think it will hurt to approach this from a slightly different angle to the plod, if we get a chance that is." There was another pause and chatter as Tara spoke in the background. Finally Mike came back on the line, "Look, Scotty, I will call you if things change, if not I will see you at Liskeard."

"Likely be in the AM," Scotty said as the motorway ended and became the A31. "It will be two AM or later by the time I arrive."

"Understood," Mike's voice crackled. "Room is booked under the name of Cross." The line went dead, not disconnected by Mike, but by the lack of signal.

Ten minutes later Scotty swung his T4 off the A31 and picked up a Big Mac, fries and a strawberry shake at the same Maccy D's that the Harrison family had used just over forty-eight hours earlier. From the drive-through, he ducked into the Shell service station and brimmed his tank. Before setting off he keyed in the new postal code. Mike's text had yet to arrive, so he'd Googled the hotel. With the route planned and not wanting to listen to the radio, he loaded the Audible App on his phone and scanned through the few audiobooks that he had on the go. He was halfway through the masterpiece that was The Stand by Stephen King, it was a long drive and just the kind of thing he needed to keep focused and awake. He hit play and pulled off the brightly lit forecourt and into the night. He didn't know why but he had a niggling and undeniable feeling that every mile turned was a mile that drew him closer and closer toward a nightmare.

CHAPTER 21

PC SHELLY ARDELL NEEDED TO PEE, THE FEELING HAD been gradually building over the last hour and now it had reached a point where the pressure on her bladder was unbearable. To try and suppress the urge and take her mind away from the increasing strain on her full to bursting bladder, she picked her phone up from the dash of the patrol car and brought the screen to life. Her face now bathed in the dimmed light of her home screen creased with frustration at the **NO CEL-LULAR SERVICE** message displayed in small text at the top. She lifted the iPhone 6 as high as the interior of her Focus would allow and did the, *trying to find a signal dance,* that had been born when the mobile phone had become a part of daily life. The dance consisted of the lifting and lowering of the phone with increased annoyance whilst moving around in whatever space you had. As she was sat in a car the space she had was far from generous, and her movement was somewhat restricted, but it did allow her to stick her hand out the window and raise her iPhone a little higher. Much to her annoyance all efforts were to no avail, not even the hint of one bar rewarded her efforts.

Out here in the back of beyond, of the arse end of nowhere as she preferred to think of it, even her police radio struggled. The spot in which the car that was to be her office for the shift was parked, was one of the few places that service on the police channel managed to leak through. It was weak though, and just enough for control to contact you or for you to call the other way if needed. Even then if you moved an inch the wrong way it dropped out. When that happened the radio beeped once in protest and the little service light on top went from happy – you're good to go green, to angry – if you get in trouble now you're fooked, red.

Shelly closed the iPhone screen down, without service she couldn't check for emails or messages. She'd already looked through her photos a few times, that you could do without network coverage. After culling a few even looking at the ones of her and her husband, John and three-year-old daughter, Grace on the beach at Woolacombe taken during leave the week before got boring. Further back in that album were photos of her looking drained and tired with Grace in her arms just minutes old. Photo's that were a showreel of the life she'd led for the past six years. The earliest ones from six years ago, and that had made the transfer from her last phone to this, were of a night out with colleagues on her police intake, a meal to celebrate the fact that they'd made patrol. She guessed that almost every person now carried a similar little showreel around with them, their life in their pocket, which is why people got so upset when their phones were lost or stolen, it wasn't the device being gone that caused distress, it was what was on it. Gadgets could be replaced, photographs that hadn't been backed up could not.

Shelly tucked the phone into a pocket on her body armour and adjusted her bum on the now not so comfortable seat of the Ford. Her shirt felt sticky below her tac-vest and soon she'd have to think about taking it off and setting it on the passenger seat. The night was far too warm and being out in the arse end of nowhere guarding an empty building she was pretty darn sure she wouldn't need it. So far in six years of frontline policing, she hadn't needed its protection, and she hoped it would stay that way until the day she retired.

For a moment she considered calling Luke Stanbey, the officer at the top of the drive. His position afforded an equally broken level of radio service and unless he too was sat in his vehicle and in the right spot she'd not get through anyway. Shelly squinted her eyes against the darkness and down the long drive. The only trace of Luke's patrol car that she could see was the interior light. It floated in that thick lightlessness like a distant star, no more than a tiny pinprick in all that black. Luke had parked his patrol car across the drive to prevent any unauthorised vehicles getting in. So far, the shift had been quiet, very quiet. When they'd taken over from the late shift at ten PM a few local press had still been lurking about, hoping to get a shot or the big scoop, but the place was on shutdown until the morning. Nothing to see but a cordoned off drive and a couple of Bobbies on point. Even the kids' parents were gone, half an hour or so away in Liskeard and Shelly guessed that finding no bones to pick from the story at the scene they'd gone in search of them. Either that or someone leaky at the hotel had given a tipoff for monetary gain, the second option was the most likely, she'd learned fast what a merciless and unscrupulous world this could be. She guessed that by the time she handed over the post to the morning shift at seven they'd be back, swarming around like flies trying to find a fresh section of turd to land on. By then a few of the Nationals would no doubt be there, too. A story like this always started small and built momentum, like a snowball rolling downhill and picking up a new news outlet as it went.

Her search for a distraction from the now painful need to make water was failing, it jabbed at her more urgently and she jiggled about on the seat a bit, cursing how her heavy body armour dug into her bladder and just made the situation worse. A portaloo had been put on the forecourt by the tree line to save those stuck out on a full shift of point duty having to use the bushes. No one wanted their picture in the local echo doing that, and it was just the kind of shot a wily photographer would snap. It wasn't far off, just to the side of the building and she knew she was going to have to go, yet she didn't want to. She'd never admit it to any of her colleagues, but the place creeped her out, the woods that surrounded it creeped her out just the same. Sure, Luke was just down the end of the drive, but there was no way she'd walk up to him and ask for her hand to be held while she took a piss. Casting the thought aside she looked longingly at the faint outline of the mobile toilet. It really wasn't far away at all, but a thin veil of cloud capped the sky, both sealing the heat of the day in and intensifying the darkness and making it seem much further. Behind the faint silhouette, she could see the line of tall oaks as they loomed above the portaloo, dwarfing the seven-foot rectangle of green plastic with its grey roof.

She cursed herself inwardly for being stupid, she wasn't afraid of getting stuck in at a job and was always one of the first to jump in to break up a fight, so what was the problem now?

It was no good, she'd have to go, the need to pee had won. It was that or she'd wet herself right there and then have to explain why the driver's seat of the patrol car was soaked in piss to the Duty Sergeant in the morning. She cracked the door and slid out of her marked Ford Focus, her feet crunched their way across the drive, the sound of her hurried steps filled her ears and give her a feeling of intense loneliness. *Maybe soon Luke will take a walk down for a natter, as he had done a few times since they'd taken on the night shift*, she told herself. It wasn't that she was afraid, a little creeped out, yes – there was something about the place that had her guard up and she didn't like it. By morning it would likely look quite serene and idyllic, and it would be obvious that it had been no more than her mind influencing her feelings due to just how bloody dark it was. The night always made things look different and sinister. Still, she wanted some company, even if Luke never stayed longer than a few minutes for fear that someone, likely a maverick reporter, might sneak past on foot. Shelly had pointed out to him when he'd last wandered down for a chat about an hour ago, that due to the woods around the building and how dark it was that you'd need a team of officers stood no more than six feet apart all around the parameter to stop someone really determined. However, Luke was always pretty by the book and after shooting the breeze for a few minutes, him stood outside her Ford bent down and talking to her through the open window, he always went back to his post.

Shelly reached the door to the portaloo and went in, the scent of strong chemicals assaulting her nostrils. She peed as fast she could, the sound of her urine hitting the foul chemical ridden mixture of the lower tank echoed up like that of trickling water in a cave. As she peed out what seemed like pints, she smiled inwardly at both her own foolishness and the blissful relief. She hadn't spooked herself so badly since she'd been a child. Back then she'd often scare herself stiff with thoughts that the boogie man would be waiting to grab her feet from under the bed, or poised ready behind the first closed door. At times wetting her bed had seemed more appealing than actually risking a midnight dash to the loo.

No mains water supply benefited the portaloo and having finally finished and buttoned her trousers she felt a little disgust as she coated her hands with the alcohol gel provided. Alcohol gel was fine, but it didn't give you that clean feeling that good old soap and water did. She wiped away the last of the gel on her trousers and followed it up with an application of a watermelon scented one she had in a small dispenser clipped to her tac-vest. Whilst it still wasn't soap, it gave the illusion of soap from its fragrant smell and that at least abated her disgust a little at not being able to wash properly.

Outside the night was as still and as silent as a mortuary during closing hours, the muggy air hung heavily and felt thick to breathe, like a gaseous soup. Shelly briskly paced the same route back, but halfway to the car something in the very peripheral of her vision snagged her attention. She paused and looked in earnest at one of the reconstruction stained glass windows at the side of the chapel, still not quite sure what it was that had alerted her. Now fully in her field of view and not to the side, it was clearer, a small light, like that of a torch was coming from the inside. It seemed to float there, back and forth between the windows, one moment a section of red glass glowed, then green, next blue and back, the calmes of lead that separated the glass gave it a slightly disjointed look. She stood, not able to quite believe her eyes and with her breath caught in her chest. Shelly looked to the radio on her body armour and cursed again at the red light blinking on top, the one that told her there was no signal, the one that told her if things went south, she was fooked. The light in the window faded, then came again, not pulsing, just moving away and dimming in intensity, then moving closer again. *Someone is inside*, she thought to herself. She considered running and getting Luke then decided that she'd take a cursory look around the building first. The only two ways in were the front door and the rear door. Both were locked, and the keys were with her, on a carabiner clip secured to her vest. From that vest, she took her LED Lenser torch and making her way to the side of the building she clicked it to life. The shaft of bright white light sliced through the darkness, birthing ominous looking shadows to each side, shadows that seemed to hide things. *What are those shadows hiding, Shelly my girl?* a voice asked in her head. For some reason, it was that of her nanna, dead now the past five years after a heart attack had taken her one day whilst she was sat getting her hair done at the local salon. She'd always used that term, *Shelly my girl!* In the day it had been sweet, endearing even, now it sounded almost sinister and there was a tone to that internal voice that made her shiver, despite the warmth and humidity of the night.

Reaching the back door, she checked the security seal, it was intact, no one had gotten in that way at least. Nonetheless, she clasped the handle and gave the door a cursory tug to be sure. Locked. As she turned away a dull *thump* came from deep inside the building, the sound of something being dropped. *Or maybe of a body hitting the floor, Shelly my girl,* the voice of her dead nanna said inside her head. *Maybe the body of the boy!*

Shelly glanced nervously down at her radio, the red light stared back mocking, telling her that she was either going this alone or walking for help. She didn't want to walk back to the car, certainly not all the way to Luke. Despite the butterflies that beat their wings of worry furiously in her chest she wanted to see this through. The scene on the front of the building was her responsibility and now as impossible as it seemed someone had gotten in. No one had yet figured out just how the Harrison kids had gone missing from the place. *If they just upped and vanished with no clue as to how, isn't it reasonable to think that someone could get in the same way, Shelly my girl,* that dead voice of her nanna said. The idea seemed preposterous, but then so did just upping and vanishing like Houdini. Shelly checked her watch, three AM. She made a mental note of the time for her report and peeled the seal off the door, then fumbled the keys from her vest and shakily unlocked the back door.

It felt a good six or seven degrees cooler in the kitchen and despite her trepidation, she felt relief at being away from the closeness of the night air. The cooler climate began to chill the perspiration on her brow and the shirt which clung to her back beneath her tac-vest began to cool rapidly, making her shiver again.

"Police," she called out. Her training took over and an assertiveness that she didn't feel presented itself in her voice. "Henry, Ellie – are you in here?" Deep silence answered, and her raised voice fell flat against the old stone producing no echo. She swept the beam of her torch from left to right searching for the source of the sound. Arcing the beam around she slid it over the breakfast bar revealing two unwashed mugs. On the drainer cleaned and waiting to be put away were two generic white plates that matched the mugs, but nothing more. Moving deeper into the building she padded through to the entrance lobby, the secured main doors lay to the front of her. She turned and followed the beam of light up the left staircase to the mezzanine level, across the internal balcony, and down the right staircase. At the bottom she paused, a large crucifix was on the floor as if it had fallen from the wall. Shelly crossed the lobby quickly, wanting to be anywhere else but here. Reaching it she shone the beam at the wall and saw the sturdy looking hook that it had been hung on. *Could I really have heard that from outside?* her own internal voice questioned. She bent and looked at the wooden cross; it was big, likely heavy too, but heavy enough to make a sound that permeated the length of the building and through the back wall? She wasn't so sure.

"How the ..." she began to mumble under her breath as she saw the equally sturdy loop of iron that went with the hook but stopped as the sound of crying echoed down from the top floor. She walked back two steps, caught between the need to get Luke and the need to investigate the sound. *Two or three minutes, that's all it will take to get to his car, tell him what you heard and saw – what you **think** you heard and saw – and get back.* But as the thought ran through her head she realised that she was somehow halfway up the staircase, her legs aching as if she'd been stood in place for some time. The cry came again, anguished, fearful, that of a child but one seemingly much younger than the missing Henry Harrison, certainly much younger than his sister. Shelly shook her head as if the mere action would erase her confusion. Moving slowly, one step at a time she reached the top of the stairs and entered the lounge. A smell hung there, one that caught her throat and threatened to trigger her gag reflex. It was a smell she knew well. Death. Not recent death, but death with the inevitable decay that followed. Another smell accompanied it, like peaches accompany cream, just far less pleasant. Hidden below the putrefying main smell was something similar to burnt hair or flesh, she couldn't put her finger on which. Shakily she placed a hand over her mouth and nose to try and stifle the fetid air, it worked a little thanks to the nicer scent of her watermelon hand sanitiser that laced her skin.

The crying came again, this time from the lower level far off in another part of the chapel, likely the kitchen that she'd just been through. Shelly spun, aimed her torch back down the stairs and found nothing but shadow and emptiness. Another cry, this one from the depths of the floor she was on. The infant wailed as if in pain and that torturous cry dropped to a guttural gurgle as if it were drowning in a viscous liquid.

She wheeled around, wishing now more than ever that she'd not done this on her own. As she turned, the smell grew stronger, thicker and the air chilled quickly as if someone had just opened the door of a large commercial freezer. Shelly felt her guts begin to churn, as they always did before she was sick. The beam of her torch had now sliced its full arc back to the lounge and now she saw it. The source of that smell. A towering mass of a man, no – not a man, more like the idea of a man, for the beam of her torch hit the robes of his tunic and impossibly came out the other side, just weaker, diffused, as if it was being shone through thin fabric.

Shelly felt her legs turn to jelly and a new and over-whelming need to pee grabbed her. With dread, she looked up to meet its face, as a naughty child might raise its head slowly to face an angry adult. Her hand instinctively reached for her incapacitant spray, not that it would do any good, it was more an involuntary reaction that six years of experience had programmed into her. The figure's head was festooned in the thick hood of its tunic, yet it had no face, not one that she could see anyway. Instead, inside that hood was darkness, a darkness so great that she felt as if it could consume her. Edging back, one hand on her spray and the other clasping her torch, the beam finally reached that nothing-face and the light her torch cast, all four hundred and fifty lumens of it, became consumed by the blackness therein. It smiled at her that blackness, it invited her in, she couldn't see it, but she could feel it. *You weren't expecting that now were you, Shelly my girl?* the voice of her dead nanna screeched in horrific glee. *You weren't expecting that at all! No, not on your nelly!*

Moving blindly back on shaky legs a scream birthed from Shelly's mouth, the need to be away from the fig-ure, from the building so strong it was palpable. Her back-stepping foot found the edge of the top step and she floundered on its edge. Her arms wheeled in the air, desperately seeking the balance she needed, desperately trying to stop gravity taking over and casting her into the dark lobby below. As she peddled her arms the torch fell from her grip and tumbled down the stairs, its beam slashing the night like a lightsabre as it fell. Be-fore it hit the floor a feeling of weightlessness took her, and gravity won. Through wide and disbelieving eyes, she watched as the figure shrunk away. For the briefest of moments, she did see a face in that dark hood, a face whose blue eyes seemed to mock her as she fell, then the face was gone.

Shelly felt her back make contact first, how far down she'd tumbled before that first contact, she did not know, but it felt as if she'd fallen forever, fallen for longer than seemed possible for the height of the lounge, down and down. With that first impact came a blinding pain as something, somewhere inside her broke with a crack that reverberated into her brain and echoed its pain through every part of her body. Falling again, down, down into the darkness; this time the impact came sooner, and she felt her neck crunch as her vertebrae were forced into impossible positions. Weightless again, then a third impact, one that drove a sound as shrill as a ship's whistle through her mind and made her head spin. Weightless again before the fourth and final impact, the one that saw her meet the floor of the lobby just by her dropped torch. This final impact was taken mainly by her head which split open like a dropped watermelon on the corner of the bottom newel post. This time there was no pain, no ringing, just the blissful blanket of unconsciousness and the oblivion that came with it.

CHAPTER 22

THE DISAPPEARANCE OF ELLIE AND HENRY HARRISON
hit the local BBC News Cornwall in time for the early
breakfast six AM broadcast that Sunday morning. By
the time the news went out at lunchtime, it had gone
national. Not the main headline story, but Samuels expected that in a similar way to that of a popular song
climbing the charts, soon enough it would hit that top
spot.

"It's countrywide news now," he said, addressing
both Carol and Rob Harrison who sat together on a
small sofa that very likely pulled out to make a bed,
thus enabling this to be called a Family Room. He
stood, for there were not many places to sit, this was
also a brief visit and he wanted to be on the move again
as soon as he could. Their faces were pallid, hers more
pallid than his. It also wore the look of a person who'd
not slept, and who'd been awake all night running
through questions in their mind that they'd not been
able to answer.

The room at the Travel Lodge wasn't cramped, but
it wasn't exactly lavish, either. The bed was unmade despite it being lunchtime, the covers were bundled up at
the foot and half hanging down to the floor, testimony
to a restless night. The air was fousty and had that shut-

in smell, not body odour as such, just an unpleasant mustiness.

Carol Harrison looked at him fleetingly, but her eyes were vacant, he smiled weakly back at her. Her face, that might once have just passed as attractive now looked sallow, her eyes were sunken back in the deep shadows of their sockets and there were worry or stress lines on her pale skin that looked to have been born long before the last day of hell that she'd no doubt endured. He tried to put himself in their position. He couldn't. No matter how hard he tried, and he inwardly reminded himself that whatever time he eventually managed to get home he'd be sure to kiss both his girls. Even if they were asleep, as they often were. So many times, they'd been sleeping soundly when he left for work and then in bed by the time he got home, but that was the job and he knew he'd never do anything else. His wife Kiera understood, or understood as well as anyone on the outside could. He guessed it was more of a tolerance than anything else. Maybe saying someone understood was wrong.

He cleared his throat, "The coverage will spread via social media faster than a bushfire. That's where people get their news from nowadays. Their pictures will be on almost every Facebook and Twitter feed on almost every phone. If someone has seen either Ellie or Henry, we will soon know."

"And if they don't show?" Rob Harrison asked him sharply. "Just how long will it be before your enquiry focuses on us and we are asked to help with your investigation, just in a more formal manner?"

Carol Harrison didn't react to what her husband had said, she just went right on looking at the TV screen where a picture of her son and daughter, taken the day before they went missing, decorated the top right-hand corner of the screen as an attractive female desk anchor relayed the story. Ellie Harrison was in a vest top, her face looking tanned and her from a bottle auburn hair worn down. Her hair shone in the sunlight and the smile on her face reached her eyes. There was no mask behind that smile, a smile that reached the eyes was a genuine one. Her younger brother stood next to her; his height elevated to that of hers by the small retaining wall on which he stood. She had her arm around him as he also beamed back at the camera. Samuels had been there enough with his own kids to recognise that the photo had been taken at the Eden Project, in one of the outside picnic areas. The headline underneath read **"Fears Grow For Missing Brother & Sister."** The TV sound was down, and the anchor's words muted to them. It didn't matter, there was no need to hear what she had to say, they were living it.

"Like I said yesterday, one step at a time," Samuels wanted to tell him it wouldn't likely be that long, a day, two at most before someone further up the chain of command gave the order, and when it came, if there were still no clues as to where the Harrison kids had gone, it would be a fair call to make. He decided to shoot from the hip, he liked the couple and despite the fact they might soon be on the wrong side of a police interview desk his gut was telling him neither had a single thing to do with where those kids were. "From a police point of view," he said slowly, "you have to look at it like this. Your son and daughter have vanished, no trace of them now for," he checked his watch, it was twelve thirty in the afternoon, "twenty-seven hours, and that's just from when your wife discovered they'd gone. We still don't know how they got out; the only other key was held in the safe of the Horners' house whose gathering you were at that night. They had people at theirs almost all night who have vouched for the fact that no one came to The Old Chapel and the last time that they saw you was when you all left and walked home. That's leaving out the fact that both doors were also deadbolted from the inside, so even someone out-side with a key couldn't get in!" He paused as his mind ran over the impossible scenario again, hoping that somewhere a synapse in his brain would fire and yield the answer. It didn't. He continued, "The only conceivable inference to draw is that either something happened to them inside that building and they were taken out, or that something happened to them outside and that either you or your wife or someone locked the door after you returned home." He'd watched Rob Harrisons' face grow redder with each word he spoke, his wife was still looking blankly at the screen and he felt that with every hour that passed they were losing her more and more, at this rate by breakfast on Monday she'd be in a catatonic state of PTSD.

The news had now moved on to the sport. Silently two pundits seemed to be conversing about the upcoming premier league season that was due to get underway next month. Samuels doubted Carol Harrison was a fan of the beautiful game, and on her best day likely didn't give a toss about who had signed for what club and at what fee, but she stared at it nonetheless. He flicked his attention from her to the screen and waited for the tirade from Rob Harrison to start, where he'd yell at him that he was a good father, and Carol a good mother and that neither one of them would ever, ever touch a hair on the heads of their kids, but it didn't. Gradually the reddening in Rob Harrison's face began to ebb as if someone had pulled a plug in his neck, one that was now draining the blood away from his cheeks.

"That's how it looks," Rob Harrison finally said, his voice as thin as a wafer and sounding defeated. "If I were looking in on this from the outside, and God how I wish I was, that's how I'd see it. I guess that's bad huh?"

"What?" Samuels asked.

"Wishing it was someone else, wishing it was me watching the news and thinking, *Oh yeah! The parents are definitely to blame, I mean what other explanation is there?*

Because that *is* what they will be saying. Maybe not to-day, but by tomorrow, and if not then the day after." A tear ran down his cheek, it was the first time that Samuels had seen Rob Harrison lose his shit emotion-ally and having held it for close to thirty hours he re-spected him for it.

"It's not bad to think like that at all," he said gently. "Rob?"

Rob Harrison looked up, his eyes were redder now and Samuels could tell he was trying hard not to break totally. "If you or your wife were anything to do with what is going on here you need to tell me, then I can read you the words and we can start to sort this mess out. So?"

"No," Rob shook his head and held Samuels' eyes. "I'm not going to get mad that you asked me, you have to, it's your job. I know your lot will probably ask it again down the station at some point, but the answer will always be the same. No. We never would, never could. It makes me sick to even think about."

Samuels believed him, not a little, but totally. It was all in the body language, there was no phony grief or false emotion on either of them, no tick or twitch that hinted a lie. What he was seeing was raw, gen-uine, true anguish; the kind that no person should ever have to suffer in their life. The fakers, of which in the past there had sadly been plenty, always thought they could act the part, but eventually they discovered that there was no acting it when it came to a situation such as this. All too soon the falseness rose to the sur-face just as surely as a bloated cadaver would. There was no doubt that if those kids didn't turn up in the next day then they would be answering tough ques-tions at the station, likely with a brief sat beside them. Those questions would hurt, shock, but in the end, he had a feeling, no - more knew that they'd lead nowhere. Rob Harrison was right though, in a case that had the potential to be as high profile as this it didn't matter if the police didn't have the evidence, the public was the jury. Trial by media, the worst kind. It was as close to the modern-day equivalent of a witch hunt that you could get because at the end of the day the media would make it a witch hunt, and someone, more than likely the Harrisons' would be the ones to burn for it, metaphorically speaking anyway.

"If we have no solid leads by five then we are going to do a full press appeal. Will you be comfortable in front of the cameras?" He directed the question at both of them, yet it washed over Carol as if her physical body was all that occupied the room, her consciousness was elsewhere.

"As I said before, Inspector, we will do what we have to do to get them back." He shook his head slowly and wiped the back of his hand over his eyes, "I've seen them before," he said in a low voice.

"Seen what?"

"The appeals, tearful parents sat between police officers at a trestle table as cameras flash in their faces."

"That's pretty much how it goes, yeah."

"You never think it will be you," he said, almost smiling now. Not a happy smile, but the way someone smiles when they accept the fucked-up situation they're in. "You never do, it's always someone else. Bit like a lotto win I guess, you never think it will be you, but then it happens, and it is you." His shoulders shook a little and he held back a sob.

Samuels thought it was a pretty shitty analogy, but he got the point Rob Harrison was trying to make and he was right. Samuels stroked at the freshly trimmed dark hair of his beard and said, "I'll get one of our family liaison officers to come sit with you and your wife within the hour." He was trying to sound reassuring, but in a situation like this nothing apart from the news that both kids were safe and well would reassure. "I think it's Becky coming out, Becky Mansfield. She is a good officer; she will be able to answer any questions you have."

"There is only one question I have, Inspector," Carol Harrison said, turning her head slowly to look at him. Her sudden animation unnerved him, and he felt a chill. "And that's where are my kids?" She switched her attention back to the TV not waiting for an answer, her neck moved slowly as if she were a mechanical doll. Her wide eyes drank in the silent start of the next programme, Diagnosis Murder.

"I'm heading out to The Old Chapel," Samuels said. He didn't mention that he'd already been out there that morning or the reason why. The Harrisons didn't need to know that last night one of the officers on duty, Shelly Ardell, had mysteriously met with a nasty accident and was now in a coma at Plymouth Hospital, her head fractured and her back all broken up, the vertebrae looking like a dropped stack of china plates. Just what Shelly Ardell had been doing poking around in the potential crime scene he had no fucking clue, but she had gone in and now no one knew if she'd ever walk again, forget walk, she might not ever wake up. Samuels hadn't known Shelly Ardell all that well, but he knew enough about her to be sure that she wouldn't have gone traipsing through a building locked down for forensics without good reason and he couldn't fathom what reason had made her go in. She'd been found at four thirty that morning by her colleague, Luke Stanbey, when he'd wandered down to where her patrol car had been parked for a leg stretch. According to what Luke had told him at the end of his shift and before heading home, was that upon finding her car empty he'd checked the portaloo. Not finding her there he'd walked to the back of the building, thinking she might be checking the perimeter and had found the back door ajar. Inside he'd soon found her broken and crumpled body at the foot of the easterly staircase. She'd lost a lot of blood, even more by the time he'd managed to get to her car, find a radio signal and call into the control room for an ambulance. The whole thing was one almighty mess, but that didn't matter, he now had an officer at death's door as a result of the investigation. The only rational explanation for the FUBAR situation was that she'd thought someone had been inside and had gone to investigate, then in the dark had lost her footing and fallen. There was no other way to explain it, he sure as shit didn't think for a second that any officer would be stupid enough to go poking around in there out of morbid curiosity. It was clear that she'd put no lights on as Luke Stanbey had found the place in darkness and her torch had been by her side in a puddle of blood that the carpet was busily soaking up. Another mystery to add to the pile. "Our CSI teams will go over the place today, see if they can figure out what happened, sometimes it takes science to solve these things."

"Do you think they're alive still, Inspector?" Rob Harrison asked flatly. "In your professional opinion."

"We can't draw any conclusions at this point," he replied, hating himself for answering like a politician. In truth he wasn't sure, probably sixty-forty to the bad, but every hour that ticked by without a sighting or them being found, the forty to the good would diminish. "Our family liaison will be with you very soon." He nodded a goodbye at them both, Carol Harrison didn't see it, her vacant eyes were locked on the silent episode of Diagnosis Murder. Dick Van Dyke was decked out in a too-white looking lab coat and chatting excitedly to his son and co-actor, Barry Van Dyke over the cadaver of a young blonde woman who was obviously the focus of this episode's murder mystery. No doubt by the time the hour-long show ended they'd have it wrapped up and the bad guy would be in jail. *If only it were that simple in real life*, he thought as he turned and headed out of the room.

In the hall he took a deep breath, enjoying the

chilled air-conditioned air that wasn't laced with the smell of sweat and anxiety. He wasn't sure if you could actually smell the latter, but there had been something there, something behind the usual odour of shut-in. Reaching the end of the corridor on the first floor he descended the stairs two at a time and at the bottom pressed the security button, the one that kept unwanted guests out of the communal halls and kept them in the lobby. As he passed the reception desk, he happened a quick look at the small restaurant come coffee shop where a few hours earlier a not so tasty buffet style breakfast would have no doubt been on offer, where eggs that were past being dippy would have been congealing on a hotplate. As he did, he done a double take, the man sat at a table facing the window he knew, the attractive blonde with him he recognised, as he did the younger well-built guy with him, but only because he'd seen them both on the TV. With a shake of his head in disbelief, he took a left at the main doors and went into the café.

PART 3
CORNWALL

CHAPTER 23

"WELL FUCK MY OLD BOOTS," MIKE HEARD A familiar voice say. He looked up to see who'd spoken, but he hadn't really needed to, there was only one person he knew or had known in his previous life that used that phrase. The last few years hadn't changed him much; the beard was a new addition to what had just been designer stubble back in the day, but it was undoubtedly Mark Samuels. "Mike Cross, how the devil are you?"

Mike stood and with a genuine smile extended his hand, "Mark," he said as his old colleague took his hand with a firm grip and pumped it up and down enthusiastically. "How long has it been?"

"Too bloody long," Samuels replied, patting his old friend on the forearm with his spare hand. "In all the places in all the world," Samuels grinned. "I never for one second thought I'd bump into you like this. A Travel Lodge, not quite the kind of place I'd have expected to see a big TV star. May I?" He gestured to the chair next to Tara.

"Of course," Mike responded instantly. "Coffee?"

"Love some, it's been a bitch of a day."

Mike poured a cup from the pot they'd been brought not ten minutes before. The steaming hot, dark brown liquid flowed freely into the white china mug.

"This is Mark Samuels," Mike introduced as he set the pot down and left his old friend to take care of the milk and sugar. "Mark was a DS on one of the general CID teams back in Sussex, we worked a few cases together back in the day."

"DI now," Samuels added, giving a firm handshake to Scotty and another to Tara. "But now down here, transferred a few years ago."

"DI," Mike said with a nod of the head, "I'd have been calling you Gov' then if I still carried a badge. As the yanks like to say."

"Bollocks," he replied. "You'd have made the grade long before me, what's it been since you left, five years, six?"

"Closer to seven," Mike answered before taking a sip of his brew.

"I know a few of the guys we worked with back in Sussex watch your show, Mike," Samuels said, blowing a cooling breath over his own mug. "I've seen a few episodes too, not really my sorta thing if I'm totally honest. How the hell did you get into that?"

"Long story," Mike replied with a wan smile. "I'll fill you in on it over a beer at some point."

"Sounds good. So, I see all your team are here, if I were a man of deduction, I'd say you were filming in the area. Am I right?"

And this is where it gets awkward, Mike thought to himself. It was sure a coincidence that Mark Samuels had transferred down here to Cornwall and bumped into him this way, a massive one. But, it was certainly no coincidence that he was here, at the same hotel that also housed Carol and Rob Harrison, and he'd likely just come straight from their room. Mike knew there'd be a police presence here, both uniform and CID, he'd just not banked on one of the lead investigators being someone he'd known. He thought quickly, not wanting to lie to an old colleague who he'd genuinely liked, but also not wanting to play his whole hand just yet as if done right it could work on their side to have Mark's help, he'd just have to play it slow. "More location research," Mike said. "We've not set our venues out fully yet for the next series." It was a lie, well a half lie. There was no second series, well certainly not with Switch-Back TV, but there was still Scotty's Youtube idea and the very slim chance that their agents would be able to jump the show to another channel. "Are you working this missing person case?" Mike asked, not wanting to reveal that he knew the Harissons were in the same hotel and the very reason he'd booked them in.

He and Tara had arrived late on in the evening, he'd booked them two separate rooms to avoid having to tackle the whole relationship thing with Scotty. There was no issue, and he'd very likely just say, *Thank God, it's about time you two booked a room!* But there were more pressing issues at hand. Last night the room he'd booked for her had stayed empty. Scotty hadn't called on his arrival, but Mike had awoken at six AM, as he did most mornings, and seen a text from him timed at just after one AM. So far the day had rated zero on the productivity scale. They'd had a light breakfast and a brief meeting where Scotty had been brought up to speed in much more detail on the meeting with the Reeds. His face was awash with disbelief and excitement as they'd recounted how the original owner had perished in a fire, how the second owner had fallen to his death whilst fixing the place up, and at the tragic story of the young estate agent, whom hours after selling The Old Chapel to Tom and Sue Reed had met his demise in a horrific crash on the outskirts of the village, then the three further suicides and infant murder.

Samuels looked from Mike to Tara and then to Scotty, his right hand ran over the neatly trimmed hair of his beard. "It's an odd one, Mike," he said in a low voice as he leaned in over the table. "I don't want to talk too loud; the fucking press are all over this like flies on shit and I don't want an overheard quote from me going in the local rag, the DCI would have my balls." Instinctively, Mike leaned in too, as did Tara and Scotty, making it appear they were all co-conspirators in some big secret.

"How do you mean?" Mike asked. "Teen girl and her young brother. I saw the news. My guess is she's abducted him, run off with him as payback for some reason or another. Could be she had a sudden mental breakdown, rare I know but it happens. Probably has no idea of the world of shit she's created for herself."

"Normally I'd be with you on that, it was certainly my first thought and that of the PC who took the initial missing persons report. But I'm not so sure."

Samuels paused, there was a pensive silence that Mike let ride out, he knew that if he said nothing then, in the end, his old colleague would feel compelled to say something, as no one liked a silence.

"Neither I, nor anyone else who has been there, can figure out just how the hell those kids got out," he finally said.

"What do you mean?" Tara asked, and Mike was glad to see she was in on the game. Mark Samuels turned his attention to her, and Mike had enough confidence in her to let her run with it for now.

"The place was locked and deadbolted from the inside, both doors, front and back. The keys that could have let them out were still hung up on the hook by the front door, all the windows were secured from the inside." Samuels leaned back in his chair and ran a hand over his face.

"You think the parents are involved?" Mike cut back in with a low voice, unable to help himself. There was a fair bit of background noise and the clinks of crockery coming from the kitchen area helped to mask their voices, but he knew you had to be careful when it came to the media. Some would use sonic ear amplifiers, a lot like the ones they used to hear real-time EVP, they could be sneaky bastards. The press, however, were fishing for a different catch, they wanted that golden nugget of information carelessly spilled by loose lips. *Loose lips sink ships,* one of his aunts used to say. And as much as he wanted the information that Mark Samuels had, he didn't want to land him in the shit.

"I can't say too much, Mike, you know that. But, no – I honestly don't. I've spoken to them twice now, this morning and yesterday. You know what I mean when I say, you get a feel for people, right?"

"Yeah, sure."

"I don't think they had a thing to do with it. I might be proven wrong, but I don't think so. The mother is one stage off catatonic."

"And the father?" Scotty asked, adding to the conversation for the first time.

"With it," Samuels said. "Far from okay but he's the one holding them together at the moment." Samuels turned his attention back to Mike and said, "The powers that be will want them spoken to officially at some point if those two don't turn up soon, as you know."

"Right," Mike agreed

"I'm just hoping I can hold that particular wolf from the door for as long as possible, I think it will be a waste of resources and time, time that could be focused on finding out exactly what happened?"

"And what do you think happened?" Mike asked, then followed it up with, "Have you been out to the place?"

Samuels frowned, "You seem mighty interested in all of this," he said.

Mike cursed himself inwardly, had he pushed it too far? He didn't think so, but then he'd worked with Samuels a few times, he always did have good foresight, went with his hunches and from what he could remember they normally played out, it was one thing that made him a good detective. "Just reliving old times through you," he replied with a false smile. He hated the lie, but here and now was not the place to go into exactly why he and his team were in Liskeard.

Samuels regarded him for a few brief seconds, smiled and said, "Honestly, I don't have a fucking clue, Mike. And that's what's bugging the hell of me. Normally, even if I don't have the evidence to hand I have a feeling, know what road to go down to get that evidence. This time, nothing. Just lots of questions and no answers." Samuels checked his watch, Mike knew this was the precursor to him making an excuse to leave. "Are you in the area long?"

"Few days," Mike lied again. "Week at the most, why?"

"Well you never did tell me just what locations you're looking at, and we have half a decade to catch up on, maybe we could grab a beer one evening. I'd love to hear all about how you got where you are now." Samuels drained the last of his coffee and placed the mug on the table before pushing it to the middle and standing up.

"A beer sounds good."

He fished his wallet from the pocket of his grey trousers, produced a card and handed it to Mike. It bore the Devon and Cornwall force logo in the top left corner and written on it in bold were the words, **Detective Inspector Mark Samuels, Public Protection Unit.** Mike read it and placed it by his own mug, then said, "Sounds like a plan to me, I will give you a call."

"Make sure you do," He nodded a goodbye to both Scotty and Tara and added, "It was nice to meet you both, but I need to head out, it's going to be a busy day and I have a feeling the press are going to be like a pack of hungry wolves if this shit storm doesn't resolve itself."

"I'll talk to you soon," Mike said, giving his old colleague a parting handshake, and with that Samuels was gone. Mike remained stood and watched him head out to the lobby and through the doors. His eyes followed him to the car park where he got into a grey Vauxhall Astra, the kind that screamed CID car to those that knew. As the reversing lights came on Mike sat back down.

"You think he knew?" Scotty asked.

"No," Mike replied. "But he's no slouch, we almost pushed it too far. Soon he will talk to Sue and Tom, of that I have no doubt, then the cat might come leaping out of the bag and I need to get to him before that happens. I respect Mark, we trust, well used to trust each other. I don't want to jeopardise that. But here, now and with God knows who earwigging us it is not the time."

"So, you're going to bring him in on why we are here?" Tara asked, her hands were clasped in front of her on the table. Mike wanted badly to reach out and take them into his and feel the softness of her skin, but he needed to tell Scotty first.

"I don't think we have a choice," Mike replied, concern on his face. "You heard him, though. Seen the show but not really my sort of thing. He may not be open to listening, but it might just buy us a visit to that chapel."

"You're actually considering the fantastic here, aren't you?" Scotty asked his eyes bright again with excitement. "Thinking that that building could have something to do with what happened to those kids? Maybe it had a hand in all those deaths, too."

"Yes and no," Mike replied slowly. He picked the card up that his old friend and colleague had given him, looked at it absently then began to turn it end over end in his fingers. "Do I think it could be linked, yes – I think there is a chance. But, I think there is also a rational explanation behind it, too. If we can bring him round to consider the impossible to reach the possible then we might just crack this thing."

CHAPTER 24

MIKE KNEW HE HAD TO MAKE THE CALL, HE DIDN'T want to but sooner or later Mark would speak to the Reeds, maybe Tom, maybe Sue, likely both, and when he did it might slip out that they'd asked him to look at their holiday home. He wasn't sure Tom would be so fast to lay the blame of the Harrison kids' disappearance on the building, but he thought, no – knew, that Sue would, no matter how improbable it might seem. After all, she'd literally told him that much during their phone conversation the day before.

"What are you going to tell him?" Scotty asked, looking back from the laptop he sat working at. Since the chance meeting with Mark Samuels a few hours ago Mike and Scotty had been going back over what Tara had found during her research, that had only been the day before yesterday, it felt as if a week or more had passed. Tara, herself was out, out somewhere following up on something that had gotten her all excited about an hour ago. She wouldn't let on what it was, Mike knew her well enough to know that was how she worked. If she thought she had a lead she'd have as much information to hand as she could before she came to him with it. He failed to see what it was she could have found, and how it might help, he was intrigued, nonetheless.

With his phone in one hand and Mark Samuels' card in the other, he looked at Scotty from the foot of the bed where he was sat and said, "The truth. That the owners asked us to stay in the building and get a feel for it, to try and debunk some of the reports made by previous guests." He began punching the mobile number in, he knew Mark would be out and about, maybe even out at the scene. He'd never been one for wallowing in the office and when a case was running, he liked, as much as possible, to be on the ground where you could get a real feel for what was happening, speaking to people face-to-face and not over the phone or via a memo or statement passed back to you from the attending officer. "He's probably going to laugh me off," Mike added, the number now complete and staring back at him from his phone screen. "But if he finds out what we are doing here before I tell him," he shook his head slowly, "that will chip away at the trust we built up when we worked together." He hit the call icon on the digital screen, exhaled a long steady breath and said, "Here goes nothing."

The phone began to ring at the other end of the line, it rang, rang some more and just as Mike began to hope that the answering machine would pick up the call, and he could have a valid reason to put this off for a while longer, it was answered.

"Mark Samuels," the voice on the other end of the line said.

"Mark, it's Mike Cross."

"Mike, good to hear from you again buddy," his voice sounded genuinely pleased. "Look I'm as keen to arrange a few beers as well, but right now..."

"Mark," he cut in, "that's not the reason for my call." Mike stood from the end of the bed and began pacing around the small room.

There was a drawn-out silence from the other end, finally his old friend and colleague said slowly, "Go on."

"It's not a coincidence that you bumped into us today, well I mean it is, but not totally. Let's say we have a common interest in The Old Chapel."

"Common?" Samuels said sounding puzzled.

"Well yes, and no," Mike knew he was beating around the bush, this was not a conversation he wanted to have on the phone, he wanted to speak to Mark face-to-face and he had a flash of an idea. "When you asked if we were location reaching and I said we were, it was a half lie, and I'm sorry, I just didn't know how to play it. We are down here in your neck of the woods for that place."

Another silence from the other end, then, "For the TV show?"

"No, Mark, not for the show, the owners asked us just before this business with the Harrison kids kicked off. Look, we have been running some background on the building and had no intention on coming down here and trampling all over a police investigation, but Sue Reed, the owner, asked us to come down early." Mike paused and took a breath, then added, hoping his plan would work. "Is there any chance we can meet and speak in person, I can tell you what I know about the building, it isn't much, and there is nothing in there that will help your investigation, not that I can see, or I'd have told you right away."

"Of course, you would, Mike, I know that." Samuels cut in.

"But I want to tell you what she told me."

There was a brief humoured chuckle from Samuels before he said, "You're not suggesting..."

"No," Mike said firmly before Samuels had a chance to say what he knew he was about to say. "All I am saying is there has been some pretty weird shit linked to that place, deaths and such, things that would not normally form part of a missing persons investigation like this. I just want you to know what I know and what I've been told, so you have the full picture. You know me, Mark, I've been in this game a few years now and so far I've not found one case I can't explain."

"Okay," Samuels said, once again slowly and sounding unsure. "Where?"

"There, at The Old Chapel, say in around two hours," he checked his watch, "Around six."

"I can't do six, there is a press appeal with the parents at four, the soonest I'll be free is seven, and Mike, that place is locked down, you know that I can't..."

"Seven is fine, and I am not expecting you to let me in, just meet me there, outside – we can talk in the car."

"The cordon is at the front gate," Samuels said. "But there will be an inner one for the building, that outer one is to keep press out and people with a morbid curiosity."

"I don't even have to get out of the car," Mike said, pushing the fact as a child might a parent.

There was another silence, this one longer. Finally, Samuels broke it and said, "Sod it, okay – give your name to the officer on post at the front, you're there as an old colleague of mine and PI, as an advisor, you hear, nothing else. None of your spook hunting shit, if it got out that we'd let a ghost hunter into the outer cordon area the press would be lapping it up. You come on your own, too. I can't have all three of you down there. You're not to chat to anyone, and I mean anyone, except for the officer at the front gate."

"I understand," said Mike. He wanted to correct his old friend and tell him they didn't hunt ghosts, they investigated the paranormal and unexplained, then tried to explain it, but he didn't. Instead Mike moved the handset away from his ear and let out a long relieved breath. "Seven PM?"

"Yes, I'm supposed to be off at five, but you know there's bugger all chance of that when a live job is running."

"It's appreciated," Mike said sincerely.

"It's only 'cos I know you and I'd be lying if I told

you you've not got me a little curious," Samuels said. "If anything changes I will call you, I'll save your number now."

"No problem, and Mark, thanks."

"See you at seven buddy," The line went dead.

Mike lowered the phone to his side and let out another slow breath as he turned to face Scotty who was now looking at him with earnest.

"That sounded promising," he said.

"I'm meeting him at seven, at The Old Chapel," Mike replied as he sat back down at the foot of the bed. "At least he didn't laugh me off the line," he added. Mile got back up, he was feeling restless and fidgety, and quite frankly a little useless that they had been sent down here and were unable to do much but sit about waiting. Waiting for the Harrison kids to turn up and be allowed into the place, waiting for them to turn up dead and – well he didn't want to think of that. "Have we got anything, anything else to take to him that doesn't sound crazy?"

"We might have," came Tara's voice. Neither of them had heard her come in but she was now stood by the trouser press, her sunglasses pushed back on her hair and acting like a hair band against her dark blonde locks. "It's tenuous guys," she continued, "but I think you need to see this!"

CHAPTER 25

MIKE LOOKED AT THE OLD, SCHOOL PHOTO ON THE screen of Tara's Lenovo Yoga, it was colour, but that washed out colour of the 60s and 70s, the kind of colour that made you wonder if everything did look as full of browns, beiges, and oranges as the image would have you believe.

"I don't get you?" Mike asked, looking back at Tara who was leaning over both he and Scotty as they all crowded around the small desk that also served as a dresser. He could smell the fruitiness of shampoo on her hair and caught a whiff of her perfume, it smelt good on her sun-kissed skin.

"That is Lindie Parker," Tara said, reaching forward and tapping the old washed out image. "She was fifteen-years-old when she went missing. She disappeared from Charlestown in sixty-nine. There was a massive search for her, but it was as if she just upped and vanished. A week after she did a Lord Lucan, a shore-fisherman snagged one of her shoes on his line a mile down the coast. That was about as much of Lindie as they ever found, with only the shoe to go on they recorded a case of death by misadventure. From the little info there is in the old Herald records they ruled that she likely fell in the harbour and tragically drowned."

"I still don't get it?" Mike said, looking at the old

image. The girl in it, Lindie, was pretty, her hair was long, and no doubt bright red. The colour of the film, film that had been transferred to a very early and rare colour newspaper print, probably didn't do the depth of the red in her hair justice. Her face looked fresh and held just a splattering of freckles that crossed the bridge of her nose, freckles that would have either faded with maturity or remained and been one of her endearing features. Sadly no one would ever know, her years cut short by whatever tragedy had befallen her on the day she went missing. He squinted closely at the old image, the only other mark on her face was a small, thin scar that ran above her right eye, likely the result of some childhood mishap. He looked away from the image and turned back to Tara, "That's tragic and all, but that's forty-nine years ago now, and Charlestown is a good ten miles away."

Tara nodded, then opened another browser window that she had minimalized in her taskbar at the bottom, this time the image was of a very attractive blonde girl, the picture was black and white. "That's Sara Capstone," Tara said. "Eighteen years old, she went missing nine months before Lindie Parker, she was from Porthpean, a little further west of here, again on the coast. Just upped and vanished one Sunday morning whilst out walking her dog. The dog came home, trailing its lead behind it, no sign of Sara, though. A week later a trawler found one of her shoes and a stocking about five miles out. Just like Lindie, they never found a body."

"Well those two cases are close enough in conjuncture to possibly be linked," Mike said, as his eyes scanned the screen. "Although they are both likely no more than tragic accidents. Her dog probably got into trouble swimming, she went in and rescued the mutt, mutt survived, she sadly drowned. Happens all the time."

"Bear with me," Tara said as she bought up yet another screen. This was a few years earlier again; the old

Herald front sheet reported the news from September 1961. This headline read,

MISSING FIFTEEN YEAR-OLD LISA SIMMS FEARED DEAD

MIKE SCANNED THE STORY, again it was headed up with a school photo of the girl. She was a fresh-faced teen, dressed in a checked skirt and blouse that looked meticulously ironed, no doubt her mother had doused it in a little extra spray starch that morning, (his own Gran had loved the bloody stuff), to ensure it kept that freshly laundered look for her school photo. Mike guessed her hair had been brown, it was hard to tell in the old black and white picture. It was held back in a studious-looking bun and a broad smile dressed her lips. Her eyes were wide and full of potential that would never be fulfilled. Lisa apparently had just vanished from the street in her home village of Duporth whilst heading home from a study session at her best friend's house. The only trace of Lisa Simms they'd ever found was her school satchel, that, according to the story, had washed up in Charlestown harbour a few days after she went missing. There was no word from the police, or theory as to just how she'd ended up drowning in the sea whilst walking home, the distance, according to the article, had been just over a mile and her route took her nowhere near the shore.

"Each case they have recorded death by misadventure, but to me, these seem linked," Tara said, her voice brimming with enthusiasm.

"It's compelling," Mike said, he was impressed with what she'd dug up over the last couple of hours, and it further enforced his belief that in a different life, with different choices, she'd have made a hell of a detective.

"But, these three cases span eight years," he continued, not wanted to quell her enthusiasm but needing at the same time to reign this in. "All in different towns and villages. I'm not sure I can take this to Samuels when I see him. Our case is, as I said, forty-nine years after the last report."

"He's agreed to see you then?" Tara asked as she closed the browser window and opened a new one, this was a story from much earlier, so early in fact that it had hardly any photographic images and consisted mostly of text.

"Yes, seven out at The Old Chapel," Mike saw a spark of excitement in her eyes and quickly added, "Just me, no hangers-on and I don't get to go inside."

Tara elbowed him in the ribs, as Scotty took control of her laptop, "This story is from 1920," Scotty said with interest as he read. "It talks about missing four-teen-year-old Lucy Harper, a resident of Penwithick, she disappeared whilst out collecting flowers for her sick mother. It says here that locals found a discarded bunch of flowers in the lane just a half mile from her house."

"Did they find any trace of her in the sea?" Mike asked.

"No, the news reports are not as accurate as they were in the sixties and seventies, and certainly not as accurate or intrusive as they are now," Tara said, closing the story down and opening a fresh screen, this was an MS Word document that she'd prepared. "These are all earlier reports, or mentions of missing persons in the area, dating back to the early eighteen-hundreds. I couldn't find any records earlier than that. Every case I've noted involves a female aged thirteen to eighteen years old who vanished without a trace and was never found. A few reports speak of possible drownings."

"I don't see any cases here linked to Trellen, or any mention of The Old Chapel, or whatever it was called back then."

Tara had obviously foreseen his question and she next fired up a Google map of the area. "These place names are old," she said scrolling across the map. "Villages and towns have grown a bit over the years, naturally, but I've tried to be as accurate as I can with where the girls went missing from."

Mike looked at the dots, whilst Trellen did not feature in any of the disappearances, in a rough kind of way it did sit in the centre of the dots, but then so did a few other tinpot villages. And if all this was somehow and impossibly all linked, why? He scrunched his face up and ran a hand over his stubble, it was bordering on hobo and he'd need to shave today, certainly before he met Mark. "It's tenuous," he said after a long pause. "Plus, all these missing persons refer to girls or young women, not one male. How do you explain Henry Harrison?"

Tara looked at him for a few drawn out seconds, "I can't," she said sounding deflated. "It's the only one that doesn't fit."

"Also," Mike added, "all these other disappearances relate to kids who went missing outside, not from inside the home. And quite how they could all be linked when we are looking at a timeline of over two hundred years is beyond me. There are similarities, sure – I will give you that, but sometimes when we look for something too hard, we start to see things that just aren't there."

"This is it, Mike," Tara said, her voice full of conviction. "I can't answer all those questions yet, I just have this feeling." Mike knew "that" feeling, it was one an investigator got when they were on the right track. Even Samuels had said earlier about often knowing when he was on the right track, even if he didn't have all the evidence yet.

He placed a hand on her shoulder and said, "It's good work, really – but I don't think I can take this to Samuels, I mean not only is this spanning over two centuries, but there's also no discernible pattern, either. I mean you get a spate of two of three vanishings over a few years, then nothing to note for thirty, then another one or two, then forty years. As I said, there are similarities in the cases, but this is a coastal region, kids go missing, kids drown. Look at any area of this size over such a period of time and you will probably find similar reports."

"It could be a cult?" Scotty said almost absently. He'd been sat quietly thinking and listening to the conversation.

"That's quite a leap of faith to make," Mike said, turning to look at him. "I know there were rumors of SRA with the upper echelons of power, Bohemia Grove for example, especially in the seventies and eighties. And sure – yes, a few people have testified to abuse, some of it pretty fucking horrific, too. But never anything like this. Cults come and go, if this was the work of a single cult it would be one that has spanned over two hundred years, abducting and abusing, likely murdering young women for that period of time and never having been caught."

"You keep highlighting the fact these cases span two centuries like that's a bad thing, what if that IS the key, the thing that has always been missed by the police."

"I just don't want us going off on a tangent, going down the wrong path with this and drawing inferences before we've even been to the place, that's all."

"There's a museum of Witchcraft and the Occult in Boscastle," Scotty said, ignoring Mike. "If there was something going on, something of that magnitude then they might have heard something, even just whispers."

Tara was now busy on her phone, "They close at six," she said to Scotty, before turning her attention to Mike. "You have your date at seven with Inspector Samuels, why don't Scotty and I take a drive out there, it's only twenty-five miles away."

"I really don't.." Mike began before Tara cut him off.

"You said yourself that our job was to look at this from an angle the police won't, and that's just what I'm doing. Maybe I've put two and two together and come up with ten, but the cult thing was on my mind as well. Before Scotty mentioned it, but I am glad he did without me influencing him. The place looks like a chapel, people who stay there either report some really fuckin' weird shit, or for some reason after staying there something goes wrong in their heads and they kill themselves, or worse, like that woman and her baby. What if that place was a place of worship, just not one that would ever be registered because of what they worshipped there? What they did there? I think we need to follow this up, Mike."

"You don't need my permission to go," Mike said with a smile. "If you have a feeling about this line of enquiry, no matter how farfetched I think it might be, you see it through."

Tara eyed him, and he found it hard to read what she was thinking, There was no doubt she was strong-willed, he'd known that since their first meeting, and he knew that trying to fight her on this was about as futile as resisting The Borg. *Scotty would like that one,* he thought.

Finally, she sighed and said, "I was just hoping you'd be a bit more, oh I don't know – enthusiastic about what I'd found."

"It's gotta be worth a look," Scotty said, backing her up. "If it leads nowhere it leads nowhere. Besides, while you're out buttering up the local plod, we will just be sat here twiddling our thumbs."

Mike nodded, knowing he was beaten. "Okay, follow this line of enquiry through as far as you can, if it goes nowhere, we draw a line under it and move on."

"Are you going to show Samuels this?" Tara asked. "I have the files on email link and PDF, I can send them to your phone."

"Not yet," he said with a slow shake of the head.

"It's not tight enough to do that." He checked his watch, it was four PM. The poor parents of the missing Harrison kids would be sitting down to a bank of mercilessly hungry camera flashes, both no doubt looking like a doomed animal caught in the headlights of a fast approaching car. *Those poor bastards,* he thought to himself. "You two best get moving if you're going to Boscastle," he concluded. "We will meet back here at nine tonight and compare notes."

CHAPTER 26

MIKE THREADED HIS JEEP PAST THE 'TRELLEN Welcomes Careful Drivers' sign at ten to seven that Sunday evening. The sun had begun its slow and gradual descent into the westerly horizon and orange tendrils of light were starting to trace their way through the deep blue of the sky, soon a magnificent fiery sunset would be issuing the last rights on the day.

Mike lifted off the accelerator, slowing the Jeep so as to take in as much of the village as possible. He passed the decaying roadside shrine that marked the spot where Winns Estate Agent, Karl Banks' life had been suddenly and horrifically cut short in a head-on collision some two years ago. Then at no more than twenty miles an hour, on past six driveways, none of the houses they served visible to him from the road.

He knew from Google Maps satellite imagery that The Old Chapel lay like an idol in the centre of the small village, making the total number of properties in Trellen, thirteen. Soon he saw a battenburged Police Ford Transit pulled across the drive, blocking access to any unauthorised visitors. A line of blue and white chevroned Police tape ran the length of the outer perimeter wall and met with a traffic cone where it broke and gave way to the van. Then on the other side, toward the front of the vehicle it began a new at an identical cone, then stretched the length of the far wall until it met a sturdy looking oak. Whomever had fixed the second section of tape had done so upside down and the words POLICE DO NOT CROSS fluttered idly and inverted in the light summer evening breeze.

Mike flicked on his left turn indicator and slowed the vehicle to a stop, drawing level with the transit and almost blocking the road. The van contained a uniformed bobby who got out of the driver's side clutching a clipboard. Mike lowered the electric window and felt the heat of the day rush into his chilled cab.

"Mike Cross," he said to the officer who looked fresh-faced and no older than twenty-five. "I'm here to see DI Mark Samuels. I believe he is expecting me."

The officer looked him up and down through the window whilst he bit absently on his lower lip, a look of slight annoyance dressing his face at having to actually get out of the van. He glanced at the clipboard, scribbled Mike's name onto what experience told him would be the outer scene log and said, "The DI is waiting for you, just pull down the drive," gesturing with his hand as if directions were needed. "Give me a sec to pull the van outta the way."

Mike nodded in understanding and craned his neck taking in his first real look at the renovated chapel, its stone walls and large stained-glass reproduction windows just visible at the end of the long, straight, shingle drive. Mike could see a further two marked cars down there, a Crime Scene Examiners van and a dark metallic grey Vauxhall Astra, the same car he'd seen Samuels drive away from the Travel Lodge in some hours earlier.

The officer jumped back into the cab, the engine was running to power the aircon and Mike saw a darkened patch on the shingle where the water expelled from the condenser had soaked into the ground. The van reversed slowly back out onto the road pulling directly in behind Mike's Jeep, allowing him to lock the wheel in a tight left and swing in between the old stone gateposts.

Samuels was stood leaning against the boot of his Astra thumbing through some papers, he spotted Mike as he approached and raised a hand lazily in greeting. Mike pulled to a stop behind the CID car and feeling a dose of trepidation, got out.

"Good to see you again buddy," Samuels said, placing the papers on the roof of the car and taking Mike's hand in his and pumping it up and down a few times. "Can you believe this weather?"

"No sign of it letting up," Mike said in agreement. "Give it a day of rain when it finally breaks and the ones complaining about the heat will start bleating on about it being the wettest summer ever!"

Samuels chuckled, "Yeah," he said still smiling, "that's about the truth of it, too."

"Any progress?" Mike asked, nodding toward the building.

Samuels sighed and adjusted the collar of his light blue shirt; a line of sweat had chased its way around the top of the collar. "Nothing, zippo, zilch," he said.

"How was the press conference?"

"Pretty shit, you know how it is buddy, a pack of hungry press and two distraught parents all thrown into the pit together."

"How are they holding up?"

"The father is doing best, putting a brave face on it all, he has to. Carol – the mother, she is bad, I mean really bad. She didn't say a word in that conference, just looked vacantly at those reporters and let him do the talking. I can't imagine what they must be going through, it always amazes me how people cope." He looked at Mike and Mike knew he was probably regretting what he'd said, Mike's own personal loss momentarily forgotten to him.

"Still no hunch then?" Mike asked, brushing it aside.

It didn't bother him, he didn't want people to pussy-foot around him, having to watch what they said.

"I wish," Samuels replied shaking his head as he spoke. "Take a walk around the place with me while we chat?"

For a moment Mike felt a pang of hope, but he soon realised that his old colleague meant around the outside and not in. "Sure," he said, hiding the disappointment. "You lead the way." His mouth felt parched, like old dried out leather and he wished dearly that he'd stopped on the way and picked up a Coke or bottle of water.

Samuels pushed himself away from the back of the car where he'd been leant and started toward the large stone structure, he cut to the right and made his way onto the lush, green and well-cut lawn.

"Reproduction stained glass fixed windows," Samuel said, gesturing at one of the larger side apertures that had formed part of the original structure. "The later ones are timber oak framed double glazing, lockable from the inside." They reached the back door, a small retaining wall split the rear lawn there into two levels. "Timber framed double glazed rear door, locked from the inside and dead bolted." He sat on the wall and looked in earnest at Mike, squinting slightly in the sun. The looming bell tower cast a long shadow across the grass to the left of the chapel and Mike tilted his head back and looked toward the de-commissioned bell. "Same on the other side and the front door is oak, solid and about three inches thick. Locked again from the inside, dead bolted as well. Both keys were hung by the door, according to the parents."

Mike knew this already, but sometimes to work the problem you had to keep going over it in your head, and sometimes vocalising it helped. Mike joined his old friend on the wall and they now both sat facing the rear door and kitchen window like two old friends just casually shooting the shit on a sunny summers evening. All that was missing was a couple of beers. Mike looked through the rear window and could see what looked to be a plush kitchen with a large American style fridge freezer combo.

"If the parents weren't somehow involved, Mike, you tell me how the fuck those kids got out?"

"I thought you said you didn't suspect them?" Mike replied, the flat stone coping on which he sat felt warm on his behind and he placed his palms flat down to his side onto the smooth stone enjoying the heat of them. A small part of him felt chilled and he wondered if it was the building, or if it was in his head from what he knew.

"I don't. I mean that. But what other explanation is there?" Samuels rubbed his eyes and Mike could see the lines of stress on his face. The powers that be would be leaning a good deal of pressure on him to get this one resolved, either by figuring out just what had happened to the Harrison kids or by finding them alive and solving this riddle.

"Have you noticed anything odd or off with the place?" Mike asked. He didn't have the answers to the questions that Samuels dearly wanted so he began to steer the conversation his way.

Samuel's looked at him as if considering the question, "No," he finally said. Yet in a way that made Mike feel unsure about just how truthful he was being. Mike put the question to bed, for now. It could come out again later once they'd chatted a bit and he had a feel for things. "What is it you think you know about this place?" Samuels asked. There was no mocking in his voice, just genuine puzzlement. "I mean you turn up here out of the blue and in the midst of all this."

Mike took a deep breath and let it out slowly before saying, "On Friday morning, before all this shit kicked off, I took a call from Sue Reed. Her and her husband own this place, but you probably know that." Samuels didn't speak, he just nodded his head. "Tig – Tara,"

Mike corrected, "and I went to see both Sue and Tom at their home in Wiltshire that evening."

Mike proceeded to tell all he knew, about the reports from previous guests and how only one stayed for the whole duration of their booking, about the suicides, and the drowning of the baby. When he'd finished, Samuels looked at the building for a few drawn out seconds, as if it would yield all its secrets to him. "That's quite some ghost story," he finally said with a wry chuckle.

"Do you also know," Mike added, "that anyone, save for the Reeds, who has owned this place has died as a result of it. The original owner, the village Minister, killed in a fire. The guy who originally tried to renovate it died doing the roof, then the estate agent who sold it to the Reeds was killed in a crash, not a mile from here after he'd visited the place post-sale?" Mike instinctively checked his phone. There was no service, but he had an email waiting from Tara that had come through on his journey before he'd really gotten out into the sticks. It had attachments that he'd not be able to open without Wifi but he knew what they were, the two centuries of research she'd done on missing kids in the area. Mike knew she wanted him to show it to Samuels but that wasn't going to happen just yet, not until they knew more. Samuels probably already thought that he was verging on madness; trying to sell him a theory which he didn't even buy into himself would be ludicrous.

"Well it sure seems to have a colourful history," Samuels said. "But I don't see what this has to do with my missing persons case."

"It likely doesn't," Mike said truthfully, "but I knew at some point you'd speak to the Reeds and I didn't want them telling you about why I am here before I got a chance to chat to you myself."

"I appreciate that buddy, I did get a feeling from our chat earlier that you were interested in the case on more than a casual basis." Samuels paused, looked back at the building then said," When you say odd, what exactly do you mean? Ghosts, ghouls, and things that go bump in the night?" He chuckled softly.

"Yeah," Mike said reproachfully. He still felt a little embarrassed at times about broaching the subject with people, especially ones such as Samuels who were engaged in a professional investigation. "I'm guessing from how you asked, and the way you answered my question originally that's a yes?"

"Maybe," Samuels replied, not returning his attention to Mike. "I'd not normally mention it and I didn't plan on adding kindling to your fire but seeing as you asked and are being upfront with me, I'll be the same. Since we started the investigation here there are two things that have struck me as strange."

"Go on," Mike encouraged, naturally leaning closer.

"Firstly, on the day the call came in we had a police dog out here to help search the woods, the damn mutt wouldn't come out of the van. Actually pissed itself right there in the cage and bit the handler. It just stayed there in the van cowering in the back. I've never seen anything like it, Mike. We got another dog out here later that day and the exact same thing happened."

"That is odd," Mike said. He knew police dogs; had known his share of handlers and those pooches usually sprang out of the rear holding cage like a jack-in-the-box as soon as it opened. "They do say animals have a higher sense of things. There was obviously something here neither dog liked."

"I put it down to the heat," Samuels said dismissively.

"What else?" Mike asked. Every nugget of information from what the Reeds had told him, to the petrified police dogs convinced him further that this idyllic looking holiday let had a dark and hidden history, one he was keen to dive into and expose. He wasn't totally sure he was ready to say the place was haunted. He did believe though, that if bad things happened enough in one place, or a singular horrific act occurred then it could somehow imprint itself on a place, as if into the very fabric of the building. Some referred to it as stone tape recordings and many believed they were the reason people saw ghosts, specifically the kind that weren't classed as intelligent hauntings, the ones where the same spirit was often seen walking the halls of a mansion at night, or the old tale of a corpse being seen swinging from a bridge having taken his life after being jilted by his lover. It certainly seemed more plausible to Mike than the spirits of the dead returning from beyond the grave. When he'd been nineteen, he'd done a little travelling in Europe and had visited the infamous Auschwitz. If ever there was a place that felt off, it was there, the feeling whilst inside the fences and halls of that terrible camp of death was almost palpable. Mike wasn't getting any particular bad vibes from The Old Chapel, but then he'd not been inside, yet.

"Last night," Samuels began with some reluctance, "The PC on night turn cordon duty, a lady named Shelly Ardell, fell down the stairs inside. She's fractured her skull and broken her neck."

"Fuck," Mike exclaimed. "What was she doing in there?"

"That, my friend, is the sixty-four-thousand-dollar question," Samuels replied with a non-meaningful chuckle. "She had no reason to be in there, not unless she thought someone was inside."

"You've not managed to ask her yet?"

"Still unconscious," Samuels answered. "It could be that she won't ever wake-up. She has a husband and a three-year-old kid," He looked down at his shoes, then back to the building. "The guy on point at the gate last night, Luke, found her body this morning when he walked down to take a piss in the portaloo and saw she was missing from her car."

"Tragedy after tragedy," Mike said. PC Ardell was

now just another name on his list of people who'd fallen foul of the place.

"Coincidence," Samuels said. "Nothing more." He looked back to Mike and asked, "What's your play here, Mike? There's nothing you can do."

"I know that, I was planning on staying away until this had all been sorted, one way or another, but Sue Reed asked me to come down, see if there was anything I could do. She thinks the building has something to do with what's happened here."

"Impossible," Samuels said in the same dismissive tone, like a parent discounting some tall tale told by a child. Mike knew he was losing him; the conversation was on the turn. "The best thing you can do is head home until the police investigation has finished, then you'll be free to do your spook hunt."

Mike felt anger flare up inside of him, he was an investigator even if he no longer carried a warrant card. "I find rational explanations," Mike defended, his voice firm. "I'm not a sideshow. What I know is there are some pretty far out reports from this place, and disaster seems to follow it like a dog does his master. I'm not suggesting those kids got sucked through the TV like the girl in Poltergeist to the nether realm. I think there is a rational reason behind what's happened, all I am doing is trying to come at this from a direction that I know the police won't."

"The reason we don't come at it from that direction, Mike, is because it's bullshit and will just waste valuable time when we could be following up real lines of enquiry."

"You don't have any lines of fucking enquiry, Mark," Mike said defensively. He didn't want to come to blows with his old colleague, but it was brewing.

"Look, Mike," he said his voice losing some of the irritation, "stay, go – it really doesn't matter. Just don't get involved or in our way, and for Christ's sake stay out of the way of the press. The last thing I need is this becoming a circus. When we finish with the place it's yours to do what you want with."

"Understood," Mike replied, glad the brewing argument had diffused itself. He didn't blame Samuels for the way he thought, he himself had been quick to dismiss Scotty when he'd made the leap of faith to all the random disappearances being the work of some undiscovered cult. Someone coming to him with tales of hauntings mixed with the pressures that he knew his old friend would be facing to solve this likely had him on edge stress-wise. Mike noticed a uniformed officer hurrying around the side of the building signalling frantically at Samuels who got up and strode over to him. Mike tried to listen, but they were too far away for him to hear. After what seemed like an age but was really no more than a few minutes Samuels walked slowly back, his face looking grave.

"Development?" Mike asked, raising his eyebrows.

"Yes, and not for the better," he paused, then ran a hand over his face. "Some tourist walking along the shore down at Charlestown has found a shoe. It's an exact match for the kind that Henry Harrison was wearing when he went missing. Apparently, it even has the poor little bugger's initials on the tongue." He looked gravely at Mike. "This is looking like it might become a murder investigation, Mike and right now the only conceivable people who could have taken those kids out of that place," he gestured at it with a thumb, "are the parents."

"You know that doesn't make sense," Mike said.

"Nothing to do with this case makes sense," Samuel said woefully. "Maybe I read them wrong, who knows. All I know is that right now it's the most rational line of enquiry and no matter what I think they will be coming in."

Mike's thoughts turned directly to the reports that Tara had dug up from the sixties and before, all those missing girls who had seemingly drowned with no real explanation or body ever being found. Also, the reports that had come before, the ones where the full details of what had happened were lost in the bowls of time. *'This is it, Mike, I can feel it,'* She'd said, and he'd dismissed her, now the possibility didn't seem quite so improbable.

CHAPTER 27

FOR A FEW SECONDS WHEN I WAKE, I FORGET, I FORGET about the cancer, the death sentence, and everything is alright. For a few precious seconds it's all okay. And then I remember. I try to go back to sleep, just to have those few seconds again, but I can't, not until the next morning, a morning closer to the day it will actually beat me and win.

Ellie remembered those words clearly, the words of her gran, spoken to her mother from the hospice bed where she'd spent the last few weeks of life, gradually being eaten away by the cancer that had riddled its way through her body. That once vibrant and full of life woman had just withered away until she was no more than skin clinging to bone beneath sterile white sheets. Ellie didn't have cancer, she'd never suffered more than a fractured ankle bone, but now she understood what her gran had meant. For now, she awoke again, and yes – for a few seconds everything was alright, everything was okay. She did forget. And then she remembered. She remembered the blackness of the room, the thin mattress on the cold and unforgiving floor and how it bit into her hip when she lay on her side. She remembered the smell of the damp stone, she remembered how she had no idea how long she'd been there, she remembered that she had no idea if it were night or day.

Her belly grumbled for food despite the fear that lay

in a deeper part of her gut, fear that twisted, turned, and felt as if it were a living thing inside of her. Stronger than her hunger though, was the thirst she felt. her tongue lay like a dirty roll of carpet in her mouth. She had no idea when she'd last drank and the fast setting dehydration had now developed a nauseating headache that threatened to morph into a full blinding migraine. The throb of pain beat a slow rhythm behind her eyes and pulsed at her temples, **thrum-thrum-thrum-thrum.**

She rolled from her side and onto her back, the stabbing pain from her hip making her wince and in the blackness of her cell, her face creased in pain. Her lips felt dry and cracked and she ran a dry tongue over them in a futile attempt to apply a little moisture to the parched skin.

Questions raced through her head; what the hell had happened? Where was she? Henry, he had been in the room with her, what had happened to him? It made her feel sick to think that he might be in danger, might be laid in a room like this, in the dark sobbing for their mother. *Oh God,* Ellie thought, *he'll be so terrified, so scared.* She fought back tears, not tears for her own situation, but for her brother's.

"Henry?" she croaked to the darkness with a broken voice. For all she knew he could be in the room with her, for she had no idea of how big it was.

"Heennrryyyy......." a multitude of voices answered, startling her on the mattress. The sound of them spoke inside her head as well as being audible to her ears. As they spoke his name, she heard insectile feet hurrying across the floor. Busy legs moving with purpose. She shuffled back but her head met the dampness of stone with a painful bump that made her eyes water.

"Elliiiieee ...." the voices spoke again en masse. She felt a spiny leg on her hair, it began to stroke at her brow with the lightest of touches, moving back and forth, the way her mother would stroke her hair when

she'd been a child. Its touch made her stomach turn and froze her with fear. Somewhere close to her ear, mandibles clicked and as they clicked the smell of fetid and burnt flesh hit her in a wave of chilled air that washed over her skin like a breaker striking a stone shore. The sounds and the smells were all too familiar, she'd experienced them before. However, this time there was no open road down which she could flee, she was trapped and at its mercy. There was no escape.

"Who are you?" she asked, channelling her fear into anger. It almost worked, and her voice sounded far more assertive than she'd expected, albeit a little croaky.

"*Weeee areee manyyyy,*" a thousand voices said in a sickening symphony. "And I am one," a singular voice said. The voice was smooth, audible silk on the ears, and yet it didn't soothe, it carried something insidious in its tone. In the darkness, something moved toward her, something not insectile, something bigger on feet that shuffled.

"I – I saw them, the girls, the babies," Ellie said, the dream that had led her to this room still so clear in her mind. It was as if each memory were one of her own, and as she remembered her anger grew. As she thought of her brother, scared, alone and sobbing for mummy, her anger grew, and she let it. The anger quelled the fear and it felt good. "I saw what happened here. How many were butchered, and for what?" she spat. She wanted to reach out to the thing on her brow but that insectile touch still froze her, as if someone had cut her spinal column in the thoracic region and totally paralysed her lower limbs.

"*Elliiieeeee .....*" the voices hissed. "*You are the key, the key, the key...*" they trailed off and died as an echo in a cave might do. "*Hennrryyy...*" they came back with excitement as if his name brought them power. "*The vessel, vessel.*"

The insectile leg ceased on her brow and she felt

something large scurry over her face and she bit back a scream. *"Elliiiee* .... *The key* .... *Hennnryyyy* .... *The vessel* .... *Vessel.......*" The voices trailed off, repeating, overlapping like ripples in a pond until they melted to nothingness.

"If you harm my brother," Ellie began, the paralysis gone with the passing of those legs on her flesh.

"You'll what, Ellie?" the silky voice spat. "You have no idea Ellie Harrison, no idea. You think it's dark in here, just wait until you're in the Abyss. It's so dark Ellie," the voice spoke faster, with passion and venom all at once. "It's so dark, so beautiful, when you feel it, when you experience it, which you will, you'll scream, ohhh how you'll scream, just like they all do. But when you scream in the Abyss the darkness is so thick it consumes it. It consumes you!"

She felt it, him. The Man. She'd seen him in the dark robes in the field. Henry – *poor Henry* – had seen him in his room that first night and now in that blackness, he drew closer. If the room were suddenly bathed in light, she knew he'd be almost on top of her, she could sense his presence, smell the rot of him, and she felt thankful for the darkness.

The stench grew and now she knew he was looming over her, likely inches from her face. The thing had no breath, for the dead did not respire, but the smell of it and the cold consumed her, she felt her skin goosebump and the frigid air chilled her to her core. "Time has no meaning there," the thing continued. Ellie could feel it bearing down on her as if his spirit had a mass that in the world and reality of the living was able to exert physical pressure upon her. "When you scream in there, and you will scream, Ellie, you scream forever!"

In an instant that pressure lifted, the cold abated and the smell cleared just as quickly as if the wave of horror that had brought it forth had just been called back by its ocean master. In the darkness, Ellie trembled and felt a tear roll down her cheek.

CHAPTER 28

IN HER DREAM TARA WAS STANDING IN THE entrance hall of The Old Chapel, the light was fading slowly as if it were losing a battle against the dark. As it fell, Tara felt panic grow inside of her, maturing moment by moment. Something felt wrong, she didn't know why but she could just feel it, and that feeling went right down into the core of her bones.

She knew she needed to find Mike, but Mike was gone. He was somewhere out of reach and she sensed he was in danger, lost somewhere and unable to find his way back to her. She tried to call out to him, but she had no voice, his name falling silently from her lips.

Slowly, from that encroaching darkness, shadows began to birth themselves in the corners, spawning in multitude in the nooks and alcoves, and when the light failed altogether, she knew then that they would truly be free, free to stalk her unhindered, the way a lion might stalk its prey on the plains of the Serengeti.

Tara turned, moving for the door, her progress felt laboured; as if she were struggling through a thick liquid, one intent on impeding her progress and not air. Reaching the door, she began to hammer her hands against the thick wood, and once again, like her voice, the blows fell silently upon its surface. She needed to get out, get away from the place and be anywhere other than there.

The light was almost gone now, reduced to a dim murk, and behind her, she sensed those shadows were now moving, they'd broken free and now they stalked her, keening as they came. That terrible sound echoed through the entrance hall, the sound the only one she could hear, and within it she could feel its hunger, a hunger that she knew would only be quenched when it had her. Tara turned and -

"You dozed off there for a while," Scotty said as she snapped awake. "We are almost there." She swallowed back, her mouth felt cotton dry and she instinctively reached for the bottle of water that was in the drink's holder, unscrewed the blue plastic cap and took a gulp. "Bad dream?"

"Kind of," Tara said, glad to be away from sleep.

"About The Old Chapel?" he asked switching his attention from the road for a split second and looking at her with concern.

"I don't know how," she replied as she fixed the top back on the bottle and replaced it in the holder. "I've only seen pictures."

"You've been focused on nothing else for the past few days," he said matter-of-factly. "It's on your mind, quite natural for it to feature in your dreams, too."

"I guess so," Tara agreed as he swung the T4 round a tight bend and down a hill that dropped them into the village. Many of the buildings were constructed from Cornish stone yet here they were washed in white, their old walls gleamed brightly in the afternoon sun. Scotty took them over a bridge then swung a left onto a road that was only really wide enough for one vehicle. The road followed the path of the river and took them toward its mouth. Beside them, shallow water sparkled and babbled its way over the small rocks and stones of its bed. Over the millennia the small river had carved its way through the land and created the natural valley in which Boscastle now lay. The place would likely flood like a bitch in the winter, but now in the midst of the long hot summer of twenty-eighteen, the water level of the River Valency barely reached the man-made walls that now directed its path to the Atlantic.

"It's literally just down here," Scotty said. "Odd little place, huh?"

"I like it," Tara replied as she looked with interest out the window. "I don't exactly live in the big city, but life down here seems to have a different pace to it."

As he nodded in agreement the satnav announced that in fifty yards their destination would be on the right, and sure enough the narrow road opened out to a carpark that lay opposite a timber and metal footbridge that took pedestrians over the river. An A-board stood beside the bridge with MWM in big white letters formed from a bespoke text font that gave the appearance of having been written with sticks. Under it read "Museum of Witchcraft And Magic".

"This is a pretty long shot," he said as he brought the VW to a stop and cranked the parking brake.

"Better than no shot," Tara answered removing her belt and opening the door. She hopped down into the car park and rounded the van smoothing few non-existent creases from her jean shorts as she went. "If this thing does have anything to do with the occult, I can't think of a better place to start."

It was just gone five PM and there were still a lot of tourists milling about, walking the path of the river to a mouth that was hidden by rolling hills that no doubt ended in ragged cliffs. Opposite the museum was a quaint little tearoom that had the appearance of being straight out of a fairy tale. Business there was booming today, and the outside seating area was rammed with people enjoying some late afternoon sun whilst devouring authentic Cornish cream teas, the scones heaped with clotted cream and topped with jam. As the parents sampled the local baked goods their kids toted various flavours of locally made ice cream; the frozen treats all perched precariously on top of wafer cones. Many ran around and generally did what kids did best, creating havoc and panic for their suffering parents and not being able to sit still.

"Place closes in forty minutes," Scotty noted already heading for the door. "We best not waste any time." The museum name sat above the door on a sign, the name written in gold lettering, a pentagram separating the words Museum and Witchcraft, the word OF written in its centre.

"Last entry was at five PM I'm afraid my loves," the lady on the reception desk said as they walked in. She looked up from a book she was reading, the cover was faced down on the wooden counter, so Tara couldn't see what the title was. "We open again at ten-thirty tomorrow," she smiled at them and removed her gold-rimmed, wire-frame glasses and gave them a polish on her light and multi-coloured neck scarf before affixing the arms firmly back behind her ears and pushed the front up and onto the narrow bridge of her nose.

Tara guessed she was in her early sixties; her hair was a greying blonde that although combed and straightened had started to go a little straggly. Save for her colourful neck scarf her clothes were black, likely a requirement of the job, worn to add a little of that Witchy appearance for the benefit of the paying guests.

"Oh, we," Tara began.

"Hold on a second," the woman said, a smile forming on her thin lips. "Aren't you?"

"Tara Gibb," Tara said with a warm smile realising this was one of those few times where she was actually recognised, "And this is Scott Hampton."

"Unexplained UK, right?" The smile was all the way across her face now, it reached her light blue eyes which sparkled with excitement behind her freshly cleaned lenses.

"That's us!" Tara exclaimed.

"I've seen every show from your first season," the woman said. "I like the style of it," she paused and then said with a wink, "No bullshit - if you'll pardon my French." She gave a cheeky grin like that of a child who'd just gotten away with saying a naughty word.

"We try," Scotty interjected, not bothering to mention that was one of the very reasons they'd been shit-canned.

"Is Mike Cross with you?" she craned her neck around them as if expecting to see him walking in behind.

"He's engaged on other business," Scotty explained as he casually picked up a flyer from the counter. It advertised their future Halloween events. The title encouraged people to, **Book Early To Avoid Disappointment.**

"Is this a business visit?" the woman asked, standing up from the small stool on which she'd been sat. "Filming in the area perhaps? If so, I can make an exception to that five PM rule. I don't usually get clear of the place until seven anyway. You know by the time I've locked down, run the tills and done a little paperwork."

Tara grimaced a little, "Kinda," she said. It wasn't a lie, but it wasn't exactly the truth either. "Do you run the museum?"

"Since the day it opened its doors," she said proudly. "June Rogers," she introduced herself sticking an eager hand out across the counter. "This is a pleasant surprise I must say. We don't get celebrities in here every day, that's for sure."

Tara took her hand for the obligatory shake, chuckled and said, "Thanks, but I hardly think we qualify as that." Scotty obliged the handshake too, smiling politely as he took in a few of the exhibits right by the entrance.

"We are working a case near here," he began taking his attention back to June and shooting straight from the hip. "A small village about thirty miles south of here called Trellen. Have you heard of it?"

A shadow seemed to fall across June's face, the smile washed away, "You mean apart from that business with those two poor missing kids?" she asked.

Tara nodded, "We were asked by the owners to investigate the place they went missing from before all this happened, The Old Chapel. We are kinda on hold until this whole thing blows over."

"What brought you to me, my dear?" June asked.

"If I'm honest," Tara said intrigued by June's reaction, "nothing more than a hunch. You see I started to look at missing persons cases in the area over the last two centuries, it's probably nothing but -"

"You found something to cause you concern?" June asked cutting her off. It was more rhetorical than a straight up question. She slid the glasses off her face and let them hang by a neck cord.

"You have heard of it, haven't you?" Scotty asked, his face forming a frown. "I mean from before this missing person case?"

She nodded gravely, "I'd imagine you know that the original owner of that place, The Old Chapel as its now called, was a man named Deviss."

"That's right," Tara said with excitement. "Johnathan Deviss."

"I believe the name should be spelled D-E-V-I-C-E," she corrected spelling it out. De-vice, but it's pronounced Deviss, I'm not sure when it changed to the latter spelling, or why."

"Device," Tara said, running the word over her tongue. "It's been bugging me since I first heard it, I know that name, but I don't know where from."

June paused and watched as a family made their way past the counter and out the door, "Thanks for coming, be sure to come see us again," she said in a cheerful voice. The father thanked her and led his two young kids, who seemed to be pretending to ride broomsticks, out into the carpark and toward the packed tearoom. "You should know that name dear if you know your Witchcraft history." June raised her eyebrows, obviously hoping Tara would take the hint.

Tara stood for a few seconds, then it sunk in, "De-vice - as in the Pendle Witch Trials?" she asked slowly.

June smiled and clasped her hands together, "You do know your Witch history." The smile wasn't as real as the one that she'd worn upon realising who they were, it fell from her lips and she continued. "In sixteen twelve, the execution of the Pendle Witches wiped out almost the entire Device family," June's voice seemed to switch into story mode and Tara guessed it was the tone she used on paying visitors when recounting a particularly nasty or juicy piece of Witchcraft history. "The family was survived by one member."

"Jennet Device," Tara said.

June nodded, impressed with her knowledge. "Nine-year-old Jennet's testimony literally put the nooses around the necks of her family. Did you know she was one of the first child witnesses to ever give evidence in a court of law, and that trial bore the way for how child witnesses give evidence to this day? Although we now don't try people for practicing the dark arts, thank goodness."

"I didn't," Tara said with genuine interest. "How does this relate to Trellen? I mean we are in Cornwall; Pendle must be hundreds of miles north. It's also over four-hundred years later?"

June checked a small bank of CCTV cameras that showed the various rooms of the museum, the walls were lined top to bottom with various curiosities of the occult from throughout the ages. "All in good time my dear," she said holding her hand up. "I think that family were the last customers," she added. "Maybe I should lock-up, and we can discuss this in private. It's not a subject I feel comfortable talking about when someone might wander in." She rounded the counter, closed the door and latched it shut, swinging the sign to **Sorry We're Closed** as she went.

"History can have a certain sense of irony," June began and she deadbolted the door, looking back at them as she spoke. "Twenty-two years after young Jennet gave the evidence that saw the necks of her family stretch, in sixteen thirty-three, she herself was arrested on suspicion of witchcraft. Yet another piece of irony was that on her incarceration and when she was tried at Lancaster Assizes, the evidence was given by a juvenile, just as she had been. On this occasion, it was a young man by the name of Edmund Robinson, aged ten, just a year older than Jennet herself had been when she was the star witness in that infamous Pendle Hill trial. Young Master Robinson claimed that whilst out picking berries he was approached by two dogs; those dogs are purported to have turned into a boy and a woman. Master Robinson then claimed the boy was turned into a white horse and the Witch, whom he recognised as a woman named Francis Dickson, took him on the horse to a place called Hoarstones. At Hoarstones he claimed that more witches arrived on horseback and some kind of ceremony ensued that produced smoking flesh, butter, and milk. I have no doubt that over the years his true testimony has been somewhat altered. It's a long and convoluted story, which I expect you will read in your own time." June said. She rounded the counter again and perched herself on the stool. "The long and short is that Jennet Device, now a young woman in her twenties, was identified as being present and one of the witches whom carried out the ceremony. She ended up being charged with the murder of a lady named Isabel Nutter, wife of one William Nutter. The boy, Robinson, later cracked under interrogation and claimed he'd made the whole thing up. Although I'm not so sure, what he described was an accurate account of a certain conjuring ceremony that was popular back then. The boy would have had no business knowing about it. Charles the first was now king of England and he didn't hold the same belief in witchcraft that his predecessors had done, his father being one. His father had been a very superstitious man. Anyway, Jennet managed to escape the death penalty that was usually afforded to those suspected of being involved in the dark arts and murder back then. She was actually pardoned for her alleged crimes but as she, as well as few of the other women accused with her, failed to pay for their keep in prison, she was incarcerated for life at Lancaster Gaol anyway." June smiled solemnly at them, "Or that's the official story anyway. Within the confines of those involved in the occult, there is a different story, one that it is rumoured leads right to your chapel, that village and the present day!"

CHAPTER 29

JUNE POURED HOT COFFEE FROM A PERCOLATOR THAT was sat on her desk into three logo bearing mugs that were no doubt available to buy in the gift shop. The aroma of the ground beans now brewed in the scalding hot water had cast away the slightly musty smell that all museums seemed to hold, replacing it with something warm and homely.

"Milk and sugar?" she asked both Tara and Scotty with a smile, she waved a silver teaspoon back and forth in front of her.

"Just milk for me," Tara said.

The office was reasonably sized, files and lever-arch folders of paperwork lined the walls on black Formica shelving that ran along the side and back wall. A small fan was clipped onto the edge of the furthest shelf, its power cord trailed down to a plug socket. The fan issued a monotonal *creak-creak-creak* as it swung back and forth, its small blades hardly stirring the warm air inside the room. On the side wall next to the led-lined window was a 2018-year planner. On it was marked the opening days and times of the museum, along with staff holidays all in varying colours of highlighter, just like you'd find in a thousand offices across the country. There were two desks, one of which was pushed against the far wall below the creaking fan, this was the one upon which Tara was half sat, and half perched. The desk was clean and in neat order, biro pens with bitten ends were stood on end in a blue plastic desk tidy, the kind that had three tubes of differing depths. A mandatory pile of coloured paperclips had been stuffed into the smallest tube, a heaped pile of reds, greens and light pinks. A red faux-leather 2018 diary lay by an HP Laptop, the screen was on and featured a picture of the museum from the air, Tara guessed it had been taken by drone. The desk at which June was making drinks was in a little more disorder, papers and letters for filing were untidily stacked in one corner and two now cold cups of tea or coffee were festering having been pushed to the back of the desk. They'd been forgotten long enough to start forming that white scum on the top.

Scotty pushed the chair upon which he sat back and forth on its coasters, his Nike trainers moving from heel to toe against the industrial blue carpet floor tiles. Tara thought he looked a bit fidgety and his large frame looked too big for the chair, he looked to June and said, "Just as it comes out the pot for me, thanks."

June nodded and made a slight grunting noise as if in agreement and doused Tara's in a hefty splash of milk, then poured Scotty's and placed both on card coasters that bore the museums MWM logo, just as the mugs did. She slowly settled herself into an identical chair to the one that Scotty was sat in, her wiry frame not filling the chair as he did. She collected up her brew and looked solemnly at them both, the way a person might look at a friend to whom they are about to break bad news. Finally, she sighed and said, "Are you sure you want to hear this?"

"We need to hear it," Scotty replied, now cradling his cup of strong black in his hands. He stopped the chair moving and now sat still and focused, the cup held just below his chin. "To be honest I am at the point where I don't know what to believe."

June nodded slowly, her intelligent blue eyes still

moving between them. "There are things," she began in a low voice, "that once a person has heard and knows can't be unheard, they can't be unknown. They are with you forever and never far from reach in your mind."

"Warning understood," Tara said seriously. "You got to the point where Jennet was imprisoned for life because she couldn't pay her prison bill." She was eager to hear what the old lady knew. Inside she felt an odd mixture of excitement and solid cold dread that lay on her like a stone slab.

"First," June said as she placed her mug onto her desk by the stacked post and papers, "I need to know what you know. Why were you asked to investigate the place? Leave nothing out, every detail my dear."

Tara looked at Scotty who raised his eyebrows in a way that she knew meant - you got this one, fill your boots! She adjusted her behind on the desk, rocked back on the heels of her Skechers and said, "On Friday just gone, Mike took a call from a lady named Sue Reed. She and her husband, Tom bought The Old Chapel from an estate agency called Winns a few years back now. They renovated it to a holiday home." Tara grabbed the top of her phone, it was protruding out of the small pocket of her shorts. She crossed the room and crouched by June's chair and began flicking slowly through a few of the internal shots she had saved to her gallery. "It's been open for a few months now," she said, talking as she perused through the images, "So far all but one guest has left before the end of their stay, and that's not the worst of it. One killed their baby after staying there, drowned the poor little soul in the bath, then took her own life. Another just straight out gassed himself in his car." Tara stood and went back to the far desk and rested on the edge of it. June nodded for her to continue. "Reports of paranormal activity in The Old Chapel have ranged from shadows that seem to move," a chill ran through her as she recalled the dream, "to doors closing. Pretty normal stuff when it comes to re-

ports of the paranormal, the kind of thing we have debunked in the past. One guest reported that furniture
moved, and one child said that a dark man had been in
her room," Tara let out an uneasy chuckle. "The last
two maybe not quite so easy to debunk, nor is the main
and most commonly reported phenomenon."

"Go on my dear," June encouraged. "You are among
likeminded here, nothing you say will be laughed at or
treated with scepticism."

Tara smiled weakly then continued, "The most
common phenomenon reported, and I will add experienced by the owners too, is the crying. Sue told Mike
and me that on an almost nightly basis the cries of infants can be heard echoing through the building. No
specific time, they just come and go. Sue Reed was
quite disturbed by it, she actually broke down in tears
and wanted to know what could have happened to
those babies to make them cry the way they do."

"Dear Lord," June said, then took a drink from her
mug as if it contained something stronger that she
needed to settle her nerves. For a moment they sat in
pensive silence, the slow *creaakkkk-creaakkkk-creaakkkk*
of the fan the only sound as it moved back and forth,
but now it somehow seemed more drawn out than it
had a few minutes ago.

Tara sipped at her hot coffee then continued,
"Tragedy seems pretty common when it comes to The
Old Chapel, too. Obviously, Minister Deviss died there,
and you have the infant murder and two suicides. But
going further back, a guy named Bough owned it before
the Reeds, he fell to his death working on the roof. One
of Tom Reed's young labourers on the site quit then
hung himself. Lastly the day it was sold the estate agent
who done the deal was killed in a head-on not half a
mile down the road." Tara sighed, "'I've tried to research the place but it's dead-end after dead-end. I do
know that the building was never officially registered as
a place of worship," she paused, her throat was dry

again and she wetted it with a swig of coffee. Tara wiped the back of her hand across her lips and continued. "When those Harrison kids went missing Sue asked us to head down and see if we could help. Before we got involved with the show, Mike was a PI and before that a cop."

"I know of Mr. Cross' backstory from watching the show," June said with a smile. "I'd imagine though, that there was not much you could do without treading on the toes of the police."

"Exactly," Tara agreed. "Knowing what we did about the place we agreed to try and come at this from an angle the police would never dream of." Tara paused and took on some more coffee. It was a good blend, maybe a five or a six on the strength chart and not a cheap one. "Did you know they still can't figure out how the Harrison kids got out of that building?" she concluded.

"I have been following the story with some interest," June replied. "But no, that's not been mentioned in detail, how interesting. Do you have any theories?"

"No," Tara said with a shake of her head. "Neither do the police. Mike just happens to know the DI in charge, that's where he is now, out at The Old Chapel meeting with him." A look of concern flashed across June's face that didn't help the way Tara was feeling. "Anyway," she continued, the windows were shut and secured, doors locked and deadbolted from the inside!" Tara paused again as June looked like she was about to speak, she didn't, instead she just nodded and accepted what Tara had told her as fact. "We can't even get in to have a look around the place at the moment, it's locked down. We came down here on the request of the Reeds but we were all starting to feel a bit useless, I mean what is there that we could possibly do? Today I got fed up with feeling like a spare part, so I thought I'd just poke around the records that are held online to see if there were any other missing persons cases that didn't add up. You know, ones that might have been over-looked by the police."

"And you found a few didn't you my dear?" June's voice was laced with knowing.

Tara nodded. June's words had made her stomach turn, her throat felt impossibly dry again. "All girls, all between the ages of fourteen and eighteen," she began. "There were other cases of course, but the ones I refer to all fit a similar, what Mike would call modus operandi. They all disappeared without a trace, all from stable homes and from what I can see were steady stable kids. Not long after going missing some piece of evidence turns up that suggests they drowned." Tara paused reflectively, giving her words time to sink in and be processed. "And yet," she continued, after a final swallow of coffee, "the disappearances are spread out over more than two hundred years, and that's as far as I could go back. There is no specific pattern to them, the last one, for example, was in sixty-nine. Sometimes a few decades pass and there are no vanishings, some years there are a couple." Tara scratched at the back of her head, unintentionally highlighting her puzzlement. "There's just no real cycle or pattern to it."

June nodded in understanding and said very matter-of-factly, "I'd imagine that if you could go further back, you'd find more, many more."

"The cases were all too far apart for the police to ever link together, but I had a hunch there was some-thing there. It was Scotty who suggested that they could be linked to the occult."

"It seemed like a logical step to take," Scotty cut in. "I mean if there is a link that's the only rational way to explain why they would span such a period of time. But still, abuse that spans that length of time is unheard of."

"That's very astute of you both," June said sounding genuinely impressed, "What does Mr. Cross think?"

Scotty laughed briefly and said, "He thinks we are barking up the wrong tree."

"He is a good investigator from what I have seen," June said in Mike's defence. "However, he is a former police officer and PI, his decision making will still be influenced by his training, and that's hard to work out of someone." June drained her cup, she let it swing by the handle on her fore and middle finger as she looked from Scotty to Tara, taking them both in once again. "There are those who move in the same circles as myself," she said, her voice now serious once again, "that think that the things I am going to tell you about that place, the Device family and the village of Trellen as a whole are no more than folk law, urban myth you might say."

"And what do you believe?" Scotty asked.

"I believe beyond a doubt that the place is evil," she replied instantly. "I believe that no good will come of you going there and investigating it. I'd go as far as saying if you do, you will put yourselves in mortal danger and I'd appeal to you to walk away now."

Scotty chuckled and leaned back in his chair, it creaked under his weight. "That's quite some speech," he said smiling. "Like the one in the horror film where the main character gets told whatever you do don't go down in the basement, or out after midnight."

"I'm being deadly serious, Mr. Hampton. This is no horror film; I say it because I mean it. Because I believed it to be so."

Tara suffered another chill, her hackles rose from just how dead-pan serious June was, she believed her, too. Right then, and at that point she both wanted badly to investigate The Old Chapel, and she also wanted badly to play no further part in this, to do just what June had suggested, get in the car and drive away from it all, leave it well alone. However, she knew that to truly uncover the secrets of The Old Chapel they would need to go there, experience the horrors for themselves and live it. Somewhere outside a car horn sounded, then another honked louder in reply, it shook her from the momentary daydream. "I think it's time you told us just what really happened to Jennet Device in Lancaster Gaol," she said a little reluctantly.

"Very well," June agreed with a nod. "As I told you Jennet was pardoned for her alleged crimes but still ended up incarcerated as she could not pay the bill for the time she'd spent in prison. History, which wants us to believe that witchcraft and occultism is all nonsense, reports that Jennet likely died in prison, but there is no official report." June smiled wryly and added, "History assumes, and we all accept. Just as most modern dumbed down people believe what the news tells them and takes it as the truth. The way we understand the truth of it is that one night a large black crow flew into her room. The crow was a physical embodiment of the demon Mamillian and he came to her after she conjured him forth from the Abyss."

"The Abyss?" Tara questioned, "As in Hell?"

June chuckled, "That's Christian dogma," she said. "Although certain religious symbols of good can be empowered to work against that ancient evil, simply from the belief that is held in them."

"You said she summoned a demon, surely that's Christian based belief?" Scotty asked.

"No," June said, with a shake of her head, it caused a few strands of her greying blonde hair to fall over her face, she swept them away with a hand. "Many religions believe in demons, things that have never lived in this reality, nor do they have any place here. It is one of the main constants that seems to be agreed upon between faiths." She halted for a second to make sure that both Tara and Scotty were with her, neither spoke so she carried on. "Although you could call The Abyss Hell, it's a fitting description for the place and without doubt the basis for it. The Abyss is much older than the idea of Hell as a place where sinful human souls go to burn. The Abyss is as old as our known universe, and as I said a place where the things dwell that have no business being here."

"I don't understand," Tara said.

"Witchcraft is about tapping into magical powers of this Earth, and conjuring things not of this realm that are not governed by the laws of the physical world, and yet can have influence here." June adjusted herself on her seat. "Some spells heal, some curse and others conjure. Some are so old that we don't know of their true origin. What I am saying, my dear, is now we understand that there are many layers to reality, more than we as mortals can comprehend. This thinking is backed up by the science, by the work and thinking of establishments like CERN, a union of the old ways and the new. I follow what they do there closely, and if you doubt me read up on it, I'm sure you will find it quite compelling. There have been many links to the occult and that establishment, and the dark arts side, too. These other realities are all around us now, like the layers of an onion, we just can't see them. However, as was found in old times, certain ceremony and sacrifice *could* help bridge that gap, *could* allow things from realms not governed by our physical laws to interact here, even cross over to this reality. I can't explain how or why they do. I guess in a way that no one understands we and they are all interlinked. I have long believed this universe to be a complicated place, it is not our job to question its workings, and the more questions you ask of the universe, the more questions it gives you in reply."

"I think I understand," Tara said.

"The spirit world for example," June stated. "I believe that is another layer to reality, it is around you now in this very room, at this very moment. It's in the air you breathe, in the space your body occupies."

"You've lost me again?" Tara said with a sigh.

"Think of it this way," June said, "You are in your car and you have on Radio One," she held up her ring-clad left index finger and gave it a waggle. "You know Radio

Two is there, but you can't hear it," June extended the index and middle finger on her right hand and held them side-by-side as Tara nodded in understanding. "It's there," June highlighted, "but at the moment your radio is not tuned in, it does not mean it doesn't exist, you'd never doubt its existence, and you know that if you change the radio to the frequency it's on you would hear it just fine."

"So, I guess," Scotty said, placing his hands on his knees and leaning forward, "that someone who is genuinely psychic has the ability to move between the frequencies of our world and the spirit world."

"Exactly," June said. "In a mental capacity anyway. Our two worlds are very close together and separated by a thin veil. We all have the ability within our brains to move between the two, just for many that particular part of the brain doesn't work. When you get reports of interactive hauntings or spirit voices, or people seeing ghosts it's an abnormality in the frequency, a shift so the two bleed over one another. I believe that to be true of what you'd class as intelligent hauntings anyway. But you must understand, The Abyss is not a place that is close to the frequency of this reality, it's a dark place where nightmares beyond your comprehension exist, a realm of pure chaos and eternal night. I actually believe its where we get our instinctive fear of the dark from. The things there, demons you may call them, it is as good a name as any for what they are, are ancient. They've existed longer than humans, but how they envy and hate us."

"And Jennet Device supposedly done a deal with a demon from this place?" Scotty asked. Tara looked at him and saw his face also held a shroud of disbelief.

"She did," said June, nodding. "The deal was that if he freed her from her cell that she would devote her mind, body, and soul to him so that he might leave The Abyss and dwell in our world."

"That seems very far-fetched," Scotty said.

"Believe what you will, Mr. Hampton," June said. "It matters not to me. Remember you came to me, not the other way around. You made that leap of faith from what Miss Gibb found to link it with the occult and you ended up here. Did you ever stop to consider there may be higher powers working here than you understand?"

"Higher powers?" Scotty questioned.

"If things of pure evil exist and can have influence here, is it not conceivable that things of pure good can do the same? That maybe there is a divine power working through you, through the three of you."

"I'm sorry, I'm not sure I can believe that," Scotty laughed, not in a mocking way, more with disbelief. "My brain made that link, by pure chance and my own free will."

"You need not apologise, Mr. Hampton," June said with a wry smile. She rolled her chair forward and patted his left hand with her right, then sat back in her chair and continued, "A year after young Miss Device just upped and vanished from Lancaster Gaol it is understood that she bore a son and that the son was the spawn of the demon Mamilian. Miss Device had fled the north and it is thought she came to Cornwall where she raised the boy and settled that village. I do not know how or when Jennet Device died, there is no official record of it, but we understand that she is no longer living."

"You're not suggesting that–?" Tara began.

"That that boy was Johnathan Deviss, or De-vice, as his name should be spelled."

"But – that had to have been – four hundred years ago?"

"Jennet Device *was* a witch," June said in that flat and matter-of-fact way of hers, the tone of voice that said her word was gospel and you'd best bloody-well believe it. "Her pledge to the dark arts would have afforded her a longer than natural life. We don't know how long true witches of the occult live, some say as long as two hundred years, some say less. Her son, Johnathan, was the son of a witch and the embodiment of Mamilian. He would have been a very powerful warlock; he would not have been eternally immortal, but he would have had longevity beyond our capabilities. I suspect that the missing girls you have found were used to breed babies for the sole purpose of sacrifice. That sacrifice of the innocent and in particular new life is a very powerful thing. It's a way to spit at the act of creation, it's also a way to transfer that pure lifeforce and extend his days."

"And what of the girls?"

June shrugged, "I believe that others in that village are part of the same coven and that the lives of the girls were also likely used in sacrifice to prolong the life of the others. I can't be sure."

"Is there any hard evidence for this?" Scotty asked.

"Just word," June said.

"And no one has ever tried to stop it? It's never been reported?" Tara asked.

"Reported to who, my dear? The police? Just how do you think they would react?"

"Yeah, shit – I guess," Tara agreed.

"And in answer to your first question, yes one person has tried, well one that I know of."

"Who?" Scotty asked.

"That fire back in two thousand and eight was no accident," June said. "It was a deliberate attempt to kill Device, to kill the beast by cutting the head off the snake."

"Who?" Scotty said again, a little more urgently.

"A man by the name of Richard Hawks," June said. One of the last of the modern day witch hunters. There are few left now, and thankfully modern-day witch hunting only involves the tracking and persecution of those involved in the dark arts, not those who practise magic for healing and for good.

"He started the fire?" Tara asked. For some reason

the sudden revelation that there were still those in society who hunted witches hadn't shocked her. She felt as if she'd crossed over a line now, one where the majority of folk stood in blissful ignorance to the darker things of this world. She and a few unlucky ones were on the other side, and now there was no going back.

June nodded, "Witches and warlocks are not immortal in this realm, they are vulnerable to attack. You don't need silver bullets or holy water, nor do they need a stake through the heart. They can be killed reasonably easily, as any person can, however, the best method and one that also purifies is fire."

"How did you know this Richard Hawks?" Scotty asked.

"I've been involved with the occult for many years. I aided him with his investigation into Trellen, he never got very far though, it is a closed sect, very powerful yet very private. That chapel is the rotten heart of that village, it's stone matriarch, and he believed that if he could kill Device and destroy the place it would put an end to it. I thought it had, I thought what he'd done had worked. Then when I saw that those kids had gone missing I felt sick."

"Where is this Richard Hawks now?" Scotty asked.

"I never heard from him after the fire, he was never seen again. I don't even want to guess what happened to him, and now what makes it worse is that his sacrifice appears to have been made in vain."

Scotty nodded, then looked a little uncomfortable. Finally he asked, "Are – you – a.."

"A what? Mr. Hampton, a witch?"

"Y-yeah?" he asked his face flushing red.

June laughed, "No need to be shy, Mr. Hampton." Her laughter was genuine and it made her eyes gleam, it seemed to lighten the heavy mood that had bestowed itself upon the office. "In answer to your question, no. Not in that sense of the term. I am a sensitive, though."

"As in psychic?"

"Yes, although I'm not what you'd call a stable one. The gift comes and goes, I have no control over it." June stood and poured more coffee into their cups, furnishing Tara's with more milk.

"And the Harrison kids?" Tara asked. "Where do you think they feature in all of this?"

"I don't know fully," June said with remorse.

"But none of the previous vanishings took place in Trellen?" Tara questioned. She placed her full mug onto the desk not feeling like another dose of caffeine. "It just doesn't make sense."

"I'm afraid I don't have the answer to that one, my dear. But, July 27th marks a very important day on the satanic calendar. Its true roots though, go back much further and predate the Satanic church. Satanists call it The Grand Climax; it occurs five weeks and one day after the summer solstice."

"That's in five days," Tara said. "What happens on the 27th?"

"Terrible things," June said with fear in her voice. "Rape and human sacrifice, acts focused on women and children."

Tara felt her stomach drop again, "This is twenty-eighteen," she said defiantly. "Shit like that can't still happen, it just can't, this isn't the fucking dark ages."

"I assure you that it can, and it does, my dear," June said seriously. "I'd wager that whatever has happened or is due to happen to those poor kids is linked to that date."

"How do we stop it?" Scotty asked.

June looked at them both, her own freshly poured coffee also now discarded on the untidy desk. "Unless you can get into that building in the next five days," she said solemnly, "and figure out how they disappeared and where they are being held, you can't. And even if you do get in, you do figure it out and you do find them you will face an evil beyond your comprehension, and I believe it will be the death of you."

CHAPTER 30

THE TYRES OF MIKES JEEP SPAN MOMENTARILY AS they bit through the shingle until they found traction on the firmer ground below. Gradually, The Old Chapel began to shrink away in his rear-view as he crawled down the long shingle drive and toward the road.

The whole situation felt like a mess, one that he had no control over, a feeling he hated, and he'd started to regret taking the call from Sue Reed last Friday. That one call had set the wheels in motion and cast him into this situation. If only he'd ignored it or just said a polite thanks but no thanks, but then that never had been his style. He figured that when this was all over, when that might be he didn't exactly know, but when it was he'd take Tara away somewhere nice. Maybe down to the Canaries, or possibly somewhere a little further afield, possibly Thailand or Malaysia. Sure, at that point there was no money coming in, but he still had a fair bit squirreled away, his emergency funds, what was left of the insurance money from Claire's death. He'd have to come to peace with spending some of it on taking Tara away later, a bridge to be crossed when it came time. It was the kind of break he felt they needed if they were going to give this relationship a go.

He reached the end of the drive and saw that the officer in the van had been replaced, a shift change had occurred whilst he'd been with Samuels. The new PC on the outer cordon was a middle-aged black man with a head as bald as that of a snooker ball. He had his attention fixed on a book that was supported by the steering wheel. Mike knew the guy was out here for the night, save for maybe an hour or so's relief break. It was the kind of duty that he'd done many a time back before he turned detective. Those hours on point could be long, arduous and lonely. Minutes often feeling as though they were hours and having something to read or focus on helped the time pass. Without it a night could feel like a bloody lifetime.

Despite reading his book the officer must have caught sight of Mike's car in his peripheral because he lay it down open on the Transit dash, gave Mike a quick rise of the hand and slid the van back, opening the way to the road. Mike knew scene protocol, he pulled out and took a right, stopping level with the driver's window he wound his own down, prompting the officer to do the same. "Mike Cross, you can log me out, I won't be coming back today," he said. He would be coming back at some point, he wasn't actually sure he wanted to or when it would be, but likely in the next few days he'd have the keys. The thought filled him with trepidation.

"Half seven by my watch," the officer replied. He wasn't actually wearing a watch, he took the time from the screen of his phone, then found Mike's name on the log and signed him out. "You have a nice night."

"How's the officer doing who took a fall in there last night?" Mike asked, hoping for a bit more info than Samuel had divulged."

"Oh, Shelly. Yeah, she's banged up pretty good but Rich, he was probably here when you arrived, reckons she come round about a half hour ago. There's a collection for her back at the nick if you're going."

Mike smiled inwardly, he obviously hadn't lost *that look* and if the guy who'd logged him in hadn't written down just who he was, which he probably hadn't, he'd look like just another CID bod coming and going. Mike didn't bother to correct him, instead, he said, "Thanks I'll chuck a few quid in. What hospital is she at?"

"They've transferred her to Derriford," he answered helpfully.

"Cheers, I'll get a card sent out," Mike lied again, then concluded with, "You have yourself a quiet one."

"Ha, yeah, well that's all it tends to be out here," the officer gave Mike a farewell raise of the hand and the window of his van slid up with a steady mechanical whine, as Mike threaded his Jeep out onto the road the Transit slipped back into place, gating off the property.

Mike drove back along the small road that serviced the village, creeping the Jeep slowly along the outer wall of The Old Chapel, peering through the trees at the structure that was just visible from the road. The lowering sun had deepened those first oranges that had traced their way across the blue sky to an almost cruor red, and it seemed as if the sun were bleeding out across that sky, its life's blood spreading out from its fiery surface. The small silhouette of The Old Chapel seemed to brood there against that haematic sky, the old stone of its bell tower silhouetted in black against it. Reaching the end of the boundary wall he sped up and took the Jeep clear of the village and out onto the windy country lanes.

The more distance he put between himself and the village the less the situation bugged him, the less it seemed a mess and he started to feel a little better about things. It didn't stop his mind working, though. It tumbled and turned over his meeting with Samuels, in particular the end, where it had been cut short due to the terrible discovery of one of poor Henry Harrison's shoe on the beach at Charlestown. *Just like many of those cases Tara found,* he thought to himself. That followed a pang of regret that he'd been so quick to poo-poo her, to tell her that there was no way those cases could be linked. He'd been the one thing he hated, the one thing he promised himself he'd never be in this game, and the one thing he'd grown angry at his old colleague for being, closed minded. He had calls to make, to both Tara and to Sue Reed but that would need to wait until he could actually use his phone.

About two miles northeast of the village he pulled the Jeep into an uneven gravel layby and clicked the phone, that had been in his pocket, into the holder on his dash and brought the screen to life. Now back in range of the nearest tower notifications began to ping through, one after the other in a varying array of tones. His mobile informed him he'd had four call attempts from Tara, this was backed up by three text messages, their urgency getting greater with each one.

Mike, when you get this call me!

MIKE! Can you call please, I can't get through?

And finally, in true Tara style, **MIKE, CHECK YOUR FUCKING PHONE AND CALL ME ASAP!!!**

He would call her, but first, he looked up Derriford hospital on Google, then felt frustration that it was thirty-seven miles east in Plymouth. It mattered not, they had few lines of enquiry they could follow without upsetting Samuels and there was precious little else to do. If Shelly Ardell had come around, he wanted to hear first-hand from her why she'd gone into the building, just what she'd seen and heard, and not some sanitised version from Mark Samuels. With his mind made up he pulled clear of the layby and headed east toward Plymouth and into that blood red sun. Before he had a chance to call Tara she rang his phone again, this time the call connected through his Bluetooth and the ringing shouted urgently at him from the Jeep's speakers. He reached forward and swiped the screen to answer.

"At fucking *last!*" came Tara's exasperated voice. "Mike, where are you now?"

"Three miles or so from Trellen," he replied with a glance at the map on his phone screen, he had a right to take in a few hundred yards and he didn't want to miss it. Before he had a chance to tell her he was heading for Plymouth her voice came back at him urgently.

"Mike, we have made the connection, we were right, me and Scotty I mean, we were fucking right!" Her words were fast, almost tripping over each other.

"Whoa, slow it down," he said, creasing his face up in confusion for the benefit of only himself. "What do you mean, you were right?"

"The occult thing, the missing girls, the whole lot. Mike – "

"They found a shoe, Tara," he said in a low and serious voice, cutting her off

"A shoe?"

"One of Henry Harrison's, it even has his initials on the tongue. I figure he probably wore them for PE at school or something."

A few seconds of silence followed, no doubt while Tara digested the information. Finally, her voice came through his speakers, but only one word, "Where?"

Mike swallowed, the next bit of information he knew he had to pass was as good as conceding that he'd been wrong. "Charlestown, a walker found it washed up on the beach this evening. Samuels is going to bring the parents in, he's now looking at this as a murder investigation."

"Fuck – Mike?" Her voice wasn't accusing or harsh, it had taken on a softness despite the curse word, as though she could sense how he felt. "Those poor parents, you think they'll be charged?"

"Protocol," he said absently. "They have nothing, not a clue, they'll get a shit time of it for twenty-four hours, thirty-six at most. I can't see them being able to get a warrant to hold them for any longer without any hard evidence. Do you have anything that I can take to Samuels? 'Cos if not in about twenty minutes if you look out front, you'll see those poor sods getting taken in."

Tara chuckled softly, "Mike, I'm not sure I can accept it all, there is no way this can be taken to the police. If they don't nick you for wasting their time you might get taken to the local nuthouse. Look, you were right to be sceptical about what I found, don't beat yourself up about it. But you need to hear what I have to say. If what we have found out today is right, this thing goes deeper and is far worse than you could ever imagine. How long will you be?"

"I'm heading to Plymouth Hospital," he replied. He realised that his heart was hammering like a drum in his chest and his hands felt clammy on the leather of the steering wheel.

"Mike, you need to get back here, what the fuck is in Plymouth?"

"A possible lead, last night one of the officers on point went into that building and almost died. I want to know what it is was that happened to her and what she saw. Samuels all but told us to leave it alone, thinks it's a waste of time us being here so I know if something odd happened to her he will just brush it off, he won't come to me with it. Whatever happened I need to hear it from her."

"Okay, Mike. What I need to tell you could wait 'til you're back, but I think you need to hear it now, so you can start processing it. I'm not sure I've fully digested it yet if I'm honest, or if I can bring myself to fully believe it, but when you look at the whole picture, from the haunting to the missing kids it all fits, like some really fucked up jigsaw puzzle."

CHAPTER 31

MIKE PULLED HIS JEEP INTO THE CAR PARK AT Derriford Hospital at twenty to nine that evening. He activated the electronic parking brake, killed the ignition and sat for a few moments, just enjoying not driving, enjoying not doing anything for that matter. He needed to get his shit together before he took another step into the rabbit hole that seemed to be swallowing him. He certainly needed to get his head straight before he saw Shelly Ardell, before he spoke to someone who had actually fallen foul of the tragedy that seemed to follow that place.

Tara's call had lasted almost the entire drive, ending only as he'd pulled in off Derriford Road and onto the hospital's grounds. By the time she'd finished, he felt an odd mixture of both numbness and disbelief. Witches, warlocks and other dimensional beings, things of make-believe, of folk law, things that had no basis or place in rational thought had been one of the main themes. And yet as hard as it was to swallow, what she'd said did fit. The vanishings of the young women and teen girls, likely pure and formally innocent from sins of the flesh and taken for the purpose of abuse and the breeding of children who were only ever destined to be used in sacrifice. Such things were certainly fitting of some of the more extreme reports of SRA, (Satanic Ritual Abuse).

Yet this wasn't SRA, not in the strict sense of the term. It was something darker than hell, something more ancient. If what Tara had told him was true this was worse, supposedly carried out to aid bridge the gap between this world and another place, a place of unimaginable chaos and evil, The Abyss.

The idea seemed ludicrous, maybe the loonies involved in the sect, or whatever the hell it was, just believed that? Hell, there were people out there who genuinely thought they were vampires, actually drank blood and avoided sunlight. Maybe those involved with the Device Church had been telling themselves they were more than human for so long they believed it, like some fucked-up placebo fed down through the generations of their members, told so often they believed it.

His brain could both deal with and accept that the cult was real, even that for the last two centuries it had managed to somehow operate under the radar of the authorities. In the past, certainly even as recently as the vanishing of Lindie Parker, the police had not been so 'on the ball' so to speak. Intelligence sharing and information recording then was not a patch on what it was now. But to believe that it involved other dimensional beings and real witches was a step too far. He could even believe that if The Old Chapel had been used as a place to practice such dark arts, and if countless infants had been slain in its walls and acts of unspeakable violence and evil indulged then maybe it was truly haunted, maybe that evil had metastasized into something malevolent that now dwelt there. A cancer that although invisible, had eaten itself into the very core of the building.

He remembered speaking to Mr. Ryan, the owner of Leap Castle, about the Elemental that supposedly haunted the place. One theory was that this insidious spirit was not that of a single person, it was an entity made up from all the evil and bloodshed that stained the history of that Irish castle, which was now a family home, albeit a very weird one. Maybe, just maybe what caused the occurrences at The Old Chapel was born from the same.

He rubbed at his eyes with his knuckles, he was getting ahead of himself. None of them had even set foot in the place yet, all they had was the word of others, accounts and stories with, by the looks of it, a fair bit of legend thrown in. Somewhere, buried in all of that behind the superstition and hearsay, was the truth.

He accepted now that the disappearances were linked, and that they, and not the police were on the right track, and if what the lady from the museum had told Tara was half right, they had until Friday to work around the police and find those kids. *This started out as a simple attend, explain and debunk job,* Mike thought to himself ruefully. He hadn't signed up for this shit, although now walking away was not an option.

Mike took a deep, steadying breath and exhaled through clenched teeth then opened the door and stepped out into the humid evening air.

Shelly Ardel was on the Fal Ward in the hospital's Neurology Department. The hospital seemed like a carbon copy of many others across the country, built in the early eighties during times of more prosperity, times where austerity and cutbacks were still in the distant future.

The soles of Mike's timberland boots squeaked their way along the vinyl floor as the smell of disinfectant assaulted his nostrils. Occasionally the clean smell gave way to something bad, shit from an incontinent patient, or vomit, it was hard to judge. Whiteboards hung on magnolia painted walls outside of each ward, patients' names were scribbled on those boards in black dry-wipe marker next to bed numbers. Mike scanned the names on each board, drew a few blanks and then found her in a private room between two general population wards. Mike knocked on the door and pushed it open a crack. PC Ardell was laid in the bed in a partially upright position, her head was bandaged from the brow up and over the skull. The bandage ran down to the nape of her neck giving the whole thing the appearance of some kind of helmet. Below the bandage her neck was held tightly in a frontal position by a very uncomfortable looking brace. An oxygen feed went in via her nose, a small, clear tube poked into each nostril. By her bedside stood the usual array of machines that measured everything from her brain function to her blood oxygen levels, they beeped and bonged in that usual symphony of hospital noise. In a large visitor chair by her bedside sat a man who Mike figured was in his late thirties. He had soft, kind looking features and a day's light stubble showed on his face. His dark blonde hair was uncombed, and it looked to Mike as if he'd not left her bedside since she'd been brought in. In his lap, a small girl or three or four with angelic blonde hair slept in a bunny onesie. He stroked at her hair with one hand, over and over, the action seemingly automatic. The other held the hand of PC Ardell, his thumb stroked at the back of her hand, working to the same rhythm as the one that stroked his daughter's hair.

"They say she might never walk again," he said in a hollow voice without even looking at Mike. "She's woken up, I guess I should be thankful for that," he smiled an empty smile and finally turned his face toward Mike who'd now slipped completely into the room and let the door swing silently shut behind him. Mike looked into the man's brown eyes, they were rimmed with a redness born from stress and tears, a look common in places of misery and pain such as this.

Mike had not even had the chance to sit by Claire's bedside or that of his infant daughter, both had been dead before the emergency services even got there, the closest he'd had to standing by their bedside was the metal gurney in the mortuary when he'd had to ID them both. He recalled momentarily, and not without a pang of pain, how the tiny body of his daughter had been no more than a small lump in the sheet that covered her. When the sheet had been pulled back he'd had to look upon a face that had been asleep and as angelic as the child who slept now in her father's lap the last time he saw it, and yet in death, had been smashed to a pulp on one side. The investigators said that she'd been flung clear of the pushchair by the impact of the car and forced headfirst into the central brick support that split the Co-op window into two panes of glass. He cast aside the image, other people's pain and suffering always brought such thoughts out of that drawer in his mind, the one he never wanted to open but nonetheless opened regularly.

"Are you — job?" the man asked, turning his face away from Mike and looking back to the woman in the bed who was obviously his wife.

Mike had formed a plan in his mind, a plan where a few lies would get him the information he needed, but here, now - and seeing the pain in PC Ardell's husband he couldn't do it. "No," he said. "I was, a few years ago now but I left it all behind."

The man nodded slowly, "You read about this stuff in the papers or see it on the news. You know, PC in hit and run, PC stabbed or attacked. It's always someone else, though. You know that it could be you, or someone you know every time you go to work, but you kinda know it probably won't be."

Mike placed a hand on the guy's shoulder and pulled the second chair around. This one was made of nasty looking orange plastic, the kind found in a school exam hall, and not as comfy as the large green vinyl one in which the man sat. It creaked a little under Mike's weight as he lowered himself onto the hard plastic. "Did you work together, too?" he asked.

"Not now, but yeah it's how we met," the man's face creased in slight confusion as the child stirred and murmured softly in her sleep, her lips parted and spoke something silently, then she settled again. "Did you work with Shelly?" he asked. "You know, when you were still in."

Mike shook his head, "No, I was Sussex," he answered. PC Ardell's eyes flickered and opened slowly, she didn't move her neck, she likely couldn't. The man took his hand from the child and took a pink sponge on a stick from a white plastic cup on the bedside table and wetted her lips with it.

"J-ohn," she croaked. "More, w-ater – please." He obliged and dipped the pink sponge lolly back into the water and held it back to her lips, this time she took the whole thing into her mouth before he withdrew it and placed it back into the cup.

"I'll cut straight to the point," Mike said, these people didn't need his pre-planned bullshit, he needed to be straight with them. "I'm trying to find out why your wife went into the building she was guarding and what caused her to have the accident."

A cloud seemed to fall over John's face, "Is this some kind of internal investigation?" he spat. "Don't you think it could wait?"

Mike held his palm up, "Hold up, John – can I call you John?"

"Yeah, whatever," John replied.

"I'm not with the police anymore in any capacity. You could say I'm, well – freelance. In all honesty, private and paranormal investigation is my new forte." John Ardell's face switched from anger back to confusion. Mike glanced quickly at Shelly, whose head was fixed staring straight ahead, yet in her eyes, he saw a hint of something, some kind of recognition.

"Before this business with the missing kids I was asked by the owner to look at the place, there have been some, well let's just say odd happenings there. Also, sadly many tragic accidents linked to it."

"You have to be kidding..." John Ardell began, his voice brimming with fury. The child stirred again in his lap, reacting to her father's voice.

"E-evi-l," Shelly croaked from her dry, cracked lips, cutting him off. "Th-a-t, pl-a-ce. E-vil," she managed as a tear broke free of her right eye and ran down her cheek.

"Shhhh," John Ardell encouraged. "You need to rest Shelly."

"Mr. Ardell, John – I'm sorry, really I am, but I just need a few minutes of your wife's time."

"I think you've done –," John Ardell began, but once again he was cut short by his wife's croaky voice.

"J-ohn – no, it's fi-fine. Mo-re wat-er, pl-ease," her words were coming a little more freely now as if the act of speech was lubricating the cogs in her throat. John lifted the small, pink lolly sponge clear of the cup, it dripped water across the bed before he popped it in her mouth. He repeated the process twice more before Shelly said in a clearer voice, "Enough – t-thanks."

Mike leaned forward, "Can you remember why you went in, Shelly?" he asked.

"A l-light," she began. "I t-thought some-one w-was inside."

"Good," Mike encouraged. "Really good. Where was the light, Shelly?"

"In t-the wind-ow," she said in her partly broken voice. "I-it look-ed like a t-torch," another tear ran down her cheek and John leaned over and wiped it with a blue tissue.

"And when you went in?"

"The cry-ing."

"You heard crying, Shelly – is that right?"

"It's a-all a b-bit foggy," she said, her face creased with pain, either pain from an injury or pain from the memory, Mike couldn't tell which. "S-sounded l-like a b-baby." More tears escaped her eyes and ran down her cheeks.

"I think that's enough," John Ardell cut in. "Just what is it you're getting at here?"

"A d-ark man," his wife said, ignoring her husband's

plea. "So, darrrkkk," Shelly's eyes widened until they looked like saucers, her paralysed body remained motionless, but her face looked terrified.

"See what you've done?" John Ardell growled, and his face didn't look so soft and kind now, a storm was brewing on it. He leaned forward over his sleeping daughter and placed his hand on Shelly's bandaged forehead and began to shush her.

"I don't want to go into that darkness," she said, her voice now perfectly clear, her words coming fast. "Please don't make me, you can't make me!"

"I think you best..."

Mike held a hand up, cutting John off, "No one is making you," Mike said in a reassuring voice. "You're safe now.

A guttural chuckle raked its way through PC Ardell's ruined body and for a second it seemed to Mike as if it rattled every one of her broken bones. Her wide eyes were on Mike now, eyes that no longer seemed to belong to the same woman, eyes that had succumbed to a darkness. A reptilian smile formed on her cracked lips, they peeled back to reveal her teeth and gums before she said in a raspy voice, "You'll die if you go in there, Mikey. You – Scotty and your whore. I've got so many beautiful things to show you, ALL OF YOU!"

CHAPTER 32

THE STEADY CREAK OF THE DOOR HINGE BROKE THE deep silence and stirred Ellie from a shallow and fitful slumber. She rolled painfully onto her side, her little-used joints and muscles shouted out in protest at the movement and she groaned in discomfort. As the orange light yawned itself into the room, she turned her face away. It was likely dim yet after her prolonged period in the choking darkness it burned at her retinas as fiercely as if she'd stared directly at the midday sun.

For the first time, she began to make out the size and shape of the room in which she was held. To call it a room was being generous, it was more like a cell. Small, cramped and square. No more than fifteen feet from one side to the next and totally devoid of furniture, save for the old grubby mattress on which she lay. Damp stone walls reached from the floor to a ceiling decked with roughly cut beams of wood. There were no windows, but that much she had already figured out for herself. The room did have two wall-hung oil lamps, yet they were unlit and looked not to have been used for many years. When it came to matters of going to the loo she'd been reduced to crawling on her hands and knees in the darkness, blindly feeling her way until she reached the furthest wall from her bed, where she'd been forced to suffer the embarrassment of defecating on the floor. At least it was dark, and no one could see, a small mercy but one she was glad of, nonetheless. Last time she'd needed to pee her own hands had found the dampness of her urine that had soaked into a hard-packed dirt floor. Hour by hour the smell of the place had begun to work its way into her skin, her own stench gagging the very air she had to breathe.

In the dimness of that orange light Ellie propped her aching body up and leaning her back against the un-even stone wall she took a steadying breath, trying to quell the fear of what was about to happen. She felt the cold and uneven surface of the stone through the fabric of her T-shirt and a shiver ran through her. Still squinting and blinking, but her vision clearing with every second, she looked down at her hands. They were filth covered from her toilet trips across the floor, dirt made damp from having to feel her way through her own urine was now caked under her nails. She'd never felt so unclean in her life and she longed for a hot shower, somewhere free of this hell where she could scrub her skin until it was out of her, if that was possible.

She still wore her Ramones tee and the leggings she'd had on when she'd gone to bed, only now the clothes were creased and smeared with the same filth that was on her hands, her feet were bare and soiled with dirt and everything about her felt unclean.

"I'd imagine you have some questions?" a voice asked. The tall silhouette of a man filled the light that shone through the open door and Ellie thought that voice sounded familiar. The man stepped into the room and she instantly knew why she recognised it. It was Seth Horner, husband to the lovely Lucinda Horner who'd welcomed them to The Old Chapel, who's bar-beque she'd been at and who she'd chatted and joked with, drank expensive champagne with and had even grown to like. "Have some water," he said, offering one of two bottles toward her. Ellie reached for it, snatched it from his hand, her thirst suddenly remembered. She had no real recollection of when she'd last drank and she unscrewed the cap feverishly then cast it aside onto the dirt floor before lifting the bottle to her lips and drinking deeply. The plastic bottle crackled and caved in as she emptied it in a few hungry gulps. A million questions raced through her head, but only one came to her lips as she swallowed the last of the cool water and dropped the now empty bottle to her lap. "Henry, where's my brother?"

Seth Horner stood over her smiling and dressed all in black. Black trousers, long sleeve black shirt with brass snap buttons, and black DM style boots. "He's just fine," he answered coldly, then ran a hand through his dark hair, it was brushed back off his forehead today highlighting the thick black frames of his glasses. The wireframed ones he'd been wearing when they first met were gone, replaced by these. "You're both our very special guests," he added. "More water?"

Ellie took a second bottle from him. Now with her thirst partially quenched her stomach began to grumble. She unscrewed the cap and drained half the bottle before screwing it back on and wiping the back of her dirt-smeared hand across her dry, cracked lips. She placed the bottle on the floor by her mattress. She doubted this was where she got set free and she'd no doubt be in need of it later; if she indeed had a later and that nasty little thought made her guts churn. "If I'm a guest," she said, that anger starting to grow in her once again, "then you won't mind if I just leave."

Seth Horner swept his arm toward the door in a go-ahead gesture and said, "You're free to go now if you want, Ellie. The only trouble is," he creased his brow, feigning regret, "that without you, Ellie, your brother will be of little use to us and we will have to kill him." His voice remained calm, almost kind sounding in some odd way, and the ease at which he mentioned killing her brother both chilled her and enraged her at the same time.

"You sick, fuck," she spat. She wanted to launch herself at him and smash his skull into the dirt floor and not stop until she felt it crack like an egg, the kind of thing that would normally repulse her, but not here, here the idea thrilled her and that scared her nearly as much she feared for her brother. Unfortunately, Seth Horner was taller, larger and not suffering from God knows how long shut in a dark cell. Instead, she opted for, "Why?" and kept a lid on her fury.

Seth smiled coldly. "I don't want to ruin all the surprises, Ellie," he said as he dropped to a crouch next to her. He reached a hand out and she flinched back instinctively, but the wall stopped her backing away. Softly he brushed a strand of her bedraggled hair off her face, then ran the back of his hand gently over her cheek and said, "And there are so many wonderful surprises waiting for you." His skin felt cold and the contact made her want to retch. "You and your little brother have a very special part to play here in Trellen in a few days, it's really quite exciting."

"I want to see him," Ellie demanded. She could feel hot tears welling up in her eyes and she tried desperately to fight them back. Inside her, fear was in a battle with anger and right now the fear was starting to win. She knew it was pointless trying to fight with Seth Horner, the smart move was to try and placate him, to acquiesce. She knew that over time some captors even grew to depend on those holding them, Stockholm Syndrome it was known as. Ellie wasn't sure she'd quite reach that point, nor ever would, but it didn't hurt to play along.

"Of course," Seth exclaimed. "Right this way." He stood, and Ellie heard his joints crack. She shimmied herself to her knees, Seth offered his hand in support and begrudgingly she took it and got to her feet.

Seth led her from the cell and out into a stonewalled corridor where she pulled her hand back. Ellie rubbed it on her leggings as if Seth were the dirty one and she clean. Her legs felt shaky, but it was good to walk again. The same wooden planking that lined the ceiling of her cell lined the corridor's, too. The same uneven stone lined the walls. Every twenty feet or so an antique looking oil lamp hung on a wrought iron bracket, their flames casting the passageway in that warm orange glow that, now her eyes had adjusted, was soft and not in the slightest bit harsh.

Ellie had no idea how long the passage was, it stretched off into the distance like a mine shaft. Here and there doors were set back into the stone on both sides, the doors were made of solid looking oak with no windows or hatches. As she walked the dirt floor beneath her feet felt cold and occasionally small stones bit into her bare soles, but she ignored the pain. The want and need to know that her brother was still alive was too strong.

"Where am I?" Ellie asked.

Seth looked back at her, those cold eyes flickered with something that she couldn't quite judge. He was a very different Seth to the one she'd met and even liked at the BBQ. A change almost akin to that of Dr Jekyll and Mr. Hyde. "Trellen, of course," he answered. "Just a part of the village that only our special guests see. Henry is right down here, he's quite fine as you will see."

"And Lindie, was she your special guest?" Ellie spat, her mind recalling the dream that had led her to this nightmare.

Seth Horner stopped in his tracks, wheeled around on his heels and took hold of her by the shoulders, his hands were strong on her and she felt the bones of her shoulder blades crunch until it made her wince. "And just how could you know that name?" he asked and fixed those cold eyes on hers, as if just by looking at her he'd get the answer.

"I know what you sick fucks did to her, too. You raped her, likely abused her and got her pregnant and then killed her baby. Just like you did to Sarah, Lucy and all those other girls in some kind of sick ritual. Is that what you want to do to me?" The anger was winning again, and she used the pain in her shoulders to feed it. "Is that what you want me for?" she cried at him. "Is your wife going to watch while you do me, Seth? Is that her thing? Does it get her off to see you rape young girls?"

Seth released his grip on her, that odd smile returned to his lips, "You have the sight, don't you Ellie?" He backed her against the wall tightly, his strong body pushing against hers. He took hold of her chin between his thumb and forefinger and lifted her face toward his and Ellie had no doubt he'd now feel how hard her heart was hammering away in her chest. "Yes, that's it," he said more to himself as he looked into her eyes. "Interesting, we've never had one with the sight." As he spoke his grin spread. "That will make your spirit all the sweeter for the darkness to consume. He nodded in agreement with himself and said, "Yes, this is definitely going to be interesting." He released her as suddenly as he'd taken hold of her, turned and then as if nothing had happened carried on down the long passage for another twenty yards before stopping outside of another of the non-descript solid timber doors. "He's right in here," he said, producing a lone key from his pocket and unlocking it.

Henry was laid on his back on what looked like a hospital bed. A three-rung metal guard rail stopped his small body falling off and dropping the three or four feet to the floor should he roll over; the other side was pushed tightly against the stone wall. A drip bag of water-clear solution hung on a hook over the bed, gravity-fed fluid was steadily flowing via a slim tube that ended in a canular secured into the back of his right hand with white medical tape. Unlike Ellie he had covers and a pillow and the room was dimly lit by an oil lamp of the same style as she'd seen in the passageway. This lamp, however, was turned down lower, the flame guttered in the air that had been disturbed by the door being swung open. Above it, the thin gossamer threads of a long-ago abandoned spider web danced on the warm air expelled by the lap. Laid the way he was on his back, his face still and peaceful looking and almost like white marble in the dim light, made him looked dead. For a few horrific seconds, until she saw the shallow rise and fall of his chest beneath the black covers, she thought he was.

"Hen," Ellie called, trying to shove past Seth and into the room. He blocked her entry and held her at the door, a strong hand on her shoulder once more.

"He can't hear you," Seth said calmly. "He has been asleep since you were both taken, we thought it would be less distressing for him."

"You drugged him?" Ellie asked accusingly. "He's five!"

"No, we have no need for such things as drugs. There is much you don't understand, Ellie. Your brother is under a sleep spell and he will remain that way until it's time. The drip is no more than a saline solution to keep him hydrated."

Seth swung the door shut and Ellie caught one last glimpse of her brother before it closed completely. "Time for what?" Ellie rubbed the tears away from her eyes with the backs of her dirty hands. "What are you going to do to him?"

Seth looked at her and smiled and for a second there seemed to be some kind of genuine compassion in his cold eyes. "Your brother is blessed, Ellie. He has been chosen for great things and you are going to help him become."

"I – don't – understand," she said shakily.

"As I said, there is much you don't understand." He spoke the words softly and took her by the wrist. "For now, you must go back to your room and wait. Patience, Ellie, patience is the key."

"No," she pleaded. "Just let us go, I won't say anything. I'll say I took Henry, we got lost, anything." Ellie's mind turned at a thousand miles an hour. Right then and there she'd have agreed to just about anything to secure their freedom. She wanted to get her brother out of that room and away from this place, she wanted to feel fresh air on her skin and the warm summer breeze in her hair, and more than anything she didn't want to go back to the blackness. She pulled back against Seth, but he tightened his grip, pulling her back toward the cell. She could see the door stood open like a gaping mouth waiting to devour her. As she pulled back, Seth tugged her along, the way a parent might drag a disobedient child around a supermarket.

"If you struggle, I will be forced to hurt you, Ellie. You don't want that, trust me!" he said, glancing back as he spoke.

"P-please," she begged, and now the tears did fall, one ushered the rest like the onset of a flood. "Just not the dark again, please let me have a light. I'll go back but not in the dark." Ellie hit out in a blind panic with her free arm, her hand forming a fist as she swung. It caught Seth square around the side of the head, her eternity ring, given to her by her mother on her eighteenth birthday, sliced the skin on his ear open. Seth howled in pain and surprise and instinctively raised his hand to the side of his head as he let go of her arm. When he removed his hand, Ellie saw that it was covered in blood. She backed up, knowing that she'd taken it too far. Her eyes scanned the long passage behind her for any means of escape but before she could break into a run, he snatched her up by the wrist, grabbing and twisting the hand that had hit him.

"Fucking bitch," he spat as he lifted her arm high and twisted it painfully behind her back making her cry out in pain. He wheeled her round so she was in front of him, then frog-marched her along the passage and hurled her forward into the cell. "If they didn't need you the way you are, I'd spend the next few hours doing things to you so horrific that by the time I'd finished you would wish you were dead." Ellie went spilling to the floor and fresh pain flared in her other wrist as it took the weight of her fall.

"Please, not the dark," she begged, her face now redden and streaked with more tears.

"You need to get used to the dark you little bitch," he fired back as spittle flew from his lips, his bloodied hand reached up to his torn ear once again, felt the sticky wetness of the wound, then withdrew it and looked at his crimson fingers with furious eyes. "Where you're going you need to be used to it," he growled, looking at her once again. "So best get used to it now!" He swung the door shut, slamming it so hard that the bang reverberated through the cell and cast out the light in an instant.

CHAPTER 33

"YOU'LL DIE IF YOU GO IN THERE, MIKEY, YOU –
Scotty and your whore. I've got so many beautiful
things to show you, ALL OF YOU!" the deep voice
growled from the throat of Shelly Ardell.

Mike creased his brow in confusion, feeling the grip
of intense déjà vu. He'd been here before. Heard those
words before. He looked in puzzlement around the hospital room, it was empty. Last time he'd lived this a man
had been here, Shelly Ardell's husband, and upon his lap
had been the child in a rabbit onesie, her face angelic in
peaceful sleep as she nestled safely in the comfort of
her father's lap.

Mike looked back to the bed. Shelly Ardell's lips
peeled back, as they had done before, only this time
they revealed black gums that held terrible jagged
teeth, teeth that would have looked more akin to something you'd see in the mouth of a shark, pointed and
razor sharp. Teeth of nightmares designed solely for rip-
ping and tearing through living flesh. He tried to
stumble back, but as he moved his attempt to get away
from the bed proved futile, for Shelley Ardell, or the
thing that had once been Shelly Ardell, but was now
something wearing her body like a suit, shot a hand
from beneath the covers. When he'd lived this before,
Shelly Ardell had been gripped by paralysis, a paralysis

brought from her broken neck. Now, here and in this version, whatever possessed her gave her the reflexes of a feline. The hand grasped his forearm and pulled him toward the bed.

Mike awoke with a start in his room back at the Travel Lodge. It had been no more than a dream. He took a deep breath and tried to slow his pounding heart, and that was when he realised, he couldn't move. His arms and legs felt numb, dull and like old rubber. He tried to will any part of his body to move but couldn't. Through the moonlit gloom of his hotel room, he saw something moving, crawling on all fours across the carpet and toward the bed. He knew what that thing was. Shelly Ardell! Former wife, mother, police officer, now a living nightmare. It reached the side of the bed and with a weirdly disjointed dexterity it sprang from the floor and landed upon his paralysed body, pinning him to the bed. The Shelly-thing was now astride him; she still wore her hospital gown only now it was smattered with blood and covered in filth as if she'd crawled all the way to his room from her private bed in Derriford Hospital. The bandage that had been on her head was gone and Mike could see the injury on the top of her head, the skull partially caved in. Through the dim light he could see the blood that caked and clumped her dark hair together, it looked black.

For the briefest of moments, the image of his own daughter's dead body took him again, the crushing cranial trauma that had taken her life not a million miles from that of Shelly's. Her pale and deathly face met his, just inches apart, so close that in his paralysed condition he could do nothing but meet her eyes, eyes that were as black as two rounds of coal. Unable to fight her off he watched as she reached up and placed her hands around his neck, the skin of her palms the ice-cold temperature of death on his own warm flesh. Their purchase on him found, those dead hands begin to squeeze and choke the life out of him. *It's a night terror, old hag,*

Mike said in his brain whilst trying to fight the feeling of blind panic that threatened to take him. *Sleep paralysis and nothing more,* and yet it felt so real, so very real. The weight of Shelly Ardell on his paralysed body felt impossibly strong and as the grip on his neck tightened like a vice, he felt his body sinking into the mattress, sinking more and more as if the bed below him was now no more than quicksand or soft soil and she had the ability to push him down through it to whatever waited below.

Slowly, surely and bit by terrible bit the room began to shrink away and now a knowing smile peeled back her pale and thin lips. Behind those lips were the same black gums, the same teeth that had no business being inside a human mouth. Her jaw widened, stretched and yawned to an impossible angle, and for the first time, he saw the blackness that dwelt within her. It transfixed him and he felt an odd separating sensation. As his physical body sank into the mattress he felt as if his soul, his very being was being drawn up and into that darkness. It wanted him. Mike felt a scream rise inside like pressurised stream. It needed to escape. He felt it rush from the pit of his stomach, up to his strangled throat where it stalled. That mouth drew closer, closer, and he could smell the fetid stench of rot now, it clung to the Shelly-thing like an invisible cloak. The scream built further, but with his throat closed off by those dead hands there was nowhere for it to go, it needed to escape, or he felt as if he would explode. That gaping hole of a mouth with its rows of razor-sharp teeth were just inches from his face now, it yawned wider still, ready to consume him, and then the scream did break free....

"NOOOOOO," Mike cried snapping awake. The sound of his own voice reverberated in his head and instinctively jolted his body to an upright position in the bed, the paralysis gone. His body was caked in sweat and the thin sheet beneath which he'd been sleeping now clung uncomfortably to him. Mike raised a hand to his throat, it hurt but that could have been from how tightly wound his muscles had been when he'd awoken. He moved his neck from left to right, loosening it, making sure this time he really was awake, and this was not some new nightmare level to the dream.

Next to him Tara slept. She looked momentarily concerned from the depths of slumber, she stirred and then settled once more. Mike took a few moments to just watch her sleep and moved a hand to her face, enjoying the warmth of her smooth skin beneath the tips of his fingers.

She'd come to him earlier that night, half an hour after she and Scotty had left for their separate rooms. Mike had been settling in to surf the channels for an action film that didn't require too much thought. What he liked to call a take-your-brain-out-and-just-enjoy kind of thing. He'd needed to try and take his mind off the hospital trip to Plymouth. It wouldn't work though, and he'd known it. For the briefest of moments back in that room on the Fal Ward, something else had been in control of Shelly Ardell, something had come through her. A phenomenon he'd read about and seen in countless horror films. One of the most famous examples being that of Janet Hodges who during the investigation into the haunting of her council house in Enfield in 1977 had spoken in a voice that many claimed could not possibly have come from the voice box of an eleven-year-old girl. Mike had never truly believed it possible, until now.

Whatever had been inside Shelly Ardell for those few seconds knew his name, that of Scotty, and *oh God* it knew about his relationship with Tara, *your whore*, it had croaked mockingly.

A gentle knock at the door had interrupted the start of True Lies, a Schwarzenegger classic from ninety-four, about an agent leading a double life, the definition of a take your brain out and enjoy film, and the bonus was

Mike had not seen it for the best part of ten years. The last time he'd seen it had likely been with Claire, one of their movie nights before parenthood had blessed them. Mike didn't want to remember fully so he didn't search for the memory that hard.

Leaving the film, he'd padded barefoot across the small Travel Lodge room and found Tara stood there, decked in a loose-fitting red Levi T-shirt and night briefs. As she'd entered the room, he'd taken her into his arms, they'd kissed urgently neither speaking a word. It was one of those times that needed no conversation, just contact. He'd led her to the bed where they'd made love, not as urgently as the first time, more sensual, both of them feeling the need to connect, to be with someone and not be alone that night.

The day had seen the investigation take a turn that according to June, the lady Tara and Scotty had spoken to in Boscastle, spelled untold dangers and they each knew that if her warnings were true, and they followed this through then there was a risk that one might lose the other. Neither were strangers to personal loss or pain, and tragedy had visited them both in the past. Mike couldn't even consider what it might do to him if he lost her now. They'd only been romantically involved the past two days, but he knew he loved her and had done for quite some time, there was no point trying to fool himself that it was anything less. Yet he knew that they couldn't walk away, the police had taken the Harrisons in on suspicion of murder, Henry Harrison and his sister presumed dead on the discovery of that shoe. The information that Tara and Scotty had learned in Boscastle, information that would never be taken seriously by the authorities, said differently. It told him that both of those kids were still alive, for now anyway. The shoe no more than an act of clever and calculated misdirection.

Mike pulled the covers back, got out of bed and walked the short distance to the bathroom where he clicked on the light. He grasped the cool white porcelain of the sink edge and looked at his sleep disturbed reflection in the mirror. His stomach dropped when he saw his neck, red marks ran around it and the skin looked inflamed and angry, yet there was no pain now. Instinctively he raised a hand and touched the blemished skin, not quite able to believe what he was seeing. It had been no more than a dream, one that had seen him have to raise through two layers of the nightmare to reach consciousness, but a dream, nonetheless. And yet there was something on his skin that told him differently, something that suggested that it had been more real than he'd thought. As he traced the marks gingerly with the tip of his forefinger they began to fade and within seconds they'd gone leaving him to wonder if he'd imagined them, if somehow a small bit of that nightmare had clung to him and made it through and out of dreamland. Mike shivered at the thought and took his eyes away from his reflection and ran the tap before palming cool water into his parched mouth. He used a crisp white towel to dry his hands and blot a few stray drops of water from his stubbled chin and then headed back to the bedroom. He left the bathroom light on.

"Are you okay?" Tara asked as he entered the room. She was sat up in bed, resting back on the headboard, the white sheet pulled up around her waist. Her dark blonde hair looked sleep-tousled and untidy, yet she looked impossibly beautiful to him.

"Fine," he lied and climbed back between the sheets. He leaned over and kissed the top of her head.

"I thought I heard you scream," she said softly.

"Just a bad dream."

"It was about that place wasn't it?" her question had a certain knowing to it.

"Not directly, no," Mike answered. He didn't want to relive the nightmare if that's what it had been, but he also didn't want to keep a single thing from Tara, so he told her, and she listened intently. Halfway through she took hold of his hand and the contact helped.

"I had one too," she said when he'd finished. "Not like that, I was inside it, The Old Chapel. I felt lost and couldn't find you," he saw her smile weakly at him. "It was getting darker and I had a feeling there was something in the shadows, something that wanted me."

"When was this?" Mike asked.

"Earlier, when Scotty and I were driving out to Boscastle. I guess I dozed off for a bit in his van. I tend to do to that when I'm not driving, something about the motion of a moving vehicle always makes me sleepy." She looked at him sincerely and said, "It's inside our heads, Mike. I don't know how but I can feel it."

It sounded crazy but at the same time didn't, he wanted to deny it, tell her that it was impossible, but he couldn't. "I think you're right," he conceded. There was no point fighting it now, the day had shown that there was more to this than any of them could understand. "I'm going out to the Horners' place in the morning," he told her.

Mike felt her hand tighten on his, "Mike, no," she said.

He shook his head, "I have to. I need to. Besides, do you really think they will risk doing anything to me? This whole thing is a media storm right now and so far, they - and the rest of that village have pulled off a great act of misdirection. They won't jeopardise risking that for me. Once I've spoken to them myself, I'll call and update Sue. She knows the Horners, I'm not quite sure how much I'm going to tell her yet, I'll just make a judgment at the time."

"If you go, we all do," Tara said defiantly.

"I need you and Scotty to stay here." Tara opened her mouth to protest but he cut her off. "If something does happen, which it won't, but IF it does you are the only ones left who know the truth. And you know where I am, so if I don't come back you have something to take to the police that they can't ignore."

"You're right," she agreed reluctantly. "I don't like it, Scotty won't either, but you are right."

"I don't like it," he chuckled. "What's to like about this whole thing? Whilst I am gone, I need you to try and find out what room the Harrisons are in. I'm guessing that by this afternoon the police will cut them loose. Even if they head back to Reading, they will come by here first and we need to speak to them."

"Is that wise, Mike? What about Samuels?"

"He can throw whatever toys out the pram he likes," Mike replied. "I'm past caring who we upset now, there are bigger and more important things in play. The police have had the place since Saturday." He looked at the clock, it was a little after three Am. "It's Monday morning now, they will be releasing the keys back to the Reeds by tomorrow I'd imagine. There's only so much of nothing the CSI teams can look at. When we go in, I want us to know all we can."

"I'm not totally sure I want to *go in* now," Tara said with an uneasy laugh.

Mike squeezed her hand, leant forward and kissed her forehead, "I'm not going to tell you not to, Tara," he said. "I respect you far too much to do that, but I will say that if you don't want to, if you want to walk away from this, I won't stop you." He knew she wouldn't, but it made him feel better to give her the chance. He would give Scotty the same option, too. As with Tara, he knew there was no way Scotty would bug out on him, but he'd lay the offer down, nonetheless.

"You're not wrapping me up in cotton wool, Mike Cross," she said sternly. "I survived that fucking twat-waffle, Jason. Taking on some cult, coven of witches, or whatever the bloody hell they are is going to be a piece of cake after him."

Mike smiled, he'd expected no less of an answer from her and he loved her for it. "In then?" he asked.

She nodded with certainty, "In," she agreed. "Now let's try and get some sleep, or neither of us will be fit for anything in the morning."

TWENTY MILES AWAY IN PLYMOUTH, Rob Harrison lay on his back on the thin, blue plastic covered mattress in his police cell. He'd not slept. The night light was on, casting the small magnolia painted room in a dim glow that would have been relaxing and homely in any other situation. This was anything but homely. In one corner of the cell was a brushed aluminium toilet and the water supply was piped in via a concealed tap in a hole in the wall. Somewhere in the cell block an angry drunk hammered away at his door, shouting obscenities and that when they opened the door he was going to, '*KICK THE FUCK OFF SO YOU CUNTS BEST BE READY!*'

Rob tried to shut it out and gazed blankly at the ceiling above where a stencil had been sprayed in black for the benefit of any Islamic occupants. It showed which way the Ka'bah was in Mecca. Rob had been a semi-practicing Christian in his university days, but he'd long since abandoned his faith. The events of the last few days were just further proof to him that there was no God, for if there was then surely, he'd not let anything like this happen.

Rob had never been one to cry, had always been good at holding his emotions in, not letting it out. Being what his father would have called a 'strong man', if not physically then emotionally. That had changed in the last twenty-four hours, his world had fallen apart and within him a chasm had opened, one so deep and wide that he knew it would never be filled again. To lose one child was an idea he found inconceivable, but two? How could he deal with that? How could anyone deal with it? The truth of the matter was you couldn't.

The sight of his son's little size 5 Clarks trainer

being held before him in an evidence bag had brought on the first proper tears he'd shed. Even being told that both Henry and Ellie were now presumed dead hadn't done it, for just the words didn't hit it home, didn't seem real. Seeing that shoe was real, HH penned onto the inside of the tongue in black Sharpie pen, the initials written in his own hand. Yeah, that had brought it home with a smack in the face, and they'd had to stop the interview to let him get his shit back together. Remembering how that shoe looked in the evidence bag made a new tear roll from the corner of his eye, it raced down the side of his face and dripped over his ear to the blue plastic mattress below.

He'd answered the polices' questions, and there had been many. The interviewing detectives going around and around, over the same things again and again, hoping at some point no doubt he'd trip himself up and an inconsistency in his story would be exposed, one they could get into and work until it grew, the way a person might keep probing an ulcer on the inside of the cheek with their tongue. Or, hoping that he'd tell them something different to that of his wife. He doubted Carol had said anything at all, she seemed to have shut herself away in her own cell, one inside her mind. He didn't hate them for their questions, in some way they were all on the same team and he knew that soon they'd have to let them go. In an odd way, the idea of getting out scared him, for in here, shut away from the world outside he didn't have to face it, the whole thing was on hold, like someone had hit the pause button. But, when they got out he would have to face it, deal with it all and in truth, he wasn't sure if he could.

He'd not seen Carol since they were taken away from the Travel Lodge back in Liskeard in separate cars. He could still see her face, pale and scared – eyes wide and filled with tears as she looked at him from the back of the unmarked police car that had been parked beside the one he'd been put in. He wanted to go to her, hold her and tell her that it would all be okay. It wouldn't, but no one ever said that. In these situations, you lied, and the lie was for yourself as much as the other person, because if you said it enough, maybe, just maybe in the end it all would be.

———

FORTY MILES away from her father and mother in Plymouth, Ellie lay in her own cell. Only this one was dark, cold and devoid of any of her rights. She too lay on her back, her right arm still thrumming in pain from how Seth Horner had twisted it around and thrown her into the room. Her left wrist ached from how it had broken her fall as she'd landed on the hard, dirt floor. The stench in the room had begun to get better, it wasn't that they'd cleaned up or been kind enough to give the place a going over with Febreze. No – she'd grown used to it and she felt sure that soon she'd not notice it all. It wasn't much of a positive, but you took what you got in situations like this. Ellie blinked her own tears out of her eyes and there was no real difference between when her eyes were open or closed, the darkness was the same.

Her mind tumbled over things, what she'd seen in the vision. She'd gone beyond thinking of it as a dream, now she knew it had been more than that. It ran over why they'd wanted Henry as well as her, for in those visions she'd never seen a male child beyond those poor wretched babies. Infants that had been slain by the dagger that had gleamed so brightly in the candlelight during all those ceremonies. Questions she couldn't answer no matter how hard she tried, yet ones she knew would be answered all too soon.

All she could do was lay there and listen, listen to the deep endless silence, listen to the sound of her own heart as it beat a steady rhythm in her chest, and wait – for what she did not know.

CHAPTER 34

THE SHRILL RINGING OF THE PHONE ON THE BEDSIDE table awoke Mike. He reached sleepily for it and through bleary eyes saw it was Mark Samuels' number on the screen, and that the time was a little after seven AM. Mike cleared his throat and swiped the screen to answer the call.

"Mark," he croaked. "What's up?"

"You were out at Derriford last night, weren't you?" barked Samuels' agitated voice down the line. "I thought I asked you to leave it alone, Mike."

Mike knew this call would be coming, he just hadn't expected it quite so early. "Mark," he began but Samuels cut him off.

"She's dead Mike."

"What?" Mike sat up in bed, the waking drowsiness gone in an instant, as if someone had just injected a triple espresso into his veins. "How?"

"Bleed on the brain in the night, it was always a risk with the kind of injury she had, they'd hoped as she'd come around that the worst was over. What the fuck were you doing out there, Mike? John, her husband was going crazy after your visit, said she had some kind of episode while you were there."

"What was the time of death?" Mike asked. He had a horrible feeling he knew the answer. The call had also awoken Tara who was now rubbing the sleep out of her eyes and sitting herself up in the bed next to him. She adjusted the pillow and leaned back on the headboard and looked at him questioningly.

"What the fuck difference does it make, Mike? I want to know what you were doing out there?" Samuels spat. Mike couldn't think on the spot of a believable reason why he'd visited the now late Shelley Ardell that would placate him.

"Mark," Mike said calmly. "It matters, I'm not expecting you to understand my reasons, but it matters."

"I can't see how it makes a blind fuck of difference Mark, but she died just after three AM this morning."

Just as he'd suspected the death had occurred right around the time of the dream, if that indeed was what it had been. Knowing it as fact sent a shiver through his body. "Mark, I'm sorry," was all he could manage.

"We go back a ways, Mike," Samuels began. "So, I'm giving you the benefit of the doubt on this one; but hear this, if you tread on my toes, or stick your oar into this case again then you and your team will be coming in, do I make myself clear?"

"Understood," Mike said.

"Go home, Mike. When the keys are released back to Mr. and Mrs. Reed they can call you and then you're free to do your spook hunt."

"Understood," Mike repeated. He wasn't going to argue the toss, it was clear that his old colleague wasn't in the mood to discuss the matter. Before he had a chance to ask if that was all the call was disconnected from the other end and Mike set the phone back on the bedside table.

"What was all that about?" Tara asked.

Mike smiled at her, "Just Mark Samuels throwing his weight around," he said. "Shelly Ardell, the officer I went to see yesterday evening is dead."

Tara's face fixed him with a concerned look, "And

I'm guessing from the one side I got of the convo that she died right about the time you had that dream?"

Mike nodded, "Samuels was quite clear that if we, well more I, cross him again and stick our noses into the investigation then we are all getting nicked."

"We can't just leave this now," Tara said. "Not with what's at stake."

Mike kissed her forehead, a big part of him wished she would leave it, in truth he didn't want her to be any part of it, but he found her tenacity endearing. "He's just flexing his muscles," he said reassuringly. "We carry on as planned, no change."

"And you're still going out to the Horners' place today?"

Mike got out of bed and crossed the short distance to the bathroom; the door was open and the light was still on. He started the shower and called back as the water began to run, "Of course, we need to do something. I want to meet them, get a feel for who they are."

———

BY ELEVEN AM and following a breakfast with Tara and Scotty in the hotel's mediocre restaurant, Mike was in the Jeep and pulling out of the Travel Lodge car park.

The arrest of Carol and Rob Harrison had stayed as the lead story on both the local and national news that morning. There was little else happening worthy of reporting on and once the story of the Harrison kids' disappearance had been gone over in detail the story switched to the upcoming Brexit negotiations. At that point Mike switched the radio off and enjoyed driving in silence with just his thoughts as company.

It was another sweltering hot late July day and the Cornish roads were already chocked with tourists moving from one scenic area or tourist attraction to another. Large family cars towing caravans kept traffic on the smaller roads to a slow and steady pace. Mike looked at the families who were enjoying the hottest summer in many years and envied their ignorance, the fact that they were happily going about their day and able to forget or just ignore the evils of the world. As June had told Tara and Scotty, there were things that once known could not be unknown. And whilst any of them could walk away from this at any point and no one would be any the wiser, they would know and Mike wasn't sure he could live with that, live with the knowledge that he - they, might have been able to do something to save those kids and yet didn't. Today's little outing to see the Horners was the first dip of the toe into the Hornets' nest, and whilst he'd not admit it his nerves were on edge.

Mike drove past The Old Chapel just before midday. He didn't stop, nor did he slow down as he passed the police tape and the marked police transit van that still gated off the property. One lone TV truck was pulled into the verge toward the far end of the chapel's boundary, the passenger side tucked in tightly against the old stone wall, leaning the BBC Cornwall van with its large dish and antenna on the top at an odd angle. Even with it pulled in as it was, Mike had to mount the verge to his offside to get past.

A minute later he reached the drive to the Horners' place and swung a tight left turn onto the drive without indicating.

Lucinda's white Range Rover Evoke was the only vehicle parked on what he found to be quite an expansive shingle forecourt. It wasn't a typical country vehicle despite its off-road capabilities, it was more the kind of lavish and overly indulgent vehicle that graced the streets of Chelsea or certain areas of Essex.

Mike span the Jeep around in one turn so the nose was facing back up the drive. An old habit from his days on the force, you'd always leave a car in a position suitable for a quick exit, and today he might actually need to make one. The midday sun was sweltering, the mercury was forecast to be topping out in the mid-thirties by the early afternoon. Not hot in comparison to some countries, but in the good old UK that was what the weather forecasters called a right scorcher.

With the relentless sun cooking the exposed nape of his neck, Mike knocked on the door, as he did, he took a steadying breath and tried to tell himself that he wasn't nervous, but he was. A feeling that he'd not felt since he'd pushed a panda car around and been first to a job whilst crewed in his own. It wasn't the fear of what was inside, it was more the unknown, not knowing how it was going to play out. Nine times out of ten it was alright, but then there was always that one where the wheel came off and it went south on you.

Mike heard footsteps from the inside on what sounded like hardwood flooring, they got louder then paused and the door swung open to reveal a tall man. He was maybe just a tad over six foot and had dark hair that was swept back on his head. He wasn't well built but he had a certain athletic look, maybe that of a long-distance runner or cyclist. He looked at Mike with curiosity from behind dark-rimmed glasses, his right ear was covered in a white patch bandage held in place with beige colour medical tape. Small spots of browning blood had seeped into the dressing enough for it to start to show through. Mike had never met Seth Horner, but he took an educated guess that this was who now stood before him.

"Mr. Horner?" he asked, and extended a hand.

"The one and only," he said with a smile and took Mike's offer of a handshake. "Look, I don't mean to be rude, but we have told the police all we can. We spoke to the DI in charge for quite some time on Saturday after we, and most of the village, helped to search the woods."

Mike smiled back, "I'm not police," he said, taking his hand back.

"If you're press, I'm gonna have to ask you to leave.

We've had them all here. TV, bloody papers, the lot. Out of respect for Mr. and Mrs. Harrison, none of us here in Trellen are going to entertain those bloodsuckers."

"Not press either," said Mike with a shake of his head.

Seth Horner fixed him with a confused look, "If you're not press or police do you mind if I ask what your business is?"

Mike was finding it hard to get the measure of him, he looked like a pretty regular guy, not the kind who'd been party to the abduction of two people, not the kind to have a penchant for rape, murder, and human sacrifice. But then guys like that didn't exactly wear it on a sign around their necks. "I guess profession-wise I'm closer to police, spent a good few years on the force. I won't burden you for long, but I was wondering if I could come in and have a quick word."

"I really..." Seth Horner began. His hand was on the door and Mike knew the sign of someone who wanted to shut it and see him gone.

"Just a few quick questions," Mike cut in, then added, "I'm here at the request of Sue and Tom Reed."

Seth's confused look turned into a smile, "You should have said sooner," he swung the door open wider and ushered Mike inside. "Although it's my wife Lucinda who mainly deals with them, she's upstairs at the moment fixing the guest rooms."

"Appreciated," Mike said as he crossed the threshold. "That ear looks sore, how'd you manage that?"

"Chopping wood down in the barn," Seth Horner replied without missing a beat. "Swung the axe a tad too high and close, damn near took my ear off."

"Prepping for the winter already?" Mike asked as he followed Seth through their entrance hall. As he'd suspected it was hard floored with what looked like bamboo. The place had looked quaint and like a picture on a chocolate box, or jigsaw puzzle on the outside, yet inside it was modern, and in a way matched the personality and style of the owner of that Range Rover. *Who lives in a house like this?* Mike thought to himself. *A witch, a mass murderer or a rapist, or all of the above?*

"It's quite remote out here, mister...?" Seth Horner paused and allowed Mike to fill in the gap.

"Cross," Mike obliged. "Mike Cross."

Seth nodded as if Mike had confirmed a fact he already knew, "One thing we learned early on was that when it comes to wood for the fire, there's no such thing as having too much."

They arrived in the lounge, the same flooring continued from the hall through this spacious room. It looked as if it had been laid throughout the entire ground floor, a costly investment but it looked good. The lounge ceiling was quite low, painted a brilliant white and crossed with dark stained beams, the beams seemed to portend that the cottage itself was in some kind of struggle to hold onto its heritage, a battle against the modern look that had taken hold. On the far wall a large and expensive looking TV hung on the wall, it had to be a good sixty or more inches. The black leather seating, consisting of a sofa and two power recliners that were positioned to afford everyone a view of whatever was on that mammoth screen. Behind the leather three-piece was an expensive looking dark oak hardboard that ran the width of the room. A large wall-hung mirror opposite the door greeted Mike with a full body reflection of himself, it likely belied the true size of the room making it seem larger than it actually was.

Seth Horner paused by the sideboard, the top of his head almost brushing the bottom of one of the ceiling beams. "And I work away for a lot of the year, the place is job enough for Lucinda to keep up on her own, can't expect her to chop firewood, too. And she has the Reeds' place to caretake now. I told her not to take it on when they asked, but you know how women are, once they have an idea in their heads you try changing it."

Mike nodded his agreement, then asked, "What is it you do?" as his eyes covertly scanned the room, looking for anything out of place, just one thing that would confirm what Tara and Scotty had been told was both true and accurate.

"Astroparticle research and Omniverse theoretical research studies," he said, looking at Mike now, the top of his dark hair just brushing one of the beams. "I'm over in Genève, Switzerland for a good half the year."

"Cern?" Mike said rhetorically managing to sound impressed. "You work on the collider, the one that the conspiracy nutjobs thought would cause the planet to suck itself into a black hole the first time it was fired up?"

"They had a point," Seth laughed, and Mike had a feeling he was loosening up a little. Mike even felt himself warming to the guy, despite what he might be he came across as likeable and pretty easy going. "None of us really knew what would happen." Seth treated him to a wide mischievous grin.

"I'd hate to have written the risk assessment for that bad boy," Mike commented.

"You and me both. Look, Mike – as I said it's my good lady wife you need if this is to do with Sue and Tom, I've only had the pleasure of meeting them once or twice when we helped Tom out with the kitchen fitment. His fitter came down sick. A friend of mine who'd fitted our kitchen the year before was free, so I put them in touch. Let me go get her for you."

"Thanks," Mike replied with a smile. "Listen I really appreciate it; I'll be on my way before you know it."

"Can I get you a drink?"

"I'm good, thanks. Just a few minutes of your wife's time and I'm dust."

Seth nodded and disappeared out into the hall, automatically ducking a little as he went through the door. Mike waited until he heard Seth Horner's foot-steps on the stairs before he got moving. First, he fished the small Sound Bug FM transmitter from the pocket of his trousers. He picked the double-sided tape off both the bug and the nine-volt battery that powered the device via a short red and black lead. The sound of Seth Horner and Lucinda's muffled voices drifted down to him from the first floor. He had time, but not much. Mike powered the device on, each bug had a frequency range between 88-108mhz on the FM band. The device was set to 90mhz, a frequency which in this part of the country was free from licenced radio station broadcasts. The bug was set to high power for maximum range. It was what Mike called a burnable asset; once deployed it stayed there broad-casting whatever was said by the unsuspecting occu-pants for two hours, at which point it became a dead duck. You then just had to hope it stayed hidden and undiscovered by the subject until the job was done, after that it didn't really matter. Mike's plan was to fire enough direct questions at Lucinda and Seth to make them uncomfortable, if that were possible. Then he'd get the hell out of dodge, park up clear of the village and see what they had to say when they were alone. It was the kind of thing he'd always dreamed of doing when he was a police detective but never did due to the amount of red tape stopping him. Now as a PI he could do pretty much what the hell he liked, and no one gave a shit. Well that was true to an extent, but he certainly had much more freedom to just get on with the job.

The large chrome framed glass mirror would do just fine. The frame was more like the kind you'd see on an-tique paintings in a manor house, only gilded in gold and surrounding some ten-foot painting of an old lord of the manor with a shotgun broken over his arm and a couple of pointers sat obediently at his feet. He ran his hand behind the mirror and pulled it gently forward. If he dislodged it off the wall, he would really be fucked - the thing probably weighed the best part of sixty kilos.

As he suspected there was enough of a recess be-hind the mirror's ample frame to hide the bug in. He palmed it to his left hand, so the double-sided tape faced out and slid it in behind the mirror. With his right hand, he pushed in the opposite direction on the frame, making sure the bug stuck. The double-sided tape was the strongest 3M made and it stuck like shit to a blanket, it grabbed instantly and by the time the sound of feet hit the stairs again he was back in the exact same spot that Seth Horner had left him in.

CHAPTER 35

LUCINDA HORNER WAS SOMETHING ELSE THAT MIKE hadn't expected. She was a strikingly beautiful woman in her early to mid-forties with clear pale skin, deep red hair and a shapely figure. The kind of woman who'd turn heads in the street, for one because of her beauty, and secondly because she had an air of a certain something about her. She wore loose-fitting white cotton trousers that were tied around the waist with what appeared to be a matching fabric belt and a pale green blouse that highlighted the deep colour of her hair and matched her eyes.

"How can I help you, Mr. Cross?" She asked as she seemed to flow into the room behind her husband. Her voice was soft and melodic and there was no hint of a Cornish accent to it or any accent that Mike could pick up.

"Could we, umm, take a seat," Mike replied, feeling a little taken off guard by her. "I promise not to take up much of your time."

She gestured gracefully to the black leather three piece and Mike settled into one of the recliners. It was large and comfy and the kind of chair he could see himself settling into with a beer most evenings, then likely dozing off before whatever film he had on was finished.

"I'm curious," she began, sitting down with her husband on the matching sofa and flattening some non-existent creases out of her trousers with her palms, her nails were manicured perfectly and painted a bright red, "as to what Sue and Tom have got you here for?"

Mike cleared his throat and said, "Well, strictly speaking, they haven't asked me to come over, it's just more part of my enquiry you could say."

"Into what, exactly?"

"The Old Chapel," he replied engaging her.

"Is this to do with Ellie and Henry Harrison?" She asked with interest. "Because if it is all I can tell you is what I – we, told the police. The Harrisons were here on the Friday evening for my annual summer gathering." She paused and smiled warmly at him. "We hold it once a year. And as they were staying at Sue and Tom's I thought it fitting to invite them. They all left around eight PM and the next I saw any of them was when Rob Harrison came around here on the Saturday morning all of a fluster because the kids had gone." Her face dropped and showed what looked to be genuine concern. "Seth, myself and most of the other villagers all split up and searched the woods, the most likely place I thought they'd be if you ask me, but not a sign. Now all this business with that shoe being found," she grimaced, and her voice lowered. "Really sad. I saw on the news that they arrested the parents last night. They seemed like such nice people, but then you never can tell, can you?"

Mike nodded in agreement, "No – you never can," he replied solemnly. If Lucinda Horner was lying, she was good, very good in fact. He'd sat across the table in interviews with every kind of criminal from petty thieves to murderers and you always got a feel for someone spinning you a yarn, there were certain tells you got to know. For some, it was a twitch of the eye, or even something as small as a flex of the fingers, the most common was the look away, the person lying unable to remain in eye contact with you. Any of those little ticks and twitches were the body's natural reaction to an untruth and they were essential if you wanted to read someone, find out where the lie was and start picking at it, the way someone might pick a scab until it comes off and exposes what's underneath. Neither Lucinda, nor her husband Seth showed any signs, there were no tells. Both seemed sincere and both looked saddened by what had happened, but Mike wasn't about to call it good on them already and declare all the evidence to the contrary as bullshit, not after what had happened out at Derriford the day before, and certainly not after that dream, if indeed that's what it had been.

"Do you mind me asking just what capacity you're here under, Mr. Cross?" she questioned softly. "I'm a little confused."

"My apologies," Mike said, bringing his eyes to hers again. They were a deep and slightly haunting green, like two emeralds on her pale skin. "I never fully explained myself, did I?" he continued without waiting for her to respond. "As I said to your husband, I was a police officer, over ten years' service, but I left due to family circumstances and since then I have been working as a freelance investigator."

"A gumshoe?" she asked rhetorically, a smile forming on her lips. "Like in those old American detective movies? How exciting."

"It's not quite that glamorous, trust me," he grinned. "My other field of work is a little more, well shall we say, specialist. I and my team of two others investigate hauntings," he paused and waited for the reaction, it usually went one of two ways, people either laughed or were fascinated and wanted to know if he'd seen a ghost and they were always eager to tell him their experience. It always surprised Mike just how many people had experienced things, seven or eight times out of ten someone had a story to tell. Neither Lucinda nor Seth interrupted so he carried on. "I will add that now my main focus is on finding rational explanations and what we, in the field, call debunking. Originally, and for personal reasons, I was looking for evidence, trying to get an answer to that unanswerable question."

"You lost someone, didn't you, Mr. Cross?" Lucinda asked perceptively, her face looking regretful.

"It's not something I wish to discuss if I'm honest," Mike said truthfully. "But, yes – you're right. Anyway, that answer has eluded me for the past few years and I've now come to enjoy finding rational answers to reports of the paranormal. Although I'd still really like to find what I set out to find."

Lucinda's face switched to an entertained smile, "Do Sue and Tom think that building is haunted?" she beamed, her green eyes sparkling. "How interesting."

"That was the main reason for their call to me on Friday just gone, yes. But since the Harrison kids vanished, I've become a little embroiled in that, too. I guess it's hard to leave that old life behind fully." She nodded in understanding. "Have you ever seen or experienced anything there?"

"Goodness, no," she said and clasped her hands together. "It was a local church, I'm sure you know that. I'd imagine a man of your experience has done his research? I also know a fair few of Sue and Tom's guests have left early, but they never said why. Just called, said they were leaving and left me the key under the front mat."

"Well two of those guests went on to kill themselves, one drowned her baby in the bath before she took her own life; and those are just a few of the strange deaths that seem to be linked to that place. I know it was never officially a church," he added. "I was wondering if you could shed some light on that?"

Lucinda shifted in her seat and glanced to her husband, possibly the first tell of a question she didn't feel comfortable with. "I knew the Minister, yes." She said tentatively.

"Deviss," Mike cut in.

She nodded, "That's right. My parents, both passed on some years back, they were never what you'd call churchy people if you get me. I went there once or twice as a child with my mother, doing the neighbourly bit — you know? And used to look in on Johnathan now and again before that terrible fire. Take him the odd meal, he was a lovely man, but he'd retired by then. As for the deaths you mentioned, it all sounds very tragic but not something I know anything about."

"And you never found it odd that the church didn't appoint a new Minister? That Mr. Deviss just kept right on living there?"

"I never gave it a second thought if I'm honest. My mother told me he owned the building, I think — if I remember correctly, it was some years ago now." She paused as if pondering the problem, then concluded, "I'm sorry, Mr. Cross I am far from an expert on the legalities of such things."

If I'm honest, quite often another little tell that whoever said it was being far from honest. "I see," Mike said slowly. "I was hoping you could help me with that, but I guess not. I was counting on the old small village stereotype, everyone knowing everyone else's business."

Lucinda smiled wanly, "We do get a little of that, yes. But I'm sorry this isn't a subject I'm that good on."

"Do you think any of the other villagers would be able to help, someone in Trellen must have worshipped there?"

"The Minister retired some time before the fire back in two thousand and eight, you could try but I really don't know. After all that has happened these past few days you might find them reluctant to talk, a thing like this affects small communities like ours, we are not used to such tragedy. The fire was bad enough, now all this business with those poor kids."

Mike nodded and took a slow deep breath then said,

"Well it seems like all that I've managed to do is interrupt your day and draw another blank."

Lucinda's smile spread and turned warm, "Nonsense," she beamed. "It's really no bother at all, Mr. Cross. And please accept our apologies if we seemed a little hostile to begin with. We have had police and press here knocking the door relentlessly since Saturday morning, so no offence taken I hope."

Mike held his hands up, "None whatsoever," he said and stood up. Both Lucinda and Seth Horner followed suit. "Look, I'll get out of your hair. The team and I will be moving in there when the police have finished with the place, hopefully, sooner rather than later. We can work on explaining some of the things that have been reported there and fingers-crossed put both Sue and Tom's mind at rest." He paused, he knew what he'd wanted to get into this conversation before he'd arrived, and the subject seemed to lead naturally on from what he'd just said. He walked out of the room and they followed. As Mike reached the front door he added, "And maybe I can figure out just how those kids got out of the building." He stopped with a hand on the black, wrought iron handle and turned back to face them. "Do you have an opinion on that, seeing as you're the main caretaker? I mean it doesn't make sense to me. The place was locked down, windows shut and latched closed, and the doors, both front, and back, dead bolted from the inside. It's one of the main reasons that the parents have fallen under suspicion. I happen to know the lead investigator on this case, and he has said, off the record mind you, that he doesn't believe for a second that the parents were responsible for whatever happened, you tend to get a feel for such things in this profession."

"It's a mystery," Lucinda answered. "All I know is what I said, they seemed like nice people. But, as I said, you never can tell. I believe occam's razor suggests that the simplest and most logical explanation tends to be the right one. I'm far from an expert but going by that rule it would seem to suggest that for whatever God-awful reason Carol and Rob Harrison took those kids out of that building last Friday night. Then after whatever happened went back in and locked and deadbolted the doors."

Mike cracked the door open and stepped out into the sun, he shook his head and said, "Nah, I don't buy it, not one bit. I've not been able to get too involved in this yet, but I know, and so does the DI in charge, even if he won't admit it," Mike smiled to himself, "that something is being missed on this one." He scratched the back of his head, the way Columbo, the old TV detective sometimes would before a big reveal. Mike didn't have shit to reveal yet, but he was working on it. "You see the beauty of being freelance and not governed by the ways and methods of the police is I can look at this in a way they don't, won't and would never dream of." He smiled confidently at them both and backed away from the door. "I'll be sure to let you know just as soon as I do figure it out."

"It would be appreciated, Mr. Cross," Lucinda said, and he detected a very mild note of sourness to her voice, so mild that he might have imagined it, but he didn't think so.

"I'll see you both again, I'm sure and thanks again to you both for your time." He reached the Jeep and opened the driver's door.

Seth and Lucinda had come out to the forecourt now and were stood with him by the car. "It's really no bother," Seth Horner said. He gave Mike a parting handshake before Mike got in, started the engine and drove off. He looked in the rear-view, they stayed out on the forecourt watching him, and he watched them until he reached the first bend in their long drive and they both disappeared from view.

At the road Mike allowed himself a steadying breath, if they were involved then that had been a dangerous move, but he'd felt confident that they wouldn't risk doing anything stupid and casting the spotlight onto themselves and the village, not when it had been so skilfully misdirected away and onto Rob and Carol Harrison.

From the glovebox, he fished out the small handheld FM receiver, the one that went with his bug. The bug was set to 90Mhz and could be picked up by any FM radio, but it had a small encryption that scrambled it for regular receivers. The one he now held decrypted it so only he could hear. Steadying the steering wheel with the back of his hand he clicked it on. The receiver was set to the correct frequency already, he'd tested it before arriving. He cranked up the volume to full as he passed by the still cordoned off Old Chapel and headed for the edge of the village.

Mike got clear of the village and pulled his Jeep into an overgrown gateway that serviced a fallow field. The aluminium gate looked as if it hadn't been opened in years. A mound of dirt had been dumped in front of it to stop trespassers accessing the field behind and over time the dirt had grassed over, weeds and large shasta daisies grew from the unkempt grass and a number of bumblebees were busy hopping from bud to bud collecting pollen. He left the engine running to keep the aircon pumping and settled down to listen. The bug had a range of just under two miles when turned to high broadcast power, it shortened the battery life considerably, but he'd wanted to be as far away from the village and the Horner place as possible. The signal strength indicator was on its last green bar, much further and it would dip to orange, then red and he'd be liable to pick up more static than anything.

He could hear the sounds of the house, feet on the hardwood floor, a door being opened, the sound of a cough. He'd been clear of the place for about five minutes but so far neither had spoken within range of his device.

"Come on, come on," he mumbled to himself in frustration and as he spoke something did come through, not a voice per se, more a humming. He adjusted the frequency a little fine tuning it, at 89.9 it came through clearer. It wasn't a mechanical hum, but that of a person, a female, a girl. It was soft and melodic, and Mike racked his brain to try and remember what the tune was, but then the hum turned to a voice, soft and sweet, and Mike felt a chill run through him that was not born from the temperature in his Jeep. He knew the ditty, Claire used to sing or hum it to their daughter when she had fitful spells of sleep, which was often.

> *Rock-a-bye baby, on the treetop,*
> *When the wind blows the cradle will rock,*
> *When then bough breaks, the cradle will fall,*
> *And down will come baby, cradle and all*

As THE NURSERY rhyme reached the last few words, that soft voice began to chuckle. It lost its silken sound and cracked like an egg into a cackle that merged with the screaming sound of feedback, like someone holding a microphone too close to a speaker. Mike cried out in surprise as the high-pitched sound assaulted his ears and he dropped the receiver into his lap. The laugh had gone, now it was all the terrible screech of electrical interference, then through it came the same voice, faint yet there, as if being picked up from a distance, from a faraway place. It was the child again, her voice soft and yet now filled with menace,

> *Run – away – Mikeyyy, - run – away – all,*
> *When – the -time -comes – you'll – scream – and – you'll - fall*

And – die – you – will – Mikey – die – will – you – all!

MIKE PICKED up the receiver from his lap, switched it off, then cast it into the footwell as if it were a poisonous animal that might render him a fatal bite. He engaged drive and gunned the accelerator, the wheels of his Jeep span on the gravel of the layby until they found purchase, catapulting him forward in a wake of dust. He snaked out onto the road and narrowly missed a family saloon heading the other way, the driver hit his horn as the two cars almost made contact. Mike raised a hand in apology and got the Jeep in a straight line, his breath coming in deep and rapid pants.

With his knuckles white from how hard he now clutched the wheel he shook his head in defiance as if trying to get the memory of what had just happened out of his brain, like a dog might shake water from his body after a swim. The incident at the hospital, in his room and now this had convinced him that whatever this was they were facing, be it Minister Deviss, or just the pure combined evil of the place born from the horrors that had purportedly happened there, it knew them. Whatever it was fucking knew them, and it knew they were close to the truth.

CHAPTER 36

ROB HARRISON LOOKED DRAINED. HIS DARK HAIR was dishevelled and messy and his face looked old and worn. The dark stubble of a day or two's growth highlighted the paleness of his skin, and his eyes were the red of a drunk who'd spent too many nights looking for the answers to all his problems at the bottom of a whisky bottle. He sat on the foot of the bed in the Travel Lodge at ten-thirty AM that Monday morning still dressed in the grey joggers and matching T-shirt that he'd been given when they'd seized his clothing at the police station. Those red eyes looked questioningly at Mike, Tara and Scotty. They were the eyes of a man who'd endured all he could. In less than thirty-six hours he'd gone from being on a relaxing family holiday to losing his son and daughter, and now, following her steady slide into a state of catatonia, his wife Carol, whom following an assessment of her mental health whilst in custody at Plymouth, had been committed to Glenbourne Hospital. Catatonic Depression was the official diagnosis, a form of post-traumatic stress disorder that caused some patients to be totally unresponsive and locked into their own minds and unable to react to stimuli.

Whilst Mike had been out at the Horners' place the day before, Tara had set about finding just which room the Harrisons had been staying in. She'd hung about in the lobby of the hotel drinking nasty vending machine coffee and feeling like, as she'd put it, a hooker waiting for her date, until the on-duty receptionist had been called away to resolve some issue with a guest's towels. As soon as the coast was clear she'd brazenly hopped behind the counter and helped herself to the information from the reception's computer terminal, that had helpfully not been locked by the young girl working at the time, and as an added bonus was on the booking screen. It had taken her less than thirty seconds to see that the Harrisons were booked into room 33 on the floor above. Then it had just been a matter of time until they were released. In that time Mike had called Sue Reed and updated her that all was well, and they were playing the waiting game now with the police. He'd not divulged to her all they had found out as he felt it may bestow further feelings of guilt on her, and that would be of no use to anyone.

Finally, and after a good deal longer than Mike foresaw, Rob Harrison had been released, not arriving back until eight AM that Monday morning, having spent a tad over thirty hours at the pleasure of the Devon and Cornwall Constabulary. Following the call to Sue, Mike had recounted more than once what had happened out at the Horners' cottage and what he'd heard on the listening device, chills goosebumping his flesh every time he went over what he'd picked up on the receiver. It had an auto-record function and would save anything to a micro SD card held in its side when on, he'd reluctantly played it back to them, only to find it had recorded nothing but the empty sound of static. Scotty had run the static through his Adobe Audition program, just in case something had been hidden behind that white noise, but there had been nothing. Still, neither of them had disbelieved him or thought him mad.

"All I want to do," Rob Harrison said, looking at the three of them stood there in his room, "is try and get some sleep." His voice was shell-like and hollow, the voice of a man with no hope. He smiled blankly at them, "Do you know I can't even remember when I last slept, can you believe that?"

Mike dropped to his knees, so his face was level with that of Rob Harrison's and said, "A few years ago my wife and daughter were killed, so when I say that I understand the pain you're feeling right now, I do understand. I know how it feels to have something reach in and tear your life away leaving you with nothing." Rob's eyes met Mike's and Mike knew that look only too well, it was the look of a man who'd been running through the unanswerable *what if's* that were prone to drive you mad if you let them. Mike stood and pulled over a chair and sat by him. He placed a hand on his shoulder so that he'd meet his eyes.

"I know you," Rob Harrison said flatly, his eyes moving between them all. "I thought you looked familiar when you knocked the door. Ellie watched your show." It wasn't lost on Mike how he'd referred to his daughter in the past tense, that wasn't a good sign, it was the sign of someone who'd already resigned himself to some terrible fact. "This is strange," he said, shaking his head from side-to-side slowly as if trying to make sense of some weird dream. "What are you even doing here, why did I let you in?"

"You let us in, Mr. Harrison because I told you we could help and that we had certain information that you had to hear." The poor guy seemed detached; Mike had seen such confusion in dementia sufferers who would do something then not remember doing it. The long-term memory was there but they seemed to move around the present time in some kind of dream. Mike guessed that with Rob it was nothing more than his brain trying to cope with what he'd endured over the last few days.

"She loved that show of yours," he continued. "Watched a few episodes with her when Carol was watching some of that trashy reality TV she loves so much. The crap that they chuck on year after year. You know the kind, I'm a Fading Celebrity, Save My Career," he chuckled dryly at his own joke but there was no genuine humour in it. Like his voice it seemed empty. "You were a cop, right?"

Mike nodded, "I was, I still investigate, private cases not just the unexplained."

"What are you doing getting involved in this?" he asked, that total shell-shocked look of confusion still on his tired, pallid face. Confusion born from stress, almost three days with no sleep and the simple fact that even someone well rested and totally chilled might be a tad puzzled as to why three people he'd seen on TV were now stood in front of him offering their help.

"I've played this out in my head, how meeting you would go, the things I'd say, how you'd be and if you'd even let us through the door and hear us out. I thought about not coming, I – we, almost didn't. But you need to know what we know." Mike stood and went to the small bathroom that was a carbon copy of his own on the floor below and drew a glass of water from the sink then brought it back to Rob who took hold of it and smiled in appreciation. He didn't drink it, though. "The people who own The Old Chapel," he continued, sitting back down, "Sue and Tom Reed, asked us to investigate it once you and your family had left. I know in the face of what's happening this sounds stupid, but please hear me out." Rob Harrison didn't speak, he just nodded for Mike to continue. "There have been some rather troubling reports of strange activity in there and many of their guests; well all but one actually, have left before the end of their stay because of it. There have been deaths, too. Suicides and one infant murder, not in the building, but acts done by people who have stayed there. It's a very strange case."

"As strange as my Ellie and Henry just vanishing into fucking thin air?" he asked with a hint of venom.

"No," Mike said directly. "Shadow figures, crying that no one can explain. One young girl said a man had been in her room watching her, a dark man."

Rob Harrison looked up from the glass and Mike knew that something he'd said had triggered the reaction. "What?" he asked. "Was it the mention on the dark man?"

Finally, Rob Harrison took a tentative sip from the glass and rubbed his lips together and Mike wondered how long it would be before the glass from which he drank contained something a little stronger than water. "The night that Ellie and Henry went missing she argued with Carol about Henry sleeping in her room. She said that he'd seen a man in his room the night we arrived and that he was too scared to sleep on his own. She dismissed it as a dream and basically told her not to be silly. I try to stay clear of their arguments, they don't have many but when they do, you'd best be out the way. I took Henry up to the lounge, but we could still hear. He never said anything to me, though."

"That's good, really good," Mike said encouragingly. "Is there anything else?"

He looked downtrodden and sighed, "No," he said.

"Did you or your wife see or experience anything strange there?"

"I really don't see," Rob Harrison began.

"It matters," Mike cut in, not wanting to lose him now. He decided to change tact. "Tell me about the night they went missing, you went to the Horners' barbeque, didn't you?"

Rob gave Mike a look that said, *how the fuck did you know that?* But he didn't voice it. "Yes," he said, in a resigned tone. Mike knew the police had probably been over this account so many times that the thought of living it again would have been unbearable, but he needed to hear it. Mike knew he had about as much chance of getting a transcript of the interview from

Mark Samuels as he did of baptising a cat. "We got there between seven and eight."

"Who was there?" Mike asked.

"From what I could tell the whole village, I never met them all, but the ones we chatted to seemed like a friendly bunch. Seth Horner, that's the husband of the lady who caretakes the place, is some hotshot scientist."

"I had the pleasure of meeting the Horners earlier today," Mike said. He felt bad that both Scotty and Tara were being left out of this, but right now he had the rapport with Rob Harrison, and he needed to run with it. "Tell me, Rob," Mike had opted for the use of his first name now, it often got people in traumatic situations to respond to you better if you spoke on a less formal level. "Did you, your wife or the two kids eat and drink anything at that party?"

"We all did," he said with confusion.

"Did they drug test you in custody?" Mike asked. Despite the dangers he knew they were facing he felt alive and on the pulse. He looked at Tara who had her voice recorder on, the red light glowed in the dim room telling Mike she was getting it all, so they could go back over it later.

"Yes, they drug tested us because of how we just fell asleep."

"What do you mean?" Mike asked.

"The night they went missing, Carol and I just went out like lights in the lounge, she woke me up just before ten on the Saturday morning when she couldn't find them. I mean I doze off on the sofa sometimes, who doesn't? But never like that and not for the whole night. I think they wanted to pin neglect on us, but Ellie is eighteen and she'd only had a few drinks and when they went missing, she was the one with Hen."

"Did they find anything with the toxicology?"

"No, I mean I don't think so, or they wouldn't have let me out?" Rob said.

"Whatever was used," Tara cut in from the back of

the room, "was obviously something that would never show up in blood work."

Rob looked at her, his pale, stubbly face confused, "What are you getting at?" he asked and then looked to Mike and Scotty, letting them know the question was theirs to answer, too. "I've just spent thirty hours locked up in a cell going over this time and again. They were on about getting a warrant or something to hold me for longer." Tears welled up in his eyes and he wiped them away. "Do you know that I'd have happily stayed. 'Cos in there it didn't seem real, it was like life was on pause and I knew that when, if – they let me out that I'd have to really face it. They should have charged me," he said with anger. "I might not have been the one to take them but it's my fault. I wasn't there for them when, when....," he trailed off and bit back more tears.

"They let you go, Rob, because they didn't have any viable evidence other than circumstance to get a warrant to keep you for longer. I'm surprised they kept you longer than twenty-four hours if I'm honest, but this is a high-profile case and heads will roll if anything is missed. But I know things have been missed," Mike said. "Not through any fault of the police mind, if we are right then this case goes way beyond anything they have ever dealt with or would ever consider. If the DI running this thing knew I was even here talking to you we'd be locked up, too. He's told me to leave this alone, but I can't leave it, we can't leave it. Not knowing what we know, which is why we are here. You need to hear me out on this," Mike paused a second. What he had to say next was a risky move, but he needed to get Rob Harrison's attention. He took a deep breath and went for it, "I don't believe that either your son or your daughter are dead," he said firmly. "I know the police do and I know that right now you probably do, but we don't."

"The shoe," Rob Harrison said, and his voice took on a little emotion now, not pain, this was more anger.

"I saw HIS shoe!" he spat at Mike and his hands began to shake slopping the water over the sides of the glass. It spilt down the sides and dripped to the floor where it darkened the blue carpet beneath. "It was in a fucking evidence bag, his Clarks trainer, the kind with the lights in the heels, only the lights won't work now because it was in the sea." Now a tear did roll down his cheek, but he didn't wipe it away. "I was with him when we bought him those shoes. I can remember the day, I can remember the shop assistant who I paid and how he had to wear them right away, and how he kept looking in the shop windows to see the lights in the heels as he walked down the Highstreet, and the look of pure joy on his face when he made them flash." Rob took a deep breath and sobbed. "And now it's in a fucking evidence bag, so don't you sit there and tell me my kids are not dead, don't you give me that false hope. Don't you dare!"

Mike let the emotion pass for a few seconds, the silence seemed longer and the tension in the room was so strong he felt as if it were a tangible thing that he could touch. He placed a comforting hand back on his shoulder, he didn't shrug it off or flinch away which was a good sign. Instead, he wiped his wet fingers on the light grey fabric of the custody joggers and looked at Mike with those red-rimmed eyes. Mike could see a pleading in them. "I don't say things like that lightly, Rob," he said. His heart was hammering in his chest, but he needed to remain sure sounding and assertive. "I said it because I believe it. Can I say for sure? No, of course I can't but we honestly believe that both Henry and Ellie are alive and likely still in that village somewhere. They are in danger; very grave danger and I need you to listen to what we have to say. When you do you will know why the police are way off the mark in their suspicions. Casting you and your wife into the spotlight of blame has been one masterful act of misdirection."

"And you think you can get them back?" Rob asked.

There was a hint of hope in his voice now and Mike hated himself for giving it because if it all went to shit or he was wrong then Rob Harrison would have the rug whipped from under him a second time, and there was no telling where that might lead. Maybe to an electrical cord tied around a loft beam and the other around his neck, or to a pile of prescription pills and a bottle of Jack, or – Mike shut the ideas from his head, this was no time for those *WHAT IF's!*

"I don't know," Mike answered truthfully. "We are going to try. The police will be releasing the keys to The Old Chapel any day now, we are going in there when they do, and I mean to get to the bottom of this."

"Why can't you take what you have to them now?" he asked suspiciously.

Mike gestured for Tara and Scotty to come forward. In the hand that didn't hold the audio recorder she had a pre-prepared file, it contained all the information and research they'd done on the place, and a fully typed account of what June had told them as well as statemented accounts of the strange experiences they'd had since getting embroiled in the case. She opened the file and began to lay out pictures of the missing girls on the foot of the bed by where Rob sat. He looked at them, his brow creasing as he pored over the many images.

"Because it's too fantastical and goes beyond reasonable thought. When Tara and Scott here brought this to me, I didn't believe it either, so I don't expect you to. Over the last day or so I have had some weird things happen to me that go beyond my understanding and now I do believe it, that's why I am here. If I thought for a second that the police would act on this then I'd be handing it to the DI in charge, but they won't."

Rob looked from Mike to Tara and then to Scotty and then from him to the images and printouts of old newspaper articles that were now spread out and taking up most of the lower end of the bed. "Who are these girls?" he asked.

Tara picked up the first image, the one of Lindie Parker and began to run through it, and Mike let her. She and Scotty had unwound the mystery and now was their time to speak; Mike just sat back and listened. Rob didn't interrupt once, not when she delved back to the history of the Device family, nor when she told of the dream she'd had or the details of the PC who'd suffered a fatal accident whilst inside The Old Chapel. He remained focused and didn't cut her off as she told him of the upcoming Grand Climax and how they felt that both Henry and Ellie's taking was intrinsically linked to the coming Friday, July 27th. The parts she missed, and there weren't many, Scotty filled in and hearing it all told out over the twenty or so minutes it took, Mike realised more than ever before how it fit together like the pieces of some fucked up jigsaw puzzle. Tara finished with Mike's visit to the Horners' place and the voices he'd heard on the FM receiver. When she had said all there was to say a silence followed, not a long one, although it felt that way. The silence was long enough for Rob Harrison to digest it all and Mike waited pensively for him to yell at them to 'GET THE FUCK OUT' and scream about how crazy they were.

"I'm going in with you," he finally said, and Mike let out a deep sigh of relief without even realising it.

"No," Mike replied.

"Yes, if that is true, I'm going with you," his voice had more body to it now, more purpose, some of that previous hollowness had been filled. He put the glass down on the carpet and scrubbed his hands over his face. "It sounds crazy," he said.

"I know," Mike replied with earnest.

"But it fits. Just how it all happened. I'm not sure I do or can believe it, but it fits. And what else do I have now?" He looked to Mike, but Mike had no answer to give. "If the people in that village did take them, then it still doesn't explain how they got out."

"I have a feeling that once we figure that bit out, we

will unravel this whole thing," Mike said. "I just need to get inside. But you can't come with us."

"They are my kids, my family," Rob Harrison protested angrily.

"I know but I need you here, you have a part to play in this, Rob. It might be an important one and the thing that saves our lives." He looked at Mike with new curiosity now, so Mike ran with it. "I'm guessing we will be in there by Wednesday at the latest. If by Eleven PM on Friday night you have not heard from us you take all of this pack to DI Samuels, you tell him to send whatever resources he can to The Old Chapel. Whatever is going to happen is going to happen on Friday. If I can't get to the bottom of this by then, you make him listen."

"And if he won't, if it's too late?"

"He'll listen," Mike said, being sure of no such thing. He could live with the lie though, for now, he'd given Rob Harrison something he felt he didn't have before their visit, purpose. And if a man as low as Rob Harrison felt he had a purpose it might just be the one thing that saves him. "We go back a long way, he knows I have a hand in this, he doesn't like it one bit, but he knows. I'm going to give you a pre-addressed envelope as well, it contains all of this information, if we don't come back then you take it to the post office and send it via first class recorded delivery. It's for the Reeds. As you probably know they own the building and they deserve to know, if only so they can close the place down."

Fresh tears welled in Rob Harrison's eyes, not tears of sadness this time, but tears of anger, frustration and maybe just a tiny bit of hope, "Okay, Mike," he said and wiped them away before they had a chance to fall. "Promise me you'll find them, you promise me that."

"I promise," Mike said. He knew it was one that he probably couldn't keep, or that by the time he found them it might be too late, but it was just another one of those things you said to stick a plaster over the wound.

Scotty collected up the sheets of paper and sorted

them into order before slipping them back into the A4 sized wallet. He passed them to Rob Harrison who nodded in thanks and sat there clutching them in his hand.

The pieces are all in place now, Mike thought to himself as he looked at the sorry mess that was Rob Harrison. *Well as in place as they can be.* A few days ago, Rob had just been a regular family man, doing the best he could for his kids, and now he'd been robbed of that. Seth and Lucinda had sat there smiling at him and feigning concern and he felt hatred for them broil inside of him. He didn't know to what extent they were involved but he had no doubt they knew. All he needed now were the keys and the game would be on. How it would play out he had no idea, all he knew was that by this time next week it would likely all be over and that there was a very good chance they'd all be dead.

CHAPTER 37

A YOUNG WAITRESS WHOSE DARK BROWN HAIR WAS
tied back in a tight bun balanced three glasses of freshly
squeezed orange juice on a circular brown tray toward
them. Mike watched her weave in and out of the
packed outer seating area of Wreckers, one of
Charlestown's many small and privately-owned eateries.
She finally reached their table after avoiding a myriad of
various obstacles such as pushed out chairs and carelessly abandoned bags and placed the three glasses
down, one in front of Mike, another in front of Tara
and finally one onto a coaster where Scotty sat.

It was a little after eleven AM on Wednesday morning, the tide was up, and the water of the quay danced
in thousands of tiny sparkling ripples that shimmered
across its surface. The day was idyllic, and the fresh
smell of the sea carried itself on the warm summer
breeze. Above, gulls wheeled a called to each other in a
deep, clear blue sky. Occasionally a fishing boat would
chug its way out to sea where it would stay until the
tide turned, then turned again allowing them back in
with their catch.

A stark reminder that everything was far from right
with the world, despite the idyllic day, was the Police
rib. It was moored against the far quay wall with a life-
jacket wearing officer at the helm, a colleague was sat

by his side holding a clipboard stuffed with paperwork. Occasionally one of the team of three divers would come up, remove their mask and cling to the rib, talking with the two officers onboard, some form filling then followed before the dive mask was fixed back in place and the diver disappeared once again below the still waters.

"The tide brings in new junk and then washes it back out every time it turns," Scotty commented before taking a deep swallow of juice and letting out a sigh of satisfaction. He wiped the back of his hand over his mouth and added, "I've seen it in Cowes harbour."

Charlestown was already brimming with tourists and more than one or two frantic looking parents were shouting pointlessly at their unruly kids to stay away from the edge of the harbour and to stop climbing on the twin metal railings that lined it to stop people falling in.

The last day and a half, since the visit with Rob Harrison, had been spent going over and re-going over what they'd learned and digging for more, but it seemed that they had already learned all they could from the public records held online.

Tuesday had been spent in Plymouth, first out at the Central Library trawling through old newspapers and microfilm. They found a few other stories relating to the missing girls that had not been available online, but nothing that helped at all, or provided a link to The Old Chapel, or Trellen in general. From the library, they'd driven to the Plymouth and West Devon Record Office only to be turned away due to lack of appointment. The portly bespectacled clerk informed them that the earliest they could return was the following Monday, but not between twelve and two PM as they were closed for lunch. He then produced a stack of forms for them to fill out covering which records they wanted access to. Mike had taken the papers with the empty promise of returning with them later that day, knowing full well that they wouldn't as by Monday this thing would likely be over.

By the time they'd got back to the Travel Lodge Rob Harrison had gone. He'd posted a handwritten note under Mike's door in an almost illegible scrawl that could have been written by someone with early-stage Parkinson's.

Mike, Tara & Scott
I've moved to the Milestones Hotel in Plymouth, it's nearer the
hospital and I need to be there for Carol. She is all I have now,
and she needs me. It's time I stepped up and got a grip on
things. I'm still not sure I can believe what you told me. Sorry.
I will honour your two requests and I have your files with me.
All the best
Rob Harrison

MIKE HAD PUT the note with the case papers, the same papers which Rob had two copies of and had referred to in his letter. In a way Mike had felt relief at what he'd written, it wasn't full of hope and Mike had a feeling that if the worst happened, or they lived but failed to unravel the mystery of just what had happened to Ellie and Henry Harrison, then the rug that he worried about being pulled from under Rob's feet wouldn't hurt that badly. Quite rightly he wasn't pinning all his hopes on them, for if you didn't expect too much then the let-down wasn't as hard to take.

That Tuesday evening they'd spent time with a tasteless Indian takeaway and two six packs of Corona. All three of them camped out in Mike's room reading what they could about the Pendle Witch Trials and the life of Jennet Device. They read varying accounts and watched a number of YouTube documentaries, but none told them more than they already knew, and all accounts seemed to reach the same conclusion, that Jennet Device had died in Lancaster Gaol. No one it seemed had as much information on the case as June Rogers, proprietor of Cornwall's Museum to Witchcraft and the Occult.

Mike swilled the ice around his glass, it clinked and chinked together, "They won't just have dumped one shoe," he said and took a sip of the cool liquid, it was sweet and acidically zesty all at the same time. "I expect over the next few days the sea will give it back, I doubt they'll find everything but...," Mike paused as a police diver surfaced. In his hand, he was clutching something. They were on the opposite side of the quay's channel but thanks to the fact the swim was quite narrow he was close enough to see it was a red adult size shoe, possibly a Converse, the exact same kind and colour that Ellie Harrison had been wearing the day she went missing.

"You were saying," Tara commented in a low voice as she watched the developments herself.

Mike drained the glass as if it had something a little stronger in it that he'd needed to steady his nerves. The helmsman and his second in command were now busy getting an evidence bag ready and suddenly Mike heard Rob's distraught voice in his head, '*It was in a fucking evidence bag, his Clarks trainer, the kind with the lights in the heels, only the lights won't work now because it's been in the sea.*'

A few tourists had noticed the flurry of activity over at the police rib and they'd now stopped, paused in morbid curiosity as one of the biggest news stories of the summer developed in front of them.

"*I can't believe they let the parent's go,*" he heard a chubby woman in a gaudy floral summer dress say to a man who was obviously her long-suffering husband. The poor guy looked to be about ten stone lighter than her as well as six inches shorter, he was dressed in plain grey cargo shorts and a yellow check shirt. On his feet were a pair of sturdy looking leather walking sandals, finished off nicely with a pair of white sports socks. The woman had a double flaked ice cream clasped in her fat fingers and she licked greedily at the cone as drips ran down it. *"I mean there's no smoke without fire, is there?"* Mike felt an insatiable urge to get up and shove the old-bat into the water. The police might not have the evidence to charge Rob or the now catatonic Carol Harrison, but the public had all they needed to brand them killers. *"I read in the paper this morning that the mother has been sectioned,"* the woman continued. *"Personally, I hope she rots in there, those poor kids. Can you imagine doing that to your own kids, Malc?"*

"Fucking public," Tara said sourly hearing the comment, too. "Read something in some shitty comic of a newspaper and take it as gospel." She raised her voice loud enough, so the woman would hear, and she did. She spun around to see who had made the comment, a look of disgust on her face. Tara met her eyes and gave her a smile; the woman tutted loudly and ushered her henpecked husband along.

Mike was about to suggest that when they'd finished their drinks they should get moving, take a walk around the town and down to the beach, just to get a feel for the layout of the place, (the scene of Lindie Parker's taking), when he felt his phone vibrate in his pocket. He fished it out and frowned at the PRIVATE NUMBER caller ID displayed on the screen. In his experience, and when working for Sussex Police, PRIVATE NUMBER meant a job call. He swiped the phone to answer.

"Mike, it's Mark Samuels," Came a familiar voice.

"Mark," he said, looking at Tara and Scotty who were now frowning at him and trying their best to listen. "How are you?"

"Under about ten tonnes of pressure to crack this thing and getting nowhere fast," came a weary reply. "Look, Mike – I am out at the Travel Lodge, but they said you'd gone out for the day."

"Just down at Charlestown, doing the touristy bit and seeing some sights," Mike replied.

"I've left an envelope for you at the reception. Sue Reed requested you have the contents right away."

Mike felt something cold churn inside of him, "You-you're finished," he stuttered.

"CSI pulled out this morning at nine. The place is all yours. I've gotta say I still don't really want you in there Mike, but I don't see what harm you can do now. The long and short is that the building has been released back to the owners and they asked me to get the keys to you, so I can't stop you."

Both Tara and Scotty had now cottoned on to where the conversation had led, and they were now sat looking soberly at him. "I appreciate it," Mike said. "Did you find anything?"

There was a pause, and Mike knew his old colleague was weighing up answering the question, "Not a fucking thing," he finally said. "The place was as clean as a whistle. It's like they just upped, and fucking vanished into thin air."

"I'll collect the keys this afternoon," Mike replied. "And thanks again, Mark."

"No problem, buddy," Samuels replied before terminating the call.

Just like they upped, and fucking vanished into thin air,' Samuels had said. Mike was beginning to wonder if his old friend and colleague might not be far from the truth on that one.

PART 4
THE CHAPEL

CHAPTER 38

THEY PULLED UP TO THE OLD CHAPEL AT A LITTLE after four PM that same Wednesday in a convoy of two vehicles. Tara rode shotgun with Mike in the front of his Jeep, with Scotty bringing up the rear in his T4, hauling all of the kit he'd loaded up back in Cowes. Much of it was theirs but a fair bit that also belonged to SwitchBack TV.

All signs that this had been the scene of a major police forensics operation had gone, save for one solitary length of police tape. It was still tied around the flaky old bark of a gnarled old oak at the far side of the property's boundary, the tape had been snapped six inches or so before the knot and the tail end fluttered lazily in the breeze.

Tara let out a terse breath through her teeth and lifted her oversize shades off her face as Mike brought the Jeep to a stop. She glanced uneasily at him and said in a nervous voice, "So this is the place." She wore three-quarter length white cargo shorts and a red GAP T-shirt, her dark blonde hair was held up in a ponytail, and for a second Mike didn't answer, he just enjoyed looking at her. "This is the place," he finally said with a wan smile.

"It knows we are here," she said sombrely, and her

words made Mike shiver. "I feel like it's watching us, don't you?"

"Maybe," Mike replied, not wanting to fully admit that he felt the same, for fully admitted it might make it fact. He felt observed as if the trees lining the grounds had a thousand eyes that were watching them and were right at that moment whispering secrets to each other. "Let's get inside and have a look round, it will take a while to get the place rigged with cameras," he said glancing in his rear-view and seeing that Scotty was already out of the cab of his VW. The rear tailgate and side sliding door were both open, and he was man-handling flight cases out and onto the shingle drive, his large arms swelling like tree trunks beneath the sleeves of his plain black button-up shirt.

"You need a hand there?" Mike asked as he got out.

Tara rounded the back of the Jeep and placed a hand on the outer casing of the spare wheel holder, "Listen," she said to them both. "Just stop and listen a moment guys."

Both Mike and Scotty obliged her and for a few moments, they all stood perfectly still with their heads cocked to the side.

"I don't hear nothing," Scotty finally said, looking at her with a mixture of puzzlement and confusion. He set the small case down that he'd been holding, placing it on top of a larger one he'd already removed.

"That's exactly it," Tara said with a little annoyance. "There's nothing to hear. Nothing!" Scotty shook his head and was about to laugh when she added, "We are in the countryside, surrounded by thick woodland. Where are the birds? This whole place should be a haven for wildlife but it's so quiet."

Scotty's face went from amused to deadpan serious in under a second flat. "Fuck," he said. "You know, you're right." And for another few drawn out seconds, they all stood in combined silence, all wanting to hear just the chirp of one bird or the rustle of wildlife from the forest. There was nothing. As he stood there Scotty scanned the treeline his head turning slowly. Finally, he returned his attention to Tara.

"There must be something deeply wrong with this place," she said to them both.

"Remember I told you about the two police dogs that they had out here to do the search?" Mike cut in.

Scotty nodded, "Wouldn't come out of the handlers' vans and both pissed themselves."

"That's right, well it seems that our K9 friends are not the only members of the animal kingdom to wanna give this place a miss." Mike looked at the stack of cases now piled up by the van. "Let's get this shit inside before we spook ourselves to the point where we are wanting to pack it back in the van and getting the hell outta Dodge," he chuckled, but like Rob Harrison's laugh the other day, there was no real humour in it.

Mike reached the swish-bang door at the side of Scotty's Van and grabbed two of the smaller cases, the ones holding their own MEL and K2 meters, as well as a few digital voice recorders. He hauled them one on to each shoulder by the strap and walked to the front door. He didn't pause there and contemplate putting the key in the lock, he did it deftly, the way a skydiver might jump from a plane, or you might tear a well stuck on plaster off your skin, for if you thought about it too long you might well back out. He crossed the threshold for the first time confidently and with both Tara and Scotty behind him.

"It's cold in here," Tara said. she dumped the two cases she carried down and rubbed her hands up and down her tanned arms as if to highlight the point.

"Old Cornish stone," Mike replied, setting his cases down by hers. "Naturally keeps the place a good few degrees cooler than it is outside."

They all stood for a few moments, taking in the entrance lobby of the place they'd been waiting so long to get into, yet all not really wanting to get into at all. The place that June Rodgers had told them would be the death of them. The place where people seemingly vanished with no explanation as to how. The place where the cries of tortured infants filled the night, and somehow wormed its way into people's heads and made them kill themselves and drown babies in their baths.

It looked lavish and not at all sinister, something pretty painted over something rotten. It was just like the pictures from the website, decorated in a mixture of natural stone and dark wood panelling. The cooled air carried a mixture of smells, oak, stone and the unmistakable scent of bleach and cleaning fluid, one juxtaposing against the other to make an odd cocktail that wasn't pleasant but wasn't exactly nasty, either. To the left by the door was a sturdy looking oak sideboard, not old, likely a reproduction of an earlier piece made within the last few years and carrying a tasty price tag. A key plaque made of rough-cut grey slate hung above it with a laminated, printed card reminding guests to leave the keys there at all times when in, to avoid losing them. There were two staircases that led to the mezzanine level, one to the left, and one to the right. They arced round in opposing curves both leading to the open plan lounge above. The place was large, but it didn't require two staircases leading to the same place, it had been done more for the grand appearance than necessity. At the foot of the left staircase, Mike could see where the dark grey carpet had been scrubbed clean, scrubbed with something abrasive and to the point where it had bobbled. There was no doubting that this was the exact spot where PC Shelly Ardell had fallen and suffered the head injury that would prove fatal. The grey of the carpet was still stained in places, where the blood had soaked in too deeply to ever be removed.

Large stained-glass windows lit the lobby, reaching up either side of the heavy oak door. They provided enough natural light to feed the lobby and the lounge, too. The lounge / living area was open plan and an internal balcony looked back down over the entrance lobby. The banisters from each opposing staircase fed round to the internal balcony rail, making one fluid sweep of oak handrail that stretched from the left stairway, up, over and across the lounge balcony and down the right. Timber beams stained the same shade as the door and banisters reached up a good ten feet from the lounge where they met at the roof's peak.

Directly in front of them and tunnelling its way under the lounge ran a corridor, panelled again in expensive looking timber from floor to ceiling. Mike could see doors set into the panelling, one of which had a brass plaque on denoting a bathroom. At the far end of the central corridor, Mike could see that it opened out into the kitchen and dining room. A second corridor ran along the right side of the building, following the original stone wall and here another laminated card was hung with the words, '**MASTER BEDROOM**' printed on it. Below the bold typed letters was a thick, black arrow pointing the way for those guests who might be directionally impaired. Toward the end of this corridor, Mike could see an opening that looked to be a third, but more basic stairway leading to the bedrooms on the mezzanine level, the ones behind the lounge. Resting on the floor, propped upright against the wall at the foot of the right-hand staircase was a large, heavy looking crucifix. Someone, likely a member of the forensics team must have knocked it off the wall and forgotten to rehang it.

"Impressive place, "Scotty said, breaking the momentary silence and making both Mike and Tara jump a little.

"Yeah, worth the heavy price tag for the stay, if it doesn't kill you," Tara said, and no one laughed.

"Let's get the rest of the gear in and have a proper look round," Mike encouraged. "We stay together, though. Even tonight I suggest that when we do turn in or feel the need to sleep, we all stay in the lounge area. It looks nice and open and we have a view of the front door. And none of that lights out shit. It looks good for TV but we all know it's bollocks, if a place is haunted it's haunted, you don't need the dark to bring it out." *Or maybe this place does need the dark,* he thought to himself. *Maybe that's what it craves.* He cast the thought aside without voicing it, turned and walked back out, enjoying the warmth of the sun and the fresh air. The inside of The Old Chapel was indulgent, corpulent even. But the sheer amount of dark timber strangled the natural light once you got past the main lobby. The internal corridors had been dimly lit despite the large windows and the brightness of the sun outside. It made Mike feel a little claustrophobic and he wasn't sorry to be back out in the heat of the day.

As he reached the back of the T4, eyes still squinting in the sunlight, Mike spotted someone coming up the drive, a man dressed in smart grey trousers and a white shirt. At first, Mike thought it was Mark Samuels but then he spotted the camera slung over the guy's shoulder and the fact he had sandy blonde hair. As the stranger drew closer he collected up the camera, it looked to be an expensive looking DSLR, the professional kind with a large lens. He raised it to his eye, and as he walked toward them he fluidly took a few snaps before letting it drop back to his side, where it hung the way a woman might carry her handbag.

"Afternoon," the new-comer called, his voice raised slightly to cover the closing distance between them. As he spoke he raised a friendly hand at the same time. "Another hot one," he added as he joined them at the back of the T4, he ran the back of his hand over his perspiration-wettened brow and let out an exasperated sigh as if to make his point.

He was in his early thirties, his sandy blonde hair was swept back on his head and his face was so smooth it looked as if he'd never breached puberty and needed to shave. His white shirt was untucked and hung loosely around the top of his trousers and Mike could see sweat patches under his arms and around the collar. "Can I help?" Mike asked, trying not to sound too short. Tara and Scotty had joined him at the back of the T4 and were also looking at the new guest with suspicion.

"Duncan Reid," the guy said and extended his hand toward Mike who shook it reluctantly. His palm felt clammy and sweaty. Mike let go and covertly wiped his hand against his trouser leg. "You's guys movin' in?" He had a slight hint of Scottish to his accent and Mike guessed he'd likely lived there in his youth, probably moving south of the border at some point where over the years his accent had become diluted.

"I'm guessing you're a reporter, Mr. Reid?" Mike asked, nodding toward the camera.

Reid smiled, and it looked friendly, but Mike knew it was false; the smile was put on as part of his hidden agenda, and that was to get some kind of scoop. "Indeed," he said. "I've been waiting for days to get a closeup of this place. I don't suppose you'd care to give me a quick quote now would you, about how it feels to stay here after it's been a crime scene?" Reid was now looking with interest at the remaining cases stacked by the back of Scotty's T4 and Mike could see he was trying to work out what they were. "Or," he added The 'or' coming out slowly as if he were still deciding to continue, "let me in to take a few snaps. I could pay you, ya know make it worth your while."

"If it's all the same to you Mr. Reid," Mike began, but he was cut off mid-flow.

"Hang on a minute," Reid said. His left hand was up now, pointing back and forth at the three of them and Mike felt his stomach sink. "I know you's three. You're Mike Cross, aren't you?" Mike didn't answer. The smile on Reid's face was genuine now and it showed his slightly yellowed teeth. "I did a piece on that case you investigated up North, it was in the Sun, where was that place now?" he paused and chewed momentarily on the tip of his forefinger before answering his own question. "That's right, Sleaford. You got a TV show off the back of that, didn't ya?" Reid was looking pleased with himself now and grinning like a Cheshire Cat. Mike didn't answer so he tried another question, "Are you's three here as part of the investigation?"

"Just taking some time out," Mike answered. He wasn't going to give Reid a single thing, but a good reporter knew when they'd stumbled on something and in that respect they weren't too far removed from cops. A good reporter had a nose for a story, just as a good cop had a nose for when someone was feeding them bullshit.

"What's in the flight cases?" he asked with interest. "Is it full of the stuff you use on the show?" None of them answered so he went with, "How about the three of you's just pose for a quick shot for me by the cars, we can put the equipment in front of you and we will get the building in behind, it'll look fab."

"How about you go fuck yourself," Tara said with a grin.

"Can I quote you on that?" Reid said confidently.

"Only if you want me to jam that Nikon up your ass so far you can taste it," Tara came back with.

Scotty stepped forward, he outsized Reid by a good sixty pounds and six inches or more in height and his mere presence caused the cocky reporter to take a step back. "This is private property," Scotty said. "I suggest you leave before I escort you off. Don't come back, either. There is nothing for you here."

"I'd beg to differ on that," Reid said, but he was now walking back as he spoke and not sounding quite so sure of himself. "Old creepy building that two kids have gone missing from and that no one can explain."

"This is real life," Mike said firmly. "Not an episode of Scooby-Doo! It's just a coincidence we booked the place for the week after the Harrison family."

"I'm not so sure," Reid added. "You's are up to something here, I can tell."

"Which paper are you with?" Mike asked.

"Freelance," Reid replied.

"A mercenary then," said Mike. "Selling your misery to the highest bidder."

"It's a dog-eat-dog business," Reid said sarcastically. He backed off a good ten yards as Scotty and Mike both closed in on him. He raised the camera and managed to get a quick shot in before ducking out of the way as Scotty grabbed for it.

"Leave it," Mike said in a low voice so that Reid couldn't overhear. "If we go wrestling that camera off him, he'll have the police back down here in a shot. And Samuels will use the first excuse he can to get us out of this place, believe me. What good will it be if one of us is locked up back in Plymouth on an assault complaint?"

"But if those pictures make the press Samuels will shit the bed on us," Scotty protested.

"I'll handle Samuels if I have to," Mike reassured. "We can't help it if some leach of a jurno took it upon himself to come snooping and got lucky. Let's focus on the task in hand." They watched Reid snap off two more shots from further down the drive, he waved a mocking hand to them before he reached the road. Mike hadn't seen his car on the way in, he'd likely parked some way off and walked back so as not to be seen.

"Task in hand," Mike said again seeing that Scotty was about as eager to go after Reid as an unruly dog is to break its leash and make a dash for the ocean. "We need to start trying to unravel this thing, and to be honest I don't have a clue where to start."

CHAPTER 39

EIGHT CCTV CAMERAS IN ALL HAD BEEN SET UP
throughout The Old Chapel. Scotty had made the
lounge the technical base and against the stone of the
left external wall he'd set up one of their portable
trestle tables. Sat upon it were two four channel CCTV
digital video recorders and into them were plugged two
twenty-inch LCD monitors feeding back images from
the eight cameras. Four of those were costly full spectrum cameras, they'd been specially adapted in the
USA. The four cameras had gone through a bespoke
modification process to enable them to see light across
the full spectrum, including that which cannot be detected by the human eye. Next to the portable FLIR
thermal imaging cameras, they'd been the biggest
outlay by the TV company, and it was only a matter of
time before they came knocking the door for it all
back.

Scotty checked his watch against the time displayed
on the CCTV systems' two clocks, it was five minutes
to seven. It had taken a full two hours post unloading to
safely install the cameras and run all the wires back to
the lounge, or what Scotty was now referring to as 'The
Bridge.' Mike stood with him and surveyed the live-
view images from around the building. Channel one's
camera was on a clamp, secured to the top of the

balustrade in the lounge, overlooking the lobby area. The wide-angle lens from this elevated position took in the whole lobby from wall to wall in a bird's eye view. The cameras on channels two and three were in the lobby, one facing down each corridor. Channel four's camera was in the kitchen area, five's was in the master bedroom on the ground floor, what was known by the brass plaque on the door as The Altar Room. Camera six was covering the upper corridor behind the lounge and a camera had been placed in the two upper bedrooms, the ones where Henry and Ellie Harrison had been staying.

"There's still a good few rooms we've not managed to cover," Scotty commented with frustration as he double and triple checked the system's settings. "Another two banks of four cameras and I reckon I'd be able to get the place so well covered you'd see a fly crack a fart."

"We'll work with what we've got," Mike replied. "Ready for a walk around and some base reading tests?"

Scotty fixed one of the team's four GoPro cameras to a head rig and strapped it on. Mike always thought that the head-mounted rig looked a bit ridiculous. As they were not going lights out on this one it did, however, provide them with full HD recording in sixty frames per second, and when attached to the body it allowed the hands to be kept free do other things, so the fact it looked dumb was outweighed by the practicality of it. Once secure he turned his attention to a large 120-watt floor speaker. It was the kind that you would often find in a gym class, used to play the music for Zumba, or Spinning. This one had a single laptop plugged into it, and into the laptop was plugged a Sonic Ear Amplifier. The resulting product was then recorded onto the laptop's hard drive straight through the Adobe Audition program and then the amplified audio was pumped out of the speaker. The idea was to catch and record the crying that so many guests seem to have experienced. With the amplification, they'd also be able to hear someone talking on the other side of the building. The hope was to see if below that crying there was more, things that the human ear couldn't pick up.

From a silver flight case laid open on the coffee table Mike took a K2 and passed its more accurate distance cousin, the MEL meter, to Tara. Both would measure any electromagnetic field disruptions; the added bonus was the MEL displayed the ambient temperature and was accurate to 0.1 of a degree. The funny truth of the matter was no one really knew, nor had fully proven that any of this kit worked, but then the investigation of the paranormal was never going to be an exact science. From a case by its side, Scotty placed six motion sensors into a canvas bag, zipped it shit, and hauled the strap over his shoulder. The motion sensors were small boxes of white plastic that were tremor activated. Once in place, they acted like mini seismographs and issued a high-pitched beep tone that lasted twenty seconds if activated.

Mike held the K2 and they moved around the lounge, looking for any disturbances in the electromagnetic field. Disruptions could occur quite naturally due to wiring or burglar alarms, Wifi and alike. Certain people who were susceptible to such interference often experienced feelings of nausea and dread, it was theorised that it could even cause some to see things in their peripheral vision, thus people susceptible people living in homes rich with EMF often reported them as haunted.

The lounge was clear, just as he suspected it would be. The building was old, but the inside was new and that meant the wiring would be, too. This would lessen the chance of it being what some in the field called 'a fear cage.' A fear cage was a boxed area of high EMF interference caused by old wiring or similar. The only place that caused the green baseline light to climb toward the red was next to the bank of CCTV recorders and monitors, but that was to be expected.

From here they went room to room covering the whole building. In each room, Mike examined the windows and their locks. He opened the ones on the first floor, the more modern double-glazed kind added during the renovations, and hung dangerously out to see if they'd been altered in any way so as to allow access when locked from the inside. None had. Scotty placed a motion sensor on the sill and then tested it by tapping his hand lightly on the wood about eight inches from the device. The tap made it beep loudly in protest.

"I hate those fucking things," Tara said seriously. "If they start going off tonight, I might just shit myself."

"We've never had one set off by anything before," Mike reminded her.

"We've never stayed in here before," she argued, and he realised that it was pointless trying to come back on that one.

"Let's keep at it, it's a big place and I want us ready to start tonight's investigation from the lounge by ten," he said going back out into the corridor.

From the bedroom that had been Ellie Harrison's they went down the stairs at the rear of the mezzanine level and into the Altar Room. Here the same readings were done, the same checks on the windows carried out. From there it was the Kitchen, Mike unlocked the door, had Tara lock him out and deadbolt it while he tried to get in. He then did the same from inside, trying to get out without removing the deadbolts or unlocking the door. Of course, all attempts were futile, as they should have been and went no way toward explaining just how the Harrison kids had managed it. After they checked the kitchen, adjoining diner and games room they were back at the entrance lobby. From the lobby they all went outside and walked the perimeter of the building, double checking all the windows on the ground floor, looking for any way that someone or something might gain both entry and exit to the building when locked down. Again, there was nothing.

By the time they'd established that there appeared to be no feasible way the Harrison kids could have gotten out, and done base reading tests in every room, it was almost nine thirty PM. The sun had all but set and the sky was a deepening blue that merged to full black in the west. They were all stood by Scotty's T4 looking at The Old Chapel as the light faded. The bell tower was silhouetted now against that bruise of a sky and as they stared at its ominous blacken outline, a murder of crows swooped past.

"Look, birds?" Scotty said, sounding relieved.

"Crows," Tara commented flatly. "It was thought by the ancient Celts that the crow escorted the sun to hell as it set on its nocturnal path and as such were an omen for evil."

"How do you know this shit?" Scotty asked.

"I read," she replied matter-of-factly, watching the birds as they wheeled across the bruising sky. "There are mixed opinions on whether they are an animal of good or bad. I've always thought the latter and seeing them here, in this place - I'd be inclined to stick with my original opinion. And don't forget that June Rodgers believed it was a Crow that came to Jennet Device when she was in Lancaster Goal. Only it wasn't a crow, it was the physical embodiment of that demon."

"Yeah," Scotty replied in a voice that was no more than a whisper, "I remember."

They watched the small flock until it became invisible against the deepening black of the western sky, then headed back inside where Mike locked and deadbolted the door.

"We have this place locked down just as it was when those kids went," he said, hanging the keys on the hook under the printed card. "We'll grab a quick brew and have an hour to chill out, sit quietly and see what comes through on that audio rig up you have done. Then do another room to room walkthrough."

"Sounds good," Scotty agreed as they made their way through to the kitchen. "What's up?" he asked seeing a look of frustration on Mike's face.

"We don't have much time, is all," Mike replied. "We have been in here eight hours and so far, we still have no fucking clue how this thing happened. And another thing, I know none of us has a single psychic bone in our bodies, but you do get a feel for a place, am I right?"

"I think you can, yeah," Tara agreed. She had the kettle in her hand and was now filling it from the large faucet. "It gave me a feeling of being watched when we first arrived but now, now - I think that could have been more psychosomatic than anything."

"And what do you feel in here, now you're settled and had a walk around?" Mike asked. "Take away what you know about the reports, forget it all and just imagine that you were here with no prior knowledge."

"It feels normal," Scotty replied, confirming what Mike felt.

"Flat," Tara agreed. "No different to my lounge at home, or any other room for that matter. We could be anywhere."

"Exactly," Mike said. He paced across the kitchen with a stern look on his face. "Is it 'cos we have gotten too close," he called to no one. "Is that it, maybe you're scared now, 'cos you know we know. You tried to put us off coming here, didn't you, you piece of shit and now we are here you're hiding like a fucking coward!"

"I'm not sure provoking it is a good idea," Tara said, grinning at his outburst.

"If it stays this way until Friday what are we going to do?" Mike asked them both. He felt helpless and at that point, he knew that in part he'd been fooling himself that this one would be an easy case to crack once he could fully get his hands on it. Because two people couldn't go missing the way the Harrison kids had without there being a rational explanation as to how it happened. There had to be one, of that he was sure. Despite everything he'd learned about the place in the last five days, and all that had happened to him he still didn't believe they'd done a Houdini and magically vanished.

"We'll figure it out," Tara said reassuringly. She clicked the kettle on and then turned to Mike placing a hand on his shoulder. "I have a feeling this might just be the calm before the storm."

CHAPTER 40

MIKE WASN'T ASLEEP, BUT HE WASN'T FULLY AWAKE either. He was in that halfway there stage, the stage where the things you hear with the more conscious part of your brain can weave the outside world into your dreams as they cross into the side that's drifting toward the land of Nod. At first, his mind thought the tinny tune was his alarm, but his semi-conscious brain couldn't reason why he'd have one set. He stirred uncomfortably in the recliner, unbeknownst to him it was the very same recliner in which Rob Harrison had slept on that fateful Friday night, almost a week ago now. As he shifted, his brain formed the words of the song

Half - a - pound – of - tuppenny – rice,
Half a pound of treacle,
That's - the - way – the - money – goes

Mike snapped fully awake, "Pop goes the weasel," he mouthed, completing the tune. The sound hadn't been coming from his phone, it had been coming from the audio rig that Scotty had set up.

Half - a – pound - of – tuppenny – rice

The ditty began again, and he rubbed the sleep

from his eyes and stared at the speaker. The room was dimly lit from the glow of the two LCD screens, their light now seeming ethereal and foreboding.

Half - a - pound - of — treacle

The metallic music-box sound came slowly, drawn out and not at the right tempo, as if it were being stretched out painfully. The speed at which it now played made that harmless child's rhyme seem terribly sinister.

MIKE CHECKED HIS WATCH.

That's – the - way – the - money – goes

It was a little after half two in the morning. They'd spent the three hours after the initial walk around going back through the building, over and over getting absolutely nothing, before in the end returning to the lounge where they'd turned the main lights down and finally succumbed to sleep.

Pop-goes-the-weasel.

An eerie silence followed, there was nothing to hear now other than the *'hissssss'* of static from the speaker. Mike waited, his hackles up, both wanting and not wanting the tune to begin again. His body felt tense and he realised that he had almost every muscle clenched. His stomach was tight, and his hands gripped the arm-rests of his chair so tightly that his knuckles were white. He looked to Tara who was laid out on the sofa, her face wore a troubled frown and he wondered if in the depths of her sleep she heard it, too. Scotty was in a regular chair to his side; his head had lulled to the right and his eyelids flickering in sleep. Mike let out a long breath that had been unconsciously held in his chest for the past few seconds, and as he did he allowed his muscles to relax.

Half - a – pound – of – tuppenny – rice

His brain filled in the words, it was an automatic reaction that he seemed unable to stop, as before the tune was slow, drawn out, coming almost one tortured note at a time. He jumped out of the recliner and shook Scotty awake, the movement and the creaking of the chair causing Tara to wake at the same time.

"What time is it?" she asked in a sleepy voice.

"Shhh," Mike prompted. "Listen!" he pointed at the speaker.

Half - a – pound – of – treacle

Scotty was up now, his sleep cast away as if it were no more than a cloak that he could dispel. He went directly to his tech setup and looked at the laptop screen. The music had caused spikes in the real-time audio graph and he looked with interest back at the first few verses that he'd missed, "How long has it been playing?"

That's – the - way – the – money – goes

"Not sure," Mike answered in a voice that was a little more than a whisper. "Not long, I don't sleep that deeply." He joined Scotty at the bank of CCTV screens. "Where the hell is it coming from?" he asked.

"On this floor," Scotty said turning his attention to the two screens and squinting at the images. "I can tell by the clarity." He rubbed his eyes and switched from four channel view to one, then began to cycle between the cameras, each now filling the full twenty inches of the screen. Each room came back in the brightly lit black and white of infrared.

Pop-goes-the-weasel!

The last bit came faster, more sped up and now too quickly for the real tempo of the song.

"There," Scotty said, jabbing a finger at the screen. "In the second bedroom on this floor. What the fuck is that?"

Half - a -- pound - of - tuppenny - rice

"That's a kids jack-in-the-box!" Tara said her voice shaking and laced with dread. She was up and now with them at the monitors. She was right, too. In the middle on the floor, in the room that had belonged to Henry Harrison was a small box that looked as if it were decorated in three or four shades of grey in the IR light. If viewed with the lights on Mike knew those greys would have been reds, greens, and yellows. An array of primary colours designed to engage the child playing with it. "I hate those fucking things," she said and shivered.

Half - a - pound - of - treacle

"That wasn't there when we did the walkthroughs earlier, was it?" Scotty asked.

"No," Mike said firmly.

"Where the fuck did it come from then?"

"There was a chest of toys in the hall outside, well more an ottoman kinda thing. I had a look inside, there were a few toys and games in there, nothing great, probably charity shop buys," Mike answered.

That's - the - way - the - money - goes

Mike leaned closer to the screen, not quite believing what he was seeing, the handle on the side of the toy was turning. The crank only just visible in the IR footage, but it was definitely moving of its own fruition, and now he understood why the tempo was off, why it kept changing. Whatever was turning it would wind it slowly for one line.

Pop-goes-the-weasel

Then as before the last line came quickly, and the handle span with speed, "Let's get in there," he said standing up and crossing the lounge to the door that led into the hall. He clicked the light on, and then light in the hall as well. The eerie tune began another impossible cycle, he could now hear the ditty coming from the bedroom and not just from the speaker.

"I don't like this," Tara said. Her voice wavered, and he could hear the fear in it.

Mike took hold of her by the shoulders and looked her in the eyes, "We will be fine," he said, knowing no such thing. "It tried playing possum, that didn't shake us, now it wants to scare us. As long as we stick together, we will be fine." She seemed to let his words sink in then nodded slowly and he knew she was with him. Scotty brushed past them, he had a GoPro on a selfie stick clasped tightly in his right hand, the record light was on and he had a look of both fear and excitement in his eyes.

"The door's shut," Scotty said as they reached it.

"I know," Mike answered. "We left it open."

Half - a – pound - of – treacle

Mike gripped the brass handle, it was cold to the touch and as the verse played out, he paused, aware of just how hard his heart was hammering in his chest.

That's -- the -- way -- the -- money – goes

He threw the door open and in one fluid movement reached around the jamb and flicked on the light. As he'd seen on the CCTV image the box stood in the centre of the room, impossibly there and the explanation as to how or why it had come to be, reachable by no rational reasoning. The air inside the room was frigid, not breath-in-the-air-cold, but chilled and they all felt it rush out as the warmer air of the hall swept in. None of them moved. They waited. Waited for the final part of the tune to play out.

Pop-goes-the-weasel

The box has its audience now and as the handle spun quickly and it hit the last note the Jack jumped from the trap. In any normal situation, Mike felt sure the Jack would have looked fine, however, when brought forth from its box by the unseen hand of whatever had been working the crank, it looked insidious. Its hair was bright blue and the red painted smile on its lips seemed to grin mockingly at them. As it sprang, and they all jumped a shrill scream of delight and terror echoed up from somewhere on the ground floor. Somewhere else in the building something, likely a door, slammed with enough force to shake it out of the frame. The shock wave set off all six of the tremor detectors and they beeped loudly in a shrill and unnerving chorus from their various places around the building.

"Fuck this shit," Tara said and stumbled back out of the doorway shaking her head. She backed off until she met the stone of the external wall. Her face was pale and washed in disbelief, the disbelief of having seen something that her mind couldn't comprehend.

Mike gripped her hand, her eyes were as wide as saucers, "Trying to scare us," he reiterated. "We are all here and we are all fine." And then the crying began.

It started low, and at first, they all had to strain to hear it. "It's on the ground floor," Tara said, her nerve seemingly restored by Mike's touch and reassurance. Scotty led the way back to the lounge, his GoPro recording the whole episode. They reached the speaker of the audio rig where the sound was amplified.

"I told you this rig was a good experiment," he grinned. If Scotty was scared, he wasn't showing it. He looked alive and as if he were relishing it all, every moment. "It's all recorded too, Mike. The whole thing!"

"This is what the Reeds heard," Mike said as he adjusted the volume. It was no more than a grizzle, the way his now-dead daughter would mither when Claire left her to try and nap in her cot. "Can you see where it's coming from?" Mike asked as Scotty flicked quickly between the cameras. Mike recalled how he'd been unable to accept that what Sue, Tom and the other guests had heard had been no more than foxes, now he knew he'd been wrong. Not only did the surrounding woods seem to be lacking all forms of wildlife save for the occasional murder of crows, but the sound now echoing up from the ground floor and through the speaker was undoubtably that of an infant.

"All clear," Scotty said, not taking his eyes from the screen. "Wherever it's coming from it's either in one of the rooms we don't have covered or," he paused as if getting to grips with what he had to say. "Or - it's coming from nowhere and everywhere at the same time."

Mike reached down and switched the speaker off, "Let's just listen a second," he said in a hushed voice. Without the benefit of the amplified ambient sound, it was harder to hear. It was there though, and it didn't take long to build in volume until it had gone from a grizzle to full wails of terror that were hard to listen to. For the briefest of moments, he wondered if there might just be an audio rig hidden somewhere, maybe a few of them secreted around the building and playing on timers. Maybe, just maybe this was all part of some elaborate scam, just as Sleaford had been. *Then how do you explain that Jack? How do you explain the missing kids and all the other shit that's happened since you started digging into this place?* His mind questioned, and he couldn't so he threw the thought aside just as quickly as it had formed.

"If that crying is a residual energy," Tara said, "then they must have tortured those poor babies before they, they," and she couldn't finish the sentence, but they all knew what she wanted to say. The ghastly sound seemed to move around them, one moment it emanated up in waves from below them, somewhere on the ground floor, then next it flooded down the corridor on the mezzanine level. Even though the speaker was off the audio continued to both record and register on the computer, the audio graph on the Adobe Audition program peaked and spiked the way a person's heart might when in atrial fibrillation and viewed on an electrocardiograph.

"Let's check the ground floor," Mike suggested, moving away from the table. "Whatever happens we stay together." Both Tara and Scotty nodded in understanding and they hurried down the stairs into the entrance lobby. Mike checked the front door. It was locked and just as he'd left it. Outside darkness pressed heavily against the two stained glass windows and no moonlight shone through.

Mike reached the first light switch and clicked it on, the light didn't abate the crying and now it seemed to be coming from the kitchen, just at the end of the central corridor that ran the length of the building. Mike led the way, beckoning the other two to follow. He reached the corridor and flicked that light on, too. It didn't help the fear that was running through him in the slightest, and halfway to the kitchen the cries reached a crescendo, they were made not of just one voice now, but many, a choir of screams reliving some horrific act over and over and as they grew the lights brightened to the point that all three of them had to shield their eyes.

"I think it's building to a peak," Mike said, almost having to shout over the noise. It was everywhere, those screams were not just audible they were somehow in his head as well, and he felt that if he had to suffer them much longer, they might drive him to insanity. Mike felt Tara grabbing his arm and he looked back at her as she pulled at him to head for the door, and for one terrible moment he heard something dark and subliminal hidden in those screams, something that wanted him to place his hands around her neck and squeeze, squeeze and squeeze until the bitch's eyes bulge and she chokes on her tongue, and –

Mike tore himself away from her and put his hands over his ears trying to shut that voice out. He knew she was right, he – they all had to get out of here before they did go mad. Mike started backing up, the light in the corridor was so pure now, such a brilliant white that it burned at his retinas and when he thought he could endure no more, when the voices started to whisper their poison once again inside his head, there was the passing of something, like the releasing of pressure. There was a sudden pop that made his ears go, the crying stopped abruptly, and the lights went out.

For a few seconds, all Mike could hear was ringing, his ears full of momentary tinnitus. He felt disorientated and in the darkness, he grabbed at Tara with his other hand. "The fuse box," he managed to say, not able to see her face. "I think it tripped the fuse box."

"Scotty," Tara called but there was no reply. Mike's head swam, and he had to rest against the wall. "He had hold of me," Tara said frantically. "He was right fucking here, and he had hold of me."

"Scott," Mike said, his voice sounding calmer than he felt. "You there, if you're there get hold of Tara and stay with us, the fuse box is in the kitchen." The darkness was thick, like being in the underground shaft of some long-ago abandoned coal mine with no torch, and from that darkness, Scotty gave no reply. He felt Tara drop to her hands and knees, she was searching the floor frantically in case he'd collapsed. In less than twenty seconds they'd felt their way all the way back along the central corridor to the entrance hall.

"Scott Hampton," she said, her voice was high and shrill and that of a person on the verge of totally losing their shit. "If you're fucking me about, I'm going to rip you a new arsehole." But he didn't reply.

Scotty was gone.

CHAPTER 41

ELLIE FELT HANDS LIFTING HER TO LEGS THAT DIDN'T feel strong enough to take her weight.

"You need to try and stand," a female voice said to her, and in the dim orange glow of her cell, the light provided as before from the burning lamps outside, she looked to see who'd spoken. It was the blonde woman whom she'd met at the barbeque, how long ago that was now she had no idea, it felt like an age and for the moment her name escaped her. Ellie could remember it began with an S, maybe Sasha, Simone or possibly Sarah.

Her blonde hair was perfectly straight and dropped to her lower back, it looked like golden honey in the fiery glow of the oil lamps. She wore a long black robe that ended just an inch from the floor and hid her feet from view. Ellie looked questioningly into her grey eyes and saw nothing. No remorse, no regret, and no emotion, just a blankness that chilled her.

"We will need to bathe you before you before the big day tomorrow," another female voice said, and Ellie knew who the other person in the room was, the one who had hold of her left arm. It was Lucinda Horner. Ellie ran a dry tongue over cracked lips and looked at her. Lucinda wore an identical robe, her red hair flowed down over her shoulders. "You stink quite terribly child," she added, her face creasing in disgust as she spoke.

Ellie felt herself being marched toward the door, on the floor of her cell lay four or five water bottles, the meagre amount they'd let her have now expended, and a couple of empty sandwich packs, the kind you get with a meal deal at places like Tesco Express or Co-op. After she'd been visited by Seth Horner, again how long ago that was now she had no concept of, they'd delivered her small amounts of food and drink. She never saw who brought them to her, the door was opened just a crack, letting just enough light in, and just for long enough to enable her to find them, before she was left to the darkness again. The food and water had been just enough to keep her functioning, and painful hunger still stabbed her belly and her mouth felt parched.

"Wh-what, wh-where a-are you t-aking m-m-me?" she managed to ask through her confusion. Her voice was cracked and scratchy and the light in the passageway hurt her eyes more fiercely than it had when Seth had taken her to see her brother.

"Not far," the blonde woman said curtly.

"I realised this afternoon," Lucinda said, "how little you know of what you are here for, and what has happened since we took you. Do you even know how long you've been here?"

"Please," Ellie croaked. "Let me see my brother." Her legs were working now, and it felt good to be moving, although to where and to what she did not know, but right at that point she had almost reached such deep despair that she didn't care.

"Your brother is still fine," the blonde woman reassured flatly. "He is just as he was when you last saw him."

"That was just over two days ago Ellie," Lucinda said as they reached a solid looking wooden door, like the one to Henry's cell, only this was almost twice as wide, and taller by a good foot. Lucinda paused outside of it. "It's the very early hours of Thursday the 26th of July, you have been with us almost six days. As far as the world outside is concerned both you and Henry are dead." Then with what seemed like a hint of mocking she added, "Would you believe that your mother and father were arrested on suspicion of killing you both? Your poor mother has taken it quite badly, she's in a mental hospital in Plymouth, or so the news is saying. Your faces have been all over the national news for days, you're both quite famous. Isn't that what every girl of your age wants these days, Ellie – to be famous?"

Ellie felt tears welling in her eyes and she tried to force them back, the thought of what her parents must have gone through now adding to her despair. "W-why?" she sobbed.

Lucinda pushed the door open, it swung inwards on old creaking hinges, "Your brother has a special purpose here, Ellie."

"A great destiny," the blonde woman said with marked enthusiasm as they led her through the door. "One that you must help him to fulfil."

The room was rectangular, yet it sank a good ten feet from the point where they stood, making a circular auditorium within the rectangle. Large black tapestries hung from the stone-lined walls, each one at least fifteen feet from top to bottom and upon them were symbols and signs the likes of which Ellie had never seen. One symbol printed inside a large circle of golden guild was an inverted triangle, the tip pointed towards the earth whilst an infinity loop ran through its centre. On another in deep red was an inverted pentagram, again inside a large circle. The centre of the pentagram, however, was not decorated with the image of Beelzebub in goat form as was a common feature for the inverted pentagram, it was empty. Instead at each of its points were strange hieroglyphical symbols. The tapestries were many, hung side by side with only a foot of stone visible between each one, and in the gap between each, a large oil lamp was fixed into the stone, a flame burning brightly inside. The tapestries and oil lamps lined the entire room and above her, Ellie saw the roof was held in place by thick beams that reached toward its apex. The design of the roof and the layout of the beams was almost a carbon copy to that of The Old Chapel, and Ellie began to wonder if somehow this wasn't the same building, just in another time and place.

From the centre of the roof hung a massive black painted iron candle chandelier, not the reproduction electric kind, this was authentic and looked hundreds of years old and Ellie knew for sure that she'd seen this roof before, just as she'd seen what was in the centre of the room; two stone altars, each large enough to hold a human body. In her dream she'd lain on one as she'd somehow jumped through time, living the last moments of each sacrificial girl, always being dragged away to the next before the dagger bit flesh.

Surrounding the twin altars were the rows of curved benches, each row elevated slightly higher than the last, creating the auditorium, they reached up around ten feet to where they now stood. In front of her, stone steps cut through the benches and down to the altars, another set of identical steps lay dead opposite on the other side of the room, and a third to her left and a fourth to the right. They cut the circular seating into four equal wedges.

"I've s-seen this p-place," she stammered. "B-but I th-thought it b-burned. I thought,"

"That's right," Lucinda said cutting her off. "Seth said you had the sight, that you knew." She looked at Ellie with interest before pushing her into a high-backed seat. Ellie felt her arms being tied to the sides of the chair, she wanted to fight it, but she was too tired, the lack of food and water had left her with little energy. "The Chapel was never truly destroyed, Ellie, as you can see it is still very much here. Just as it has been since Minister Device founded it all those years ago."

Ellie felt her head being strapped to the back of the chair; the material used to bind her felt velvety yet the ferocity with which Lucinda tied her forced her skull painfully against the timber frame back of the chair. "You know," Lucinda said, dropping down to meet Ellie's eyes with her own cold green ones. She brushed Ellie's dirty, greasy hair off her face as she spoke "It's a shame, you would have matured into quite the delectable creature. if things had been different then you'd have made a wonderful addition to our community, our coven."

"I'd never, never be like you," she said, mustering defiance into her voice.

"Shhh," Lucinda cooed. She smiled softly and brushed her thumb over Ellie's dirt-smeared cheek. "You don't choose the darkness, Ellie. The darkness chooses you. Your brother has been chosen, chosen so that the Minister might once again dwell in this world, dwell in living flesh, as he did for so many years. He will still be Henry, only he won't be Henry. Your death will enable that transition, Ellie. So, you see as much as we'd like to keep you, alas - destiny has other plans. Through your death, he will live."

"He will become," the blonde woman said enthusiastically. "Through your sacrifice, he will become and once more our father will lead us."

Ellie's head span, all she could think to do was plead with them, plead with them to let her go, plead with them to just end it all for her quickly and painlessly if that's what they meant to do. The girls in her dream had birthed children to these monsters, which meant they must have been incarcerated here for months and months at a time. She'd spent just less than six days confined to her cell and already she felt as if her mind would crack. Before she could speak there was a commotion from the passage outside the door through which she'd just come. She was unable to turn her head, but soon the door was pushed open and a small crowd surged past her. At the front, his legs bound at the ankles, so he could do no more than waddle, and his hands tied behind his back, was a tall and well-built man in his twenties with jet black messy hair. His face was ashen, and cloth had been tied in a gag through his mouth. He saw Ellie tied to the chair and his eyes widened in recognition, he tried to mouth something, but it did nothing other than cause blood filled saliva to run from the corners of his mouth and drip in long stringy stands down to his black button-up shirt. Behind him a group of ten or more people shoved him forward, shoved until he reached the edge of the stone steps where, with a final push, he lost his footing and fell. His body tumbled all the way to the bottom like a ragdoll, where he came to rest by the base of the nearest altar. Ellie thought he was dead, but as the first of the group reached him, he began to stir, began to sit himself up. Ellie saw his face now wore a fresh cut, just above his right eye and deep red blood flowed freely down the side of pallid cheek, the crimson liquid all the more brilliant in colour against his ashen skin. Ellie knew the guy, but in her confusion, she couldn't place just where from. Had he been at the barbeque, too? She didn't think so, but his face was definitely familiar. Just as she couldn't fully recall the name of the woman with blonde hair, it was lost to her for now, just out of reach, yet her mind continued to try and grab for it.

The group who'd bundled him into the room and cast him down the stairs all wore identical robes to that of Lucinda and the blonde woman, only their faces were covered with white featureless masks of porcelain. Three of the masked figures manhandled him onto the altar nearest to where she sat, he kicked his bound legs out in protest and muffled groans of pain and anger came from behind the fabric of his gagged mouth. Once in place, the same three held him down onto the stone while two others worked deftly at binding his body, legs, and head in place, so he was fixed looking at the beams of the roof, just as Ellie had been when she'd been a passenger to all those girls. Once he was bound in place his shirt was torn open exposing his bare chest, and even from her elevated position, Ellie heard the small plastic buttons as they tinkled to the floor. She wanted to look away, but the binding on her head meant she was looking directly at the nightmarish scene. Unable to do anything else to shut it out, she closed her eyes.

"Open your eyes, Ellie," Lucinda said. "Open your eyes or I'll have them dig one out with a spoon and feed it to you. You look pretty hungry, maybe you'd like that." The calmness in which Lucinda spoke chilled her and Ellie had no doubt that Lucinda Horner meant every word of it.

"P-please," Ellie sobbed. "I don't w-want to s-see this, make it s-stop."

"He's been meddling Ellie," Lucinda said in a low voice as if it were a secret. "Sticking his nose in where it is not wanted. His spirit is not pure like yours so it's of no use in main ceremony, but the darkness will still devour his soul nonetheless, and he needs to learn a lesson, Ellie. One he will never forget. And trust me he won't forget this. You see, Ellie when you are killed in any ceremony to the Lord of Darkness your sole goes to his realm, just as yours will. The human soul never really dies, so it becomes trapped there where the demons feast on you forever."

"You-you're crazy," Ellie sobbed, but Lucinda didn't give her the pleasure of a reply, she was now stood upright, still and focused on the horror coming from the centre of the auditorium.

Other robed and masked figures were filing into The Chapel now, they moved around the lowest level of the auditorium where they stood as still as statues, their masked heads bowed toward the man on the altar. *They're going to kill him,* Ellie thought to herself. *Oh Jesus, they're going to kill him and they're going to make me watch.*

And, *You need to watch, Ellie because the next person on there is you, the next life to be taken on that stone will be yours!*

Only one robed figure was now left by the altar, the others had joined the faceless congregation and now all of them stood, their blank faces of porcelain bowed.

"Lord of night, Lord of Darkness," the faceless figure began. The voice was that of a female. "On this, the eve of the Grand Climax we give you this man's soul in sacrifice so that you may feast upon it." She reached under the altar, on the side that Ellie could not see, and as her hand reappeared Ellie recognised with horror what she now clasped. The golden dagger.

"Eo die festum," came a chanting reply from the group of twenty or so and although they spoke, they remained statue still.

"Lord of the Abyss we offer you this man's soul so that the shadows may devour it." On the opposite side of the room, Ellie saw what at first looked to be no more than the shadow of a man's cloak, but it formed quickly and purposefully, and soon she knew what it was. The thing that had been in Henry's room that first night, the thing that had stalked her in the field the next morning, the thing that had visited with her in the cell. The others didn't seem to notice it, or if they knew of its presence, they ignored it. Despite the fact that it had no face, Ellie knew it was looking right at her and grinning.

"Devorabunt," the group chanted as the figure conducting these unholy last rites removed her mask. The woman was older than Lucinda, maybe in her late sixties. She had jet black hair that was cut to a bob not too dissimilar to that of her own and Ellie recognised her as one of the villagers that she'd met at the BBQ. She'd even spent some time kicking a cheap plastic ball around Lucinda's garden with Henry, whilst he ran and laughed with delight, and the memory of it made her feel sick.

. . .

THE DAGGER WAS high above the man's bare torso now, clenched tightly in a two-hand grip and beneath it, his body writhed against the restraints in anticipation of the blade. The dark man on the opposite side of the room watched on from his faceless darkness. The robed figures still stood statue still, waiting, anticipating. And above her, in the murk of the roof, the shadows stirred.

Beneath the fabric of the gag the man tried to speak, maybe to beg or plead for his life, but what he was trying to say was lost. Elie wanted to close her eyes again. She wanted to shut the horror out. Wanted it to end, but both Lucinda and the blonde woman were stood guard by her, so she watched, feeling nauseated and helpless as the sacrificial dagger sank into his stomach, sank and sank, until it reached the hilt, all seven inches of the glinting, golden blade eaten by his flesh. Ellie heard him scream with pain and she saw his large muscular body tense. It went rigid before it tried to double over, but the restraints held fast and prevented the natural movement. The black-haired women, the master and architect of this nightmare, kept both hands on the dagger, she paused for a second, waiting until the poor man's thrashing had subsided a little, then proceeded to cut him from stomach to sternum.

"We send his soul to the Abyss, so that you may feast on it for eternity," the black-haired woman cried in glee. She removed the knife from his chest and held it aloft in blood-soaked hands, and as she did Ellie saw the skin on her face mould, as if melting before her eyes. The skin rippled and twisted before her face came back.

"Nam aeturnum," chanted the group as his body convulsed and blood flowed down over the stone. The muscular spasms caused a section of his intestine to spill from his body, it slid from the slit in his stomach and fell to the floor like some oversized piece of limp spaghetti, but it wasn't over yet. As he lay dying, the shadows began to drop from their hiding places among the beams and like birds of prey, they swooped down sinking their ethereal forms hungrily into his fatally wounded body. As each one penetrated him, a fresh screaming cry of pain erupted from his now bloodied lips. It went on like that for what felt like an age but was likely no more than a minute. Gradually the spasms began to ebb, the way an epileptic might stop convulsing at the end of a grand mal. Eventually they stopped altogether, as did his screams.

In the final moment of death, his head, the restraint holding it now loosened from how viscously he'd fought against it, gave way, and lulled to one side. His lifeless eyes locked onto Ellie's. At that moment, she knew where she'd seen him before and why he'd looked so familiar.

CHAPTER 42

MIKE FELT HIS WAY ALONG THE CENTRAL CORRIDOR,
leaning his body lightly against the wood panelled wall
for direction. Tara gripped his left arm like a vice and
after the brightness of the light and the crescendo of
screams the darkness and the silence that now followed
felt both perpetual and disorientating. The only sounds
that now befell his ears were his own laboured breathing, the sound of their feet as they shuffled along the
thickly piled carpet and the occasion sob from Tara.

"He's g-gone, Mike," she sobbed in a voice that was
no louder than a whisper. "He had hold of m-me, then
he d-didn't and now h-he's gone."

The central corridor came to an end and Mike knew
that now they were in the kitchen. No moonlight came
from the windows or the half-glazed panel of the back
door and he had to rely on memory and touch to navigate his way along the granite worktops to the gas hob.
He sighed in relief as his fingers found the dials and
Mike wasted no time in turning one and depressing it.
The hiss of gas emanated from the burner and filled the
room. With his other hand, Mike found and clicked the
lighter to life. It was one of those long ones with a
clicker button on the end and shaped like a match, designed for the sole purpose of getting the stove on
when the electricity went. As the flame found the gas

the burner fired, finally providing some light to see by. He repeated the process with the other three hobs and soon the kitchen was bathed in an ethereal glow of blue gaslight. He turned and took Tara in his arms, pulling her close enough so that he could feel her trembling. She buried her head into his shoulder and he enjoyed the faint smell of shampoo on her hair, it was something real in this seemingly impossible situation.

"I'll get the lights back on and then we will look for him," he reassured her. "The fuse box is in the utility cupboard by the back door."

"And if it's not the fuse box, what then?" she asked.

Reluctantly he released her from his arms, "One step at a time," he said, reaching the cupboard and opening the door. The fuse box was at head height, a white rectangle with a smoked plastic cover. He flipped it up and ran his eyes along the bank of switches, feeling relieved to see that the main breaker, the one that killed power to the lights and the sockets, was in the down position. "See?" he said. "The fuse tripped." And then a new and terrible thought crossed his mind, *what if when he turned it back on the lights stayed off?* The power had surged massively and there was a chance it had fried the entire breaker. If that had happened, they'd be stuck with the light from the cooker hob until dawn, and that was still hours away. He scrubbed the thought and promptly flicked the breaker switch up. There was a heavy and deeply satisfying **CLICK** and instantly the lights in the central corridor and beyond in the entrance lobby sprung to life. In the kitchen, the brushed aluminium microwave beeped and 00:00 began to flash slowly on its green display. Mike closed the cupboard door and immediately turned the lights on in the kitchen, too.

"We need to find him," Tara prompted, already pulling Mike by the arm and back in the direction of the central corridor. Mike went with her and they retraced their steps back toward the lobby. Halfway down the passageway they found the GoPro, it was on the floor and still attached firmly to the selfie stick. Mike bent and picked it up, the screen was dead, so he tried to turn it on. The screen briefly flashed on, gave Mike a battery symbol with a red line through then beeped twice and turned off.

"The battery is flat," he said with confusion. "Odd, it had only been recording for ten minutes at most." He tucked the camera into the pocket of his cargo pants and carried on to the lobby. The front door was still locked, the key still on the slate hanger below the printed and laminated note reminding guests to leave the key there at all times when inside. From the lobby, they climbed the righthand staircase to the lounge. On the trestle table, the two twenty-inch screens displayed a NO SIGNAL message in blue. "When the power went it knocked everything out," Mike said. "The CCTV base units need to be manually rebooted." Mike flicked the two units to life, the equipment whirred quietly to itself and one by one the cameras came back. Mike scanned through them as Scotty had shown, all the rooms were empty. Mike hit the record option on both systems. Things had already gone south in a way that was far beyond reasonable and CCTV footage might prove vital in trying to explain it later. Satisfied the camera system was working he crouched down and picked up the battery-operated Sonic Ear Amplifier, he worked the dial with his thumb. "Battery is flat on this as well," he commented before placing it back down. The laptop had been plugged into the mains, but the screen was blank. Mike fired it to life and saw that its internal battery too had died.

"Mike," Tara prompted, she was pacing behind him anxiously. "Please, we still have half the building to search."

"I'm trying to figure this thing out," Mike said, and he reached his own trembling hand out and took hers. "He can't just have blinked out of existence." *But that was exactly how it had happened,* Mike thought, and, *That's how those Harrison kids went, here one minute, then pooof, gone the next.* "What do you remember?"

"The screaming," Tara said. "I'll never forget that. I think in ten years' time I'll still be hearing that when I close my eyes to sleep at night. Then the lights got bright. I had a hold of your arm and Scotty had a hand on my shoulder. I looked around at him, then looked back to you. It was so bright by then, and then I felt," she paused as if searching for the right term.

"Like a pressure drop?" Mike asked.

"Yes, like when your ears go. The lights went out and I felt a bit, I don't know – sick. No, not sick not that bad, more a little nauseous. It all happened so fast; this was all over no more than two seconds. When the lights went out, I felt his hand move off me and then he was gone. Mike, he was just not there."

"Well I guess now we have to accept that the Harrison kids likely vanished in a similar way, and if we can find them - "

"We find Scotty," Tara said hopefully, for a second there was hope in her eyes, but then it washed away. "But we've been around this fucking place three or four times this evening and - "

"We will figure it out," Mike said, but he could hear the lack of conviction in his own voice.

From the lounge they went room to room, Tara calling Scotty's name as if they were searching some expansive area and not the inside of a building. In the bedroom that had been Henry Harrison's, the Jack was still out of his box, his painted red smile grinned back at them knowingly from the centre of the room. Mike shivered looking at it and after a sweep of the room and the ensuite he shut the door, glad to be away from it.

Within five minutes they were back in the kitchen, "He can't have just vanished," Tara said as if trying to convince herself of the impossible situation, her voice was wavering, and Mike knew they both needed to get out of the building, if only for a few minutes. "What do we do now?"

Mike took the key from the hanger by the back door, "I don't know," he said feeling defeated. "But I think I'd like to get out of here and get some air for a few minutes while I try to figure it out, you look like you need some air, too." He unlocked the door and they both stepped out onto the rear patio area. Mike turned his face toward the sky and inhaled the mild air deeply, the air caught in his chest as he noticed something that didn't compute. "Look at the sky," he prompted. The sky was still black, yet in the east, the first tendrils of orange dawn light were threading their way like veins of amber through the darkness, and at this time of year it would be fully light before long.

"I don't understand," Tara said sounding confused.

"How much time has passed since you woke up?"

"Ten, fifteen minutes. Twenty at the most," she replied.

"It was half two when I heard the music box, I looked at my watch, I remember it clearly. I remember it all clearly," he said. Mike backed into the light coming from the kitchen window and checked the hands of his Timex. "It's four in the morning, Tara. What the fuck happened in the hour and a half we seem to have missed?"

CHAPTER 43

MIKE YAWNED, TOOK A SWIG OF THE SEMI-COLD instant coffee and grimaced at how bad it tasted. He needed the caffeine, though. The footage on the screen from the lower lobby, the one from the camera pointing down the central passage showed them heading into it, toward the kitchen. As Tara had remembered, Scotty had been behind her, his hand on her shoulder. The brightness of the lights got to the point that it whited out the camera and the screen became bleached in white triggering a contrast warning in the recording. As it whited out the recording suddenly stopped, the point where the breaker had tripped. Mike ran it back and played it through again at half speed and dropped the brightness to its lowest setting, hoping to find something, anything at all in the last few seconds before the power went, but there was nothing. He'd also checked the Go-pro which Scotty had been carrying, yet that had failed to yield any results. It appeared from the footage he had managed to download from the SD card that the battery had suddenly and inexplicably died at the point where the lights had reached their brightest.

It was almost nine AM now and he'd been trawling through every camera going over and back over those last few minutes before the darkness came and stole

Scotty and an hour and a half's worth of time from them.

He drained the last of the foul coffee and set the mug on the trestle table. Behind him on the sofa Tara slept, her ash blonde hair had fallen over her face. Mike left the screens and went to her and brushed it back off her face, enjoying the warmth of her skin on his fingertips. She murmured something and stirred so he left her, not wanting to wake her yet. She'd laid down just after they'd come in from the garden, she'd protested that there was no way she could rest, not when Scotty was missing. Yet within ten minutes she'd been snoring lightly and as yet hadn't woken, but that was okay because while she was asleep, she wouldn't be blaming herself. There was no way any blame could be apportioned for what had happened, but the mind is a funny thing and has a way of torturing you. Mike knew that only too well. And he knew that she'd be going over those last few moments in her mind, as he had on the screen, breaking them down and looking for something she could have done differently to bring about a different outcome.

Mike was about to check the audio through again when there was a purposeful knock at the front door that made him jump. He didn't rush to the lobby to answer it; instead, he crossed to the balcony over the lobby and placed his hands on the balustrade and looked down at the door, almost as if he could see through it to who was on the other side. The knocking came again, louder a bit more of a thump, and Tara who'd been woken by it rushed past Mike and began down the stairs.

"It might be him," she said hopefully.

Mike went after her and caught her arm as she reached for the keys, "And it might not be," he said warily. Mike turned to the door. "Who's there?" he called.

"Mike," came a voice he knew. "It's Mark Samuels, we need a chat." Mike removed the deadbolts and unlocked the door. Samuels was dressed for work in smart grey trousers, shiny flat-soled shoes, and a white short sleeve shirt. There was no tie, not yet, and his top two buttons were undone. He looked pissed and as soon as the door was fully open, he thrust a copy of the Daily Mail into Mike's hand. "Front page!" he said sternly. "Front fucking page, Mike. How the fuck did that happen? You tell me."

Mike didn't need to look at the front page, nor did he need to read the story, he knew what would be on there. He looked anyway and read the headline to himself silently.

SPOOK HUNTERS AID POLICE IN INVESTIGATION FOR MISSING BROTHER AND SISTER

It was printed in bold black headline text across the top of the page. Below it was an image of himself with Tara and Scotty to his side, taken by that cocky reporter the day before.

"Look, Mark," Mike began, but he cut him off.

"Read it!" he prompted.

Yesterday afternoon the Daily Mail learned that Mike Cross, Tara Gibb, and Scott Hampton became the new tenants of The Old Chapel in Trellen, Cornwall, where last Saturday morning parents of Ellie Harrison (18) and Henry Harrison (5) found them missing from the room they'd been sharing. The missing person enquiry became a murder hunt when one of Henry Harrison's shoes was found by a dog walker on the beach at Charlestown. A shoe belonging to Ellie Harrison was recovered by police divers from the harbour Wednesday lunchtime. Both parents were questioned by police but later released without charge. In the latest twist of this strange case, our reporter photographed the team of SwitchBack TV's Unexplained UK unloading flight cases at the building on

Wednesday evening, only hours after the police stood it down from being a crime scene. Mike Cross, a former Detective Sergeant with Sussex Police, became well known for his work as a private and paranormal investigator when he exposed a fake haunting in Sleaford, Lincolnshire back in 2016. Off the back of that case Cross became the lead investigator for the TV show, aided by his researcher, Tara Gibb and tech specialist Scott Hampton. None of the team offered comment on what they were doing at the scene of the summer's biggest crime story but with the amount of equipment being unloaded, it doesn't look like they're on their summer holidays. Story continues

page 8 –

MIKE DIDN'T BOTHER to head to page 8, he lowered the paper and looked first to Tara who'd been reading over his shoulder.

"I said I didn't want this becoming a circus and now look at it, Mike. It's a fucking mess."

Mike was tired, more than a little stressed out and his nerves were frayed like old rope. It was all he could do to stop himself either just closing the door on Samuels and hoping it would all just go away, or punching him on the nose. He held back both temptations, sighed and said, "That prick of a reporter was waiting out here yesterday, probably had been all day, hoping to see who turned up. And guess what, it paid off, he got lucky. None of us asked for this."

"I told him I was going to ram that camera so far up his ass he could taste it," Tara said dryly. "So don't blame Mike for this. The only thing to blame is the freedom of the press in this county to make life hell for whomever they choose."

Samuels stood there for a few moments but the pissed off look refused to budge. "You both look like shit," he finally said. "The spooks been keeping you up all night?"

"I don't have time for this Mark," Mike said firmly. "Did you come round here for anything else, or just to have a go at us for something we had no way of avoiding?"

"If you insist on being here," he replied curtly. "Try and stay out of trouble." Mike handed him back the paper. "Keep it," he said, turning and heading for his Vauxhall. Before Mike could offer any further comment, he was in the car and had it started. Samuels gunned the engine and the wheels spat shingle before he disappeared, firing up a rooster tail of dust behind him.

"Were you that much of an a-hole when you were a copper?" Tara asked. "Or is it just him?"

Mike closed the door and leant his back against the sun-warmed timber. "He's under a tonne of pressure, he's a good guy really."

Tara took the paper from him and gazed at the photo, taken not twenty-four hours ago when they'd all been together. He could see the pain in her eyes and knew they were focused on the part of the picture that showed Scotty stood by one of his flight cases. They'd all become close friends over the last few years, and he knew she thought of Scotty as the little brother she'd never had. "How are we going to find him, Mike?" she asked, her eyes not moving from the front page. "How are we going to find any of them when this place can just swallow you up like some fucking monster?"

Mike smiled at her weakly. "I don't know," he said. "I just don't know."

CHAPTER 44

JASON PAXMAN CLUTCHED THE COPY OF THE DAILY Mail in both hands, his fingers gradually tightening in anger until the pages began to crease.

"This is not a library," the voice of the shop assistant said in a heavy Indian accent. "If you want to read it, you buy it."

Jason ignored him. The image of the guy who'd broken his nose was staring back at him from the front page. Beneath the white strapping holding it back in place, the sight of him made his busted nose throb. Just to the side of him was Tara, the fucking bitch, and another guy who over the last few days he'd seen on the show she'd been involved with. It had aired whilst he'd been locked up in The Verne, but catchup TV had allowed him to watch the entire run of shows in one long marathon. It was utter shite but he'd watched it nonetheless, enjoying the anger that brewed within at seeing her actually making something of her worthless life while his was being wrecked. He'd known she was into that load of hokum, but he'd never envisaged she'd get to where she had. Had she not ratted him out after he'd been good enough to leave her a phone, so she could call an ambulance after dishing her a beating she well deserved for fucking up a six-hundred-pound rug, things would be different. He'd have put a stop to that team of idiots she'd started hanging around with. He'd dealt her a few beatings about it back when all the nonsense had started but he'd not had the time to knock it out of her properly.

"You want the paper or not?" the assistant said.

"Fucking idiot," Jason mumbled under his breath, but loud enough for the assistant to hear. Of course, he wanted the fucking paper. He'd been round to Tara's twice since he'd fallen foul to Mike Cross, hoping to catch the little bitch on her own and deal her his own special Jason Paxman brand of justice, but the bitch had seemingly been gone for the last few days. Now he knew just where she was. Some piss-pot village in Cornwall doing fuck knows what at the place those kids had gone missing from. Jason was vaguely aware of the news story; it had been on the TV enough over the last five days and even when pissed it was hard to ignore. His alcohol-fuelled mind couldn't quite grasp why Tara was there though, and judging by the report in the paper, neither did the reporter who'd snapped the shot.

Jason bent and picked up the twelve pack of Stella that he'd actually come in for, placed the paper on top and set both on the counter. "I'll take a bottle of Jack, too," he said. "Not the small one, the litre one."

The assistant ran the three items through, and Jason could see how he looked at him with disgust. It was a little after eleven in the morning and it was obvious from his appearance that this little party pack of booze was for one, and due to be consumed not long after getting home. It didn't matter, it was always noon and drinking time somewhere in the word. His old man had been partial to getting on the sauce and that's what he'd always said, *'Grab me a beer, son, it's after twelve somewhere!'* And often after he'd had enough he'd find some reason for Jason to feel the bony side of his hand, or if he was really sauced, his fist.

"Thirty-seven fifty," the clerk said with a noticeable hint of disdain in his voice bringing him back from the memory. Jason handed him two crumpled up twenties that had been stuffed into the pocket of his jeans. He snatched the change from the clerk's hand without talking and headed out to his Audi, where he tossed the purchases onto the passenger seat.

He'd been drinking a lot since getting out, drinking every day if he was honest with himself, it should have mattered to him, but it didn't. The sauce had been pretty widely available inside, as well as a few other tastier drugs that really blocked out the monotony of prison life. He didn't care for the harder shit that much, but what had been mild alcoholism before his incarceration, was now a much more deeply rooted addiction. One he relied upon to numb the pain of all he'd lost and fuel the anger that burned inside him.

That bitch had cost him close to three years of his freedom, and his business, which thanks to his absence had gone to shit. All he had now was his car, the flat which thankfully he'd managed to pay off in full by the time he was thirty-four, and twenty grand in savings. Ten grand of that he'd taken out of the bank and put in a safe back at his flat in Blandford. It was enough for him to live on for a few months, enough to keep him inebriated and the world shut out. When it was gone, he still had another ten left, then there was the car, that had to be worth another fifteen still. Then when the time came there was the flat. Yeah, he was good for a while, the slope to oblivion was long and the fact that at some point he'd likely piss the lot up the wall didn't matter a jot to him.

He drove the short distance from the twenty-four-hour garage and convenience store back to his flat just outside of the town centre. All the way he kept eyeing the picture on the front of the paper that lay on the passenger seat and as he glanced at it his eyes kept falling on the building behind Tara and that prick, Cross. Jason knew he shouldn't be driving, that he was still way over the limit from yesterday and as he pulled to a stop outside of his flat his hand shook setting the parking brake. He'd woken up on the sofa at a little after ten in a dry house and his body was aching badly for more sweet liquid poison.

He fumbled the key into the lock of the communal door then managed the stairs to the second floor. One more tricky keyhole later and he was in. The place stank. He'd not really noticed it on waking but having come in from the outside it hit his nose and for the briefest of moments, he felt disgusted at himself. Stale beer, sweat, and dishes left piled up on the drainer, many still containing the remnants of takeaways. Some of which had been there long enough to start growing a thin layer of mould on that a few small flies now buzzed and circled over. He'd run out of crockery a few days ago and the more recent meals lay in messy remains in their styrofoam containers.

In his previous life, before that fucking bitch had taken it away, just walking into such a shithole would have made his skin crawl. Now it didn't matter to him, nothing did, except maybe for the booze, that mattered because it made everything else not matter. Well, there was one thing that sure as shit did matter and that was dealing a little payback for what she'd done to him, but apart from that he didn't really give a flying fuck about anything.

In the kitchen he dumped the goods on the breakfast bar, reached into the thin, blue plastic bag and took the bottle of Jack out, cracking the top off and taking a deep pull, all in one needy movement. The hot liquid felt like pure relief as it burned his throat and after two or three deep swallows, he set it down on the worktop with a bang and let out a sigh of relief. Craving quenched, for now, he took out the paper and stared at the photo again. That cock sucker, Cross had to have been fucking her, why else would he have been at her flat in the middle of the night? Or if he wasn't fucking her, he was trying to. No guy would stick up for a worthless little slut like her unless he was tapping her, or trying to, that was just the way of the world. From Mike, Tara and the other guy with them, who he seemed to recall from watching the show was called Scotty, his eyes fell on the building again. The Old Chapel it was called according to the paper, and the more he looked at it the more he couldn't look away.

Aside from the booze, getting even with Tara had been the only thing on his mind since getting out, and now by some twist of fate he had the chance to not only settle that little score but at the same time he could dish a little payback to the Cross guy, too. And as he looked at the photo a voice inside of him agreed. It whispered dark things to him that both terrified and excited him, and as it whispered like a vile worm inside of his head, Jason listened. By the time he finally managed to take his eyes away from the paper he knew what he had to do. If he got caught for it there would be no short stay in prison, no this would be a long stretch. It should have mattered to him, but it didn't, and the voices had agreed, nothing mattered now apart from the sweet feeling of revenge.

Jason picked up the bottle of Jack, took another long drink from it and carried it, and the paper through to the lounge where he set both on the coffee table that was still littered with the remnants of last night's binge, and the day before, and the day before that. He rooted around the piles of crap in a frustration that only fuelled his anger until he found his phone.

Tommy Wojcik had been his cellmate for the first six months in The Verne. Tommy was a badass fucker from Poland who'd been on the back end of a five stretch for an armed robbery in Bournemouth. He'd fallen foul of some ballsy little fuck of a cash in transit driver who instead of handing over the money had swung the metal armoured case at his head and got lucky, knocking him clean out. The two other goons with him hadn't had the chance to sort the prick out as some other do-gooder had called the police as soon as shit had started to go down. The sound of approaching sirens had likely saved the driver's life. Tommy was a good guy, not the kind he'd have mixed with in his old life, but then prison was apt to change a man, and often not for the better. Tommy never ratted out the other two in his gang and had taken the time on the chin; in much the same way he'd taken that cash in transit box on the chin. Tommy had proven that there was honour among thieves after all. By the time Tommy got out they'd become close friends. More than once Jason, or the Pacman, as Tommy called him, had needed to have his back when it got nasty, as it often did inside. Tommy had not been coy about his connections with the criminal underworld outside and had been keen to let Jason know that if he ever needed anything when he finally got out, then just to call and he'd sort it. For a price of course, nothing was free in this life.

Jason drank from the bottle of Jack as he scanned the phone. He found Tommy's number and hit call, the warm feeling of the booze settling into his belly, mixed with the notion of how that bitch's face would look when he showed up. As the phone rang his eyes fell on the picture again and the building.

"Pacman," came Tommy's heavily accented voice after only three rings. "Is good to hear from you, my friend. I heard you were out and was hoping you'd call, how are you?"

"Things have been better," Jason said, and wasn't that the fucking God's honest. He set the bottle on the table and ran a hand through his hair, it felt greasy and in need of a wash.

"The first time you go inside, it take a while to re-adjust. Soon it become easy."

"I need a favour, Tommy," Jason said, cutting straight to the chase. He liked Tommy, but he wasn't in the mood to shoot the shit with him over this and that.

"A favour I can do - well sell maybe more the word, no?"

Jason explained to him what he wanted and when he'd finished there was a brief silence before Tommy said, "No problem. Why you ask me for this? Is no problem of course for a man of my means. Are you missing it that much that you keen to get back to your cell?"

"Just some shit I need to take care of," Jason replied, his eyes fixed on The Old Chapel. Despite the fact it was no more than a printed picture he could feel the darkness inside that place, it called to the darkness inside him.

"I understand," Tommy replied. "Some things are best not discussed, no? I can get your merchandise by Monday; the price is two thousand pounds."

"Monday is no good to me, Tommy. I need it today, by this afternoon at the latest."

"You are hard man to please, Pacman," Tommy said. "I can arrange something, but it will cost more."

"No problem, you name the price."

"That is a very dangerous thing to say to a criminal my friend," said Tommy with a rattling laugh. "But you had my back more than once, so I will not, hmm - how do you English say it, take the piss."

"Thanks."

"I can have for you by five, and the price will be extra five hundred. Do we have deal?"

"We have a deal," Jason answered seriously.

"You must come to me, I text you address in a minute."

"No problem, see you at five bud."

"I shall look forward to it," Tommy said happily, then the call was disconnected.

Jason had become quite apt at functioning whilst drunk, but he knew that he had to kerb it as much as he could if he were to stand any chance of seeing through what needed to be done, so he drank sparingly, just keeping himself topped up enough to stop the shakes.

At three he showered, shaved and put on fresh clothes. The redness of his eyes was one thing he couldn't fix, and they belied his freshened-up appearance. Once dressed he went to the safe that was fixed into the wall at the back of his built-in wardrobe, he punched the code, 020716 and looked in at the money stacked there. A few months ago, right after he'd gotten out it had been ten grand square, now it was probably closer to six. He didn't try to work out how long it would last, it didn't matter. He took out two pre-counted stacks of twenties, then took another and split it in half. He tucked the two-five into an old envelope and took another two hundred for the road. He likely wouldn't need that much but it didn't hurt to be prepared.

At four he left the flat, the remnants of the bottle of Jack in a hip flask that Tara had given him for Christmas a few years ago. There was a certain irony about it enabling him to stay functioning long enough to reach her and do what needed to be done, and he liked that, he liked it a lot. On the passenger seat was the paper, and when traffic permitted, his eyes wandered to The Old Chapel and he let the voices in.

The summer evening traffic was pretty shitty heading into Bournemouth, but to be fair trying to get anywhere in Dorset during the summer months sucked balls, the roads were all rammed full of fucking tourists, many of them dragging their shit-box caravans.

It was a little after five when he finally pulled up outside of Tommy's place. It was an old Victorian townhouse, typical of the kind that had once housed the wealthier families in Boscombe, a town that made up part of the general Bournemouth area. Times had changed somewhat, and the area had become run down, those old, once grand Victorian houses now converted into bedsits and flats.

Tommy's place was a top floor loft converted apartment just off the main Boscombe High Street. The communal area reeked of damp and cannabis smoke and the red floral carpet looked like it had been laid when the place was new. On the stairs, the pile had worn down until the aged wooden boards below showed through. Jason had thought his place was bad, but it was like a palace still compared to this stinking shithole.

"Pacman," Tommy said with joy as he opened the door letting the smell of cigarette smoke join the general stench of the communal landing. Jason could hear the monotone beat of some euro dance baseline and behind it the chatter of voices. Tommy was dressed in three-quarter length white shorts, no top and his slightly paunchy belly hung over the waistband. His body was covered in various tattoos of varying quality. They ran down both his arms and were jotted about his portly frame in no particular order, seemingly fitted in here and there wherever there was enough virgin skin to ink on. "You bring money?"

"Of course I brought the money," Jason said and handed the envelope over.

"You should not carry this in the open, around here they rob you for Big Mac." Tommy laughed and took the cash, opened the envelope and thumbed through the notes. "I need to count?" he asked with a smile.

"It won't offend me if you do, but it's all there, you can trust me," Jason replied.

"I no need to count, you are a dear friend, Pacman. I know you not screw me over." He grinned again showing his slightly off-colour teeth. One of the incisors was missing, lost – according to Tommy during a bar fight in Warsaw. "You want to come in, have drink?"

A drink sounded good, but time was ticking, and Jason needed to get going. "I'd love to bud, but time is not on my side."

"Another time, maybe?" Tommy said with genuine disappointment.

"Once I'm done with this," Jason agreed and Tommy ducked into the flat, coming back a few seconds later with a zipped-up holdall. Tommy unfastened it and reached inside.

"This is sawed-off Beretta A400 Semi-Automatic Light," he said, weighing the weapon in his hand. "Is lightweight, and deadly as fuck, especially at close range. Gun hold three cartridges. Two in receiver, one in barrel. When you fire it has a gas reloading system, next shot is ready in under a second. This is a good shotgun, understand?" Jason took the shotgun; the barrel had been shortened to just past the length of the receiver. It felt good and tactile in his hand and the matte black stock gave it a purposeful appearance. "Aim at close range, once you use all three shots is not fast to reload, you understand?" Jason nodded. He had a little knowledge of such firearms, his uncle, the more successful one in the family whose business acumen Jason seemed to have been blessed with, ('cos his old man had been a useless sack of shit), had taken him shooting a few times. "Police catch you with this," Tommy continued, "even if you not use is big trouble, you know this, you are not idiot are you Pacman?"

"I know," Jason said blankly.

"And if police catch you, where you say you get?"

"Not from you. Tommy it's cool. I'm grateful."

"Then we are good, no?"

"We're good," Jason confirmed, and Tommy embraced him in a quick back-slapping hug before they parted ways.

Back in the car, Jason nipped the flask, he wanted to drain the lot but if he did his driving would suffer, and if he got pulled over pissed and packing a semi-automatic sawn-off, he'd be more fucked than a prom queen in a football team locker room.

Slowly, through the traffic, Jason headed west,

around the outskirts of Poole and toward Dorchester. Just before seven, he passed into the county of Devon. He'd never been to Trellen before, he'd never even heard of the fucking place, but he didn't need a map. So long as he kept looking at the picture the voices would guide him, and soon that bitch, Tara, and the cock sucker, Cross would be treated to a lead supper. The other guy in the picture, the one they called Scotty, would likely need to be taken out, too. He was a big bastard and Jason, although handy enough in a fight thanks to his prison time, didn't fancy his chances without the gun. Yes, he may be an innocent in this, but he'd have to die regardless. Jason now knew that there'd be no prison cell for him after this, it was a one-way ticket, and after he'd killed all three of them the voices would demand his own life. It should have scared him, it should have mattered that he lived, but it didn't. Nothing mattered, nothing at all.

CHAPTER 45

DRIED, BROWNED AND BRITTLE LEAVES BROKE UNDER
their feet like bone china as they walked through the
wood. The day had turned from a dry scorching heat to
a humid one and the air now felt thick and heavy to
breathe. Mike stopped and placed his hand on the
trunk of an ancient Oak, he let out a long-exasperated
breath and ran the back of his hand over his brow, it
came away sweat and dirt-smeared. He checked his
watch, it was a little after eight PM and the light of the
day had just started to change, the way it does when
night begins to creep across the land from its home in
the East.

The day's activity had been focused on going back
over The Old Chapel, room by room, inch by inch,
looking for something, anything that would give them a
clue as to where Scotty and the Harrison kids had gone.
It was an arduous and repetitive task, one that built
nothing but frustration as blank after blank was drawn.
Mike still found it incredulous to believe that the place
could have swallowed them up whole and that there
was no rational explanation as to how they'd gone. But
then how did he explain the missing time? And the fact
that all that was left of Scotty was the GoPro he'd been
holding. Anything could have happened to them in the
passing of that hour and a half, and when exactly it had

passed, he did not know. Mike had come to reason that it had most likely been when the screaming had stopped and the pressure had changed, but he didn't know for sure. Thinking about it and trying to work the problem made his temples throb. He knew that the time was close where he'd have to consider the fantastic, he'd have to consider that the things you saw on the movie screen and read between the covers of a book were real and that somehow the impossible was possible. But not yet. He still felt as if they were missing something, the final piece of the puzzle that would make it all fall into place.

"These woods are too big for two of us to search," Tara sighed. She joined him by the oak and cocked her hip to her right side, taking the weight off her left leg.

Mike looked at her, her blonde hair had darkened with the perspiration on her brow and her eyes still held the fear that had set in when Scotty had gone, only they were redder now, redder from the crying that she'd done. "I think it's just a short way up this path," Mike replied, "then we should come out back at the rear garden of The Old Chapel." Neither of them were that keen to get back, but the night was setting in, the light within the wood was murkier than out, and there was no way he'd want to be caught out here when it fell completely.

They'd been in the woods for the last few hours and had since established for the third time that The Old Chapel was nothing but a blank canvas of clues. They'd entered on the easterly side of the garden and followed a small path that wound its way through the trees until it reached the courtyard at the Horners' cottage. Once there they'd stayed hidden, using the cover of the trees but after half an hour of nothing both had grown impatient and felt the need to get moving, get looking, even if deep down they both knew it was a futile search. It just felt good to be doing something.

From the Horners' they'd headed north, sometimes

losing the path and having to pick their way through the woodland until they found another. The village of Culden lay in that direction, and Mike had been keen to see if someone lost in the woods could reach it on foot. The going was hard, the further north they pushed, the thicker the woodland grew, thorn bushes making the way hard to pass. In the end, they'd come to a stream, the water was low due to the extended heatwave but near to its banks, the ground had become soft and apt to take your foot, and likely your shoe if you tested it too much. They'd followed the small babbling stream, the brackish waters racing and bubbling over stones and small rocks, back in a westerly direction until they felt they must be level with the grounds of The Old Chapel, and then dropped back south leaving it behind.

"And then what, Mike?" she asked. "When we get back, then what?"

He took her hand in his, "You think we should call someone, don't you?" he replied.

Tara screwed her face up in confusion and he could see the conflict inside her. "He's been gone for over seventeen hours, Mike. I mean I don't really like that Samuels guy, but if you speak to him, tell him what happened and show him the footage then he will *have* to believe, won't he? I just think this whole thing has gotten too big for us, that's all."

Mike knew she was right, not only right but they had a duty to report him as missing. But then the circumstances around how he'd gone were far from normal, "You're right," he agreed. "But not yet. The Grand Climax is tomorrow, Friday the 27th, that gives us tonight to figure this thing out and if by eight tomorrow morning we don't find him or the Harrison kids I'll call Mark Samuels."

"It's not done with us yet, is it?" Tara said, and her words made Mike shiver.

"No, I don't think it is," he agreed. "When we get

back if you want to take my Jeep and drive to the nearest hotel, I understand. I'm not asking you to stay."

"If we do this, we do it together," she said and forced a smile. "Let's get moving."

They walked in silence for the rest of the way back. No sound accompanied their walk, save for the sound of their own feet on the dried and fallen foliage of the forest floor. For during the hours they'd spent searching not a single rustle had come from a single bush, nor the call of a bird other than that of the crow from the trees. There were some insects of the flying kind, but they'd not encountered one bigger than a bee. Finally, and a little after eight thirty in the evening they broke clear of the dusky wood at the very bottom of the rear garden. During the last half hour of that walk, Mike had been trying to get right with himself in his own head. He knew Tara would be feeling blame for what had happened, for Scotty had a hold of her, and she felt as if she'd allowed him to become lost. However, Mike had taken the job, had brought them all down here and ultimately if there was blame to apportion then it was his to take. Had he hung up the phone on Sue Reed back there in Manchester, a day that now felt so very long ago, Scotty would still be here. If when he and Tara had visited, he'd politely refused, maybe lied a little and said that despite how intriguing it sounded they were a little busy and thanks but no thanks, then Scotty would still be here. If he'd heeded that warning that had come inexplicably through his FM transmitter after his visit with the Horners, then Scotty would still be here. They hadn't taken that road though, and no amount of going over it would help, nor would it bring him back.

Mike reached the back door, slid the key in the lock and paused, "Before we go back in, I need to tell you something," he said to Tara.

"You're scaring me," she said uneasily. "If it's possible to be more scared than I already am."

"I think I know why those people who stayed here

did those terrible things after they left. Why that woman drowned her baby in the bathtub, why that man, seemingly happily married and successful, shut himself in his garage and ran a length of hose from his exhaust and just sat there breathing it all in until he died."

Tara placed her hand on the stone of The Old Chapel, "You think it made them do it?" she asked.

"I do believe it's like a virus now," Mike said. "I know we mentioned it before, but I couldn't believe it. Now I do. It doesn't affect everyone, but some are susceptible to it, some it can speak to. And if you let it in, if you listen, it makes you do terrible things." He looked into her frightened eyes again. "It spoke to me last night. In the seconds before Scotty vanished, it spoke to me, Tara."

She swallowed, and Mike heard the click of her dry throat, "What did it say?" Her voice wavered as she spoke.

Mike shook his head forcefully and felt tears of anger and pain coming to the corners of his eyes, "I'd never – never," he said firmly.

"Mike, what did it say?" And she took hold of him now, by the upper arms.

"Strangle the bitch," Mike replied. "Strangle her, choke her until her eyes bulge and her tongue swells."

"But you didn't listen, did you?"

"It wanted me to listen, and – and, a part of me wanted to let it in, Tara." Mike felt her arms around him now and he embraced her back.

"But you didn't, Mike. You fought it; you didn't let it win."

Mike reluctantly broke the embrace and handed the keys to his Jeep to her. Tara looked at them with puzzlement. "I thought I said," she began, but Mike cut her off.

"I did, I shut it out, but what if next time I can't? What if when this fucking place comes for us tonight I can't? If I look odd, different, if you see anything in me you don't like you take those keys, get in my Jeep and drive until you're clear of this place, until you're out of danger. Do you understand?"

"Mike, you – "

"Do you understand?" he almost shouted.

Tara was crying now, tears rolled down her reddened cheeks, and he hated himself for it, "I – understand," she sobbed.

He took her in his arms again and hugged her tightly, kissing the top of her head. In the sky above, heavy, pendulous clouds had begun to roll in from the west, encroaching their blackness on the golden amber of the dying day. They covered the falling sun, that now was no more than a half ball on the horizon, and bit by bit began to seal a lid on the coming night. In those clouds furthest west lightning flashed, portending the vehemence of the storm to come.

CHAPTER 46

JASON SPED THROUGH THE DARKENED LANES OF RURAL Cornwall, he used no navigation other than an internal one, one that told him which way to turn when he approached the appropriate junction. He nipped the last of the Jack out of his hip flask and tossed it into the passenger footwell. He could have done with more; his body was operating on the least amount of booze that it could before the shakes would set in. He knew that if they came on at the key time it could be the end of his plan. He was close now, a few miles at most, and he knew that once he'd shot all three of those fucks, the building, or that sweet darkness that dwelt within it, would require his life too, and that was fine, that was okey-dokey with him.

On the seat next to him sat the zipped-up holdall that contained the three-round Beretta sawn-off semi-automatic shotgun. Within the bag were two boxes of twenty-five cartridges. With the three in the gun ready to fly it gave him fifty-three rounds in all. Likely fifty more than he'd need, but it didn't hurt to be prepared. He reached across from the steering wheel and rested his hand on the stock of the gun and stroked it affectionately through the canvas of the bag. Far in the west lightning chased through the clouds. It had been moving around him and getting stronger the further west he went. Soon the storm would cycle around and end up right overhead, but that was a few hours away yet, and before then another storm would break upon The Old Chapel. His storm. And he would bring his own lightning, lightning birthed from the barrel of the sawn-off as he pulled the trigger.

Just after ten PM, Jason passed a sign welcoming him to Trellen. The voices had grown stronger mile by mile and now their whispering filled his head completely with their beautiful poison. He didn't slow as he crossed into the village, he kept going until one of those voices rose above all the others and said, *"HERE!"* Jason jammed the brakes on and swung his Audi left onto the drive, the front-end understeering as he caught the shingle a little too fast. The tyres dug through the stones and bit, giving him back control. At the end of the drive, he could see a white Jeep and a VW T4, the kind someone had half converted into a camper. The T4 had been in the picture that had led him here, and in the dimly lit cab, Jason glanced at the paper sitting on top of the bag. This was the place, the photo confirmed it, and the voices confirmed it. He pulled around, close to the treeline and so the T4 hid his car partially from view. He unzipped the bag, took the gun out, a smile forming on his lips when he thought about the look on that fucking bitch's face when she saw him there pointing a gun at her, then the disbelief as he pulled the trigger. Maybe he'd shoot her in the chest, let the bitch bleed out on the floor while she listened to him hunt down and kill the other two. Maybe he'd shoot her in the face, he expected that at close range the shot in the cartridge would likely take half her pretty face off and that would be fuckin'-a- cool to see, too! *Decisions, decisions,* Jason mused to himself.

Gun primed and in hand, Jason got out of the car and stood with the driver's door open where he emptied the two boxes of twenty-five cartridges into a small canvas shoulder bag that bore the Beretta logo. In his haste a few dropped, they bounced off the driver's seat and vanished from view under the car. It didn't matter, he had more than enough. He guessed the bag could hold maybe sixty rounds. It had come with the gun and was designed to carry spare cartridges for when people were on a shoot. He himself was on a shoot, only the game wasn't pheasant or duck, and the thought brought an amused smile to his face. Ready, or cocked-locked and ready to rock, as he preferred to think of it, he fixed his attention on The Old Chapel and let the darkness in. It was stronger than it had been in the picture, sweeter, purer and less diluted. As he looked another blast of lightning flashed fiercely in the sky a few miles west, presenting him a momentarily lit view of the whole building. For the briefest of moments in that electric light he thought he'd seen a man in a cloak stood on the lawn watching him, then the lightning flashed again, and he was gone.

———

MIKE WAS in the kitchen boiling the kettle for a cup of tea that neither of them really wanted when there was a knock at the door. Just as with the previous night, this evening was turning into a waiting game, waiting for something to happen, yet at the same time half hoping it wouldn't. All morning and since getting in from searching the woods, and spying on the Horners' place, The Old Chapel had been shrouded in a pensive silence and thoughts on what they should do next had been tumbling around his head all day.

"Samuels?" Tara asked uneasily.

"Could be," he said and grabbed a large carving knife from one of the drawers. "You can't be too careful, though." Mike headed down the passageway where Scotty had vanished from the previous evening, the knife in his hand. Whoever was on the other side knocked the door again before Mike reached it.

"Who is it?" Mike demanded, one hand on the key that was still in the lock, the other clutching the knife.

"My car broke down about a mile away," came a male voice from the other side of the door. "I can't get my phone to work out here, I was wondering if you had a landline I could use to call for recovery?"

Mike turned the key in the lock thinking it was likely a shit house story thought up by some reporter who thought they'd get the scoop on just why he and the team were there. He had the door unlocked and half open before he heard Tara screaming for him to not open it, he couldn't make out what she was saying exactly but somewhere in there was a name he knew, Jason, but it was too late. As Mike registered the name and pushed his weight back against the door, Jason crashed against it on the other side countering his effort. There was just enough space between Mike and the door for it to gain enough momentum to knock him sideways and off-kilter. Mike stumbled back into the entrance lobby, the knife spilled from his hand and tumbled out of reach. He watched in a mixture of shock, surprise and pure horror as Jason came confidently over the threshold with a sawn-off shotgun in his hands. The barrel was aimed at him and his finger was on the trigger, already taking up some of the poundage. For a split-second, Mike looked directly into the shotgun's eye of death and he felt it wink at him.

"Well, well," Jason spat, taking them both in with eyes that looked both predatory and wild with anger. "Look what we have here, a ratting whore and her master!"

Mike regained his footing as Jason spoke. He knew that if he didn't get the gun from him, they were dead. Mike didn't know what Jason expected, maybe he'd expected them to freeze, maybe he'd expected them to beg for their lives. What he didn't expect was for Mike to rush at him, and it seemed to take him a little by surprise, for his reactions were a little slower than that of an average man. Mike sprang forward, crossed the few feet between them in the blink of an eye and managed to cut below the barrel and come up below Jason. He got a hand on the gun, forced it up and began trying to wrestle it from his grip. Mike had been faster, but Jason was stronger, and now he could feel him winning the tug of war, only this wasn't the kind at the village fete, whoever lost this would likely lose their life.

"Get down," Mike shouted at Tara, only too aware that in such a struggle it was easy for a gun to go off and hit a bystander. Jason's face was locked in a grimace of fury and exertion, it was damp with sweat and Mike watched a single bead of it run from his forehead down the bridge of his misshapen nose where it then fell to the floor. His breath stank sourly of booze and now Mike knew why he'd not been so fast to react, he was pissed.

"DIE!" Jason screamed through clenched teeth as he began to get the better of Mike. The gun barrel went from high to low as they struggled, and the barrel was now aimed at the floor behind him. Mike could feel Jason countering his efforts and soon the gun would come back up, only at this angle, it would end up under his chin in a suicide shot, and if that happened Mike knew he'd be dead. "BOTH, DIE!" Jason screamed again, and then there was an ear-splitting bang as the shotgun went off, the kick of it jarred Mike's his arms. Somewhere behind that deafening sound, he heard Tara scream, and for one terrible moment he thought she'd been shot, but that was before he felt the lancing hot pain spreading through his left leg.

———

TARA WATCHED in horror as Mike wrestled Jason for the gun, it swung left, right and each time it swept its deadly gaze across the lobby she dived out of its way. To begin with it looked as if the swiftness of Mike's action had won him the advantage, but Jason was stronger and slightly taller, and it didn't take long for him to begin regaining that advantage. His powerful arms forced the barrel to the floor, taking Mike further off balance, then using all his strength he began to bring it back up in an arc that would end directly under Mike's chin. Mike fought against him and there was a sudden flash from the muzzle and an ear-shattering bang as the shotgun went off. Tara screamed and watched as Mike instantly let go and stumbled back, the sudden release of pressure caused Jason to stumble the opposite way and for a moment he looked kind of dumbfounded as if he couldn't register what was happening.

Behind both Mike and Jason, out on the forecourt headlights swept the drive and Tara watched as a what looked like a Toyota Yaris did a U-turn and pulled to a stop level with the door. Mike was on his back, clutching at his leg, his face pale and sweat covered. The car drew Jason's attention for a split second and he turned to see who the latest person joining the party was. That split second of distraction was all Tara needed to act. She rushed across the lobby and picked up the heavy wooden crucifix from the floor at the foot of the stairs, where it had been resting since they'd arrived. With it clasped in a two-handed grip she rushed at him, bringing it up like a baseball player about to take a pitch. Jason must have sensed or heard her coming because as she got to within six feet of him, he turned and raised the gun at her. Tara cut left as another shot rang out, she'd moved quicker than Jason and the round hadn't spread enough for the buckshot to get her at that close range. She heard it splinter the wood of the panelling behind her and as it did, Jason screamed in rage. Before he had the chance to fire again, Tara was on him and she swung the heavy cross high and hard and caught him with the arm of the crucifix up under his chin. The momentum and weight behind it instantly shattered his jaw and snapped his neck back with a sickening, *Crack.* Blood and shattered teeth flew from his mouth and hit the carpet, the impact of the blow knocked the gun from his hand, and he staggered back two or three paces, his neck at an impossible angle. At the door, he wavered briefly before he fell backward through the frame causing the back of his head to hit the stone of the doorstep with a nauseating *thwack*.

Tara stood for a few moments, the cross still in her right hand and her chest heaving. She looked from the front door, where Jason lay not moving, to Mike who was now trying to sit himself up, pain creasing his face and a blossom of blood staining his grey cargo trousers. Eventually, the weight of the crucifix got too much and it dropped to the floor with a heavy *thump*. Tara's head span and nausea swept over her causing her to double over and vomit onto the carpet.

"My, what the devil has happened here?" a female voice said from the porch.

Tara looked up and saw the concerned face of June Rodgers. She was dressed in loose-fitting black trousers and a matching short sleeve top, around her neck was the same lightweight scarf that she'd been wearing when they'd met back in Boscastle. Behind her in the sky lighting flashed, igniting the tree line and briefly turning her figure into no more than a silhouette. Tara wiped the back of her hand over her mouth and straightened up. "June!" she said in surprise. "Wh-what the fuck are you doing here?"

June stepped over Jason's body, seemingly not fazed in the slightest by it, "I've been getting feelings all day that I needed to come," she said seriously. "And that if I didn't, your team and those poor Harrison kids would all be dead by morning."

"But the Grand Climax is tomorrow?" Tara said questioningly.

"I'm afraid not, Miss Gibb. The ceremony for the

Grand Climax begins at midnight," she said. "That is in a little over two hours."

"My God," Tara said, realising their mistake. "We never factored in that it turns the 27th at midnight, how could we have been so stupid?"

"Let's not worry about that right this second, my dear," June said, crossing the floor to Mike, "Could you give me a hand here with Mr. Cross, he appears to have been shot."

CHAPTER 47

THE LOBBY WAS FILLED WITH THE CHOKING, ACRID smell of gunpowder from the two discarded rounds and the sound of the blast still rang in Mike's ears like tinnitus and made his head feel like cotton wool. That smoky metallic smell caught the back of his throat and made him cough, the cough then jarred his body and further ignited the fiery pain in his leg, causing his face to crease in pain.

"Let me see him," June said, striding over and dropping down by his side.

Mike smiled weakly at her, "I don't think we've met yet," he said.

"It's a hell of a first impression, Mr. Cross," she said. Her voice was serious and yet there was the slightest hint of dry humour in there and it made him chuckle. "I wasn't sure what I'd be coming into by turning up here tonight, but the Cornish equivalent to the Gunfight at the O.K Coral wasn't it!"

"Jason?" he asked.

"If that's the name of the fellow in the doorway I'd say he was quite dead. Now, let me get your trousers down so I can take a look at that wound."

"I – wait," Mike protested but her hands were already unlacing his Timberlands.

"In a previous life I was a veterinary nurse," she said

as she loosened the zipper. "Not quite the same I know, but I once treated a German Shepherd who'd caught the wrong end of some buckshot, so as experience goes, I'm all you've got."

"I killed him," Mike heard Tara say in a hollow voice. She was crouched by his side, next to June watching her work, but her eyes, which were rimmed with red from the exertion of vomiting, looked distant and her face was pallid and sheened in sweat that glistened in the lights of the lobby.

"Was he one of them?" June asked.

"One of who?" Tara questioned.

"From the village?"

"No, he was an ex. I don't know how," she paused a second and Mike saw realisation dawn on her face and that realisation brought her back. "He must have seen the newspaper, Mike. My God. I knew he was crazy, but he was here to kill us."

June's hands stopped working on Mike's trousers and she looked at Tara with genuine puzzlement before she said, "I suggest you re-think your choice in the opposite sex, my dear. You have enough to contend with here without ex-boyfriends turning up and trying to kill you." She turned her attention back to the job in hand and fixed her grip around the sides of his waistband. "This is going to hurt, possibly quite a lot but I need to see how badly you were hit and if any of the shot is still in you. Tara, I need your help, you support his lower back and lift his backside. Ready, on the count of three, one-two."

On two June tugged his trousers down, taking care as she lifted them over the wound. Thankfully they were lightweight, loose in the leg, and came away easily. It hurt, but not as badly as Mike feared it would.

"Is it bad?" he asked trying to see past June's head. When she moved, he got a first look at the damage caused by the blast. His skin on the left side of his calf looked gouged and angry like someone had hit him repeatedly with one of those spiky hammers that chefs use to tenderise steak.

"It could be a lot worse," June replied as she surveyed the damage. "I'd say the buckshot has grazed the skin, well most of it. There are likely a few bits of it still in there." She looked at Mike and smiled, "Good news is I think you'll live. I can patch you up, but we need to get this looked at, at the hospital."

"We can't," Mike said. "There isn't time. Patch me up and I'll worry about the rest later."

June's face frowned with concern and through the open door behind her lightning lit the car park with a series of staccato flashes bringing with it the smell of ozone. it mixed with the metallic smell of the discharged shots and made the muggy air hard and chemical-like to breathe. "You need medical attention, Mr. Cross." She added seriously. She removed her neck scarf, balled it up and handed it to him and said, "Press this on the wound, it will stem the bleeding a little before we dress it."

"Mike, call me Mike."

"Mike. Very well," she looked from him to Tara and then around the lobby. "Where is Mr. Hampton?" she asked with puzzlement.

Tara's face fell into a solemn look, "We don't know," she said helplessly. "He vanished last night."

"Vanished?" June asked sounding bemused. "How did he vanish, my dear?"

"We were experiencing some major activity," Mike added in trying to get over the fact that he was now sat in his boxers in front of a lady he'd only just met. "It started in the upstairs bedroom with a Jack-in-the-box playing to itself, then culminated in the crying that has been so widely reported. Only this time it was different, the lights glowed so brightly that it almost blinded us, then it just stopped, the fuse tripped, and the lights went out. Scotty was gone, as were around an hour and a half of the night."

June looked at him confused, and Mike knew he'd spilled it all out like an excited toddler. She stood, and Mike heard her joints crack, her face looked pained, but she didn't voice it. Instead, she bit it back with a deep breath, then said, "Take me through it one step at a time, 'cos I'm still not quite sure how Mr. Hampton vanished on you. And am I right in believing that you lost over an hour of time?"

Mike moved his bum on the floor and got his leg more comfortable and winced as he pushed the scarf down onto the wound. It felt better now that the fabric of his trousers was away from the skin, but it still throbbed deeply. "Yes," he said. "I awoke to the sound of a nursery rhyme coming from one of the upstairs rooms. Scotty had rigged up some sound amplifiers, so we could hear the whole house. Turned out to be a Jack-in-the-box playing to itself in one of the upstairs bedrooms. That was about two AM, give or take. Then we heard the crying, it started low, barely audible but it soon built. Then as it built the lights brightened, like I said we could barely see it got so bright. Then something happened, like a pressure change – I even felt it in my ears, Tara, too. After that, the lights went out. I think the power surge tripped out the main fuse. At the point, the lights went out Scotty vanished. He had hold of Tara one moment, then the next he was –"

"Gone," Tara said for him.

"Yes," Mike agreed, "Gone! The whole incident was no more than ten minutes from beginning to end, then say another ten while Tara and I fumbled around in the dark trying to find him, then me getting the power back on. Once I got the lights on, I just needed to get out into the fresh air and get straight about what had just happened; if you can get straight about such things. That's when I noticed the sky, it wasn't light, but the first signs of dawn were there. It was almost four AM."

June's face looked troubled, but Mike could tell she knew something, or thought she did. After a long pause while she considered what she needed to say she said, "I believe the fabric between our version of reality and that of the Abyss is thin here, very thin. I can feel it in my head, in my bones. It's one of the reasons this place feels so wrong. Not everyone will feel it, but those with the slightest bit of psychic inkling will. Tell me, have you heard any animals in the woods?"

"None," Tara answered. "I noticed that. They had two police dogs out here when the Harrison kids went, but they couldn't get them out of the van."

June nodded her head thoughtfully and said, "At night when our world is shrouded in darkness that fabric is thinner still. You see, in the Abyss there is no time. Time is a constraint on our world, it's a thing of this dimension. The fact that the two places are so closely bonded could mean that at times there exists a state of flux between here and there, and when that happens those of us bound to this reality, to this world, could experience time loss. Hours flicking past in the blink of an eye. The ones who reside in this village are unlikely to be hampered by these time losses. I'd say that whatever happened to poor Mr. Hampton, happened in that lost time."

"I find that," Mike began.

"What, Mike?" June cut in standing over him and fixing him solidly with her bespectacled eyes. "Hard to believe? Yes, it is, but you need to believe it, and when you do then we can get on with this thing and try to find those kids, and your friend. Do you have another explanation?"

Mike shook his head, "No, I don't."

"Good," she said curtly. "Now let us get on with patching you up." She turned her attention back to the wound and moved Mike's hand away from it. "Well it's ruined a perfectly good scarf, but the bleeding seems to have stopped enough for me to take a proper look. I'll do what I can tonight but tomorrow we need to get you down to Derriford."

"Understood," Mike replied. June was the kind of person he instantly liked. She was straight to the point and there was something school ma'am-ish about her. Something that said she wouldn't stand for bullshit and woe betide anyone who got in her way.

"I have a good first aid kit in the car, I will sterilise the wound, bandage it and pump you with enough painkillers to get you moving." And with that she went out to her car, stepping over Jason's dead body as if he were no more than a sleeping cat.

"I killed him, Mike. I fucking killed him," Tara said again as if saying it over and over helped it to sink in.

"You don't need to feel bad," he reassured. "It was a kill or be killed situation. If you hadn't done what you did, we'd both be dead now."

"That's the thing," she said. The colour was back in her face now and she both looked and sounded like the Tara he knew and had come to love. "I don't feel bad, Mike. Not one bit." She paused as if she needed to let what she said sink in. Then with a hint of foreboding in her voice, she added, "It's this place again, isn't it? It likes death, it likes chaos and violence. It doesn't care who dies, just as long as it gets its blood." Tara took a deep breath and shook her head. "I tried to tell you, Mike," she said regretfully. "I tried to tell you not to open the door. I recognised his voice, but it was too late, you already had the door unlocked."

Mike placed a hand on her leg and said, "You don't feel bad because that bastard deserved it. He had it coming. If and when this is over you start to feel differently, which you might, you keep telling yourself that."

Before she could answer, June breezed back into the lobby. she had on a fresh and seemingly identical necktie and in her hand she carried a medium sized green canvas bag which she placed by Mike's side before getting to work.

Ten minutes later the wound was cleaned and bandaged. She'd found three bits of buckshot embedded in his leg, those she'd dug out with a pair of medical tweezers while he'd bit back cries of pain. She'd told him there might be more and that was why it was important he get it looked at by a professional. She'd then cleansed it, that had hurt like a bastard too, but not as much as having someone digging about in your flesh with tweezers and no anaesthetic. With Tara's help, they'd bandaged it and June had made him take two Naproxen. Painkillers prescribed for her arthritis yet strong enough to make the injury manageable and thus enable him to function.

"You said you had to come?" Mike asked her as she pumped alcohol gel over her bloodied hands and wiped them with some spare bandage.

She nodded, dropped the now bloodied bandage into the packet from which it had come and said, "The feeling has been building in me all day, Mike. I tried to shut it out, but my gift can be quite strong when it's working, and today it's been on overdrive. By this evening I literally couldn't focus on anything. Every time I tried to this place came back to me. In the end, and as much as I didn't want to, I knew I must come."

Mike smiled up at her, "I've never been much of one for trusting people with gifts such as yours, but then my beliefs have been tested more than I'd care to admit over the last few days. We need all the help we can get, and personally I'm glad to see you."

June smiled at him but didn't speak, and in her sparkling eyes, Mike could see fear. After what felt like an age she said, "I was asked to help before, by Mr. Hawkes, the witch hunter I told you about. I turned him down, I was too afraid to come to this place. I've lived with myself for not helping him because after the fire it all died down and I thought that it was over. I've been fighting a lot of my own demons since those kids went missing," she sighed deeply, and her eyes were sad now. "I was a younger woman then and I made a mistake, it's time to make amends for that."

"Are you not scared now?" Tara asked her.

"My dear, I'm terrified," June smiled shakily. "But sometimes we need to be brave."

"It's not just the kids going missing," Tara added in. Her voice dropped and sounded regretful. "One of the police officers guarding the place earlier in the week took a fall down the stairs inside, she's dead now as well. Not to mention all those other peculiar deaths. This place is rotten," Tara continued. "It gets in people's heads. No matter what happens tonight, if we find Scotty, Ellie, and Henry or not we need to destroy it."

"Not just the building," June said with certainty. "That didn't work last time, the whole village must go."

Tara sighed hopelessly, "I don't know how that's even possible," she said.

"One step at a time," June said reassuringly. "And talking about steps it's time you tried to take a few Mike. How about we see if you can walk?"

Mike nodded and with a little help from Tara he got to his feet. The leg hurt but the pain was manageable, and he knew he'd been lucky. The Naproxen were fast workers and they'd already taken the edge off. He knew that if the gun had been half an inch in a different direction his leg would have taken the whole round and if that had happened, he'd be out of the game.

Mike limped over to where Jason lay, his legs were over the threshold, his torso out. He wasn't sure if it had been the blow from the crucifix that had killed him or how the back of his head had hit the stone of the porch stoop, possibly and quite likely a mixture of both. His jaw was disjointed and his mouth no more than a bloodied looking maw of broken and shattered teeth. Thick, dark red viscous blood leaked from the back of his skull in a thick and slow-moving river that ran down the stone step and into the shingle. Jason's eyes were open but had rolled up into the top of his head, and now only the whites showed. For a brief moment, Mike imagined those eyes rolling back into place, a smile forming on Jason's lips and a hand grabbing his leg. But this wasn't Jason Voorhees, who'd stalked and killed his way through countless horror movies. This Jason was just Jason Paxman, an abuser of women - most definitely, a total arsehole – without doubt, but that was all, and now he was dead and Mike felt sure that no one, save for maybe his mother, would miss him.

"We need to get his body inside," Mike said, looking back at Tara and June. "Give me a hand, once he is in, I'll get a sheet or a duvet from the master bedroom on this floor and cover him." Mike slid the canvas bag that Jason had been carrying off his shoulder and looked inside. The bag was full of shotgun cartridges, how many he couldn't count, but there had to be more than forty in there. He placed the bag by the gun and made a mental note to reload it once they were done with his body. There were no doubt unexplainable things in motion here, but Lucinda and Seth Horner were human, or at least in part he thought they were, and he felt sure that if it came to it the gun would dispatch them, and anyone else from this fucking place just as surely as a stake through the heart killed a vampire.

Between the three of them, they struggled Jason's limp and lifeless body over the threshold and into the lobby, the back of his head left a thick smear of crimson behind as they dragged him, as if someone had roller painted red Halloween blood across the floor. They left him laid level with the sideboard just inside the main door, the one which the slate key plaque hung over. Satisfied, Mike limped back to the gun and gave it the once-over. In his early days on the force, he'd done the initial firearms course, quitting on the last week when he decided it wasn't for him. It had been many years since he'd last held a weapon, but he still knew the basics. This was a Semi-Automatic Shotgun, the chamber held three rounds, the gun had a gas-powered reloading system meaning the next cartridge was loaded with lightning speed. It was a nice weapon, light and no doubt deadly, and there was a part of him that saw Jason's intrusion as a stroke of luck, for it had brought him the gun.

"Are you planning to use that thing?" Tara said.

"I don't know," Mike replied as he snapped two more rounds into the receiver and readied it. "All I know is we have a weapon now, and I feel a whole lot better about having it than not." He crossed the lobby, realising how ridiculous he must look in his blue boxers with a bandaged leg, socks and toting a shotgun. At the door, he shut then deadbolted it as more lightning flashed brightly, igniting the stained-glass windows in reds and greens. A few seconds later a deep rumble of thunder rolled across the sky. Mike rested the gun on the sideboard above where Jason lay, the whites of his eyes were now staring blankly up at the roof. "My bag is in the master bedroom at the back. I'll grab some more trousers and a sheet to cover him." Mike turned to June, she was stood by Tara at the foot of the stairs down which PC Shelly Ardell had taken her life ending tumble. "Then I think we will have a walk around with you, see if you can pick up on anything that might help us figure this thing out."

CHAPTER 48

MIKE CROSS, STILL IN HIS BLUE BOXERS, THE FRESH bandage tied tightly around his left lower calf and with the Naproxen ebbing the pain away bit by bit, made his way down the passage to the master bedroom, or the Altar Room as the Reeds had named it. In his hand he clutched the ruined pair of light grey cargos, the left leg torn and bloody.

At the end of the passageway he opened the closed door and went in, the room was cool and dark and the first thing he did was click the light on. Their bags and all the now empty kit cases were stacked by the far side of the large bed where Scotty had left them the day before. Mike only had one holdall with a few emergency bits in he'd bought from Go Outdoors in Plymouth on their way down. When he'd left home to head to Manchester, he'd had no idea he'd be away for so long.

He was no more than halfway across the room when behind him he heard the door click shut and instantly he had the undeniable feeling that he was no longer alone.

"You've been a busy boy," a female voice as soft and smooth as honey said from behind him. Mike tossed the ruined trousers onto the bed and turned. She wore a long black robe, it began at the shoulders then plunged at the front to reveal a little of the woman's cleavage before it flowed down over her thighs, ending just an inch from the floor, hiding her feet from view. The robe had a hood that was up, and her face was hidden from view by a blank, white mask of porcelain, the kind muses sometimes wore, only this was more sinister, and it set a ball of ice in the pit of his stomach. Long, deep red locks of hair framed that faceless white mask, they cascaded like waves of fire from the hood and over her shoulders. Mike didn't need the woman to remove the mask to know who she was.

The ball of ice was fear, but now a larger one formed in him, one of fire and it melted the fear, the way the sun might melt a child's ice-cream dropped onto hot tarmac on a scorching day. Inwardly, he cursed himself for leaving the gun on the sideboard in the lobby because he felt pretty sure if he had it, if it was in his hands then he'd just shoot the hateful bitch right then and there and worry about the why's and wherefores later.

"Where is Scotty?" he said. His voice was both calm and assertive. "I know you took him, I don't know how but I know you did."

Lucinda Horner sleeked forward with the grace of a feline stalking its prey. She seemed to glide across the floor toward him and as she came, she raised her hands to the mask and removed it, revealing her pretty face. Her skin was as smooth as alabaster, her full lips painted deep red, "Shhhhh," she cooed, raising a finger with a nail manicured perfectly in gloss black to her lips. "You don't need to worry about him, Mikey, he's already dead. The lord of the Abyss demanded it." She cast the mask aside and it landed on the bed by his trousers.

Her words brought him an instant pang grief, anger, and sadness and there was no doubt in his mind that what she'd said had been the truth, but for some reason the news of Scotty's death hadn't hit him as hard as it should have done. He didn't want to strike out at her anymore, the anger was being quelled by something and now he wasn't even sure that if he held the gun that he'd so badly wanted not ten seconds ago that he'd use it. In an effort to hold onto himself he turned his thoughts to Tara and June. What was happening to them whilst she was here? Somehow Lucinda seemed to sense this, she glanced back at the door and said, "It's only me, Mikey, just me. They are quite safe, for now anyway."

"Where is your husband, where's Seth?" Mike asked, but even his own words sounded distant, as if spoken by someone else, and second by second, he could feel the fact that Scotty was dead not mattering more and more, neither did June, nor Tara. Those feelings, that hate-filled fear and anger slipped away as easily as sand falls through spread fingers.

Lucinda chuckled, she was stood in front of him now and she raised a hand to Mike's face and touched him softly, "Oh Mikey," she purred. "I don't need old Seth to fight my battles. You see the men in this village, save for the Minister who is father to us all, are no more than servants to our coven. Worshippers of the Dark Lord who wish to live in service by serving his daughters. Powerful men, yes, brilliant men, yes, but only men. And tonight, we will bring the Minister back to this world in human form, and once more our father shall lead us." Her face was just inches from his and he could see the fullness of her lips as she formed the words, He could smell the intoxicating scent of her warm, moist breath and at that point, even the pain in his leg was forgotten. "I can feel how much you want me, Mikey," she coaxed, and as she spoke, she placed a hand on the front of his shorts and squeezed at his growing hardness. "You heard the darkness last night, didn't you Mikey? It spoke to you and you wanted to listen, you wanted to give in." And at that point he did want to give in, he wanted to grab the back of Lucinda's head and force those deep red lips against his, he wanted to kiss her and drink her in, he wanted to tear the robe from her body and expose the smooth, pale skin of her breasts and he wanted to –

"No!" he cried, forcing Lucinda back. A feature of her face had triggered a memory and that in turn had held the last piece of his sanity, of what made him, him and allowed him to keep clinging on before it all went over the precipice and into that Abyss. She had a thin scar above her right eye, not really a scar, more the memory of one, of an injury suffered long ago when she'd been no more than a girl. Below that scar, and those deep eyes of emerald green was the faintest hint of childhood freckles that long ago had likely been more pronounced and had dressed the bridge of her nose. Now those freckles were so faint that they were only noticeable at close quarters. As his mind came back, he knew why they looked so familiar. The image of the missing girl, Lindie Parker, and how her youthfulness had suggested beauty in adulthood, and how she'd had that same scar over her eye, and freckles that at just fifteen had been all the more prevalent, and as he looked, as he remembered, the horror and meaning of it all came to him, the jigsaw slotted into place.

"You're – Lindie - Parker?" he managed to stammer out, as Lucinda staggered backward from the force of his push. it was as much a question as it was a statement and for a moment confusion at his rejection washed her face. "You're Lindie," he repeated. The idea seemed impossible, Lindie Parker had been taken at just fifteen-years-old from the Charlestown Harbour way back in 1969. It was now 2018 and Lindie Parker would be sixty-seven, almost sixty-eight years old. Lucinda Horner was no older than forty-five, and to say she was that old was a push. But he knew it, he could feel it was true, "I don't know how, but you are," he added.

Lucinda stared at him, her head cocked slightly to the side and something about how she looked at him made Mike feel uneasy. A cloud seemed to pass over her green eyes and without warning, she sprang for him with feline agility, the robe flowing out behind her. Mike felt her make contact, his leg jarred and pain flared, the force knocked him backward onto the bed where she straddled him, pinning him to the double mattress like some dominatrix in a palace of pain, her hands on his forcing them back behind his head. "What's the matter, Mikey?" she spat. "I thought you wanted to fuck me!" As she spoke flecks of her spittle hit his face. Any lustfulness in her voice was gone, and what replaced it was venom. "Most of what made Lindie, Linde left a long time ago, part of her is still with me, but such a small part it's insignificant now." And with that she threw back her head, like a lover in the throes of an intense climax, then before his eyes the skin on Lucinda's face morphed and for a brief second it was as blank as that of the mask which she'd been wearing. As it came back to human, she was no longer Lucinda, she was Lindie or something that had once been Lindie. The scar was more prominent, the freckles more visible and the hair not quite such a deep shade of red. The anger left her and what replaced it was that childhood innocence he'd seen in the picture. "They took me, Mikey," she said sadly. Her voice had changed too, and now it matched the look of a girl in her mid-teens, one who should be stressing about exams and boys and if she had enough money to buy those shoes she wanted so badly. "They took me from my mummy and daddy and held me here, held me in The Chapel where the men raped me. Beat me and raped me, over and over, giving me their seed until I was pregnant. After I'd had my baby, they sacrificed her so that I could become." Her green eyes changed as she spoke, blackness flooded them until she regarded him with no more than two bottomless pools of darkness. "Your baby daughter is down there with my Hope now, Mikey. Your precious little Megan." And now her voice changed, too. It lost that childhood innocence and became that of many, many tortured voices speaking to him from somewhere far beyond this world. "Down in all that darkness," the Lindie-thing continued. "She cries for her daddy, Mikey. She cries for you as the demons devour her pure flesh, and your slut, whore of a dead wife can do nothing but listen, listen to her screams! They're waiting for you there, Mikey, all you need to do is let the darkness in." She bent forward to kiss him and Mike knew that if her lips touched his he would be lost to this world; the darkness would come flooding in, filling him up until all that made him Mike Cross, was gone.

"Wherever my wife and daughter are," he said with indignation, "they are not in your hell!" And as he spoke Mike rammed his knee up between her legs in a move that would bring any good man down. The impact caused the Lindie-thing to let go of his arms and he bucked his body up, and hit out at her with both palms, forcing her back off the bed and causing her to tumble to the floor. The Lindie-thing looked up at him now, and the blackness had gone, once again she looked at him as a child, eyes welled with tears as if she'd just been scolded by a parent and for a moment, he felt guilty. Then she came at him once more, springing at him from the floor like an attacking animal with agility that seemed so inhuman. Mike dove right, rolling off the bed as adrenaline flooded through him, plugging the gaps in the pain that the Naproxen had not managed to find. The Lindie-thing landed right where he'd been not a second before where she crouched on all-fours ready to pounce. Her red hair had fallen over her face, the black eyes were back, and they drank him in, regarded him with pure and unfiltered hatred.

Outside the room he could hear Tara banging on the door, the handle rattled but wouldn't move. He heard her crash her body against it, but she didn't have the strength nor the size to break it open.

"Get the gun!" Mike managed to scream as the Lindie-Thing came for him again. It pounced off the bed and landed on him, legs wrapped around his, hands clawing for his face. He stumbled back, hit the closed curtains and pulled them down, the wrought-iron pole crashed to the floor and struck him on the back of the head and shoulders.

"She screams, Mikey, she screams for her daddy," the Lindie-thing cried triumphantly as he felt nails digging into the flesh of his neck. Her breath was on his face, only now it wasn't intoxicating, it was rancid and smelt of decay and of things dead and buried. The futile banging on the door continued, and somewhere Mike could hear Tara screaming his name. He fought the Lindie-Thing off him again, and with his back pinned to the wall, he managed to get his good leg on her stomach and kick out with all his force. Her body was light, maybe even fragile and she tumbled away from him, his weight and size besting her, but he wasn't sure how much longer he could continue to ward off her relentless attacks. Blindly he grabbed out behind him, found the wrought-iron pole from the curtains and whipped it around, tearing the fabric from the loops. As she came for him, he swung it at her, the pole hit the side of her face splitting open her right cheek. She – it, whatever it was screamed in a mixture of pain and frustration and Mike knew she would come again and unless he could stop her, she would keep coming until his strength wavered and she got the better of him.

The pole was about four feet long, half an inch thick and finished in what looked like a spear, giving it that slightly gothic effect that bestowed itself upon the whole place. As he knew she would, the Lindie-thing sprang forward in another attack and as she came at him, he went for her, driven on by no more than the involuntary will to survive. He thrust out the pole with all his strength. If she saw his move she was too late, her body had too much forward momentum and the decorative spiked end struck her hard in the chest. There was the slightest moment of resistance before the bones in her breastplate gave way with a sickening cracking sensation that traversed down the pole to his hands. The strength of her own attack paired with the force of Mike's counter assault meant that it kept going right through her body until it breached her back, impaling her completely. An ear-piercing shriek of pain and surprise filled the room and her eyes fell on the appendage now jutting out of her body. From the pole, her eyes turned to Mike's and the blackness drained from them, replaced now by their natural greenness. She looked at him, as if looking at him for the first time and then just like there had been the previous night there was the passing of something, not pressure this time, something else, something he could not put his finger on, and as it passed the door opened and Tara rushed in followed by June.

Mike felt the weight of her slight frame on the curtain pole - turned deadly weapon for a second, maybe two, before he released his grip on it, and as he did, she dropped to her knees, then fell to the floor. Blood flowed from the wound, pumping out steady spurts of deep red from around the pole. It looked black against the fabric of her cloak until it hit the cream carpet. Mike looked from Tara to June and back to the girl, who was still a child, still that girl in the photo from so long ago, and he knew she'd not change back. Whatever had been Lucinda Horner was gone, cast out in death. She looked at Mike for a few seconds, and in her eyes, he read not pain, but relief, and it stayed with her until she closed them for the last time.

CHAPTER 49

MIKE DROPPED TO HIS KNEES BESIDE LINDIE'S BODY, A mixture of emotions running through him, one juxtaposing against the other. Part of him felt relief, yet at the same time, he felt a deep sadness in the knowledge that the girl's torment hadn't ended in 1969 when she'd been taken. They'd assumed that Lindie Parker had been the victim of some gruesome murder through the act of sacrifice, yet they'd been wrong, and in a way, what had happened to her had been worse.

Just how much of that original girl had been trapped in what had been Lucinda Horner he did not know. Had they shared a consciousness? Lindie there all along like some silent passenger, a prisoner in her own mind. Or had she been no more than a memory to Lucinda? Like the previous tenant of a flat you might rent and have met only once on the day you moved. Mike had no idea, it went far beyond what he could comprehend, but he hoped it was the latter, for to consider that Lindie Parker had been trapped in there for the past forty-eight years was inconceivable to him. And yet at the point when she'd died, he'd read relief in her eyes, those eyes had almost seemed to thank him, and he knew that in those last few seconds, in death, the girl who had been Lindie Parker had been with him in that room.

Mike touched the scratch marks on his neck, his

hands came away with only the faintest traces of blood on them. It was enough to tell him that she'd only managed to inflict superficial scratches to his skin with her nails and the pain was hardly noticeable next to the steady throb from his leg. He'd been lucky, lucky for a second time and he wondered if he could chance that luck for a third.

Tara was stood the other side of the body; her eyes were fixed on the girl's face and they were eyes full of disbelief. "She was Lucinda Horner," Mike said, his voice sounded taught and strung with the stress of having to fight for his life twice, against two people who'd generally wanted to kill him, and all in under a half hour.

"But, how?" was all Tara could manage.

"I don't know," he replied, staying on the floor by the body. For a few moments, he just wanted the weight off his legs, both the good and the bad one. On the floor by his side, a tide of red was slowly spreading out, soaking into the woollen carpet, the fibres absorbing the blood as eagerly as a sponge does water.

Mike looked at June, her grey bob of hair framed a serious expression. "She told me that they beat and raped her, got her pregnant and then sacrificed the baby so that she could become."

"Then it's likely that all of the women in this village, who make up this coven," June began.

"Are on that list of missing girls I put together." Tara finished off.

"They are using the act of sacrifice to promote one of possession," June said thoughtfully. "Witches, true witches, live far longer than humans. Device was part human and part demon, a very powerful Warlock. Through ritual and sacrifice, he has enabled the witches in that coven to live even longer. Be almost immortal, just that immortality is of the soul and not the body. When nearing the end of their already unnaturally long lives they are literally ported into a new body. Fascinating, quite fascinating."

"She said they were his daughters," Mike added, understanding now why Lucinda Horner had looked so young, why at sixty-eight she had looked more early forties. "That the men in this village are nothing but men, men who wish to serve the Dark Lord by serving his daughters."

"Did you know this?" Tara asked, looking at June.

June shook her head which in turn swayed her grey bangs, "No my dear. Mr. Hawke, the man I told you about when you came to me at my museum, had no idea of this. In all my experience I have never known anything as unnatural." As she spoke a deep crack of thunder shook the sky and reverberated through the building. "If Tara's research is right, she was the last one, back in 1969." June pointed to the dead body of Lindie Parker, her face even paler in death than it had been in life, highlighting the redness of her hair. "The next time one of the witches in this coven reaches the end of her life, that is when another girl will go missing, of that, I have no doubt."

"Which explains why there is no pattern to it," Tara jumped in with, then paused. "But that doesn't explain Ellie, Henry, and Scotty."

Mike stood, took the weight on his leg, winced a bit but then it got easier. Grimacing and feeling like some zombie slayer in a horror movie he placed his left foot on Lindie's chest, grasped the curtain pole and pulled it out of her small body. It came free with a horrible sucking sound that made him want to vomit. "Scotty is dead," he said, hating how callous he sounded saying it, almost nonchalant. And as he spoke, he avoided Tara's eyes, for he knew that if he looked into them and saw her grief then her pain would bestow itself upon him and add to his own, and he wasn't sure he could handle that.

"You can't know that," she said with noticeable

anger. "If you think he is dead then so are the Harrison kids, and if that's the case then what is the fucking point of us being here?" And now he did look at her and he could see tears welling in her eyes. June placed a hand on Tara's shoulder which she didn't shrug off.

Mike threw the pole aside, took one of the curtains he'd torn down and covered Lindie's body with it. "They killed him, Tara," Mike said, his voice softening. He went to her and she slid from June into his arms. "I don't need to see his body to know what she said was true."

"Why," she sobbed. "Why would they do that?"

"I don't know," Mike answered, talking into her hair as he held her, as he spoke he could feel individual strands of it sticking to his lips. The physical contact felt good and he realised that right then they needed each other, and only together could they get through this. "But now is not the time to grieve for him. There will be time enough for that if we live through this thing. We need to find Ellie and Henry and end this, make sure he didn't die for nothing."

Mike felt her move her face away from his chest, he looked at her. Her eyes were red, and her lashes wet with tears. "You think they are still alive?"

"I do," Mike nodded. "And I know what they want them for, or at least I think I do."

"Maybe you should enlighten us then, Mike," June said. She'd stood aside and allowed them both their moment of pain, but her voice told him it was time to get on with the job.

"Lindie, Lucinda, whatever it or she was said that tonight the Minister would come back in human form and that their father would lead them again." Mike looked at June as he spoke. "Now I'm guessing that they sacrificed those babies to enable the mother to become because she was firstly, a blood relative, and secondly the child offered was pure."

"A virgin," June added nodding. "Pureness of the

soul is very important in occultism, and you're right on both counts."

"So, am I also right in assuming that would work if the one being sacrificed and the one being possessed were brother and sister?"

A look of realisation broke like the dawn of a stormy and cloud-capped day on June's face. "As long as the sister was a virgin then yes, it would be no different," she said hurriedly. "But Ellie Harrison is eighteen-years-old, Mike."

"Ellie was not taken to become," Mike said, speaking to them both. "She was taken because she is a virgin, it is the only explanation. The one who is going to become is her brother. Tonight they will kill her in a sacrifice and Henry will become Device, only not the ancient Device who died in the fire, Device reborn in the form of a five-year-old. Other kids stayed in this place before the Harrisons, and whilst one of them was killed by its mother after staying here, they were not taken. They have been waiting, waiting for the perfect combination, and Henry and Ellie were, are it." Mike had that feeling, the one he used to get when he was on the force and working a difficult, yet high profile case. One that had the team stumped. That feeling came when you had a breakthrough when the answers to all the questions that had been puzzling you were answered.

"But that doesn't make sense," Tara cut in. "That fire was back in two thousand and eight? If they wanted him back in ten years, why wait for ten years, why not do it right away?"

June smiled at her, "You are thinking three-dimensionally again my dear. Time does not have the same meaning to the dead. The time is immaterial. I believe that Mr. Cr – Mike, has hit the nail on the head as they say."

Mike frowned, looked about the room and said, "What I don't understand is this. If this building was where all those atrocities took place, if this was their chapel then where is it going to happen?"

June looked at him knowingly as more lightning strobed the de-curtained window behind her. "This building is the heart of this village," she said. "And heart has many chambers."

"I don't follow you?" Mike said.

"Okay, let me try a different metaphor. When you look at an iceberg what do you see?"

"Why can't you just tell me?" he asked in frustration.

"Because, Mike you need to figure it out and understand," she replied. "Now tell me what you see?"

"A fucking iceberg," he said, starting to feel anger at her mystical shit.

"The tip," Tara said, "You see the tip."

"Quod superius, sicut inferius," June said seriously, then translated, "As above, so below."

Mike looked at the floor as if it would suddenly turn translucent and allow him to see into the bowels of the building. "You think that this is just the tip of the iceberg, that there is a below to this place."

"Mr. Hawke only spoke of this building, this was a chapel, they held certain ceremonies here, and it was also the home of Device. He never got to the point where he learned all of the secrets of Trellen, though. And until now I have never had a desire to find them out. I can feel it, though. The energy coming up through the floor of this place is so strong it's flooding through me like a tuning fork. Why, if we listen I may even hum," she grinned at them, but the grin was a façade that hid her fear. "The term *as above so below* holds prominence in many religions, it appears in the Lord's prayer in the lines, *on Earth as it is in Heaven*. It is also important in the occult. In witchcraft, it is denoted by the mirrored tree, adjoined by spiralling roots that symbolise the gateway between the physical world and that of the spirit world. I believe that this building is its own symbol, one above, and one below. Only for this place the below is its own metaphor for the Abyss, and the below is where the worst atrocities will take place, where this village hides its deepest secrets, and that below is where we will have to go to save those kids."

"There must be another way into The Old Chapel then," Tara said excitedly. "Which would explain how Henry and Ellie went missing from a locked building, how Scotty vanished and," Tara pointed her finger toward the covered body of Lindie Parker, blood had started to blossom through the fabric of the curtain, "how queen fucking bitch there got in!"

More lightning flashed, and thunder cleaved the sky, it seemed to shake the foundations of the building as if in some kind of divine confirmation of their deductions. "It's not inconceivable," Mike said, picking up his bag and placing it on the bed. He unzipped the top and spoke as he rummaged inside for a clean pair of trousers. "I mean it's more likely than them just teleporting in here like something out of Star Trek." The mention of Scotty's favourite show sent a pang of grief through him and he glanced from the contents of his bag to Tara and saw it in her eyes as well.

"But wouldn't that mean, Sue and Tom Reed were a part of this?" she asked, thinking the question over for herself as she spoke.

"Unlikely," Mike replied. He found a pair of dark blue, almost black walking / activity trousers and slid them on, taking time to go carefully over the wound. A few small spots of blood had started to come through the bandage, but they were minimal. "The Horners caretake this place, they – the village for that matter, could have quite easily filled in a hidden entrance to a lower level long before the Reeds took over, then they'd have had plenty of chance to un-fill it and hide the opening after the work was finished." Mike fastened the button and checked his watch, it was ten to midnight.

"It's almost the twenty-seventh," he said. "Do you have any idea what time they'd carry out the ritual, June?"

"Not exactly," she said. "Some point between mid-night and three AM I'd imagine."

"And that's counting on there being no more periods of lost time," Tara added in. "Where do you think this entrance is?"

"Well you were in the lobby," Mike said thought-fully. "I came down the side passage and she followed me into to the room. She never came through the door whilst we were dealing with Jason, which means she must have gotten in somewhere." He paused, lost in the memory of his brief meeting with the Horners and how he'd complimented the place and how Seth had men-tioned something about helping out with the fitment of the kitchen. "The kitchen," Mike said as the synapse of memory fired. The CCTV was still recording, but to review the last twenty minutes of footage would cost them time, time they didn't have. Mike trusted his hunches, and when on a case they were rarely wrong. "They helped out with its fitment, Seth mentioned it when I paid them a visit." Mike limped across the room, he found it easier to be moving as he pondered a problem. The kitchen made sense, certainly as the Horners had been involved in its fitting, but where? The floor was solid stone tile, there were no breaks or drainage covers. He looked at the body of the dead girl, a girl who had once been Lindie Parker, somehow laid here now a corpse and not looking a day older than when she'd gone missing some forty-eight years ago. Suddenly, and like the clicking of a lightbulb it came to him, the eureka moment and he knew they'd answered the one question that had hung over this case since day one. Just how had they gotten out? "The utility cup-board," he said, turning to June and Tara. "It's the only place big enough and hidden enough for someone to come through."

"But the floor in there is tiled, just like the rest of

the kitchen." Tara protested, but Mike was already out of the bedroom door and on his way through the rear passage that led along the back of The Old Chapel and came out in the kitchen. Tara and June followed behind him, the Naproxen had worked wonders and he hoped June had enough on her to keep him dosed up until this was over.

In the kitchen he crossed the tiled floor, his socked feet moving silently on cool stone. At the cupboard he flung the door open, half expecting to see whatever trap door he'd imagined standing open. It wasn't. The cupboard was empty save for the fuse boxes, gas, water, and electric meters and a large canvas bag that hung from a brass hook on the back wall stuffed full of plastic bags for guests to take shopping.

"See," Tara said from behind him. "Tiled, solid. We need to rethink this Mike."

"Not so fast," he said and backed out of the cupboard. "There's no threshold between the two rooms, and look, a small gap where the threshold or grout should be. The two sets of tiles are almost flush.

"What are you planning to do, Mike?" June said as he began to rummage feverishly through the cupboards. "You could get the gun, sit by the door and wait for someone to come looking for Lucinda, I am sure she will be missed soon enough."

"That's not a bad idea," Mike said, as he found the cupboard he was after. It was full of heavy, cast iron pots and pans. One of them was a griddle, the Le Creuset logo imprinted onto the blue metal handle. The Reeds had spared no expense on anything to do with this place, and the cooking utensils were no exception. Mike took the heavy griddle from its home; the other pots and pans clanked loudly in protest and fell from their neatly stacked pile. A small milk saucepan spilled out onto the stone tiles with a *clang*. Mike left it where it was, every second was precious now.

"What are you going to do with that?" Tara asked as

he brushed by her. Mike didn't answer, she'd see soon enough. As he reached the threshold of the utility cupboard he dropped to his knees, ignoring the pain in his leg. He raised the griddle pan high and swung down hard, the edge hit the tiles with a crash that reverberated painfully through the griddle, up the handle, and to his hands. One or two of the tiles chipped but didn't break, they were thick and likely not cheap.

"Come on, come on," he muttered to himself feverishly as he swung the griddle pan high again, he brought it down with more force this time, causing more pain to vibrate through his hands. This time tiles broke, and he felt sharp pieces of masonry hit the skin of his cheek, luckily none went into his eyes. "Turn your faces away," he said urgently, not stopping to check if they had. He swung high for the third time and with all the force he could muster he slammed the griddle pan back onto the damaged tiles. He was right on target, striking the ones he'd already shattered, smashing them away revealing plywood, and as the pan struck the wood it gave a hollow sound that suggested a cavity below. Mike paused as lightning flashed, he looked at both Tara and June and he saw it on their faces, too. They had heard it. He didn't speak, he went back at it, striking the tiles over and over again, so many times he lost count, hitting and hitting until his arms ached and his hands felt sore. He kept at it, through the discomfort until all the tiles were no more than a shattered pile of expensive rubble on top of the plywood to which they'd been affixed.

Mike cast the pan aside, it clattered noisily along the kitchen floor behind him as he went to work scooping out handfuls of the broken floor, clearing it off the ply. The space was small, but Tara was with him now, and together they kept going, looking like two desperate prisoners trying to tunnel out of a cell, until all that was left was the plywood and a few small pieces of tile that still clung defiantly to it by whatever adhesive had been used at the time of fixing.

Mike drummed his fist down onto the ply, a deep hollow sound echoed up. "It's a door," he said triumphantly. "It's a fucking door!" He felt with his hands along the threshold and wall, there was a gap there, but it was small and there was no handle from which to lift it, meaning it likely had a one-way latch. "Knife," he called to June who was at the entrance to the door, watching them both work. "I need a strong knife, something to prise it up with."

"Right-o," said June and he watched over his shoulder as she busied herself at the draws, sliding them open one after the other, not bothering to close them before moving to the next. On the fifth draw, she found what she was after. "Will this do?" she asked, holding up a lethal looking carving knife. The blade was sharp, but more importantly, the steel of the blade was thick and a good eight or nine inches long.

"One way to find out," he said. He ushered Tara out of the cupboard and backed out himself. Mike took the knife from June and dropped back to his knees, his clean trousers were already filthy and covered in dust, his hands were white, and he guessed his face was, too. Tara was no better; her jeans were dusty as was her hair and dirt smeared her face.

Knelt at the entrance to the utility cupboard, Mike wedged the point of the knife into the thin gap at the threshold. "The griddle?" he said, looking behind him. He wanted a lump hammer or a mallet but in situations like this, you had to make do. June bent down and passed it to him. Mike spun it in his hand, so the flat bottom of the pan was pointing toward the handle of the knife. He hammered at it a few times, wedging it further into the gap. Once the blade was a good six inches in, he dropped the griddle and applied his weight in a downward motion to the handle. There was a moment of resistance and a point where Mike thought that the blade was going to snap, but it held and finally with a splintering cracking sound the trap door came loose and sprang up. Mike let go of the knife and got his hands under the plywood. The knife slipped through the gap and he heard it clattering downward, the steel blade striking on stone as it fell.

"Fuck," Tara said in no more than a whisper as Mike held the door in his hands. It was open just a few inches and he paused that way for a split second, both wanting and not wanting to know what was beneath.

Mike took a steadying breath and lifted the hatch slowly. The ply was thick, someone, whoever had done this alteration after the Reeds had signed off on the place, or had the kitchen fitted, had stuck two sheets of inch thick ply together, ensuring that once tiled over the floor sounded and felt as solid as the rest of the kitchen. As it opened, he peered in, half expecting an attack from below and once again wishing he had the gun.

Below the hatch was an ancient, steep stone spiral stairway that dropped God knows how far into the ground. Mike squinted down, the bottom had to be a good eighty to a hundred feet below them, and down there he could just see the faintest traces of orange light and some kind of passage.

CHAPTER 50

THERE WAS LIGHT WHEN ELLIE AWOKE. IT WAS NO
more than gloom, but the gloom was better than the
darkness to which she'd become so accustomed. She
could see the timber lined roof of her cell, and as she
rolled onto her side, she felt a protest of pain on her
neck. The compacted dirt floor was still littered with
its drained and crumpled bottles of water that they'd
brought to her, the empty packets of sandwiches, far
too few in number to have fully quelled her hunger, but
just enough to keep her from starvation.

Not only was her room dimly lit, but she felt clean,
she could smell shampoo in her hair and shower gel on
her skin, and that was when she noticed her clothing.
Gone was the filthy Ramones T-shirt and three-quarter
length leggings. Now she wore a white robe, the fabric
of which felt silky on her skin. It began at her shoulders
in two straps about an inch and a half thick that joined
the material of the garment at the chest. It had no
arms, making it more like an old-fashioned nightie than
anything. It ran the length of her body ending around
her ankles in a band of intricately woven lace. With
dawning abhorrence, Ellie knew she'd seen this nightie,
dress, robe – or whatever it was before. Every girl she'd
been passenger to had worn one identical to this, which
meant one thing, tonight she'd be on the altar again,

only this time she wouldn't be passenger to the girl, she'd be the girl. She'd feel the blade of that golden dagger as it plunged into her stomach, she'd feel it slice up through her body to her sternum, just as she'd seen happen to the poor guy the night before. The guy whom right at the moment of his death, she'd realised was Scott Hampton, tech manager for the Unexplained UK Team. What the hell he'd been doing there she still hadn't figured out. A small part of her wasn't entirely sure that she hadn't dreamt the whole thing. It seemed real to her, and yet also very unreal. His muffled screams, the sound of his shirt buttons tinkling off the stone as they'd torn his top off. And – oh Christ – the way the face of the woman who'd kicked the cheap plastic ball around Lucinda and Seth Horner's garden with Henry had changed. Morphed and changed, that had been just before the shadows.

It had been real, of that she became surer the more she remembered it, and tonight it would be her, with Henry on the neighbouring altar, and through her death, she knew that the Dark Man would take him, and what made Henry, Henry would be gone.

Ellie propped herself up, feeling violated at having been undressed and washed by God knows who, and that somehow once again they'd moved her without her knowing, sent her to sleep with all the ease of an anaesthetist. That was when she noticed the door. It was the source of the light in her room, and it was open. Ellie stayed that way, propped on her elbows for long seconds, listening, waiting for them to come for her, no sound befalling her ears but that of her own heart beating fast in her chest.

How long she lay propped up like that she did not know, a minute, two, maybe ten but when no one did come for her she struggled to her little-used feet and gingerly picked her way across the floor, movement becoming easier with each step. At the door, she looked around the frame, outside was the same long passage down which Seth Horner had taken her days before, down which Lucinda and the lady with the blonde hair whose name began with S, and could have been Sasha, or Sara, had taken her. This time it was empty.

Somewhere, exactly where she did not know, she could hear banging, crashing, like someone was trying to break something down. The sound was faint, but it was there, coming from above and further down the passage to her left, the way they'd taken her when she'd been led to The Chapel. Ellie counted the blows, one, two, three, then four. They got faster, more frantic and she felt sure that soon whatever it was that was trying to break through would, and then it would be upon her, and when it came, when it got her she would be taken to The Chapel, strapped to the stone and then she'd feel the knife.

"Henry," she whispered to herself. She turned from the direction of the noise and looked down the passage-way, it stretched as far as she could see, dimly lit with the guttering flames of countless oil lamps. Ellie got moving again, out of her cell now, and toward the one where Henry was held. His door was open, and save for Henry, who still slept peacefully atop the bed, it was empty. The sight of him choked tears to her eyes. His angelic face pale and innocent in sleep, and just how peaceful he looked and the fact that they wanted to take that away, replace his shining light with something so dark enraged her.

His clothing had been changed, too. Now he wore black trousers, a white shirt and his light blonde hair had been combed back off his face, giving him the ap-pearance of a page boy. And if not a page boy then a child dressed for the casket, put in his best clothes be-fore being cast into the ground years before he should have been returned to the earth.

Ellie entered the room, reached the bed and touched her hand to his face. His skin was warm and smooth to the touch, his chest rose and fell shallowly, and she recalled how at first when she'd been here with him days before she'd thought him dead. Ellie looked for the cannular, the one that had fed saline solution into his veins, hydrating him in his induced coma-like sleep. It had been removed, and now the back of his left hand was dressed carefully with a plaster. The cannula itself was still attached to the drip. it hung by his bed, a bulbous drop of blood pooling on the end. Whoever had removed it had done so not long before her arrival, the discovery made her halt and with breath caught in her throat she looked behind her, sure that someone would be there, but the room behind her was empty.

"Hen," she said, dropping the guard rail on his bed and shaking him. "Hen, wake up!" her voice was no more than an urgent whisper but in the silence of the cell, it felt to her as if she'd shouted it out at the top of her voice. "Hen, it's Ells, time to get moving kiddo, wakey, wakey." But he did not stir, his eyelids didn't even flutter in recognition of her voice. Seth Horner had claimed he'd been under a sleep spell, she didn't know if that were true or just some metaphor for whatever medication they had him drugged with. Whatever the truth Ellie knew that if she was going to get him out of this place, she'd have to carry him. Ellie had carried her brother many times, often following after-school trips to the park where he'd declare his legs were too tired to walk, and being the soft touch that she always was with him she'd collect him up, his school bag on one shoulder and him on her hip with a hand under his bum for support. But then she'd been fed, she'd been hydrated and not confined to a darkened cell for the best part of a week.

Knowing she had no other choice she slid one arm under his legs and one under his upper back, gripping him with her hand under his right armpit. Then hastily and feeling like at any moment she'd be discovered, she lifted him clear of the bed. He was small for his age, his clothing, most of it handed down from his cousin, was still a year younger than his age, yet in her dehydrated and malnourished state he weighed more like a boy of ten.

Out in the corridor, the distant banging continued, the blows coming in faster succession. The noise of it, the not knowing what it was scared her, so Ellie turned right and kept going. Adrenaline and hope now along for the ride, Henry began to feel lighter and she managed to set a pace that was more like a gentle jog.

How long she traversed that passage for she did not know. Occasionally she'd reach a door, one identical to that of her cell, and each time she passed one she felt sure that someone would spring from it, yet no one did. Finally, the passage kinked to the right, and as it did she noticed a spiral stone stairway, the kind you'd see in old castles. It led up, how far she could not tell but stood at the foot of it she felt as if she were at the bottom of a deep well. Ellie paused for breath allowing the wall to take her weight and that of her brother.

"Hen," she whispered again, looking down into his unconscious face. "Please wake up, I'm not sure I can carry you much longer." But she knew that she would, she knew that she'd carry him until she collapsed from exertion if she had to, until her legs gave out and she could walk no more.

Her arms burned with lactic acid, she'd not be able to burden his weight and climb the steps with him cradled as he had been, so she lifted him up, until he was slumped over her shoulder in a fireman's lift, then with one hand steadying herself against the wall she began to climb.

Legs like jelly, lungs on fire and with her back both aching and running with perspiration and after what felt like an eternity, Ellie finally reached the top. What awaited her was a closed hatch. It was set no more than four feet above the top step, which was three or four times the size of the others, creating a landing type platform. Crouched awkwardly she slid Henry off her shoulder and sat him against the concave stone wall.

"A little help here, kiddo," she panted, allowing herself a moment's rest. She placed her hands on the underside of the wooden panel above, then with her leg holding her brother in place pressed an ear to it and listened. Nothing. Ellie both wanted to try it and didn't, for if the hatch was locked she'd be faced with the climb down, and she wasn't sure she could make it without falling, and if she fell then so would Henry and she'd be powerless to stop him tumbling all the way to the bottom, and such a fall would undoubtedly kill him. Knowing there was no other option than onward she summoned what strength she had and pushed.

She'd expected it to be locked, expected to be met with resistance, yet the hatch sprung open with ease, it flew back and crashed to the ground on the other side, showering her in dirt and dust, enough to suggest that it had been hidden from view in the room, or whatever it was above. Ellie coughed and spluttered, shook the dirt from her freshly washed hair and gingerly poked her head through, her right leg still holding her sleeping brother in place below.

The room was dark, it smelt of grass, of dirt and of oil and fertiliser, and although there was no light by which to see she knew it must be some kind of shed or barn. Her grandfather's large double shed had smelt just like this, and it summoned within her childhood memories of being with him in the garden whilst her gran prepared a Sunday roast. She had no idea whose shed or barn this was, yet she knew that going on was more favourable than going back, and whilst she was moving, whilst she was free, she had a chance.

Ellie dropped back into the stairway and with renewed energy, she lifted Henry up under his shoulders and with her face grimaced in effort she managed to lift him through the hatch and climb out herself, before swinging it shut.

For long moments she just lay there on the ground in the darkness beside her brother, her chest heaving, her bare feet throbbing and her heart hammering like a drum in her chest. Sweat ran off her face, down her back and caked the silk fabric of her ceremonial robe to her tired body, losing precious liquid that she couldn't spare. She reached out a hand, found Henry's and clasped it tightly, just enjoying the contact for a second. Outside, lightning flashed, briefly igniting the barn through dust-covered windows. The brightness stung her eyes and as the following thunder split the silence, she sat bolt upright. *I need to move,* she thought to herself, but her limbs ached, and she didn't need to be able to see her hand to know it shook as she held it before her. *Just a little further, Ells. Just a little further.* Lightning came again, this time she used it to get her bearings, the main doors to the barn were directly in front of her, the passage to them was clear, save for a large ride-on mower parked just off to the right. Driven now by the thought that she might get out of this, might be able to save her brother, and in doing so save herself she managed to stand and lift him once more over her shoulder. Ellie staggered forward in the darkness, with her right hand outstretched she found the mower, leaning on it for support as she passed it by. As she neared where she thought the door was more lightning flashed and in that split second of light, she thought she saw someone by the doors. She paused, waited for the attack, another flash came, she found the figure and almost laughed at herself. It was no more than a long wax jacket hung over a stack of old patio chairs. As thunder boomed overhead, shaking the barn's roof timbers her hands found the door handle, she turned it again expecting to be locked. It wasn't. It swung open on rusty hinges and Ellie felt the warm, muggy breeze of the outside world wash over her face.

CHAPTER 51

STILL BUZZING FROM THE DISCOVERY OF THE HIDDEN trap door, Mike reached the lobby. The air had cleared and no longer smelt of the discharged round that had mashed the side of his leg. Surveying the room, he breathed two sighs of relief. The first was at the sight of Jason's body still laid out at the base of the oak sideboard, a very small part of him had half expected this place to reanimate him, bring him back as some unkillable zombie hell-bent on retribution. Luckily it hadn't, and that kind of thing at least remained a thing of fiction and Hollywood movies. Secondly, was the Beretta Semi-automatic three-round shotgun and ammo bag. It was still on top of the sideboard by which Jason lay.

Mike found his Timberlands, they were still right by where June had treated the wound, the tan nubuck of the left was spotted in blood. He slipped them on, laced them tightly and then collected the gun up before checking the chamber was full, which it was but a lot had happened since he'd loaded the weapon and he wanted to be sure. Happy with the gun he shouldered the kit bag and turned to Tara.

"If this is where you tell me that I'm not going with you then forget about it," she said sternly.

"I'd tell you if I thought it would do any good," Mike replied. He leant forward and kissed her on the forehead, it was smeared with dust and dirt from breaking the floor in the utility cupboard. "June, I'm hoping you have more sense, you don't need to be here."

"That's very presumptuous, Mike. This is my area of expertise and I think you might find that when the time comes you will need me more than you know."

"Okay," Mike said with frustration and knowing there was no point in fighting it. "We only have one gun, and we can be thankful to Jason for that. If you both insist on coming, then grab what you can as a weapon and stay behind me."

Back in the kitchen, Tara searched the draws and found another carving knife, similar to the one which Mike had used to jimmy the hatch door with. She tried to pass a slightly smaller blade to June, but she refused. "I have no need for one of those, my dear," she said.

"If you're coming down there you go armed," Mike reinforced.

"I have all I need right here," she came back confidently. From below her black, short sleeve top, she produced a large pewter pendant. In the centre was what looked like a three-bladed propeller and at its centre a six-pointed star. In the three sections separated by the propeller-like symbol were ancient hieroglyphs, more decorated the pendant's outer rim. She reached back under the shirt and produced on a second necklace; a small bottle of liquid held in a jewel-encrusted bottle. "When the time comes this will prove far more useful than your shotgun," she said with certainty.

"Is that holy water?" Mike asked.

June regarded him seriously and said, "This is not a Christian ritual, Mike. What we are fighting here is older than the Devil, older than any religion. The pendant contains an ancient spell for the banishing of evil spirits, the symbol denotes the spell. The bottle contains a potion for the casting out and banishing of witches and demons."

"Eye of newt, tongue of frog," he smiled.

"Blessed water, ragged robin, dragon root, St John's wort, mustard seed, mandrake root, and henbane, if you must know."

Tara lifted the bottle from where it hung on June's neck and looked at the content with interest, "Does it work?" she asked.

"Supposedly if it touches the skin or clothing of a true witch who practices in the dark arts she will burn and be vanquished," June replied. "Cast a protection spell with it upon a person and the witch will not be able to glamour or harm them. As for if it works, I don't know. I have never faced evil such as this."

"I've seen enough to test my beliefs over the last few days so I'm not mocking anything," Mike said flatly. "Do you know how to cast such a spell?"

"Happens I do," June smiled. "But I thought you'd think it all nonsense."

"I was just attacked by a sixty-eight-year-old woman who looked forty then turned into a teenager who's been missing for the last forty-eight years. If you're telling me that might work, then I'm on board. We can use all the help we can get."

June nodded, then without speaking she unclipped the bottle from the neck cord and wetted her finger with it. She stepped forward and on Mike's forehead he felt her draw the same propeller-like symbol onto his skin, as she drew she murmured under her breath, "Nos defendat, ut intra in tenebras, et non faciem mortem, defendat. Immundorum ut eicerent eos igni tueatur."

"What does it mean?" Mike asked, astounded at the natural beauty and silkiness of the Latin as it rolled off her tongue.

June smiled and placed her hand on his arm, "It's one of my own spells," she said. "It basically casts protection over those going up against evil. It just sounds better in Latin." She winked playfully and turned to

Tara who stepped forward, then repeated the process before carrying it out on herself.

Tara looked at her questioningly and said, "When we saw you in Boscastle you said that you weren't a witch?"

"We don't exactly advertise ourselves," June replied. "Especially not to strangers. Much like the poor Jewish people, history has not been kind to us. And be under no illusion I have no powers compared to what we might come up against tonight, below this place." She turned her attention to the open hatch and added, "Who wants to go first?"

The stairs down were steep, the stone of each step worn from years of use, and Mike found it hard going on his leg which continued to beat a steady rhythm of pain. By the time they reached the bottom his brow was wet with perspiration, perspiration born from both pain and heat. Down below the building and in the earth, it was cooler still, and he leaned against the side of the passageway, resting the stock of the gun on his foot whilst enjoying the feel of the chill on his brow.

"It's like a mine shaft," Tara commented reaching the bottom, and she was right. It stretched off to the right as far as he could see, the same to the left and a cool breeze trickled its way through the air. Oil lamps lined the wall on both sides, their flames all dancing to a different tune.

"It must run under the entire village," June said in amazement. "It appears The Old Chapel is not the only thing to have both an above and below, Trellen itself symbolises it."

"All this time they were looking for those kids and they were right under their feet," Mike noted shaking his head. "Let's find them and get out of here." The first door he came across was just to the right of the stairs, it was large, made of oak and similar to the front door of The old Chapel. It had an old heavy looking slide bolt which was in place, he slid it back and pushed the door open, his gun at the ready.

"Dear God," Tara said as she followed him in, "this must be where - "

"Here is your Chapel, Mr. Cross," June said cutting her off and not bothering to correct herself to his first name this time. The room was easily the size of the entire building over which it sat. The upper tier on which they now stood ran around the perimeter, then a circular amphitheatre dropped down a good ten to fifteen feet in rings of pews giving the room the appearance of a circle within a rectangle. At the centre of the room were two stone altars, one clean and one soaked in dry blood, much of that blood looked fresher and had no doubt been spilt in the last day. Mike wondered with fear and disgust if it was Scotty's. The thought that he might have met his end here at the hands of those monsters enraged him and he felt his grip tighten on the stock of the sawn-off. The walls around the ceremony room were lined in rich tapestry art, each depicting a different symbol, the likes of which he'd never seen. In between each piece of evil art that had to be a good fifteen feet tall, hung larger oil lamps. They were all lit and cast a deep orange light across the room and darkled the beamed ceiling to shadow.

"Do these mean anything to you?" he asked June.

"They symbolise the darkness and sacrifice," she said, her eyes scanning one to the next. "Some I have never seen before." She clutched her hands to her head and for a moment Mike thought she might pass out. "So many," she said in dismay. "So many have suffered here, I can hear their cries, feel their pain." June's eyes brimmed with tears. "He keeps them here," she said. "Those poor babies, they are so afraid of him, they cry when he is close, they scream and his spirit drinks it in, it makes him strong." She moved her hands from her head and her right clutched at the amulet and bottle of potion. "Finding the Harrison kids is not enough, Mike. We need to put an end to this place."

Mike nodded, he knew what she said was true. There was no way they could just leave this place, for if they did then it would only be a matter of time before more innocents were taken. "If you want," he said to her placing a hand on her arm, "I will take you back up."

"No," June said, shrugging him off with defiance. "You'll do no such thing. We see this thing through together."

"This doesn't feel right," Tara said uneasily looking around with wide eyes. "Where is everyone?"

"They are close by," June said. "I can feel their energy, their darkness. I believe that this ritual is not just about the sacrifice. I get the feeling there is another part to it in play, but soon enough it will find its way to this room where it will culminate in the sacrifice of that poor girl, and the becoming of her brother."

Mike ducked out into the passage, checked left and right but saw no one. "There are more doors down there," he said pointing left. "We search them all, those kids have got to be down here somewhere." Gun pointing out in front of him he led the way, his finger on the trigger and almost hoping he'd be given the chance to pull it.

The first door he came across was partly open. It was smaller than the one to the ceremony room, more of a traditional size, yet arched at the top. He kicked it open with his good leg, the door swung wide and bounced back on its hinge as he went in, the sawn-off barrel leading the way.

The room stank and the smell hit his throat almost triggering his gag reflex. Littered about the floor were crumpled drinks bottles and empty packs of pre-made Tesco sandwiches. The far corner of the small room was the source of the smell, it had been used as a toilet, but not even a hole had been dug and faeces lay scattered about on wet soil that he knew had been made that way by piss, like some human-sized cat litter tray. He held his breath and edged into the room, then started to breathe shallowly, letting his sense of smell adjust to the place just as he used to when he'd been a cop and attended the scene of a body that had lain undiscovered for a week or more. June and Tara followed behind, hands over their mouths and noses, trying to filter out the stench. Mike spotted a grubby red T-shirt abandoned on the floor at the head of a small, dirty mattress that made up the only piece of furniture.

"She was wearing a red Ramones top when she went missing, am I right?" he asked, turning to Tara and holding it up.

"That's hers," Tara said.

Mike crouched down beside the mattress on the floor, he ran a hand over it, the centre was still depressed from where a body had lain upon it and the faintest hint of body heat was still on the fabric. "She was here, not long ago, either," he said in frustration.

"Mike," Tara said urgently from the door. "Mike, I think someone is coming." She moved June back out of the door, Mike crossed the room in a few strides and took up the other side of the jamb.

"She was going to take care of them," Mike heard a voice say. It was a ways off and came to them in an echo that bounced its way down the passage.

"We should have taken and killed them all last night when we had the chance," another male voice replied. They were closer now, and he could hear their feet on the tightly packed dirt of the passage floor.

"Too risky," the original voice said, and now Mike recognised it as that of Seth Horner's. *"Lucinda was confident that she could glamour Cross into doing the rest of the job for us."*

Mike knew they were talking about what had happened in the bedroom, how she'd been in his head and how he'd been so close to letting her all the way in, and the thought of what she might have had him do if he'd let that happen, made him shudder. He glanced around the jamb, the three figures were dressed in identical black ceremonial robes, male versions of the one that Lucinda had worn. Each one had a white mask, held in the hand and not worn. One of the three was indeed Seth Horner, the other two Mike had never seen. One was shorter, fatter with a round redden face, like that of a boiled sweet, and a piggy nose. He was maybe fifty, fifty-five years old, his greying hair had thinned to bald on top. The other was younger, tall with dark hair and handsome features, no older than thirty, and Mike wondered if this guy was a hopeful, a prospect for the future, hoping to cut the mustard and make it to be the husband of some future incarnation of one of the witches here.

Mike readied the gun, he knew what he had to do, it differed from what he wanted to do, and that was to pop out into the passageway and unload all three rounds into them one at a time. Sadly, no matter how much he wanted to, it was not an option. The report from each shot fired would be deafening down here and would bounce off the walls of the passage and travel for God knows how far, thus alerting Christ knows who. At the moment the element of surprise was on their side and he meant to ride it as long as he could.

Both June and Tara looked at him expectantly, Tara with the knife clenched firmly in the right hand, the orange of her nail varnish chipped and cracked from where she'd helped him clear the broken tiles from the floor. He raised a finger to his lips as one of the males said, *"She likely got carried away with them, whatever is happening up there best be good, we will miss the start at this rate. Mind you, if she's not finished with them and that blonde bitch is still alive, I wouldn't mind having some fun with her, she's so hot she is practically on fire!"*

Mike took his eyes from the opening and looked at Tara, her face was creased in disgust at his statement and he hoped that she'd be able to keep a lid on her temper long enough for this to play out as he needed it to. She sensed him looking and as he caught her eyes he shook his head and mouthed a silent, "NO!"

Mike waited, pensive and ready, the echoes in the passage belying their true distance from him. As soon as he felt certain they'd reached the right side of the door he rounded the frame and raised the gun. He'd judged it almost right; they were still a good fifteen feet back but close enough that if he needed to discharge a round the narrowness of the passage would ensure one of them would take a hit. "If it's Lucinda you're going looking for," he said firmly, "then she is up in the master bedroom under a sheet, dead. Only she isn't Lucinda anymore, how's that for fucked up?" All three faces were locked onto him, they wore a look of sheer surprise, to begin with, but as Mike spoke, they twisted in anger and hate.

"Do you have any idea what you've done?" Seth Horner spat, foam forming on his lips, he balled his fists but let them relax a little when he saw Mike's finger twitch on the trigger.

Mike nodded coldly, "Ended the torment of a girl taken over forty years ago," he answered sweeping the deadly eye of the gun between the three of them, back and forth, back and forth, as if willing one of them to test him. "Where are Henry and Ellie Harrison?" he asked seriously. "Tell me and maybe I won't shoot you all where you stand."

The chubby-faced guy chuckled defiantly and said, "It's too late, the night has begun and there are too few of you to stop it. Kill us if that's what you want but you can't stop it."

Mike wanted to shoot him, he didn't need the voices in his head to want it, either. This was him and no one was along for the ride. Instead, he strode forward and closed the gap between them, all three started to back off but he was too fast. Reaching his target, he whipped the butt of the gun around and slammed it into his piggy nose. The guy cried out in both pain and surprise, staggered back and fell to the floor as blood gushed down over his chin. "In," Mike said to the other two, gesturing into the room with the shortened muzzle of the gun. "Any more shit and I'll just shoot one of you and to hell with the consequences."

Piggy nose, now piggy broken nose picked himself up off the floor with the help of Seth Horner and one by one they filed into the cell, further surprise dawning on their faces as they saw June and Tara stood by the grubby mattress. "Is this where you held them?" Mike asked, his voice full of anger. None of the three spoke so Mike slammed the butt of the gun into Seth Horner's kneecap causing him to drop to the floor. "I said is this where you held them?"

"You'd best answer," Tara said coldly, the knife looking purposeful in her hand. "If he doesn't shoot you, I'll gladly cut your dicks off and make you eat them. If I can find them that is."

"The girl," Seth Horner said, his voice creased with pain. "Just Ellie."

"And the boy?" Mike asked.

"A room down the passage," the young guy said. "He's been kept sedated, so he knows nothing about it."

"You're all heart," Mike scoffed. "Where are they now?"

Seth Horner, his hands clasping his smashed knee looked to the ceiling, "Up top," he grimaced.

"What do you mean, up top?"

"In the woods," he replied. "They're in the woods."

"What are they doing in the woods, Seth?"

"Every becoming starts that way," he said. "They make them think they've escaped, gotten away, but then the village brings them back. It's the final test."

Mike thought of Ellie and Henry up there now, in that storm. Lost in the woods full of false hope that they'd escaped and Ellie likely comforting her brother, telling him it was all okay and he'd soon see his mummy and daddy again, and not be afraid. As he thought about it his anger and disgust threatened to boil over. "And is that where everyone is now? Save for you three, up there enjoying the game?"

Piggy broken nose guy laughed, it rattled from all the blood in his throat making it sound as sinister as he'd likely intended. "You don't understand," he said.

"No," Mike said with disgust. "I understand. I understand that this sect has been taking young girls for hundreds of years, raping and beating them, making them bear children who are then sacrificed so that the mother can become. I understand that you men are no more than sick freaks who choose to live your lives in service to the fucked-up evil that allows it. Now give me your robes, all three of you."

"Go fuck yourself," the younger guy shouted and spat a wad of phlegm at Mike's feet. Mike was too far gone to negotiate, his anger, hate and want to end them too much. Without talking he swung the Beretta at his face, stepped forward and pulled the trigger. At close range, the shot disintegrated the right side of his face, from the eye socket to the back of his head just vaporised in a mist of red that sprayed out over rough cut stone wall behind. The report from the gun was loud, and both June and Tara yelped in surprise as it went off. "Anyone else going to argue?" Mike said, swinging the still smoking barrel between the remaining two men.

CHAPTER 52

ELLIE HARRISON, WITH HER COMATOSE LITTLE brother over her right shoulder and every muscle in her weakened body crying out in protest, cleared the barn. She looked back as lightning scorched the sky with a horizontal fork of white-hot electricity. Now outside knew the building which she'd just left, it was the Horner's place, and she'd been in their barn, the one screened from view at the bottom of their large garden, the one the forest had seemingly been intent on reclaiming for its own.

Only a week ago she'd been in this very garden, laughing and joking with both Seth and Lucinda, laughing and chatting with the other villagers, villagers who all along had plans for her and her brother, who in a way had been doing no more than grooming them for this very event.

Across that darkened sea of a lawn, lights glowed in a few of the windows, denoting where that chocolate box cottage stood, but Ellie had no desire to go there, she wanted to be as far away from it as possible, as far away from the entire village as she could get. Turning her back on both the barn and the cottage she found an opening in the trees, and then using the darkness as cover she slipped silently into the forest.

The going was hard, visibility literally zero and

every step pained her feet as sticks and brambles poked at her bare flesh. To make matters worse Henry seemed to grow heavier with every passing minute until it felt as if she had a fully-grown adult over her shoulder and not a five-year-old child. After a few minutes, and only when she was sure she was deep enough in and away from the house did she collapse to her knees and lay her brother down on the dried leaves of the forest floor.

"Hen," she shouted in his ear, whilst shaking her brother's body. "Come on Hen, please snap out of it!" But he remained comatose, only the tickle of his breath on her cheek when she placed it by his mouth told her he was alive. Lightning strobed, thunder rumbled, and a warm breeze blew through the trees, igniting them in a thousand voices that called to her, "*Elllieeee,*" they whispered as they rustled, and suddenly she was transported back to the vision in her dream. "*Where are you, Elllii-ieeee?*" they mocked. "*Come back to usss Elllieee, come back to usss sooo that your brother can becomeee.*" Ellie looked at her hands, half expecting to see them filled now with a grizzling infant. They weren't. Her burden to carry through this nightmare wasn't a baby, it was a five-year-old, and she knew that every girl who'd been in the wood as she had, had ended up in that room, ended up hearing the cries of her new-born infant as the blade sliced its skin. Only she didn't have an infant, and this time the blade was intended for her.

"Leave us alone," she screamed into the night as if it were a living thing that she could scare away. She pulled Henry's still body into her arms and cradled his head in her lap. "Just leave us," she sobbed. But she knew they wouldn't, this was a cruel game of cat and mouse, and the village, it's people, and The Old Chapel all made the cat, she and Henry the mouse. Sitting still wasn't going to outrun it, so she rolled Henry from her lap and stood, her legs protested but she quelled the pain enough to bend down, then through the agony and driven by her will to survive, she hauled her brother back over her shoulder. Cruelly she made it no more than ten paces before her bare feet found the underside of a log hidden by both leaves and darkness. it pitched her forward, sending Henry crashing to the floor and her spilling over on top of him, yet still, he did not wake.

"*Ellieeee,*" the trees called again, and now she felt things crawling, many things, things that just now were leaves, only now they could move. They scurried over her hands, up the backs of her legs and through her hair. As if working with the nightmare three brilliant flashes of lightning made day of night, and for a second she saw that the forest floor was crawling and alive with bugs. They squirmed and scurried, their busy bodies and feelers clambering over one another, and over her brother who slept on oblivious.

"*Elllliieeee,*" the wind called. She got up frantically brushing the insects from her hair and arms. More lightning showed her the forest floor, but now and once again it was no more than dried, dead leaves, the bugs were gone, as were the ones scurrying over her flesh. She lifted Henry and staggered on, the voices on the wind taunting her as she went.

She turned north, knowing that Trellen ran in a line along its road from east to west and that eventually if she headed that way for long enough, she'd breach its limits and be free of it.

"*Ellieeeeee,*" the wind whispered, but it was fainter now, behind her and she allowed herself hope, and the further she pushed the less the voices came, and the less the voices came the more she hoped.

Finally, and after an untold time on pained and cut feet with the weight of her brother burdening her weak body, she broke free of the trees and collapsed onto the soft grass, sweat drenching her body and her lungs gasping for air.

"The Lord of Darkness brought you back to us," a female voice said. Ellie felt her stomach drop and reluctantly looked up to see the face of the woman who'd taken the life of Scott Hampton. She smiled at her, "Come, child," she added, holding a hand out for Ellie to take. She wanted to fight, wanted to strike out at her but she was spent. Instead, she rolled onto her back as they lifted Henry from the lawn.

"Hen," she croaked, reaching out a hand toward him, but the effort was futile, for a second later he was gone, back toward the barn they'd surfaced in and escaped from, what now seemed like hours ago.

Ellie felt hands lifting her tired body, they didn't make her stand, instead they carried her, one person on each arm and one on each leg. As they took her toward her death the sky split open in a white-hot flash of lightning so bright it made negatives of everything for a moment, it cleaved down from the heavens and split a tree behind the barn in two with a hail of sparks. The faceless crowd behind her gasped in shock as the tree began to burn and for a moment the hands which held her wavered and she felt their grip relinquish, but only for a second. As if the heavens themselves were crying out in protest at her taking, more lightning rained down into the woodland behind, sending flames and sparks jumping into the air that now reeked of ozone and discharged electricity.

"Get her below ground," she heard one of the voices say, and now the hands had her true again, carrying her into the barn. As they manhandled her back through the hatch from which she'd escaped the smell of smoke hit her nose and she knew that out there, behind the barn the forest was on fire.

CHAPTER 53

SETH HORNER'S INTELLIGENT BLUE EYES REGARDED Mike from behind his black-rimmed spectacles and in them, Mike saw fear and he liked it. Following the sudden and brutal execution of their younger friend both Seth and Mr. Broken Piggy Nose had both relinquished their ceremonial robes without further argument. Mike had handed both to June and Tara, then taken it upon himself to wear the one from the dead guy, because after all, he'd been the one to make a corpse out of him. Luckily the blast had distributed most of the brain matter, skull and other gunky crap over the wall, leaving little to soil the garment.

"You're supposed to be a scientist," Mike said to him. "I can't figure out how you got involved with all this?"

Seth, now sat in the lightweight black lounge style trousers and a nondescript black T-shirt which he'd had on beneath the robes, half chuckled and massaged the knee that Mike had whacked good and hard with the stock of the A400. He had managed to stand on it to de-robe and sadly Mike didn't think he'd broken bone. "Science and religion are more related than you can imagine," Seth said. "And I don't mean like cousins, they are more brother and sister. I'm not tanking Christianity, Buddhism, or any of that shit here, they are just ideas, but the basis for those ideas comes from a common source. Good and evil, black and white, the Ying and yang – the above and the below, call it what you want."

"And the work you do," Mike began, his voice clearly wearing disgust.

"You wouldn't understand the first thing about what I do," Seth Horner scorned. "We have learned how to open doorways between realities," he marvelled. "Began to understand how those realities influence our world, how our physical bodies tie us here, but in death, we become free and move off to other realms."

"Why choose this, why evil, tell me – I need to understand how you can justify what you do. How it didn't tear you apart to know that thing which masqueraded as your wife was no more than pure evil in the shell of a girl who was stolen from her family, who was robbed of her life!"

"The fact you need me to explain it means you will never understand," Seth answered coldly. "And the coven made her life far more meaningful than anything she would have ever accomplished." He paused, stretched the knee out, his face wincing before he continued. "The world is rotten, Mike Cross. You must feel it, chaos is taking over. Famine, war, chemical weapons, riots, people mowing others down on the streets in acts of terror, financial unrest, the list is endless. All the while the masses feed on the propaganda being fed to them on their TVs and in the papers. The revolution is coming, Mike. Darkness is coming. And when it does, when it spills out over the planet then it's best to be on the right side."

"Bullshit," Mike spat. "You are a part of it because you like it because it gives you free rein to do what you want. Well, guess what? That ends tonight."

Seth laughed as if he'd heard the funniest joke in the world, "This coven is eternal," he said. "It's existed undiscovered and pure for over three hundred and fifty years, and you think you and your two whores can come in here and stop us with a knife and a shotgun? You're delusional, whacko, fucking crazy." Spittle flew from his mouth as he spoke, and his face turned red with anger. "You're all going to die down here tonight," he continued with furious passion. "Just like your friend did yesterday. When they tear you apart later, which they will, they'll do it slow, nice and slow so you feel every ounce of pain, every cut and as you scream, just like your friend did as the High Priestess gutted him from stomach to sternum. You'll wish you never set foot in our village."

The mention of Scotty being disembowelled that way drew acidic bile into Mike's mouth and he drew the gun down on Seth Horner, letting the barrel sit point blank between his eyes.

"Mike," Tara said urgently from the door. "Don't!"

"Why the fuck not? You heard what he just said, how they killed Scotty."

"They're coming, the others. There's a group heading this way."

Mike glanced at Seth as a bead of sweat ran down his forehead and ran into his thickset eyebrows. Seth wiped it away calmly with the back of his hand as Mike lowered the gun. He glanced at the door and looked as if he wanted to open his mouth and call out. Mike couldn't fire for fear of being heard, but he could use the gun as an expensive and fancy club. "Your sick world ends tonight," he said, and with that, before Seth could call for help, he smashed the stock of the gun into the side of his temple, knocking him unconscious.

"W-wait," Broken Piggy Nose stammered, he held a hand out and tried to scoot back, but there was nowhere for him to go. Mike swung the butt of the sawn-off hard, it connected with the side of his head producing a satisfying *crack*, knocking him to the floor and Mike wondered if he hadn't killed him with the force of the blow.

"Masks on," Mike said to June and Tara. "File in behind, stay together and don't do anything until I make a move." They nodded in agreement, both sliding on their masks, all three becoming anonymous.

It was a risky move and Mike hoped that there was no magical number to the coven, for with Lucinda dead and the three in the cell the congregation would still be one person shy. He didn't have time to worry about it, it was a shit or bust situation and the fact they'd got this far was nothing short of a miracle. Whatever was going to go down would have to go down at some point and if they got as far as the ceremony room and they figured they were one short or did a roll call, or whatever the fuck they did, then the gun would come out and the game would be on.

Mike chanced a look around the frame, the group were about forty feet down the passage and coming their way. In the dim, dancing light of the lamps, he could see the robed figure at the front had a small child in their arms. They were too far off to see clearly, but Mike knew it was Henry Harrison. He looked dead, but then the words of the younger guy, who now only had half a face came back to him, '*We've kept him sedated,*' he'd said. Behind the boy were two more masked figures, they held a girl, one at each of her arms. She wasn't so much walking with them, more being dragged, her feet scooting along the dirt.

"Ellie," he whispered to himself, and just the sight of her alive filled him with hope. Behind were more masked figures, he could tell the women by the lower cut robes, but with his fleeting glances, he couldn't judge the ratio of them to the men. In all, he guessed there were fifteen to twenty, certainly no more than twenty-five. He had enough rounds to see them all dead, but the chamber only held three and if he unloaded them all he'd have to get the first shot back into the main chamber which was time-consuming. Firing two rounds meant he could just reload into the bottom of the receiver, a much quicker option.

The arms of the male version of the ceremonial robes were baggy, lots of room for movement and to dive your hand inside was easy. Mike adjusted the ammo bag, so it ran across his chest, he practised the motion of going for replacement shells and found it simple enough. Next, he lowered his right arm, the one holding the A400 into the garment and hid it from view. It wasn't ideal, but it wasn't bad, either. As they drew closer, he pushed the door to the cell closed until the light from the passage was no more than a thin lance penetrating the room. Further anger brewed in his gut knowing that Ellie Harrison had likely been subjected to this suffocating darkness for the week they'd had her, and it made him wonder what kind of psychological damage the girl would have suffered if they did manage to get her, her brother and themselves out of this place alive.

One by one the figures darkled that lance of light as the procession passed by. Mike waited, bode his time until he felt sure the last one had passed, then he slowly opened the door and slipped out behind the group with Tara and June right behind him.

They dropped in unnoticed, the group focused on the passage ahead. Despite the robe and the mask, Mike felt exposed, felt as if he wasn't wearing the robe nor the mask, and as if at any moment they'd all turn to face him, all those blank faces looking at him with a knowing that their porcelain frozen features could not fully express. And when they did, they'd fall upon the three of them and they'd be overpowered. The thought made his breath come heavily, the inside of the mask growing wetter each time he exhaled. *Get your shit together,* he told himself. *Get your shit together or this will be over before it's begun.*

They reached the door to The Chapel, and as the door opened the line of bodies halted briefly before they filed in. He followed the figure directly in front, down the steps and one by one they filled the lower circular pew, the one closest to the twin altars of stone which sat in the middle of the amphitheatre a good twenty feet in front of him. As Mike took his place, with Tara to his side and June to hers, the small body of Henry Harrison was lifted to the stone of the clean altar. He was dressed in black trousers, a white shirt, and black shoes. His clothing was dirtied, but as he lay there the stillness of his small body and the pallid complexion of his angelic face made him look more suited to a casket. *He looks dead,* Mike thought to himself, and through the narrow slits in the mask, he squinted trying to see the slightest rise and fall of the small boy's chest. Despite being on the lowest level, the one on which Henry now lay was still too far away to see such shallow movement.

His sister, dressed in a body length white nightgown-come-dress, also dirtied and torn, sobbed defeatedly as they lifted her to the blood-soaked one. She put up a futile struggle, but one of the masked figures who had her drove a fist into her stomach, making her double over in pain. At the sight of the assault, Mike felt his hand tighten on the gun once again and it was all he could do to stop himself whipping his hand out through the arm of the robe and shooting the bastard who had her. Broken, beaten and spent they forced her down onto the stone, bound her legs with a purple rope made of velvet to manacles of iron set deeply into the stone. Next, her arms were fixed the same way so they reached above her head, which was then fixed in place with a strap so she could do nothing but look at the ceiling. Ellie was closer to him, still a good twenty feet away but he could see her wide eyes darting left and right, trying to see what was going on but unable to move head. Trying not to look out of place he took in as much of the scene before him as he could. There were three of them, three against twenty or more and it began to dawn on him with cold reality what a suicide mission this was.

Ellie's mouth was gagged with a rag the same colour as the ropes, and beneath it, he could hear her, she was either sobbing or trying to beg, he couldn't make out which. He had seen such things in movies, read about them in books and seen re-enactments in documentaries, but the horror of the real thing was something that if he lived through this night, he knew he would never forget. It would stay with him forever and never be far from reach in his mind, stored in the same drawer as Claire and Megan's death. As the last of the restraints were fixed, the two who'd bound her filed into the pews beside June, and now only one remained. Stood at the foot of the altars, between brother and sister she removed her mask. The woman had a bob of black hair, she was older than Lucinda Horner, much older, maybe in her seventies, yet she looked physically fit and close to an imposing six feet tall. Her yellowish eyes seemed to dance in the glow of the oil lamps as they looked with a sickening glee at the two offerings laid before her. If Lucinda had looked no older than forty-five at sixty-eight Mike had no idea of this woman's age. He thought back to the images of the missing girls but couldn't place her. Whoever she was he had no doubt that in the absence of the Minister she held supremacy and was the High Priestess that Seth Horner had mentioned.

"Ten years ago," she began, her voice booming through the large room and her eyes now scanning the faceless congregation. "Our father was taken from us in physical form, cast from this world by fire, but as you know he who can dwell between worlds can never truly die."

"Numquam mori," the group chanted.

"Tonight, on this Grand Climax, he shall come back to us in the form of a child. Through this child, he shall be born into this world for a second time." The woman walked between the altars and now stood between the heads of Ellie and Henry. She reached down and when her hand came back up Mike saw she held a golden dagger. "Lord of the Abyss, we summon you here tonight, we summon you with the blood of the girl, with the life of the girl who is pure, who gives herself to you so that you might live through her brother. Come and be upon us now, be upon us in your dark glory, be upon us and may your darkness cover the world." At the foot of the twin altars, as she spoke the shadows began to pool, they swirled and slid, dropped from the roof and writhed in ecstasy, like black ethereal serpents. From those shadows was born the figure of a man. Not a solid man, more the idea of a man, for although he had shape and form, he had no substance. Mike readied the gun, his mind racing over how the hell he was going to stop this, how the hell he was going to take on the entire room of twenty odd with a three-round shotgun, a knife and a bottle of potion; the idea seemed absurd.

"Lord of Darkness," the woman said with feverish delight. "We give you this girl so that the brother might become."

"Esset facti," the crowd chanted.

As she raised the dagger, Mike began to raise the gun. He began to slide his hand through the arm of the robe, his finger taking up strain on the trigger. Then behind him, the door through which they'd come, burst open.

CHAPTER 54

"Cross," Seth Horner shouted as the door flew open. "He's among you, there's three of them!" A murmur swept around the faceless congregation that now turned toward Seth who was propped against the door. His face streaked with blood. His glasses were gone, and his right eye was swollen shut from where the stock of the Beretta had hit him.

"Masks," the High Priestess screamed from the centre of the amphitheatre, "get your masks off!"

Mike had the Beretta halfway down the long baggy sleeve of his robe when Seth had burst into the room. He glanced quickly from where he stood at the door to the High Priestess as she screamed for the masks to be removed. The golden dagger was in her hand a hand that was over Ellie's stomach and ready to begin the sacrifice. At the foot of the altar the shadows broiled angrily, they formed the shape of a man, one clad in ethereal robes, before twisting and churning like an angry sea as if they yearned to form fully but couldn't decide which form to take.

"Gun," Mike heard a male voice shout from the other side of the amphitheatre. Those filling pews on the opposite side of the room would have a clear view of it, the ones directly to his left not so much. He

twisted on the spot, confident that not all the congregation had made him, and many still hadn't, for they
began to move breaking the circle and helping him to
blend in. There were too many targets and not enough
rounds in the A400 to dispatch them all, he knew he
needed to create a diversion, something to draw their
attention away from the fact there were three outsiders
in their midst. Knowing the shot would give his position away to everyone, yet needing to act, he raised the
gun over the heads of the coven and shot at the oil
lamp on the opposite wall. The gun kicked back, but
again it was minimal thanks to the recoil diminisher
built into the stock. As the blast drowned out the room
the Beretta spat the spent cartridge from its side and
instantly reloaded the next round.

The shortened barrel spread the shot faster, making
the weapon less accurate, but enough of the shot
slammed into the large lamp nonetheless, shattering the
oil tank just below the collar. Flames and oil sprayed all
over the two tapestries either side, instantly igniting
them in a **WHHOOMMPPHHH**, that sent a cry of
surprise through the congregation who bristled back
from the flames, moving as if one animal.

Mike looked to Tara. Her mask was still on, as were
many others, the words of the High Priestess forgotten
in the confusion. Save for the knife which she held low
she blended in perfectly. Mike watched her move behind one of the congregation and bury the lethal steel
blade into the back of a robe-clad figure with stealthy
deadliness. All this, from the door opening to the
shooting of the oil lamp, had taken place in no more
than ten seconds. Mike knew that with the gun in his
hand he'd be the main target, and now the first of the
coven came for him, a female with long blonde hair that
spilt out around her mask and from the sides of her
hood. As she came at him, she tore the mask off and
Mike saw rage in her haunting grey eyes. The mask cast

aside she went for the gun, intending to grab the barrel and tug it from his grip, but Mike was faster. He raised the barrel up a few inches and pulled the trigger. The shot hit her at close range square in the neck. It tore through her throat and obliterated her spinal column, causing her unsupported head to drop to one side. She regarded him like that, a look of sheer surprise at her own mortality on her face, before she fell forward and face planted the floor, dead.

Mike needed room so he clambered back, up onto the next row of pews behind. The action made his injured leg shout in protest, but he ignored it. Another came at him, the figure, possibly a man; it was hard to tell in the melee, stumbled forward onto his knees as Mike moved back out of his way. As he fell Mike's hand was already inside the robe, he clutched two more cartridges and slammed them deftly into the loading point at the bottom of the A400's receiver. They were now around twenty seconds in, twenty seconds since Seth had burst into the room and prompted it all to turn to shit. Gun reloaded Mike aimed at the guy as he tried to stand and fired, the blast from the shot punched his body into the floor. To his side fire had engulfed both tapestries, the flames had eaten ravenously at the rich fabric and had already reached the top where they licked with hungry orange tongues at old dry wooden beams that supported the stone roof.

Below him he spotted Tara, she'd been made, her ruse was up and now two masked figures went for her, one grabbed her around the neck and pulled her to the floor where they fell upon her like rabid animals with a lust for blood. He aimed the gun but hesitated, the shot would spread too far from this distance and he'd risk it hitting her, too. He grabbed two more rounds, span and shot out another oil lamp, spitting flame over two more of the fifteen-foot tapestries, wanting the place to burn, wanting to make sure that if they failed and all died here tonight then so did as many of the coven as possible. With the fresh fire now spreading behind him, he went to Tara, loading the two fresh rounds as he dropped back to the lower pew.

Thirty seconds in now, the room was a cacophony of hellish noise, of shouts and the crackling of flame that seared at the skin of his exposed hands and heated the fabric of the robe to the point where it felt hot on the nape of his neck. The fact the room was underground with only one door in and out meant the heat was sealed in and the temperature was rising fast. The air was already become hot and noxious to breathe and Mike knew he'd underestimated a little how fast the fire would spread. He didn't know how long they'd have before the air became too hot and smoky, another minute, two at the absolute most, but that was okay, for by then this thing would likely be decided.

He reached the two figures on Tara and kicked one square in the side of the face with his blood splattered Timberland and groaned as the impact pained his injured leg. The force of the kick snapped the attacker's neck back and the momentum caused their body to roll off her and onto their back on the stone floor where he instantly shot them in the chest. The next round slammed into the chamber ready, thanks to the weapon's gas-powered reloading system it was there in under a second. Mike turned the gun on the second figure, a woman, she was on top of Tara, clawing at her face while Tara's hands reached blindly for the knife that had been knocked out of her hand and lay just an inch out of her reach. Mike jammed the barrel into her side so that her body would take the entire round and pulled the trigger. Her body jolted as if hit with a violent burst of electricity. The shot went straight through her slim figure, spraying blood as it exited via her back. The blast threw her off Tara and with a shrill scream of both pain and surprise she rolled onto her back, wide eyes staring at the ceiling. As she drew her last two breaths, that came in a wheeze of blood which bubbled at her lips, she grew younger until she was no more than a girl of fourteen or fifteen once more. Mike knew that despite the violent horror of what he'd done, he'd freed another soul from the turmoil of its possession.

JUNE KNEW what she needed to do, the moment Seth Horner burst into the room and Mike made his play. She used the confusion to move anonymously through the panicked congregation as they lost their circular form, her eyes fixed on the High Priestess as she screamed for the masks to come off, and the abomination of shadow that had no rightful place in this world. As pandemonium broke out in the crowd, and the sound of Mike's gun filled the air, the High Priestess stood in the centre of the amphitheatre, guarding the restrained body of Ellie Harrison and that of her sleeping brother with defiance and almost in total oblivion to the fire that burned behind her. She saw June coming and she raised the golden blade in warning, sensing she was an adversary. Flames danced up the walls behind her making the blade shimmer as if it were no more than golden liquid held in place by some magical spell. As June reached her, she cast aside her mask not needing its anonymity, just needing to get the job done. Glad to be free of it, she reached her hand inside her robes and pulled out both the bottle and amulet, tugging the vessel of liquid free as she went.

"Projiciam vos a facie mea es, mitte te tenebrae est, de quo egressus es," she said with calm certainty as she doused it over the robes of the High Priestess, (which roughly translated to), "*I cast you out to the darkness from whence you came.*" The moment the potion hit her robes they began to smoulder, the High Priestess let out a scream and launched herself at June, the dagger raised high. June moved to the left; the Priestess' robes had already turned from their initial smoulder to fire that began to engulf her with an equal hunger to that which ate at the tapestried walls. The dagger flashed down as she stumbled forward and sliced June across the top of her arm. Pain flared, stronger than that which any normal dagger or knife could summon, for this was no ordinary dagger. It had taken many lives, the metal, although no doubt priceless though age and gold content was cursed, and June felt her blood become tainted by it. Screaming she fell painfully to her knees and clutching the wound she dropped the bottle to the floor. Beside her, the High Priestess writhed and shrieked in her robe of flames until they overcame her, and she lay still and burning at the foot of the altar which held Ellie. The flames licked dangerously at the base of the stone, creeping and flicking higher as if having tasted flesh, they now sensed more and were eager to devour it. They quested up, further and further until they were close to the silk of Ellie's gown. June, now on the deck too and clutching her bloodied arm shifted her weight onto her backside, her arthritic joints crying in pain as bone ground on bone. Ignoring the searing heat, she kicked out with stiff legs, thrusting her feet momentarily into the blaze. With one strong effort she moved the flaming body away and clear. Frantically her eyes now sought the man of shadow, the one who had been Device. Somewhere in the room, someone was shouting for Mike to drop the gun, the coven had grouped together and now stood one side of the circle, Mike and Tara on the other. June caught Mike's eyes, he was about to shout something to her, but a terrible sound drowned it out, it was the sound of something breaking and giving way.

———

MIKE LIFTED Tara to her feet, reached below the robes and took a fist full of cartridges from the ammo bag. His hands shook with adrenaline and he dropped two to the floor before he managed to load two more into the A400's receiver. The congregation had become one mass now, they'd backed off as if deciding there was safety in numbers, and for a few long seconds a standoff ensued. Mike and Tara on one side of the room, the remaining members of the coven on the other, the twin altars between them.

"Drop the gun," a voice demanded from the group. "Drop it and we will end you both quickly, disobey and we will overpower you."

They were still too many in number and Mike knew that if he didn't obey, if he kept the gun and they did rush him then he'd be forced to fire all three shots, if he was lucky he'd kill one of the coven with each, but he'd then have no time to reload and the gun would be reduced to no more than a fancy club, and that eventually they'd lose.

On the floor in the centre of the room and at the foot of the nearest altar was June, her robe had been sliced open on the left upper arm and blood flowed from the wound beneath and dripped steadily to the floor. He caught her eyes and was about to call out to her, tell her to get to his side of the room but before he could speak one of the gigantic tapestries broke free from its mounting. The fire had eaten away the thick rope which secured it to its anchors in the stone wall. The remainder of the congregation stood below it. Mike saw what was about to happen at the same time as the group did.

Sensing their imminent doom, the remainder of the coven drove forward, as they did Mike aimed at the fifteen or so remaining bodies and discharged two rounds, leaving no more than a second between each shot. Two spent cartridges flew from the gun and three more went down before the second cartridge hit the floor. In the final second the group halted, caught between the gun and the flame, but it was too late, the tapestry dropped with a beautiful yet deadly display of dancing flames onto them burying them all under a sheet of fire, which simultaneously set the wooden pews ablaze.

———

TARA WATCHED as fire engulfed the group, and as the blaze drank them in, the screams of those beneath began. From the edge of the downed tapestry, one of the group managed to break free. The burning figure ran like a flaming dervish toward them, she couldn't tell if they were male or female, but they made it no more than ten steps before the flames overcame them and they fell to the floor, twitching and writhing.

"Ellie and Henry," Mike shouted, snapping her out of the moment's transfixion on the scene of horror.

They rushed forward together, the heat inside the room was suffocating, it mixed with smoke that stung her throat, burned her lungs and made her head spin. Mike struggled forward beside her, his limp now more pronounced and she could read the pain on his face from each step he took.

"Device," she heard June shout as they reached Ellie, and beside where June lay Tara saw the shadows begin to form.

———

JUNE WATCHED the shadows take shape, like a swarm of intelligently controlled miniature bugs, each no bigger than a microbe of dust they span until they formed the shape of a man. Tara and Mike had reached the girl and as they began to cut the ropes June grabbed the half-full bottle of potion from the floor and struggled to her feet. Amulet in one hand, bottle in the other she faced it down.

"Jam tibi impero et praecipio maligne spiritus!" she chanted, then stepping toward it she repeated in English, "*I command and charge you, O evil spirit!*," and as she uttered the words the shadows came for her, seized her up and lifted her into the smoke-filled air as if she were no more than a ragdoll. "Qui immunda est - *He who is unclean*," June continued, the amulet held before her. She glanced down, Mike had the boy, the girl was free of the restraints and with an arm around Tara's shoulder, they were making toward the steps which led to the door and away from the fire.

"Qui hoc non habet locum in terra - *He who has no place on this Earth.*" She thrust the amulet into the thing's body, a body that still had no solidity and yet could lift her with ease. As her hand plunged into its unearthly form, she felt it burn the flesh, searing her fingers and the back of her hand. "Unde veni et mittam te abyssum irent - *I send you back to the Abyss from whence you came.*" And with her final words, she thrust the hand containing the bottle forward gripping it in her fist until it broke, spilling the contents over her burning fingers and through the thing's shadows.

———

ELLIE'S HEAD swam with confusion and fear. Just as she'd anticipated the blade of the dagger and a pain worse than she could imagine something happened, something went wrong. Her head was fixed in place, looking at the beams of the roof so she'd been unable to see exactly what, but she'd heard the sound of a gun followed by a **WHHOOMMPPHHH,** as something somewhere in the room caught fire. Things had happened fast then and she'd soon been certain that this wasn't part of the ceremony. The whole thing played out in no more than a minute or two but laid bound to the altar and unable to do anything but listen to the screams and the shots going off around her, it had seemed much longer.

"Let's get you out of here," a female voice said, just as Ellie felt certain that whilst she and her brother had escaped the horror of the ceremony, they'd now burn to death instead.

As she watched the relentless flames dancing across the beams of the roof, she felt hands working to free her. "My brother," she rasped, the stifling air scorching her windpipe with every struggled breath.

"Mike has him," the voice said. Who Mike was she had no clue, but these people were obviously here to help so that was fine by her. Suddenly Ellie felt the straps holding her head come free and she was being pulled to a sitting position where she finally saw who'd spoken. She recognised who it was immediately. Despite the bruised and swollen cheek and the skin of the woman's face that had been reddened by the heat, she recognised Tara Gibb, or Tig as they called her on the Unexplained UK show. Ellie's head was too far gone with the trauma of the night to even process how it was possible, why Tig was here setting her free and dressed in the same black robes as all the others. She felt Tara place her arm around her back, supporting her under the arm and lifting down off the altar.

"It's time to go," Tara said urgently.

———

ALMOST UNABLE TO BREATHE MIKE REACHED THE stairs, he had Henry Harrison over his shoulder and the gun in his other hand. Tara was in front, supporting Ellie and helping her up the steps and toward the door. Mike looked and saw with horror that the thing of shadows had June, she was a good ten feet in the air and at the mercy of its grip. Words formed on her lips yet under the roar of the fire they were lost to him. He saw her thrust the bottle into the thing's body, causing it to scream, but it wasn't just one scream, it was the scream of many and they reached a crescendo that drowned out the roar of the blaze. As those screams filled the room the shadows that made it churned in turmoil, it lost its human form and she crashed back to the floor, landing in a painful crumpled heap at the foot of the sacrificial altar, the one that not a minute ago held Ellie Harrison. Above her broken body the thing that had once been Device span like water going down a plug-hole and as the last of its impossible form disappeared, the screaming finally stopped.

June rolled onto her side, looked directly at Mike and smiled and he knew that she meant for him to leave her there. Before he could decide either way the sound of cracking and breaking came from the roof, Mike looked up in time to see a section of the mid-beam break away, taking with it a chunk of the stone above and the massive iron chandelier. The whole lot crashed down in a hail of sparks burying June beneath and killing her instantly. *I have a part to play in this,* she'd said to him, and she'd been right. She'd known she had to come, and he wondered if she'd known it would be a one-way ticket.

Mike could feel blood running down his injured leg now, he knew the wound was open and every step was agony, yet with Henry Harrison over his shoulder and with the sight of Tara and Ellie in front he found new vigour.

"The roof is coming down," he called to Tara. "We need to move."

"June," she said with dismay, looking back.

Mike didn't speak. Tara had not witnessed her death and right now there was no time to explain, instead, he just shook his head slowly, and he saw tears begin to run down her dirty face.

Broken, burned but somehow still alive they reached the stairs that led back to the utility cupboard in The Old Chapel. Tara went first, still supporting

Ellie who was struggling to walk on feet that were battered and cut from whatever had happened to her in the forest. Smoke from the blaze crept along the roof of the passage and chimneyed up the spiral stairs making it hard to breathe. Finally reaching the top, coughing and gasping for air, she pushed Ellie through and into the kitchen before Mike stumbled through with the still sleeping body of Henry over his shoulder.

He wanted to rest, he wanted to lay down on the tiles and just take five to get himself together, but outside he could see more fire raging in the forest, and above the blackening trees the electrical storm still raged, strobing the sky in flash after flash of brilliant white light, yet no rain fell.

"Mike, the forest," Tara said, and as she spoke, below their feet the ground gave a tremor.

"The – storm, there – must – have been – a lightning strike," he panted. "We, we need to – get to the – the cars." The smoke pouring up the hidden stairwell in the utility cupboard and continued to flood the kitchen and before long the air would be toxic to breathe, with the hatch broken there was no way to close it and stop the smoke. Mike slammed the cupboard door shut, it helped but smoke still poured out from under the door. *Move,* Mike thought to himself, *you need to get moving or all this will have been for nothing.*

"Just a little further," Tara said to Ellie, who nodded and looked at Mike with petrified eyes.

"He won't wake up," she said to Mike. "I tried but they have done something to him."

"We need to worry about that later," Mike replied, already feeling the fast building toxic smoke choke his lungs. The ground shook again, stronger this time and Mike knew that with the roof to the chapel below them collapsing that soon the whole place might come down. He put the Beretta on the side and span all six of the gas burners on the range cooker to maximum flow, before collecting the gun back up.

"What are you doing?" Tara cried.

"This place ends tonight, once and for all," he said firmly and hobbled toward the central passage and the lobby, where propped against the front doors, battered and bruised they found Seth Horner, a knife in his hand. On seeing the four of them his face twisted with rage and he staggered forward, the blade slashing the air in front of him.

"Nooooo," he screeched. Mike still had the Beretta in his left hand, there was just one cartridge left in the chamber. As Seth struggled inanely toward them, he raised the gun and with a one-handed grip pulled the trigger. Without the stock resting on his shoulder the recoil kicked hard and cast the A400 from his hand, but not before the buckshot hit Seth Horner square in the chest, it jarred his body back with a whack that sent him to the floor where he fell upon Jason's dead body.

"You told me earlier," Mike said with disgust, "that only in death are we truly free." Seth Horner looked at him, his face battered, his body broken, and his breath coming in rattling rasps. "I guess you're going to find out." Mike didn't bother picking the gun up, as the ground tremored again, he threw the door open and went outside.

THERE ON THE shingle forecourt in the glow of the encroaching fire stood Mike's Jeep, Scotty's T4, June's Yaris and behind the VW was an Audi that Mike guessed belonged to Jason. Smoke hung on the air, but compared to how it had been below ground and in the kitchen, it was still much easier to breathe.

"Key's," Mike said helplessly patting the sides of his robe. "We don't have any fucking keys, they are inside." He looked back at The Old Chapel with frustration, it sat against the glow of the forest fire and seemed to shimmer in the heat. "I'm going to have to go back in."

He went to set Henry on the ground but as he bent there was a deep rumble from the ground and the bell tower at the back of the building gave way and came crashing to the ground. As the decommissioned bell hit the deck it sounded out what would most certainly be its last monotone ***BONNGGGG***.

Tara grabbed his arm, "Jason's car," she said and Mike saw that the driver's door sat ajar, meaning that if he'd not closed it in his eagerness to get to them, then he might just have left the keys in the ignition, or the electronic fob thingy inside, whichever it used.

Mike reached the Audi, the door was partially open and sure enough, in his haste to begin his murderous rampage good old Jason, who by some twist of fate had brought them the gun, had also left them their means of escape, for in the centre console sat a keyless ignition fob. Mike opened the back door and lay Henry across the rear seat, Ellie climbed in after him and cradled his head on her lap, tears streaking her reddened face.

"Can you drive?" Tara asked as Mike dropped into the driver's seat, just taking the weight off his leg felt like bliss. She cleared the newspaper showing the article that had led Jason here off the seat and into the footwell before getting in herself.

"I'll be fine," he replied as he set his right leg on the brake and hit the ignition button, the car started instantly. Mike knocked the auto-shifter to drive and launched them forward in a hail of shingle that spat up from the rear tyres.

———

ELLIE HARRISON WATCHED The Old Chapel sink away through the rear window. In her lap she cradled her brother's head, stroking his blonde hair affectionately and still not quite able to believe she was one, alive and two, free. The car reached the road and swung right. Behind her the night was aglow with the oranges and reds of the fire, the lightning that still flashed across the sky silhouetted the cloud of smoke that hung above the trees giving it the appearance of some great beast, maybe a dragon that lay over the village, one intent on smoting it until all that remained was ash.

"The whole village is burning," Tara said in amazement, and then as if on cue an explosion bloomed from where The Old Chapel had been. A great ball of fire spawned into the air, it reached high over the burning trees and into the smoke-stained sky above. Even from the road they felt the ground tremor as the below that had been the dark, hidden secret of Trellen collapsed and swallowed the building. As the ground shook, no one spoke. Each knew with their own quiet satisfaction what had happened, and each knew that this time there would be no rebuilding, The Old Chapel was gone.

FROM THE BACKSEAT Ellie felt the strong acceleration of the Audi, Mike redlining every gear before he clicked the paddle-shifter on the steering wheel. Near to the edge of the village the headlights briefly illuminated the now dishevelled roadside shrine that marked the very spot where Karl Banks had met the tipper some two years ago, then it was gone, swallowed up by the amber glow of the burning night. As they sped past the sign that read **'Trellen Thanks You For Driving Carefully'**, Ellie felt Henry move his head, she looked down and slowly his eyes flicked open.

"Hen," she cried out. "He's awake."

Ellie saw his eyes looking at her with puzzlement and for a terrible second, she thought that he may have no memory of her.

"Ells?" he said sleepily. "Is it time to go to the beach yet?"

The beach? She thought, and then she remembered that they'd been due to go to Charlestown, and how excited he'd been about it. Henry had been asleep through the entire ordeal and to him no more than a regular night had passed.

"I think so, Kiddo," she sobbed, leaning down and kissing him on his dirt-smeared forehead, her tears now ones of joy and relief. "I'll even buy you an ice-cream."

PART 5
AFTER

MIKE AWOKE TO THE SMELL OF DISINFECTANT AND the steady beep of medical apparatus. The blinds in the private room were drawn, yet two intense shafts of deep light lanced through the dimly lit room thanks to a couple of slats that were slightly askew. They picked up otherwise invisible dust motes that span and swirled it the deep light until they passed into shade and out of view.

Stood at the foot of his bed, dressed in grey trousers and a light blue short-sleeve shirt, collar open and wearing no tie was Mark Samuels. In his left hand, he clutched a notebook and pen, the kind of notebook Mike used to take everywhere with him when he'd been on the force.

"What – where," Mike croaked in confusion from his dry mouth and through dry lips. The last thing he could clearly remember had been the massive bloom of fire raising into the sky as they'd fled the village.

"Relax," Samuel said. "You're in Derriford Hospital. You've got a gunshot wound to the leg, you're suffering from smoke inhalation and you have some third-degree burns, nothing too serious. Plus, a mild concussion from the accident."

Mike tried to prop himself up in the bed, but his

battered body ached and protested too much. "Accident?" he questioned, suddenly feeling panicked.

"The Audi A4 you were driving, a car registered to a Jason Paxman from Blandford, Dorset, crashed around eight miles north of Trellen, on the Bodmin road. The ANC system on the vehicle, that's the clever bit of kit that detects an accident, automatically informed the police and ambulance when the car went off the road and into the hedge."

Despite the pain, Mike did prop himself up now, "The others," he said. "Tara, Ellie, and Henry?"

Samuels smiled, rounded the bed and placed a hand on the shoulder of his old colleague, "Mike, relax. It wasn't a bad accident, Tara thinks you passed out, maybe from blood loss, or just plain exhaustion. The vehicle was only travelling around twenty miles an hour, you were approaching a junction, you went right across it and into a hedge. The airbag on the driver's side failed and you took a blow to the head on the steering wheel."

"They're all okay?" Mike asked, the moment of panic still prickling his skin.

Samuels removed his hand and stood back, "They're fine. In hospital, not from the accident I add, you were the only one injured. Tara has some third-degree burns, minor smoke inhalation, the same for Ellie and her brother."

"Oh, thank God," he sighed and allowed his aching muscles to relax into the bed a little. "What day is it?"

"It's a little after six on Saturday evening July 28th," Samuels replied, taking an automatic glance at the Casio on his wrist. "They've fixed your leg up, dressed your burns and given you a bit of blood." He paused and pulled the visitor chair over. It was mint green with a high comfortable back and furnished in a wipeable PVC type material. The legs scraped over the composite tile floor with a bone-chilling screech as he dragged it. "What happened, Mike?" he asked seriously as he sat. "How the fuck did you find those kids?" Then before Mike could speak, he added, "The entire village of Trellen is gone, Mike. The fire took it all, buildings the lot. Some sort of sinkhole opened up where The Old Chapel stood, they think there must have been an old forgotten mine shaft or undergrown cavern down there. It seemed the fire caused a gas explosion in the building, that in turn fractured whatever was below it. Fire crews have been out there since someone in Culdon raised the alarm at around two on Friday morning. The forest fire is under control and all but out now, but there is no sign that anyone got out of the village other than the four of you. The whole thing is all over the news, Mike. It's a media shit storm and no one, not even the police have an answer as to how the fuck you not only got out but got out with two persons that were the victims in a murder investigation." He rubbed his forehead with the hand that didn't hold the notebook and then concluded, "I tried to talk to Tara while you were out, but she said I needed to talk to you. That it wasn't just for her to tell."

Mike gestured toward a glass of water with a straw that sat on the bedside cabinet, Samuels picked it up and held it to Mike's lips while he drank, draining the glass in a few long pulls. The water was lukewarm and had a slightly metallic taste to it, but it still felt good on his parched mouth. When all the liquid was gone, and his throat didn't feel quite as dry he said, "You wouldn't believe me if I told you the truth."

"Mike, yesterday morning at a little after half two a double crewed police unit found you and Tara in a crashed car with two missing persons who'd been presumed dead. You all looked like you'd escaped a fire but neither Tara, nor Elle would tell the officers what happened, I am not expecting a simple explanation."

Mike took a deep breath and coughed a little, his chest was still a bit rattily. He knew why they'd not said anything, they'd wanted to make sure the place burned.

As it was the alarm had already been raised, but they'd been right to hold their silence. Mike tried to work the timing in his head, had they inexplicably lost an hour or more again while below ground? He wasn't sure and trying to work it out just made his head pound, so he left it alone, it didn't matter now. "Very well," he conceded. "But off the record."

"Mike, something is going to have to go on the record, you know that as well as I do."

"I know, Mark, but not this. I'll tell you, you take it away and have a sleepless night while you get it right in your head, because you will have a sleepless night, maybe more than one. Then work out a version that will appease the masses. Come back to me, we will go over it with Tara, Ellie and her father as well. When we are happy, we'll call it good and I'll sign whatever needs to be signed."

Samuels nodded his head slowly in consideration, "Okay, Mike, okay," he finally said. There was no mocking tone as he spoke, not like there'd been before when they'd last chatted in the rear garden of The Old Chapel, now he was serious, so Mike began.

It was just after a quarter past seven by the time Mike finished recounting what had happened, and as they both sat in silence for a few seconds Tara slipped into the room wearing a pair of red joggers and a yellow T-shirt. She had a light, duck egg blue hospital dressing gown over her shoulders, it was untied and hung loosely on her slender frame. Her hair looked freshly washed and still a little damp. Her face was reddened from the burns and there was a bruise on her left cheek, it ran up as far as her eye that looked slightly swollen, yet she still looked beautiful to him, and now maybe more so than ever, and in that evening light she'd never looked more alive.

"I was waiting outside," she said before crossing the room to Mike's bed where she leant down and kissed him on the head and took hold of his left hand.

"Is it true," Samuels said. His voice was little hollow and his face was the pale of someone who'd just been delivered life-changing bad news.

"Every word," Tara confirmed. "Scott Hampton and June Rodgers," she added.

"I'm sorry?" Samuels said, looking at her with confusion.

"Write those names down," Tara said, nodding toward the notepad in his hand that he'd not opened since getting there. "Scott Hampton and June Rodgers. Whatever account goes out to the public make sure those names are in it. They died in that fucking place in the process of saving Ellie and Henry, and they need to be remembered for being the heroes they are. Tell the public what you want but they need to be remembered."

Samuels looked at her for a few seconds, then said, "Okay Tara, understood." He got up from the seat and walked to the door, opened it, looked back and said, "Rest up Mike, I'll be in touch."

CHAPTER 56

MIKE WAS RELEASED LAST OF THE FOUR TRELLEN survivors on Wednesday, August the 1st. The name, Trellen Survivors, had been given to them by the media who'd received the official report around the finding of Ellie and Henry Harrison, as well as the fire in the village the day after Samuels had visited with Mike at Derriford Hospital.

The official report was that Mike, Tara, and Scott, as well as their mutual friend, June Rodgers whom they'd met through work in the paranormal field, had been staying in The Old Chapel on a short break when fire caused by a number of lightning strikes from one of the worst electrical storms on record had taken hold of the forest that surrounded the village. In a heroic effort to save others the four of them had gone to a neighbouring house to try and alert the owners. Finding no one in and fearing them asleep they broke into the home of Seth and Lucinda Horner only to find the missing brother and sister being held in the cottage's basement. The four had then been attacked by both Seth and Lucinda Horner who'd been part of some unknown satanic cult. In the fight, Mike got shot in the leg and tragically both Scott Hampton and June Rodgers had died. Mike, Tara, and the Harrisons had then fled the burning village, only narrowly escaping the fire. As for Jason, well he'd been omitted from the account altogether.

It was a half-truth laced with a good dose of semi-believable bullshit, and one played out on the news and written in the papers. As such it had been swallowed totally by most of the public who don't think to question what the main news outlets tell them.

The day of his release Tara met him at the hospital, she'd been released on the Monday and had been staying just down Derriford Road the past two nights in a hotel. In truth, she'd not been at the hotel much, save for showering and the evening meal. Choosing instead to sit and sleep on the visitor chair in Mike's room, neither of them really wanting to be alone.

From the hospital, they were taken back to Tara's place in Dorset in a private hire taxi, booked and paid for by Mark Samuels with Mike promising to pay him back when he finally got home and was in a position to sort out a few personal affairs. Samuels had told him not to worry, that it was on him for bringing an end to the biggest case of the summer and as his way of apologising for not taking Mike or the team seriously. Mike didn't argue.

He spent the first night out of the hospital at Tara's, he had no real yearning to go home to that empty house in Arundel with so many memories of his old life, one that seemed now to belong to a different version of him. He knew he'd have to at some point, if only to pick up a few bits and start sorting things out like the insurance claim for his Jeep. Maybe then he'd see about getting the place on the market, there was nothing for him there now but memories. It seemed like an age had passed since he'd left that house for the meeting at the SwitchBack TV offices in Manchester and his life had been a rollercoaster pretty much since then. Now he was off the ride it all seemed different, the events of the last few days had changed him, they'd changed Tara, too. He guessed it would get better with time, the trauma of what they'd been through would ease, but a small part of it, and the guilt at the loss of Scotty, would stay with him them forever, of that he had no doubt.

Mike woke at seven on the Thursday morning and lay for a few moments in the dim light of the bedroom, the sun held at bay by Tara's thick drapes. As she slept soundly, he got up and showered, then re-dressed the wound on his leg. It was healing but still pained him to stand on, it was getting easier with each passing day, though. In the kitchen, he wrote her a note to say he loved her and that he'd be back in the afternoon after he'd taken care of a few things.

Tara's A2 had been left in her bay when they'd driven down to Cornwall in his Jeep and now between them, it was the only car they had. He found the keys in her handbag and took a drive, heading out of Shaftsbury and picking up the Salisbury Road.

He pulled up outside of Sue and Tom Reed's place a little after half nine that morning. The day was already uncomfortably warm as the great heatwave of 2018 continued to bake the country, and most of Europe, too.

Sue Reed must have been in the kitchen and had to have seen him coming as he made his way up their long path, and between the two weeping willows that still hung their branches down to that perfectly cut lawn.

By the time he reached the front door she was stood there with it open, "Mike," she said with a melancholy smile as he reached the door. "I was wondering when we would hear from you, come in."

"Things have been a little odd," he said as she ushered him in. "Considering what happened I should have called sooner. I'm sorry."

Sue gave him a light hug, the contact surprised him a little, but it was also welcome. "Nonsense," she said. "You should have called ahead and warned me you were coming though, Tom just left to head into town. Insurance stuff to sort at the bank."

"How is he?" Mike asked, going through to the lounge.

"Not bad," Sue answered, looking at him from the living room door as Mike took a seat on her floral-patterned sofa. "He says we are officially out of the rental business now, and that when the money comes through its going back in the bank and staying there."

Mike nodded, noticing one of those old family photo albums on the pine coffee table, the kind that looked like a thick book, the cover made of black laminated card and from a time where digital photography hadn't even been a consideration.

"I thought I should come and tell you what really happened," Mike said, taking his eyes away from the album. "The full story."

"I did wonder if what the news reported was the full story," and as she spoke, he saw tears well in her eyes. "When I heard that Lucinda had been involved, and that your friends had been killed, do you know how," but she couldn't finish the sentence.

Mike stood and went to her, put an arm around her and said, "No one could have known." Then changing the subject, he said with a gesture toward the coffee table, "I've not seen a photo album like that for a good few years. Most people keep all their memories on their phones nowadays. My mum has a box full of them in her loft."

Sue wiped her eyes with the backs of her hands, sniffed back a little and said with a forced smile, "Yes, silly really. I never mentioned it before, I was from Cornwall originally, moved across to Wiltshire when I was in my early twenties for work. A long time ago now," she said as if reminiscing in her head. "That's when I met Tom, at a concert." Mike nodded, letting her talk had distracted her from the guilt and that was a good thing. "I had a sister," she added. "Died when she was fifte, drowned in Charlestown harbour. They never found her body, though. There's a grave for her, a little churchyard just outside of St Austell. They buried an empty casket. When they were still alive my parents went there regularly, put flowers on the headstone and that. I've not been there in years, I doubt anyone has been," Sue said sounding guilty. "Thirty or more I'd say. I don't think I could even find her grave now. When they thought that those poor Harrison kids had drowned there it brought back a few memories and I realised that no matter how hard I tried, I couldn't fully remember what she'd looked like. I tried to remember, but time had fogged it over." She looked at Mike with sad tear-filled eyes. "That sounds bad, doesn't it? She was my sister, but I couldn't remember her face?"

"It was a long time ago now," Mike said, not quite able to believe this was going where he thought it was going. "Practically a lifetime ago," he added.

"Yes," Sue said a little distantly and Mike could see that her eyes were staring blankly at the album as she spoke. "I suppose it is. Would you like some tea?"

"I'd love a cup," Mike lied, not really wanting the tea, wanting instead a chance to look at the album that sat on the coffee table.

"I'll bring some through," She smiled, and with that, she disappeared off into the kitchen.

Mike went back to the sofa, sat and with shaky hands picked up the old photo album. The pages smelt musty as he turned them, the scent of something long stored and not often brought out. The first image was a black and white one of a baby in a christening robe, *Sue aged six months,* was written below in the kind of handwriting that people no longer used. The next image was of two old people stood on a promenade somewhere, the woman held one of those old-fashioned parasols and Mike put the picture somewhere around the early 1920s. He kept thumbing until he found what he knew he'd find, no matter how impossible it seemed.

The picture was black and white, it was of two girls taken on holiday, both in bathing suits and stood on the beach clutching ice-creams. One of the girls was a young Sue Reed, only then Reed hadn't been her last name. Her black hair stood out in the colourless photo, it was tied up in a bun, she had a broad smile on her face and her eyes seemed to sparkle with youth. She was maybe nineteen or twenty years old in the snap and it had likely been taken just a year or so before her move to Wiltshire. The girl beside her was younger, thirteen maybe fourteen years old. Her hair was lighter, and Mike didn't need the benefit of colour to know that it was red. Freckles dressed the bridge of her nose and Mike knew that if the camera were a little closer, as it had been in the school picture used on her missing persons newspaper article, then he'd see that scar above her right eye. Below the image in that same neat calligraphy-like handwriting was printed, *Lindie and Sue, Woolacombe Bay - Summer 1967*.

Mike gripped the album tightly in his hands and stared at it in utter disbelief and with a deep sadness until he heard Sue putting the tea makings on a tray, then he closed it and placed it carefully back on the table. Sue came through with the drinks, balancing them on a tray with a plate of Garibaldi biscuits, and in that instant, he knew he'd not tell her. She carried enough guilt about what had happened. Her sister was a distant memory, so distant that she'd had to dig out an old album to fully remember how she'd looked. What would he or she gain from the telling of that terrible truth? Telling her that Lindie had not drowned, that she'd been taken, beaten, raped and tortured, made to bear a child that had then been killed so that she could become. That she'd been the thing that was Lucinda Horner, and he felt sure that somewhere inside that woman a small piece of what had been Lindie had remained, imprisoned and in constant torture.

Nothing.

There would be nothing for Sue Reed, once Sue Parker, to gain from the knowledge other than more pain, and everyone had had enough of that, enough to last a few lifetimes over. So, as he sipped at his tea and the Garibaldi biscuits sat untouched on the plate, he ran through what had happened, but he left out the part about the Lindie and the other girls, meaning that only he, Tara, Ellie, Mark Samuels, and Ellie's parents knew the full truth of it. And was that such a bad thing? Some truths were so bad, so rotten that the fewer people burdened with them the better it was.

When he'd finished and Sue had sat in stunned silence for a while, she looked at him with reddened eyes clutching a tissue and said, "What now, Mike? What are you going to do now?"

"I'm not sure," Mike answered truthfully. "I think – I think maybe I'm just going to take a little time to heal."

CHAPTER 57

THE SNOW CAME IN EARLY FEBRUARY OF 2019, plunging the whole UK under a frozen white blanket of ice that threw the country into public travel chaos. As Mike and Tara pulled off the M4 at the Reading exit, large flakes drove at the windscreen of his new Jeep like a myriad of tiny phantoms intent on breaking through, only to be thwarted away by the wipers.

"Might get snowed in up here," Tara said as she cranked up the heater. "Weather says it's only going to get worse. Beast from the east two they're calling it."

"We can get a room," Mike said with a grin and she punched him playfully on the arm.

The sat-nav took them from the motorway, around the town and past the Madejski Stadium, home to Reading FC, then out to one of the residential districts. The Harrison residence was a typical detached family home, built in the 1920s and as Mike pulled to a stop outside, the snow picked up its pace and began to wheel from the sky in flakes the size of twenty pence pieces.

"This is it," Mike said as he killed the engine. "I've not seen the Harrisons since Derriford."

"Six months ago," Tara noted. "Time flies," she said with a sigh before getting out of the car. "I've been in contact with Ellie on WhatsApp but it will be nice to see her again."

The house was on a slight hill and as Mike headed for the door a rear wheel drive BMW struggled by, the smell of its burning clutch filling the frozen air as the driver tried desperately to keep the car moving.

Rob Harrison answered the door less than ten seconds after they'd knocked it. He wore thick, warm looking tartan lounge pants and a T-shirt that declared he was Number 1 Dad. He looked like a totally different man to the one they'd visited with at the Travel Lodge the day he'd been released from custody and had told Mike, Tara, and Scotty not to give him false hope. When they'd seen him at the hospital after his tearful reunion with Ellie and Henry, he'd looked better, but he'd still been broken at that point. Now he looked mended.

"Mike," he said with a wide grin, beckoning the pair in and taking his hand for an enthused shake. "How are the pair of you?" The smell of pizza wafted through from the kitchen and the house felt wonderfully homely and warm after the frigid air outside.

"Good, Rob. How's Carol?" Tara asked as she took off her coat and gave it a shake, casting the melting snow to the hardwood floor of the hall.

"Better every day," Rob answered. "She's upstairs taking a bath; she'll be down later."

"And Henry?"

"He doesn't remember a thing, wondered what all the fuss was about in the weeks after, why everyone recognised him. Thankfully by late October, it all started to die down."

"It's for the best he doesn't remember," Mike said. "And Ellie, how is she?"

Rob's smile dropped a bit, "Still sleeps with the light on," he said, and Mike wondered just how long she would, maybe for the rest of her life. "Other than that," he continued, "pretty good. She's been excited about your visit all day, was worried you wouldn't make it due to the snow."

"Four-wheel drive power," Mike said with a smile. "Gets you through."

"She is in the lounge. Can I get you guys a coffee? You look like you could use a hot drink."

"White with one and white with none," Tara said. "I'm sweet enough already, he's not quite there yet but I'm working on it."

Rob chuckled and took them through to the lounge where Ellie was vegged out on the sofa in baggy joggers and a red GAP hoodie reading a well-thumbed copy of The Shack by WM Paul Young. On seeing them she put the book down, stood and treated them both to a hug. "I'll give you guys some time," Rob said and left the room.

"Good book that," Mike said, looking at the tatty cover now face up on the sofa's middle cushion.

"It looks at religion and life from an interesting perspective," she said. "The author is quite the theologian. I've read it like five times. Seen the film twice, too. The book is better."

"How's you holding up, Ells?" Tara said as they sat.

"Getting there," she said with a smile that said differently. "I still sleep with the lights on."

"Your father tells me that you're taking a year out before you go to Uni," Mike said, sitting forward. "Is that right?"

She nodded, "I just felt I needed a little time to take stock of things. Maybe psychology isn't such a hot topic to study when you're a little fucked up yourself," she chuckled. "How about you guys?"

"Getting there," Mike said. "Time heals as they say."

"After all the media interest in what happened we have had a stock of offers to get the show back on the air," Tara said.

"You should do it," Ellie encouraged. "Your show was great, much better than that Haunted Happenings shit."

"That's kinda the reason we came to see you," Tara

replied. "We are a member down since events at The Old Chapel, and rumour has it that you might have a touch of the old psychic gift."

Ellie smiled, "Turns out I have," she said. "Always had a bit of it, but after that place, it's stronger. I don't know why, just another thing it's left me with. I thought you didn't endorse that kinda thing?"

"Times change," Mike said with a melancholy smile. "Beliefs change, too."

"What are you offering here?" Ellie asked, her eyes now wide with excitement.

"They want us to do a new series, not SwitchBack TV, this is Channel 4, mainstream and nine PM on a Sunday. Not just the UK, we are going to the States, too." Mike replied. "The first episode is St Augustine Lighthouse Florida. Filming starts in April. What I'm saying is, if you want a place on the team it's yours. I think Scotty would have wanted you to have it."

Ellie sat in silence for a moment, looking between them both and for those few seconds Mike couldn't read her, he was starting to think that it had been a bad idea, that maybe she wasn't ready for it, that maybe she was still too broken from the events of the summer. After all she still couldn't sleep in a darken room, maybe a show exploring the paranormal wasn't the best idea and would make her worse.

"Yes," she said excitedly.

"Are you ready for this?" Tara asked as if she'd read Mike's mind. "There is no pressure, say no if you want. It just felt right that you took the place, if you want it. We spoke to Morgan, that's Scotty's brother, he said the same."

"Of course, I want it," Ellie beamed. "What else am I going to do for the next year, sit around here sponging off my parents? And you know what they say? Kill or cure! Sitting around here is doing me no good anyway. Maybe this is just what I need to help me get my shit in order." And with that she leapt forward and hugged

Tara so tightly she fell back into the chair, both of them giggling.

When the laughter finally stopped and Ellie, now smiling more than she probably had since the relief of escaping The Old Chapel, had taken her seat Mike said, "We can sort out the legal and contractual stuff over the next few weeks, but for now allow me to give you a warm welcome to the team."

THE END

THE END

FROM THE AUTHOR

Well, here we are, you made it to the end! If you want to know a little about me, and my inspiration for this book then read on.

As a writer, albeit a small time and pretty much unknown one, I still get asked the question that all writers get – Where do you get your ideas? Now I'm not blessed with a mind swimming with inspiration like some of the greats of our time. Honestly, I really don't know how they do it. However, I thought, and wanted, to take a little time to explain where my idea for The Chapel came from.

Having finished the two Watchers books, I thought I was about done with writing. It's not that I don't enjoy it, it's the time it takes. Time, I don't always have with a full-time job and a young family. The thing with writing is, it's a bit addictive. Once you know you have the commitment to write a novel, and you've had some good reviews you feel compelled to write more. So, being a glutton for punishment I soon found myself yearning to write again and this time I wanted to write horror. I was a big fan of horror novels growing up and still am now. My main literary diet to this day consists of books by the master of horror himself, Stephen King, and the beautifully written works of Dean Koontz, and of course the great British master of horror, the late James Herbert. The trouble with the horror genre, both literary and on the big screen, is that it's been done, done, picked up, revived and fluffed up and done again. The point I'm trying to make is, it's really hard to be original. That aside I was determined to have a go. I'm not sure how well I accomplished that, I will let you, the reader, be the judge.

I've always thought that the scariest horrors, the most disturbing works, are the ones that could be real. Ones that take a perfectly plausible scenario, (the vanishing of a brother and sister whilst on a family holiday), and then introduce the paranormal. I've tried to live by this rule for The Chapel and I hope you agree.

Now here is where my inspiration came from.

Back in the late 2000s and early 2010s, I helped to run tech for a TAPS Family paranormal investigation team, Southern Paranormal UK. Now those of you familiar with your ghost hunting shows will know The Atlantic Paranormal Society, or Ghost Hunters as the program is called. We didn't have the pleasure of being on the big screen like the front runners of the organisation, or like Mike, Tig and Scotty in the novel, but we did investigate some pretty cool places. Many of which feature in the book. Places such as East Drive, Jamaica Inn, Leap Castle, and Moot Hall are all places I've experienced first-hand, and even the "I hear you," EVP that introduces Scotty's character is something I really recorded. The scenario around that chapter is actually based on a real event.

Now you'd think that as a former investigator of all things that go bump in the night, I'd have a myriad of ideas spinning through my head worthy of a novel, well you'd be wrong. Annoyingly for me, those little sparks of inspiration don't come easy, they have to be worked at, nurtured and grown. So, during my long daily commutes to work the ideas began turning over and over in my head, the cases I'd worked with the team, the things I'd experienced. One place above all the rest kept coming back to me, one location wouldn't budge, and that place was The Old Chapel. Yes, it really exists, it's real and I can honestly say that in the numerous places I've investigated, and the hours I've spent trying to find the answer to that unanswerable question, nowhere scared me like that place did.

I have applied a certain amount of artistic licence and changed the name of the village and the outer description of the place, however, it seemed kind of fitting for it to retain some of the original detail.

So, let me tell you a little about the real place that inspired this book. Back in 2010 it really was a holiday home, a converted chapel that had been beautifully transformed into a multi-bedroom let. The Southern Paranormal UK Team rented it out for a weekend, treated it as a busman's holiday you might say. A little R&R and some investigating. Obviously, the majority of this book is a work of fiction, but things such as the banging on the bathroom door of the Altar Room, as experienced by Carol Harrison in the book, really happened. So did the dryer jumping off the radiator and crashing to the floor. We had a ton of other strange goings on there that we struggled to explain. Just moments prior to the radiator dryer incident I heard on my own Sonic Ear Amplifier rig someone or something in the room with us. I heard raspy breathing as they, or it, passed me by. I can say without any embarrassment that it scared me, and when you spend your nights searching for the unexplained you don't tend to scare easy! If you do, then you need to find another hobby.

Lastly, and before I sigh off I'd like to say a big thankyou to our friend Kim, who worked her way through this manuscript, asked the questions that needed to be asked and went to work with an HB pencil and highlighter on many of the pages.

Anyway, I've bored you enough and this is where I will leave you. I sincerely hope you've enjoyed the book, if you did please leave a review, if you didn't then tell me why. We are nothing without a little honest feedback.

S.T Boston

Dear reader,

We hope you enjoyed reading *The Chapel*. Please take a moment to leave a review, even if it's a short one. Your opinion is important to us.

Discover more books by S.T. Boston at

https://www.nextchapter.pub/authors/st-boston

Want to know when one of our books is free or discounted? Join the newsletter at

http://eepurl.com/bqqB3H

Best regards,

S.T. Boston and the Next Chapter Team

———

You might also like:
Watchers by S.T. Boston

To read the first chapter for free, head to:
https://www.nextchapter.pub/books/watchers

The Chapel
ISBN: 978-4-86750-458-1
Mass Market

Published by
Next Chapter
1-60-20 Minami-Otsuka
170-0005 Toshima-Ku, Tokyo
+818035793528

5th June 2021